Charles Reemelin

Life of Charles Reemelin

Charles Reemelin

Life of Charles Reemelin

ISBN/EAN: 9783744662758

Printed in Europe, USA, Canada, Australia, Japan

Cover: Foto ©Raphael Reischuk / pixelio.de

More available books at **www.hansebooks.com**

❀ LIFE ❀

— OF —

CHARLES REEMELIN,

In German:

Carl Gustav Rümelin,

From 1814—1892.

Written by Himself, in Cincinnati, between 1890 and 1892.

There is a history in all men's lives,
Figuring the nature of the times deceased:
The which observed, a man may prophesy,
With a near aim, of the main chance of things
As yet not come to life.

2 Henry IV., iii. 1.

CINCINNATI, O.:

WEIER & DAIKER, Prs., 356 WALNUT STREET.

1892.

INTRODUCTION.

I wrote my life, chiefly for the purpose of completing my life-long pursuit of self-knowledge; hoping at the same time, that members of my family and surviving friends. may also read it with profit. I had made preparations for this purpose. nearly all my life, by preserving letters and papers, as well as keeping diaries; but had not, until my seventy-fifth birthday, read them collectively, nor taken a succinct review of them. It then occurred to me that, if this were to be done at all, it had better be done at once; and accordingly, I began the volume now before the reader, in the Fall of 1889.

It grew, under my hands, more than I intended, because the facts, as I narrated them, seemed to require some explanations as to causes and reasons; a circumstance, that, as I take it, is apt to be the case with autobiographies of emigrants, who become immigrants or settlers; since they are likely to get into unusually complicated relations as to their native and adopted countries, their usages and institutions, as well as their own social and political courses. Both a native land and an adopted country claim of them love and esteem, and that requires honest discrimination.

Such a complication met me at the very beginning of this my work; for I had to decide: whether I should write it in German or in English. I presumed, that most of my fellow countrymen would claim, that I should compose it in the language of my native land, whilst my native American compatriots would insist on English. I decided to follow the rule, I had long before adopted under similar circumstances; namely: to employ that language, which would suit most of the probable readers of such a compilation. In the case before me, the decision had, under this rule, to be made in favor of English; for that language was familiar to nine-tenths of those likely to peruse these pages, even among my German friends.

It suggested itself to me besides: that, at my age and the state of my health, the question really was the completion of some *one* manuscript. in English; leaving the translation into German for after-consideration. As the biography is, most likely, not to be published, while I am alive, the readers of it will be the judges, whether this my course has served the purpose expressed. I must state, however, in justice to myself, that I adopted the English language reluctantly, because I knew, that I could have expressed many of my ideas better in German. I refer here to all the words, which the authors of Germany use for bringing out their much more definite conceptions of modern political economy. I can name here but one such: "Vermögen," which is so much more useful in defining the word "Value"; than the word the English use for it, viz: "Wealth," and the French: "Richesse." They have really no adequate word for the purpose.

To these remarks, I now ask leave to add, a few reflections, that arose in my mind, on re-reading my autobiography. They seem to me to be necessary for a full understanding between the reader and myself.

The main fact of my life is: that I became an immigrant, and had two countries to love and cherish, and both from ever shifting standpoints. I came alone. Now my family consists of my wife, seven children and eighteen grandchildren. I left Germany when our family consisted of parents, and twelve brothers and sisters, of whom but four are alive. My patriotism cannot, therefore, be a mere nativism. With me, judgment tempers the emotional, and often the misjudgments of others engender in me ill feelings that chill fellow feelings. For instance, nativists treat immigration as a suspicious element of the population of this country, though themselves are descendants of immigrants. They cast a slur on folks, whom they really do not know; they do it from pride, that is the opposite of self knowledge, and they do, for, that reason, only stigmatize themselves. My best answer to such a defamation was, in my opinion, the straight story of my life, written by myself, and so published, that it shall not be lost, nor misrepresented.

This my life shows, that I came here neither as a beggar nor a fortune hunter. I had speculative views in my head, but for them I was personally responsible. I claimed no preferences or excemptions, but I was rather proud of being one of millions of equals in a common fate, who wanted no guarantee, except those, that flowed in the air we breathed, to-wit: that we would never be subjected to invidious distinctions nor reservations, except the one in force everywhere, which says: that all communities may object, within a year and a day, to any immigrant, of whom it can be legally proven, that they are likely to become a township charge, or a disturber of the public peace. With this reservation goes universally the law of humanity: that immigrants are entitled to temporary relief, against unforeseen poverty; and are not to be rejected for barbarian chimerical reasons.

I still believe, this ancient law is better, than all the laws since passed or proposed. It secures the country and the immigrant. It rests on general rules of humanity and justice, and shuts off colonization, that begins in false presumptions of power for the authorities of the mother country, and equally false ones for the duties of the colonists. All such were deemed, by all free-minded persons, as having become defunct by the establishment of independence, in 1788; but traces of it lingered in prejudiced minds, who claimed, that England should remain the mother society of the United States, and its politics should be their model, minus always the King and the aristocracy and the official clergy. Acquiescence in this claim took this country at once away from the old Solonic standard, that the true way to organize and to perfect Government is to aim continually at being positively right, according to the rules gathered by the historic experience of mankind. And thus being without standard, the nation fell into negative rulings, that precluded it from pursuing any normal course at all. It adopted the old English make-shifts, to-wit: political parties, whose struggles for power were to act as sifting processes for arriving at some conclusions in public affairs. It was doing, what is proverbially called: "hunting a needle in a hay stack." I mention this here, because it states the leading fact in American Politics. It explains: why there is so much prevarication in our public conduct; and, as to myself, it is the circumstance, that made me always appear as a heretic, for amidst all my support of certain public bodies, I always reserved my right to differ on this point even with friends for cause. I never forgot, that I was, in America, a Citizen of the World, whose first and last duty it is, to be a fellow worker in the general progressive civilization now going on. I never was a comrade of nativistic self-worshippers; and emigrated to prove it. And I was ever an admirer of Solon's standard of positive right, and I never failed to show it, when I saw it about to be violated, for I always defended it. I did this in the midst of partisan associates, and became often unpopular among them, to the surprise of friends and foes. They could not reconcile, how I, an ardent supporter, of the causes I had espoused, should at times again become their opponent; I could not reconcile, how they — free citizens — should become party slaves ?

This point is indeed the riddle of American public life. And again and again I have found it exceedingly difficult, to determine how to act. It was ever so plausible to mistake Party fidelity for patriotism; and I know of thousands, whose only claim, to popular fame, is, that they absolutely ignored all distinction between the two phrases. Some even pride themselves on this their oblivion.

I do not mean to claim, that the reader will find all these points discussed extensively in this, my life; no! I believed it proper only. to present so much of it, as might explain my participation in the courses of events going on. for the last sixty years, in the United States, for the establishment of a confederation of States and civic order therein, and thus be useful to intelligent searchers for historic details. And I have, for that reason, been diligent in pointing out. where to find the public documents, reports, speeches, lectures and papers that have been delivered, written and published by me. I deemed this proper, because my own experience, while composing my autobiography, where I had to reread all these papers, had convinced me, that they have some public interest. Their perusal in close consecutive order and retrospect, all together, has cleared my views on many questions, and made me drop errors and confess mistakes, but it gave, I think also, to my reflections a wider scope and deeper insight. I saw, for instance, much more distinctly: what a mass of crude speculation and self deception there is in our finances; and how almost irretrievably defective and wasteful our public administration is; and why it is so. I perceived too the mischiefs, that lurk in all our tax laws and public debt systems; viz: that they are largely mere spoliations of the respective parts of society by other parts, in which the sharpers are the beneficiaries, and the producers the victims; but I understand too. that there are here the most gigantic false distributions of wealth. that now exist in the world, because the larger accruings of wealth are here not the outcome of labor, skill, industry and economy, but they represent speculative values, privileges, and concentrated corporation power and management of public affairs, that should in a Government, that claims to be right, be carried out through public administration, that gets only payment for actual services.

These observations, all led to one general conclusion; to-wit: the people of the United States are now hemmed in by a most tyrannic absolutism, but are not fully conscious of it: and need more than any other people on earth self knowledge. And the test to be put to every publication, my autobiography included, is therefore: does it conduce to this end? The United States need self-knowledge most. because it is the cornerstone of their institutions; in spite of their refusal to see it. Their wonderful much misunderstood prosperity.has blinded them. as to their land and their people, and prevents the mental and moral research, that is most necessary to *their* welfare. They have, relying upon the impunity with which they have hitherto committed the greatest of political errors; that of allowing their public affairs to be conducted under party motives: surrendered not only present government to party rule, but also the future reformation of it. All correct public policy must now be first sanctioned by the respective party; but that sanction it will never receive, because, in parties, there are no checks and balances, in other words, no wholesome reactions, that might enforce some reform. Every party yet formed, has before long, been sunk in its own corruption. Parties are now, in the United States, but struggles between the factions within them. And between themselves, they are but wastes of energy; they but

"Lend corruption lighter wings to fly."

In conclusion, we can but hope, that our labors shall not have been entirely in vain. And, if our life should be spared long enough to see yet a United States Government, in which an efficient public administration redeems past wrongs and mischiefs; then I should esteem it as the greatest blessings that could be bestowed upon me; for, if it is not my native land, it is that of my descendants, and I can say to it and its people in all sincerity:

"With all thy faults I love thee still."

August 1st, 1892.   CHARLES REEMELIN.

Life of Carl Gustav Rümelin.

CHAPTER I.

MY ANCESTRY AND CHILDHOOD.

I was born May 19th, 1814, in the town, now city of Heilbronn. It was up to 1806 a free city of the German Empire. Since then it has been annexed to Württemberg, one of the States of the Germanic Union.

My father's name was Gottlieb Benjamin Rümelin. My mother's maiden name was Caroline Boettinger. He was a wholesale grocery merchant; she grew up in a similar business, carried on by her mother. The ancestors of both were well to do people. The fact that my father was an immigrant into my native city, whilst my mother belonged to one of the old established families, caused early manifold reflections in my mind. In some respects it intensified my home feelings, in others again it unsettled them. Indeed I saw in the fact frequently, and do still, a foreboding of my future. I saw the light of day in a large establishment, that had extensive accommodations for dwelling, pleasure and business within its mansion. There were fine outhouses and a large garden. It had formerly been a Carmelite Convent. Historic inquiries seemed therefore to be born with me. I made many inquiries and insisted on full answers. but did not always get them. It perplexed me often to reconcile the extreme contrasts between our family life and the life of the old monks. My inquisitiveness found new nourishment at every step I took in life. I often asked how could both be right? My life had always more or less incongruities with surroundings from the past. I never therefore could be a strong believer in the permanency of human institutions. even when a divine origin was claimed for them. What I learned about my name added to this versatility. It belongs to that uncertain class, as to which folks alternate between misspelling and mispronouncing. I have met the name very frequently in other lands; but never twice spelled alike in two places. and so too have I heard it from many lips, but never with like pronunciation. I have still intimate friends, that express my name every time with a variation.

Let me state some of the more prominent versions: Rümelin, Rümmelin, Remelin. Römelin, Rönilin, Rimeli. Remele, Rämlin, Remler, and I write it in America Reemelin. Kossuth told me, that he knew of Rümelini in Roumelia. He said also, that he had no doubt, that our family came formerly from the Province of Roumelia in Turkey. In D'Aubigne's "History of the Reformation" Peter Rümelin is mentioned as a valuable supporter of Zwingli. And in Basle a public place is called "Rümelin" after him, and as further confirmation of the variableness, inherent in my family name, I may state, that at this time I know of Rümelins in Berlin, Odessa, Basle, Roschach, and of course in the United States and Württemberg, who like me are pestered by the variability with which their cotemporaries express and write our name in the respective languages; but seldom twice alike.

As already intimated, the antiquated Carmelite Convent, with its inner arrangements, for the abbots and monks, as to house room, garden work, the storage of food and drink in granaries and cellars; the fine promenades, with the stories told us children about their modes of living and culture, formed the rudiments of my earliest education; so that I became quite an inquisitive character. The circumstance, that the street, on which our house stood, bore, up to 1825, the name "Jew Street," gave my curiosity a further field of thought; for it was certainly a queer historic conjunction: this Carmelite Convent and the Jew Street. Both their folks came from Palestine to Heilbronn, to be there first honored, but afterwards despised and ejected. I troubled my father for explanations and got them from him, including the statement: that while we were talking, there was a public movement going on for the emancipation of the Jews, and that my uncle, my father's brother, who was Judge and Legislator, was its prominent supporter. Quiet inquiries showed me, that my mother and her family did not coincide with this movement, and that among native Heilbronners it was generally unpopular.

The measure passed, because the majority had other opinions, then the folks in Heilbronn, of the historic memories as to the Jews. The name Jew Street was abolished and it was named after the Crown Prince "Carl," that is its name now. How long? These vicissitudes made a deep impression on my mind, and in after life, when I had to meet public questions, in which the same principles were involved. I recollected them, and they formed standards for making up my mind in the new cases I had to deal with. I knew that popular local prejudices are an unsafe guide in public issues.

I grew up also amidst waning antipathies to Napoleonic overbearing courses. The old Emperor had, as stated, turned over my native town in 1806, to the King of Württemberg. So great was the outcry against this act at this time, and whilst I grew up, that I had not the least conception, up to 1820, that there could be any excuse, much less a good reason for this high-handed act. I attended with my father and mother jubilees over the expulsion of the French, and believed it to be my sacred duty to yearn for the old liberty of my native town while I lived. My mother's relations applauded this my youthful patriotism, and I wore with special satisfaction caps that indicated, in color and make up, my anti-french propensities. One day my grandmother, on my father's side, who resided in Ludwigsburg, and was a regular visitor at the old Queen's Court there, warned me against these my proclivities, and told me besides, that the annexation of Heilbronn to Württemberg was very beneficial to it, and that it should have taken place centuries previous, by the free consent of the people there. Her remarks struck me then as very unreasonable; but I had to realize their truth afterwards by wholesome experience. So I passed from my ancestral conceptions and those of my childhood, to maturer age, with mixed feelings; but on the whole with no regrets, for either, after I dropped them.

One of my bitterest memories is the famine year 1818. Long I remember the diminutive size of the pieces of bread we then got to eat, and I used to talk of them, as if, my sharing them, had been an act of heroism. And at the same time I would mention, that I was said to have been one of the children on the festival wagon, that was drawn into the town by six horses in 1819 with the first ripe sheafs of grain of that year. Of its arrival on the city's large market space, a picture had been got up, of which I had and carried a copy to America. On it I could point out one of the children's faces as mine. I lost the picture, and am less positive of my memory about it. That such a wagon came 1819 to Heilbronn is certain, but my presence on it is, to say the least, doubtful.

The reader is by this time, as I presume, prepared for me to mention the fact, that the author of the Chronicles of Heilbronn was a relation of mine. His name was Carl Jaeger. He was a Clergyman. He composed the Chronicles in 1822 to 1827. One of my most delightful places of visit was his parsonage at Bürg near Neustadt, where the big Linden tree is. The book appeared in print in 1828. I have a copy of it in my library, and I love to use it for refreshing my memory about my native city. Most interesting to me is the following clause of the book:

"We have now related historically this city's life from its insignificant beginning—a millenium ago—through its different periods of happy prosperity and flourish, to the moment, when, not without our sorrows, we had to note the tribute it had to pay to time by losing its independence. It may be true, that during the history of our city, as of all cities, there were evidences of littleness and narrow-mindedness, and that in consequence thereof much progress was retarded; but we must not forget, that, what here is called narrow-mindedness, bears, in the history of the larger States, the honoring name "Policy." Let us trust, therefore, that this city's life may continue to flourish and prosper also in the new relations, and that providence may bless the industry of its citizens and the circumspection of those trusted with its public welfare. With this wish we lay down our pen."

I never read this passage, in America, without a pang of home-sickness for my birth-place; but neither without reflecting, that my views, as to Cincinnati, and its prospects, were formed by taking into account historic data learned in the Chronicles of Heilbronn.

CHAPTER II.

HAPPY CHILDHOOD TURNED INTO UNHAPPY YOUTH.

THE brightest of my recollections are about my native city in my childhood, and I think that my affections for Cincinnati grew out of the general resemblance of the two; every item in the latter being on a larger scale. Heilbronn has the river Neckar, Cincinnati the Ohio, on its Southern side. Both are situated in a valley surrounded by hills; but I remember every thing about the first and its vicinity with a distinctness which I could never attain as to the latter. I ascribe this to the deeper impressions, which the scenes, passed through in youth, make; and it is the same cause, that gives in every human heart precedence to ones native land over an adopted country. And as I write these pages, and bring to mind event after event of my life, I am of nothing more certain than my belief, that I enjoyed myself more during the first six years of my youth then ever since. I think that I slept sounder, eat my meals with greater gusto, played with a freer zest, and held all I possessed with more gratification. Never again did I meet with a family, that had as much harmony and did each other such manifold good. And there is no void nor exception in this cheerfulness nor in the gratitude it wrought in me. From early morn, till bedtime, I can thing of no wrong or harm within our family circles, and if there were any, they were so trivial as to be entirely forgotten. It was the outer world, the outside eventualities, that marred our general home happiness; for on our visits to relations, we found there only evidences of a desire to give us an opportunity to witness, in the best light possible, the inherent superiority of our kind of social life. And this confirmed in us that thing called: family pride. We attributed the good we enjoyed, to our parents and to their ancestors on both sides; for we knew of no evil they had ever caused either to ourselves or any body else.

This my contentment, with all my surroundings, received a rude shock one morning in the Fall of 1820. I heard a shriek, and recognized my mother's voice in it. I rushed toward the room from whence it issued, and as I came to it, the door flew open, and out of it came my mother, pushed by my father, until she fell swooning to the ground, in the hall. I fell down beside her, weeping bitter tears. She soon recovered and looked intently around. Seeing me alone beside her, she embraced me: then said: "Forget! O forget! what you have seen!" I made no reply; for the chambermaid appeared and with her my mother reentered her room, leaving me alone in the hall. I went down stairs, and there met my father, who gave me a look, that I could neither interpret nor forget. I lost the sense of implicit obedience, to my father, then and there.

The request of my mother I could not comply with; for, instead of forgetting, I thought of the occurrence again and again, and in endless reflections, but never could arrive again at definite conclusions about my filial duties to my parents. The hired girl spread the incident among our relatives, and even strangers, and my aunts and uncles talked to me enjoining secrecy, as if their talk was not a violation of their own injunction. I felt my childhood gone as if by magic, indeed I was at a loss what to think and how to act. I was afraid to speak to my father, and turned away from my mother, for fear she would see my tears and weep herself.

In 1821 my mother began to have spells of illness, and they became more serious and frequent every month. The birth of my youngest sister Sophie in 1822 aggravated mother's disease; and we children realized now more and more, that we were not only losing a mother's care; but also a father's guardianship. The former daily walks with both our parents, with the highly instructive conversations, ceased gradually and our father's communicativeness diminished even faster than our mother's; our infantine society became evidently less attractive to father, as our mother was confined to her room, or was sent away to sanative establishments. The family ties were evidently being loosened, and, toward us, father became markedly reticent.

I had good instructions in the schools, and by special private teachers besides; but the education which a mother imparts, under a father's promptings, I was losing every day more, after 1821. I passed then, from the common, into the latin school, much too early, and without the finish, in German, which I should have had. My private teachers did their best to make up for my deficiencies; but while they supplied me with extra information and stimulated me in the special learning; they could not, or at least did not, give me that connected full training which I needed most under the circumstances. The latin schools of Heilbronn were then still under the old gymnasial system of the city, that existed in 1803. It had its five classes, Prima, Secunda, Tertia, Quarta, Quinta. In them were still the teachers, which the free city had; they taught upon obsolete methods. The punishments were largely a mixture of cruelty and farce. The school rooms were in the basement of the former convent called Santa Clara; they had neither good light nor air. I remember, as largely lost time, the 18 months I spent in Quinta. In the Fall of 1823 our mother died. As we children stood weeping around her deathbed, father said weeping to us: "You cannot know how great your loss is." I felt it to be the bitter consummation of a series of irreparable losses. Our family had been moved away from the old Carmelite Convent, to a new dwelling, that fronted on two streets called—translated into English—respectively: "the Great and Little Uprightmen's Street." The house had no side-yard nor garden. The dwelling part was roomy and excellent, but the rooms for business and play were very narrow as compared to our former home. I always believed that the removal to this house hastened my mother's death; and the funeral looked like a family break-up, and so it proved. We all met at the grave, and were never again all together until over a quarter of a century afterwards. My eldest sister Lina was taken the next day to our grandmother in Ludwigsburg, and my eldest brother went to Carlsruhe, in Baden, to an apprenticeship. We five younger ones kept looking around for somebody to be a mother to us, and we found it in our mother's eldest sister Nanny, whose husband kept, with her assistance, the first Hotel in Heilbronn.

We were an impulsive set. We were oftener to our aunt's establishment, than was pleasing to our father. He said: "You are acting like intruders." We had heard of disagreements between father and aunt, on account of her standing by my mother in the difficulties she had with him. Our aunt's wise discretion and firmness prevented the breaking out of serious discords with father, and in the course of time he acquiesed in adopting our dear aunt as our foster mother, to stand by us in all our troubles. I for one can say: that I ever felt in thus attaching myself to my aunt, that I had the direct sanction of my mother for it. Again and again I had, during my mother's life, seen that her sister Nanny was to her, in all her troubles, the person on whose advise she relied explicitly. Not to acknowledge her as my protectoress would have looked, as I thought, like a denial of affection to my dead mother. There were daily incidents, in which her interference smoothed over, bickerings with father, as fast as they arose. He found it indeed soon very proper, that we all should use aunt as our peacemaker and regulator; for to her we were all obedient.

But what she could not prevent was our discontent with everything about home as to household affairs. There were frequent changes of female servants. Father himself often took his meals at public houses. The contrast between the housekeeping of our mother and the hired servants, was too marked not to be noticed by us all. And the comparisons we could not help making, with the dozen of domicils of intimate relations, confirmed our dissatisfaction. On the whole there was a tendency to insufferable conditions.

For a while household affairs worked fairly well in the hands of the servants who had charge of them while my mother lived; but soon this ended in disorder and they were dismissed. Then special housekeepers were hired; but they failed in regular succession. I read the cause of these failures in a book that treated upon political economy as follows: "No housekeeping that has not the welfare of several generations in view can be a success." Fair conditions were, however, reached in our household by the appointment of the daughter of a french Hugenot clergyman as "*femme de menage*." At once, without regulation, we fared well in every respect, including the teaching of our lessons for school. We younger brothers said to each other: "mother has come back." On several Sundays she took us along to the village where her parents lived. There we were tested in our capacity to converse in French, and listened to her father's french sermons. The last time we were there, a scene took place which I must relate:

The King had forbidden further french service on the ground: that the whole congregation understood German, the language of the county, which was true. The minister complied; but, at the conclusion of the service an aged Frenchman arose and asked: "May I myself pray aloud in French?" The pastor answered: "I suppose so." Then the Frenchman spoke the Lord's Prayer in French aloud, and the congregation sung a hymn in French, and all then joyfully adjourned. We children repeated both, in French loudly with them. I sympathied with the French, and pitied the King, for giving such an illiberal order. Often this scene rose to my mind; when I heard folks insist in the United States on German immigrants using English exclusively, I have ever since believed, that tyranny in language is the meanest of tyrannies.

Causes unknown to us children brought the retirement of the young french lady. We regretted it deeply. I, as usual, went perplexed, to my dear aunt for explanation; and complained, while doing so, of my father's severe judgment on his servants. My aunt told me, that "it was improper in a son to criticise his father," and that she at least would not listen to me. I asked her: "whether my mother would not have listened to me?" She replied evasively: "No such case would then have occurred." I saw plainly, how much poorer an orphan is, than a child, whose mother is alive. After our French guide and instructor left us, we were for a while left to our own promptings as to conduct, and to our own relatives hospitality, for good eating. Soon after, in 1826, we heard that two of us —my brother Theodore and myself—would soon be sent to a boarding school, about twenty-five miles from Heilbronn, for our better education. We were glad of the news, but regretted the necessity.

CHAPTER III.

BROTHER AND MYSELF GET AMONG STRANGERS.

SOON after our mother's death, we noticed, that our father visited his own mother more frequently than he used to do previously, and he always took one or two of us children along. I learned soon, that to know my grandmother meant more than loving her; for she was a superior woman and inspired *reverence*. When I saw how meek my father was to her, and how firmly she gave him advice, it opened my eyes as to my home relation. I felt what an advantage a great female character is to a family, if she is capable of, and allowed to govern.

To her our father went, when our French governess left, and my wise grandmother discerned quickly, that taking us away from the parental roof and placing us in a boarding school under teachers, whom we would have to obey implicitly, would be the best way out of the awry situation we were in. She directed my father to a nephew of hers, Waechter by name, who was deacon in Marbach, (the birthplace of Schiller,) for finding such a school. And as luck would have it, there was then just such a school in that town, with an opening for two scholars like my younger brother and myself. And father at once entered us; for he saw the advantage it would be to us to learn under the supervision of so near a relative and distinguished a person. The name of the keeper of the boarding school was Richter. He was preceptor of the Gymnasium of the town, and to it and the messuage and the garden attached we had free access. There was enough conventuality about it all, to make me very willing to accept it as a sort of second-hand copy of my first domicile in Heilbronn. We were taken to it in the Fall of 1825 by our father, and we took readily to the preceptor with his blue eyes and blonde hair that were turning gray, and also his wife with her motherly appearance.

Deacon Waechter introduced us to the preceptor in the presence of our father. He made me blush on hearing some of his recommendations; they described us both as much more docile than we really were. And soon after father's departure we demonstrated this point; for we went right down to the river Neckar and there experimented with the miller's boat, until the fastenings broke, and we escaped an involuntary return journey down the river to Heilbronn, by jumping out and swimming ashore. Our utterly drenched condition told our mishap to the preceptor and his family. It informed them also of some of our capacities, that had not been mentioned before. They did not take them very seriously, but thought we should take our experience as a lesson.

Our cousin, the deacon, kept us from being reported to our father, and being otherwise punished for our infraction of the Sunday laws; but the fact that I was chiefly to blame, and had indeed seduced my younger brother into the scrape, settled the question in the preceptor's mind, what my father had spoken to him about; namely: whether I was fit to be a student of theology, and eventually a candidate for the ministry? He decided, soon after, that that was out of the question. So I was relieved from studying Hebrew and Greek, but was continued in French, and as I loved the language, I liked the change.

In Heilbronn, brother and I, had been thoroughly trained in gymnastics. In Marbach there was no such discipline in the schools, and we had to apply for leave to keep on, in our own physical acquirements, through some drill through good walking exercises and frequent swimming. We had proved, and kept on proving, our capacity in the latter particular, by bold exposures; and, though this gave us a bad name among the adults in Marbach, it gained us the respect of the younger generation.

There were with us, at Preceptor Richter's, several fellow students, who were sons of pastors in the neighboring villages. They invited us to visit them on Sunday, and when we did, their parents welcomed us heartily. There our manners were much improved through the good female society we met. The households of these clergymen were model households for us afterward through life.

Every other Sunday we were invited to our grandmother's at Ludwigsburgh. There we met our aunt, my father's sister. She resided with our grandmother, and had two sons and two daughters with her. Our aunt's husband "Lohbauer" had been captain in the army and a poet. Some of his poetry is still quoted. He was killed in battle, and his children were entitled to a gratuitous education in the respective public institutions. His widow enjoyed a pension besides. The eldest son had chosen a military education, the younger passed for the ministry. Both daughters had enjoyed instructions in the royal Art Schools, and were very proficient in music. Both sons and daughters were enthusiasts for the then great question: *Helenic Emancipation.* We, their younger cousins, caught the fervor, for the cause, from them. We knew a little less of what was really wanted for the Greeks, than they did. Neither of us knew much.

Our grandmother, with whom they lived, enjoyed the large fortune left by our grandfather. She had the title: "Frau Hofräthin". She too was imbued with the feeling for Grecian Independence and its leader "Ypsilanti". Among them I received my first introduction into modern politics and its liberties, or should I say: liberty?

This generally favorable development in studies, discipline and enjoyments received an unforeseen interruption in January, 1826, through the arrival of our father in Marbach. It was Saturday afternoon. Next morning he took us with him to Ludwigsburgh. We thought it to be a mere visit to grandmother. About half way to our destination we met two ladies, and I recognized in one of them my cousin. Pauline Lohbauer; the other I did not know. They got into the carriage with us. and as soon as seated, father introduced the strange lady as our "future mother". Brother Theodore received her tender embraces quietly, but affectionately. I averted my face, turned round, as if I meant to jump out of the carriage. My father held me down, but could get out of me neither a friendly word, nor a kind gesture. And thus repulsively I acted all day. Grandmother alone could get me to speak out frankly; but what I said: was but an expression of my wish, to be allowed, to return to Marbach. It was granted, and I ran the five miles back to Marbach without dinner, and there locked myself in my room.

I have ever since regretted this my conduct. It was both foolish and improper; but I could no more help it then, than I could have helped from crying out, if I had been beaten with a cane. My behavior annoyed my father sorely. It was to him an unpardonable impropriety; and I doubt if my father ever fully forgave me for it.

It seems my father meant to tell me that day how he had arranged it with grandmother: that my eldest brother and myself, with the intended husband of my eldest sister, should be taken into father's business as full partners as soon as we should, respectively, arrive at the proper age and be otherwise qualified. I was, with this understanding, to be placed one year into the upper gymnasium in Heilbronn, and then in 1828 to be apprenticed in my father's business. Of all this I heard a week after, only of that part —the upper gymnasium. I accepted it with pleasure, as it coincided with my own purposes, as will be explained hereafter.

I attended with brother Theodore, on father's special invitation, the wedding. Step-mother embraced us both tenderly. It was for us a strange situation; but I had become master of my feelings, and concealed my repugnance. That sharp inner conflict between the memories of my mother and the present sight of my step-mother, no longer existed.

I had ceased to regard the second marriage of my father as a sacrilege. In short, I had reasoned out the distinction between religious and social morality, and had come to the conclusion: that the ideal single-hearted love of the first wife was not incompatible with the faith that is pledged to a second wife at re-marriage, But nevertheless I could not avoid feeling my own mother and myself as wronged by the second marriage. I regarded my mother as defrauded, and I held myself for months as an utterly unhappy being. The head may *reason*, but the heart will *feel*. Each has its rights.

CHAPTER IV.

MY RETURN TO HEILBRONN FOR EDUCATION.

IN the summer of 1827 my father recalled me to Heilbronn and placed me into the higher grades of instruction. And he himself took an active part in my education, both by conversation during walks, and reading with me at home. My father really did at that time too much toward my instruction. He supplemented himself the excellent tuition I got in the gymnasium, and then added besides: private teachers. One of these, a Jew, gave me lessons in history and geography combined on the idea which Professor Bryse in Cambridge has lately recommended. The other, also a Jew, instructed me in double-entry book-keeping, combined with political economy. He added, unbeknown to my father, practical lessons on financial plans for State Lotteries. I called them "slippery finances."

In the winter of 1826—1827, and again in 1827—1828 there was added, according to law, religious instruction to prepare me for confirmation. This instruction was by a regular Lutheran Clergyman – Dentzel. As in Marbach, so now in Heilbronn, we had to attend church on Sunday during morning service, and several days in the week we were taught in the catechism. My private teachers gave me also their religious views. And besides we had morning and evening family readings of prayers from Witschel's prayerbook, father being the leader. I got thus religious instruction in three-fold form besides philosophy in the gymnasium. At the instruction, by the clergyman, young ladies were present; and this awakened among us young gents, sentiments of love, that were not in the catechism, though they were in the bible. My love went toward the burgomaster's daughter, Bruckman was her name. It was never declared to her outright by me, but I gave her many significant signs from a distance, and I think she understood them, from signs she gave to me in return. Our love was certainly pure, so far as abstinence from personal contact went. And our religion was liberal; for its orthodoxy was well mixed with free thought and liberal sentiment. Our religious teacher had been instructor of the Queen of Westphalia, who was the wife of Jerome Bonaparte. I have warm recollections of all my public teachers of that time, including Rector Tscherning, with his readings of Homer's Iliad. I remember still more vividly Conrector Roth and his lessons on history and classics generally. Very useful to me were Professor Dörners explanations of Greek literature. Most interesting were Professor Kiessling's chemical experiments. And best of

all were Professor Kapff's lectures on phylosophy, though his mode
of speech was very hard.

It may be well to add here: that my grandmother made me a
present of that fine religious work by Tschokke: "Hours of Devotion." It wandered into my father's library, where I left it, when,
in 1832, I went to America. I recovered it afterwards in 1843, and
brought it, without asking leave, to this country, where it is now in
my library. I have there also a copy of our family prayer-book. I
keep there also the bible in Latin, English and French, as I brought
them from Germany. I regard them as the anchors of my religion.
I mention this for no other purpose, except to state facts, that are a
part of my history, and necessary to its understanding.

I read at that time also books of a very different kind and tenor;
for instance: the cheap editions of Walter Scott's novels, translated
into German; also Rousseau's and Voltaire's writings. Most pleased
was I with Fenelon's works. My father had several large atlasses
and historic works. I accompanied my father day by day to his
garden and vineyards, and there imbibed, beside a zest for literature,
the love for grape culture, which years afterwards made me an
amateur vinedresser and author on grape culture.

In the winter of 1828, my father met with a severe mishap by
being thrown out of his carriage, on his return from a visit to his
mother in her mortal illness. His left arm was broken and he was
for weeks confined to his room. He never saw his mother again
alive; could not even attend her funeral. He made me at that time
his constant attendant, and showed me much affection. We became
intimate under entirely new relations. He would even mention to
me my mother, as if he wanted to reinstate her between us, and
himself with me. He read with me, or rather, he made me read to
him, history and geography, and conversed with me on political
economy, all in an advanced spirit, which surprised me. I found that
he had imbibed his taste for literature while clerk at Basle, Switzerland, in a banking house. His mother's death no doubt rekindled
in him memories of former affectionate ties. I was but too happy
to be the recipient of these, and of the ripe politico-economic counsels
he gave me. Then was it that I imbibed, what some would call:
free-trade ideas. In fact, I was learning: how much mischief is
caused by false government, and incompetent administration. My
aspirations then were to finish my studies in Heilbronn, and then
go to higher schools and be a scholar forever.

CHAPTER V.

DREAMS TURNED INTO SHARP REALITIES.

IN the Fall of 1828 this leisurely course of my life was rudely interrupted, and a life forced on me of a very different nature.
The death of grandmother brought to father a large inheritance in

cash. He could now, for the first time, do business without paying heavy interest to bankers; and he extended his trade. That made an opening for an additional clerk. This enabled my father to promote an apprentice, he had, to a higher place. To the situation thus vacated—the lowest apprenticeship—he ordered me; and that meant copying letters, running errands, and doing light work. I had to do this according to the then prevailing custom: that business employees must enter at 14 years of age into the lowest place, gradually rise through merit, and serve at least four years before they got into the higher positions, such as book-keeper. This involved, my being taken out of the upper gymnasium. at a time, when I had but one more year to attend to secure my promotion to a college course. I felt, my being made an apprentice in the grocery business, to be a degradation, and a denial to me of a literary career, that included the espousal of a profession. I begged my father on my knees to let me go on with my studies, but he flatly refused. He hinted at my past conduct, as having precluded myself therefrom. He told me that he knew better than I, what was best for me, and that I had to submit. All he conceded, was, to let me continue to take my lessons with my private teachers, the Jews. He promised also to continue our joint readings, and did it; but it was not the reading of a student, is was light literature chiefly. I had to go into the counting room, copy letters, help pack goods, get the mail and dispatch business generally. I looked on myself as *degraded*. My father regarded me as promoted. I suspected in all this a stepmother's improper interference; while she told me, that by my opposition I stood in my own light. I held myself a doomed individual; thought, that my schoolmates derided me. Most of them entered into the very career I had desired, and were successful in it. They looked on me as a failure. I had to seek my comrades now among youth in business, and make them my confidents of the desperate plans that were now addling my brains. I could not consult my mother's relatives, because they would, being business people, have looked. upon my objections to being an apprentice, as contempt for a business occupation. They would not have understood my complaint: that I had been taken away from the literary career. which I had a right to expect.

How often have I since seen, that my stepmother meant well with me and judged truer than myself. But I could not arrive at any such conclusions at that time; nor would, I think, anybody else, in my situation, then have done so. The situation was certainly unsatisfactory to me, and it did not take long to make it disagreeable to my father and the rest in the counting room. I was, as stated. still taking lessons from private teachers, early in the morning. On my way to them I had to pass the place of departure, on the river Neckar, of emigrants to America. Seeing them, it suggested to me as a remedy for my troubles to emigrate also. I recollected then, that a cousin of mine, Eberhardt Plank, son of my mother's deceased sister, in Augsburg, had emigrated five years previous to America under similar circumstances, and had done well there. All my comrades applauded my purpose, and the clerk, in my father's counting room, asked to be allowed to join me whenever I went. But when I applied to my father he refused to furnish money for the journey, and declared my object to be a wild idea, which he could not sanction.

I had learned from my eldest sister, that we children of the first wife had by law a fixed portion secured to us as our inheritance of the wealth our mother brought to father at marriage. She also told me, that as to this inheritance the full amount had not been reported to the law officers. The amount of the inheritance was said to be equal to about five hundred dollars ($500.00), enough anyway to pay my way to America.

I took courage in the Fall of 1829 to ask my father to let me have enough out of this my inheritance, and to let me go to America. He admitted that there was such an inheritance, but that it was payable only at his will, or after his death. He thought it was mean in us children to talk about such matters, especially when, as in my case, we were only 15 years old. He notified me also, that if I persisted in my refractory course and continued to cast reflections on his integrity. I would hear of something that would make me regret forever of having annoyed him. Under the circumstances I concluded to appeal to my aunt. When I told her, what my father had said, she asked me: whether I had to fear any disclosure of any great wrong I had done? On my answering: no! she turned to me and said: "Do not irritate your father; but do not fear any disclosures. I know what they are about. But I know also, that they are untrue. If your father again threatens you, then tell him; that you have spoken to me, and that I want him to come to me with his old stories; and that from me he will hear the truth." What all this meant, was a marvel to me. I wanted to ask her for more explanation, and yet something within me forbid me. My aunt begun speaking in tears; next she took my head between her hands, and looked squarely into my face. Then she burst out laughing, and cried: "How absurd! There! What a tell-tale Rümelin face! Go! Go! Send your father to me!"

Several weeks afterwards my father had me called to appear before the family council. I knew, that a severe trial awaited me; but was not afraid after the interview with my aunt. I went there determined to be firm, but respectful to my father, under all circumstances. I had hardly got into the room, when I noticed besides my father, my stepmother was present. He announced: "That he had me called for the purpose of hearing the final conclusion he had come to as to my future." He said this in so threatening a way, that I felt bound to speak out at once and bring on the crisis. I told him, that I had seen my aunt, and that she had bid me to tell him, that he ought to see her before proceeding to extremities, as she would inform him of the truth in the whole matter. My father was struck dumb by my remarks, and looked as if about going into a swoon. He kept, however, waving his hands at me, as if bidding me to leave the room. My stepmother came up and whispered in my ear, "that I had better go away and she would pacify father, and all would be right."

I called on my aunt the next afternoon; she informed me, that my father had been to see her already, and there would be no further trouble with me. She begged me to have patience, as measures were in progress, that would be satisfactory to me. She would not disclose their nature. I asked her to assist me in my intended emigration to America; as I was sure my mother would if alive. When I mentioned my mother, my aunt wept profusely, and I went away. My aunt shouted after me: "O, that your mother could see you."

Soon afterwards a shipper who had heard of my desire to go America, offered to take me, as a deck hand, to Amsterdam, and secure me a passage to Philadelphia, for a very small sum. And I accepted his offer, feeling sure to get the small amount in time in some way. I communicated the offer to the clerk in my father's counting room, and consulted him on the subject. He at once advised the acceptance of it, and said: "The sum required is so small and the plan so feasible, that you need not trouble yourself, as I myself have means enough for both of us." I had, however, some money in my saving's box, and a small sum fell into my hands from business transactions, which I felt myself entitled to use as part payment of what was due to me from my mother's inheritance. I did not like anyway to be dependent on others for such outlays. On the night of May 14th, 1830, we left Heilbronn, with the understanding, that we were to join the shipper in his boat at Mannheim. Our conveyance was a slow one. We reached Heidelberg next day only at noon. There we were retained unexpectedly by one of the horses becoming sick. So we were overtaken at a village between Heidelberg and Mannheim, and were taken back to Heilbronn the same evening, as captured fugitives, that deserved punishment.

CHAPTER VI.

INSTEAD OF, TO A NEW COUNTRY, I GET INTO A NEW BUSINESS.

I was taken to my father's room. My companion, the clerk, was turned adrift. He went to Mannheim and the shipper took him to Amsterdam, there he fell into the hands of the recruiting marine officers of Holland, and was taken to East India. I never heard, what became of him there.

My arrival in Heilbronn was an eye-opener all-around, as to the false course that had been pursued by us all. When I was brought before my father, he asked me in a dispairing tone: "What in the name of God shall I do with you?" I answered: "That I had come back to submit to his decision, whatever it might be." I begged him, however, to let me leave Heilbronn. For two months I was left unemployed. I was, however, allowed to take private lessons with my teachers, and thus took up again my former studies. This my return to literature reconciled me to my defeated wild attempt at emigration.

In July I was told, that a new most promising career was open to me; namely: my entry, as a cadet, into the Beet Sugar factory about to be established, under the auspices of the King, in a place called Denkendorf (Thinking Village). I accepted the proposition heartily, but thought, that my father's wishes were the main cause of its being made. I found out that I got the place with the understanding that my father would join in a company to carry on beet sugar making, if the experiment in Denkendorf should prove a success. I was to qualify myself at once in chemistry, so as to pass the examination for the Cadetship. I passed the examination with honor. I left home with a sincere determination to learn the manufacture, but believed quietly that a better solution would have been, to have let me go unhindered to America.

When I bid my aunt farewell, and stated this my belief, she cried: "What! Still thinking of America." I asked: "Why not? Am I not going to Denkendorf (Thinking Village), and why not think there of the country, to which I am destined at last?" I added: "Denkendorf is but the round-about way for me to America.

My father took me to Denkendorf. On the way he told me for the first time: that he and his deceased brother Charles, after whom I was called, had been in the place forty years previous as students of Theology at the, then, Royal Academy. On arrival we found a room in which they had lodged, and there, on one of the window panes, both brother's names were still as they had scratched them in with a firestone. He regarded this as a good omen, and then told me, as far as he knew it, the history of the locality. It seems: that five centuries before, a large congregation of Cistercian monks occupied the convent, and enjoyed its many comforts and conveniences; especially the fine lake with its water power near by it. In the middle of the eigtheenth century the convent was converted into a Lutheran Theological Seminary, and my father and uncle entered it as students. My father gave up his studies on account of ill-health, and became a merchant. As I listened to my father's narrative, the thought struck me: what a part old convents played in both our lives. He was born in one in Maulbronn, and so was I in one in Heilbronn. He was taken to one for educational purposes, so was I.

Whatever this was? call it: coincidence or fate! It confirmed in me historical inquiries and a habit to reason on events and their logic.

Father arranged for my board and lodging with the parson of Denkendorf and his lady. The parsonage stood very near the factory. I soon let them know, if my father did not, that they were not entertaining an angel unawares; but a youth, that was rather worldly minded.

I itched, to ask my father during the journey to Denkendorf, or as he departed for his return to Heilbronn, for some explanation of the former still unexplained matters, but failed to do so. Why? I could not tell. So too could I never press my aunt for a further statement. I concluded to drop the matter, and so it has remained to this day in the main.

The clergyman volunteered to teach me further in the classics, and he did. His good lady promised to take good care of me by furnishing good board; and she kept her word. I can say, in truth, that I was an apt recipient of the favors of both. The reverend gentleman's teaching in Latin, geography and history, revived in me the instruction I had received in my youth. He found me deficient in mathematics, and so left me. His good lady bore testimony to my good appetite for all that she, and her maid, cooked for us. I certainly stood well in her graces, if not in those of her husband.

I staid in Denkendorf one year and a half. The most useful instructor, I had, was the chemist of the beet-sugar factory, Mr. Waldbauer. He strengthened me in the natural sciences, and enjoyed my zeal for that kind of knowledge. Very useful was to me a Mr. Spring, the chief manager of the business of the factory. He had been long the head of a silk establishment in Lyons, France, and had grown rich there. He expected to become a large stock-holder in the contemplated beet-sugar factory. On the royal domain, connected with Denkendorf, was a royal forrester with the name of Vischer. My grandfather's first wife's name was Vischer, it did not take my father long to make out the relationship. The forrester had a son of my age, I became his companion and learned of him matters, which my father would hardly have approved, if he had known of them. When my father left on Sunday evening, he doubtless believed me fully surrounded with good influences, and left me to myself, as he gave me very few instructions or injunctions. I thought myself for the first time entirely free. The good parson and his wife took evening walks with me and their son. The latter treated me as an elder brother, and we both enjoyed each other. He was my first application of the doctrine of affinities; both in the chemical and social sense. Goethe meant it by the word: "Wahlverwandtschaften." In our age it goes by the name of hypnotism. I met my young friend fifty years afterwards, as cashier in a railroad office. He recollected me, but his affinities were changed.

More and more my sense of independence grew; but also my sense of responsibility. The chemist, the supervising engineer, and the chief manager, trusted me as fast, indeed a little faster, than I acquired capacities. I was seldom blamed and often commended, which was the reverse of what had been the way with me at home. The king visited occasionally the factory, and he too was told of the advances, we volunteers, made in the business. He was pleased with us, sought explanations from us, and let us very clearly understand, that he came, like ourselves, to learn.

We took up the work from the storing of the beets, to the grinding, pressing, boiling and the evaporating of the sap, including the chemical treatment, seriatim. It took us several months, before we obtained presentible sugar. It was not refined sugar; but of the kind called "brown sugar" here. Being the first sugar made of beets in Württemberg in large quantities, its defects were overlooked, while its virtues were overpraised. The first specimens were, of course, sent to the king's table, and received undeserved praise.

But in spite, perhaps in consequence, of the sample we sent, the conception grew apace: that, while it was a wise act in the king, to give a part of his royal estate for *starting* the manufacture of beet-sugar, it would be neither prudent nor practical, for an individual or a company, to undertake it as a business, with no more data to go on, than our experiment had brought out. We could not get out of a hundred pounds of beets, more than five or six pounds of brown sugar; and the molasses and other offals had then very little value. By the middle of winter, 1831. it became very evident, that the starting of beet-sugar making, had to have a very different basis from that then in vogue in Denkendorf. There had to be more chemical knowledge and better technical capacity. This perception at once decided an elderly gentleman, who had come there like myself, to learn the business; but behaved very mysteriously to me, to quit. Before he left he acquainted me, for the first time, with the plans upon which he had come there. It was: that he hoped to win my sister Lina, and then to start a beet-sugar factory in partnership with me. I told him, that, in my opinion, Lina would rather marry him, without the beet-sugar factory and partnership, than with it. He asked: "Why did not your father tell me so." As I knew no more of the plan than he told me, I could not tell him. I found out afterwards that my sister had never been consulted, and became aware, that both she and myself were waifs in our father's speculative propensities. The disappointed candidate for my sister's hand—plus a beet-sugar factory—left Denkendorf abruptly, without bidding me farewell. I remained, gladly, until late in the Spring, and learned all about beet-sugar and starch-sugar. Often we visited the Royal Agricultural Academy, three miles off, and gained much practical information. In July I returned to Heilbronn, and helped in my father's grocery business, until an opportunity would offer for a clerkship. My father took very kindly to me, and treated me more as if I were to be my own master. He often questioned me on matters in Denkendorf. And once he even hinted, that he had changed his mind about my going to America. His own memories of Denkendorf had made him more lenient to me.

CHAPTER VII.

I BECOME A MERCHANT'S CLERK ON SALARY.

I found out, on a visit to Stuttgartt, to whom I was indebted for this change; namely: to Mr. Spring, our chief manager in Denkendorf. He told me himself, that he had written a letter to my father, in June, 1831, to this effect:

"Your son has learned to make beet- as well as starch-sugar; and has generally increased his knowledge in the natural sciences. His technical capacities are also considerably better. He understands the subjects of "fermentation and evaporation." He has a practical insight into mechanical forces, and knows much about the construction of fire places for heating purposes. He needed, when he came to us, free social intercourse with persons of mature experience, who would treat him as their equal, or at least as one, that is not to be hectored like a pupil. I made him my friend by being to him "frere ainee." Give him the best position in your business, he will be equal to it. And if you can't do that, send him out to see the world. Place him in a large commercial house, even if he gets no salary."

My father did not follow this advice fully, but he carried it out enough to send me away from Heilbronn, and out of Württemberg; but only to Wimpfen, six miles from Heilbronn, on the river Neckar. It is a separate possession of Hesse-Darmstadt, with about 5,000 inhabitants. The town is surrounded by Württemberg and Baden. There my father had an old merchant friend by the name of Langer, and with him, he got me a place as clerk, in a wholesale and retail grocery store, at $60.00 a year, with boarding and lodging. In connection with the regular grocery business, he carried on an oil mill and a snuff factory. The main trade in the grocery line, was: selling groceries to smugglers across the frontiers. These neighboring states levied about three times as high duties as Hessen did. A smuggler could make $2.00 a night by carrying sixty pounds, on his back, over the frontiers. This was high compensation for them.

Mr. Langer's business was really on all points a good one, and any branch of it was sure, in a life time, to yield a fortune; but all four branches together were, as everybody told me, before I came a gold mine. I took it for granted, that this was so as to Mr. Lar but I asked, what will it be to me? I tried to get some information from the clerk, whom I superceded, but failed; and nothing was left to me, except either to decline, or come at very low wages. I chose the latter, and found that the place was, though it payed me poorly, otherwise pleasant enough. I succeeded in pleasing both, Mr. and Mrs. Langer, by getting up a set of double-entry books, with a balance sheet each month. They had had nothing, like that, before.

The retail business perplexed me, because several important articles were unknown to me. But Mrs. Langer was indefatigable in teaching me, and soon I was declared to be a good retail grocer. The custom increased, if not much, at least some, under my hands. The oil mill I liked as means for getting knowledge in mechanics, which I was glad to acquire, and so it was in the snuff factory. My knowledge in chemistry was considerably amplified, and so was my knowledge of a variety of idle tastes, adult men and women have. In spite of myself I got a taste for snuffing, and it stuck to me long afterward in America, when, by actual weight, I snuffed one pound a month. The smuggling trade, my part being only to sell to smugglers, did not trouble me by any compunction of conscience. I was a free trader, and held firmly to the principle, that any and all antagonisms are fair against a government, that levies an exorbitant tariff on imports or exports. To be sure, it was not pleasant to get into antagonisms with my own State, even indirectly, but I got over that, by remembering, that my State lost nothing by any goods I sold to smugglers, which really it had a right to take. And as I now think of this matter, it is a consolation to me, to know, that my State reduced within two years afterwards its exorbitant duties, and thus broke up further smuggling. I certainly loved it more as a free country.

It was the government that taxed too high, that was wrong, not the smugglers. I learned at Wimpfen how general a practice smuggling was then. Even the best reputed commercial houses bought smuggled goods, if they did not smuggle directly. I had adopted the rule, from my private teachers in political economy, that this disproportionate taxation was *per se* dishonest; that the censure for smuggling should fall on the dishonestly taxing government. This conviction was strongest as to articles of necessity such as salt. Moreover: had not my father procured me this my place? Did he not know, that it meant my participation in the very business of smuggling? The reader sees, how fallaciously I then argued!

What was less clear in my mind, was the issue: whether we were justified in bribing customs guards and thus facilitate smuggling? As I was often in my native town, I asked myself: could the authorities dare prosecute me as accessory? I was told, by good the lawyers, that no such prosecution could be instituted, since I acted as clerk in a town, outside of the jurisdiction of Württemberg, and payed no money out myself, nor smuggled personally.

Thus, in many ways, I found myself moving in anomalous circles. Wimpfen had better and cheaper goods, food, wines, etc., and it was the resort of pleasure for the whole surrounding country, and strange folks of all kinds gathered there. All life and intercourse was freer. And this showed itself most at fairs, markets and balls. For instance, it happened to me one afternoon, that an old gypsy woman approached me with her daughter and offered to tell my fortune. I carelessly held out my hand, and was told: "You are a charmed person (gefeite Person). All that injure you, will be unfortunate." At this I wanted to withdraw my hand; but she said: "Stop, hear the balance: Beware of those whom you aid thoughtlessly and help undeservedly. They will prove your bitter foes. You will cross the ocean several times. Don't use the same ship twice." She let my hand go and held out hers. I gave her a gratuity, and she disappeared. Her prophecy has often plagued me, and prevented me from being charitable, because I experienced many times ingratitude from just such folks as she warned me against. I never learned the real truth in her prophecy, until late in life I read in the "Choice Sayings" of Publius Syrus the adage : "Thoughtless charity breeds ungrateful people." I was also forcibly reminded of this prophecy, when reading in Italy on a college wall the inscription: "Do not think to win the love of others, by rendering them service. You only acquire their envy." I now saw, that the gypsies are not really prophets, that read our destiny from our hands. They but utter from memory traditional wisdom, which they learn from their wise women.

The first effect of the prophecy on me was, that it reminded me of America, and I strongly thought of it, in the early part of Winter 1832, by several circumstances. My salary was really inadequate to my wants. I thought I needed finer clothes than I had brought from home. I had not enough money to buy them. A Jew suggested to me, selling him the old ones and have new ones made, by adding my money. Mr. Langer did not like my trading with the Jew, and said so. That was my first disagreement with him; I could not see, why Mr. L. should meddle in my personal affairs. And still less, why, on my giving him the true explanation, he did not offer me an increased salary ? At that time some Württemberg merchants, that bought smuggled goods, stated to Mr. L., that they thought it unfair to them, to have me, a son of their rival in business, in his store, and thus be made acquainted with their purchases. They threatened to withdraw their custom, unless I was discharged. It needed but a slight provocation to make us fly apart, and this happened early in 1832.

CHAPTER VIII.

AT LAST I GO TO AMERICA.

January, 1832, my father requested me, to spend my Sundays in Heilbronn, and to make out for him the final account, he had to render as guardian of a certain "Rund." This, his ward, was an illegitimate child, born from a Heilbronn damsel, that had too intimate connection with a Russian officer, when the Russian Army passed through Heilbronn in 1813. Amongst the papers submitted to my inspection was a book with the title: "Report of a Journey to the Western States of North America, by Godfrey Duden." It had induced "Rund" to emigrate to Missouri. He had done well. Why not I? I bought me a copy of the book, and have it laying by me, as I write. Rund's letters from America were also among the papers submitted to me, and they corroborated Duden's book. Indeed, I have ever found it to be a reliable guide as to America. It revived and intensified my longings for America. I told my father of the ill feelings, that were gathering around me at Wimpfen, and how my stay became more and more uncertain. After I had made out the account, I handed it to my father, who paid me well for it. Then I told him, that I was more than ever determined to go to the United States. He opposed it, but less peremptory than formerly. I persisted, and finally he yielded on condition, that I should repeat my determination before all the members of the family; and upon an allowance of 500 guilders, and an out-fit, relinquish all further claim for support during my father's life. I did so, and he gave his consent with his blessing.

This blessing he wrote out, and handed me the paper now laying by me. It contains first an account of the money he furnished me, as follows:

50	Prussian Thalers, @ Guilder			1¾	fl.	87.30
12	Five Frank	"	"	2.20	"	28.00
22	Holland Ducats,	"	"	5.87	"	123.34
2	Holland gold pieces,	"		10 00	"	20.00
8	Napoleon D'or,	"		9 30	"	76.00
10	New Louis D'or	"		11.09	"	111.30
9	Kremnitz Ducats	"		5.36	"	50.24
					fl.	496.58
				Change		3.02
				Total	fl.	500.00

Under this account he wrote:

"To my dear Gustav, for emigrating to America, with my heartfelt wishes for his welfare in this life and eternity. May the omnipotent, all good God, take him under his gracious protection, and be with him with his blessings.

I recommend to my dear Gustav, daily prayer, in the morning, on getting up, and ask him as high as I can ask him, to have God in his eye and heart. May he consider, that God only can help, advise and protect; that all good acts have good consequences, all bad deeds bad consequences. I shall not see thee any more in this world; but I shall pray for you in eternity, joined with thy blessed mother, that has long ago preceded me.

BENJAMIN."

This paper, in his own peculiar hand-writing, has gone with me since, wherever I have been. I have it now. I showed it to my aunt, and she shed tears of joy on this recognition of the righteousness of her aid to me in my troubles with my father. I then asked her, to tell me, what the old story was about, with which father had threatened me. She declined, and then added: "All is well that ends well. Keep this paper with his blessing. It is all you need." I followed her advice. I afterwards obtained, without asking for it, a full explanation through my brother Edward, and then understood, that my father wrote that last paper for the purpose of causing a mutual oblivion of the many disagreeable episodes in our intercourse. He never expected to see me again, as he states in the paper, and he apprehended, that I would have to pass through much trouble in America. So he took extra pains to place me in good condition before starting. He really overdid his care, and I had to learn, before I finally wept a good-bye to him, that there is such a thing as parental love, that over-does things. It is the one, that forgets the rule: "Let well enough alone."

Wherever my father would hear of an emigrant, he brought me to him, to take counsel with him, and to see, whether he could not give me some information. In nine cases out of ten we found, that I knew more of America, than they did. To be sure, it was not much; but it came from more reliable sources. Finally my father thought, he had found the right way for my safety. It was: to make me a member of an Emigrant Society, started under semi-official patronage. I was taken before one of their meetings, and was cordially received. My father, however, now shrunk from a final consummation; because it would have entangled me with the society's plan more, than he desired. He did not want to place the whole 500 Guilders into the general purse. *Neither did I.* So we traveled back to Heilbronn. My father had, however, become acquainted with a tailor, named Gremminger, who was about to emigrate to the United States; and he had, somehow, made my father believe, that he had made very practical arrangements for getting to Philadelphia cheaply and safely. So it was agreed, that I should be let in under the same arrangements, and accordingly my passage money, fl. 75:00, from Heilbronn by Emigrant boat down the Neckar and Rhine, to Amsterdam, and by sea to Philadelphia, was paid. All the rest of my money except about 50 Guilders for pocket money, was to go to Gremminger, who was to board and otherwise care for me on the voyage, and account to me finally in Philadelphia. I was amazed at the blindness of my good father; but had to submit or to throw up the sponge. Under Gremminger's advice and according to his list, a whole lot of things were now bought, and were gradually put into a large iron-bound trunk. There were in it shirts, drawers, stockings, flannels, boots, shoes, coats, vests, pants, etc., enough to last me for a quarter of a century. Strength was their main recommendation. Besides the trunk, there was prepared for me: bedding, including a fine hair mattress, feather pillows and quilts, also Russian blankets and linen sheets of any kind and number to go to house-keeping. I had to carry besides, a fine gun and a leather hunting pouch to hang around my shoulders, filled with combs, brushes, knives and forks, towels, and other things, too numerous to mention. Thus fully acquipped according to Gremminger's rule, I had at last the satisfaction, to hear my father say, that nothing more was wanted; and that my outfit was complete.

Left now to ourselves, that is to say, my father and I being alone, I was informed, that my pass-port had been arranged without Gremminger's knowledge for special reasons. And they handed me a general traveling pass-port for six months, such as traveling clerks for commercial houses get. I should have had a pass-port *with leave to emigrate.* So I expostulated; but was told, that an emigrant pass-port could not be obtained for me, as I was subject to military enrollment. I was assured, that letters of recommendation to merchants, all along the route, including Amsterdam, would be given to me, and that they would relieve me, if I got into any trouble; so I acquiesced.

CHAPTER IX.

MY JOURNEY TO HOLLAND.

MY final departure took place April 27, 1832. Seven sloops, each containing about fifty emigrants, left the wharf. Thousands of friends and relations were there to bid us good-bye. My relations, especially on my mother's side, thronged the Neckar's front. They took my going as a final adieu. Emigration was then taken to be a sort of penance, and many a pitying tear was wept for me, "the unfortunate Römelin," and again and again I was told: "This would not have happened, if your mother had been alive." Father was not there to hear these left-handed compliments. He had broken down in a flood of tears after he had blessed me, and said his last farewell. Step-mother, also weeping, had to lead him away, when I crossed the threshold of my paternal roof, and stepped out into the wide world, accompanied only by my eldest sister. None of my brothers were then at home. As I mingled with other emigrants, I saw plainly, that, being made their equal, took me down a peg or two in the social scale. I felt this sharply, when the hired girl, who had nursed me in my cradle, fell over my shoulder crying: "Had it to be? Bear up! Bear up! Your mother is with you after all!" As her tears fell upon my hand, they felt like mother's tears. It made me almost light-hearted, that she should have come in her old age, and see me off. Two other leave-takings affected me very differently; namely: those from two women, that were passengers in another boat from ours, but were also bound to America. They had been servants in our house while my mother lived, they were liked by her, but left, under a cloud, after her death. They pressed forward toward me with great animation, then cast down their eyes and simply wished me a happy journey and joined their boat. We never met again. Many of my school-mates flocked around me, and greeted me warmly. They accompanied me to a special farewell meeting with my teachers, and there joint adieus, most grateful to my feelings were said.

As we floated down the river, I bid farewell to one after another of the scenes, that were so familiar to me. I now realized: that my departure meant, that I was now a cut off limb of a very numerous family, and that I need not look hereafter to it for aid or support. This consciousness of all my steps to myself, weighed heavy on my mind; but nothing daunted. I remained firm to my purpose to emigrate. I passed Wimpfen without a regret for leaving it behind. I thought my going to Wimpfen, as a clerk, was after all a mistake. I took with me knowledge, that steps had been taken, to establish the Zoll-Verein, and that smuggling had ended forever from Wimpfen, and I rejoiced at this.

When I awoke the next morning, I realized, for the first time, that every hour was taking me further from home, and that I became more an alien to all around me. And yet, an inner voice told me, as I passed Heidelberg, Mannheim, Mayence, Coblentz, Cologne, that going abroad, and gaining knowledge of the world, was following a correct impulse, and that I need not give up a particle of my patriotism in becoming cosmopolitan in my principles. What perplexed me most, was the social promiscuousness of my fellow passengers. Very few were well born, and fewer still well educated. In all, there was something, that interferred with their being a steady, conformable member of any strict society. And yet most of them were obtrusive with their claims for universal equality. They got angry, whenever any one declined, to associate with them. They were bitterly opposed to paying any deference to any one. Some were doubtful characters, and they were most tenacious, for receiving equal respect from all. One I knew from Marbach. He was a well-to-do miller there, when I knew him. Misfortune overtook him, his wife died, and he failed in business. On our boat he acted as if he were rich. He had a woman with him, whom he claimed to be his wife. I made up my mind, to treat him as a casual acquaintance; but he determined to claim me as an old acquaintance, and gave me much trouble on the whole journey. Another annoyed me even more. He had been a day laborer in the beet-sugar factory in Denkendorf, and then I had to reprimand him for negligence. On the boat he took extra pains to let everybody know, that he owed me no deference. As I had never claimed any of him, his insolence was very offensive to me. The reader will see, that it was as difficult to keep one's proper distance, as to be duly intimate. I thank my stars to-day, that I succeeded in avoiding all quarrels, as well as all close intimacies. My getting to rights was much aggravated by the subordinate relation, which Gremminger wanted to assign to me, as to himself. He would order me, to bring to the boat, purchases he had made for our meals; and he assumed the right, to direct me generally, which I was just as determined, not to yield to him, I was much aided, in my resistance, by the shippers, who knew my father, as a merchant. They came to me for advice, in business matters, and would, in case of trouble, ask me to go with them to merchants, to whom I had letters, for aid and advice. They backed me up, and defeated Gremminger's attempt to play the master over me.

My journey, down the Rhine, was to me, on the whole, a most agreeable passage. I had made it before, but the peculiar surroundings, under which I was making it then, assisted me to see the countries and the people better than before. I felt every step to be an advance in knowledge and correct behavior. The richer food, the better wines and greater comforts, we met everywhere and shared in, were all so many encouragements, to go further and further into the wide world. We were treated, everywhere, as future Americans. Some of our passengers got involved with the public authorities, for using their firearms too freely; but on explanation, all passed off, without serious trouble. As we had no paupers among us, we were well treated everywhere.

I have already referred to the irregularity of my passport. On the journey I ascertained, that there was another passenger in the same predicament. As we approached Arnheim, the town at which our boat left the Rhine, and went thenceforth, by canal, to Amsterdam, we were advised, by the officers of our boat, to get out, two miles above the town, and to walk on foot to Arnheim, where we might go to a hotel, and wait for our boat, and then go to it next day. The reason for all this, was: that Holland had passed a law: requiring every one, entering Holland, to give security, that he would not become a public charge. This had been done for all the passengers, except us two. The purpose of our disembarking was, therefore, that we should not enter Holland as emigrants, but as travellers. We followed the advice, feeling confident, that we would not be molested. In the hotel, in which we lodged, we were, according to law, asked for our passports, which we handed over, and they were sent to the police, for visa. The police director had heard of the arrival of the boat, and suspected that we had come in it, and had got out, to evade the law of Holland. He called us before him, and on my showing my letters of introduction, to bankers in Amsterdam, in which they were asked to assist me, in getting a place, as clerk, he visaed my passport to go to Amsterdam, but added a proviso: "In case the bearer of this passport makes an effort to emigrate to America, he shall be returned to Arnheim." The same was done to my companion. Next morning we left for Amsterdam, and reached there in 24 hours. We stopped at a hotel that bore the name: "The Prussian King." Soon after, our companions, down the Rhine, arrived, and we expected to be able to embark at once, in a ship to Philadelphia; but we were detained 30 days. Our complaints, to the authorities, were not heeded, and we were not compensated, for our losses, nor for the delay. To get our passports visaed to Philadelphia, we had to pay, each of us, a bribe, to get them from the police. Holland was, then, a meanly governed State. The emigrants, passing through Holland, were fleeced on every occasion. All the government did, was to pass the law, already mentioned; but it led to chicanery against the emigrants. The consequence of this false course was, that the very Holland, that used to have the benefit of thousands of emigrants per day, was now evaded by them entirely. Since 1880, wiser counsels have prevailed; better laws have been enacted, steamer lines provided, and reasonable regulations exist for the police; but it will take many years, before Holland will recover her former position. We embarked from Amsterdam, in June, 1832, for Philadelphia, in the bark Isabella, Captain Kurtz.

I spent many happy hours in Amsterdam, in the family, with which my brother Edward boarded, during three years, from 1827 to 1829, both inclusive. I took some pains to learn Hollandish, and visited the theaters and churches for that purpose, but the longer I tried, the more repugnant it became to me. I disliked the language for its false German, but also for its bad anglicanisms.

More offensive, than the language, was, however, the strict Calvinism on the one side, and the grossest Libertinism on the other. Whole streets were occupied by houses of prostitution. And the navy was largely supplied with sailors through these bawdy houses. Several of our young men were so enticed; I myself was saved from a similar fate, by a too revolting behavior of the keepers of the house. Gremminger left me to myself in Amsterdam. He paid the bribe to the police, also my hotel bill, and after we got on board, he wanted me to board with him again, during the passage. This I accepted, on condition, that I might quit at any time, on three days notice. Thus I perfected my father's contract, and was able to quit at pleasure.

CHAPTER X.

CROSSING THE ATLANTIC.

OUR ship, Isabella, was an American vessel. It was a heavy rigged Brig of 500 tons burden. When the Star Spangled Banner waved over us, as we sailed out of Texel, the outer harbor of Amsterdam, I thought the flag beautiful; but I must say, that any banner, that floated westward, away from Holland, would have looked grand to me at that time.

Our journey, to Amsterdam, had taken twenty days; we were detained thirty in Amsterdam. We were therefore forty days on the way, since April 27th. We went to sea in the evening of June 7th, with 211 passengers, all in the steerage. Each family cooked for itself on the fireplaces on deck. The ship supplied wood and water. We went out of harbor with a stiff north-west breeze. Sea-sickness soon set in. And as the storm increased, and night came, I became a helpless invalid. I could not make up my mind to anything. If there had been an opportunity, I would certainly have gone home, and asked my father's forgiveness, for ever troubling him with my craze for emigration. When, at a terrible lurch, I saw the supercargo of the ship pitched overboard. I could not tell, dark as it was, whether the fall was due to the shock, the ship had received, by a heavy wave, or to his purposely leaping overboard. He disappeared, and was seen no more. I fell too, but gathered myself up, and retreated to my bunk. I would have considered the sinking of the ship a gain. Next morning it was cold, with a clear sky over head, and a fair north wind driving our ship toward the British Channel. As I stepped on deck, having had my breakfast, I felt like being born again, and was ready to stick to the ship, even on emergencies.

I met the captain, who inquired, in German: "whether I could write English, and would undertake to keep the ship's books?" On my replying, that I thought I could, if he would have patience with me. I was informed, that he proposed to appoint me substitute for the supercargo, who had fallen over board, and that my services commenced at once. So I stepped from the steerage to the cabin; eat a full English meal on top of my previous German breakfast. I was shown the books, that I was to keep; they looked rather unintelligible to me, and the captain could not fully explain them. I turned over a leaf or two, and began making a record, using as my guide the previous pages of the book, and in that way familiarized myself with all the books. Then I made some entries in them, and they proved satisfactory.

Gremminger's tutorship over me now took an abrupt conclusion. He did not know, at first, how to take it. The removal of my luggage, including mattress, blankets, sheets, etc., to the cabin, deprived him of conveniences for the younger members of his family, whom he had quartered with me on my bed clothes. When I asked him for the moneys placed by my father with him for me, he declined, pleading, that he needed more time for consideration. I gave him a week, and the end of the week he played offish again, and now I spoke to the captain, who at once ordered Gremminger, to hand over whatever he had of mine, including a diamond breast-pin, I had from my grandmother. He again plead for time, but the captain ordered him to surrender, and said, the settlement could be made at any time afterwards. He handed over 325 guilders, and my other property. We settled on a fair basis afterwards, and he treated me respectfully during the rest of the voyage, and I reciprocated with interest. At Philadephia we parted, and never saw each again The gypsy's prophecy came to my mind. I learned through inquiries, that he settled near Pottsville, in Pennsylvania, as a grocery keeper. That he got into trouble there, with his wife, for being too intimate with another woman. He became very poor, and so died. His family recuperated, through the earnings of the children. Since 1860 I have not heard of him.

Our passage, to the United States, lasted nearly three months. We passed through every maritine disaster except shipwreck. Our vessel leaked from the first, and we had to become adepts in pumping out bilge-water. We were thrown beam ends, our sails were often split, and our ropes snapped; but we had plenty of time to repair damages. Our ship was well supplied with everything necessary for a long voyage. Evidently the captain and officers were used to long voyages. Mending sails and cordage, as well as fixing masts and rigging, was continually going on, and all hands, including myself, were getting to be practical mariners in these portions of naval economy. I am glad to-day, that through steamships, we have learned. to largely dispense with such excellencies. Captain and myself had some confidences together, as I kept the books, including the log-book, under his direction; I knew, for instance, why our captain was so very anxious to exchange signals with other ships. It was: because he was never entirely sure of his own reckonings. This he did not want the second mate to know. So we kept the log-book by double entry. First on a scrap-book. on which we entered our own observations, and second in the regular log-book, in which we entered the result, after we had exchanged signals and compared results. The captain was of a generous disposition, and not disposed to be jealous, as to his authority. He liked the first mate, Thompson, who was, like himself, an old tar, that learned navigation by long practical experience, but he disliked the second mate, Pike, who was proud of his academic learning and knew the captain's deficiencies.

Our fare in the cabin was conducted on the process of gradual simplification, by which we learned, in the process of time, to do without milk, eggs, fresh butter, meats and bread; for we ceased to have them in our larder. We were reduced, finally, to the four original solid elements of marine cooking, viz: crackers, bacon, lard and flour, with some water, much gin, and dried prunes for liquids and luxury. A similar reduction, to a minimum, was going on in the steerage. They finally made pan-cakes, out of a dough of mixed flour and water. Crackers and mess pork they bought out of the ship's supplies, I acting as commissary. As to our and their water, it was kept in large casks on deck, and we had, for obvious reasons, ceased to be particular as to its looks, taste, or smell. We, in the cabin, used to filter it, but dropped the habit, for the same reason. The officers had some access to a lot of Selzer water, in stone jugs, of which we all used sparingly, but had to do it so long, that the whole lot had to be reported as spoiled, when we arrived. Who paid for it finally, is still a question; I did not. The jugs were empty.

CHAPTER XI.

MY FIRST MONTHS IN AMERICA.

WE saw land in the morning of August 27th, and cast anchor on the same day, about six o'clock, at Cape May, on the Delaware River. There we were informed, that the cholera raged in Philadelphia. We had left Europe, fearing that cholera would soon get there, never thinking, that the cholera would ever get to America; and here it was, in America, before us. To our astonishment we were put in quarantine for 48 hours. We asked, whether this meant to protect us against the cholera, or the cholera against us? For we certainly had none ourselves. We had departed from a healthy port three months previous, had no disease, except sea-sickness, of any kind on board, and brought three persons more to land, than we had taken away from Amsterdam. We could not see therefore, what putting us into quarantine meant? We were told, that some of our passengers had eat some watermelons, that they had bought on shore, and that there was some fear, that this would bring on the cholera. We never reached Philadelphia until the 31st of August. I was allowed, by special permit, to go ashore, and take my room-mate with me. He had a brother in Philadelphia, and he wanted to see him at once. He took me with him to his brother's house, and there I was invited to stay. I was wrong in accepting this hospitality, but also unfortunate in it, for the brother's rent fell due that same day, and he borrowed the amount of me; viz: thirty dollars. I never saw the money again. It was my first experiment in America, to see, whether the gypsy prophecy would hold good here also? It certainly did do compoundly.

I changed my quarters the Monday following, and boarded after that at Hotel Mannheim, kept by persons that came very near from my native town, Mr. and Mrs. Betz. They were nice people.

Mrs. Betz had an eye to mutuality. She saw very soon that I had a good many things I did *not* want, but which she *did* want; for instance: my hair mattress, my Russian blankets, my sheets, my pillow slips and comforts. I knew the cost in Germany, and she offered to give me that amount, I accepted it, believing it to be a fair bargain; and such it was, in the sense of an emigrant boarding house. So I had a credit for my board at the hotel for several weeks. The board was $2.50 a week. It took me a good time to hunt a situation. Mr. Betz found, that I understood cellar work, bottling wine and beer; so, to make me begin to earn something, he engaged me, to help him in such work, at the rate of ten cents an hour. I regarded it as good pay, and nobody gainsayed it. I earned in that way, if not my full board, at least some of it, and had time yet to go around the city, and hunt me a place, without drawing on my cash. The first place I secured by my perambulation was in a stone yard. It was early in the morning, and I was put to work immediately, on my assurance, that I was willing to perform any labor I could do for reasonable pay. I was told, that I should have one dollar anyhow, for doing my best at one end of the handle of a sand-stone saw. I held out the whole day, getting a lunch at noon of bread, cheese, and beer, and a good silver dollar in the evening. I left, without stipulating to come back the next day. And he let me go, without inviting a return. This result was evidently satisfactory to us both. Mrs. Betz, when I told her about it, and showed her my dollar, exclaimed: "You are getting to be a full American."

I was perhaps over anxious to obtain work and pay, but I have now no regrets for my zeal, because experience has taught me, that those emigrants, who take matters leisurely, and wait for big wages and light work, prosper least; whilst those, who lose least time in the beginning, are most certain to succeed in the end. I may be asked, why I did not keep the place in the stone-yard? I answer: first, I felt sure, that the excessive heat would kill me in a short time; second: that I believed, that the owner did not want me to come again. The hired man that handled the saw on the other side, was evidently displeased with much of my work. I pulled often, when I should have shoved, and visa versa; and every time I missed, he would mutter: "God damn, that Dutchman!" I was willing to become an expert in stone sawing, but not in swearing. I learned, however, that day a useful political lesson. It is: "that there must be a common proficiency if you want effective co-operation."

The next place I obtained, at my own solicitation, was in the sugar refinery of Bute & Troutwine, on Seventh Street. I had to work at $9.00 per week, under the rule of a skilled workman, who was very considerate of my labors. He added, after every correction: "Never mind. I see you are learning fast. You will soon be an expert." I stuck two weeks, but had to give up, because upon consulting a physician, who informed me: that the atmosphere was too moist and warm for a young man growing as fast as I was, to continue work in it for even twelve or more hours each day. My employees told me to come back later in the fall, if I did not get a place to suit me better. I got such a one, and did not go back.

Mrs. Betz took me now again under her motherly wings. She had no children of her own, and it was a pleasure to her, to be useful to youth generally. Her endeavors with me were doubly successful the first day. She found two open places for me, one in a white lead factory, the other in a glue factory. I promised to examine both next day. I went early to the first named, thinking my chemical knowledge would serve me there. The owners were frank people. They informed me of all the precautions against disease I would have to use, and expressed besides apprehensions, that I was too young yet, to stand it. I then called at the glue factory. The owner was a Swiss, and he explained to me the work I would have to do, and the wages—$6.00 per week, with board,—I would get. The smell in the factory was indeed an objection, but, nevertheless, I promised to come the following Monday on trial. Then I went back to my hotel.

There *my* news came athwart those of Mrs. Betz, and hers athwart of mine. On seeing me, she exclaimed: "I have engaged you, for the very place you want." I retorted: "But I have accepted the place in the glue factory." She insisted, that I must keep my promise. I concluded, that I would appeal to the glue-maker's generosity, and went at once to him. On explaining to him, that the place taken for me, by Mrs. Betz, was in a grocery, a business I understood, and rather preferred, though I would get much less wages, than with him, he acquiesced with me at once, and gave me back my promise. And when he learned, to whom I was thus engaged, by Mrs. Betz, he joyfully exclaimed, in his Swiss dialect: "Why, that is Mrs. Bald, the widow lady's grocery, on the northeast corner of Poplar lane and Second; I buy my groceries there and will now continue to be your customer." Thus I escaped being a glue-maker, and succeeded in returning to my original vocation. On Monday following October 1st, 1832, I entered into my new service. I found Mrs. Bald still weak from a recent illness. She introduced me to her chief clerk, a Mr. Beamish, from Cork, in Ireland. She asked us both to come, in case of any differences, to her. When I looked surprised, and asked: "why she anticipated differences?" She smiled, and said: "Why, you are from different countries, and it is commonly understood, that Germans and Irish don't get easily along together." We both promised, that it should not be so with us; especially, if she would be the peace maker between us, if war were to break out.

There was, unbeknown to Mrs. Bald, a dangerous element to the peace of the family in the house. It consisted of the Irish hired girl. She soon let me know, that she could not see any reason, why an additional clerk was engaged, and he a Dutchman. I took her words as fair notice, that my permanent employment would have to receive her approval, and that I held my place on good behavior towards her. The form, this would have to take, Mrs. Bald, on inquiry, informed me of. It was: to keep the kitchen well supplied with kindling wood, and to reserve for cooking and the table the best from the store. I laughed to myself, when I was notified of the items, for I wondered, what face my father would make, if he would hear or see this, my sub-service in the ladies department. We shall see later, that the presence of the Irish girl had other bearings besides.

My employment, in the *store*, worked detrimental in quite an unexpected quarter, to-wit: that of the negro porter—Peter—, I never heard another name. He and his wheel-barrow occupied, by tacid concession, an indefinite space on Second Street, behind some empty barrels and boxes. He paid nothing for the license; but agreed to make himself useful, when occasion offered. To have all the delivery arising from the store, was also included, those that wanted it, to pay for it. With my coming, there was to be free delivery of goods, and it by me, on our own wheel-barrow. I was not aware of the presence of this transporting agency, until the third day, and then I made as large eyes at it, as Peter had made at me. For several months afterwards, Peter was an independent wheel-barrow man for the whole neigborhood, but, for the store, I had the job to myself. I got no pay for it. I was, therefore, not a competitor with Peter, in the paying part. Two months afterwards, Peter was reinstated in all his old privileges. Mrs. Bald found, that it did not pay, to have me do the transporting business. My services *in* the store were more valuable.

I must now bring up a point of my life, that proved a great benefit to me; namely: I had letters of introduction, from Amsterdam merchants, to Messrs. J. & A. Ritter, a dry-goods house, on Market street, in Philadelphia. They were descendants of Dutch Quakers, that gave stamina to William Penn. The elder partner spoke German fluently, and treated my introduction as more than matter of form. He invited me to his house, one of those attractive simple brick dwellings, on Seventh street, that testified to the civic and personal virtue of its inmates. There I met both elderly and young Quaker ladies, that were, in spite of their Quaker exterior, patterns of cheerful propriety. They were handsome too. There I also met, early in October, Mr. Bald, the owner of the principal bank note engraving and printing establishment, of that period in the U. S. He was the brother-in-law of Mrs. Bald, the widow lady, whose clerk I was. He told Mrs. Bald of this meeting, and my free intercourse in the Ritter family. It was introducing me to her in a new character, and with consummate female tact she let me know, that she now had a better appreciation of me. She told me, that she was a descendant of a Saxon family, named Braun, changed here into Brown; that came here under the auspices of those half Quakers, the Herrnhuters (Moravians); and that, through them, she still maintained an exchange of civilities with many Quakers, such as the Ritters. From that time I felt sure, that Mrs. Bald trusted me, and that she had the same assurance as to my trust in her. Both were soon afterwards put to a severe test.

Mr. Beamish surprised me one Sunday, whilst driving out into the country to an Irish friend of his, and a good customer of the store, by telling me that he would be married, that evening, to Mrs. Bald, and that I need not expect him to occupy, as heretofore, the same room with me. He informed me, also: that his driving with me to the country, was a feint, to put Mrs. Bald's brothers, who were opposed to the marriage, off their guard. He suggested, that if I would shape my course that evening, so as to avoid, all evening, even the appearance of acting by appointment, it would facilitate his and Mrs. Bald's plans very much. I told him, no such caution was necessary, as I had made out already, not to go home for supper, but to call on the Ritter family, and spend the evening with them. He handed me the house and store keys, as well as that to our room, and I carried out my programm. I came home late, found nobody up and about the house any more, and closed and bolted the house and other doors. I was, before I fell asleep, rather dubious, whether my course was altogether right toward all concerned?

Next morning, on coming down stairs, with the view to opening the store, I found the Irish girl already up, and Mr. Brown, brother of Mrs. Bald, with her. They each put so many questions and so fast to me, that I was relieved from answering any. Finally they both left, and I saw clearly, that I would get no breakfast, unless I procured it elsewhere; which I did, from Mrs. Betz, whose hotel was only a few doors west. Mrs. Betz was amazed at the news I brought.

For a day or two there was much crimination and recrimination by the brothers of Mrs. Bald, now called: Mrs. Beamish; the Irish girl also playing a part. The latter claimed that Beamish had led her to expect marriage from him; but he denied all such imputations. A German girl came forward, on the recommendation of a townsman of mine, and took charge of the household affairs. She cooked a good dinner that very first day, which even Mr. and Mrs. Beamish relished, and we soon forgot her Irish predecessor. Mrs. Beamish was thenceforth a very thoughtful woman. Her relations and friends were rather shy of her. My course was simply to assume, that her marriage was a matter, about which I had nothing to say, or do, than to remain respectful to her.

My German descent, and capacity to deal with German customers, was of great advantage to Beamish's business. When I first came, nine-tenths of the customers were Irish, whilst at the end of six months, full half of the customers were German mechanics and farmers, and the average receipts were trebled. I had picked up, in my English, some Irish brogue; and I understood the Irish names of many things we kept for sale for them. One Irish woman told me once: "You are the queerest Irishman I ever saw."

CHAPTER XII.

WESTWARDS I HAVE TO GO.

At the end of six months my employers doubled my wages. This increase of wages was very gratifying to me. I had known, all the time, that my wages were not at all commensurate to the services I rendered.

Near the end of my first year in America, I was tempted, by offers of much higher wages, by rivals of Mr. Beamish. I told them, that I regarded it as improper, for me, to accept such offers, as for them to tender them. They thought it strange in me, to have such ideas, and said: "I would have to give up my Dutch ways, if I wanted to succeed in America." I replied, that at the end of the year I meant to appeal to Mr. and Mrs. Beamish for a more generous compensation. If they then refused, I would, perhaps, call on them. And so I intended to do; but an unforeseen incident brought on, an entire rupture between Beamish and myself, that revived my wish to go further west.

Mr. Beamish would often get unduly excited, and then act improperly. While in this temper one morning, he gave me, in very rough words, a peremptory order, to do an act, that I was about to perform myself. I told him so, but he contradicted me insultingly, by denying, that such was my intention. This hurt my feelings, and I begged him to wait and see. He now insisted, in the most exasperating way, on my doing the work at once, or quit the place. I asked him for my wages; he tendered me first pay only up to the day; but on slight reflection, he paid me for the whole mouth. I thanked him for the money, and he relaxed his bluster and bid me a friendly good-bye. I called on Mrs. Beamish to bid her farewell. She said: "I had expected some such an occurrence, and am only glad that it came with so little exasperation in the end. She wished me all possible success in my journey west. I returned to the Hotel

Mannheim, still kept by Mr. and Mrs. Betz, and there prepared for my journey westward.

It is but proper, that I should state here, that my year's stay in Philadelphia, with Mr. and Mrs. Beamish, added largely to my knowledge of goods proper to be kept in an American grocery. I learned also much, as to the best sources of supplies, for the articles necessary for a good store. And I had become acquainted with the methods of treatment, best suited to the different variety of customers, likely to have to be encountered in America. I had also improved in my English. So we parted, though offended at each other, still with a fund of kind feeling, that would outlast all temporary ill-feeling. Mrs. Beamish's: "Good-bye, Charles!" testified to this, and I have it in my mind still.

While forming my plans, for my western journey, I had several offers, from countrymen of mine, to form partnerships, or, at least join enterprises; but my experience, as to such entanglements, upon mere conjectures, stood me in good stead here. I escaped becoming the partner of a cattle-dealer, between Ohio and Philadelphia. So, too, I missed a peddler-partnership, with a two-horse wagon. I determined: to go alone, to settle upon my own judgment, and to my best ability develop my individuality. I knew that I would have to pay for my experience; but it was a satisfactory thought, that I had to pay only for my own errors, and not for those of others, and that others would not suffer for errors and mistakes committed by me. I wanted to travel free and untrammeled for once. I soon made my arrangements, having none but myself to consult, to go west. I had my choice of route between going direct west, via: Lancaster, Harrisburg, Laurel Hill and Pittsburg; or, via: Baltimore, Frederick, Hagerstown and Wheeling. I preferred the latter, because I was told, that I would more likely, find a steamer at Wheeling, for Cincinnati, than at Pittsburgh; the Ohio River being reported very low.

I carried with me the old trunk I brought from Germany, and in it was much the larger part of the clothes and other materials, that were in it when I came. I wore around my left shoulder also the identical pouch—knap-sack they called it—and on my right the silver inlaid gun. Very snugly stored in an inside vest pocket, I had one hundred and forty-two dollars; ($142.00). My cash had increased $45.00, but my luggage was minus the mattress, blankets, pillows and sheets. I kept, carefully wrapped up in a portfolio, a circular letter from Messrs. J. & A. Ritter, to their business friends in the larger western cities. I have it now among my papers as an heirloom.

I went to Baltimore, in the latter part of August, 1833, by the fine Delaware and Cheasapeake Steamers, then running between the two cities. I stopped at Belzhuber's Hotel, the one that Jefferson was said to have frequented. I was shown the hitching-post, to which he was reputed to have tied his horse when he journeyed to Philadelphia, and in going to and fro as Vice-President and member of Washington's Cabinet. I appreciated these facts, being a Democrat.

At Baltimore, I called on a cousin of mine, who had married a Mr. Megenhardt, after her lover, Captain Miller, a hero in the war for Grecian Independence, had been killed at Missolunghi. Her maiden name was Pauline Lohbauer. She was the daughter of my father's only sister. She was the affianced of Miller, and a devotee for free Greece; and was the object of admiration for her beauty in very extended circles; she had a wide reputation as a singer. My father, who disliked her mother, loved her; and she was often, for weeks, at our house. She was the companion of my step-mother, when I was first introduced to her. She was my eldest sister's dearest friend. When I called on her in Baltimore, she had resided there three years, and had grown corpulent. She had had one child. She lived in humble, but comfortable circumstances, and was glad to see me. Her younger brother, the preacher, had followed her, and given her much trouble, by his erratic course. He had been confined in a lunatic asylum, and had troubled her exceedingly.

At Baltimore, I could not help noticing, that it was a city, that would not fulfill the high expectations, that its earlier friends, Washington included, had formed of it. I found too, that Cheasapeake Bay was overrated, when its 350 miles of water frontage was made the criterion of their preference. I questioned then, whether it was of great advantage to Baltimore, to have the seat of the National Government placed so near it. Washington City, and the whole policy of having a Union Capitol, as well as State Capitals, was adopted without a full consideration, of the effect it would have, on Baltimore. And to-day, it is hard to tell, whether Baltimore is more in the way of Washington, or Washington more in the way of Baltimore. The events in our civil war, brought Richmond also in use, and raised many new questions as to these three cities. Baltimore is, however, but one of thousands of instances in the history of the United States, when localities had to undergo, after a first quick growth, the test: whether they would have a permanent happy development. There always comes, sooner or later, a re-action from a first exotic price paid for real estate, to a much lower rate, and then the question arises: will it get a persistent self-growth, with its now proximities.

From Baltimore I proceeded, the third day, at 7 a. m., westward, by railroad, the cars being drawn by horses to Frederick, where we arrived a little after noon. From Frederick, I went by stage, towards Wheeling. We reached Hagerstown at about 7 p. m., and were there told, that we could not proceed further without repairs, which would detain us at least until next morning. We took rooms at the State Hotel, where we had a good supper. Before going to bed, I took a walk, and witnessed, incidentally, the whipping of a female slave. I regarded this as barbarous, and went straight to the stage office, asking: whether I could not exchange my Wheeling ticket for one to Pittsburgh. As the Wheeling stage had nine passengers engaged, and that to Pittsburgh only three, the exchange was granted, and I proceeded forward at once, so that by 10 o'clock, I was outside of slave, and inside of free territory. The second day I arrived at Pittsburgh, via: Uniontown. On the way, we were driven some two miles along roads, on which the woods were afire. The two front horses suffered severely. We were driven very fast, and altogether I got quite an exalted opinion of American stage-coach traveling, as I sat with the driver, on top of the stage. My fellow passengers declared: that they wanted no more of that kind of fun; neither did I.

On my arrival at Pittsburgh, I presented my circular letter to several of the firms named, but received, from all, the reply, that I need not expect employment for several weeks. So I looked for traveling facilities to Cincinnati. There were no direct stage lines, but on the river there was a steamer, the Allegheny, a stern-wheel boat. On the bulletin board was the inscription: "Starts to-morrow." This "to-morrow" had daily renewals for several days. I paid my $10 upon the promise, that in three days, or less, I would be in Cincinnati. The three days were extended to fourteen days, and these were, considering all things, a speedy arrival. At Pittsburg, and afterward on the route, we were everywhere told of the cholera raging along the river, and especially in Cincinnati. An old gentleman advised me, as I was going on board the steamboat, to provide myself with a "coffin". I treated the advice as a joke, and replied: "Never mind, I shall find, if nothing else, a coffin in Cincinnati. And, sure enough, my first employer's name was "Coffin". It proved to be more than a play on the word.

Of the 112 passengers, we took away from Pittsburg, 37 died, on the passage, of cholera. and were buried,—without coffins,—in sacks in the river. We suffered much, for want of wholesome food. The supplies of fresh meat on the boat run out after the third day, and the reputation, of having cholera on board, went ahead of us, and at our several landings, folks declined to have any dealings with us. The captain had laid in a good stock of whiskey, pork and crackers, and he furnished from it liberally. Toward night, we managed generally, to land near one of those fine orchards, on the river bottoms, for which the Ohio was then famous. There we would land, and supply our boat, gratis, with apples and other fruit, and also with chickens, that roosted on the trees. Sometimes, when detained by shallows, we passengers went out hunting and secured plenty of game. My fine duck gun proved a valuable instrument.

CHAPTER XIII.

MY ARRIVAL AND EMPLOYMENT IN CINCINNATI.

We arrived in Cincinnati, on the last Sunday morning of the month of September, 1833. We were glad to leave our steamboat. I took my iron-bound trunk on a dray, and went up the wharf, at the foot of Broadway, and stopped at a coffee-house, called "Orange", kept by a German, and asked him, to name a fair-priced hotel. He pointed, after selling me, for five cents, a glass of good real French wine, to the Washington Hotel, on the south side of Front street, between Main and Walnut. I was told, that my fare, at the hotel, would be $1.00 per day. This price was low, considering the excellent meals and good rooms they provided; but it was high, when judged by the contents of my purse. So, after eating my dinner, I took a walk over the city, and ascended Sycamore street, up to the top of the hill, near to where then the Catholic Bishop's mansion stood. I was delighted with the fine view over the city and surrounding hills. I had been told, that Cincinnati then contained at least 40,000 inhabitants. I predicted, in my mind, that it would soon have 100,000, and concluded: that, as the river was low, and as I could not proceed further west, that I would make Cincinnati my home. Coming down, I took Main street, and on inquiring for a good German boarding house, was pointed to one near Sixth, on the east side of Main, where the fare was $2.00 per week. I went there, and agreed to come next morning. I went back to my hotel, took my supper, and retired, feeling quite pleased with my arrival and conclusion to stay.

After I awoke, next morning, and had my breakfast, I sat down, in front of the main entrance. Soon I saw a small crowd gathering, on the opposite side, around an object lying on the pavement. I went over, and found the object to be a dead man, besmeared with blood, mud and molasses. A young man recognized the man to be a person commonly called "Driftwood Johnson". He got this name from the fact, that in earlier times, he had dragged driftwood out of the river, and used it, for his own use, as well as selling it, for fire and building wood. Word soon came, that he lost his life in falling down the hatchway, in the wholesale grocery store, in front of which he was lying. Soon the discovery was made, that the man had been an habitual burglar, and had, the night previous, broken into the store, where, on being pursued, he fell through the hatchway and was killed. This led to a search of his premises, and there were found lots of other goods, which were all taken to the Mayor's office, and there identified as goods stolen from stores, by the said "Driftwood Johnson". It was found, that he was rich, and had really no cause for his robberies. His family was humbled, but not disgraced, because they were proven to be guiltless. The daughters were well married, into good families, that still live about Cincinnati. I participated in the excitement, and lost several hours, so that it was 11 o'clock, when I got back to the hotel, paid my bill, got a dray and moved to the boarding-house, I had selected the day before. It was a well-kept house by a Rhine-Bavarian, whose name I have forgotten. Immediately north of it, Ferdinand Bodman kept a tobacco store and wholesale wine house. All the surroundings were German, which made me feel quite at home.

Whilst in that boarding-house a day or two, an elderly gentleman, who claimed to be a physician, informed me bluntly, that he had observed my looks and movements carefully, and was sure, that I had an incipient attack of the cholera. He advised, nay, he ordered me, to my room and bed. He gave me medicine several times, and instructed a stout North-German girl, to procure hot brick, to wrap them into a blanket, and to rub my feet hard with them. Between her rubbing and his medicine, I got asleep, and slept for thirty-six hours. When I awoke, I was, as the saying is: "weak as a cat". Soon the doctor came, whose name I now learned to be: Oberndorf, the most popular German doctor of Cincinnati. He then gave me some more medicine, and ordered a regular nourishing diet for me. I gradually recovered. The good doctor would not take any fee from me at that time; and years afterward, when I insisted on paying him, he charged me only $2. He was my family physician for several years after I married, and remained my friend until his death. Afterwards I wrote his life, for the "German Pioneer", and therein redeemed his character, from the charge that troubled him very much; to-wit: that he had not graduated at a college. I had procured proof, from the French college at Montpelier, that he had passed with high honors. I sincerely wished, he had read this vindication of his, while alive.

As soon as I was well enough, I went to work to see: whether I could not secure employment. I called on the persons, to whom I was recommended, by the circular letter of J. & A. Ritter, to-wit: Messrs. Isham & Bros., a dry goods house, and Bellamy Storer, a very prominent attorney. The first offered to take me, as an apprentice in the dry goods business, with but small pay, at first, but with a gradual increase. This I declined, as it involved the learning of a new, to me disagreeable business. The second tendered me the place of office boy, with the prospect of becoming, in a few years, an atttorney at law. This proposition was still more disagreeable to me, than the first, and I ceased my visits. In both cases I acted too hasty, for they each had prospective advancements, that would have suited me. The fact is, I allowed my German prejudice against dry goods stores and lawyers, to rule me. I must confess, however, that I apprehended also my inability, to ever become a dry goods merchant, or a first class lawyer.

I secured the most suitable place for me then,—a grocery store clerkship,—in a round about way. I had seen, in the "Gazette", an advertisement for a young man that understood the seed business. and spoke both German and English. And as one part of my father's business was: to purchase and export seeds, I went to the address given, on Lower Market, Mr. S. E. Parkhurst. and asked: whether if I might not suit him? He expressed his belief, that an arrangement might be made, if we could agree upon the wages; he asked me to call again, the next day. I had learned, from his conversation, that the opening for me, at Parkhurst's, came in consequence of the resignation of the young man he had had for years; he had resigned. because his brothers, who kept a grocery, wanted him in their grocery. Putting this and that together in my mind, I thought I understood, why Mr. Parkhurst. Yankee as he was. had not closed with me at once. I guessed, that he reasoned thus: "Here is a young man, that understands the grocery business, and speaks German and English. He is the better clerk for my clerk's brothers, and my clerk is a better man for me. I will suggest this to them, and prevent my clerk leaving me. At the same time, they will get this young German for lower wages, than they would have to give their brother."

When I came back, next morning, my presentiment proved correct. I was now introduced to the brothers of Mr. Parkhurst's clerk, Messrs. T. B. & H. B. Coffin, and asked to hear, what they had to suggest. They explained: that they had concluded, that neither of them being grocers themselves, they ought to employ a clerk that understood the business, and that they had been told, that this was the case with me. I nodded assent, and they added: "Our business is small; but we expect an increase. If you will come at low wages, with a prospect of an increase, we will employ you." I asked for more definite terms. and then they offered me $6.00 per month, with board, for the first six months, and then $12.00 for the following six months. After some reflection, I accepted the offer. I reasoned: that I was dealing with sharp, but open-minded men; and that, in becoming connected with them. my future was sure to be progressive, and the present small prospects would grow in a compound ratio. I thought the proposition was an act of good sense all around; though hard on me.

The reader will now recall to mind, what occurred on my leaving Pittsburg, about the "coffin", and see, that my prophecy came to be doubly true. for I had found not only one "Coffin", but three. The only circumstance in the transaction, that puzzled me, was: that the young Coffin, that remained at Parkhurst's, got $15.00 a month, with much lighter work, than mine was. I felt this to be a sort of Yankee doubling on a German, that was hardly fair. The Coffins would have had to pay their brother the $15.00, why not me? I took the matter phylosophically. and was never a moment less zealous for Messrs.

Coffin's success, than I would have been at higher wages. I had brought with me, from Germany, the axiom: "present wages are not as important, as man's accumulative future earnings. Those that get more wages than they merit, accumulate ill-will against themselves, whilst those who get less than they deserve, accumulate credit for merit."

CHAPTER XIV.
MY MEAGER BEGINNING HAS A FAT OUTCOME.

Events ran, at any rate, with this reasoning. I was, to Messrs. Coffin. of ten-fold value, compared to the wages, they paid me. When I entered their service, I saw from the books, that the sales of the previous week were $27.56. In my first week they arose to $147.60. At the end of the first six months the sales averaged $100 per day, and at the end of the year they averaged $150 a day. This increase was not all due to my personal abilities. Much of it was caused by the conjunction of Yankee with German faculties. I was fully aware of this fact, and stored it away, in my memory, as an important item, in all calculations. as to my present or future relations with Messrs. Coffin. Others, that had noticed the growth of this business, judged more superficially. They thought, that all they had to do, to secure the same results to themselves, was to secure me; so they offered me higher wages. I declined, for the same reason I did in Philadelphia. But, when a countryman of mine, who belonged to one of the oldest families of my native town, and who had, as peddler, made about $1.000, came to me and offered me a partnership in a new grocery store, with a bar in the rear, I accepted it, on condition, that I should consult Messrs. Coffin, and that, only, if my leaving would not cause any detriment to them, might I agree to his proposition.

When I informed Messrs. Coffin of the offer, and the conditions, upon which I accepted it, they objected, to my withdrawal from their business, then. They said: "We have had under contemplation, for some time, a project, for starting another store, on Fifth street, near the Middle Market House, and to have you in charge of it, either as chief manager, on salary, or as partner." They informed me, of the house, they had in view, and explained to me their negotiations. for renting it. The owner was sick, and not expected to live, which was the only reason, for the proposed selling out. The stock on hand, was very small, and it and the fixtures were offered at low prices. I asked Messrs. Coffin, to allow me, to state to my countryman, their offer, and to confer with him, about the affair; which they conceded promptly. When I mentioned the subject, to my townsman, he got angry and advised me, to stick to my "Coffins". He treated me, as if I had deserted him. and that this was mean in me, as a townsman of his. I assured him, that he was mistaken, in thus impugning my motives; and that my conduct, toward him, had been fair and open throughout. But he would not listen to my explanations, and left me in a huff. He re-assumed his peddling in Kentucky and Tennessee, and never returned to Cincinnati. His folks in Germany never heard of him either. He was 40 years old, when he left Cincinnati, in 1834, and if now alive, would be 97 years old. I assumed him dead years ago. I published, as editor of the "Pioneer," a sketch of his life, under the head: "Nameless Pioneers." I refer those, who take an interest in Weissert, to that publication.

I reported to Messrs. Coffin, what took place between my townsman and myself, and steps were now taken, to perfect our agreement. We concluded, to make the business a partnership; my share of the partnership to be one-third of the net profits, to be annually ascertained, by an inventory. They to advance $500, and myself $100; I to devote all my time to the store; they to aid me, by occasional assistance; and by securing credit and recommendations. The name of the firm was to be, for a short time, Coffin & Co.; but it was soon changed to Coffin & Rümelin. We started the business in October, 1834.

The partnership brought, to a head, certain differences in our respective ideas of business, which had often been a subject of discussion between us; but in which I, as clerk, had simply to carry out, what Messrs. Coffin thought best. Now, when I was partner, the case was different; and I took early occasion, to assert my intention, to carry out, in the new business, my own ideas. The difference between us, was this: they believed in carrying a large stock, and that included the policy of buying large lots of goods, whenever offered at low rates, on credit. My rule was, to use credits sparingly, if at all, and to conduct business as near on a cash basis, as, under the circumstances, was possible. Neither of the Coffins had been merchants in their youth. The elder, Henry, had been a steamboat engineer; the younger was, as a young man, a carpenter; and had gone to Buenos Ayres, where he had been connected with business operations, and acquired considerable means thereby. My close habits of business, my adherence to the principle, that the least possible use and grant of credit was the true basis of a safe business, never suited either of them. When now the concrete question arose, whose ideas should prevail, as to the new store, the Coffins, with their practical turn of mind, asked: "What objection is there, to our pursuing, in Lower Market business, our way, and you going on, in the Fifth street business, your way?" I answered: none whatever, if the business of the two stores is kept separate. They then suggested, it would certainly be a benefit to the Fifth street store, to have the use of their large purchases at cheap prices; and I admitted, that goods from the lower store, at prices paid by them, might be used at the other store, provided the amount due, at the prices named, should be paid, by me, within a fortnight. To this I assented, because it enabled me to have use of a larger stock than I would have had without it, and the prices, I had to pay, were not higher than I would have had to pay anyway. In sperm oil, mackerel, salmon and Nantucket goods generally, the Coffins had special arrangements for lower prices, than I would have had to pay in cash, There was, therefore, in the relations of the two stores, a beneficial mutuality, that gave the combination fairness and consistency.

The lower store lost some German customers, by my leaving; but gained by the increased sale in all those articles, in which they had a specialty. Our then differences, as to the basis of conducting the business, disappeared in practice: but, in the course of time, others arose; for instance: it was found, at the inventory, made at the end of the first year, that there had been about $2,500 made. Messrs. Coffin claimed the right, to withdraw their share (about $1,500). I denied it; because it was contrary to the original agreement, and interfered with the steady development of the business, on a cash basis. But I acquiesced, when they agreed, that thereafter, they would get one-half the profits made, and I the other half. My capital and theirs, was, after the $1,500 were taken out by them, now about equal.

Then there was another disparity, to-wit: My being a cash purchaser of goods from them, which they bought on credit, gave them a large command over the cash of the upper store. This deceived them, as to the realities of their own situation, and they expended, for personal use, more money, than was compatible with a sound business. They actually spent, in building and living, more than they made, including the profits of the upper store. This course operated, in making firms, whose credit they were using, more shy, to sell to them, on credit, large lots at wholesale prices. I soon found, that I could buy, for cash, even small quantities, at less prices, than those charged by Messrs. Coffin, and thus the original relation, in the partnership, was more and more reversed. They admitted this, and accorded me corresponding preferences, so that, at the end of the third year, I got two-thirds of the profits, and they but one-third. At the same time, their own original business, on Lower Market, got weak, as to credit, by common report. I, on the other hand, had long before dispensed with all credit operations, for the store on Fifth street. The upper store had increased in capital.

The thought, that I was able to carry on the business alone, could not fail to occur to me frequently. And after I married, on October 2nd, 1837, it ripened into the conviction, that I was, in duty bound, to secure the business to myself alone. This feeling took the shape of alarm, when a friend, who was a lawyer, informed me, that partners were under unlimited liability for each others business debts. I know how difficult it would be, in our case, to prove separateness in the transactions of the two stores; and I saw, therefore, the pressing necessity, of coming to a final separation. Acting under the advice of my attorney, I asked, in September 1839, for a dissolution of our partnership. They expressed a willingness to yield it; but wanted first, an inventory made, so as to have some basis, to either sell out to me, or to buy me out. I told them, that I had such an inventory, and that I was ready, to make or accept an offer. They asked for time, to compare it, which I yielded. We then arranged for a meeting, a few days subsequent, at which to see, which of us. and to what extent, would agree to pay a bonus over and above the inventory and account. The understanding was besides, that the amount so ascertained, was to be paid in cash, or secured by short indorsed paper. I prepared myself, with the necessary money and paper, to meet the emergency. I felt pretty sure, that I would become the purchaser, and as I had foreseen, so it ended. Messrs. Coffin bid first $50 bonus, then I bid $100; then they bid $200, whereupon I bid $500, and declared it my last and final bid. It made the whole amount, to be paid by me, about $3,000. They accepted it, and I paid $1,400 of it down in cash, and agreed to pay $1,600 more in two weeks. They signed the paper, I had prepared, by my attorney; and the store now was mine. I have the paper, giving the details of the transaction, among my papers; it is dated: August 15th, 1839. It was high time to end the partnership. Had the publication, of the dissolution, been delayed but a week, it would have involved me in liabilities, that would have periled my solvency; in fact, ruined me.

CHAPTER XV.

POLITICAL BEARINGS.

The five years I was with Messrs. Coffin, either as clerk or partner, were eventful to me, in every respect, besides business, and as some of them had also bearings with Messrs. Coffin, I will now relate them.

I had come from Philadelphia, a confirmed Jackson man. I was made one, on my first arrival in Philadelphia, in 1832, by the abuse heaped on Jackson by the Whigs. I had read, in Germany, of the hero of New Orleans, and admired him. I compared the Whig opposition to him to that of the Thebaans against Epaminondas, and called it "base ingratitude".

Soon after I became Messrs. Coffin's clerk, I got into a dispute, with their father, about Jackson. I felt very bitter, against the venom, he exhibited, toward my hero. They bid me, not to talk politics, in the store, and I agreed not to do so, if no one else began the controversy, as their father had done. The agreement was faithfully kept, by both of us, and no doubt, our connection was prolonged by it. Nevertheless, it was an open secret, among us, that we differed in politics. I saw very plainly, that they were deeply offended. when, in the Spring of 1834. I adhered to Jackson, on the question of the removal of the deposits from the U. S. Bank. I had deposited my few dollars in the U. S, Bank, and they wanted to know, why I did not, according to my politics, withdraw, my money, from that institution? I reminded them, for answer, to our mutual agreement, and they admitted their hasty breach of it. But politics remained an impediment to a close intercourse on all points. After I was taken to the upper store, as partner, the customers, of it, consisted largely of democrats, and in a sharply increasing ratio. Messrs. Coffin, could not, if they would, prevent our customers talking their politics to me, and showing their joy, with my agreement with them. I had been the main cause, of the inglorious defeat of the notorious "market-wagon tax," and the farmers, who were mostly democrats, liked me, for my opposition to the said tax, and they increased their custom. In 1834, I was also the most prominent supporter of the German society in Cincinnati, and thus became known, more generally. among the Germans, who were mostly Jackson men, and that, too. operated in giving me more political strength, than was agreeable to my partners.

My kind of support of the new German Democratic paper, in 1835, first: under the editorship of a Mr. Hartman, and then: under his successor. Benjamin Boffinger, was fully appreciated by the Germans. The two editors had directly opposite difficulties; namely: Hartman could not come *down* to the lower journalism, which was asked of him. here; while Boffinger could not come *up* to the higher grade. Hartman resigned the editorship. and left, without compromising himself; but Boffinger sold out to the Whigs, who thought, that any German paper, provided it was printed in "Dutch," could carry the German vote. This idea might have proved true, if we emigrated Germans had not interposed, in 1836, and rallied the more intelligent Germans of Cincinnati, in favor of starting a new paper, the "Volksblatt", which spoiled the whole game of the Whigs, in buying out Boffinger. The history of this movement has been published again and again, the last time in much preverted form, by F. A. Rattermann. I do not think it necessary. to renew the controversy here. The fact is, that the purchase of Boffinger was not a success for the Whigs, that tried, under Gen. Harrison, in 1836, to win the Germans by money.

I was made a citizen of the United States, October 9th, 1837; it is evidenced by a certificate of that date, now before me, signed by William Henry Harrison, as Clerk of Hamilton County Court of Common Pleas. From the same paper, it appears, that I made first application for naturalization, in February, 1835. Judge Este administered the oath, after making the usual inquiries. Gen. Harrison interrogated me sub-officially, on handing over the papers, drawn up by his deputy, D. Gano, and receiving the customary fee of $2.00. We new citizens, paid this fee cheerfully, under the federal law; indeed, I may say, that I never was for the subsequent cheapening of citizenship to fifty cents or a quarter. The interrogatories, put to me by Gen. Harrison, arose chiefly through a desire, on his part, to be certain, that we applicants understood, really, the full import of the act, we were passing through. He wanted to know of me: whether I understood the oath I gave, to mean, that I had become a citizen of all the States of the Union? And when I affirmed his inquiry, he handed me the papers. When however, I told Gen. Harrison, that by the German way, the federal citizenship was kept distinct from that of the State, and that I believed it to be the better proceedure, it seemed to annoy him, and he denied, that there was any distinct State citizenship. I now referred him to the naturalization papers, he had handed me, and showed him, that I had sworn off allegiance to Würtemberg, and then asked: "Why did you not ask me to foreswear the fealty to the Germanic Union?" He dismissed me then, without further question; but he often afterwards would talk with me on the subject and finally acquiesced in the German idea.

About the time of my naturalization, I resigned the commission of Captain of the German Rifle Co., given me on the 8th of February previous, under the signature of Wilson Shannon, then Governor of Ohio. That resignation closed a very disagreeable episode of my life. I had joined, several years previous, the Lafayette Guards in Cincinnati, and was chosen Secretary of the company. I withdrew from it, on account of certain quarrels, between Captain Roedter and Keppner, that were too repulsive to me, to remain a member. The Lafayette Guard was the only volunteer company, that was ever organized in Cincinnati, and mustered, on its first and several subsequent parades, the full number of one hundred officers and privates. It was also the only company, of whose members over two-thirds were drilled soldiers before they mustered. Their bearing, at the reception of Gen. Jackson, in March, 1837, on his return from the Presidency, was noticed by him and many persons that had seen service in the field. They pronounced them superior to any soldiers ever seen by them before.

In 1839 I was asked to assume the Captainship of the German Rifle Co., with the expectation, that I would raise it to like efficiency with the Lafayette Guards, and I made a strenuous effort to that effect, but did not succeed. One afternoon, at sharp-shooting exercises, held in Wade's Woods, a mob was got up against us, by certain low characters, that bore the nick-name: "Fly Market Rangers." Our order of proceedings was violently broken into, and everything was thrown in such disorder, that no other course was left open, than to form the company into a hollow square, and retire to our armory, in good order. This was done, and then I announced my resignation at headquarters to Gen. Hales, who accepted it. The disturbance, that compelled us to withdraw, was the logical outcome of the divisions among the Germans, in reference to military organizations. Their numbers had, in both organizations, dwindled to less than the lawful number of gun-bearing members. The expenses had become unbearable, to the active members, and modes of raising means, to defray ordinary outlays, had to be resorted to, that were really censurable. My resignation was a great relief to me. It saved me from further useless waste of time and means.

I now turned my attention to matters that were of more practical importance to me and my family. The reader will remember, in what a crooked relation I got, with my passport, in consequence of our failure to take the strictly legal way, as to my military duty, before my departure for America. This crookedness came up again, in Germany, when I reached my twenty-first year. I was then enrolled in Heilbronn on the regular list of those, that had to draw lots, as to military duty. My father informed me, that he had been notified of my being on the list, and that he had concluded to draw lots for me, and that if he drew a free lot for me, it would end the matter; and if not, he would answer, that I refused to come. If, then, the government would attempt to seize on what was coming to me from my mother's estate, he would answer, that I had received the full amount of my mother's inheritance. To enable him to say that, beyond dispute, he asked me to state, in documentary form, the full amount. The request surprised me, for reasons, that will readily occur to the reader; but I transmitted the document, with an inner smile at the fact, that this matter had already led to three crooked transactions, whilst my father regarded them as all perfectly straight; and as doing me a favor, every time. Parental affection covers a good many crooked items. Subsequently my father sent me 400 guilders, which was the sum, he said, that had been saved, by me sending him the aforesaid document. Now it appeared to me, that it was placing me and him into a false position, to be a volunteer soldier here, while I stood in the recusant attitude in the Old Country; and placing myself, besides, in several misleading written and verbal statements on file there. I was liable, if I ever returned to Germany, even as a visitor, to be summarily arrested and punished. As soon as I had my resignation effected with Gen. Hales, I wrote to our Secretary of State, in Washington—Forsyth— and asked: whether steps could not be taken to protect me against attaching my inheritance from my father? After some delay, the reply came, that the department had no diplomatic representative in Würtemberg, nor any other means to protect me there. Forsyth recommended our then representative in Congress, Bellamy Storer, to say to me, that I had better pursue the way of appealing to the King's clemency, and thus relieve myself of all further troubles. I com municated this to my father, and asked him, to bring the matter, through persons of our family, who stood near the King, before that Potentate. It took several years, to reach a favorable decision. It came, however, in 1842, and amounted to this: That on payment of 400 guilders, for a substitute, all fines and penalties should be remitted and I fully pardoned. I remitted this sum in 1843, to my father, and he sent me back my receipts aforesaid. I was thenceforth free to go and come between Germany and America, and felt, that I had now attained also my full American Citizenship. I asked myself, whether it would not have been the better way, if this whole business of military duty had been arranged, in 1832, according to law.

CHAPTER XVI.
GRADUAL LEARNINGS IN POLITICS.

As already mentioned about Gen. Harrison, I carried into my political reasoning, as to State citizenship and the elective franchise, perceptions, that I had imbibed in my native land. I believed, that it was an error to assume that U. S. Citizenship, and the right to vote at State elections, were tantamount. I had voted in Ohio four years before I was a U. S. citizen, and paid my annual head-tax, on the ground, that the Constitution of Ohio, conferred on all white male inhabitants, 21 years old, that resided in the State one year, and paid this tax, the right to vote. Some urged, that I might be arrested for this, others advised: that I had better see the State Attorney. They called on him, and he told them: "By the Constitution Rümelin is right, by usage he is wrong." They abandoned their attacks on me, and I carried with me through life the knowledge, that in the United States, Constitutions and usages often contravene each other.

I cast my first vote, after my naturalization, for the whole Democratic ticket, in October, 1837. I had made speeches at public meetings that Fall, and for two years previous. I placed, however, proportionately small value upon work at elections, in fact it was more or less distasteful to me. I thought the advocacy of honest principles and wise measures, should precede the elections, so that no electioneering work should be necessary at the polls. In 1835 already, I saw the necessity, of holding up, high before nominating conventions, the standard of hard money and free trade as a check on the propensity, of all our parties, to reduce party contests to a machinery for office seeking. We kept at that time and for a dozen years afterwards, the Democratic party pure through cultivating a high-toned political spirit. It was high-toned, because it rested on free religious and political inquiries and convictions. A free Sunday had at that time been secured, through Richard M.

Johnson's report against stopping the mails on Sunday. It was declared to be a Democratic victory over the sinister efforts of bigoted religionists, that aimed to impress, upon American society, their obsolete sectarian doctrines, and the casuistries, by which they were advocated and promulgated.

I came to America with the idea, that here liberty had its last refuge, and that, if it were lost here. it would never be recovered. I believed therefor, that its defense was the first and highest duty of immigrants, that had come here from countries. whose liberty had been destroyed by Kings, Nobles, Priests and Nabobs. Soon after I arrived, I was told, that there were here Churchmen, Politicians and Speculators combined, in, what was then called, the Whig party, which meditated the overthrow of liberty; and unrelenting resistance to this combination, and persistent support of the Democratic party, was therefore esteemed by me my highest duty.

When, therefore, during the latter part of Jackson's and Van Buren's administration. certain reforms were introduced in the Post Office and Treasury Departments, we Germans supported almost unanimously the Democratic party. The Whigs, on the other hand, were equally unanimous against the Democratic party, and its political measures. We thought, that they did this, because it affected not only the leaders in politics, but also the leaders in money matters and the larger speculations. We believed the adoption of the Sub-Treasury to be tantamount to guarding the government against prostitution to corporation and clique rule in the country's finances. Our rule was, that Banks and Bankers should not have the use of public money. and that public credit should not be used: "To lend corruption lighter wings to fly."

Such use was so repugnant to us, that it is a marvel to me to-day, that a law, allowing such use of public money and credit, was ever adopted or carried out. We believed, it never would have been done, if the Sub-Treasury policy had been persistently carried out, and the policy of Jackson, Van Buren and Benton had been adhered to with sterling integrity by the country. We know now, that the full value of the policy, that was then called Democratic, was never realized, because it was, in fact, never thoroughly understood, and therefore never embraced as a symmetric and comprehensive regulation of money, coinage, and all institutions that mediate the payments and exchanges over the whole Union, and facilitate credit transactions; but we know, also, that the world has gathered experience since, and that we may learn it from financial scientists; provided: we do not lock up our minds with partisan prejudices and falsehoods, and thus give our demagogues free scope to perpetuate systems of coinage, paper issues and banking, that mean the most gigantic spoliations of production, trade and industry, which the world ever saw. The worst feature of it. was the continued use of the public money, for private speculation. Indeed, we might call it *peculation*. The monstrous land speculations, between 1833 and '38, were chiefly caused by these wrongs. They included the subjugation of the West by land-pirates, that could enter large portions of land at one dollar per acre, and re-sell them to farmers at ten dollars per acre. This was: subjecting the real productive wealth of the country to the fabrication of nominal wealth; and thus the inequalities, caused by the social forces, were never properly counteracted by wise political measures, such as a public administration, that produces public wealth, for the benefit of all. Seeing all this, I begun to realize, that my reliance on the Democratic party, as the only purifying and reforming element, was leaning on a broken reed. Its press and popular teaching, on the stump and in Congress, appeared to me, as growing more and more worthless, and at the same time, there were unclean plottings, for securing offices and jobs. Lower and lower characters, succeeded in pushing themselves into the front ranks.

At this time, early in the Spring of 1837, my brother Paul arrived. He brought me the latest works of the Political Economists of Europe. This gave my studies, reflections and political conduct a new start and direction; I re-examined all my political assumptions, especially those in regard to the several parties, in this country. This could not fail to make me less ultra in my partisan likes, as well as dislikes.

My brother's admonitions were not always pleasant to take. He eulogized too highly the improvement that had taken place in public affairs in Germany. And he was often rather hard in criticising our modes of carrying on politics. He even took sides with the Whigs. Nevertheless, I admit, that he was a great help to me, in re-considering my political ideas, and adopting clearer views.

CHAPTER XVII.

MY INDIVIDUAL SOCIAL AND COMMERCIAL LIFE.

I expect, the kind reader has arrived, by this time, at about the same apprehensions, at which I did myself, in the beginning of 1837; to-wit: that I was about sinking my individual, social and commercial standing, in the demon of American Politics. And there was really some danger of this. I was then unmarried. I had formed attachments to certain young ladies, but none endured. There was no anchorage in my social life. The male friends I had, could not supply it. Those of them, that might have attempted it, had left Cincinnati. My business had prospered, as far as I could carry it, by my single exertions. I was very much in doubt, whether I could rely entirely, on those in my service. Employees are, in the United States, as often a peril, as a prop, in business. I obtained, in 1838, a good clerk in Michael Goepper, but we had, at times, hitches together, that indicated his unwillingness, to be clerk any longer, and that he meant to be boss. My brother's arrival was therefore opportune. He brought with him a better knowledge of goods, in the modern sense. His address to customers, was superior to mine; he made it possible, that I could go from the business, to other places, and extend its trade; and he and Goepper were fully competent, between them, to conduct the Cincinnati business.

Reflections on these points brought the conviction, that I needed a wife, and the result was, that I succeeded in winning the affections of Louisa Mark, my present dear wife. It came in this wise: Goepper's father had made me his agent for selling a lot of fine imported Cherry and Prune Liquors, which he had brought with him on speculation from Germany. I went to Louisville about the middle of June 1837, for the purpose of disposing of these liquors, and stopped at a German Hotel, kept by a countryman of mine, with the jarring name : "Schnatterer." He approved himself to be an excellent assistant in disposing of liquors, and his wife a still better assistant in forming a match between a couple, predisposed to marriage. Mrs. Schnatterer was a native of Cincinnati, and she attracted to her husband's public house in Louisville, all that came there, that had formerly lived in Cincinnati. A Swiss family, by the name of Mark, was such an acquaintance, at that time, and I met at that public house, one afternoon, their two daughters. I was introduced to them, and before we parted, that evening, I was head over ears in love, with Louisa, the younger of these two daughters. I did not in words announce my love, but I believed, myself understood by her, and carried this idea back with me to Cincinnati. From there I communicated my wishes to Mr. and Mrs. Schnatterer, and requested them, to make inquiries in the right quarters: whether my presumptions were well grounded. I received an affirmative answer two weeks afterwards. And, confiding in it, I went August 1st, — my father's 57th birthday — to Louisville, and made a formal offer to Miss Louisa Mark, and was affectionately accepted. We fixed our wedding day for October 2d, 1837, and it was consummated accordingly.

It may be said, that our union was quickly formed, and rashly carried out; but, all, that I can say, is: that all, that was done, was done well; it had the blessings of my wife's and my own parents. Some persons intruded at our wedding, without being invited, which increased the expense of our wedding largely; but this sort of American liberty seemed an inevitable part of a marriage in this country, and we soon forgot the mishap. We went, next day, to Cincinnati, and were soon domiciled, in the third story, above our store, in apartments, specially provided. We owed our married happiness, before all, to the aid and advice of the Schnatterers, and next to Mr. Rehfuss, but first and last to ourselves. We brought but little wealth together for housekeeping, but it satisfied us; and, what more did we want? The question of our probable joint possessions had once great importance. It has much less to-day, It was at that time more essential to us, to *make*, than to *have* money. We were married, on due license, by a regular minister of the Presbyterion Church, in Louisville. We are still carrying our wedding rings, and with them the tokens of our Golden Wedding, just 50 years afterwards. It was a good ratification meeting, seven children and fifteen grandchildren were present at the celebration, in *Dent*, on our farm. I had so named the town.

At that festival many old recollections of my life were brought to mind; they may as well find a place here. And first I have to state, that Goepper left us soon after our marriage. He found a place more suitable to him, with higher wages, as clerk in Billiod's Brewery. His getting there led some years afterwards to his establishing a Brewers' supply business, and be became wealthy. He went into county politics, became County Commissioner and County Senator. He did not like to have it mentioned, that he owed his popularity to having been my clerk. He played a sorry part toward both, my brother and myself, in 1854; and a still meaner one, in some dealings, he had in the assignment, made to me by C. Wolff & Co., in 1861-62; but shabbiest of all he behaved during the civil war, when he attacked me, ostentatiously, for, what he called: "my pro-slavery politics." As Senator in the Ohio Legislature, he claimed, nevertheless, to be my successor. I was frequently reminded, by his conduct, of the gypsy's prophecy at Wimpfen.

CHAPTER XVIII.

GERMANS PLAY THE MARPLOTS ON ME.

Between 1833—36 I entertained the project for a full University in the U. S. I believed, that such an institution should originate with Germans, and be modeled after the Universities of Germany. My main reason was: that there were no real Universities then in the U. S, and that, without a direct connection with the higher European culture, there could never be the right integrity in religious, scientific, political and economic culture here. My project took definite shape about 1835. I did not claim, that my idea was new, on the contrary, I asserted again and again: that, in the history of the world, younger nations established institutions of learning for mankind at large, for the purpose of having mental culture freed from fetters put upon it by existing establishments, that were bound up in some special orthodoxy. I pointed out the schools, that Pythagoras established for progressive Greek philosophy in Southern Italy; I adverted to the higher culture given to the Romans by the Grecians; I claimed also, that calling professors into foreign countries, with the view to have them teach — internationally —

scientific truths, was always the means of advancing the views in general knowledge. I asserted, further, that an interchange of scholars of distinction, between the great schools of a period, is positive evidence of a high degree of advanced intelligence. The very conception of a republic of letters rests on the axiom, that national frontiers do not and should not exist in it. I expressed my belief: that our example would be followed by other nations, represented in the U. S., and, that thus the U. S. would, eventually, have the completest educational development in the world. I published my general programme in the "Volksblatt", but forgot to keep a copy, and have to make my present statement from memory. The article in the Volksblatt attracted the attention of most of the German scholars then in the U. S. And my call for a delegate convention, at some central point in the U. S., like Pittsburgh, composed of representatives from respective localities, was welcomed by all. In Cincinnati an underhand movement was entered into, by which I was not chosen as a delegate, but Walker, who was a theological graduate of Tübingen, was elected. Walker was always a spoiler of the plans of others, just as he wasted his own life. He asked me for my financial scheme, including the land contract, on which it was based. He never returned the papers to me, nor even presented them at the convention. I will now explain this my plan:

I had made an optional purchase of 937 acres of land in Colerain Township, about 12 miles North of Cincinnati. The cost of the land was to be $27,000; it was held by Judge Este, a brother-in-law of Gen. Harrison. The land lay in one body. Very little of it had been cleared, most of it was upland, full of healthy localities. I proposed to reserve 37 acres in the center for the University grounds and buildings. The remaining 900 acres were to be sub-divided into acre lots, to be deeded, in a lottery drawing, to 900 German subscribers of a $1000.00 each, in cash, for the University. The $900,000, thus obtained, were to be a fund, from which the professors were to be paid. It was to be placed with the City of Cincinnati, as a perpetual debt, bearing six per cent interest annually — $54,000.00. The professors to be appointed by trustees, chosen by the subscribers to the fund, and residents on the lots. The buildings on the land to be paid for by cash subscriptions, and the sale of scholarships generally.

This plan and contract I gave Walker, who took it with him, to the convention, at Pittsburgh. The convention met; Walker was present. After some discussion, the German University was abandoned, and in its stead, it was "resolved", to establish, at Philipsburg, on the Ohio river, near New Harmony, a Normal School, for educating teachers in the German language. The Normal School never came into active operation. There were some Academic Buildings bought in Philipsburg, that had been erected for another purpose. But no real start was ever made toward carrying out the Normal School scheme. It killed, for the time, my plans, but it was also a suicide, so far as their plans were concerned. My own view, has been for some time, and is now: that the failure of my project. is another illustration of the truth of the couplet:

"A lost moment, eternity itself cannot bring back."

As to Walker himself, his subsequent sad fate, is but one instance, of dozens of men, that went to rack and ruin here, who, if they had remained in Germany, would have had, if not an honorable, at least no such a pernicious career, as Walker had here. I wrote his life, under a fictitious name, for the "German Pioneer", and there I leave him, adding only Bismarck's remark as to such men: "A journalist is generally a man, who has lost his vocation." Walker had lost his career as a clergyman, and he died in the gutter. The gipsy's prophesy, to me, had, in him, its illustration: after the wrong done me, he never again prospered.

CHAPTER XIX.

FAMILY JOYS AND FAMILY SORROWS.

The first child, a son, was born to us May 5th, 1839. We called him Henry. We then lived in the third story, on Fifth street, north of the Middle Market House, between Vine and Walnut. My wife's sister, Elizaeeth, was living with us. And my wife's parents had moved from Louisville to Cincinnati. The child made, by its very presence among us, a great change in our way of living, thinking and acting. Some of our young social friends dropped quietly away; political associates became less intimate, whilst we formed closer ties with other families, that had children, such as Mrs. Miller and her daughter, Mr. and Mrs. Molitor, neighbor Wolffe, Mr. and Mrs. Bouche, Duhme, Hanna B. Krenking and others. We had also more country acquaintances, to-wit: the families Daudel, Heath, Vaihinger, etc. My best, indeed, I may say, my only bachelor friend, — Cronenbold — who had done me more good by elevating my tastes, and getting me to quit lower associates, had just left Cincinnati, and gone to St. Louis. He was, for several years, the only type-setter of musical notes in the city, at Messrs. James & Bros.' Printing office, on Walnut St. The loss of Cronenbold's society made us cherish the more our acquaintance with Mr. and Mrs. Bouche. They gave me much advice as to my mode of living, and presented me finally, with the work of Dr. Hufeland. Its title is "Macroby", which means "The art, to live long". I estimate, that this book has lenghtened my life at least 30 years. I have the book now in my library. The parents of my wife, Swiss people, from the Canton Aaran, that had lived in Louisville, when we were married, were then also living in Cincinnati, on a small piece of land, and to them the birth of a grand-son was also very gratifying.

This birth was followed, in the fall, by my purchase of the business of Messrs. Coffin. It increased in volume and profits, as I stuck closer to it than ever. Everybody took this as a special blessing of providence, and so did I, when a year afterward, the inventory, made by my brother Paul and myself, showed me to be worth at least $6000.00. I then bought me a house and lot, 100 feet square, in Wade's Woods, within the corporate limits of the city, a little West of Freeman and South of Eighth St., for $2000.00, and moved there, intending to use it for our suburban residence for life. It was to us, for a while, quite an enjoyment. We kept a horse and spring-wagon. I had plenty of opportunities to enjoy horse-back riding. My brother Paul attended well to the business. But, in the Fall following, our first-born son fell a victim to the Malaria of Mill Creek, and died November, 1841. Caroline, our first daughter, who was born yet on Fifth st., in the Fall of 1840, came very near dying of the same disease. We had the two best German physicians, Drs. Schneider and Paul; but in vain. The burial of that child of ours, was the bitterest pang I ever felt in my life. I regarded his death as proof, that my own constitution was weak. I could not bear to continue to live in that house; I sold it. My cravings about my own health in the presence of Dr. Paul, who had known me for years, made him upbraid me. He predicted, that I would outlive him, and reach my 80th year. Mr. Bouche gave me the already mentioned work of Hufeland. I read, nay, I studied it, and followed its precepts as gospel truth. A paradox, that occurred during the illness of my two children, troubled my mind a good deal, as to medical science; namely: Henry, that died, took implicitly all the medicine, prescribed by the Doctors; Caroline, that recovered, refused, to take any. She persisted in asking for milk, which the Drs. had denied her, until she got it by my orders, the Drs. finally acquiescing in it. The query, raised by me, was: did *not taking* the medicine, save Caroline? Or, *taking it*, kill Henry? I believed then, and do now, that the milk worked the difference. A year or so afterwards, when we lived in the country, Caroline again became ill, she again got milk, fresh from the cow, morning and evening, and nothing else; it again saved her life.

We moved back to the dwelling over our store on Fifth Street, much tried by the question: What was my life really to be? My father, when I wrote to him the death of my first born, reminded me, that he too had lost his first born son, Julius, when but a year old. He begged us both, to take our loss as an admonition, from the chastening hand of Providence, to be prepared for sorrows, and not to be too reckless in our enjoyments."

CHAPTER XX.

MY PARTICIPATION IN THE ELECTION OF 1840.

Early in 1840 I declined, deeming myself too inexperienced, to be nominated as a candidate for the position of Representative of Hamilton County in the Legislature of Ohio. I recommended John Myers, the oldest German Democrat of Cincinnati, in my stead. I took nevertheless a very active part in the campaign, both, in the press, and on the stump. I made speeches in Ohio, Indiana and Kentucky, paying my own expenses, travelling mostly on horseback. The Democratic ticket in Hamilton county was defeated, with the exception of G. W. Holmes (for Senator). The year before, —1839— the Democrats had a 1000 majority for their whole ticket. It was immediately charged: that the change had been effected by imported voters; but, it was also contended, that Gen. Harrison's popularity caused the difference. I believed, that both causes had something to do with the result. I knew Harrison well, was on friendly terms with him, although differing with him in politics.

Harrison had been up to 1828 a Republican, which was then the name of the afterward called Democratic party. The old Jeffersonian ideas, modified by Madison and Monroe, were then his fundamental political conceptions. What he objected to, in 1840, in the Democratic party, were the changes from the old Jeffersonian politics, which Jackson, under New York inspirations, had effected in Democratic politics. Harrison was in 1840 really at sea in his political ideas. He had not the progressive knowledge of his age. He had an unbounded faith in his own popularity, and he asserted, that he knew of no purchases of voters for him. These were, however, proven, to have been perpetrated by the corrupt men, that conducted the campaign, for him, in their own and associated moneyed interests. Harrison had disavowed some of the measures of the Whig party. The investigations in the Senatorial contest, between John C. Wright and George Holmes, showed this. The voters were imported from the River counties in Ky. No direct proofs of Harrison's connivance were submitted. Then, as now, the parties were corrupter, than their leaders.

I gained, during the canvass of 1840, considerable reputation, as a public writer and speaker; the latter by an extemporized discussion at a meeting in Whitewater Township, on the Harrison Turnpike, 18 miles from Cincinnati. Early in the morning, on the day of the meeting. Gideon Ayers, the Secretary of the Democratic Executive Committee, came to my store, and insisted on my going with him to the meeting, that was to be held, at 11 o'clock, and continued all day. I went with him, and found, on arrival, the Democrats dejected, not only for the want of speakers, but still more for the lack of Democrats on the ground. The Whigs were elated, for they had on hand four, so called, "big guns"; namely: Southgate. Wright, Johnson and Pendleton, Sen., the latter being the candidate for Congress. There was a large concourse of their partisans. My appearance raised the temper of the Democrats a little, but it raised that of the Whigs still more. They were proud of their speakers, and thought, the "little Dutchman", as they called me, only a convenient victim for their onslaught. They tendered me a *free and equal* discussion. This meant: that their speakers would open, and that I should follow each respectively, half an hour about. I being the only Democratic speaker, would have been sandwiched between their four speakers, and would have been made mince-meat of. I told them, that I had come to talk to Democrats, and would address a mixed meeting. only by the consent of the Democrats. I suggested, however, that it might satisfy both, if I addressed the crowd. left. after their speakers were through, and take my own time to reply to what had been said. Then they might select a speaker, to follow me. if there was any time left. This they accepted promptly, expecting, to have both the Whigs and the Democrats to speak to. and to load me so heavily, for any after reply, that I would break down in attempting it.

I cannot give the whole of the proceedings; it suffices, to state, that their speakers had their say, in a continuous flow of oratory, for four hours. I took brief notes. About four in the afternoon my time came. I had much easier work, than I anticipated; for, all I needed. for a complete victory, was, to play off the inconsistencies of their several speakers on each other. It was a peculiar characteristic of the Whig party. then, to combine, within itself, all the heterogenious elements of American politics, that were outside of the Democratic party. The speakers. that I had to reply to, represented this motley partisanism. Wright was an old Federalist; Southgate. a Henry Clay Kentucky Whig; Johnson, a Quaker; and, Pendleton, an old Virgininia Republican. Each was eloquent on his own special ground. and it was a masterly array, as long as nobody exposed the fact, that each embodied a censure, on his fellow speaker, for entertaining erroneous views of his own, such as National banks, Protective Tariffs, Encouraging Land-speculations and catering to Puritanism. I, on the other hand, attacked this mongrelism. and showed the integrity of the Democratic party, and argued, from both, that the Whig party was unfit, to be the country's public authority, because it was a retroactive party, and wanted to revive old wrongs. while the Democratic party tended to reform, to advanced ideas and measures. I used. especially, the utter confusion, there was in the Whig party. as to public improvements, and called them the political loiterers of the time. When I was through, the feeling of the audience was reversed: the Democrats were exultant. the Whigs despondent. No regular reply to my remarks, was even attempted. And now, to everybody's surprise, arose Othoniel Looker, a former Senator and Lieutenant-Governor, of Ohio, whose old personal friendship for Harrison was known. He accorded to my remarks a complete vindication. I left for home amidst excited hurrahs for me.

The news, of this, reached the public soon, and I had, thenceforth, my hands full of electioneering work for the rest of the campaign. I have already given the result. Harrison's election and inaugural address were but verifications of the position, that I had taken. This became the more clear, after Harrison died in the Spring of 1841, and on John Tyler becoming President. Tyler's veto of the National bank project, was offensive to nine-tenths of the Whigs. The suspension of the State banks, in 1842, under the lead of Nic. Biddle; the wild courses pursued, as to the public lands; the defective public administration of the Post Office Department, etc., all these alarmed the public mind, and satisfied the country, that the Whig party should not have been placed in power. Some said, jocularly: Reemelin is no longer the "Little Dutchman", he is a "Little Prophet."

CHAPTER XXI.

EVENTS — NOT WILL — DIRECT MY COURSE.

The expenses caused to me, by the election of 1840, pointed with unmistakable force to a return to my business. My brother Paul had done well for me in the management of my affairs. He now urged, that our business be enlarged, and arrangements made, to have more direct connections with the sources of the supplies of our trade. I saw very plainly, that he aimed at such a conduct of our trade, as would engage us both to our full capacity. I agreed unreservedly with this idea. And, with that in view, I made early in 1841 a journey to New York, for the purpose of securing there the services of several commission merchants, that had been the purchasers for the Coffins and myself; namely: Messrs. Baldwin, Mitchell, Fail and others. When I arrived in New York, I found, that they were more than willing to come to free, definite arrangements with me. They hinted, that they would prefer to act for me, and drop Messrs. Coffin, because they liked my business ways, as to the use of credit, better. I arranged then with them, that they should buy for me, at the wholesale auctions, as I gave them orders; they to charge me no commission, provided: I remitted the cash within ten days from the date of the purchase and forwarding to me. Thus I got Tea and many other articles at lowest wholesale prices, and got clear of the necessity to keep a bank account to any extent in Cincinnati. This gave me cheap prices and secured my own safety, for the western banks were very unsafe then. I arranged, at that time, also for a German commission house, E. & T. Poppe, to expedite the goods I imported from Europe. such as Dutch herrings, Succory, Wine, Prunes, etc. I returned to Cincinnati, expecting a very decided enlargement of my business. My brother Paul thought so too. and it pleased him decidedly, because, he believed, that it would necessarily tend, to take me out of politics.

I had. however, hardly got home, when a letter came from my father, with orders, that one of us should come home. The reason for this extraordinary order was. that father wanted a son in the home business, so as to relieve him of overwork and annoyances. Father was then 61 years old. Paul held, that I better go. I thought otherwise, being a married man, and having a child, besides owning property and the business here. I suggested, that we should draw lots. to which Paul agreed. At the drawing, Paul drew the ticket: "to go home." It did not take long. to arrange for his home journey. He went. by stage, via: Columbus to Cleveland, thence by steamer to Buffalo, and thence by canal and Hudson River, to New York. He crossed the Ocean by a Paquet-Ship to Havre, and then went by stage, through France, to Heilbronn. My father received him gladly. and soon made him partner, which enabled him, to marry an excellent wife. with means. and settled him. to all appearances, for a long life in Heilbronn.

My own condition would now have been rather forlorn, if my wife had not proven a most capable business woman, and practical help to me. in every way. Her assistance made it possible. to transact my business with the kind of clerks and salesmen, that I had then. We lived all through 1841 in the third story over our store. My sister-in-law — Elizabeth — assisted my wife some in the household. up to the time of her marriage to Seifert. We carried on, in the rear of the store and the second story. a rectifying Establishment and Vinegar Factory. Our business went along prosperously. I was making between \$3.000.00 to \$4,000.00 a year. I gave politics but little opportunity to interfere with my business.

I lost some time, that Winter. in attending to a special business. which I will now explain. I was early in 1841 made agent of the estate of Reimer Ruge, deceased. His lands were situated in West Virginia. near Parkersburg. He had bought them about 1770. A Mr. Testdorf. of Hamburgh. Germany, who had been temporarily in Cincinnati. in 1841. had recommended me for this position, to Dr. Bruns. a lawyer. in Lübeck, where Miss Caroline Ruge, the principal heiress, resided. I went to Parkersburg. to learn all I could, about the lands. early in Spring of 1841. There I found General Jackson — not *President* Jackson — who was the attorney of Miss Ruge. Jackson had had charge of the lands for years. His representations did not sound favorable to me. for an early disposition of the estate, such as I was directed to make. Nothing daunted, I instituted inquiries into matters generally. and they brought me information about the purchase of the lands in West Virginia, by Ruge, about 70 years previous, including Washington's journey and land purchases there, in the middle of the XVIII. century. The fact, that the latter were adjoining my client's lands, interested me, of course, specially, and I became thenceforth an intense inquirer into the earlier American history, and its realities. I had to give up many of my, formerly acquired, romantic ideas.

CHAPTER XXII.

MY CLIENT'S DIFFICULTIES.

I soon found out, that Reimer Ruge's heirs would have considerable difficulty in disposing of their lands. Their ancestor had purchased them and occupied them before the Revolution; but had left them, and became a non-resident proprietor, which gave him a questionable attitude under Virginian ideas of natural law. Non-resident ownerships, especially those of Europeans, were hard to establish and to maintain. Attorneys worked for *them* reluctantly, but for the *squatters* cheerfully, because the so-called "Relief Laws", and popular prejudices, were all in favor of the squatters. The surveys and records were, any way, carelessly made and kept. I concluded, to use my letters of introduction, to merchants in Parkersburg, to find some young attorney, that was as yet free from any entanglements on the subject, and would at least advise me in my first provisional steps. Such a one I found in Mr. Spencer. After comparing notes with him, I concluded, to employ a guide, and to go with him into the country, on horseback, and hunt out the lands, by the aid of old papers, which lawyer Jackson had called: Surveys. They covered about 30,0 0 acres of land, that had cost Ruge about 20¢ an acre. We were given the names of the persons residing on the lands, under some possessory title. After much trouble we found, that about 27,000 acres might as well be considered as lost to us, as those, living on them, had secured, what was called: "*adverse possession*", under the laws of Virginia. The remaining 3,000 were represented to us as about half still recoverable. The kind of ever wild, ever land-hungry, and never settled inhabitants in our Southern and Western States, confronted us, as resident proprietors, on our entire examination. And, I saw very clearly, why formerly the Indian, much like them, as he was, went under before them. So I had very little hope for Ruge's heirs, non-residents and foreigners, as they were. I employed Mr. Spencer to ascertain all the necessary facts and to report to me. I then returned to Cincinnati. After a few months I got a full report from Mr. Spencer, that corroborated, in the main, the statements already made. Eventually I found a purchaser, who was willing to buy for $6,000 the 3000 acres, with the risk of getting only 1500 acres. After careful inquiry I concluded to sell, subject to the home heirs. I transmitted to them Mr. Spencer's report and my own explanation, and they concluded to accept the proposition, in the Fall of 1842. It was the only definite offer they had had for years. A year afterwards I paid them the money.

In the Spring of 1842 I bought of my father-in-law the 14 acres of land he owned and lived on in Green township. I had had all my life a wish, to have a rural residence. I got the wish from my grandfather, on my father's side; and the purchase therefore gratified me very much. I paid my father-in-law $1400 for the land. In the Summer of 1842 I bought 160 more, that were adjoining, and paid $4,000, making a total of $5,400, for the 174. The 14 acres had a good dwelling on them, of which the middle part was a first class two-story log cabin. I had the building repaired and improved, and then we occupied it. My good "business" wife now proved herself to be a good farmer's wife. She did, for a while, the work without female help. I rode every week-day on horseback to the city, to attend to my business there, and returned at night. These daily rides improved my health, but made me rather lean. After a while I procured a spring wagon, and made my daily journeys in it, with much more convenience to myself.

September 5th, 1842, another son was born to us. We called him Mark Foster. Mark being for my wife's father's name, and Foster for my wife's mother's maiden name. He was a beautiful boy and looked health itself. We regarded his birth as an assurance, that he would be the son that would perpetuate our joined name in America.

I will now return to a few political matters. The main evil in the election result of 1840, was not so much the defeat of Van Buren, as it was: that the leaders of those Northern Democrats, who meant to cure American politics of certain mischiefs, were thereby deprived of the power and influence to do so, in a critical moment. They became either disheartened, or disconcerted. The mischiefs consisted principally in the subordination of National politics to local, social potencies; that had grown chiefly of Southern ultra pro-slavery propensities. This had the effect, that the mainspring of all individual participations in politics, now became personal ambitions, the obtainment of office and great wealth. Personal party services gave the preemption to the offices, both as a question of official patronage and of popular election. The easier acquirements of wealth, passed under the control of privileged corporations, such as banks of issue, factories and other companies, so that unbiased, unselfish and truly patriotic voting at elections, in the Legislature or other representative bodies, became almost extinct. These evil tendencies were recognized gradually by more and more observing minds, after 1840; and Van Buren and his friends were their embodiment. When in 1842, under the lead of Nic. Biddle, ex-president of the defunct U. S. bank, all the state banks except five, suspended specie payments, it confirmed these issues with the Democrats, and brought conviction to nearly all; that combinations, if not conspiracies, of social interests and ambitious men, were possible now in the United States, to an extent, that would render it, if not impossible, yet exceedingly difficult, to purify thenceforth, American politics from the corrupter social influences.

Any person might see, with half an eye, that the establishment of solid integrity, was the aim of the hard money, free trade and sub-treasury Democrats—like Van Buren, Blair and Benton; whilst loose extravagance and privileges were the object of Clay, Ewing and Webster. I do not mean to assert, that, if Van Buren had been re-elected in 1840, there would have been an immediate and perpetual solidity in American politics; but I assert, that Van Buren's defeat, gave to the opposite tendency, a strength and intensity that rendered it nearly impossible to renew efforts to counteract it. Had Van Buren been elected, and we would never have had the war for the annexation of Texas, nor the repeal of the Missouri Compromise, nor the Tariff of 1842, nor the wholesale chartering of banks, nor other extravagancies, too numerous to mention. Such demagogues, as Stephen A. Douglass, would, then never have swayed the Democratic party and made it a mere Mutual Insurance Co. for office. And Lewis Cass would never have befogged it, by his dubiousness, as to all public questions.

I belonged, between 1839 and 1843, to every organization in the Democratic party, that had for its object a re-awakening of the solid American economic sense, that existed under the lead of Jackson, Van Buren and Benton. I was, with other Democrats, always particularly zealous to counteract the false notions, which the Whigs advocated at that time, as to public and private credit. There were men then, as now, who asserted, that going into debt were acts, creating capital. The multiplication of banks of issue was advocated on that very basis. Some persons went so far, as to claim, that large amounts of indebtedness were evidences of prosperity; and whoever asserted, that money, saved and accumulated, was the true way to create capital, was laughed at, as an old fogy.

The Democrats were divided then into "hards" and "softs." The excitement was great, and every election turned on this point. And so it came, that every Legislature, that passed a bank or other special charter, was considered, by Democrats, a traitor to popular rights. One winter the great issue was: whether certain banks, eleven in number, that were about expiring, should be re-chartered? We "hards" won; that is to say: the charter was refused. Thereupon, we resolved to hold a celebration meeting; then the "softs" resolved to hold a condemnation meeting. Each party claimed the Court House as its place of meeting. We "hards" took possession early, and made Postmaster Burke our Chairman.

The "softs" now made a demonstration, to dispossess us, but we held on : and then the "softs", seeing many persons in the Court

House Yard, adjourned to the yard, thinking, to get up a meeting there. But, we "hards" stuck to the Court House, believing, that there alone the meeting would be regarded as the regular authentic place. We then read our resolutions, and spoke in favor of them. Soon we had the crowd with us. Seeing this, the "softs" re-entered the meeting in quads, and threw packages of red pepper at our speakers. The "softs" expected, that this would disperse us, but not so. On the contrary, we stood our ground, and finally passed our resolutions, without further molestations; and then adjourned. The crowd was with us, and hurrahed for us. That was the celebrated "*Red Pepper Meeting*", at which William Corry, Burke, Dawson, and others, myself included, vindicated gloriously the integrity of the people through the Democratic party. There were many similar encounters, but none as racy or as fiery, as the meeting just described. The eleven resolutions, which passed, were drawn by me. The brevity, sharp cogency, and pungent language, made them specially suited for passage by this boisterous crowd. Those assembled could and did repeat each, as it was read, and the loud repetition by the meeting, in the chorus, gave the whole thing an eclat and enthusiasm, which secured us the victory. It being but a victory of a part of the Democracy, and not, as those between 1836 and 1840 were, embodiments of ideas in the whole party, under a recognized leader, made the situation precarious. This left the question, of finally giving it National recognition, still open; and all efforts to that end, were interfered with, through Tyler's intrigues with Texan politicians. And similar cross purposes were played at other localities. It always meant a postponement, of true National politics, to mere local social movements. In fact, we had then species of *Politics*, that were the opposite of honest public conduct.

CHAPTER XXIII.

FIRST RE-VISIT OF MY NATIVE LAND.

The re-call of my brother Paul, and his success in father's business, in Heilbronn, caused two movements here, that neither of us had contemplated; first: a revival of a longing in me, to see Germany again, and my folks there; second: making arrangements here for carrying out this purpose, without too severe a burden on my wife, and without serious jeopardy to my business.

The marriage of my wife's sister to Francis Seifert, made him a possible person in such an arrangement. His business in Jeffersonville, was a retail grocery, which, *if* dissimilar to mine, was still suggestive of S. having a general experience in the grocery business. He got, to some extent, an insight into my business, when first in Cincinnati. At least, he saw its success, and, of course, compared it with his. His wife, as well, as he, had inclinations toward Cincinnati, and they increased, as his business in Jeffersonville grew not as successful as they wished.

When, therefore, after my brother's departure, I was troubled with more or less incompetent clerks, and this became a serious matter on our removal to the country, as my wife could not be in the store during my unavoidable absences; the suggestion arose, like a matter of course, that Seifert's giving up his business in Jeffersonville, and entering mine in Cincinnati, would be the proper measure all around. His relationship was deemed as a sort of security for his fidelity. Thus, what was first an idea, became a fact. Seifert and family moved into the dwelling above our store, and he became my clerk, with a share of profits, which is called in German "tantieme". He evinced considerable zeal, for fully qualifying himself for the business, and showed some fine capacities; but certain observations, as to which I cannot speak explicitly, convinced me, that his coming was a misjudged undertaking all around, so I severed the connection, paid him $400, and this enabled him to start a grocery business of his own, on Canal market, where he remained about a year. Afterward explanations of his previous conduct, while with me, were made, and this led to his re-entering into my business, and conducting it, with the assistance of his wife, during my visit to Germany in 1843. I thought of the gypsy's closing prophecy, but not deep enough.

Thus I was prepared to close up my arrangements for the journey. It was from the first understood, that wife with baby and Caroline, should stay on the farm. When this was determined upon, my father-in-law announced his desire to accompany me, and this I gladly accepted. That led to my mother-in-law staying with my wife on the farm, which was very satisfactory to myself and wife. All this was fixed definitely by March 20th. I now ordered in New York the purchase of a ticket over the Ocean, and otherwise prepared for the journey. Between March 20th and April 1st, there was extreme cold weather in and around Cincinnati. The thermometer on our farm March 27th was 23 degrees below zero. We left our farm on April 7th for Cincinnati in a sleigh, and departed the same day for Pittsburgh by a regular river steamer. Ice was floating in the river. I sold the sleigh, horse and harness for $40.00. The horse was the best I ever owned for horse-back riding. We left the farm in charge of Mueller, a good farmer. My wife and family resided on it as stated; my mother-in-law also living there. We reached Pittsburgh, April 10th. Our passage up the river cost $5.00, each, including board. The fare was good. There was much drinking and card-playing on board. My father-in-law and myself kept aloof from both. I was specially interested, to see the towns and scenes again, which I had passed in 1833. They had much improved, but many things remained the same and were easily recognized. The

Ohio was then, yet the main thoroughfare for Eastern travel, from Cincinnati to New York. At Pittsburgh my father-in-law went to his younger brother, who had joined the most absurd religious sect, I ever heard of. The meeting of the two brothers was not an agreeable one, as I soon saw. We meant, to leave for the East immediately, but the canal travel had not been opened. We heard very contradictory rumors, as to the probabilities of the opening of the canal. Some said, that the canals were free from ice, others contradicted that. We were to start April 15th, at noon; but did not get away from Pittsburgh before late in the evening. We had, therefore, time, to attend the public meeting, for the celebration of Jefferson's birthday. We heard much florid oratory, but no clear views, as to what Jefferson really meant. Indeed, I may as well state, that the U. S. were then, as now, very much at sea, about the real character of their public men. They are so, for the reason, that they are divided into parties, and are, therefore, in the habit, of either using too much eulogy, or excessively sweeping vituperation, as to their public men.

We departed from Pittsburgh in the dark, and, as we could not really see anything on the outside, we went to our berths, and were soon asleep. We had been told, that we would make 60 miles by day-break. But, when we awoke, we had made only 20 miles, and were retained, for repairs, at a dock. And thus, it went on all the first day. We travelled between good and bad news, and were frequently in danger of our lives. We reached Johnstown on the second, instead of the first day, and were there told, next morning, that the inclined plane over the mountains was under repair, there having been a severe accident; we would be detained for a week or two. This news broke my father-in-laws patience, and he determined, to go back to Dent, to his wife and daughter, by the first returning canal boat. He had this opportunity that same evening, and, he took the return track, and bid me good-bye. I wrote through him to my wife one more adieu. I got pretty fair lodgings at a small hotel in Johnstown; but I had to remain there only thirty-six hours. Then we crossed the mountain by railroad to Hollidaysburgh, whence we went, by canal, to Harrisburgh, and from there, by railroad, to Philadelphia. Part of the way, the rail roads were inundated, whilst part of the canals had not water enough. "But, all is well, that ends well", and so I got safe to the "City of brotherly love", and there lodged at Krafft's hotel. The latter proved to be a fair boarding house, as to eating; but the rooms were disagreeable on account of stinging lodgers, that were not entered on the Hotel books. They stuck most tenaciously to us travellers. At Krafft's hotel, I got wine from my native land — Neckar wine — at 5 cents a glass, about half a pint. I enjoyed it as advance welcome from Vaterland.

My first visit was, to my former employers, Mr. and Mrs. Beamish. On going there, I met on the street, unexpectedly my first debtor in America, Weisser. He recognized me as quickly as I did him, and instantly crossed the street, to evade me, but I was too quick for him, and confronted him. He was non-plussed, but I put him at his ease, by announcing to him, that, "our meeting was not by my desire, but, having met, I wished to say to him, that all the payment I was going to claim, was: to tell him, that I did not want any: that his borrowing gave my whole course in America a good turn, because I went to work without delay, and have done well by it ever since. Give my regards to your fair lady, and accept my hearty farewell." "Stop! said he, my wife is dead. I am not able to work much, but do about get along; you shall be paid." "No, sir, said I, keep it! as a keepsake; good-bye." I left him, and have never met him again. The Wimpfen prophecy came to my mind.—

When I got to my old store, I got still more distressing information. Beamish too had died. Mrs. Beamish (to me she was Mrs. Bald still) was carrying on the old business with the help of her two sons, one by her first husband — Bald — the other by Beamish. The oldest daughter, Miss Bald, had got well married. The younger, Miss Beamish, was as lovely, as Irish-American girls are usually in this country. I spent several hours with them all. They enjoyed my visit, but there was something, that I did not talk about, and they did not mention: Beamish's conduct and death. I learned it from others. He often forgot himself in drink, and then shrank from his usual intercourse with his family. He finally concluded, to re-visit Ireland, and the old homestead, near Cork, on Bantry Bay. He came back, but his conduct was unchanged; he lived but a year or two afterwards, and then died. I had sincerely wished him a long life of usefulness, and was sorry, that I had not met him again.

I visited, of course, my Quaker friends, the Ritters. The two gentlemen I had letters of introduction to, in 1823, had died. The young ladies, I had the honor to know, were well married. The young gentlemen were doing a moderately good dry goods business. When I told them of my journey to Germany, they thought it a fine enjoyment, and expressed a wish to see Holland, their ancestral home. My special friends, Mr. and Mrs. Betz, I found alive, but retired from business. Their hotel was kept by another person. I called, of course, upon the glue manufacturer, Mr. Mark. He was infirm, but through his son, I heard news from my wife's relations in Switzerland. He insisted, that I should make their house my home, but I excused myself, as not having time. On the 25th of April I went to New York, part by railroad, and part by steamer. There I stopped at Lovejoy's Hotel, a good lodging place. My business acquaintances were hospitably courteous. My countrymen, the bankers, E. and T. Poppe, of Cologne, introduced me to prominent Germans; and among them to: Baron Von Eichthal, who, in publishing the "Schnellpost", gave to the United States the first newspaper conducted on the best possible plan, then pursued by the "Allgemeine Zeitung" in Augsburg. The editorials were written by persons, who had a first class university education. The example, he set, led to decided improvements among the German newspapers. Baron gave me letters to his correspondents in Europe, and they were of great advantage to me in various ways. They gave me outlooks as to European politics, which I could not then have received in any other way. I saw then, what I have often noticed since, that the best new political developments in the United States, have ever come from Europe. I then came to the conclusion: that as Americans are likely to be in the future, so there will always be an interdependence of America and Europe for a higher culture. The thought arose then in my mind: whether a stoppage of blind emigration, such as now exists from Europe, would not be a blessing to that continent?

On the evening of the first of May, I left for Boston, by the Stonington route. I arrived there next morning, and after a good breakfast, at the American Hotel, I took a good ride over Boston, and saw it pretty thoroughly. In the evening I went by railroad, with snowbanks on both sides, to Portland, and got there next morning. There, after breakfast, I called on the brothers of my wife, at their shop, near the Exchange. They were cutlers by trade. They took me to their family homes on Telegraph Hill. Each had a house and lot of of his own. Their wives were good Yankee women. They had not seen their sister, nor she them, for 15 years. They and their families were members of good standing in the Presbyterian Church. They were not rich, but comfortably situated. I enjoyed two days with them. That our religious views were different, they saw, as well as I. And we both understood, that so it must remain. That perception was not an annoying thought to me, but it was to them, as I saw very plainly.

Portland was to me of great interest. While I was there, a public meeting was held, in favor of the railroad to Montreal. Mr. Fessenden, a very able man, spoke. I corresponded, at that time, for the "Cincinnati Enquirer", and in my letters gave my views for the railroad project. The letters were copied into other papers. I felt certain then, and feel certain now, that in the course of time, both the people of Maine and the United States, will see more and more clearly, that populations raised in New England, are not and cannot be congenial elements of an American society, that is to combine a mixed population; neither can New England ever be the fair ally of the rest of the present Union. The Yankees must ever aim at a command in a union with us, which is not their honest due. Their natural necessities will make them use their religious tenets as a convenience for advocating political measures, that cannot be successfully argued on square argument. They will want to regulate

American society religiously, and will have all those for foes, who want to be free in that respect. My brothers-in-law in Maine, being Swiss, should have studied Basle's History. That Canton does not enjoy the good will of Switzerland as fully as they might, if they held more liberal views. And the same fate awaits Maine and Massachusetts to-day. At the railroad meeting I spoke of, I learned from the maps, that were exhibited: that Portland is a natural seaport of Canada and not of the United States. I mentioned these my views to a Canadian Frenchman, a clock repairer in Portland, and he extended them, by claiming, that Maine, New Hampshire, Vermont, and part of New York, should be annexed to Canada, and then the whole made one Northern Empire, from the Atlantic to the Pacific. I asked him: how he could reconcile such thoughts with his fealty to the United States? He answered: "O! losing that part of New England, would be no loss to the United States."

I returned to New York May 5th, and embarked in the packet ship Ashburton on the 7th. We rode, as stated, on the railroad between Portland and Boston, along snowbanks three feet high. And on May 7th we sailed down New York Bay with snow on all the heights. There was an overplus of cabin passengers, and I had to accept a berth in the cabin of the first mate. It was no loss to me. My quarters were roomy, my meals excellent in quality, correct in time, and abundant in quantity. The officers were communicative and free in all their ways to me. I might have taken a full share of their grog, but preferred to have, for myself, a very good Bordeaux wine at two shillings a bottle. We arrived in Liverpool June 1st, after a passage of 24 days. By the recommendation of the first mate, I took rooms at the Angel Hotel, and found good fare at reasonable prices; the bed was clean and excellent. I stopped two days in Liverpool, and formed a high opinion of British commercial integrity.

Passing out of Liverpool June 3rd, by the tunnel, I shall never forget: how cheering to me was the sight of the beautiful green, bathed as it was in dew, that met my eyes. I had not seen green nature for six months, and was now rushed, so to speak, into the greenest country in the world. It was a bright, lovely morning. A Cornwall mine owner had become acquainted with me at the Angel Hotel, and he took me, on arrival in London, to King's Arms Tavern, on Cheapside. The tavern suited me exactly; for I wanted to live like a well-to-do sensible Englishman, that associates with trades people. The roast beef, the mutton chops, dumplings, bread, pies and ale, were rich, cheap and in full supply. I asked for no extras and was fully satisfied. The prices were $1.25 per day, and much less than I expected, having heard so much of things, being dear in England. The location was very suitable for my main object: to see London quick and to see it well. It was my first visit to London, and I wanted to board central'y, so as to have it easy going and coming to my hotel. The first day I saw in rapid succession: St. Paul's Cathedral, the docks, the tower and the tunnel. At the latter I obtained, by coincidence, a fair sight of the Queen and Prince Albert. I was in one of the middle arches, getting a miniature model in lead of the tunnel, when we noticed a commotion; ushers rushed by, not noticing us, bidding everybody to get out; but we did not. Soon the Queen's party came near to where we stood. They received copies of the miniature in lead. I saw nothing very startling in the Queen or her consort. Why should I? Still, I was gratified, to have had so near a view of them. After going back to my inn, and eating a good dinner, I went up the Thames in a steamer, and saw all along the river front the fine sights it presented. Next day I visited West Minster, the new houses of Parliament, Hyde Park, Kensington Gardens and other sights. One day I spent at Windsor, and realized there most fully: how mean a man Henry the VIII. must have been, to have had killed Anna Boleyn.

For going to my native home, I chose the route through the North Sea, to: Ostend, Aix la Chapelle, Cologne, up the Rhine, to Mannheim, and from there up the River Neckar to Heilbronn. I started June 7th, by steamer on the Thames at 4 A. M. We reached Ostend in the evening. Having just crossed the ocean, I did not get sea sick; but numerous persons did, though there was a light sea. On arrival, we had a fine dinner at Hotel du Baines. On board I had made the acquaintance of a son of Lord Lyndhurst, and we were neighbors at the table. Next morning we were thrown together on the railroad, and stopped also at the same hotel at Colonge. He was glad to have found some one, to whom he could talk English, and to hear something of America, his mother being an American. He accompanied me up the Rhine, and we finally became frank and free with each other. I took the liberty to call his attention to the fact, that his bills were always much higher than mine. He thought it extortion. but I reminded him, that his English ways caused the landlords and waiters more trouble than my German ways. I pointed out to him, too, that his signing himself, a nobleman, inevitably led to his being supplied with costlier things. He was a very sensible young man. When I met him three months afterwards, in Switzerland, he had improved on my advice, and now thanked me for it kindly. It reminded me of an observation I had often made, to-wit: that Englishmen have ever been learners from Germans. King Alfred learned from the cotemporaries of Charles the Great; Cranmer from Luther; Melbourne from Prince Albert. Insular protuberances seem to need German trimming, and English speculations corrections from German economists.

CHAPTER XXIV.

MY ARRIVAL IN MY NATIVE LAND IN 1843.

In the middle of June I arrived, in my native city, early in the morning, by the Mail Coach; it stopped at my uncle's hotel. Breakfast was just ready, and I sat down as one of the passengers. My dear aunt, my mother's sister, waited on the table, and handed me my coffee, without recognizing me. I felt like kissing her hands. Soon my uncle came out of his office, the way-bill in his hand, and, looking around the table, walked up to me, he slapped me on my shoulder and cried: "O! you scamp, still playing truant? But it is no use, I know you." This of course, brought me quickly into the embraces of my aunt, who wept for joy. After breakfast I skipped off for my father's house. There also at first, no one know me, but soon the old servants recognized me, and the news spread. I was subjected to a very boisterous reception. My father alone was very reserved in his treatment of me. His first words were: "This surprise is not right, you ought to have written, and announced the time of your arrival. He fell now, however, upon my neck, and wept like a child. What he thought, I never knew. My step-mother and her children, looked on me as a welcome, but still new addition to the family. I had a similar feeling. Soon, however, all stiffness wore away. Other members of the family came, and it rained questions on me. I too had queries to make. I then concluded to go into town, visit relations and friends. After dinner my brother Paul, who had been on a tour to customers, returned, and he gave me my final re-introduction, by declaring: that I looked exactly, like I did, when he was with me in Cincinnati. My elder brother, Edward, who had married a wealthy lady in Gailsdorf, came on purpose, to see me, and to take me off with him to his home. My step-sister Ottilia paid me the queerest compliment. She told my father next day: "Why, father, he is of all your sons, most your son; for he talks with his features, just like you." My father was not as complimentary to her, he said: "You are a goose."

One thing was very plain to us all, namely: in the family, as it was in 1832, there was but one set of children; now, there were two. My two real sisters were both married, and had their own households. So too had my brothers. It took me some time, to pay them all visits. My first call, after I had gone to my eldest brother's home in Gailsdorf, was to my eldest sister Lina, who had married a captain in the army. She had an elegant home in Ludwigsburgh, and she suited it. Would, that my mother could have seen her in it! My youngest sister, the one, that is still alive, had married a rich elderly merchant. She, the beauty of the family, had met no beauty in her husband. And yet, she was well mated.

Among my brothers, Edward had done best, but was least satisfied; he would have liked to have been chief of my father's business, and his successor too. My father was still in the business, with brother Paul and Cousin Richard as partners and assistants. The business was in a very prosperous condition. My brother Theodore, who had studied theology, was now preceptor in the gymnasium of Hall. He was married to a clergyman's daughter and had one child. He had abandoned being a clergyman., and expected to be teacher for life.

I found, then yet. the rector of the gymnasium I attended in my youth. Also my preceptor in Marbach. I called on both, to express my gratitude. They thanked me for my call. I called on all my schoolmates, that were alive; the one, whom I loved most. showed me the least attention. Indeed, he was rude to me; and it hurt my feelings sharply.

It was at "Hall", 1843, on our father's 63rd birthday, that we five full brothers, to-wit: Edward, Carl Gustav, Theodore, Eberhardt and Paul, met all together, for the first and last time in our lives. We were all born in the same house, but were never all together under its roof, nor in any other, except then in Hall. As I write this, I am the only one of them alive. We had five rings made, and on them were engraved the names of all. and the occasion. that brought us together. We had a good collation and talked over the history of the "Rümelin" family. All at once, silence overcame us all; our eldest brother brought out a toast upon our dead mother, which was received in dead silence. Then we added jointly: "and father too," and then we drank the double toast in silence. My elder brother said afterwards: "It is queer, that I should bring out mother first; she is twenty years in her grave, yet we all join with her in our toast, our father, who is alive, but absent. We represent a re-union of our parents. I added: "Yes, but it is our reunion, that has brought it about."

I had promised my wife, that I would go to Switzerland, and there call upon her near relations, especially on her father's brother and family, at Aarau. She had been there, two years, in 1829 and 1830. as a child. with her parents. She still had some acquaintances there. that. she thought, would remember her. Accordingly, I went, by stage. in July, from Stuttgardt to Tübingen, thence to Tuttlingen, Schaffhausen. and then, along the Brunig, to Aarau, where lived my wife's uncle and aunt. and their daughter Henrietta, who was married to a merchant by the name of Billwiller. I spent a week with them. and became half Swiss myself. I called upon the other relatives of my wife and did it in company with my wife's charming cousin, Henrietta. I was always well received. I returned to Würtemberg through Lenzburgh. Zürich. Winterthur, Constanz and Friedrichshaven. In Aarau I saw the spoils. that had been seized in the Convent "Muri" from the ultra Catholics, in the so-called:

"Sonderbund War," or as we would call it: "Secesh War." The seizure was said to be worth ten million francs. At Friedrichshaven, I met my schoolmate and cousin, Ferdinand, son of my dear aunt Schmalzigaug. My cousin was the chief administrator of the royal estates there, which are very extensive. He took me over the entire domains, and they were of intense interest to me, because I saw there, for the first time, a large body of agricultural land, gardens and forests, attended to on *rules of highest culture;* including a dairy, fine cattle and horses, as well as all necessary buildings, barns, stables, hot-houses, including a fine palace. My cousin was an agricultural scientist and a finely educated gentleman. His explanations awakened a new range of study and experience to me. It revived in me many things I had heard of my grandfather, who had been an amateur farmer, vine-dresser and gardner, like myself, but had been, beside, a large stock raiser, especially of fine Spanish sheep. I became aware, in all humility, how small all *my* agricultural work and aim had been, and I resolved to make up for lost time and opportunity. My cousin saw my enthusiasm with pleasure; but he cautioned me against riding hobbies; by saying: "It takes a king's purse to do all that is done here. He aims to make it an incentive, to be followed by others. If it had to be done for profit, it would require a very different economy from the one you see here." I took the hint and stuck to my common sense husbandry.

At Friedrichshaven I witnessed a most sorrowful scene. A German, who had emigrated to Brazil, as I did to the United States, but had never fulfilled the law as to military duty, as I had, came there with his wife, a fine Brazilian lady, and two children. He was arrested on arrival. At my request, my cousin made inquiries, of the law officers, whether the severest of the penalties, penal imprisonment, could not be then and there avoided. We were told, that, as the case stood, there was no way, except for him to be taken to the fortress of Ulm, and after submitting, for a while, to imprisonment, to apply to the king for pardon. They advised the disconsolate wife, to go with her husband, on the same train, to Ulm, herself; there to go to a hotel, and then take such steps, as, after consultation with lawyers, would be deemed best. This course she pursued. I heard, on inquiry: she did apply, with her husband, for pardon, and received it, after paying about double what I did, to-wit: $320. He had, when the pardon came, served a month and a half in the penal class of military delinquents. I felt, at first, as if all this was severe injustice; but on subsequent reflection I asked myself: whether a person, that owes military duty, on the basis of a very reasonable law, and leaves the country, well knowing the penalties of an invasion, is really, unjustly, treated, if he afterwards comes back, in defiance of the law. Does he deserve much commisseration, if he is taken up and punished? To answer this question correctly, it is necessary to bear in mind, that another man was serving in his stead all this time. I was glad I had duly settled my delinquency, before I returned. Besides, I wish to add: that I am now convinced, that a military service, based on universal obligation, as most of the German States now have them, is a much truer way to keep up a proper military establishment, than the recruiting service, now prevailing in the United States. Our "bounty" systems, during our civil war, were still worse.

From Frederichshaven, I went, by stage, to Ulm. I took my seat, as is my custom, on the top of the stage, and, as we drove out, after dinner, I had a fine rear view over Lake Constanz, into Switzerland, with its gorgeous mountain scenery. And as I looked and drank in the scenes, a feeling of pain, that I thought must be something like what is called the "Swiss home sickness" overcame me, and I sighed for the good persons and things I had enjoyed in Switzerland; but mixed with it a longing for my good Swiss wife in America. At Ulm, I stopped at a hotel formerly kept by a brother of my uncle, but new parties had then acquired it. I visited the Münster tower, over three hundred feet high, and took a good view of the surrounding country. I made now a detour to Munich; via: Augsburgh, where I stopped at the hotel called "The Mohren," known for the many Emperers, that lodged there, and the fine wine, kept in its cellars. Here I tried to find again the person that had tried to escape with me, to America, in 1830, but found, that his father had died, and that he then left for the lower Danube, and was said to be then in Bucharest. He emigrated eastward, I westward! I hunted up there also the descendants of my two uncles—Plank and Zeller, and I found, but two of their descendants alive. They received me kindly, and showed me the nice "Fugger" buildings, or tenement houses, that were really of most interest to me in Augsburgh. Of great importance to me was also the Council Chamber, where many sessions of the imperial diet were held. The axioms in Latin, affixed to the portraits on the wall, of the great men, took my eye, and I copied them all, and entered them in my scrap-book; they were often useful to me. The family mansion of Catherina Welser, who, as is well known, made a love-match with an Austrian Prince, also engaged my attention. In short, Augsburgh quite re-germanized me, and made me read up in German history.

At Munich, the grand buildings, already built and building, by King Ludwig I., were great sights to me; and I reflected on the fact, that according to the doctrines of the Democratic party, in the United States, such expenditures of the public moneys are unconstitutional. I was not strengthened, in the doctrine, by my reflections; on the contrary, my faith in it was weakened. At Munich, I enjoyed, as may be expected, the good eating and drinking at the restaurants. Toward the close of July, I hurried back to Heilbronn,

At my native town, I participated in the celebration of my father's 63rd birthday. I engaged my return passage in the packet ship Oneida, running from Havre to New York. She was to start August 24th, and I had, therefore, but three weeks to close my sojourn in Heilbronn and to reach Havre. Every day brought a new family entertainment. We visited the neighboring villages and places of public amusement. Among other persons of interest we visited, was *Dr. Justinus Koerner*, whose works on somnambulism are well known. The sweetest hours I spent with my father, in our family garden, just outside of the town. The most enjoyable places were the hills encircling Heilbronn; I could not take in the grand views often enough. My good uncle, Dr. Seyffarth. was then alive yet. He had been married to my mother's eldest sister. They had four beautiful daughters, one of them was married to the great manufacturer of modern superior paper: Schaüfelin. His house and fine gardens were the rendezvous for all our relatives on my mother's side. Art and advanced knowledge had there a hospitable home. My uncle, Seyffarth, was then. as he had been for over fifty years, the fostering mind of every progressive development in Heilbronn. He was then near 80 years old. He had received his medical education at Vienna University. when it was at its best, and kept up his studies with unabated zeal. He was the official physician of the town. and had a most extensive practice. In our family, he was regarded as the unerring doctor, that could cure all curable diseases.

When I bid my father farewell this time, both he and myself thought of the departure in 1832. He said now several times: "I shall see you again." The whole family was assembled, as I left the house. There was too much cheering for me, and it was suggested to me, that most likely a great misfortune was hanging over me. I left for America. on the 11th of August. a very sober man.

CHAPTER XXV.

MY RETURN VOYAGE IN 1843.

In this return voyage, I allowed myself to be imposed upon, by saddling myself with two youths. One was the foster son of my brother-in-law Faulhaber. I knew, that in taking him along. I removed an obstacle to my sister's full happiness. Taking him, led to my taking also a young Mr. Seeger, son of Col. Seeger, an intimate friend of my brother-in-law. Fritz, my brother-in-law's son. travelled with me as my relative, the other as a favorite friend. The first went with me. to my home, near Cincinnati. Of the second I was relieved. soon after my arrival in the United States. We made the journey in the middle of August. by stage to Havre; via: Carlsruhe. Strassburgh and Paris. At Carlsruhe. Frederick was brought in by his father. Seeger came along in Heilbronn. At Strassburgh I stopped two days. I met there. by appointment. the father of Mr.

M. Werk, of Cincinnati, and brought him the daguerrotype of his son. He entertained me hospitably. From Strassburgh to Paris, we went by stage in 48 hours. In Paris we stopped a week, at Hotel Violet—passage Violet.—We went, diligently sight seeing, under the guidance of a commissioner, who was a devoted Napoleonite. I had excellent advice from a Mr. Pitrat, to whom I had letters, from his father and brothers, that resided in Buffalo, West Va. They had crossed the ocean with my brother Paul, in 1838; and we had business and other friendly intercourse with them ever since. They expected to possess here about half of 20,000 acres, sold them, as a part of old French claims. of the XVIII. Century, but were glad to compromise on about 3,000 acres, on which the family now resides. It is an ugly story, this American-French-English land jobbery. I have neither the inclination, time. nor the space. to discuss it here. It reminds me of the trouble I had with the property of the Reimer-Ruge's heirs. There were, in 1892, several deaths in the Pitrat family in the United States. We mourned for them sincerely.

Another very useful friend, was a dry goods broker, who did business in Paris, for many of the larger New York dry goods houses. I have forgotten his name, but owe him a debt of gratitude. Through his suggestion, star candle manufacture was introduced into Cincinnati. I gave him the addresses in Cincinnati. He was a fully Frenchified German, and his business capacities were most extensive. He had great forecast as to the saleability of goods, in the United States, that came very near infallibility.

About August 19th we arrived in Havre. We travelled from Paris to Rouen, by river steamer, starting early and arriving in Rouen about noon. We had a fine dinner at Hotel d'Admiraute. In Havre we arrived by stage in the evening. We stopped at Hotel de L'Europe, and fared well at reasonable rates. August 24th we went on board the ship Oneida, and left for New York August 25th. We crossed the Atlantic in 24 days. Our captain's name was Funck. He was one of the oldest captains, having been across the ocean 186 times, which, counting 10 voyages per year, would make 18 years. The captain had one very good quality, to-wit: care for *safety*, and he had two contradictory qualities—inveterate whist playing and frequent prayers. Our negro cook disliked the first, and had un-bounded confidence in the other. So whenever the captain was off duty and playing whist, the negro prayed. that God would forgive the captain. Between the two, we had incessant prayer. The captain could hold his countenance even with a hard joke, which the following will prove: Just when about parting, an elderly lady, a Miss Wheaton, of the family whose most distinguished male mem-ber, wrote a book on international law, came in haste on board; she was indeed somewhat late. A servant brought. with other luggage, a neat basket full of fine French eggs. The lady had the steward—

our negro—brought before her. She handed the basket, with the eggs, to him, and then said to him: "Please understand, that these are fresh French eggs! Boil of them every morning, for breakfast, three or four soft. I want no other than French eggs! They are better than your American eggs, and I want to be sure to have none but French eggs served to me!" The steward promised, and then took the eggs down to the provision room. On the last step he stumbled and fell, hurting himself badly, and breaking most of the eggs. He had the captain brought to him; and asked: what he should do in the dilemma? "Do? Why, there is but one thing to do, and that is: to keep your mouth shut, and serve Miss Wheaton with *our* American eggs; she will never know the difference, unless you tell her." Every morning Miss Wheaton got American eggs, and ate them for French, right after the captain's blessing of the food. Often since, when I saw Americans fanatical for some special measure, for nativistic reasons, I thought of Miss Wheaton's eggs.

We arrived in New York September 15th. There I received, as soon as I had landed, the sad news of the death of my second son, Mark Foster, through a letter from my grief stricken wife. He had died August 2nd. I had anticipated great joy in meeting and caressing this my second son. Now every step toward home was a pang. I made but few visits in New York, and hastened home. There even the sight of my wife, and the fine state of the crops, could not put me in the joyful spirits I had promised myself.

My father-in-law and mother-in-law were with my wife and Carrie. My business in the city appeared prosperous. My brother-in-law, Seifert, had done well, as far as amount of sales went. I discovered some disappointments afterwards.

The politics of Hamilton County I found in confusion. Party spirit had borne its fruit once more, to-wit: Dissensions between the ambitious;—David T. Disney, whom in 1837 the better part of the Democracy had shelved, had succeeded, by the help of the Volksblatt, under Roedter, to revive himself, and to secure the nomination for Senator. The offended elements resented that. Under the lead of Moses Dawson and Elwood Fischer, they organized a vigorous opposition. On my arrival, they called on me, to join them; but my grief, over my dead son, was too recent, and too severe, to allow me to take an active part in politics. I confined myself to voting against D. T. Disney, which was my first break with party fealty. It was not an agreeable act for me to do. Affiliations, in sects and parties, have their ties, that none can break lightly, if his character has that sort of fidelity, that may be called: "well tempered" at all. We join sects and parties, from motives of public good, and this motive elevates us within ourselves, and raises our associates in our estimation. Differences of zeal for the cause arise afterwards. The selfish motives, but also the casuistic reasoning for the cause grows, and soon we have three kinds of associates: the ultra zealots, the sluggards, and the men who act in everything with due measure and agree. This complicates every act of severance. And so it was then in Hamilton County. The question was: Shall we split the Democratic party and render it impotent? Behind that stood another: Shall the party be potent at all? And surely it should not, after it has lost its pristine patriotic spirit. My uncle. Rümelin, the Judge, told me in the Summer previous, in Germany: "Political parties are but attempts to supply, by inorganic institutions, the public virtue, which should be evolved through organic institutions. Parties cannot be the country's public authority, because they cannot have the proper action, interaction and reaction within themselves. That can only be done where the entirety is embraced in one organism. This truth, all parties have at last to find, because they are but a part of a respective society, and not its whole. Happy the nation, whose partisans are wise and virtuous enough, to know, when to start parties and when to disband them." These well meant words of my uncle, made a deep impression on me. I remembered them on my arrival in Cincinnati. I pondered on them, and asked myself: "Is not the Democratic party getting into the condition when it should be disbanded?" It perplexed me.

CHAPTER XXVI.

EVENTS AFTER MY RETURN FROM GERMANY IN 1843.

Bringing Frederick Faulhaber to our house, with the understanding, that he should become a permanent member of our family, was a misconception of proper relations, from the first; and every after step was a misstep. There was no place for him, in our household, nor on the farm. His father's desire, that he should become a gardner, was not practicable with us. Nobody about our house, knew how to treat him, and of course he was in everybody's way. The servants were at a loss how to treat him; they looked askance at him. Incidentally Sherman, one of the trustees of the Shakers at Whitewater Village, in our county, with whom I was well acquainted, and knew him to be a fine gardener and nursery man, seeing Frederick with us, made some inquiries about him, and suggested, that he should be apprenticed with him, live with the Shakers, and become a good farmer and gardener. I accepted the offer, on condition that he should be left free, as to his religion. He went there, and has remained ever since. He is esteemed among them, as one of their most useful members. He is a confirmed Shaker and usefull man.

The male help I wanted at that time, came to me in the person of a hired man, that knew all about the best kind of farming and gardening. His name was Frank Frohndorf, my now, rich neighbor. He was excellent in the treatment of horses and cattle. He milked the cows, saw the milk in the cellar, and was always ready to assist the women, in relieving them from severe hard work. And, with it all, he could teach others, which was valuable to *me*. I added some book learning, and I have now the agricultural books, that I had then, and were my favorite reading I thus united practical with theoretical farming Under Frohndorf's direction, I then planted several acres of vineyard. We kept four horses and about half a dozen cows. We made considerable butter, and sold it at fair prices. We took in considerable money for wood, which we hauled to town, and so too it was with hay, corn, apples and other farm products. The best thing I did, however, was to reduce the size of our farm, by selling off, part on credit, for $50.00 per acre. I saw clearly, that the chief difficulty in American agricultural development, was the ever increasing want of expert hired labor. None such was being raised in this country, and fewer and fewer of the kind was, and is coming from Europe. Obviously then: the kind of farming I carried on in 1844-48, had no future. So I sold off, first 9 acres on the southeast corner, then 11, next 23, followed by 80 acres, and so on, until my farm was reduced to what it now is: 32½ acres. With the money realized, I bought city property, and improved it for renting out. This secured me gradually an income in rent, that made me, with what my farm yielded, an independent citizen. We exercised, as was then the custom of the country, much hospitality. This bore hard upon my wife, as she could not always procure the needed female help. I must add here, that we were often *imposed upon*, when least prepared for it, by *self invited guests*. I still kept up in 1843 and part of 1844, my going and returning from the city, and attending to business, while there. My experience taught me, however, more every day, that it would be best for my health, my purse and peace of mind, to sell out my business. Seifert was, as already stated, an eager business man, but he was of the kind, that should have things to themselves. Such persons are not good partners. Seifert met my inclination, to sell, half way, by offering to buy me out, if I would give him credit. I did so at fair prices, and was paid at the dates named. And thenceforth I lived on my farm, and became more and more an adept in rural pursuits. Seifert changed the business almost entirely, after he had it to himself. He preferred to deal in fancy goods, that yielded large profits. I had stuck to the, so called, staple goods. He prided himself on a large stock of goods. with which to make a fine exhibit. He gave and he took credit, freely. I had adhered to quick sales of goods for the common wants of my customers, and was backward both in granting and receiving credit. I need not state other differences. It suffices to state: that, as I predicted, his business swelled up a while, in amount and profit; but then came a change, and finally it dwindled into a small concern. He sold out at auction, losing on the stock he had, at the close.

After I sold out to him, we were friendlier together, than before. He did all he could, to appear grateful to me; our path run in harmony, being much apart.

The sale of my business, to Seifert, enabled me to be much more at home, than before, and it was tacidly understood, that both my father-in-law and mother-in-law should remain with us, on the farm. But family emergencies, at Seifert's, in the city, first drew my mother-in-law to the city, and soon my father-in-law followed suit. Of these moves, that of my mother-in-law was the most proper, and worked the best; but that with my father-in-law never became very agreeable. She remained well liked until she died. He had left long before. And then, he made himself generally impossible, by marrying again, an unsuitable wife. With her he moved to Harrison,—had one child,—a daughter. It was painful to my wife to associate with her step-mother, and it even interfered with her filial feelings toward her father. I sympathized with her, remembering my own feelings, under similar circumstances. These were unhappy hours for us all!

I had, during my visit to Germany, many conversations with persons, chiefly relatives, of whom I could not help seeing, that their remaining at home, had given their literary education, both technical and general, a higher finish and more thoroughness, than mine had. On the other hand, I discerned readily, that my being an emigrant, necessarily made me a more self-instructed and self-made man, and that my mental faculties, had more adaptation to circumstances, than theirs. I concluded, that, if I added my advantages to theirs, it would make my life much more satisfactory to myself, and to all dependent on me. I took counsel with friends, and they advised me to get more into regular connection with the higher current literature, through the reading of good books and pamphlets; and that this would soon fill up any voids and defects in my education. I did so, and from that time dates the gradual filling up of my library and a higher aim in my studies. Goethe remained my main literary treasure. I became also a writer for the papers in a much more comprehensive sense. I used to write for the German papers in Cincinnati; I contributed to Moses Dawson's paper and to Sam Medary's "Statesman". I wrote on grape culture for the "Ohio Farmer".

These articles met the eye of a New York publisher, with the name of "Orange". He requested me to revise them, for being published in book form. I did so, and I received about $700 for the book, under the title: "Vinedressers' Manual". The book made me known in circles that had not known me hitherto. It proved a good speculation to the publisher, and I was fully satisfied with my pay, and the good the book did. I found this kind of writing a much better operation, than my gratuitous contributions to newspapers. In the first, I gave my opinions, in the latter my knowledge; in these I had to be definite and certain, in the other only plausible; for the books I had to study and test my learning, for the papers only strain my talents a little. I wondered then with myself: whether there was not a literature on the subjects, I used to write about for the papers, in which knowledge had to be equally definite and certain? Inquiries now brought me the perception, that there were in our age progressive publications of scientific works, embracing these subjects, and that it was my duty to become familiar with them. I did so, commencing with works on Political Economy, and gradually extending my studies to jurisprudence, State Science and Socialism, as well as the Natural Sciences. I then took up the idea, that *the education of adults* is most necessary, in our age, *in the United States.*

CHAPTER XXVII.

POLITICS IN 1844 AND 1845.

The defeat of Martin Van Buren, for renomination, for the Presidency, in 1844, after his visit to Jackson, and the popular demonstrations in his favor, on the journey, was to me a bitter disappointment. I saw in it a treacherous combination of a minority in the South, to wrong a Northern Democrat, and to antagonize progressive Democracy. The nomination of Polk, known for his sterling Democratic convictions, smoothed my anger, and I supported the ticket zealously; but it was the conjunction of Texas and Oregon, on the flags in Ohio, that healed the breach, and carried the Democracy through that election. I was peculiarly placed, because I had been nominated to the Legislature, which forbid my opposition, unless I resigned my nomination. That would have been a preposterous step during a Presidential election. I acquiesced, therefore, for reasons stated. After the Fall election, I went with Moses Dawson, on invitation, to Jackson's home in Tennessee, and there the question came up as to Texas and Oregon. Jackson mentioned: that good faith would be kept toward Northern Democrats in this matter. Dawson asked: whether Calhoun would not perhaps play foul? Jackson, however, asserted that Calhoun was not to be feared. The forebodings of 1844 proved nevertheless correct in 1845, to my sorrow, when Polk, led by Calhoun, truckled to England and surrendered those parts of Oregon, which are the most important to the future of the United States. I held firmly: that the American Statesmen, that could surrender Queen Charlotte's Sound, Van Couver's Island, the mouth of Frazier's River, and the adjacent territory, betrayed the best interests of the United States;

and I never forgot this in my subsequent political conduct. I have adhered to it all my life.

This matter played an important part during my first term in the House of Representatives in Ohio. I was on the committee, that had to report on the question of the annexation of Texas. In my minority report I asserted squarely: that I did not support the annexation from love of slavery, but in *spite* of it. I insisted: that the question was geographical in its main point, and not social or institutional; the population being small, as that of Ohio was in 1802. I said this on purpose to indicate the fact, that I was not only no slavery propagandist, but the contrary. I supported, the same session, the report, that exposed the impudence of the claim of Virginia and Kentucky, to the north side of the Ohio River, up to high water mark. My object, in these steps, was: 1) to signify my determination, that I, for one, was not in accord with any of the movements, that would convert the United States into an agency for furnishing lands to slave-holders, and for colonizing them with negro slaves; 2) my willingness and desire, to have a territorial extension policy for sound national geographical reasons. My position surprised the Whigs; for they had taken me for a partisan zealot, in favor of any step, that might be insisted upon by my party. I was equally decided in my opposition to making the government of the United States an agency for securing lands to Northern land speculators for gaining wealth and offices. And when I stated these views, I surprised the friends of the Free Land Policy, for they too had mistaken the nature of my partisanism. I then became aware, that a party-free man is always misunderstood here. I had taken my nomination and election by the Democratic party for a seat in the Legislature of Ohio, more, as a means to continue my efforts to bring and keep the Democrats of Ohio on the higher level, already spoken of, than as a reward for my party services. And the higher level meant, coming up to, and falling in with. the general progress of the age on questions of philosophy as well as politics. I took early occasion to indicate this, by opposing the antiquated, merely ceremonious, and therefore really irreligious, opening of the daily sessions of the Legislature with prayer, by a regular clergyman. I quoted, for the purpose of showing my opinion of the main motive of such public conduct, the words of the German poet:

> "You pray as robbers pray,
> That God may bless your stealings."

I was denounced for this, as an Atheist.

What alarmed me most in Ohio's public affairs, was the utter want of any well considered enlightened public policy as to the administration of public affairs for the State, the Counties, the Cities and Townships. I once startled the House, by asking: How can a government be republican, that transacts all its business through private corporations and their partisans? I also frequently inveighed against entrusting public functions to special commissions, and showed this practice to be a relic of British subjection to its conquerors. In short: through my course in 1844, I initiated the Constitutional Convention of 1850.

Special mention, may be proper, of the fact, that in the session of 1844, I established, in a Whig Legislature, the custom of printing public documents in the German language. My speech on this subject, rested on the principle: that Ohio should publish in any language, in its public papers, whose publication is necessary to reach a reasonably large portion of its population. My speech was extensively published in Ohio, and also in Germany. Its main point, to-wit: that questions of language must not be decided by nativistic or linguistic prejudice, but by the reason, that causes the justified publication. I said: "Employ that language, that is alive among your people, with whom you wish to communicate. A right State, forces no language on its people! Nor will it try to suppress any.

A question of personal integrity arose toward the end of the session. A member had introduced a joint resolution to pay the members of the Legislature $3.00 per day, instead of the $2.00 named in the Constitution. I opposed its passage, because it worked retroactive. The resolution passed, and all the members of the Legislature, except myself, took the $315, for 105 days of the session, when they were entitled, by the Constitution, only to $210.

CHAPTER XXVIII.
PUBLIC EVENTS BETWEEN 1845 AND 1849.

I was elected to the Senate in 1845, by an increased majority. I took this as evidence, that some, that had voted against me in 1844, because they deemed me too intense a partisan, had seen their mistake. I appreciated this, because it did me no more than justice; for I was pro-Democratic and anti-Whig, not, because I had *party* principles, but because my convictions, as to the public welfare, made me respectively an opponent or supporter of certain public policies.

The unfair preponderance of the Legislative over the Executive and Administrative power, was the great defect of the Constitution of Ohio in 1802. I favored every step toward the formation of a new Constitution, with a view of rectifying that defect, and secure better symmetry.

During the season of 1845, my most effective act was my minority report on the Morgan County contested election case. I proved, that, while single districts were right in principle, they were unconstitutional under the State Constitution of 1802. This distinction, between abstract right and constitutional legality, was then, as now, very often lost sight of. I made it prominent, by showing, that while the election of Morgan County was in accordance to the Constitution, and could not, therefore, be contested, as the Constitution then stood, still it was not right by abstract reason; and my view was sustained by the majority of the Legislature. My speech brought me a letter from Salmon P. Chase, in which he approved my position. I was gratified at this evidence of appreciation from such a distinguished personage; but it was not unalloyed pleasure; because I had to notice, that I was not fully understood by him. He supposed me advocating single districts from personally ambitious motives; and assumed that I meant to make the country portion of Hamilton County into a single congressional district, in which I could have myself re-elected for life. He evidently underrated my judgment, and misrepresented my moral sense. I knew that nothing is so precarious, as local or personal popularity. I knew also: that I was too free spoken, and not complaisant enough, to hold any temporary popularity, that I might ever acquire. I was sincerely opposed to all gerrymanders, from my sincere conviction, that they are wrong in principle; and all I wanted single districts for, was to make representation in Ohio consistent with the ideas of fairness, on which representation is granted. Each representative should represent not only a distinct territory, but also a distinct constituency. In Hamilton County, each voter had then four members in the House, that were each his representatives. This exceptional relation is unfair under honest representative government. It has, for years, led to combinations for carrying the delegation of Hamilton County with a view of securing improper persons for United States Senator, and also for securing, to certain special interests, the power to have such laws passed as they desired. We shall meet this question again later on.

The prominent measure of 1845 to 1846 was Senator Alfred Kelley's Tax Bill. It was introduced by a set of joint resolutions, that declared it necessary and proper to reform the abnormities, that had grown up in Ohio, as to taxation, by defective valuation laws, and wrong practices under them. They also declared, that the proper way to provide means for *all* public purposes were: "To levy taxes on *property*, both real and personal, according to its true value in money."

The latter principle I attacked in the House, and contended: that it was not proper, on the contrary erroneous, upon the general principle: that, having but one tax object and measure, would inevitably lead to special overburdenings and unfair exemptions, as well as financial inadequacies. I showed: that in many cases personal taxes were the right measure, and excises were best; and that so too, it was as to fees and similar exactions. To my surprise, no reply was made to me. And I had to make personal inquiries for the reasons of thus ignoring my remarks. I learned, that I was absolutely misunderstood as to my argument, as well as to the theory, that underlaid my remarks. They said to me: "Your views on taxation are outlandish." I found thus, that certain prejudices were in vogue, resting on the assumption, that having one country, and settling in another, induced the person so settling, to have certain special tendencies inconsistent with the new country, and that these tentencies were therefore necessarily wrong. And this presumption included another, to-wit: that whatever laws new countries adopt, are necessarily right; as they would be free from certain *ancient* wrongs. I asked those who thus argued: How about *modern* wrongs?

I discovered, however, a further weakness in the minds of members; towit: a fancy for generalizations, such as: insisting on a single tax basis and tax method; they called this Republican simplicity. These false directions of the public mind had stuck fast for years. They got even into the new Constitution, and plague us to-day. Even our National Government is kept from comprehensive reforms in its Revenue Measures, by this frenzy for shallow pated simplification. Discriminations for reasons is the true rule in taxation.

Senator Kelley's resolution passed, and the Tax Bill, according to its tenor, passed the Senate. In the House, it was referred to the Committee on Finance, of which I was a member. There I labored assiduously and sincerely, to perfect the Bill, by removing its grosser anomalies and defects. This our chairman, Mr. Cowen, a Whig, noticed, and suggested, that I was inconsistent. I explained my position, and its sincere objects, and from that moment he was my friend, and confided implicitly in me. He finally said to me, in his dry, jocular way: "Reemelin! I feel some compunction in reporting this bill as the committee's work. It is really your bill, and you ought to father it." Putative!? I asked. He laughed and reported the bill. The bill passed the house and became a law. It was Kelley's bill, with my corrections. I voted against it nevertheless.

In 1846 I was elected Senator for Hamilton County, and was made to feel, that certain Democrats regarded it as an act of great generosity, to allow me to be a Senator, being only 32 years old, and but 14 years in the country. I felt that there was a tendency in our party politics, that would make it, sooner or later, very difficult, for me to have a public career reconcilable with my ideas of public propriety. To have it, I would have to be an odedient member of the party, and sustain every exercise of power by it, on the ground, that it continued to conduce to the continuation of power in its hands. I doubted my ability, to be thus implicitly obe lient, to my party.

For years the apportionment laws for Senators and Representatives were gerrymanders; that is to say: there were allotted members to counties not strictly by population, but with the view to secure to the party in power a majority. These gerrymanders did not always work to order, because there were fluctuations, and such a one occurred in 1846. Instead of having a majority in both Houses for the Whigs, as was calculated, the Senate was a tie. Then came a further mishap. A Whig Senator got sick, and this gave the Democrats a majoriiy. This accident the Democrats took advantage of, and organized the Senate with Democratic officers. Edson B. Olds was chosen president, and had the appointment of the several committees. He made me the chairman of the Committee on Finance. As such it became my duty, to pass on several questions, that grew into great importance in the Constitutional Convention in 1850. The most important of these were questions of taxation of banks and their assets, of which more hereafter.

In the session of 1847 and 1848 the Whigs had a majority, but not large enough to have a constitutional quorum, of two-thirds, without the Democrats; and they were therefore unable to pass any party measure obnoxious to thirteen Democrats. Such a one came before the Senate for the apportionment of Senators and Representatives. That bill contained many wrong clauses; but this bill had in addition a provision for single districts, that was then, for reasons already explained, clearly unconstitutional, although abstractly right. I took early the ground, that I would adopt any and all means to prevent this bill from passing; because I believed it my duty, as a Senator of Hamilton County, to oppose the bill, with all the strength I possessed. Among the powers open to me, for that purpose, was the seceding from the Senate with other Senators, and thus break up a constitutional quorum. This power had been frequently exercised. The Senate had the power to bring in the recusant Senators by force, through its sergeant-at-arms. That, of course, all absentees had to risk. Thirteen Senators agreed with me, and when our longer presence would have passed the iniquitous measure, spoken of, fourteen of us Senators left the Senate and adjourned to room No. 18 in the American Hotel, immediately opposite the old State House. The Senate made several efforts to force us back into the Senate, but recoiled from using force outright. Finally they resorted to a parliamentary trick. They claimed, that, if the Senate receded from its own amendment, then pending, it would remove all disagreements and pass the bill. They would recede, and thus effect their purpose. The falsity of this assumption appears at once, when it is considered, that the Senate had never yet passed a bill, without the amendatory clause—the said clause being for single districts. The Whigs forced this issue into the election of 1849, much to their sorrow, as we shall see.—The year 1848 brought mischief untold, not only upon Ohio, but also elsewhere in the United States, not to speak of Europe; because there was then a furor over the world, for liberty, whose real import was little understood. Men ceased to be leaders, that should have been continued; and men became leaders, that were inadequate to the situation.

In this country it was Presidential year; Louis Cass being the candidate of the Democrats; Zacharias Taylor of the Whigs; Van Buren of the Free-soilers. The Free-soil element split, in Ohio, the Whigs more than the Democrats; and the result of the election was: that the Whigs lost their preponderance in the Legislature, and were unable to organize the House or the Senate, except by surrendering to the Free-soilers. They could do that in the Senate, by voting for a man for Speaker whom they could trust, but in the House the single district question brought a contest, in which the U. S. Senatorship, in the person of S. P. Chase, became the main question, and finally led to a discomfiture of the Whigs in Ohio for a long time, indeed forever, as the Whig party was disbanded.

I had declined, in the Fall election, a nomination for Senator, upon the ground, that we recusant Senators, should avoid being a disturbing element in the election. This was an error. When men raise an issue, they must support it personally. In my place, a Democrat, weak in his support and his opposition, was nominated and elected. I should have run and been elected, for that would have been better for the country and wiser for me.

In Ohio, slippery politicians became the leaders of the new Democratic party. It called itself the reform party; because it wore a new coat. The actual change was, that it had become a more intense spoils hunting and office distributing party. It combined with the Free-soilers, to repeal the black laws and to elect S. P. Chase to be U. S. Senator. It received, for these acts, numerous offices, which the Legislature then could confer, and this gave the whole affair a stamp of venality, that took from it all the glory, that might have otherwise been in it. As it was, it gave to the Democratic leaders that could *trade*, but not *think* in politics, the upper hand, and they run the machine for personal ends. The main leader was Alexander Long, an intense partisan.

In Federal politics the result took a different course. The election of Zacharias Taylor brought an element into power, that had one good character, namely: political independence. It killed the biggest of all political humbugs: "popular sovreignty," in the territories. It placed the Democratic party out of power, and it is a pity, that it did not prevent forever the reorganization of another party in its place. The Free-soil party called itself the People's Party; but *there was no People* in this new party.

The Legislature of Ohio of 1848 and 1849 started out in storm-clouds. Both the Whig and the Democratic members attempted to to take violent possession of the House. The Democrats got ahead, because two Whigs,—Morse and Townsend—had turned Free-soilers and had an understanding with the Democrats, that they would assist in seating the two Democrats elected from Hamilton County. I was in the midst of that struggle, at the risk of my life; for I was determined, that, that single district grab, should not succeed and disgrace the principle. I cared nothing about the repealing of the black laws; I regarded them as an issue, in which both parties played the demagogue. Chase's election for U. S. Senator I preferred to that of any regular party-man, and I was glad that the appropriations for building the new State House was continued. I liked also the prospect of a call for a convention to form a new Constitution, because, as already explained, I expected many reforms from such an Assembly.

CHAPTER XXIX.

CALLED TO EUROPE FOR MY FATHER'S SILVER WEDDING.

In the Fall of 1849, I received from my father, an invitation to attend. at his expense, his Silver Wedding with his second wife. He wanted my whole family to come, but we thought that Carrie and I would suffice, as it would entail too much expense, on my father, to take the whole family. The festival was to be held January 9th, 1850; all the children and grandchildren of Benjimn Rümelin were to be present. So we got our ticket for crossing the ocean to Europe in the packet ship Havre, Capt. Ainsworth, that left New York November 20th. Caroline had, as companion in the Cabin, a Mrs. Kratzer, a lady, who kept an excellent eating house in New York, where we eat while there, at the daily table d'Hote. We crossed the ocean in not quite 20 days, arriving in Havre, December 12th. We were detained several days in the channel. Louis Napoleon was then President of France.

In Paris, Mrs. Kratzer asked me December 18th, to accompany her, in her inspection, to the eating houses most noted for their fine cooking. I got that day more delicacies to taste, than ever before in weeks of luxurious living. I heard explanations on making coffee, cooking sauces, preparing vegetables and other fine dishes, that made me a sort of connoisseure in cooking, a knowledge on which I set great store ever since; but when I ventured to speak upon the subject afterwards to my sisters, they called me hard names and refused to listen. I have since kept the knowledge discretely to myself; but may say: that the explanations were all simple injunctions: not to neglect certain proprieties, that good cooks never neglect. And I enjoyed the good eating even with its plenty. I know, since, a good meal when I get it.

In that Winter there were great snow-falls all over Europe. We went from Paris by railroad to Chalons sur Marne; but thenceforth made all our journeys over France, Baden, Würtemberg, Bavaria and Switzerland, by sleigh over fine snow tracks. I arrived in Heilbronn in an elegant Mail sleigh December 21st.

The silver wedding took place on the day stated. There were thirty adult Rümelins present. Several of us children read poetry.

which we had prepared; I among the rest. My piece of poetry is preserved, but I shall not quote it here. Letters from many relatives at a distance were sent in; one from Odessa, from a grandson of my uncle. It was a feast of unalloyed joy. Other family entertainments followed. My youngest full sister, that then lived in Heilbronn, rather surpassed the rest in hospitality. We were truly grateful for the pleasures afforded us, and to me the enjoyments were especially pleasing. The presence of my two sisters, and of four brothers, at this wedding, recalled memories, that I could for the first time again enjoy. Both my sisters talked to me of our dead mother, her kindliness and beauty; and we all shed tears over her early death. She might, had she been alive, have celebrated her 44th wedding day.

One evening I attended, by invitation, in Stuttgart, a social gathering of liberal minded literary men. A gentleman brought out a toast in my honor. He briefly introduced me as a person that had emigrated 18 years previous, and had now returned to participate in a family celebration; and was glad of the new advance of free ideas in Germany. He invited those present to drink my health, which was done very enthusiastically. Of course I responded. I laid stress on the fact, that what I had written from Stuttgardt to Cincinnati, in 1843, had become true, to-wit: "That those reforms were the most successful in our age, that, in accordance with the technical and scientific improvements of the age, reformed, by freeing commerce and trade, and securing better and freer international intercourse." I also bade them to understand that, "only in this respect, and so far as it was done, did America really progress faster than Europe.' Next morning I left Stuttgardt by omnibus, to visit my brother at Metzingen. During the journey I saw, what purported to be a report of my remarks, on the previous evening, in the Democratic organ. They were somewhat distorted, but there had been interpolated into it invidious remarks on my cousin, Gustav Rümelin, who was then rector of the gymnasium at Nürtingen, and had been a Representative at the Congress in Frankfurth, in Germany, and voted for electing the King of Prussia, Emperor. My Democratic views were contrasted with his. A historic fact in our family was also brought in: Our great grand-father, August Rümelin, had, one hundred years previous, been the chief officer of the town of Nürtingen, and been elected its Representative. As such, he had refused to vote taxes for the reigning Duke, and for that act he was arbitrarily arrested and kept in prison for some time, but was finally honorably released and exhonorated by the action of the Duke, who had regretted his injustice.

At that very town I was reading the distorted report of my speech the night before. I had arrived by the morning coach, and put the report in my pocket, when the stage stopped. I was told there would be 15 minutes detention for a change of mail and refreshments. As I went into the tavern, I noticed a man, having an excited crowd around him, vociferating: "Hurrah for the people! Thank God, we have driven out all of the Rümelins." I stepped up and asked: "Are you sure, that there is no Rümelin about?" He replied: "Dead sure." I inquired: "Will you bet on it?" He answered yes, certainly. "How much?" he asked. I replied: "The wine for the crowd." I put up $2.00 in the hands of the tavern keeper, and the man put up the same amount. The wine was brought in. I now handed the Postmaster my passport, and told him, that I was the person named in it. He glanced at it; then shook hands with me and said: "Why, sure! you are a Rümelin, and must be the one that made the speech last night." He handed me my money back, and the mail coach being ready to start, I jumped into it, and as we drove away the crowd shouted many adieus to the American Rümelin.

By noon I arrived at Metzingen and stopped with my brother, who owned the drug store of the town. I related to him and his wife my encounter in Nürtingen. We of course drank to the memory of the *old folks in Nuertingen.*

CHAPTER XXX.

WIDE AWAKE TO THE CHANGES IN EUROPE.

During my entire journey in the Winter of 1850, through Germany, Switzerland and France, I was much annoyed by excited discussions, whose shallowness I saw but too clearly. I was the correspondent of the "Volksblatt," and expressed therein my views, which I venture to quote here. I wrote:

"I find here all the towns and villages much beautified and enlarged. The evidence of a slow progress in greater comfort and more intelligence are unmistakable. Old walls and ditches, with ancient fortifications and edifices, and obsolete institutions, yield, one after another, to the current of time. City walls and towers disappear. Why not expect the same of the old walls of wrong and prejudice? There used to be formerly many seats of baronial prowess; where are they now? Shall cold stone alone feel the new age that has come? Shall not the human heart also be penetrated by the warm breath of better laws, of freer rights and higher aims? Surely it will be so; not through single persons, so-called great men, as is so much believed. No! In thyself! thou! the kernel people of Europe! lies the needed vigor. I witnessed, lately, tho spectacle of an icebreak in the River Neckar. It looked to me like the foreboding of the future of my native land. Frigid was, but a little while ago, the surface of that river; it was a sheet of ice; it invited bold skaters; only here and there was an opening. But there came a pushing up from below, the outer air softened the cold ice, and the water beneath got a freer flow, and piece after piece broke off. There was a rushing and a crushing, and many a bulwark, erected by human hands, had to yield to the throng of the river. Gradually the flow became quieter and clear like a mirror; and the river, that was, but a little while before, icy and dangerous, now was smooth, and again ready to serve the shipper, and through him mankind. So it is now at thy surface, my native land! Icy and chilly above; below the surface it throngs, from various causes, upward. Light and truth are mellowing the upper crust; and soon the ice will break, and pure and glorious Germany will stand before us, affording bread, enjoyments, and all the progress, which a lasting welfare brings. The poet says:

"Von Unten ist der Druck; nach Oben ist der Drang."

"From below comes the pressure, upwards is the impulse."

In another part of that letter I wrote: "Now polit cal matters look somewhat dreary in our fatherland, but in the midst of bad conditions, I think I see traces of a new blossoming; Germany has acquired out of its so-called "March gains" one thing: to-wit : an *active public life*, and out of it must soon come blessings of many kinds. The public eye sees now the weakness of the country, and every heart feels the desire, that Germany must be *one* land, *one* people. I say: Quit disputing, whether the country shall be Austrian or Prussian? Insist upon it, that it shall be *German.*" This correspondence opened the minds of many, in the United States to Germany's future.

I staid with my brother Eberhardt, and his good young wife several days. His wife's money enabled him to make the first payment on the Drug Store, which he had bought, and he was making enough to pay principal and interest, as it fell due. Had he but remained there for life, as he then purposed, and as we all approved; and what a prosperous family he would have raised. We shall see, to our deep regret, the contrary.

From Metzingen I travelled, in mid-winter, over the Suavian Alps, via: Urach, to Biberach. In the coach with me was a Government officer. We travelled through the night, and could converse, but not see each other. After he had found out, that I came from America, by seeing my name on the way bill, he became very taciturn, and soon I turned over, and fell asleep, never waking up until we got to Biberach for breakfast. There I found out, that my traveling companion was one of the prominent supporters of the aristocratic party.

At Biberach and Ravensburgh I stopped just long enough, to take a good look around the towns. Both the places are beautifully situated towns; they present, from their respective church towers, fine views over the surrounding country. At Friedrichshaven I called again on my cousin Schmalzigaug. whom I have already mentioned. Thence I crossed Lake Constanz, by steamer, to Roschach, in Switzerland; from there I ascended by railroad on a grade of 150 feet per mile, then regarded as very steep, to St. Gallen. There I paid a visit to a cousin of my wife, Henrietta Billwiller, whom I had met in Aarau 7 years previous; and now I also learned to know her husband, Ulrich Billwiller. I never in my life met a couple, of whose future there was then less question, than of theirs· They had a well paying trade in laces and fine cotton goods; and his mercantile capacities were recognized by everybody. Every act of theirs had the imprint of the strictest propriety. They had no child, but being yet young, that happiness was still to be theirs. Mr. Billwiller's mother lived in the same house with them. She was a very intelligent lady, and being the widow of a merchant, of much assistance to her son in business. I made a most enjoyable excursion with them into the Canton Toggenburgh. The mountains were covered with snow, and the pine forests stood in snow several feet deep. I do not hesitate to say: that Switzerland is fully as beautiful in its white Winter dress, as in its perennial Summer covering. On the higher points, we could feel the warm southern breezes: "Foen" winds, they were called. I paid a visit to the great manufacturing town Tüffen. The Queen of Würtemberg was there at that time, and I heard there the frank reception and address of the daughter of the principal manufacturer, to her. It was difficult to say which to admire most? The ingenuousness of the Swiss maiden, or the affability of the Queen? It was to all alike a neighborly visit among honest friends. How easy is the flow of kindness from the lips, when the heart is right within!

From St. Gallen I went to Zürich, where the relatives of my wife lived, that wanted to see me, specially, as they had some intention, to emigrate to America. I advised them against it, but they seemed to have made up their minds for it. They requested me to secure them an option on a good farm, such as I esteemed suitable for them, and, I promised them my assistance, though I disapproved their purpose. They were well-to-do farmers, but I deemed it very unwise for elderly people, to undertake such an adventure. We shall meet this matter again further on. From there I went to Burgdorf in Canton Bern, where other relatives of my wife lived. They were publishers of a paper, and book-sellers besides. The head of the firm was an influential politician. At Bern I met my cousin Rudolph Lohbauer, son of my father's only sister. He was then an exile at large in Switzerland; but, soon after, he got a position as a Professor in the Swiss Military Academy. He showed me the Swiss Diet in session, and I heard their proceedings in German, French and Italian. I was also introduced to Gen. Dufour. My cousin was cured of all his ultra political and eccentric views. He knew well my wife's relations in Burgdorf, and they knew him also. He was of much use to me in introducing me to Swiss statesmen, and their conversations gave me much knowledge of Swiss affairs and Democratic institutions. From Bern I went, via: Freiburgh and Lausanne, to Geneva. At Freiburgh I saw the grand Cathedral and other objects of interest. Also at Lausanne. At Geneva I spent several days and heard some lectures at the University. I was glad, I had made this journey, as it let me see Switzerland and especially Geneva. in an entirely new aspect, — that of its French affiliations. I must admit: I liked the German Swiss the best. I returned to my native city by way of Iverton, Biel, Neufchatel. Basle, Strassburgh and Carlsruhe. I brought Spring weather with me, and was therefor the more welcome among my folks. I there met my daughter Caroline again, who had felt somewhat lonesome, while I was away. There was also some little misunderstanding with my father in paying our expenses in coming to the Silver wedding.—I never expected mnch, if anything, and was therefor not very much disappointed, when I got less than the other children.

CHAPTER XXXI.

OUR RETURN VOYAGE TO AMERICA IN 1850.

On the eve of my departure a most disagreeable circumstance arose. A servant girl of my parents had formed a strong inclination to go to America with us; my daughter seemed to have brought it on, by telling her of the wages, hired girls get in America. My father had opposed the plan,· as the girl was of special service to him. When spoken to, I declined to bind myself, to employ her, or to take her with us on the journey. Moreover, I wanted to leave my wife perfectly free, to take her or not, after seeing her. The girl solved the initial question, by going off, on her own hook. She arrived safe in New York, and took temporarily a place as cook. She came finally to our house, and my wife engaged her. But her service did not last long, after she accepted the addresses of our hired man, and married him; both left our service. He lost his life soon afterwards by a fall of a tree. She did not remain a widow long. She married again, and we lost sight of her. I must add, that all precontracts for employing emigrants to the United States, are illusive transactions, because they are not based on fair relations, on either side. In the case just mentioned, a good girl was thrown out of a situation, she was especially fit for, and thrown into relations, for which she was rather unprepared. She came with false expectations to the United States. She was less happy in America, than she would have been in Germany.

A young man, son of a near relation of mine, was, about that time, also sent to America, at the instigations of persons from America. His father came to me for advice. I told him, to send his son, if at all, perfectly free to America; and, to tell him pointedly; that he must go on his own individual risk, with no hopes of preengaged support in America, nor any of after-support from Germany. I wrote down on a sheet of paper, so that he might refer to it hereafter: "Selfpoise is the quality, which emigrants need most. No extraneous support can supply this. Indeed every promise and every hope, that weakens self-reliance, is an injury to the emigrant; it prevents him or her, from ever becoming the truly free emigrant, they ought to be." My advice was not heeded, the young man came here with expectations of after-support from home, and on promises of special assistance here. He was a plague to American society while here, and a vagabond and swindler, after he returned to Germany. He died about five years ago on the lower Danube, under very unfortunate circumstances.

Myself and daughter finally got away from Heilbronn in March. Our route home was through Frankfurth, Cassel, Göttingen to Bremen, where we took the steamer Herman, Capt. Crabtree of New York, stopping over a day in South Hampton and seeing Nettley Abbey. We arrived in New York in the first week in April; and there I was informed by the papers, brought on board by the pilot, that I had been elected a member of the Constitutional Convention of Ohio. The election gratified me as a high honor, but when the details of my election came, I hardly knew how to take it. I found, that my nomination by the Democratic Convention took place under circumstances very compromising for certain persons, that had always pretended to be my friends; chief among them was Molitor. He had supported me awhile; but then abandoned me for a special candidate of his own, that was really a very objectionable person. At a critical moment, the enemies of that candidate turned in for me and defeated him. It looked now, as if I was not chosen, because I really had the majority, but because my name was adroitly used to defeat another. There was one fact to counterbalance this, and that was: that I had really enough votes from staunch friends at all times to prevent trickery against me from succeeding. I found besides, that certain prominent Germans, among them J. B. Stallo, who pretended then and since, to be liberal men, had organized a clique of fanatical Catholics to oppose me; and if there had not been then about three hundred really liberal native Americans, I would have been defeated. I evidently made a narrow escape. All this being done during my absence, it gave to the efforts against me a sinister hue; but to my success a hallo of glory. I saw this on my arrival in Cincinnati, and simply denied the false charges that they had made, then let the galled jades wince. My position was a very puzzling one, to-wit: I should have thanked some persons for my nomination, who were really my foes. Was it not under circumstances best for me to simply accept the situation and attend to the duties of the office conferred upon me?

Quietly I remembered the prophesy of the gypsy. In this connection, it may be well to state, that in my political carreer in Cincinnati, I received more opposition than support from my countrymen. A few were true friends; but others again were envious of me, and blocked my career all they could.

Affairs at home in Dent had, thanks to my good wife, gone agreeably and profitably, and I was very glad to turn from slippery politics, to squarely honest domestic affairs. Much of the Spring work on the farm was already done. Preperations for our new house, on the highest ground of our place, were going on, and I saw every day more: what a standby in life, especially in America, is an intelligent loving wife.

The Constitutional Convention was to meet the middle of May. The latter part of April, a son, whom we called Frederick was born, he lived only a year. My own health had been impaired during my winter's journey by irregular ways of living. On the steamer already, I had an attack of Bilious Fever. On arrival in New York much was said about Cholera, and I ought to have had myself critically examined by a good physician, as soon as I got home. But being elected, and having to meet the Convention within a month, the examination was put off. Besides, the birth of a son made my good wife's health more important than mine. I attended the opening of the Convention at Columbus, May 6th, 1850, and continued there until July 9th, when in consequence of the Cholera breaking out as an epidemic, the convention adjourned to meet in Cincinnati, on the first Mondry in December ensuing. I had soon after I got home, a light attack of the Cholera, several of my neighbors died with it. By careful living and kind nursing, I soon regained my health again.

CHAPTER XXXII.

STUDIES ON CONSTITUTIONAL JURISPRUDENCE.

During the Summer and Fall, of 1850, I took, besides assisting on the farm, garden and vineyard, into serious consideration the points at issue in reforming the Constitution of Ohio, as they had been brought forward during the two months we were in session in Columbus. I felt certain, that my carefully elaborated proposition for, what I called: a selfacting apportionment of Senators and Representatives, would, in the main, be adopted. And that I regarded as a vital point, because, with it, the arbitrary manufacturing of a spurious public will, would be, if not entirely, at least so checked, that the formation of an intelligent, virtuous and wise public will, which is the basis of all correct politics, would have some chance in the future.

During my visit in Europe, and in consequence of my election to the Convention, I had reflected deeply upon the subject. It presented to my mind the paradox, that both Europe and America should have constitutional troubles at the same time. The first had them about reforming institutions, that were Centuries old, the second about organizations, that had hardly existed 50 years. I asked: Have not like causes like effects? There was evidently a likeness of causes, but on closer examination it proved otherwise. Europe took up the question of public administration as a matter of repairing the old one; while in the United States it was largely taken up as a question of original organization. The trouble in the U. S. was: that the people, that talked reform there, had no experi_ ence for their guidance, and their patriotic sense was therefor continually jostled out of its integrity by ingrained partisan feelings. In our public conduct time and facts were anamolies, and I certainly felt this most keenly myself. Selfresearch seemed the first duty for us all. I, at least, so accepted it.

I begun then, primarily for my own benefit, to make up a book, now by my side, and entered into it. whatever, while reading or thinking, struck me as true and important, always naming the author. I quoted from, in the margin. I entered most of its contents during the recess of 1850. It contains now, besides, a large number of aphorisms from various sources. The work of noting down was rather troublesome, because it put in question so many of my favorite ideas; but, I felt sure, that, what was unsettled, became resettled on a clearer basis, and by better impressions on my mind.

I comprehended, better, than ever before, that the great point of a Constitution is: after correcting existing wrongs; so to organize the government for the future, as to keep it free from attempts to enslave society. That, I believed, would be best done in Ohio: 1) by provisions, that counteracted the self-perpetuation of parties, and, 2) by keeping our people steadily on the path of a truly politic self-development. A people's best liberty is freeing itself of its own errors.

At that time the country was agitated by the arrival of Kinkel and Kossuth. I assisted largely in raising $100,000.00 for Kossuth, and got personally acquainted with the eloquent Hungarian. He caputed us as an exile. We identified him with our Democracy, which was a mistake for both of us. I had not then seen Hungary, as I afterwards did, and Kossuth was to me an ideal character; ideal in his conception of himself and of persons and things around him, and his idealism, he impressed others with. He came near imbuing the United States with it, and to impart to us an excitement, that would have changed intirely our international relations. He failed, because his political conceptions mean, that his nation worships itself, and imparts that selflove to its politcians, so that, very few of them, have considered seriously enough the inevitable destiny of Hungary. Kossuth might have drawn it away from its intense selflove, and its momentary enthusiasm, for a liberty, that was hardly skin deep. But Kossuth's lead, in America, could never amount to sound advice to us, as to our international policy. He was not fully informed, that in our postal and other commercial relations, we always had arrangements and understandings with other nations, and had therefore, practically, recognized, that isolation is not our correct relation to the rest of the world. I saw very clearly myself then, that the time had come, that we should have, besides national, also international politics; but, that we would then, as now, have to understand, that it is not a Kossuth, that can lead us in such matters. What we needed, was and is: to have practical men of our own, as well as of other nations, for leaders, such as acted in framing our international postal treaties. And these kind of men must take the several subjects in hand, with that common good sense, which, while it yields to necessities, as they arise, looks beyond the wants of the moment, and provides for the better future, by an improved international intercourse. For that we need statesmen, that are above national partisanism. *Deak*, whom I met in Pesth, in 1865, was of the true type.

CHAPTER XXXIII.

THE CONSTITUTIONAL CONVENTION IN OHIO.

The convention met, in Cincinnati, in December 1851. I attended it in good health. It continued in session three months, and finished its work March 9th, 1851, when it adjourned sine die. The two published volumes of debates contain a full record of the proceedings and discussions. Events have since passed upon much of the work done. Of us, who did it, only a half dozen are alive. I now fully realize, how hard a task it is, in the United States, to make a lasting written constitution. Instability is here inherent in all constitutional work. Our constitution was a much better one, when we passed it, than it was, after amendments to it were added by popular vote. These amendments were demagogical tricks, by which gross political errors were smuggled into our constitution, and untold mischiefs were thrown upon society; besides preventing true reform in the future. The temperance clause, written by Sam. Carey, is the worst of these interpolations.

Think of it! Since the constitution has been adopted, the pages of our Statute Book have grown from 1500 to over 7000 pages, and they are the abbreviated collations of over 10,000 pages of enactments. We have besides over 3500 pages of Judicial decisions. And all our taxes, assessments, fines, fees and amercements, are a tangled mass of spoliation. We have no rightful, competent, public service, not a shred of proper municipal government, we possess not a particle of check on public corruption, except of that mushroom sort, which arises in pursuance of partisan quarrels over the public spoils.

This state of things humbles us constitution makers, for we are so far responsible for it, as we might, had we been more fully bent on it, have prevented much of the wrong. I accept my part of this responsibility, but plead, that I sincerely labored for a more perfect constitution. What counteracted my efforts in this direction, were indeed, first of all, my own shortcomings; but, still more potently worked the spurious public will, with which our parties had inflated themselves. And from this has flowed a very confused public mind, that has made our society go into a social war, which has given to all our public affairs a corrupt tendency. It is bred daily in our partisan public press; for there every falsehood finds dissemination; every error its casuistry, every wrong its support. It is there, where the adults of our population are misinstructed, miseducated, and misdirected, continually.

It may be well to remind the reader, that the year 1850 was, not only for Ohio, but for the whole Union, the embryo year for changes in our constitutional policy. The compromise measures, sometimes called "the Omnibus Bill", were at that time being discussed. They were to be, if not a constitution, at least an adjustment of difficulties engendered by false movements, then going on in society about slavery. There was then a general, underhanded onslaught on our constitutional law. Sumner's election in Massachusetts, gave to our entire National Government a new twist. It meant: that Massachusetts, at least, did not want peace. It was the same, as if Saxony would to-day send an Anarchist into the German Bundesrath. Sumner's remarks: "Slavery is sectional, liberty national", was, in every sense, a perfidious play of words; it was throwing down the gauntlet of New England to the Southern States. The first part represented a false Northern sentiment, the second, a false Southern. Fillmore was then President, Daniel Webster his Secretary of State. Both knew Sumner to be a dangerous man, and they regarded him as a public enemy. I heard it myself, in Benton's room, from Sumner's own lips, that Webster regarded him in this light. He foresaw then, that the entire construction of the U. S. constitution was at stake, and that hereafter the logic of events, and not the logic of statesmanship, would rule. And just so I felt, when in the Winter of 1852, I stood in the Legislature of Ohio, and heard bills read and discussed, that had been introduced under the pretense, that they were to carry out our new Ohio constitution. It was plain to me, that in that Legislature, though it had a Democratic majority, breathed another public spirit, than that in our convention. And so I have had to feel since. Why should I not tell it in this, my last work? I write it, because, it is a most essential thing for our people to know: that the government in our constitutions is not the actual government under which we live, but, that there has been substituted the fiat of party caucuses, that meet in the dark, and have no principles, except the loaves and fishes, and their prejudices, as to religion and politics. That wrong did not arise out of our new constitution.

The new constitution engaged my time, after it was ratified by the people. A resolution had passed the convention, ordering the constitution to be translated into German, and written, out in fair hand, on parchment, for depositing it in the archives of the State. This writing out of a constitution in two languages was done through me in the United States, only in Ohio. Molitor and Stallo were named as translators, in co-operation with Blickensdoerfer and myself, as members of the Constitutional Convention. I had to have some correspondence with B. as to the right translation. He wanted, what he called a "free translation", like that of Shakespeare's Macbeth, by Schiller. I insisted upon a strict translation, in the sense of a State paper, that followed the terms used and gave their exact meaning. B. consented to this view, and after several conferences at my house in Greene Township, the Constitution, in German, was a perfect transcript of that in English, and so deposited in the State House. In Europe most constitutions are written out in Latin and the respective language of the country.

After the Convention adjourned in March, private matters claimed my attention. Among them was my agency for the estate of the heirs of Reimer-Ruge in Lübeck, which I mentioned before. I was informed that Leavitt, to whom I sold the lands, was in default. I ordered my lawyer to bring suit at once, which expedited the final settlement; and enabled me to remit the money to Lübeck in due time for final settlement.

The death of my son Frederick brought deep sorrow to us, but also sharp regrets, that we were not entirely clear of having a share in his death; because we had from feelings of kindness to a young doctor, called Schroen, that had married a distant relation, taken him as the physician. The gypsy's prophecy arose most sharply to my mind; and I wished the young doctor far away, forever out of sight, but he persisted in visiting us, and to renew our sorrow by every visit. He lost his excellent wife, and then removed from the neighborhood. About ten years afterwards he went into the Civil War and then disappeared. We at least never heard of him again.

CHAPTER XXXIV.

OUR VISIT TO NEW ENGLAND IN 1851.

The circumstances, related in the previous chapter, made it proper, to gratify a long entertained wish of my wife, to see her brothers in Portland, Maine, and, at the same time, let her see again the place, where she got her education, 20 years previous. The idea, once entertained, became a fixed idea. July 7th, 1851, myself, wife and my son Edward, who was then five years old, left Cincinnati by railroad, stopped over in Columbus, and next day went to Cleveland, where we took the steamer for Buffalo, arriving next morning; and there we took a day, to see the Niagara Falls. We were of course delighted with the great natural sights, we saw there.

From Buffalo, we went to Albany, by night train. Next day we went from Albany to Boston in one day, and from thence through the night to Portland. My letter, announcing our departure from Cincinnati, and probable time of arrival in Portland, never reached my brothers-in-law; hence our arrival was a surprise to them. They got over it, after they recognized their sister, which at first they did not do. Our son Edward soon became a good companion to his American cousins. My brothers-in-law lived in the two houses, already described. Their families were entirely assimilated with the Yankee ways. We alternated week about, between Godfrey the elder, and Gabriel, the younger brother. They lived on what was called Observatory Hill, a very healthy location. We heard from each other, in good humor: that, though we were all three original Lutherans, by baptism and confirmation, neither of us had adhered to their original faith. They had become Congregationalists; I a so-called Free Thinker. I noted their modes of living and their household and general peculiarities in my diary. As to Portland, its people, and their political and religious status, etc, I presented that, in my correspondence to the Cincinnati Enquirer, then under Faran's and Robinson's control. The first gave me letters of introduction to prominent persons in Maine, that had been members of Congress with him; also to the editors of the Portland Argus, the Democratic organ. During our six weeks' stay at Portland, we made many excursions. Among them was one to Bath, were I met at a festival of the Presbyterian church, Professor Stowe, husband to Harriet Beecher Stowe, whom I had known in Cincinnati. He was the main speaker and presented orthodox views. He was very polite to me and my wife. My sojourn in Maine, and my mingling with folks of both the Democratic and Whig party, gave me a better knowledge of New England, than years of reading or talking about it, would have given me. My correspondence with the Enquirer contains much of my views, as they were then published by me. I hope, it will not be deemed immodest, if I state, that I received many verbal, and written congratulations on these letters. I have not seen them lately, but have them among my papers, which I expect to deposit in the rooms of the public library of Cincinnati. We left Portland for home on the 18th of August.

We went home via Boston, New York, Dunkirk, Cleveland, and Columbus. In Boston we saw the city thoroughly, and were delighted with the historic information, our stroll over it, had imparted to us. The Hotel, we stopped at, was not pleasant; it was the Merchants' Exchange Hotel. In New York we made a few visits to my Bankers, Poppe & Co., and also took a drive over the city, and enjoyed the signs of growth, it exhibited everywhere. The Erie R. R. in New York, with its magnificent scenery, gratified us highly. But at Dunkirk, the utterly neglected floor of the connection depot, between the railroad and the lake steamer, came near costing my son Edward his life. I snatched him away from a pitfall, just as he was going over an opening left by a missing plank. It sends a thrill of sharp pain through my body, even now, as I think of it.

CHAPTER XXXV.

THE SEVERE POLITICAL STRAIN ON ME IN 1851—52.

In the Fall of 1851, I made 450 gallons of wine in my vineyard. It was the last large wine crop, I made in Dent. From that time on I reduced my vineyard. In 1851 I had 9 acres of grape vines; in 1861 I had but one half acre left. It was best so, though I disliked to give up, what was once my ideal object. I sold also gradually my stock of wine, and invested the money in property. I had to admit, that American natural and social conditions were stronger, than my immigrant will.

At this time I received also the last installment, which was coming to Frederick Faulhaber from his inheritance from his mother, from Germany. It was $1600.00, and I sent it to the Shakers at Whitewater Village, where it went into the general fund. I asked myself: Was this consummation the end of German beginnings; or the beginning of an American end?

American politics now again received my attention in spite of my inclination to have nothing more to do with them. I had very decided opinions as to what should be done by the Democratic party. I believed, it should be the medium for correcting American politics. But the idea of our leaders was, to make the party the dominant power of the Union, and to secure the offices to their subservient partisans. In 1851 I was asked to make speeches at Democratic meetings, with perfect freedom, to express my own ideas. And I did, thinking I could do so, consistently with my sense of public propriety. And I made my speeches accordingly, but I could neither satisfy the public nor myself. What I said was more an admonition towards, what ought to be done by the party, than what I believed would be done by it. I noticed, however, that the very remarks, which the candidates disliked, pleased the audience. I drew, from this, the inference, that there was a schism in each party, between the great body of it and those, who wanted to work it for personal gain. The election of 1851 went Democratic, because, that was the general tendency at that time. I took from this, that the Democratic party was not in a condition, to be the best possible organism for the good of society; it subserved personal ends.

When I started out in 1852, I had no idea of the busy year, I would have to lead. The months of January and February were almost entirely absorbed in forwarding the cause of Kossuth and Kinkel. I continued this, until I secured, by collections, about $90,000 for them. On the 18th of January my son Louis was born. About three days afterward, my wife became very sick, with the disease, called: Milkleg. She had to undergo terrible sufferings. I felt them, really, myself, as I saw her suffer.

I was, that Spring, too much away from home, and left my household affairs too much to hired folks. I determined, that on this subject, there should be a change. But often as I resolved to abstain from politics, just as often, something or other, not foreseen by me, would call me back, and embroil me again in some public matter. I saw then very plainly, that, what made it so difficult, to stick to resolves, in such affairs, were the entanglements, that were unavoidably there for members of political parties, between public and personal considerations, and arriving at correct determinations. There was the further difficulty, to decide, whether I could in honor abandon the Democratic party, at a time, when my leaving it, would, in Cincinnati, have given the preponderance to the untrustworthy elements of it? And, of course, with this came the further question: whether this would not be the opening of the door to the Whig party, the one I believed to be my chief duty to oppose. None knew the perplexities, I then passed through, except myself.

I got some relief in the Winter, of 1852, by reading Blackstone's Commentaries and other law books. This gave my reading and acting a better tone.

One of the meanest popular crimes was perpetrated in Columbus, in 1852. The legislature was backward in appropriations for the new State House. The public] was determined to hurry them up; one night they — nobody knew, who *they* were? — burned down the old State House. A repetition of a similar crime was perpetrated in Hamilton county, when they burned down the Court House, to force the County, to build a new one. The worst of these matters was, that the perpetrators of the crimes always escaped punishment.

During April, my name was frequently mentioned as a candidate for Congress in the Fall. I knew, that I would have a determined, both secret and open, opposition. So I determined, to state publicly, what would be my conduct under all circumstances; and in the the first week of May, I had my card to the voters of the Second Congressional District printed and distributed. I said at the close of the card: "I am determined to keep aloof from practices, too common of late, which are turning the Democratic party, from a band of brethren, into a camp of enemies, and whose seeds of discord must bring a fearful harvest of disaster and defeat. I will not by any act of mine, prolong the existence of this lamentable state of things. I am anxious, as one of the Democratic family, that those good times shall be revived, in all their purity and brightness, when the Democrats met in their primary assemblies. as conscientious citizens, and not as personal partisans. Falsely ambitious men, singly and in cliques, then always met their deserved rebuke." The first answer to my card, came in the shape of a call, for me, to a pretended interview for settling difficulties in a friendly way with my opponents. In the call it was stated, that my *not* attending would lead to a bitter quarrel. I went there June 1st, in good faith, alone and unarmed; as I knew of no cause of any settlement, at that time being needed between me and anybody else. The real purpose of the call was, as I learned afterwards, to confront me with a man, that would tell me to my face, that I had accused a certain opponent of mine of a crime; and that, unless I disproved the charge, they would fall upon me, to beat and crush me, assisted by rowdies, especially hired. I came, fearlessly. The man, that was to confront me — Earhardt — also came; but, instead of charging me, as expected, he denied, promptly and squarely, the imputation on me. He admitted, that the whole matter arose out of a mistake, *he* had made, as to a remark of his wife's. Roll, my competitor for Congress, now sneaked away with his rowdies; so did Wash. McLean fail to explain his connection with the matter. I learned, thus, most dedidedly, that with a certain class of American politicians, Shakespeare's reflection is still the dominating sentiment: "Hate'st thou the man, thou would'st not kill?" I should not have come on an anonymous call.

June 7th, I delivered an oration, at the German Musical Festival, in Columbus. Galloway, Secretary of State, and Dennison, afterwards Governor, also spoke. This brought my name prominently before the public. June the 14th, I spoke in Cincinnati at the ratification meeting of the nomination of Pierce and King. The mass of the Democrats, including myself, regarded Pierce's nomination, as an escape from trouble, which would surely arise, if either Buchanan or Cass would receive the nomination. We were mistaken. The main danger was in Douglas, and Pierce, the dark horse, proved even worse than either of the Gentlemen named.

June 20th: Timothy C. Day, former editor of the Enquirer, called at my place in Dent, with William Myers, his and my friend, and stated to me definitely, what I had long suspected, to-wit: that there existed then, in Hamilton county, a *secret political society*, for the distribution of the offices among themselves. And what they told *me*, privately, at my house, they published, five days afterwards, in the public papers. The public soon saw, that the organization of that secret society. was chiefly for the purpose of defeating my nomination for Congress. As the list of members thereof, was published, it was discovered. that Roedter, a distinguished German.

also belonged to it. Molitor's name, another prominent German, was *not* found on the list. The people had thus to learn: that politics were running evidently in Hamilton county to odd ends.

The Whigs had nominated Gen. Scott for President. This was followed quickly by the death of Henry Clay, the founder of the Whig Party, and it became evident, that there would be no very strong opposition to Pierce's election. The nominations for Congress became thereby of greater importance to the politics of the county, than was, at first, supposed.

Invitations to speak for Pierce, came in to me from all sides, and I complied frequently. July 4th, I spoke at Aurora, Indiana. I was everywhere regarded as the defender of public integrity, and liked or disliked accordingly. I saw very plainly, that the meaner elements of the Democratic party had injured their prospect of success, by the exposure of the Miami Tribe. I was the most prominent denouncer of this and all secret political societies.

A most dastardly attack was made on me at this time, in the papers, by a Catholic, P. D. Warden; he was the hired tool of Roll. For a while Warden played a big part in the Democracy, but the attack on me, and his subsequent meanness, drove him away from Cincinnati. He went to Washington and found more genial quarters, and loitered about the Courts and other public places. He died lately. regarded universally as a sponge on society. He met me afterwards once in Washington and apologized. It humbled me to hear his hypocrisy.

August 4th, came the meeting for the election of delegates in Green Township, the place of my residence. The corruptionists showed their hands at once. by using the split as to two delegates, so as to defeat the will of the majority, that was decidedly on my side. They got up personal fights and quarrels, which disgusted the elder part of the audience, and they left before the final vote. The corruptionists took advantage of this, and secured two of their delegates from the minority that remained. These, surrepticiously obtained, delegates were early on the ground of the convention at the Brighton House, next morning, even before the Convention met. They at once re-commenced their brutalities: One person, a supporter of mine, was assaulted and wounded, in the very face of the delegates. I thought, the time had come, to decline any further candidacy of mine, under these circumstances. My opponents were there, prepared for any mean act to defeat me, even blood would have been shed, if I had not declined. I thus saved from actual violence the better elements of the people, that were supporting me.

Roll easily secured the nomination, although there was a weak effort in favor of Mr. Groesbeck. During the canvass before the people, I was asked to run before the people against Roll, but I thought. this would be unfair under the circumstances; so Scott

Harrison was selected, and made the canvass. During it, I made an independent campaign against the Miami tribe. My life was endangered several times, while making public speeches, but I persevered, nevertheless. My wife was my staff in all these dangerous moments; for she kept up her courage on all emergencies, and I owe her eternal gratitude, for the moral support, she gave me.

I wrote in my diary, as the lesson of the whole matter: "A life, spent for a party, is a life lost." And so it is in every way, even as to money. It was my farm life, to which I could retire in convenient intervals, and recruit my strength, and moderate the draft upon my purse, that was being drained by heavy expenses, that gave me the selfreliance I needed. And it is a pleasure to me, to be able to state to-day: that not a copper was ever contributed to me, either directly or indirectly, in this struggle of mine, by others.

Wednesday, October 13th, was the day of triumph. All the candidates upon the ticket of the "Miamis", who were known to be secret conspirators, were defeated, and, what is more, were disgraced, for all their villanies were exposed during the canvass, and thus rebuked. It was also a personal victory to me. As I passed along the streets, I was hailed as the vindicator of the public honor. The change in one day was astounding. On Thursday following a city delegation came out to my country home, and congratulated the country and me on our success. They took me to the city in triumph, and made me address a mass meeting of thousands, at the head of Main street. My speech was applauded, and the resolutions, I had drawn up, were unanimously adopted. I had been warned of intended violence, but evidently there was now a public spirit abroad, that prevented any such attempt. I felt, however, how high toned a man must be, to speak fearlessly, with death thus in his mind. The sense of it, really buoys one up, so that he can stand the pressure, he otherwise could not confront.

CHAPTER XXXVI.

THE TREACHERY OF THE PIERCE ADMINISTRATION.

I voted for Franklin Pierce in November 1852. I labored and spent my money for him, upon the frequently expressed ground, that he would secure us, through a model national administration, against the rascals, that had stolen from the people of Ohio their local, municipal and state government, by getting up secret political societies. But, Pierce was hardly elected, before indications multiplied, that the rascals had secured his favor, and would have all the more prominent positions. We had therefor to yield gradually to the conviction, that we were all grievously mistaken, in assuming, that we had to deal, in the Miami Tribe, with a special local evil. And we erred also, in taking Buchanan, Cass and Douglas as individual types of bad men. We should have inquired: whether there was not a general cause for these evil developements? And we would then have found, that there was such a cause; and applied remedies for the disease. The cause could be no other, than a half century of party government, that found support in the various corrupt elements in society, and had therefore a tendency to drive out of the public service all those, who were zealous in the public cause. This party spirit had imparted to all lower American politicians, a peculiar subserviency to special interests. At the same time, it caused more and more of shrinking among certain persons, from asserting their personal integrity. Those of us, who tried to counteract this false current, found our labors more difficult, and less availing every day.

The comfort of my family, my personal inclinations, and my inner convictions, all pointed to an entire severance of my life, from what is called "politics" here. And this I made up my mind to do. But Messrs Day, Molitor, Gurly, Myers ,and others, urged me to assist them, at least so far, as to see, whether influences could not be brought to bear on Pierce, from New York, to form a Cabinet, that would revive our confidence in the possibility of regenerating the Democracy. I agreed, after long hesitancy, to go with Mr. Day to Washington, and, if necessary, to Concord, to see, what could be done in that direction. I left home, with a heavy heart, in February, 1853. We went to Washington, taking Cleveland by the way, and soon found, after arrrival, that our journey would be a failure, because Pierce was a trickster, and had made up his mind, to associate himself with the corrupter elements of the Democratic party. I returned therefore early home to my wife and family, and was glad to throw off, for some time at least, the bitter feeling, that had been engendered in my mind, as to prospects of a better status of things, in the country, from my mind.

All through the Fall of 1852, there was much emigration from Ohio, to California, and it took an extra rush immediately after the Presidential election. Several of my neighbors moved away. I noticed, in conversation, that most of those movers, gave as their reason for going, that the country was changing, in pursuance of emigration from Europe, in such a way, so that they could not stay. Not one stated the real reason, to-wit: That they were unfit to live in a country, where actual merit and actual earnings, were to be the conditions of prosperity. They had, by their farming, ruined the lands. They had so far lived in apparent affluence, and could no longer go on in that way, after the lands were no longer fertile. So they emigrated, but were too sharp, to state the real reason. I was sorry, to see them go, because I knew, that, at least half, that went, would rue it. And so they did, and a great part came back, some years after, much poorer. Many died on the shores of the Pacific Ocean.

In that general rush to California we may note the current upon which the growth of the United States was then running. It run on the presumption, that the great right of the people of every State, was, to push westward, and to occupy the new lands; to despoil them of their fertility, and to grow rich through the rise of prices afterwards. Nobody admitted the great duty of a people of a country, to be true to their land, and the society, settled upon it. They talked a great deal about State rights, and very little about State righteousness.

That Fall I had several accidents with my children; but none had any serious consequences, and this was a great relief to me. In the political arena there were several unhappy incidents. The wotst one was, on September 15th, the attempted assassination of Dr. Albers by Klauprecht, for slandering his wife and mother-in-law. Klauprecht was convicted and sentenced to the penitentiary, but pardoned by the Governor, after getting there, before we was put into a cell. It was queer, that every cause, like the one, we were engaged in, bred fanatical persons on both sides, and actual bloody conflicts. All that Fall, after the October election, I studied law every spare moment, that I could have, so as to qualify myself for assuming the practice of law, if ever I should finally conclude, to take that step. I kept at it, because I was certain, that such a study is, in itself, a good occupation; but, I knew all the time, that there was within me, an inner aversion, to be a practicing attorney. Such disinclinations cannot, at last, be set aside, as we shall see.

I allowed myself, to be persuaded, to begin the year of 1853 with an effort, to secure my township's vote to the Democratic State Convention, to be held January 8th, at Columbus. I was elected by getting 56 votes of the 86 cast. I was drawn into this to help my old friend and honest Democrat — William Medill — who was a candidate for the nomination of Governor. He was the President of our Constitutional Convention in 1851, and that, of course, made him my friend. When the convention met, he was nominated for Governor.

When I got to Columbus, there was great excitement, whether Medill or Manypenny should be nominated for Governor. What was the criterion? There was absolutely none. Yet — *Stanton*, the future Secretary of War, under Lincoln, started one, to-wit: *Hard* money versus *Bank* money; and a fight on the floor of the convention, between Cook — the father, and Cook, the son — ensued, and furnished the test, by which Medill conquered. But the real question was ignored by all. It was: whether intelligent men, that meant the country's welfare, should not put on their studying caps, and ask themselves and others: whether there was not something seriously wrong in the Union and every part thereof? That question was not put. It was jesuitically asked: "Have we not met and voted? Have we not been victorious over each other? Aye, we had! But what kind of government is that, in which every good effect must be secured by victories over each other?

There was then a man, to-wit: S. P. Chase, who put another question to us — slavery? It became the issue afterwards, but was it a real issue? No! It was like the rest of the issues, fictitious, and made for a factional purpose. So, we still ask: What was the real issue? And, I answer: It was, as already intimated: whether American society was organized on political realities or partisan fictions? As to it, we have to answer: Society in America was then encased in institutions, that were neither real nor ideal in any true sense. And for proof of this assertion, we point to the State convention in Ohio, in 1858. Both Medill and Manypenny were fit for Governor, if only the routine of the office were to be the criterion; but neither were fit to be a Governor, of a state like Ohio, by the real criterion, — their personal fitness as statesmen for the office. Chase was every way the superior of both, except from the standpoint of the then current politics. And, as to them, he was as unfit as the others. All three committed a common mistake: to dispute, which party was right? They should all have known, that all parties were then really wrong. Wrong! because, they were false public organs, organized upon specious pretexts, that rested on casuistries, just as doctrinaires ever do, when they want to rule over society. They extenuated their own evil ways on the pretense, that they are preventing worse ways by others. On that plea the Missouri compromise was repealed, and for months there were undercurrents in every State, to secure pliant tools to fasten the meditated treachery. Douglas was the master partisan leader in this iniquity.

CHAPTER XXXVII.
ODDS AND ENDS IN OUR POLITICS.

In 1853, in calling upon the Governor, Ruben Wood, I was surprised, by being handed by him, at the close of our interview, a commission for Director in the Harrison Turnpike Co.; the road, that run past my farm. It was a mere compliment, and as such I took it home. Others regarded it as a favor from the Governor, that implied an obligation on my part, to support him. I served several years on *my* understanding. The next surprise was the suggestion of one of the Judges of the Supreme Court, to me, to have myself examined for admission to the Bar, as proper for me in my public position. I agreed to it, was examined rather rigorously, and passed, as the document, now before me, signed by Kendall Thomas, Clerk of the Supreme Court, sitting in Franklin County, January 7th, 1853, certifies.

On Saturday, January 29th, 1853, I made a speech at Harrison, for a railroad from Cincinnati, to run over the hills from Green

Township to the State line between Ohio and Indiana. The meeting was unanimous and enthusiastic for the plan, but not for furnishing the necessary means. My speech was afterwards published. At that time building railroads was a universal desire, but there was no squarely honest plan, for building and running them. The law gave carte blanche to speculators. There was nowhere any fair public authority, to pass upon projects, nor to raise the ways and means on squarely honest terms. It was all volunteer work, in which the most audacious had the most success. Our project had true merit, it has it yet; but, it is still in the air, whilst other undertakings, that have not half the merit, have been built, and gone into operation. The history of the latter tells of long struggles, much waste of money, and the final success to tricksters, that really advanced the least money; often, indeed, none at all.

Let us return to party politics. Februa y 1st, 18 3, I started with Mr. Day for Washington, by railroad, via Columbus, Cleveland and Pittsburgh. At Cleveland we had an interview with Mr. Gray, editor of the Plain Dealer. He frankly told us, that, though he voted for Pierce, he was then inclined, to doubt his fitness. Gray thought it significant, that our late Democratic State Convention first nominated Medill, then repudiated the Baltimore platform, on which Pierce was elected. He said: "Discord is evidently ahead!" At Pittsburgh we called on "Stanton", and I saw, how intense he could be in cases, for which he acted as attorney. Self-intensification was evidently the main point in his character. His partner Umbstaedter was an old acquaintance of mine, and personal friend, and from him I learned much about the character of Stanton, that afterwards came out publicly, during the civil war. The further we travelled, the more we conversed, the clearer it became to me: that our way to secure a place for Mr. Day, and to meddle in politics, was really a dubious way. From Pittsburgh we went to Baltimore, and both, Mr. Day and myself, called upon some of our friends. I again visited my cousin Pauline. Her husband had become the General-Agent of the main omnibus line in Baltimore. She had many inquiries to make of me, as to our old homes.

At Washington we called upon Mr. Disney, the Representative of Cincinnati. He told me frankly, that he was not for Mr. Day for Postmaster of Cincinnati, but for his brother-in-law — Vattier. I refrained from discussing politics with Mr. Disney. He was, however, outspoken himself, as he always was, when we were members of the Legislature together, in 1845—46. I had become his successor in the Ohio Senate: and he said: I ought to have been elected to Congress, in 1852. Disney was evidently not favorably disposed to President Pierce. He expected no favors from him, being an outgoing Congressman. I called upon Benton, as an old acquaintance, from Jackson's time; also on Chase, and with him on Sumner. I then became acquainted with Butler of South Carolina, Bright of Indiana, Armstrong of the "Globe", and also Sam. Houston. Pierce was evidently proving a marplot to Democracy. Mr. Day had an offer for becoming a partner in the "Globe." I advised him to accept it; and it would have been, to him and the country, if he had done so, an advantage. The "Globe" would have been, a much better paper, and Mr. Day a much more successful man, than he was, in running for office. He declined, and took the wrong path on the dividing line of his destiny.

After a week in Washington, I got disgusted with what I saw and heard. Cabinet making, office seeking and political intrigue was upon everybody's lips. I told Mr. Day so, and begged him to go home with me. He concluded, to stay a week longer. I left for home, February 10th, with Dr. Fries. We took the Baltimore and Ohio R. R. to Wheeling, thence by river to Cincinnati. February 13th, I was at home again, and very glad of it. I wrote a letter to Pierce, explaining the situation in Ohio, and warning him against the Miami tribe. I say in my diary of this letter: "Glad it was no application for office." I took up Spring work on my farm.

I was gaining in my law business, but saw nevertheless, that, turning lawyer, 39 years old, is too late for much real success in the legal profession.

I had then several applications for trading my farm for other property, but always in the end, failed to come to terms on any offer. Once I came near becoming an owner of a thousand acres of land in Kentucky, but $100.00 divided us, and we came to no trade. I am still glad of the failure.

April 19th, 1853, my mother-in-law died. She became 73 years old; all her five sisters died before the 67th year of the same disease she died of: Dropsy. She was buried in the Lutheran burying ground on Walnut Hills. Wife and myself attended the funeral. My father-in-law was now indeed a lonesome man. They had lived separate before, as my mother-in-law persisted in living with her daughter, in Cincinnati. My father-in-law could not get along with Siefert, and preferred, to live apart. I informed the relatives in Switzerland, of the death and burial of my wife's mother. I took occasion, to testify to my deep sorrow at her death.

Seifert showed to me during the burial, and afterwards; that he was angry at me, because, I had not cooperated with him in getting the Pension Agency. He was seemingly unconscious, that it was improper, both in him and me, to take any office from the Pierce administration, that meant to be a sop to the Anti-Miamis, so as to propitiate them, and to get them to support the administration. I could not agree to any such compromise, directly or indirectly; and especially could I not support Vattier, who had been a defaulter in the county, and a prominent member in the Miami tribe. My

difference with Seifert was one of the instances, that brought home
to me the disagreeableness of the prevailing politics. I was expected
to drown all my inner sense of right, and to fall in with the current
political misconduct!? I could not do so. Seifert might easily have
seen the false position, he was placing himself into; if he had looked
at the conduct and fate of Roedter, who had gone to the support of
Vattier, and the administration generally, and was paid for it. in
receiving money support toward establishing his paper. He too was
complaining of me daily, because, I had not abandoned my opposition to the Miami tribe. Roedter's opposition paper was finally un-
successful, and both he and his supporters, lost large sums of money.
When Roedter's paper went down, it was known, why he accused
me. This should have opened Seifert's eyes, but it did not. He
shut his eyes to the misconduct of Vattier in the Post office and his
final insolvency, and became my adversary in many ways.

In May, 1854, the two Railroad companies, in Indiana and Ohio,
that were to construct the railroad, already spoken of, from Cincinnati over the Hills to Harrison, and thence to Indianapolis, met at
Brookville. They elected E. M. Gregory, Joint President, after I
had declined the position. I thus escaped a task of great responsibility and risk, and remained a much freeer man, than I would have
been, if I had accepted the place.

CHAPTER XXXVIII.

MY THIRD JOURNEY TO GERMANY.

Toward the latter part of May, 1854, myself and wife took up,
for general benefit and health, the plan of a journey to Germany
with our children. We begun early to make our preparations. Before our departure, I made a round trip to Madison, Rushville, Indianapolis, and Dayton, for our railroad project. At Indianapolis, I
had the Governor and other high officials for my audience. I met
there also many old Cincinnati friends; namely: Myers, Nicolai and
Dr. Homburgh. At Dayton I fell in with Judge Stillwell. who had
been a member of the Constitutional Convention with me. He
begged me, to take to Cincinnati for him, and place with Ellis &
Morton, bankers in Cincinnati, a package of $20,000.00. They were
brand new issues of a new Bank in Illinois, that had lately been
established, by his aid. I complied with his request, thinking it,
however, funny that I, a hard money democrat. should be colporteur
for an issue of new born bank notes, of a very questionable character.
The thing gave me much trouble, because the train to Cincinnati
was delayed to 11 p. m. I had to wake up Morton, the cashier, at
his house, to hand him the package, and thus got clear of the package on saturday night yet. When I got clear of it, the gypsy,s
prophesy came to my mind.

We left for Germany on the 13th of June, my father-in-law

stayed on the farm. I had a good renter and householder with him, so that he was well employed at his own leisure and useful to his daughter and myself besides.

My neighbors, with one or two exceptions, behaved, as little towns-people are apt to do, mean toward us before our departure. They came running in with all their small claims, as if we were about to run away. When we came to settle our accounts, it was found out, that most of them owed me, and they no longer were anxious to close the account. This conduct of my neighbors showed me, how necessary it is, in country towns, to have the cash system in all transactions between neighbors. We never had any hard feelings with our neighbors on the subject, and soon forgot all about it. I was reminded of it, by my diary, in writing this, my auto-biography.

Of political friends, Mr. Day was the only one, that upheld me in going to Germany. He saw, that it would settle my mind, to get out of the country and among persons, that would talk to me on new subjects in new ways. Seifert was a bitter head to the last. He even forbid his wife to bid us farewell. Van Hamm took my promise, that I would be his law-partner on my return, and agreed to attend to all my cases in court, or elsewhere during my absence, as the first step toward the partnership.

I had great hopes of the success of our railroad to Indianapolis; but I felt sure that Gregory, would at least not injure the develop-ment. Railroading was then a game of words, played with a view to gain supporters by plausible arguments, and he certainly was as likely to be successful, as any one in that line. I was sure, there would be no great rush to subscribe to the stock.

So we bought our tickets, for six of us, to-wit: Us two old folks and our children, Carrie, Eddie, Tilly and Louis. On the 12th of June we packed up, and got started after the usual annoying delays. We journeyed from Cincinnati to New York by railroad via: Cleve-land, Dunkirk, Binghampton and went at once on board the steamer Washington, Capt. Fitch. We reached Bremen in 15 days, stopping only for the landing of passengers at South Hampton. We had fine weather all the way. The Captain was a good officer as far as navigation went; but he was a scamp as to women, whom to call ladies would be a misnomer. He would also indulge, on occa-sion, in wine. On the night previous to our arrival at South Hampton, this was the case at the festivities given in the Cabin. Then the following interlude occurred. I heard the captain speak of "star-light" as likely to be seen by night fall; then to call him. When this time arrived, I went on deck, and looked ahead for the light. I did this, because I saw, that the Captain had a little too much wine in his head, and was not paying any attention to the ship. As I stepped on deck and looked forward over the bow of the ship, I saw "Starklight" dead ahead—within about a mile. I rushed down into the cabin and whispered: "Starklight dead ahead," into his ear. He arose quickly and rushed on deck, he gave one look forward, and as quickly run to the helmsman, crying: "Helm to port, or you are a dead man!" The helm was put as ordered, and the steamer quickly obeyed, and we passed the rock on our left, so close to shore, that in a few minutes more we would have struck and been wrecked. The captain thanked me, but he remained on deck, and left the company in the cabin to their own hilarities. A certain lewd woman thus lost her companion, but the ship was saved. I was left to my own sober thoughts and reflections on the possible situation for my wife and four children, that were sleeping quietly in their berths.

At Bremen we stopped at Hotel l'Europe. The owner, a Mr. Schultze, had come down to Bremen Haven to induce us to go to his hotel. We liked it very well, especially my wife and children, for its good fare and cheap charges. The next day I left my wife and children there, and went to Lübeck, via Hamburgh. There I settled up finally, with the Reimer-Ruge heirs, already mentioned. I enjoyed my visit to Lübeck exceedingly. It is an excellent relic of the free hanseatic cities. On my return journey to Bremen, I stopped over a day at Hamburgh, and took a good look at that city. I called on Messrs. Testdorf, wholesale druggists, whom I had met, when they were on a visit to Cincinnati. They had recommended me to the Reimer-Ruge heirs. They were very glad to hear of the successful settlement of that business, and took great pleasure in showing me their native city.

At that time the Schleswig-Holstein question was the chief topic of conversation. All saw, that great changes were impending as to German politics. The several claimants were about equally alarmed as to their respective titles. It was difficult, then, to foresee: how these were to be reconciled with international law. I saw: that the ones most firm and most patient in their claim, would finally succeed. Prussia pursued that policy, and for that reason gained her case. The question was not so much: what independence was due to the Dukedoms? But, what dependence had better be placed on them? A people that can not be properly independent, had better be made properly dependent.

We remained in Bremen but a day after my return. We went to Heilbronn, via: Cologne, Mayence and Mannheim. Between Bremen and Cologne, our luggage was subjected to a sharp examination by the custom house officers. They found a half made up silk dress of my wife's, which, by the delay of the milliner, in Bremen, she could not get finished. The custom house officers claimed a heavy duty and a fine besides. I was amazed at their demand, but we had to submit. All our annoyances and delays came to us from having the dress in that condition. We were told, that Bremen merchants told us untruths, just to sell the silk to us. My wife's expostulations were also of no avail. The incident revived in me memories about my time in Wimpfen, when I hated custom house officers and high tariffs, and enjoyed nothing so much, as playing them a trick. I told the German custom house officers, that annoyed us, that I regretted ever having spoken a kind word for them, as to their conduct toward strangers. I found afterward, that there was then spite work going on, between Bremen and the Custom's Union, and that we were victimized by it. I have since entered Germany from all parts of Europe, and must say: that I found the officers always polite and fair. I hold our then loss as a misfortune. My wife's judgment is not so lenient; she is positive still, that it was downright robbery.

The fine weather we enjoyed going up the Rhine, and the good treatment we got in hotels, on railroads, and on the river steamers, soon took away the sharp stings we had received by the inspection of our luggage. And when we got to Heilbronn, we soon forgot the whole matter. We forgot even the severe loss, our little son Louis had to submit to, when his fine white beaver, that he had brought from America, was blown from his head into the Rhine. It was an advance payment he made, for the many joys that awaited him afterwards. We did not like to have him go bareheaded, so he got a good new hat, about three hours after his landing at Mannheim. And all called him a fine boy, dressed up as he was, when we arrived at my native home, and was welcomed by all our relations.

CHAPTER XXXIX.

OUR SOJOURN IN GERMANY IN 1854.

On arrival, my father was very marked in his kindness to my wife, and, as I came to gratify my wife, I was glad of my father's kindness to her. The only hard feelings arose in me, when I was reminded, that this visit would be the last, most likely, and that we would never see each other again. Then I could but weep in secret. The conditions in and around Heilbronn were also somber enough. My brother Paul had had a stroke of palsy. He was a mere wreck, and his wife felt hard her sorrow. Everybody. my father included, foresaw, that this would lead to his parting out of the business, as he was becoming more useless every day. That was a sore point with my father; it brought memories of former attempts to secure the business to several of us children. He had always feared and disliked the possibility of only one member of the family inheriting the business. The whole family was against it. And yet all saw, that such would be the case, unless brother Paul were speedily cured.

Paul had, for years, been the leader in the family's enjoyments. It seemed impossible to have any family reunions without him. Our step-mother did her best to bridge over the difficulty, but it would not work in all instances. Having a common family garden, where grandpa was the grand-signeur, enabled her to accomplish much. The garden was fully supplied with all kinds of delicious fruits, that made Heilbronn, to the young Americans we had brought, a sort of Paradise. It had no forbidden fruit for them, except so far as I instructed them, not to exceed the proprieties of life. My father wondered, that these young Americans behaved so much better, than other children he had seen, and this too gave my step-mother great encouragement.

It was on several occasions a delicate question, how far it was proper, to take our children along in our journeys to other relations. Grandma always solved this, by deciding promptly, that they should stay with grandpa, and sister Ottilia generally seconded the motion. It carried thus by a majority of two-thirds over my head. Our children however got the benefit; they were popular for their sticking to grandpa.

Our first visit was to my brother Eberhardt, who then lived in Ehingen on the Danube, and carried on a Drug Store. He had, against everybody's advice, sold out his Drug Store in Metzingen, being tempted to do so, by the profits he made in selling out. The purchase at Ehingen more then absorbed the profit. The population of that town were nearly all Catholics. My brother Eberhardt was not only a protestant, but a free thinker. He had, besides, a Catholic for a rival. It was easily seen, that his position in Ehingen was precarious, while that in Metzingen had been assured.

We came there to stand as "God-parents" to his new-born son Alfred, and our time passed very pleasantly. We saw no bigotry among the folks we met, on the contrary, they were liberal. They met us frankly in their rural festivities, in which the Priests mingled and drank wine and beer with us. Our American Puritan Clergymen would have denounced this as sinful enjoyments. I mingled freely with the Priests in their public schools, and witnessed, on invitation, the Scientist — "Professor Krause" — giving lessons by experiments in electricity. The examiner was a Catholic Clergyman, who was evidently quite interested in the instruction. I had no fear of Catholicism for my brother, but I apprehended, that he would again fall into his old error, of not letting well enough alone.

From Ehingen, we went to Switzerland, and visited my wife's relations in St. Gallen, Zürich, Aarau and Burgdorf. It gratified me very much, to see how my wife enjoyed this coming back to Switzerland and her relations. I enjoyed, with her, specially a visit to *my* cousin Rudolf Lohbauer, who was Professor in the Military Academy, at Thun, in Switzerland. He was very much respected as a military instructor. He afterwards wrote a good review of our Civil War in 1861–65.

In Switzerland, we received, unexpectedly, the news: that one of our children in Heilbronn, Thilly, had taken the measles. We hastened back, but soon found, that there was very little use in that, because the main point was to let the measles have their regular course, by keeping the children as quietly as possible. As we had bought our return tickets, and fixed on our departure from Havre, it was important, that the children should get well as soon as possible. All, but our son Louis, got fully well before our departure, and even as to him there seemed to be no likelihood of any relapse.

My wife enjoyed, of all persons she met, most, the society of my sister Lina. It did me good, to see my wife so affectionately intimate with my eldest sister. The whole surroundings in my sister's house were cheering to my wife, and she met there a number of ladies, that she liked also, and was liked by them.

My brother-in-law, being the Marshall of the King's Palace, was useful to me in aiding me to carry out a commission, given to me by our Cincinnatian Nicholas Longworth, viz: to present to the King a basket of his sparkling Catawba. I had the wine handed in to the King on his birthday, in September, and learned next day, that the wine had been enjoyed, not only by the gentlemen of the Court, but also by the ladies. I had sent the wine, with a letter of mine, explaining Nicholas Longworth's object in sending the wine. I soon afterwards obtained a letter of thanks from the King's secretary, containing respectful greetings to the wine culturists in the United States. This royal letter I handed to Mr. Longworth, on my return to the United States, in October, and it gratified him very much.

In Stuttgardt I was confronted by a German-American, who had returned permanently to his native land, and who knew of my associations there, by the rather pointed question: "whether I thought it proper, for an American citizen, who had been a Legislator, indeed a Constitution-maker there, to be connected with establishments and persons, whose royal splendor and power must confront him every moment." I answered: affirmatively. I then mentioned to him myself: that I had, by invitation, attended a session of the Central Board for the promotion of trade, in which a Prince of the blood would also be present; that there I hoped to learn much sound political economy from the mouth of a distinguished author. I asked him now: "what wrong there was in my thus sitting in the same room with the Prince?" I argued: that there was not only no harm, but much propriety in such conjunctions. He made no reply. I can now add, that in the year 1873, I sat as a student, in the University in Strassburgh, alongside of the Crown Prince, now Grand Duke, of Oldenburgh, and heard, *with* him, Professor Laband on Financial Science. I saw, that the Crown Prince was a good student.

But besides Political Economy, I was also then enlightened and instructed as to the Science of Government, Public Administration and Taxation. For instance: A cousin of mine, Eugene Rümelin, the eldest son of my father's brother, who was then Judge of the Court of Public Administration in Stuttgardt, explained to me the principle and practice in that Court system. It was previously unknown to me, and I am certainly very much obliged for the information then given to me. It has been very useful to me, and I know of no more important subject than this, to the people of the United States; they should have such Courts in every State of the Union.

From my step-brother Otto I derived much instruction as to Financial and Fiscal Administration. He was then assistant in the Auditing Department in Stuttgardt.

In such intercourse, I learned also the fundamental distinctions between what we call here "the American way of filling public offices," and the provisions "for filling up the public service," prevailing in Continental Europe. The first is a corruption of the old English system of official patronage, which even England has now largely abandoned. The second is the product of a number of wise reforms and perfections, adopted in the course of a century, on the suggestions of master minds, like Turgo, Stein and Hardenberg. The criterion between the two may be expressed in two words: favor—merit; that is to say, in the one: office comes to men by favor and arbitrary action; in the other, through proven merit and regular promotion.

I exchanged views also with jurists, political economists and higher public officers; and thus obtained all the technical and specific knowledge that I thought would, at some time, be useful to me. And I may close this chapter by adding: that through relations and acquaintances of my wife in Switzerland, who explained to me the laws, government, public organization and administration in that republic, I was confirmed more than ever in my views; that: what keeps the United States from sharing fully in the present general advance in civilization, is the hide-bound partisanism, with which we conduct our public affairs. We are, in consequence, unable to form a legitimate public will; we are, on the contrary, experts in originating bastard public wills, through party platforms. They act as blindfolds to our people, and mislead them.

CHAPTER XI.

RETURN TO OUR AMERICAN HOME.

Towards the end of August, we had all gathered together again in Heilbronn. The children were getting along fairly as to the measles, so as to justify us in fixing upon September 15th for the day of our departure. My brother Paul, who, as stated, had a paralytic stroke, announced now, to my sorrow, that he had made up his mind to go with us to America. Father had wisely opposed it. He doubted the propriety of the step, but *I* could not speak with that decisiveness, which was needed, to make my counsel to have full value and import. I had to admit the incompatibilities there were between my brother Paul and my brother Edward, but neither could I keep from realizing, that there were likely to arise in America much greater ones. Still I hoped, that Seifert would find Paul useful in acquiring better commercial knowledge, and in this my wife coincided with me. Both of us paid too little attention to Paul's utter decrepitude, and therefore unfitness for America. We became, however, aware of it, as we journeyed along; for Paul showed, on closer contact, that unfortunate disposition of persons broken down in health; they want to rule and direct the more, the less fit they are to do so.

In the beginning of September, I made a flying trip to Munich. I there called, with letters of introduction, on the relations of the wife of my friend Molitor. They held high positions under the Bavarian Government, and were finely educated people. The young ladies were charming and very happy to meet somebody that knew their American aunt. They had heard much more disparaging reports, than the facts justified. I told them the honest truth, and they informed me of what I had long presumed; to-wit: that Mrs. Molitor lived in the United States under much lower circumstances, than her early raisings and surroundings entitled her to. The young gentlemen were assidious in their attentions to me. They showed me Munich with the fervor of standing admirers, and I learned of them much as to art.

On returning to Heilbronn, and about to leave, a farewell re-union of some forty relations gathered from all parts of Würtemberg, at Bietigheim. We had there a fine dinner, with the best of wine, singing, brief addresses and conversation. I could not get out of my mind the old proverb: "That joyous and noisy farewells are the forerunners of coming afflictions." Father and mother had remained alone at home. Next day we left Heilbronn for Paris and Havre.

My farewell from father and mother affected me deeply. My father had had hard work to get into the right equanimity toward me, but he had succeeded. He took me aside, into a room alone, by ourselves; he checked me, when I was about to ask him, to allow me a last word; and said, with flowing tears, in German: "Werd' nicht irre; ich hab' dich immer geliebt. Ich liebe dich noch. Gott segne dich und die Deinigen." This means, translated into English: "Do not mistake matters; I have ever loved you. I love you now. God bless you and yours." He kissed me and embraced me, and I returned his affectionate caresses. With faltering steps I left my father's house. I wept as I passed along the streets to the depot; I weep now as I write. I never saw my father again.

Our journey to Paris, by way of Mannheim, Forbachand Chalons sur Marne, took us about two days. At Paris we got remark-
ably well along in sight seeing. At night, on the 18th, we went to
Havre. All the way on our journey, we saw more and more the
great mistake it was, for Paul to go, in his condition, to America.
On the 20th of September we departed for New York.

We had a rough equinoxial passage of 15 days in the steamer
Humboldt, Captain DeLines. Brother Paul suffered hard from sea-
sickness, and his diseased body showed signs of the deepest pains
in his illness. We saw now, to our dismay, that his going to
America was a sad mistake.

My wife and children suffered much also. I kept up to my own
astonishment. We got to New York, October 5th, and stopped there
two days, at Hotel Earl, where we were well located. We went to
Cincinnati by the Erie Railroad. Paul troubled himself unnecessarily all along the route, and thus complicated the situation.
Eventually he fell, just as he was trying to get on the train, while
it was beginning to move, about 40 miles east of Dunkirk. We tried
to have the train stopped, so as to ascertain, whether he was really
injured, but we were refused; but assured, that he was not injured,
and that he would be along in the next train. For three hours we
suffered the agony of uncertainty, at Dunkirk. At 11 o'clock P. M.,
brother Paul came along, badly bruised, but not dangerously hurt.
We stopped over night at Dunkirk; next morning we left for Cincinnati. I reached Dent time enough, to cast my vote for the Democratic ticket. I was saved, however, from taking part in the contest. and regarded this as one happy deliverance among so many
mishaps.

After arrival home, I took a stroll over the farm. and felt good,
at the orchard full of apples, the vineyard full of grapes, and the
corn crib and the barn filled with food for common use. I sold
my wine crop for $580.00. The apples we put on shelves in the cel-
lar, nearly every week we sold a load of hay, thus we replenished
our purse, and I had soon a thousand dollars deposited to my credit in the Citizen's Bank. I felt like dropping politics, and all other
public matters, that would take me much from home. But I
reckoned without my host; there were still several personal connections, from which I had not been severed sufficiently to adhere
to this purpose. Whenever I came to town, my friend Day had
some enticing plan for me. One time he wanted me to go with him
into a new paper, and at another time into a new bank. I had to tell
him at last, jokingly: "Mr Day, through you I have lost many days,
but still," I admit: "unreservedly: you are one of the few good
public men in the United States."

CHAPTER XLI.

AGAIN IN POLITICS IN SPITE OF MYSELF.

In the early part of November, 1854, Governor Medill came to Cincinnati, and sent for me, to the Burnet House. And then and there he insisted, on my taking dinner with him. After a good dinner, with wine, he disclosed his object, namely: That I should prepare the main part of his forthcoming message: that on the finances of Ohio. I told him, that I feared, it would be a very difficult work for me, to write the leading items in his message. He asked: Why? I replied: "Because the Governor has now to consider the interests of the party, who elected him, and cannot recommend measures and subjects, merely from the standpoint of right and propriety. He insisted, that the very reason, why he wanted me to prepare his message, was: that he was determined to speak out frankly to the Legislature on taxation and expenditures. When he had stated that, I agreed, to write out a general draft, and, as soon as done, would send it to him. This I did, and, as I expected, it was too outspoken for tax reform. At his request, I went, however, to Columbus, to have verbal explanations. There he said, deftly: "I want the language a little more dignified." I asked him: "Do you not mean: softened? He laughed: "Well, have it so." Accordingly I re-wrote it; but still he wanted it softer. This re-writing was done several times. At last, he said: "I think, we had better take the first draft, for the oftener you re-write it, the more pointed becomes the language."

We then sat down together, and went over it word for word. He made several excellent suggestions, and I found him a fine English linguist, and clear in his judgment on the financial question. By New Year his whole message was prepared and ready, to be sent to the Legislature, when it met. We had kept our secret so well, that none of the Democratic papers knew, who wrote the message. And it now happened to some of those, who disliked *me*, that on the same day, on which they lauded the *message* to the skies, they had squibs, abusing *me*. The merit of the message was: that it apprised the people of Ohio, that they had, for half a century, been penurious to their State government, and careless to their Local and Municipal governments, and that, in consequence, taxes had in the latter increased disproportionately; in other words: Government in Ohio had not its equilibrium nor proper comprehensiveness. Ohio had, for that reason, at no time a financial public policy: There was no general budget; and of course, no systematic economic public conduct. The worst of it was, that there was no rightly subordination in the public administration, and no financial unity. Every thing was at loose ends, and the result was, that, whilst sharpers got much money, undeservedly, out of the respective treasuries, for their special purposes, other more meritorious public persons and concerns were suffering for want of means and proper compensation.

During my labors on the message I was harassed day and night by two sorrows: 1) by the very dangerous illness of my son Louis, and 2) by the perplexing troubles of my brother Paul. Thus, while I was trying, to bring Ohio to its equipoise in taxation, my own home was without its peace in its domestic concerns. Louis' disease yielded finally to Dr. Crookshank's skill and my persistent nursing. The latter consisted chiefly in singing my old mother's lullabies, with a heavy heart, but in cheerful sounds. I shall never forget my joy, when, one of these, awakened Louis to a smile. It was the harbinger of returning health. My brother Paul had failed to satisfy Seifert in the store, and I had not succeeded in finding him a business place among my friends. Nowhere else is it so difficult as in America, to bring an abnormal person into normal employment. Paul was such a person. In a weak moment he thought of my former clerk Goepper, and called on him for help. That person had a debt to secure at a Tobacconist by the name of Berndt. He suggested to Paul a partnership with B. It took $400.00 to secure the debt. and (by coincidence?) the same sum to become partner. Paul took the bait, and, who so convenient, to furnish the $400.00, as his brother, my humble self? He asked me to look into the matter for him. I did, and found the situation as given. I told Paul of Goepper's double-edged dealings; but instead of thanking me, he got angry, and accused me of raising difficulties, so, as not to have to come to his aid. I handed him the check for the $400.00 without a word. Paul paid it to Berndt, Berndt to Goepper, and Paul was partner of the firm of: Ahem! "Berndt & Rümelin." By the middle of May the firm broke up, and Paul lost every dollar of the $400, he. —or shall I say, I—put in By June, Paul tried, whether Shakerism would suit him. He went there. It did not suit him; and in the Fall he returned to Germany; having spent for nothing in that year of his life, about $1000.00, of which I contributed $400.00. When he arrived in Germany, he must have stated the matter to his wife. my father and brothers in a way, that made them think, I was to to blame. They wrote upraiding letters to me. My replies failed to correct the impressions, Paul had made. In 1856, on my journey to Europe, I learned, that Paul had, at last. admitted to my father, how Goepper had inveigled him, and how he. without fair inquiry, had misjudged me. I then gave up all claims for the half of the $400,00, and was paid the remaining $200 00, without interest, out of funds, left by my father. Paul's widow educated Pauls three sons, and made three good men of them. She deserves great praise for her wisdom and kindness in the premises.

During 1854, and for several years afterwards, I was correspondent of the New York Evening Post. Mr. Day had introduced me to John Bigelow, who was editor under Mr. Bryant. My first article was on the Pacific Railroad, the last in 1861 on questions, connected with our Civil War. The latter did not suit the Evening Post people, and that stopped the correspondence.

The year 1854 was to me what they generally call: an off year; that is to say: I labored *much* with *little* fructification. Medil's message, and its favorable reception by the public, might be said to mean the reverse, but I would ask: Is it really a gain to read yourself praised for your work, under the name of another? Medil paid my expenses. I refused to accept more. I was glad to see, that the people of Ohio appreciated the advice contained in the message, but regretted, that the Legislature failed to pass any reform measure at its session; and to this day Ohio's entire financial policy it still at fault and disjointed.

Much of my time was devoted to the Cincinnati, Harrison and Indianapolis Railroad. I was its general agent, and the only officer, that received no more pay, than he actually earned. Part of it was in stock, which I traded afterwards for land, at higher prices than it was worth. I finally sold the land at a loss. The road was never established, and I may consider all the money and time I put in, as investment, as lost. It is near $2,000.

On request I wrote for the "National Era" letters on general politics. My article on: "Mixed make-up of nations causes superior developments," was favorably commented upon by many other papers. This my correspondence brought me the reputation of being an abolitionist, which I certainly was not, in the then prevailing sense; but I took no pains to contradict it.

In the year 1855 I allowed myself to be tempted to plant five acres of vineyard on the American subsoil plan, against my own better knowledge. It cost me much money, and proved an entire failure in the end. I eventually rooted it out, without having a single good crop. To have good vineyards, we must *plant* good ones.

I entered heartily into the anti-Nebraska movement, and rejoiced unreservedly over every popular rebuke that Pierce got. I enjoyed the popular detestation of Douglass as a traitor to liberty. I made speeches in German and English for this cause, and received nothing for all my labor, except dark looks from some pro-slavery democrats. The cause of liberty would have been sustained without the subsequent losses it caused to the public: if nativism had not then, under the name of "Knownothingism," slipped in insiduously, and besmeared the whole subject with its daubs and froths. As I look back to-day, and call to mind how near the opposition to the repeal of the Missouri Compromise came to arousing a sound national indignation, that might have united all the sincere lovers of honest political reform, if only Benton, Blair and Chase had been the leaders. I cannot, however, help sorrowing, for the lost time and labor it all cost me. I stood utterly confounded before the political chaos that was then spread over the United States, through a false Americanism, and a spider-webbed abolitionism.

CHAPTER XLII.

KNOWNOTHINGISM WITH ITS DISINTIGRATIONS.

With Knownothingism as the illusion of some of the brighter men of the South, who were beginning to find, that things were absolutely going wrong in the United States, and with opposition to the repeal of the Missouri Compromise, as the point upon which Northern minds, that had made the same discovery, could unite,—it was evident, that there never could be a wholesome development out of such divided counsels. Ambitious men got an opportunity to intensify and corrupt the public mind, and to mislead it. The country, instead of being rescued from the inclined plane, at whose ends stood civil war, slid down the plane and went over the precipice into it.

My own private affairs claimed a large part of my attention, but I was debarred, from a heart-felt participation in politics, by the forebodings of my mind, caused by the false direction men and things were taking, as just now explained. I sold my old log-house-homestead, and 19 acres besides, at $200 per acre. It left me in Dent but 32½ acres. I bought, part cash and part stock, 200 acres in Whitewater Township, believing it likely, that my wife's relations from Switzerland would want such a piece of land, when they arrived. These relations, soon after my purchase, informed me however, that they had concluded to remain in Switzerland; and I then took steps to sell these 200 acres again. I finally got clear of them, at prices that amounted to a complete loss of my stock investment, and, the getting back of my invested money, in dribs, without interest. I became aware, at that time, that the United States were, in consequence of a lack of good farm laborers, drifting toward a diminution of the value of landed property, excepting only a few special localities, that were situated on the highway of speculation. I should have acted on this perception of mine, but failed to do so, to my regret.

In June, Morgan, the Auditor of State, Trevit, the Secretary of State, and Cook, the Attorney General, appointed me Examining Commissioner of the Independent and Free Banks of Ohio. This was a generous act on the part of these democratic officers, for it looked like an endorsement of my opposition to the Miami Tribe and the repeal of the Missouri Compromise, as well as to corruption generally. My friends Molitor and Day, thought the public woul1 regard my acceptance of this position as a willingness on my part to resume my old relations to the Democratic party, and that it would compromise me with my best friends. I regarded it as a way out of a whole lot of misunderstood tendencies toward compromising situations. It seemed to me: that the examinations of the banks would, besides employing me in work congenial to my feelings and education, also furnish an excuse, for dropping forever all the others that were uncongenial to me. Accordingly I accepted the position, and was engaged actively in it for five months. I sent in special reports, as I proceeded in my labors. I made my general report in December, and it can be found in the State Documents of the session of 1854. I permit myself to say: that I read it lately, and still feel, that my labors as Bank Commissioner have not been entirely in vain. I exposed many of the then prevailing abuses, and many of the better bankers thanked me for it.

I perceived by July, that I was getting out of politics by the surest way possible in the United States; namely: that of having made myself an impossible politician. The Knownothings had caused a disintegration of both of the standing parties of the country, and a large portion of the citizens had lost their way and were seeking to refind it, through some of the new reorganizations of old matters, that were going on. To very many of our people, a man standing on his own integrity, as I certainly then did, was an incongruity; and some came to me and suggested, that I ought to rally around myself all Democrats, that wanted the regeneration of the party. I agreed to this, at least so far, that I was willing to be the delegate from my township to a convention, in which such a regeneration was to be effected. I was elected delegate; but was immediately set upon, as if I was trying to subjugate the Democratic party. I was threatened with violence, if I went to the convention, and was advised to go there armed. I attented the convention at Carthage, nevertheless, August 12th, unarmed. Then, right there upon the ground, with no guard known to me, except my son Edward, then eight years old, friends came to me and warned me again and again. Among these was my old Democratic friend, Johnson, of the Third Ward, who begged me to go home, for he assured me, that he knew my life was in danger. I refused to go. He then informed me, that he at least would stand by me, and defend me, if necessary, against certain persons. I took my stand in the convention in the afternoon, after I was tricked by the committee in the morning, and expressed my opposition to the fallacious and weak platform, reported by the committee. I denounced it in firm language, as a fraud upon the promises that had been made to me, as to a regeneration of the Democratic party. As well known, I was then brutally assailed by Joe Talbert with curses, and by others with clubs. Against the latter Johnson protected me; and nothing saved me from being killed, except this my friend. He parried the blow, that would have killed me; and he bid me to not risk another, but to go home and save myself to my family. The man that meant to kill me then, was not

Joe Cooper, as was generally asserted, but a much meaner man, to-wit: Joe Talbert. I was subsequently asked, by Geo. E. Pugh, to return to the Convention, but I declined, believing, that I had done my full duty, and no more could be asked of me. I drove home with my son, and was glad to be once more in the peace of my own family. My deepest sorrow came the Monday following, for on that day, the true-hearted Democrat Johnson, who defended me at the risk of his life, from the assaults of Talbert, died of the cholera. I asked then, and I do now: was this Providence? I am carrying to my grave a weakness in my left arm from the blow I got from Talbert. It was for me the hardest illustration of the gypsy's prophecy.

That day's treacherous assault made it impossible for me to have any further connection with the "regulars" of the Democratic party. I adhered to Democracy as a principle, but very few understood me on this point. Many wanted me to become a Republican, and, when I declined, they were offended. They would continue to come to me. and suggest this or that proper movement for me to lead in. Some said: there can be no politics in Ohio, in which Charles Reemelin is left out. I told them all: to determine their own course, and leave me to mine. I thought, the first thing for all of us to do, was to regain our individual independence, and to wait patiently for the situation, in which we could properly cooperate.

That conjunction came, in my opinion, by a call for a mass meeting, in the yard of Turner Hall, on the evening before the election, and believing so, I attended it. I was called upon for a speech, and made one, based upon the significant illustration: "The Arkansas Fiddler." I made, by it, my attack upon the corruptions of the Democratic party, irresistible. I pointed out the misery that was brought upon the country by the eternal playing of the old party refrain, about "Democratic party!" As I walked away from the meeting, I saw, that I had defeated the combination, that was then the most dangerous to the peace of society. Next day my friend Day was elected over Pendleton, and Harrison over Groesbeck. As to my own fate? Well, and what of it? Did I not stand there before the whole people, as the free exponent of their cause? Yes. I did. But who understood me fully? Not a dozen!

CHAPTER XLIII.

SOME PRIVATE MATTERS.

The knowledge I had gained as Bank Examiner, made me cautious, as to my deposits in the banks. The failure, of these so-called: banks, really brokershops, on the 8th of November, 1854, caused me no loss, for I kept small deposits in banks anyway, and none at all in slippery ones.

From Germany the sad news came in September, that my stepmother had died, and that my father would be henceforth a lonely widower. My brother Paul, who had left the Shakers and was living with us, treated the news with cold indifference. I felt, how lonely father would now be. Of my step-mother, I preserved nothing, but good memories. I felt truly grateful to her, for the 30 years, she had been the efficient head of my father's household. I think my own mother would have coincided with me in these views.

Just before the close of the year, the City Council, of my native city, honored me by making me the guardian of the children of my deceased schoolmate, Louis Linsenmayer, and ordered the money to be sent to me, for them, to Cincinnati. This was, however, not done then. I ordered them to invest the money in Germany, and to remit the interest to me, for my schoolmate's wife and children. This step proved eventually of great benefit to the heirs, when, during the war, I got the money upon the gold basis, then converted it into greenbacks, at a premium, which doubled the amount of the inheritance, so that they gained some $1,600, in our money.

During the year 1855, I got clear of my troubles about the Cincinnati, Harrison and Indianapolis Railroad. But I allowed myself to be persuaded into assuming the Presidency of the Dayton Short Line, commonly known as the Tunnel Co. March 22nd I was elected President, and remained such for several years, really receiving but little compensation in money, though the expenses incurred by me were paid to me regularly. It kept me much from home. I wrote, for the Road, in 1855, the pamphlet "Financial Exhibit," and others, that explained to the public this enterprise. They attracted attention enough to make it probable, that the tunnel would be adopted by the respective companies as the main railroad entrance from the East into Cincinnati, and if that had been the case, it would have been a blessing to the city. The main impediment to success was however, the unreliable characters of the men that were, originally, the leading characters in the tunnel project, whom I need not name. They let every opportunity, to affiliate with other railroads, slip away, and the leaders in the other rival roads: L'Hommedieu and Strader, took advantage of this and secured the connecting railroads, as contributors to the success of their projects. My action was, therefore, to a large extent forestalled, and my efforts had to be directed to gain after-affiliations with later projects. I never underrated the difficulty of my task, but it spurred me on, to persist in my endeavors. All throughout 1855 and 1856 I devoted all my spare time to this subject, as will be explained hereafter.

February 28th, my youngest son Rudolf was born. I say of him in my diary: "He was born under the sign of the lion, may he prove a lamb." I can say now, that he was, several times, a lion in my path, and that there is but little of the lamb about him. But he has proved for us all an excellent family physician.

In April, 1855, the country was rudely awakened to the sad realities of the Knownothing riots in Cincinnati; and still ruder, by the riots in Louisville, in August following. These riots gave an entirely false direction to American society and politics. The task of the statesmen of the country was: how to bring harmony into the various separating tendencies of the populatory elements, that flowed together in the United States. The purpose of the Knownothings was: to bring discord and quarrels upon these same elements. There were many causes in operation, that were producing these political difficultes; and to them, ingrained as they were, in the false political education, our office-seekers had then received, as to ambition, our public speakers and writers should have paid attention and caused their exposure. But they did the contrary; they prevaricated on the subject.

Cincinnati had, in July 1855, at least one trial of that corrupt clique, that had organized the Miami tribe, in 1852, and had generated, that immense amount of corruption, that then disgraced the county for years. The man, that was tried, was the noted County Commissioner, John Patton. The Court and Jury did their duty, but the condemnation and penalties came several years too late. Our history illustrated then, that the old adage still applied to the United States: "When the cow is stolen, they shut the stable door." The popular mind had become callous, and much of the good effect of the conviction, was lost by the leniency, with which the culprits were treated by the public generally. Unfortunately a great portion of the rogues got away with their booty.

August 1855 my earliest friend and companion in Cincinnati, died, namely: Louis Rehfuss. He was the groomsman, it will be remembered, at our wedding. I never knew a man, with whom it was so difficult, to remain a friend; he had so many antagonisms in his character, and yet he deserved friendship as well as anyone, for his integrity. I attended his funeral and was, I believe, one of the few sincere mourners there, outside of his own family. He was in 1833, when I first became acquainted with him, much the healthier man of us two, and for years he remained a hearty man. We expected him to live to the end of the century, but a cancer in the stomach developod, to the surprise of everyone, and he died, when. he was but 45 years old.

In the latter part of August, I went, for the first time, to New York, for the Dayton Short Line. I met there old Vanderbilt, and presented to him my "Financial Exhibit" about the tunnel. After reading it, he frankly admitted: that, if he had seen that paper of mine five years before, he would have taken up with the project and thus have secured, for his affiliated roads, the tunnel, as their railroad entrance into Cincinnati. He appreciated my argument: "that possessing common entrances into large cities was the prime necessity for them and the railroads." He suggested to me, to move to New

York, and he would find me a proper position. When I declined, he advised me to quit public employment altogether; because, he prophesied: "that I would not have the success I deserved in Cincinnati, on account of my sticking to what I bel.eved to be the *right* way to carry on public affairs." He thought, that "yielding to common custom," was true wisdom *here.* I held "true wisdom" applicable *everywhere.*

My father-in-law distressed my wife at this time, by marrying, 75 years of age, a 25 years old woman. She proved a very inferior character. That error was the commission of the ultra folly there is in nearly all such late marriages; to-wit: a wanton unsettling of the filial feelings his children had for him. The high ideal of a father's love was lost. He had no corresponding benefit. New Year in 1856 had thus a very sombre aspect for my wife.

CHAPTER XLIV.

NEW POLITICAL WORK.

When I returned to Cincinnati, in September, 1855, two public men claimed my support, both candidates for Governor; to wit: Medill on the ground of fidelity, that I owed to my old party, the Democracy; and Chase for the good feeling, I owed to the *future* party — made up by anti-slavery or libertymen. I put off both, by asking them squarely, whether I did not owe a prior relation to the country and its people. Chase was the more reasonable of the two. He admitted, that Governor Medill, and still more, Auditor Morgan, had claims on my consideration, as personal and political friends. He conceded also, that there was something due to those Democrats, that had defended public purity in the Democratic party, in square antagonism to the corrupt elements in the party. I may as well, however, in justice to us all, admit the fact, that we had, without exception, much trouble to keep in view, as the true standard:—the duty we owed to society. Each party endeavored to substitute party zeal for patriotism. And the America-born intensified this error, by their insisting on nativity, as the more reliable source of patriotism. This assumption gave to existing nativism a prestige, to which it had not only no title, but was absolutely fallacious. Wrong partisanship — the worst defect in our public conduct—is America-bred; it infects both native and adopted citizens.

I claim in this matter, no more nor no less merit, than that, with so much to lead me astray, I never lost my way as entirely into any of the respective blind alleys, as most natives did. I was thus surely patriotic. I spoke therefore for Governor Medill and Auditor Morgan, but let it be distinctly understood: that it then looked to me, as if I was much in the situation of the duelist in Capt. Maryatt's three-cornered duel, who was fired at from all sides, with no chance to return the fire. "Popular sovereignty" was then the two-edged sword that cut everybody's fingers. I made a speech at Mt. Pleasant on the subject in November, that cleared the fogs in many a brain. I demonstrated it to be a popular humbug.

Among the Germans, a quarrel between Molitor and Heman, respectively "Volksblatt" and "Volksfreund", raged, in which I became involved, from a sincere desire, to stop the disgraceful billingsgate, with which the two German papers were conducted. I had mediated for a final peace between them, and had the terms written out, which both were to publish simultaneously. Neither acted square, for each added, editorially, some remarks that changed the general idea. Molitor went further, he altered the manuscript itself; and *I had to state this fact, to avoid being misjudged by the public.* Some insisted, that no matter what the facts were, I should have supported Molitor against Heman, because Molitor had been my early friend. I thought otherwise, and Molitor became my bitter foe. Only shortly before his death he relented, and we got on visiting terms again, and then re-discussed public affairs.

CHAPTER XLV.

STILL CAN NOT KEEP CLEAR OF POLITICS.

The year 1855 died out, and 1856 came in, under the political excitement about the speakership in Congress, in which Banks succeeded after a long struggle. He was much assisted in his success by my old friend Timothy Day, who had been elected to Congress at great cost to him. The House of Representatives had been in session, nearly a month before New Year; January had also gone by, and not until four days had passed in February, a speaker — *N. T. Banks* — was elected. I said: "This is the prelude of the com ng war." Nobody believed me. Their hearts were too full of mutual hates and prejudices, to see ahead.

Banks had the tenacity, intrepidity and suavity necessary under the circumstances, and the Republicans perceived, that no time was to be lost, to secure the future. So they worked persistently for the National Convention, called to assemble in Pittsburgh, on the 22d of February. To my surprise I was chosen a delegate to it by a German meeting in Cincinnati. I had taken it for granted, that Hassaureck was to be the German Representative from Cincinnati in that body; and had therefore paid but little attention, to what was going on. But I had misjudged the very composition, that was wanted for that occasion. It was not, to make the Convention up, out of pronounced adherents, with already fixed political tendencies; but, to induce persons with open minds, to enter it and to co-operate in the preparation of a wise policy, and thus to prepare for success. Had they known early, that I had arrived at the final conclusion: that the abolishing of all party government, and the establishment, in all its integrity, of the Constitutional Government, should be the definite policy, and perhaps, they would not have elected me; for the German meeting aforesaid, meant the establishing of a *new party*, and to get it as soon as possible into power, which was not my object.

I regarded not only one, but both of our old parties as failures. I held, besides, that, in time, all parties, that might be formed, would eventually be failures. This I felt bound to explain to those, who had made themselves my constituents, and to ask my discharge. I did so, at the general meeting, but, on Hassaureck's motion, I was retained as delegate nevertheless. Under the circumstances, I felt bound to attend the Pittsburgh meeting. That convention discharged its functions, according to current opinion with consummate ability. It left the question, as to who should be the Presidential Candidate, fully open, while it declared for the formation of a party on such terms, that it avoided the point of danger, that of being a *standing* party. It took, however, very definite issue against the continuance of the Democratic party in power, and so expressed itself. As to the new party, it took grounds in such a way: that it could well be claimed, that it was formed for a mere temporary purpose; namely: the re-enactment of the prohibition of slavery in the territories. Mr. Blair, who drew the resolutions, conceded this point, on my suggestion, and it made my free co-operation possible. When I was called upon to address the convention, I could, without compromising myself, express my confidence in the new movement. I actually believed: that it would reinstate the old policy of : "Freedom assured in the territories", and that then, by the very logic of its course, it would become an agency for the correction of all the other party wrongs, that existed in our public conduct. A rather eccentric member of the convention, whose name I have forgotten, followed me in some playful remarks, on my having called myself and constituents — Germans. He claimed, that according to his septennial transsubstantiation, we had all long ago been transformed into Americans. The audience, that should have *reflected* seriously, laughed; and consequently it lost sight of the most important point in its action; to-wit: the restoration of the Nations government to its full Republican integrity.

CHAPTER XLVI.

FROM THE POLITICAL WE DROP INTO THE SOCIAL.

From Pittsburgh I proceeded to Baltimore. There I wrote out, by request, my speech in the convention for the National Era, and sent the manuscript to Washington. At Baltimore, I met Governor Marcy and urged upon him, to allow himself to be brought out for an independent candidate for President. I desired to afford to all, that desired to place into the Presidential chair a man of undoubted executive ability, an opportunity, to vote for such a man. To my astonishment he agreed promptly with me, in the general views. which I expressed to him, but declined to be that candidate himself, He said: "My relation to Pierce precludes my being a candidate, as long as Pierce is in the field." He informed me, that Benton would accept to become the candidate on my basis, but he did not want to be nominated by a new party. I could not see much executive ability in Benton's character.

From Baltimore I went to Philadelphia for our Tunnel Railroad, and there sought to induce Thompson, president of the Pennsylvania Central, to consider earnestly our tunnel project. I saw him with Jewett of the Steubenville Line, who united with me in my proposals and approved them; but Thompson was obviously bound faster to the Little Miami policy, than either of us knew. I left for New York, fully convinced, that, I had to find *there* the connections, through which our tunnel project would have to be carried out. I got to New York on February 29th, and stopped at the Prescot House.

In New York I was apprised of the political situation, as to the most prominent candidate for Republican nomination, Fremont. I had free intercourse with this gentlemen's friends; having been, as stated, for sometime, the Cincinnati correspondent for the New York "Evening Post", whose principal editor was John Bigelow, and he was just writing Fremont's life. From all I heard and saw, I concluded, that nine-tenths of the Republicans of New York, believed, that Fremont should be the nominee, and that all other candidates were out of the question. I thought them mistaken, and think so still. Mrs. Fremont would have been the better candidate of the two.

In my railroad negotiations, I acted under the advice of German Bankers, who did not then see their way clear, for definite operations, either in New York or in Germany. They thought, that my arguments would soon effect an interest being taken in my plans, in Europe.

At this time I received the sad news of my father's death on February 15th, 1856 My eldest brother, who was the sole owner of the whole business and family mansion, expressed the idea, that my presence in Heilbronn would soon be desirable. I concluded to go, but first returned to Cincinnati; there to determine, after consultation with our directory, on the best course to pursue under the circumstances. March 22d, I was re-elected President of the Dayton Short Line. The Board of Directors met, and very decidedly voted in favor of my going to Europe; I was still in doubt. April 13th, Governor Chase nominated me, as one of three Commissioners, whose duty it was, to investigate Reform Schools, and to report on the subject to the Legislature of 1857. The Senate confirmed me, before I had time, to consider my acceptance. I could not well decline after that. My colleagues were Messrs Ladd and Foot. We met April 18th at Columbus; with the Governor, who exercised a good deal of hospitality towards us, and took great interest in the subject. Chase was a model Governor in this respect. The Governor's office was insignificant so far, as the Constitution prescribed his duties. He magnified the office in the best sense. He spent more than his salary, and his home was a Gubernatorial mansion, which his, then unmarried, daughter adorned. She was then, just coming out, as the phrase is. Her conduct to her father's guests was charming, and an honor to the state.

I had read upon the subject of Reform schools, and was, after visiting the institutions in Ohio, and other states, satisfied, that, whilst they were fair schools of their kind, they were then still inadequate to the wants of the State and its necessities. I expressed these my impressions at the meeting of the Board of Commissioners, and suggested, that it was to be regretted, that the Legislature had not provided for one Commissioner, at least, to go to Europe, as I was sure, that he would there find institutions, that would answer as examples, for what we needed here. Chase at once remarked, that such a visit was, *not forbidden*, and that the only question was, whether an after-appropriation would be made. if any expenses were incurred, and, that, if I would go there, he would give me a commission, with the broad seal of the State attached, that would make me the State's Representative abroad. We all took the offer at first as a good joke, but it grew in our minds; and, as I was likely to go away to Europe for railroad and personal reasons, it became a fixed idea with me, that the three might be combined, without any expense to the State whatever. It was thus finally carried out, including the Governor's grand commission, as will be seen hereafter. I thus became the first foreign Minister, that Ohio had abroad.

CHAPTER XLVII.

MORE INDUCEMENTS TO GO TO EUROPE.

I had missed, that Spring, for the first time, spending my birthday at home; and when I arrived at home, on May 24th, I was upbraided by my family for my absence. I apologized and promised that it should never happen again.

June 2nd the National Democratic Convention met in Cincinnati. Being at that time much in the city, and knowing many of the delegates, I was thrown into their company frequently. Everything about the body had a sinister look. The friends of the respective candidates hated each other, and charged on each other respectively: what was true of all; to-wit: "that they had the spirit, of cliques, and ignored entirely the reasons of State." I saw early, that neither Douglas nor Pierce had a chance to be nominated, but it was clear to me also: that no new man could possibly get a majority. The fates, that always run toward evil, thus made Buchanan the nominee. Benton, who had come to Cincinnati, with vague hopes of receiving the nomination, soon gave the matter up, after the Missouri delegation, that was for him, had been expelled. Friday, June 6th, Buchanan was nominated. Mr. Bigelow, who had used our railroad office for his headquarters, kept me advised of matters as they developed. He, as correspondent of the Evening Post of New York, knew all along of every important step that was being taken. He left for New York on the 7th of June, after Buchanan's nomination had been effected. We were both convinced: that Buchanan, was of all candidates, the worst possible.

I had made up my mind definitely, that under no circumstances would I support Buchanan. I regarded him as the worst sort of president, that could be elected. I believed, that he would be a Democratic Federalist, and that we would have from him the most vicious politics possible in the United States. I was too full of my impending journey to Europe, to make much calculation upon the probabilities of the election.

June 13th, the People's Theater burned in Cincinnati, and my old store, now kept by my brother-in-law, was in much danger. The firemen, however, got the fire under, and my brother-in-law escaped without much loss.

The National Republican Convention met June 13th, at Philadelphia. I gave Hoadly a letter, stating my reasons, why Fremont should be nominated against Buchanan. He read it before the convention, and it had its decided effect. Fremont was nominated. No other candidate could have received as large a popular vote as Fremont did receive. I still adhered, however, to the opinion already expressed, that an abler and more experienced statesman, like Marcy, would have been far better.

Invitations to ratification meetings and for speeches then came pouring in upon me. I see it stated in my diary, that I declined seven such in one day. Democratic papers, of the Enquirer kind, abused me daily. They were the *more* virulent, the *less* they knew about me. I was urged for Congress by the Republicans, but there was never a particle of willingness on my part to accept the position on any other terms, than to be *party free*. That was, however, then impossible, as it always is, in heated party contests. My wife agreed with me in this determination. Fremont suited me as a candidate against a democratic party, that was ruled by Buchanan, but I could not be a member of Congress of a party, that, like the Republicans, wanted to rule the country permanently as such.

Preparatory to the journey to Europe, I had to visit, with my fellow-commissioners, the other Reform Schools in the United States, and we attended to this duty by visiting the institutions of Rochester, N. Y., Westborough, Mass., and other State institutions in Boston, New York, Maryland and Pennsylvania. None of these institutions suited me fully. I wanted one, that was in no way a *prison*, except for temporary punishment. I was told, that I would find none such anywhere. I was sure, that I would find them!

June 30th I left Cincinnati for Europe, and concluded to go, first of all, to Philadelphia, for consultation. I met again the officers of the Steubenville & Pennsylvania Railroad; and we agreed, July 2d, on the preliminaries of a union contract between our roads. Then I went to New York and laid these preliminaries before the bankers, who were to frame the financial policy thereon, in consultation with me. It may be proper to state here, that my programm, for the joint use of the tunnel entrance into Cincinnati, was the first elaborate plan of such a combination, on the basis of each company paying a definite sum of "rents", similar to the French public debt system. Several French, German and Swiss banking firms in New York approved of this plan. I must refer to my report, issued in pamphlet form, for the particulars. Had the Steubenville Railroad, or rather: had Sam Jewett, dealt square, and I would have gone to Europe with an income, secured for the tunnel, for more than treble the amount of interest than was necessary to pay that on our bonds. I carried with me unquestionable proof, that the million of bonds we proposed to sell, would cover the cost of the tunnel, but I could not get a contract signed direct by the Steubenville Railroad. All I could obtain, was the signature of Thompson & King, as attorneys of the road. When I arrived in New York, I was handed private letters, from a strong bank in Germany, to their agents here, assuring me, that upon proper showing, it would undertake the negotiation of our bonds; so I concluded to go there, and prepared for the journey.

Before I left New York, I was in frequent interviews with the chief leaders of the Republican party, and especially with the intimate friends of Fremont. His life was being published, and I was asked to take an extra copy of it to Alexander Von Humboldt, and to try to get from him a letter, speaking in favor of Fremont's election. I had a card, introducing me to Humboldt, from a friend of his in this country, who was a literary admirer of him. I disliked the mission thus assigned to me; but I presented the copy to Humboldt, August 24th, and asked him: whether he would not express himself friendly to Fremont's election? He frankly declined to have anything to say as to American or other elections. He had spoken of Fremont as a meritorious explorer and traveller, and could do no more. My own inquiry: whether he deemed party government proper *in any case* as the normal condition of a nation's politics? He answered: "That his brother William had always held the negative on this point, and that he accepted that as correct; never having seen cause to change his mind."

My preparations for Europe were now complete, including accounts for keeping apart the respective expenses incurred for special public and private objects: during my journey.

I left New York, per steamer Asia, for Liverpool, on July 7th, and arrived, after a fair voyage, on July 20th, going the same day to London. There I stopped at London Coffee House, a very good lodging house, at very moderate prices. My friend Day recommended it to me. At London, besides sight-seeing, I devoted my time to railroad business, and also to the matter of Reform Schools. Mr. Robb, of New Orleans, whom I met on the steamer as a fellow-passenger, introduced me to Bayard Taylor, another fellow-passenger. I had letters to Mr. Martin, partner of Peabody, in London. To him I explained the objects of my visit to Europe. He at once informed me, that a new railroad project had no chance in London, as bankers were full with existing bonds of American railroads, and not well pleased with results. He tendered me letters to bankers on the continent, which I accepted gratefully. As to my Reform School mission, he presented me to Mr. Peabody, who received me cordially. I saw that Mr. Peabody understood the subject fully. He gave me a list of institutions to visit. At the same time he gave me a card, that secured my seeing, at once, the best reputed English institution—Red Hill—near London.

CHAPTER XLVIII.

MY JOURNEYS THROUGH EUROPE IN 1856.

From London I concluded to go to Paris, as the best initial point, for my several purposes. On the way, I visited Red Hill, the English Reform School, to which Mr. Peabody had given me a card of admission. He had designated it as the model institution, he would prefer. It was under the government of Reverend Turner. From what I had been told, I expected an every-way-superior institution; but I found it to be of the class, where much ceremonious praying, and stiff piety, was assumed to be the best reformatory education. Personal cleanliness and good manners were neglected, and so were habits of economy and propriety, the proper handling of tools and nice behavior in the rooms and on the play grounds. The rural openness gave the institution, indeed, the appearance of kindliness and freedom, which I regarded so necessary to Reform. There was less horticultural instruction than I expected, and only small indication of fruit and vegetable culture. Nourishment, in the solid sense, was the main point, in what the boys got to eat. Nice behavior, at the table, was little thought of. The managers said, that they pursued *practical* objects. I wanted to see more attention paid to comfort and enjoyments. I believed in Plato's two rules: "Early education should be given through amusements." — "True education means improvement of the body through Gymnastics, and of the soul through music."

July 25th I arrived in Paris, and next day I presented the letters of introduction, I had from a gentlemen in New York, to Count Morny, who received me kindly, and after hearing my statement, as to the purposes of my journey in France, said, that he would give me a note to Fould, then Louis Napoleon's Minister of Finance, and leave me to explain the subject matter of my call. I accepted the note and presented it to Fould the same day. He permitted me to explain the purpose of my call in German. I had hardly begun my statement, when Fould interrupted me, and declared vehemently against American railroad bonds. His angry tone appeared ludicrous to me, and so did the deep lowering of his bushy eyebrows. I smiled. He saw it, and asked me pointedly, what I meant by it? I begged his pardon, and told him: that I could not help it, because an anecdote of a similar occurrence, between a former French Minister and a retired Captain, had come to my mind. He looked friendlier, and asked me to relate the anecdote, which I did, It was the story of the poor Captain, who came to Paris to the Secretary of War, and asked for active employment, with some pay. He was told, very pointedly, that his request could not be granted. The Captain smiled and thanked.

Fould now interrupted me, and wanted me to explain: wherein lay the similitude? I said: "First, in the rebuff and the smile; but secondly, in the similarity of the explanation; to-wit: The Captain and myself may be classed as poor, and therefore neither of us could stand to be long about Paris on expenses; a prompt reply was to the Captain and to me a relief from waste of time and money." Now we both smiled, but not for the same reason. Fould now offered some excuses for his abruptness. He said: "The sales of American railroad bonds are absorbing French capital, to the annoyance of French public interests." This emboldened me to ask him: whether my surmise, that I had met him about 20 years before in Frankfurth, had any foundation? After a few inquiries he admitted our former meeting. I was then page to a Strassburgh merchant, a friend of Foulds, who was called Ehrman. His tone now became friendly, and he asked me to explain my railroad business anew. It interested him, and he thought, that for a city, surrounded by hills, a tunnel entrance was eminently the best for railroads. He gave me confidential letters to a French banking house in Geneva, Odier & Co.; also an introduction to Mettray Reform School. From his remarks, I judged, that such letters were his way out of an unpleasant situation. I presented my other letters to other bankers; to-wit: Charles Munroe, Allier, Grand & Co., but could not obtain any positively favorable answer.

I remained in Paris eight days. During that time, after giving up my attempts to sell railroad bonds, I visited, with a card of admission, secured to me by Count Morny and Foulds, the institution, called: "Colony de Mettray," which was, in my opinion, the best Reform School in the world. *There* are not only the true ideas of philanthropists carried out, by a man like Colonel Demetz, but also the finest household economy possible is kept up, through clerical supervision. The boys become good gardeners, fine mechanics and trusty laborers very soon, because their characters are reformed, void of hypocrisy. There are also systems of reward and punishment, that are the best promptings to virtue, and the truest checks on vice. I talked with many boys there and found, that, with most of them, being taken there, was in itself a reform, because it effected a liberation from prison air and discipline.

In the first week of August, I went from Paris, via Cologne, to Osnabrück, where, by appointment, made in New York already, I was to confer with the bankers: Westerkamp & Fortlage, as to the possibility of negotiating our tunnel railroad bonds. Our conference was a severe test of my financial programm; they inquired into every detail, and had a young railroad engineer, who examined the figures, and expressed himself freely on them. Their final approval of our project, gave me more confidence in its success, than I had before. They agreed to take the matter up at once, and see the other bankers, whom they expected to enlist. They advised me to call upon the bankers in other cities, to whom I had letters, with a view of sounding them, and to keep them advised of my progress. This I did, and visited Cologne, Frankfurth, Stuttgardt, Augsburgh and Munich. At all these places, the bankers, most of whom knew me through connections with my father, were polite to me; but some of them deprecated American securities, on the ground that the methods employed had no right financial basis. They declared, for instance: that selling bonds at 20 and more per cent discount, was very wrong.

CHAPTER II.

AT MY NATIVE HOME IN 1856.

On reaching my native city, I went, first of all, alone, to my father's grave. It was adjoining that of my step-mother. More reflections, on the vicissitudes of human life, rushed through my brain, the minutes I stood there, than ever did before or afterwards in my life. The history of three generations of relatives, with countless scenes and memories, thronged my mind; but one figure, was most present there: that of my mother. She was there as an intense spirituality, but in no embodied form. I turned to hunt her grave, by the record, as well as my recollections, but only to find, that in pursuance of the entire rearrangement of the graveyard, since her funeral, her grave had, in pursuance of law, been disturbed, at least it could not be found. Nevertheless her memory has lived on, and she lives still, in her children; and this memory is the only grave she has. It exists to-day, and is the only "after-life" she has got. O! Dear mother! Am I wronging you in this view of after-existence? Or: Do I owe you a faith in a heavenly existence, which I cannot work out in my mind? I think not!

After I had been in the graveyard, I called on my brothers and sisters residing in or near Heilbronn, and with them visited other relatives. My inheritance was also settled. It was 4250 Guilders, about $1700.00. It gratified me more, than ten times the amount acquired otherwise would have done, because it embodied a father's *and* mother's indisputable blessing. I disappointed by my prompt action, in accepting my father's will as the final settlement, the Notary, a Mr. Mayer, that wrote the will for my father, and calculated, that I would, being beyond Seas, when the will was made, object to its validity. He looked very much disappointed, when I accepted it unreservedly, as a settlement, not to be questioned by a son. He had calculated on a prolonged lawsuit.

I made at that time also visits to reformatory institutions in South Germany, Switzerland and Belgium; often they were right on my other journey's way. I soon became convinced, that the vaunted superiority of English and American Institutions, consisted chiefly in spending more money, having more showy buildings, and giving the inmates, in quantity, more food and clothing, than is usual in Continental Europe. I perceived, that public benevolence must not be judged by any such standard; that on the contrary, strict economy and higher morality furnish the better criterion. I believed too, that disciplination, taken from military regime, secures truer order, than that adopted from partisan or sectarian conceptions. The latter carry into public institutions an unnessary strictness on the one side, and undue indulgences on the other. The most noteworthy economic feature in Continental Institutions is: that the feeding, lodging and furnishing for the inmates is kept separate and apart from that of the officers and employees. This keeps out of European institutions the questionable practices, that prevail in English-American Institutions, namely: the excessive costs of lodging, housing and feeding of the officers and employees and their families in them. These expenses are generally extravagantly high, because they include luxuries, that are really not wanted by them, and do them no good; they cause invidious comparisons.

The custom, of these European Institutions, of employing therein the sub-altern officers from military positions, brings into them a punctuality of conduct, that sets an excellent example to the boys.

Among the best institutions I visited, was the institution of Rev. Werner at Reutlingen, in Würtemberg. I was made acquainted with Werner through my brother Edward, who was one of his patrons. Werner had been in his early life a travelling preacher. The fundamental idea of Werner was: that Reform Schools must be instituted and maintained by voluntary services and gifts of philantrophists, and the productions of their inmates; all resting on God's blessing. To me the reverend gentleman appeared like an ancient apostle or saint. He induced some dozen persons of wealth and piety, thirty years ago, to devote, with himself, their all to the original institution at Reutlingen. They started with their own means and work, gradually enlarged it into factories; some were paper mills. But Werner could not, on this basis, always make both ends meet. He was in debt considerably, when I was there. The total wealth, his institution represented, was much more than the debts. My coming there, as Commissioner for the State of Ohio, suggested, that I should be used to represent to the Queen, and other high personages, the actual situation, and thus to cause a reorganization, by which the then accrued debts were satisfied, and the whole institution placed beyond all peradventure. When Werner was told of the success, he turned to me and said: "You see. My foundation was after all sound. God's blessing, charity and our labor, have sustained it all." I left him with his faith, and he died with it, about three years ago.

Werner was certainly a more successful organizer of labor, than any I have ever known. He came very near solving the problem of having production of the best kind and largest in amount, without paying wages, or any other personal compensation. His "Communism", as well as "Socialism", was so compounded (I came near writing confounded) as to defy distinct separation. I was certain, that it could not be congenial in the United States, and therefore said, but little about it, in my report. I published, however, his letter to me, which is an excellent document.

Much more practical, for general adoption, were the institutions maintained in Switzerland by Mr. Zellweger, then a banker in Paris. He was a native of Switzerland; but had emigrated quite young to Paris, and there found a career of success, after many previous failures, that carried no reproach on his character. I had drafts on his house from New York, and was introduced to him, when I presented them. Being informed of my commission, as to reform schools, he pressed me to visit his affiliated institutions in Switzerland. He gave me a list of them, going by different names, about a dozen in number, in the various cantons. He explained to me his views on the subject. He was against large institutions, and none of his had over 50 inmates, including managers. He said: "Large institutions are, in nine out of ten cases, for the inmates, on first admission, a misplacement, that needs afterwards correction. Small institutions afford opportunities to fit them to individuals, and to make the best start towards a good end. They give also the opportunity to vary the manager, according to necessities. On visiting Mr. Zellweger's institutions, I found the greater part of his statements correct, but cannot here go into details.

As already intimated I looked upon Mettray in France, as the model, for us, in the United States, to follow. I so reported. But I did not state in my report an incident of my visit at Mettray. It was a remark made to me by a German Catholic Bishop, whom I had accompanied to the Institution. He said on parting from me: "You will never succeed in establishing a Mettray in the United States, because you will not have the requisite persons for the right economical administration, or the right religious education." And when I looked surprised, he continued: "Don't mistake me! I do not say this as a Priest, opposed to Protestantism. I express it to you, because I want to caution you, against the too high expectations, which I see, you have. In the United States they have not yet learned the value of especially capable public administration, by *servants* in the best sense; to-wit: that of well disciplined persons, animated by a stern public spirit, that has its best reward in accomplishing high moral good." The good Bishop's advice had more truth in it, than was pleasant to admit. I think, however: The United States will sometime reform their public administration.

CHAPTER L.

CLOSING UP MY WORK IN EUROPE IN 1856.

August 19th I returned to Osnabrück, and there closed up with Westerkamp & Fortlage, for the sale of the bonds of the Tunnel Railroad. The contract, that I made, would, if promptly complied with, have secured the building of the tunnel. It was never carried out, because the stockholders of the Tunnel Co. never subscribed the $250,000.00 for the interest fund, which would have secured the selling of the bonds. That failure was a great disappointment to me, because it rendered nugatory all my labors for the Railroad Co. in 1856. It was, I think, an irreparable shortcoming on the part of the stockholders. Speculators now hold the franchises, hoping to induce somebody to pay them a large sum for surrendering them; but I guess they will wait in vain, because the railroads now entering Cincinnati, have entered into arrangements for their convenience, which they can not well abandon any more. Besides, locomotives now overcome much higher grades than thirty years ago.

From Osnabrück I went to Berlin, with a view of explaining to Bleichröder and other Bankers, who were expected to cooperate in the sale of the bonds, our entire Railroad project. I did so, and made I think, a favorable impression. At that time I called upon Alexander von Humboldt, and presented him the life of Fremont, written by John Bigelow. Humboldt declined to write the letter, for Fremont, suggested to him.

At Berlin I learned of the birth of my daughter Lizzie, in Dent, July 26th.

I then went to Dresden and Leipzig. At both places I had interviews with bankers about our railroad bonds. I then reported at Hanover to our agents. I delivered them the bonds, and consummated the agreement, as far as I could. Then I went back to Heilbronn, and bid farewell to my relatives there and my birthplace. When I left, I never expected to see my native town again.

I made a quick tour through Switzerland, calling on all of my wife's relatives. At the larger cities, I also visited the bankers, to whom I had letters; and examined some of Zellweger's Reform Schools. From Switzerland I passed through Strassburgh to Paris, where I called upon some of the gentlemen, that I had called upon the July previous; thence I went to London and renewed my acquaintance with Mr. Peabody and his partner, Mr. Martin. I left Liverpool for New York, by steamer "Africa" September 20th. October 3rd I arrived in New York, and October 7th I was in Cincinnati, and found all well at home; thanks to my wife.

I had hardly got home, before I was importuned for making stump speeches in favor of Fremont. This was disagreeable to me, because the republican party and Fremont had placed themselves in such a position before the people, that I could not take ground for them in all the integrity, which I deemed to be proper. I was unreservedly opposed to Buchanan; I was also positively for Fremont; but was not, and could not, be a member of the republican party. I apprehended therefore, that my public remarks would do more harm for Fremont, than good, because I could not state too emphatically my determination to be party free. I did make stump speeches in Hamilton and Butler Counties, and I was glad to feel, that I at least did the republicans no harm. The people were indeed less partisan, than was presumed.

Fremont was defeated in November. Buchanan was elected. I feared that such would be the result, when I cast my vote: but I foresaw also: that Buchanan's election meant, in the end, a precipitation of the country into chaos. The old saying came to my mind: "that when the masses of society are distract, they want to know and hear naught, except what favors their special eccentricities." When, therefore, on the night before the election, I was applauded at the meeting, I never mistook it for a deserved approval of what I said. I understood it to mean gratification that I agreed with them. They applauded themselves, not me, nor my way of saying things.

CHAPTER LI.

NEW REFORM SCHOOL IN OHIO.—1857.

The Board of Commissioners for Reform Schools heard, soon after my arrival, my verbal report of what I did in Europe, with approval. They authorized me to draw up the report to the Governor, for the General Assembly, in accordance with the conceptions I had drawn from my observations at European institutions. These were: that the State of Ohio should institute a Reform Farm, in accordance with the "Family system", in operation in Mettray, in France. I so drew the report, and it was adopted by the Board and presented to the Governor. He sent it, in January 1857, to the Legislature with his recommendation. At the then session, the necessary legislation, for establishing the institution as above described, was enacted. Our Board of Commissioners were continued, and we were authorized to purchase the requisite land, and to erect some buildings, for the starting of the Reform Farm. My continuance on the Commission, as resident chief officer on the farm, after it should be established, had not entered my mind, until the Governor mentioned it to me, as if it were a matter of course. I at once begged him to reconsider his view; for I knew, if no one else did, that for the new institution a specially fitted man had to be found; and that I had not the needed qualifications, nor was I so situated in my private relations, as to permit me to reside on the State Farm. I noticed then, for the first time, that Chase was at last still more addicted to the political habits that came to this country from England, than I had believed. My appointment included, evidently, in his mind the presumption, that it carried with it a certain mutuality of confidence and support, such as there was between an English Minister and his appointees. My ideas left both to Chase and myself more personal independence; and on that basis alone could we be officially connected.

Upon that idea I accepted the appointment, April 22, 1857, confident that, after the farm should be purchased and initiated, my connection, beyond that of an occasional advisory member, would cease; and that then a head officer, competent to administer the affairs of the institution, would be readily found. My salary, for 1857, was to be $1,500, besides travelling expenses.

I am sorry to have to admit now, that I was mistaken as to my expectations. The offices that attracted then, as now, the aspiring men in the State, were those that promised a future prominence in politics, and a much larger salary than the one named. This one offered neither the one nor the other. The office was made desirable, several years afterward, by increasing the salary, and adding pay for the wife's services, and board for a numerous family. How different in Mettray!!

During May, June and July, 1857, I visited many places, tendered, as per our advertisement, for the State Reform Farm. Often I had to meet the Governor for consultation, and I always found him wide awake to public interests. According to law, we were charged also with providing for a Reform School for females. It gave us much trouble, because it was an unnecessary burden and complication. We made a tender to the House of Refuge on the subject; but the directors, who evidently feared State interference with their institution, rejected it. Perhaps it was best so, under the circumstances; it led, as is well known, to a separate State Reform School for females.

After visiting many farms, I decided finally to recommend to our Board, the purchase of 1,100 acres, situated near Lancaster, Ohio, for $10,000. My main reason for this purchase was: the unquestioned healthy of the locality. The only objection ever made to it was: that it was not land rich enough to raise corn. Everybody conceded its suitability for fruit culture and vegetable gardening. Our Board ratified my recommendation. Governor Chase had heard, previously, the reasons, as well as the objections, to the purchase. He besides, had asked, for the grounds, upon which the other farms tendered, had been refused. Being told that, though being more fertile, they were objectionable, because subject to malaria, he asked: Whether that was not a common disease in the State? He was answered in the affirmative, and then he said rather jocularly: "I do not think, that State officers should object to land in Ohio, because it has the common disease of the State." A bystander remarked: "Neither should land be chosen for this institution, because that disease prevails!" It was then seen: that there was a special reason for choosing particular land, and such as was specially healthy, for the State Reform Farm, and soon it was agreed, that the Governor should postpone his decision, until he had seen the proposed 1,100 acres. He was taken there on a bright July morning. The first words he uttered, after being taken to the highest point on the farm, from which there is a fine view over the surrounding country for 40 miles, were: "Why, gentlemen! The air is so pure here, that I think we might hear the angels sing."

The purchase was consummated in the Fall of 1857. Steps were at once taken to erect the first family building for housing 40 juveniles, the house to cost not to exceed $2,000. And it was unanimously agreed, that the building should be a good double *log cabin*. A Mr. Jaeger, a young man of excellent character, born in Columbus, Ohio, and just married, was chosen to be the superintendent, and to move at once on the farm, into the family buildings, that were then upon it. Mr. Jaeger had received an excellent education, both in this country and Europe. His wife was also a highly educated lady, and well qualified for attending to the household functions. I was glad to get the couple.

It is proper for me to state here, that I could not devote much time to politics in the Summer and Fall of 1857; but when the contest developed into a rivalry between S. P. Chase and H. B. Payne, I supported Chase, on my lifelong policy, that between a mere partisan of my own party, as Payne was, and the man of principle and devotion to the country, like Chase, I would always vote for the latter

CHAPTER LII.

SAD EVENTS RECALL ME TO MY HOME AFFAIRS.

Blow after blow came on my head about this time. In July, 1857, I received the news of my brother Paul's death. In June previous. September 15th, my darling daughter Thilly d e l. These events warned me, that my public employments were both too many, and too intense, to allow me to be all, I should be. to my family. My own individual life was neglected, my family life wasted, and my culture dissipated. I was three-fourths of my time away from home. I yearned every day for my old habits of work, interspersed with reading and writing, and visits to and from friends in Cincinnati and elsewhere. But I could not attain it. The Tunnel Railroad was then less absorbing of my time, since the Hannover Bank agents, had thrown up the contract, I had made with them; when they found our stockholders dilatory in the stipulated subscription: but I still had to keep up for the sake of the tunnel, my connection with the Zanesville and Lebanon Railroads. Certain bankers in New York took hold of my combination plan, and came out to inform themselves as to it. It fell to me to attend them, during their examination for this purpose.

Politics were to me then very unsatisfactory. Those older politics, I would have liked, were unattainable; whilst those, that prevailed, were all, only *new wrong* ways, to get out of *old wrong* public conditions. And I begun to realize, in my own mind at least, that under our social sources of politics, these wrong processes would prevail for some time, if not forever. What could I find in politics, except to be a waif, in a current, that could be no channel for me. I remembered the old saying:

"Incidit in Scyllam, qui vult vitare Charibtim."

My private affairs did not, in fact could not, receive at my hands, the attention I should have given them. And so was it also, as to the education of my children. Formerly I instructed them much myself at home, and learned myself in doing it. Now I had to leave it largely to private and public schools, and learned less myself. And I felt often, when in the midst of visiting acquaintances, that there was a fruitlessness in my conduct for my family and myself, that was, on reflection, very painful. My health was also gradually giving way, because I lived, too irregular. The Winter of 1857 was very hard on me, being mostly very cold, with sudden changes, from extreme freezings, to the softest thawings. Thus I was brought to self searchings, not only, as to my private relations, but also my public affairs. I saw how much we lacked of having any correct political organization. The defalcation for $750,000 in the State Treasury, that was found out during 1857, with its triune depravity of the three treasurers, that were respectively Whigs, Democrats and

Republicans, namely: Bliss, Breslin and Gibson; was followed afterwards, in August, by the failure of the Ohio Life Insurance and Trust Co.

And, if we now bring before us the pusillanimity of party politics, as carried on by President Buchanan, and we have before us the disheartening situation, that the country then was in. It informed all, that wanted to know the truth: that there was in American society and American institutions, under the upper surface of prosperity, an inner degeneration going on, that was likely to become incurable. In our parties, bad men controlled good men, through their social connections in banks, railroads, insurance and other companies. In a word: our government was not a government of the people, by the people and for the people, but a government of inner party circles, that took their cues from the party press, party caucusses and corporation officers. It was a government run for great ambitions and pecuniary interests, without the proper checks on corruption. Hence it bred crises, breakdowns, bankruptcies, which again led to combinations for pretended relief, that did no good.

These several courses were so many painful reflections to my mind, and I wrote about them in the press. I continued my correspondence for the N. Y. Evening Post, and tried to arouse public attention to the various attempts to revive former abuses; for instance: the proposition by Alfred Kelly to perpetuate, in Ohio, old fashioned gerrymanders under new forms. My letters prevented that abuse at least for that time, but with me it was a harrowing thought, that every reform seemed to be but temporary here, in the face of persistences in old iniquities.

CHAPTER LIII.

MORE PUBLIC EMPLOYMENT.

I never thought, at the end of 1857, that the events of that year, would bring me into further public employment. I labored hard to get the Reform Farm into fair working order, so as to bring in my successor. In October, we got the first family building ready for raising. On November 4th, the evening previous, we had yet fine Fall weather; next morning came a severe snow and rain storm, that forbid, those assembled there, from raising, and all attempts to undertake it. We raised it, about a week afterwards, by the assistance of regularly employed mechanics, who used pullies, ropes and other machinery, for we could not undergo the old log rolling process. We had the satisfaction to be confident, that this brought a safer erection and better job. The estimated cost of $2,000, for the building, was exceeded only 48 cents, and we officers paid that out of our own pockets. Afterwards the Reform Farm Commissioners met, and agreed to the annual report I had prepared. They also approved the appointment of two students from Oberlin College, to act as elder brothers, for the first "family", as soon as the respective inmates could be brought to the farm. After an interchange of views, with the directors at the Penitentiary, and also the House of Refuge in Cincinnati, we selected from juveniles. confined in them respectively, about a dozen inmates, and took them, unchained and with only two unarmed guards, I being one. in open wagons part of the way, and in common railroad cars. through the country, to Lancaster. We had not the slightest attempt at a run-away, but brought them all to the farm, and there we put them into an open house, with unlocked rooms and unbarred windows.

It was the VIII. wonder of the world; and mark it, for a Reform School in America. Chase remarked: "This is a good model for reforming slavery." I was less sanguine; for I could not forget, that the task was still before me: to find the man, that would be the honest wise head for the Institution.

The guards in the penitentiary and the House of Refuge had loudly predicted, that we would not get a single youth to the farm; for they would all run away. As to holding them without locks and bars, on an open farm, they laughed at the idea. Well. We had faith in our system. It rested on human nature, that was helped: by square kind treatment; and human nature vindicated us. Not one of the boys ran away; though boys. brought afterwards, did escape. In all, but two cases; they were easily recaptured; in fact, several came back themselves. and never again attempted to run away.

The two young students from Oberlin University. remained but a short time. Their enthusiasm. for an idea. oozed all out before practical public services. We then took one from Cincinnati, and one from Cleveland, and they stayed longer. Our report gave great satisfaction to the Governor and the Legislature, and made us. the Commissioners, popular, which had its sweets, but also its bitterness, for me at least; for, at that time, men, popular for some merit, besides partisanism. attracted the notice of party leaders. They saw in popular men only opportunities to use them as tools for their ambitious schemes. I had never, so far as I was concerned, severed my affiliations with those Democrats, that wanted, like myself, a reforming Democracy; but they were now giving me, with few exceptions. the cold shoulder. Among the exceptions was Morgan, the Auditor of State.

When in the Winter of 1858. the Democratic majority in the Legislature got into the reformatory mood, and proposed the appointment of a commission to investigate the defalcation in the State Treasury. Morgan suggested my name. indeed. he insisted. that my appointment was indispensible. to give the Commission. the prestige of impartiality. which it needed. Morgan informed me of this, and begged me, to do nothing for or against my selection; but to confide in his political and personal integrity in the matter. I followed his advice; but could not fail to hear conversations, between the Republican State Officers, including Chase; and to learn, that the investigation was distasteful to them. Why? That was not so easily ascertainable, and I did not find it out at that time. I assumed, they were opposed to it, because it was to be carried on through Democrats.

There were then in the Legislature Democrats, such as Saffin, that were secretly opposed to the investigation, especially, if I was to be one of the Commissioners. Saffin concluded to entrap me. He telegraphed me over his own signature: "Have proposed you as one of the Commissioners for investigating the defalcation in the State Treasury. Will you accept?" I remembered old Virgil's proverb:

"Timeo Danaos et dona ferentes."

I telegraphed back: "See Morgan and Chase. What they agree to, is acceptable to me."

I heard no more about it that day. May 10th, 1858, the law for the Commission passed, with Edgerton, Morgan and myself, on it as Commissioners. Chase had declined to say anything in the matter; but, when he found Morgan in favor of my appointment, he advised the retention of my name. So the trap set for me by the corrupt Democrats, snapped into their faces, and I had one more labor to perform for the State.

I found, that the time had now come, to find a permanent head officer, for the State Reform Farm, and I notified the Governor, both in writing and verbally, of this necessity. He had delayed this matter for nine months, and had, in the meantime, lost an opportunity, to appoint a very suitable person from Sandusky, whom I had suggested to him. That person had accepted another call, and soon after died. Chase eventually appointed, on January 1st, 1859, Geo. E. Howe — a much less qualified school teacher. Howe was known to be a good school-teacher, but as to his other qualifications, but little was known. He had, however, a jewel in his honest and truly excellent wife, and that covered a multitude of defects on his part. I can only say now in conclusion, as to the State Reform Farm in Ohio: that it has always lacked that, which has made Mettray the model institution, and which I ever proclaimed as indispensible, to-wit: men for head officers, that know, how to organize a public administration, and to keep the service therein on strict discipline and efficiency. The men, that had been appointed, have possesed some good qualities, but they lacked military direction and precision, including disciplination.

CHAPTER LIV.

SOME AFTER-JUSTICE.

And now it is but fair, that I should do justice to my wife, and state, that she was the better half in my conduct of the State Reform Farm. In an emergency, when we needed a head, for the household, she volunteered, left her own household and took charge, without compensation, of the kitchen, the house-work and dormitories for several months. The boys felt, that they had now, what they needed so much, a mother; and all the officers and employees understood now better, the leading idea of the Institution they were engaged in. She had given them the practical illustration, and many visitors, who had doubted before, the possibility of such a free reformatory institution, admitted, after they saw it under her management, that it was feasible.

I hope I will be excused, if now I state the fact, that I drew only two-thirds of my salary as Commissioner of the State Reform Farm, whenever I received pay for my time in other State employments. I never took double pay. I would have regarded doing so as a dishonesty. For a while I continued to perform the functions of acting Commissioner; but when Howe entered upon his duties, I resigned. Occasionally I have since been a visitor there. I must admit, that the farm was then a much finer institution, in buildings and such like matters, than I would ever have made of it. My ideal was Mettray, with its rustic cordiality and plainness; where the aim is: to have the institution self-sustaining as near as possible. That aim was early, after my resignation, abandoned in Ohio as impracticable. It had been kept up in Mettray and Reutlingen. The Ohio State Reform Farm costs, in my opinion, much more than it should; but is it not so in all our State institutions? And so we come back to the question, propounded by Governor Chase: whether we have a right to blame one institution for the common fault of all? I have concluded to rejoice quietly, within myself, that so many youths, that would have been sent to County Jails, and State Prisons, if there had been no State Reform Farm, have enjoyed the country air, the rural work and the freer disciplin of this Reform School, whose model I have carried from France to America, and from the Loire to Belle Riviere. My expectations may have been too high-strung for American use; but I hope I will be forgiven for it, if for no other reason, certainly for the one, that I have stepped aside, to let a native American adopt his own methods, and to establish them in Ohio.

I need not go into the details of the transactions of our Board of Commissioners for the investigation of the defalcations in the State Treasury; for they have been reported to the General Assembly and extensively published. I owe it, however, to my colleagues and myself, to state, that there was no partisan shrinking by any of us, from exposing party friends, that had involved themselves in criminal acts, or indeed any improprieties; nor was there any partisan sharpening of our pens against political foes. The fact was, that the entire society and body politic was then permeated with false finance, that approached frequently to felonious practices. The Government had, in the United States, failed to provide efficient public ways and means for the necessary financial and fiscal reforms. Whilst there should have been system, order and integrity with strict economy, there was chaos, haphazardness, dishonesty and waste; and it was all intensified by mean party politics. The final exposure came; because the wrong had grown too big, and too all-pervading, to hide it any longer. My previous action as Bank Examiner in Ohio, gave me much previous knowledge, and this aided us in our investigations. I soon perceived, that several of the republican State officers, that had formerly warmly cooperated with me in reference to Reform Schools, now looked askance at me. It was, because I frankly stated, that the democratic party was not the only corrupt party in the United States.

The investigation of the defalcation of the State Treasury demanded my attention to the close of 1858. We expected to make our report early in January, but it was not handed in to the Governor, until March 7th, 1859. It was published in the daily papers on March the 9th. The regular printed report did not come out until several months afterwards. The public had, by that time, become indifferent to it. It looked upon it as a story of spilt milk. There were, however, quarters in which the exposures, made in the report, were held to be pointed at a certain class. In these quarters there was more or less displeasure against the report. They pretended to see in it an attack on certain prominent republicans on the one side, and the shielding of certain democrats on the other. I know that both accusations were untrue; for my colleagues had erased out of the report, on my motion, every word of which either of these tendencies could be suspected. As already pointed out, the defalcation was committed by three treasurers, and each belonged to another party. Obviously no one party was specially guilty, nor any one specially innocent. The report was strictly impartial.

CHAPTER LV.

MY ASSIGNEESHIP IN THE O. L. I. & TRUST CO.

In the beginning of the year 1859, I was appointed, by the Superior Court of Cincinnati, in conjunction with J. P. Kilbreath, one of the assignees for the O. L. I. & Trust Co.; the bank that had failed several months previous. The appointment was made on the motion of Messrs Hoadly & Mills, attorneys for one of the largest creditors. I was required to give $50,000 security. To make this a mere nominal responsibility, for my sureties. I gave real estate security, by executing a mortgage to them, on my real estate, with my wife's dower released. And on that basis I solicited Messrs. Werk, Brachman, Billiod, Klotter, Deckebach, C. Wolff and Graselli and Eckhardt, all old German acquaintances of mine, to go my security. They all refused, though fully secured. They had pretended to be my friends all through my life. Their reasons were too pitiful to state them now. I left them and applied to comparative strangers, towit: Messrs. Thorp, Gest, Day, Bell, Adae, Duhme and Roelker; and they signed my bond without a moment's hesitancy. The Court accepted it promptly. Judges Spencer, Gholson and Storer said to me privately, that they were pleased with my securities, because they were not on other bonds before. The refusal of the former had humbled me very much. I had supposed, that no citizen of Cincinnati would decline to go security for me; and here were nine old acquaintances that refused it, after each of them had represented themselves to me as my special friends.

My duties, in the affairs of the Trust Company, being chiefly performed in Cincinnati, gave me more time with my family. I had to be absent, however, several times in New York for weeks. I was warned against my co-assignee as an intriguing officer, but I found him an excellent accountant and astute business man. I had examined, in the State service, the Trust Company thoroughly, and made a report, on its connections, with the State finances. I now had to familiarize myself with its general business in Cincinnati, and its branch in New York. I found that, so far as the Bank confined itself to its legitimate home business, that is to say, to discounting business men's paper, as it arose in trade, there was an unbroken prosperity. Its failure was due to questionable transactions with railroads, land and stock speculations, and tricky manufacturers of the high tariff class.

My separation from the assignment took place in 1860, through one of those untoward events so common in the United States. The newly elected Judge of the Probate Court, a Mr. Hilton, who was known for his trickery, took advantage of a law, passed the Winter previous, to call us assignees of the Trust Company before him, and to require us to qualify before him. At that time the Probate Judges got all the fees made in legal proceedings before them, and everybody knew at once, that the obtainment of fees from the Trust Company, was the motive of this call upon us. I at once concluded to resign, rather than submit. My associate concluded to surrender. By the advice of my attorneys, Messrs Mills & Hoadly, I tendered my resignation to the Judges of the Superior Court. They accepted it and finally discharged me and my securities. I thus kept myself from the grasp of a fee-hungry judge. By the Spring, 1860, I was clear of all further connection with the assignment of the O. L. I. & Trust Co.

Thirty years have passed since, and the matter is still pending in the Probate Court, though a final report has been made by Kilbreath. During the year, in which I was co-assignee, about half in amount of the whole business (six millions) was settled, and we had resolved on measures, that would have closed the business in another year. The unfair interference of the judge named led to procrastination, that could never be fully overcome. I looked, therefore, then and do now, upon the act of the judge, as hostility to the Trust itself.

CHAPTER LVI.

A REVIVAL OF AN ALMOST FORGOTTEN SUGGESTION

I was known to retain a deep interest in the State Reform Farm, even after my official connection with it had ceased. This brought me before the public several times in reference to it, when some special measures, about it, engaged public attention. I had urged with my colleagues on Governor Chase, in 1858, that the project of a model farm in Ohio, under the management of the State Board of Agriculture, should be connected with the State Reform Farm, as a part of the policy to make it self-sustaining. The proposition was then unfortunately postponed; but in 1860, it was taken up again by the Commissioners of the State Reform Farm, and brought before the Legislature. I was asked to make a speech in favor of it. I deemed it proper, to suggest to the State Board of Agriculture, that they ought to be present, and that my address to the Legislature should, at the same time, be one to their Board, and that was, as we shall see, a mistake.

I had been for years a contributor to the "Ohio Farmer," and I had furnished also articles for the report of the Secretary of the State Board of Agriculture, of which the one, in 1851, on the Climate of Ohio, was much quoted by other papers, both in this country and in Europe. I presumed, therefore, that my suggestion for combining the project of a model farm, garden and nursery for Ohio, with the State Reform Farm, would be agreeable with the State Board of Agriculture. This assumption was my mistake. The Board wanted authority for a State model farm, under *its own exclusive* management, and on its own grounds. It did not believe in a joint management, and still less in any project that would be under the general supervision of the Governor. The members of the Board and its secretary, attended the meeting of the Legislature, and heard my address; but not to agree, on the contrary, to disagree. I soon found this out, by the postponment of my proposition. It lives, however, nevertheless in my mind, for I have seen the thing done in Mettray, and I still believe, that the Ohio State Reform Farm will ever remain a semi-work, as long as the reform of the juveniles confined there, will not have, as in Mettray, definite utilitarian objects of general value to the State and its society: in other words: the Reform Farm must have a beacon light before the minds of its officers, as well as its youth, that ennobles their thoughts, by letting them feel themselves of special service to the State and its people. Only after they shall feel themselves to be of clear benefit and progressive advantage to society, will their feelings rise to the full conception of their rightfull relations to the State. This would have the further benefit, to-wit: the boys would be taken more readily by the farmers of Ohio and adjoining States as hired hands, and this would release the State Reform Farm from its present embarrassing surplus. I must add, that the State Board of Agriculture is entirely mistaken, when it labors to keep up the present isolation of their Board, and that of the State Farm, from the other institutions of the State. They thus perpetuate one of the worst evils in Ohio, towit: Its general incoherence in its public administration.

I must now say a few words with reference to another proposition of mine, that was put off in 1858. It was: to have steps taken to do away gradually with the present U. S. Recruiting Service, and to supply, in part, the wants of the regular army, from State Reform Schools. I had seen, in Mettray, military exercises carried on, that prepared a certain number of the inmates for being received into the regular army, as their fitness for the same was proven. I had met also, on my journeys, frequently, officers and common soldiers, that had served in the Crimean War, with honor to themselves, and great benefit to the country, and were proud of the fact. It suggested to me, that a similar preparation and drill, for entering into our military service, might be made in the new Reform School, we were about establishing in Ohio. I had mentioned this to my fellow Commissioners, and urged upon them, the adoption of such a proposition, into our report. They, however, would not listen to it, and they rejected it, being the majority. I have long deemed it a mistake, that our army was still the only one, that received, through a hireling recruiting service, its common soldiers and sub-altern officers. In every presidential message, from Washington to Jackson, it had been urged: that we should have a national militia, and that meant, in effect, that our army should emanate from the main body of society, and not be enlistments from the streets, and social incidents. I thought the use of reform schools in this matter, would serve a double purpose; first: it would do away with the present false recruiting; second: it would familiarize the public minds with reform schools and their main idea; to-wit: that the juveniles sent there are not criminals, but simply youth taken out of false surroundings, for the purpose of returning them to society in a reformed condition. I have since talked to military men, and they all agreed with me, that this idea should, as soon as possible, be adopted, and practically introduced.

CHAPTER LVII.

MY RETIREMENT TO PRIVATE LIFE.

In October, 1859, I sold to Mr. Oliver, my farm in Green Township for $10,000.00. This sale led to my purchase, of Doctor Vattier, the property I now hold on Vine St., between Ninth and Court. I purchased it for $10,600.00, which was then considered a high price. It was understood, that Mr. Thomas, who was then occupying it as a renter, was to give me possession. Afterwards Vattier and Thomas prevaricated. Thomas claimed under a prepayment of rent, a further years' possession. Being all three of us Freemasons and Democrats, we left the matter to Masonic arbitration. V. and T. being older Masons and ancient officers, got the decision in their favor, and I had to rent a house on Ninth Street, which cost me the sum of $720.00, and great inconvenience besides. I learned the lesson, that both Freemasonry as well as Democracy, are often used, by sly dogs, like Vattier and Thomas, to get the advantage over their trusting brethren. Moreover I remembered, that I had not had. in my life, for some time, an example of the gypsy prophecy. So, as stated, I had to rent at $60.00 a month, a house on the south side of Ninth, between Race and Elm; I moved into it in mid-winter, risking the health of my family and myself. In it we exercised for several months a free hospitality, as country folks are apt to do, when they first become towns people. We never got into our own house, until the end of 1860. Vattier and Thomas have had no luck since their perfidy to me, and are both in their graves. The gypsy prophecy seemed still to be in force.

Among the happy events, of this period, was the birth of our youngest daughter Lulu, August 4th, 1859. She was born yet in Dent, and closed the family birth account.

I took up my law business again in 1861, but found it, as others had done, very difficult to resume an abandoned business, and do well in it. My law partner, Mr. Van Hamm, had faithfully attended to the cases I had, but not being a German, he could not be the attorney for some of my customers.

My time would now have hung very heavy on my hands, if during my journeys to Germany, I had not picked up habits of reading and studying, that made me capable of enjoying literary leisure. It is, however, always a hard problem to solve, in the United States, how to be inactive, after a lifelong activity. It is here, where society changes, so rapidly in its elements, most difficult, to keep up an agreeable acquaintanceship into old age. The extreme difficulty lies, however, in keeping up proper public convivialities, in which good wines and plays act an important part. Elderly folks are apt to pick up new habits from a mere desire to pass their time pleasantly away. I remember, as I write, how billiard playing grew upon me, at one time. I recollect also: how certain friendships, that were really no benefit to me, stuck to me in spite of myself. I appreciate still the great enjoyments I have had, and still have, through the companionship of persons, whose tastes were literary like my own. Their small number rendered them more precious.

CHAPTER LVIII.

I GET INTO THE INSURANCE BUSINESS.

Under these circumstances, it seemed like a God-send, that the President of the Germania Mutual Fire & Life Insurance Co., in New York, tendered me the agency of that excellent company in Cincinnati. My only reason for hesitating to accept the position, was: that I believed rather in Government administration of such affairs, than that of companies. I held, that, whilst to all appearances the United States were rapidly exceeding in progressive developments all other Nations, they were by all true standards of comparison, really falling behind. The U. S. had no properly organized civil public administration for the purposes named. There was therefore in the United States a very costly competition between Companies and Corporations in the Insurance business. This made the business more competitive than seemed suitable to me. It had a roughness and a grossness in its conduct, that made it contrary to my ideas of transacting such business.

In answer to my statements, I was told: that the Germania was started on a very different basis; namely, the mutual plan, and that its main object was, to secure to those who insured, a much larger net result, than the usual Insurance Companies. I agreed, to introduce the President — Mr. Wesendonk — to persons, who, I thought, were likely to insure, and did so. I heard the arguments presented, and the calculations, submitted by W ; and they certainly bore out the statements, made to me. I therefore accepted the agency, and remained in it for about 24 months. There were, however, several disagreements between the Company and myself. My way of conducting business, had been hitherto such, that it would recommend itself, and need very few of those artifices, that consisted in making great show and address. I did in my former business very little advertising nor importuning or hunting for customers, and I presumed I could do an Insurance business on the same basis; but I found myself entirely mistaken. This business requires quite different processes, and to get them up was very expensive and laborious. To do it like others, I would have needed clerks and agents, and would have to make personal calls on customers; such, as were not at all to my taste.

At the Home office they had a very big idea of the line of business, that might be gotten up in the city of Cincinnati in a very short time. They expected it to be soon large enough, to secure their agent $5000 a year. It became soon plain to me, that I was really in their way. Soon a Mr. Hartmann came to me with letters, from the New York office, suggesting, that he should become the agent; he paying me for the expenses, I had incurred so far, which was about $270. I agreed, to resign in his favor, and upon that basis the transaction was closed. He remained the agent of the Company, until he died about eleven years ago. The Germania entered afterwards into a combination with two other companies, and had a joint agency in Cincinnati. This conjunction was but one step among many similar ones, and out of it had grown the general tendency to bring the matter under general State regulations and guarantee. The State of Ohio has now an Insurance commissioner, whose duty it is, to bring the whole subject into better order. When I had stepped out of all insurance business, I thought of my old teacher, the Jew, — with his lottery plans and explanations, with my interlocutions; and these memories brought reflections on the fact, that in the United States, more people live on these kind of extra services for society, than anywhere else; and I had to regard it as an indication of a defect in our political developement, and believed, that I had no business in it.

CHAPTER LIX.

THE ELECTION OF 1860.

This election excited early my attention. Of the four Presidential candidates, Douglas, Bell, Lincoln and Breckinridge, none could receive my unhesitating support, because none of them deserved it unreservedly. Douglas I regarded as the most dangerous man in the United States, he was, what Benton called him, "a contemptible demagogue." I knew him personally, and believed, that his ambition was of that sort, that would not recoil from any political crime to insure success. I soon became convinced, that I could under no circumstances vote for him. Bell's nativism precluded my supporting him. I had been at his house in Nashville, Tenn., and there saw, that he and his family were, so far as their social propriety and dignity were concerned, unexceptional. I do not believe, that his election would have brought any serious trouble upon the country. The only objection I had to Lincoln, was his partyism, though I admitted, he had it in a very mild form. There was left only Breckenridge, him that fate had marked for its victim, both in its favors and hates; who was made to agree to the repeal of the Missouri Compromise, when he was really against it; Buchanan's Vice President, Douglas' counterpart. What more fatal positions could there be? It involved antagonisms, which he could not solve, and of which he had to be the victim. In them there was, however, no direct wrong.

I had concluded to vote for Lincoln; for I was charmed with his signal defeat of Douglas in the celebrated debate on slavery, but his utter heresy, as to Federal Law, or, as we call it in German: "Bundesrecht", raised insuparable objections to my mind. I saw indeed plainly, that if there were no Constitutional objection, that he, as an individual, was the man to trust implicitly; but there *was* a Constitutional objection, and, what is more! there was a lawful interpretation of the United States Supreme Court against his ideas. I asked myself: what shall I do? And I said to myself: neither of them have all the fitness for the office; but with Breckenridge we shall have peace, and gain time to effect an inter-state compromise. I knew personally, that Breckenridge was no pro-slavery man, that he desired a settlement, which would have left us the integrity of our constitution, and saved personal liberty; all without war and its bloody and other false solutions.

The prominence given me in the support of Breckenridge in Ohio, by putting me on the ticket, as one of the two Senatorial Electors, was thrust on me against my desire. I would have gladly avoided it, without appearing to flinch from facing the full consequences of my views. I saw very well, that it was not to be a pleasant job, to go before the people of Ohio with nine-tenth of them against you. There was even personal danger in doing so. I knew, however, if anybody could do it, I could, and so it turned out. In some counties, gentlemen of opposite politics to me, came forward and assisted me, in organizing my public meetings. At some of them, opponents of mine presided, and stated, that they did it out of personal respect to me, and I venture, to affirm here, that only at our meeting were then, the public questions involved, fairly stated and discussed, on both sides.

After the election I was drawn into a discussion with Mr. Boswell Marsh, of Steubenville, and we exchanged ten letters. They were published in the "Crisis", and I have preserved copies of them among my papers. This was before the inauguration of Lincoln and the war proclamation.

After Lincoln's inauguration, the situation was entirely changed, Soon we got into war measures, and the question was one of obedience to constituted authorities, in which, questions of *right*, soon sunk out of sight. I deemed it my duty, to assume, as to the war measures, an acquiescent attitude; without, however, surrendering my right, to vote at all elections, my convictions against the war. I could not, after thirty years adult public life in America, fall into a childish implicit submission to party rule of any kind. And we certainly then had no other! My independence did not arise from any wavering disposition, as some had charged on me. The reverse was true. I was too tenacious of rules of action, I had sincerely adopted and could not easily change. I knew too much of party rancor, to believe, at one single bound, into the pretended patriotism of the heated partisans, that had got into power under the success of the Republican party. Nor could I believe, that all these partisans had all at once become enthusiasts for liberty. In brief, I did not shut my eyes on purpose, to deceive myself in reference to the facts that were going on. I was determined to keep them open, and to judge men and events according to the truth that was in me.

And as I write this down, a quarter of a century later, I must say that I do not regret my course in the election of 1860, nor during the administration of Lincoln and his successors. I am to-day as sorry for the infatuations, both North and South, that brought the war, when we ought to have had peace. The true future historian will form, and pronounce a very different judgment of the events between 1860 and 1868 than that, which had been laid down by cotemporaneous narratives in our partisan press.

I was then still entangled with some public duties and functions, because I could not at once sever my peculiar personal relations from them. I did my best to close them up as rapidly as I could. At the same time I quietly prepared myself, for re-assuming my farm in Green Township. Mr. Oliver, the gentleman who had purchased it of me, had got into family difficulties, that made it impossible for him to remain in the United States, and he so stated to me, and asked me to hold myself in readiness to come with him to some agreement by which I would retake the farm and live on it myself. I promised him to do so; and carried out my promise.

CHAPTER LX.

THE WOLFF ASSIGNMENT.

Unexpectedly I was then called upon by Charles Wolff, whom I had known for 40 years, and asked me to become his and his brother's assignee, for closing out their iron and stove business. I could not well refuse, and qualified, in January, 1861, before the Probate Court of Hamilton County. I continued as such assignee until December, 1862, and then closed up the business, by my report to the Probate Court, of which I have preserved several copies. I must refer, for the details of that assignment, to this report, and can now only make a general statement of the results.

It was: that all claims were settled in full, and that, to the assignors their individual and family possessions and homesteads were saved, without their having to claim them under the Exemption Act. This result was secured, through my early assumption of the responsibility of settling with creditors, by their taking the assets placed in my hands, at fair prices. Thus I closed the business in 23 months, at a cost of less than 2 per cent. The creditors lost nothing on the assets they took, at the prices charged.

In disposing of the affairs of this assignment, I made some very humiliating discoveries; because I had to meet with persons, that claimed to be steadfast friends, while really they were my perfidious enemies. I have mentioned one of these already, to-wit: my former clerk, Goeppert. Another was a former grocer, by the name of Klotter, who kept his business up, chiefly on my credit, between 1830 and 1840. In the final closing of the account, my attorney, Mr. Stallo, played also a very questionable part. He insinuated to the Wolff's, that I was claiming more than I was entitled to. This compelled me to raise this question before the then Judge of the Probate Court, Woodruff, and to have it argued. I had claimed $5,000. In the final allowance, the Judge gave me $7,500, and to my lawyer, Whitman, he allowed $600, a sum that need not to have been paid, if I had not to discharge Stallo. Of the $7,500 allowed me, I relinquished $1,000 of my own accord, and so did my lawyer relinquish one-third of his, at my request. I carry to my grave a deep regret, that I was not permitted to go out of the Wolff assignment, without making such bitter experiences with pretended friends. Honor required me to state them.

In the Summer of 1862, I took from Mr. Taafe my old farm, which he had purchased from Mr. Oliver, and found himself unable to pay for. In nominal money value I made, by this transaction, about $2,500, but the loss by deterrioration, in the actual value, far outweighed this nominal gain. I had not deemed it possible, that a man could let grow up, in two years, such immense quantities and varieties of weeds. And this forced me to take cognizance of a big fact in America; namely: that the biggest success in America are the weeds, which we allow to grow up on both our lands and in our politics. Still I was glad to get back to the little world, that I had created in Green Township, and to which I had given the name of Dent. It brought about, what I most needed, a coming to myself, my best work and my family. The greatest boon was to bring my younger children back to their birthplace; for to children it is of the greatest benefit to be country-raised. I now took up with new scenes, the restitution of my home place to cleanliness and order. I took up my vineyards and gardens, my friends and my pasture, my barn and my dwelling, and made it again a place for higher enjoyment. I spent some $5,000 in improvements. The receipts for the money are among my papers.

CHAPTER LXI.

MY RELATION TO THE CIVIL WAR.

The four years of my life, from 1861 to 1864, both inclusive, have for my recording pen but little employment. The main items I would have to write about, would relate to the war. And what good would that do? I would have to tell of wealth destroyed, and of suffering and of humiliations endured; and that would read like a contradiction of the public records, for they speak of wealth *created,* and of benefits conferred, and of exaltations caused; and of paper money issued, and the immense increase of revenues from taxation, lent probability to these very statements, for there was an enlarged *nominal* amount of value. There are some plain facts, that must, however, be mentioned to destroy the illusions, under which the world is laboring, and to bring out the real truth. We have an annual pension list of over $165,000,000, which is at least $40,000,000 more than Prussia spends on her army and navy. I think this single fact can serve as a beacon light, with which to examine into other dark spots, and to bring out fully the great injury, the war has done to the Union. As soon, in 1861, as I felt war to be certain, I took steps, so to place myself, as to public affairs, as to keep easily out of the toils of war, both my family and myself. I had passed my 45th year, and was therefore not subject to enlistment by law. I was too well versed in the history of my native land, to ever become personally involved in a civil war by my own free will. My first step was, therefore, as stated, to give up my city residence, and to go back to my former country home. I refrained from writing for the Press, to make public speeches, or to hold public conversations. Still I was attacked, through the Press and in social intercourse, even in going and coming for my mail I was molested, and saw others maltreated. After my removal to the country, I was there better treated, but on the evening and during the night following the announcement of the assassination of Lincoln, my house was threatened to be burned down by an infuriated countryman of mine. I was saved from injury, through an American neighbor of mine, with whom I had, in former years, had many differences on the political subject. Both facts had their humiliations, the wrong of my countryman most!

The fact, that such things had occurred elsewhere, led to the observation, that bad men had acquired, in American society, a control, through pretended patriotism, which they in no wise deserved. This fastened itself on my mind, and I saw that no seclusion could protect me from their violence. I accepted, therefore, in 1863, a position in the C. W. & Zanesville Railroad, with a double motive: to bring me more into general intercourse, but also with a hope, that I was reviving the probability of the completion of the tunnel, that old favorite project of mine.

I had one satisfaction then, which but few enjoyed; to-wit: I associated with several good families, among whom current party politics were, if not entirely ignored, at least a very unimportant subject in conversation; the topics being there literary and scientific. One of these families was that of August Eggers, and the other that of Mr. Hartman, Sen. I esteemed the hours spent in these families, especially happy; for they contributed largely to our higher culture, and were thus a great relief to me from the prevailing general brutalization of society. I must mention: that the ladies of these families contributed largely to our enjoyments. At our interviews, we read law, history, geography and political economy, as well as the natural sciences. I also continued then, the keeping of the book already mentioned, in which I entered every citation or remark from ancient or modern persons of note. I also kept up scrap-books, for preserving therein printed slips of contributions made by me to the Press. I also preserved copies of works I published in pamphlet form.

On my frequent journeys to New York, on railroad business, I was brought there in contact and renewed acquaintance with many persons that were, in the best sense, the leading minds of the country. I met also some, that were leading men in the worst sense, and was thus kept from falling into the common illusions, that were prevalent at that time. 1 recoiled, through the light I was getting, from the better sources I had access to, from falling into the entire misunderstanding of current events, that was then promulgated by the Press and most of the public speakers. I saw that our tax laws caused more private gain than public benefit. I understood, that our borrowing of money, and our regulations of the value of money, were in every case deceptive tinkerings with money and credit; that they caused fluctuations, by which wealth was falsely distributed, and the producers of real wealth were robbed through ficticious prices. Those, that produced least, got most. I saw too, that the standard of public virtue was becoming every day more corrupt, so that selfishness passed for patriotism, and even for public wisdom, and that taking advantage of popular errors, passed for financial capacity.

There were several attempts made, to place the Democratic party into its true position before the country, but they were not effectual. The old split against Douglass, in the election of 1860, was still controlling popular feelings, and these were aggravated, by the friends of Douglass assuming more or less false attitudes, in reference to the Civil War. Most elections were farces, though we had many tragedies. In Ohio especially, the contest between Valandigham and Brough, for Governor, were such. It began in a tyrannic arrest of Valandigham, by soldiers. I saw it accidentally, while on a visit to Dayton. Valandigham's subsequent conduct placed everything into a false position. I urged then, as I had done before and since, that our intense partisanism, had driven both our great parties, into false relations to the Civil War; in this: that both fought in it for party supremacy, and persisted in this error, while they denied it in words. The South's secession was really not a secession from the Union; it was an act of desperation, to protect themselves, against being victimized, by party powers. This act of desperation took a false direction, because the South was all the time conscious, that the North had committed the same wrong in foisting on the country as rulers: Pierce and Buchanan, both being the heads of their respective parties, and not the chief magistrates of the Union. Whenever democrats met, in 1864, the old wrong of 1852 and 1856 loomed up and acted like a deep shadow on all their attempts to get right again. Very few of them rose to the comprehension, that public affairs, in the United States, could then no more be righted by party organizations, old or new, and least of all, by any that claimed to be a continuance of any that existed before the war. Those of us, that saw this plainly, and claimed that the country could get right only through a constitutional government, entirely reconstructed, were, if not brutally assailed, at least villified, and we could do no more, than quietly persist in our views. Such is, at least, my belief.

I have always held, that Abraham Lincoln had an inner consciousness: that, being a party president, was the only obstacle to his solving the difficulties, under which he became President. I think he said to himself the truth. He must have felt in his own mind: that in his heart he was not a party president. I read this assurance out of his letter to Alexander H. Stevens, of December 22nd, 1860. He wrote:

"The South would be in no more danger in this respect, (interference with slavery,) than it was in the days of Washington."

Lincoln wrote this, in reply to a letter from Alexander H. Stephens, on December 18th, 1860, in which he had said:

"Washington, Jefferson and other presidents are generally admitted to have been anti-slavery, in sentiment. But in those days, anti-slavery did not enter, as an element, into party organization."

I think these extracts bear me out, in my statement, that Lincoln did not mean to be a party president.

And now I may speak the word, that has been at the point of my pen, all this time; it is: *the war came, because: as parties were then, they could not trust one another.* Lincoln could trust Stevens, and Stevens Lincoln; but neither could trust the other, when they spoke as leaders or subjects of a party. I think Lincoln would have kept his word, as he wrote it to Stevens. The trouble was: that Lincoln could not trust the South; nor the South Lincoln.

I have carried this conviction in my mind, ever since I had an interview with Stevens, at his own home, after the war. I had it indeed before, and stated it in various publications.

An old friend of mine, Wm. M. Corry, with whom I had co-operated 20 years before, in the anti-Bank meeting, at the old Court House, when it rained red pepper on us, for giving nine good reasons for our opposing the re-charter of thirteen banks, published, during the war, a paper, that he called: "The Commoner." He asked me to write for his paper, and I did so, either over my own initials: "C. R.," or the assumed name: "Clamito." I coincided then, in a general way, with my friends, but could not do so in everything. He so took it, and gave me and my pen entire liberty. We, who wrote for the paper, were understood to be free lances, against the "regulars" of our parties. I have kept copies of the articles, which I wrote. They are in the Cincinnati Library.

CHAPTER LXII.

SOME PRIVATE MATTERS IN 1864—65.

My father-in-law, John Jacob Mark, died in May, 1864. He made me his administrator by will. He left a small estate; his second wife got more than her share, by an error in his will, which we left undisturbed. His daughter by his second wife, received her equal share, with the children of the first wife. He was an eccentric, but an honest man, and true patriot, to both his native land Switzerland and the United States. I learned much from him, and bless his memory while I write. I have forgotten his few foibles. He is buried alongside of his first wife.

In 1865 I was brought, unexpectedly, into new relations to the German Press. I received from Mr. A. Brush, the editor and owner of a new German Monthly in Chicago,—the "Monatshefte"—that were devoted to German literature in America, an invitation to write for his paper a series of articles on Political Economy. This was evidence to me, that the German Republicans in America, were disposed to give up their ruder patriotism, and to look with a more friendly eye upon us German democrats. I wrote the articles, and they were favorably noticed in this country and in Europe. I think myself: that they were useful, because they were written from the pure scientific aspect, and presented several points, that were new, then, in the United States. One of my points was: to bring out the immense advantages German authors have, in writing on questions of Political Economy, through the use they have of certain words. They can, for that reason, write much more definitely, and at the same time much more comprehensively. I instanced this through the word "Vermögen," and otherwise illustrated it. I have copies of the several numbers, in which the articles appeared, in my library; and I must say, that I find them frequently useful to me, in questions of Political Science. The Chicago Monthly has been discontinued. Such a Monthly is much needed *now*.

Occasionally the Commercial Gazette yielded me its columns. And frequently I published my own writings, at my own cost, in pamphlet form. Generally I preserved copies among my papers. I have now filed them with the City Library.

At the election, November 8th, 1864, I voted for McClellan, and even made speeches for him, during the canvass, but was careful not to have myself taken for a regular party stump-speaker. Lincoln was re-elected, as everybody anticipated, and nobody really regretted. All through the Winter of 1864 and 1865 there were baffling news of a coming peace. The Emancipation Proclamation of Lincoln had evidently made the South inclined to give up a hopeless strug-

gle. The anti-slavery zealots of the North, had attained a definite
point, as to the terms of peace, that would satisfy them. And so
came, with the fall of Richmond, the conclusion of a peace, that was,
whatever we may think of it now, then much better for all, than the
continuance of the war. The assassination of Lincoln, by Booth, was
as absurd an act, as the killing of Caesar by Brutus, but meaner in
every respect, and more disgraceful to all the public authorities, connected with it. This assassination gave to events a fatal turn. It
might have shown, Democrats and Republicans, Northerners and
Southerners, that our Civil War meant the cessation of the old legitimate government, and the surrender of the country to infatuation.
How much better it would have been, if Lincoln had had the making of the ultimate peace, all in his hands, He could have been
generous. Johnson had to appeal to the generosity of his party, and
as we know, he failed miserably.

I must say a few words of Andrew J. Johnson, who became
President, by the death of Lincoln. I knew him personally, and had
visited him in Nashville, when he was Governor of Tennessee. His
nomination, as successor of Hamlin, was a mistake. It was intended,
as a compliment, to the democratic element, that joined in the war,
with the understanding, that when the war was over, they might
resume their previous relation to their old party. Such understandings are always delusions. They are never kept. Events set them
aside. It was so in 1865. On the part of the democrats, as well as
on the part of the republicans, new understandings had to be made.
Andrew Johnson was a Southerner of the class that succeeded, in
gaining high political positions, in spite of their richer fellow citizens. He was, what they call, a self-made man; it means: that he
ascended the ladder of ambition, unaided by the prestige of parental
wealth, or college education. He obtained his high positions in the
State, through a sort of oratory, that flourishes on the stump, because it indicates a fertile brain and a good memory, of political
catch phrases. Johnson was, in the popular mind, a second Jefferson, plus Jacksonism. I saw him in Nashville, about 40 years ago,
as Governor of the State of Tennessee. I rather admired him; for he
had overcome passions and proclivities, that other weaker men
would have failed under. He loved to tell, that he started out in
life, as a tailor. His wife was a lady in the best sense, and stood
alongside of him: as the pledge of a finish to his reformation.
The war of 1861 upset both his morals and his politics; and
when he was inaugurated as Vice-President in 1865, he was on a
spree, and instead of honoring, degraded himself. When the Presidency fell to him, by the assassination of Lincoln, his character
stood low, in the popular mind. The great body of republicans,
tender-footed, as they were, as to intoxication and other grossnesses,
never had any confidence in him. And when he attempted to

straighten himself up, in 1865, every act in his public policy was misconstrued, and these misconstructions finally culminated in his impeachment. That went too far; it reacted in favor of Johnson. Johnson never was, never could be a traitor; neither could he be an obsequious party tool. And the end of it was, that the breakdown of the impeachment, saved him from contempt, and re-established some of his old reputation. And he retired finally, with the restored respect for the good in his character; the bad being forgotten. I was glad of this, for the sake of his good wife. That wife's biography should be written by some Southerner, that can appreciate, what a heroine she was, in being that man's wife; both when he held high positions, and honors, and also when she had to be it in sorrow and with wounded feelings.

CHAPTER LXIII.

I GO TO EUROPE WITH MY ELDEST SON.

I attended in the early summer of 1865, the convention at Philadelphia, in which it was intended to cement, the reunion of the States, through a reunion of the Democratic party. I remembered my attendance on a similar convention in Pittsburgh in 1856. Then partisanship was unable to keep the Union intact. Now it proved equally futile, to attempt to fasten the Democratic party together. *Wedges* split logs and *parties* split nations. I concluded, that all labor and outlays incurred on Andrew Johnson's post-bellum politics, were waste of time and means, for which we should have had better employment.

I had had in the Fall of 1864 a good vintage, and I realized a good price for the wine, so that I had a snug sum for any special purpose I might have. And that culminated in my long cherished plan, to take my eldest son to Europe for finishing his education at one or more of the Universities there. We left for Europe, August 20th. In Columbus, Ohio, I lost my gold watch in changing cars, early in the morning from a sleeping car. Evidently a pickpocket had relieved me of it. My son called it a bad omen: I said, it was "a farewell kick, that meant a hearty welcome when we came back." I advised my son to let it be a lesson to him anyway, and it might save him from other bad luck, and so it did. We got well to New York, embarked there in a german steamer, the Weser, for Bremen, and got well there in good time. There I renewed my acquaintance with my old friend, Eggers and his good wife. I showed my son, on our further journey, Hannover, Göttingen, Cassel, Frankfurth and Heidelberg. We arrived in my native city the day afterwards and were well received. They took our coming, as a burnt offering on the altars of Germany. I thought, I was doing my duty to my son and my adopted country. After introducing my son to all the relatives, I took him, in October, to the University of Tübingen, where so many of our ancestors had studied. I felt sure, that his name would secure him a hearty welcome. My brother Theodore, who had graduated there, as a Theologian, was with us, and he introduced my son Edward to several Professors, and especially to the celebrated Dr. A. E. F. Schaeffle, with whom we have kept up a correspondence ever since. His writings on political economy have now a great reputation, and he is the editor of the principal journal on political economy. I have contributed to it an article on the Monroe Doctrine, and also one, on the history of Green Township. The rest of the year 1865, I spent in travelling over Germany and visiting my relatives. I again went to Switzerland, but found there sad changes, in the Billwiller family. The head of it had become an unscrupulous speculator in mining property, and he was seriously involved, He tried to draw me into his speculations, but I declined. He succeeded, however, in borrowing some money of me, which I had much trouble to get back, and only succeeded, by making, in Zürich, a peremptory demand. His utter failure, and death several years afterward, showed me, how closely I had escaped severe losses. His good wife had to undergo severe sorrows afterward.

From Switzerland. I extended my travel to Lyons, in France. There I met, for the first time again, since 1828, my cousin Theodore Böttinger. He was the eldest son of my mother's elder brother, who had died in 1821. My father became Theodore's guardian, and he sent him to the same school in Marbach, which my brother and myself attended. Afterwards, my father apprenticed him to the Herrnhuters in Saxony. There he learned silk culture, and that knowledge secured him a good place with a Russian Nobleman, who was also engaged in the silk culture. Through that place, he became acquainted with French silk merchants, and they made him the head of their silk establishment at St. Ettienne, near Lyons. He became, subsequently, partner and principal owner of it, and when I met him in Lyons, was one of the wealthier men in Lyons.

Our meeting was a queer coming together. I had heard but once, of him, since I left him in Marbach, in 1828. My father told me, he had sent him to Russia. When I parted from him, in '28, we did not like each other, but we had had no open quarrel. Our parting may be likened to the parting of Abraham and Lot. When, in 1865, I arrived in Germany, I met, at my father's, his sister Alwina, my favorite cousin, because she resembled my mother. She mentioned, in her letter to him, my arrival with my son, and he promptly sent me an invitation to Lyons, which I, for shame, accepted and carried out.—We met, on arrival at the depot, and he insisted on me going with him to his house. I found him living, as a bachelor, in an elegant suite of rooms. He had a good looking housekeeper, and to her kind mercies I was delivered, and she proved a superior attendant on me. At our meals, we had all the delicacies of the season, fine wines and liquors, and all luxuriously served. We had breakfast at the best restaurant of the city, and there I was introduced to the several business friends of my cousin. At dinner, we had as guests, select friends with their ladies; showing that his bachelor life gave no offense to them. In short, during my visit, all my former coldness toward my cousin, melted away, and we became very affectionate friends. I might have assumed, that an entire different person was with me, but the family likeness was too striking, to entertain any such ideas. He had a fund of information on every subject broached. As to the housekeeper: I saw more and more, that the relation was honorable, in the very best sense of the word. His sister, a most excellent lady, visited him frequently for weeks. This kind relation lasted to his last hour, and when he died, he left her a large fortune by will. One of the most pleasant days I spent with him, was in going out to his country house. He carried on there, through expert employees, a first-class incubating establishment,—eggery, we would call it, at which he raised chickens and eggs for the London market, and kept a nursery for fine fruits and flowers. It produced him a large income, and raised in me the idea: that such an establishment and nursery would be a perfect gold mine in Cincinnati. I certainly would go into the business, if I could be a young man again. The high wages, that have to be paid in the United States, would be the only impediment.

My cousin and myself exchanged narratives of our histories, and that brought up questions as to our two adopted countries, Russia and the United States. We both saw, how many of the conditions are similar in these countries, and, yet again, entirely dissimilar. I cannot here enter into the details of our discussion, but I may give his general observation. He said: "Neither of the two countries have any politics in the sense of their pursuing, their respective courses, from premeditated, well reasoned public policy. The Governments of both are fatalisms." He gave as a reason for this: "that in both countries the social impulses sway political conduct, and are introduced, before they have matured into a well formed public will, as law." He added: "With your American social fatalism, you have its elder brother, religious fatalism, and you have it almost as much as the Turks and Persians had it, only in a different form; because the great body of the people of the United States believe in a divine interference, for their special benefit." I asked him: "whether he had not imbibed these his ideas at the Herrnhuters?" He replied: "No! Their religious development is much more humanitarian and intelligent, than that of the English and American Puritans; and so is the history of their treatment of the Indians in America, as compared with that of the English-Americans." I did not continue the controversy, but wrote down his remarks, when I got to my own room.

Of course we discussed also the topic: how it came, that I emigrated westward, and he eastward? and this again led to our noticing it similtaneously: how queer it was, that we, who had mutually disliked each other, now sat together in friendly confab, without a trace of former antagonisms. My father's different treatment of both of us, and the difference of a father's and a guardian's policy, was discussed. He laughed at it, that his character had to be corrected, by being sent to Herrnhuters, with their strict discipline; whilst I had to undergo that of the loosely governed American society. It pleased him greatly, when I pointed to his garden and nursery, and complimented him on the fact, that he had got much further, in gardening and chicken raising, by learning from the Herrnhuters, than I had, by picking up information from my neighbors and agricultural journals. He himself, brought up the delicate question of bachelorism, by raising the question: "whether, if I had been sent to the Herrnhuters, I too would have remained a bachelor?" He added quickly, when I was about protesting against the idea: "Now, don't misunderstand me as admitting, that bachelorism is in itself wrong." "On the contrary, I hold, that I choose the wiser part. Just look at my sisters! what a help I have been to them?" Then he named a dozen nephews and nieces, and then asked me: "Don't you admire the unruffled home life, that I enjoy, through my excellent housekeeper?" He said: "All my relations look at me as a benefactor." I did not deem it necessary, to debate with him, the distinction, between children inheriting from parents, and bequests to nieces and nephews, but called his attention to a point, he seemed to have overlooked; namely: that children have much more cause to love and respect their parents, than nieces and nephews have their rich uncle; because: children enjoy a father's wealth and tuition, while he is alive: and his death is a loss, while to the others it is a gain. I pointed out to him besides: that I had been raising a family for 34 years in America, and, while his money outcome was larger than mine, he had been all this time a "solitaire." He saw the point and laughed. I left for Heilbronn, and reported to his sister, that we had become loving cousins to each other. This gratified her very much. As to our conversations, she obviously took no interest in them. I fear, it will be so too, with most of my readers.

CHAPTER LXIV.

MY TRAVELS THROUGH GERMANY AND HUNGARY.

After placing my son Edward at Tübingen, and arranging his studies, and having passed Christmas at Heilbronn, I went, by way of Nördlingen to Nüremberg, on the first day of 1866. At the first named place I saw again, the last time, a well preserved ancient free city, that had its entire stone circumvallation in tact, and I took special pleasure, in going 'round upon the covered wall around the whole city. At Nüremberg I met my brother Eberhardt as a clerk in a drug store. With him I spent several days in sight-seeing all over Nüremberg, and I enjoyed myself socially very much. Then I went by railroad to Regensburgh; another ancient city of great historic interest, both modern and ancient. I walked and strolled about, feeling as if I were in a dream, that I, a citizen of the newest nation, should be making a tour of cognizance in a town, where the conditions of the middle ages are still prevailing. Here the Congress of old Germany used to meet to elect Emperors, and decide on many vital questions Here Charles the V. had his love scrape with his landlord's daughter, of which Juan d'Ausria came, of "Lepanto" memory. It seemed that the princely personages of old did not, like the late Crown Prince of Austria commit suicide, when caught in such a difficulty. I went up also to see that glorious home of Art, "Walhalla," which the good taste of King Louis, of Bavaria, created. Between old things and new, and still more, between them both and the future, the mind is intensly occupied, when one walks about between the history of a thousand years, the statutes, pictures, and other works of art, that we never forget our journey again.

I may as well state, that I enjoyed greatly the social pleasure at the hotels and in the old cathedral of the town. I also had a very interesting conversation with an engineer, who had become captain on a steamer on the Danube, who had formerly been clerk on a steamer on the Ohio. We both enjoyed the coincidence and the views it suggested. From Regensburg, my journey's programm took me toPilsen, in Bohemia, where I had an opportunity to enjoy, drinking the real Pilsener beer, brewed in Prinz Windischgraetz's brewery. Au Austrian officer, whom I met at the hotel table, became at once my boon companion. He introduced me to the head manager of the brewery. I was to him a *rara avis*, because I was a German and American combined. They pumped out of me, by numerous inquiries, considerable information, that was entire news to them. They took me kindly to the convivial meeting, held by the chief officers that evening. Some of their merchants were also present. Next morning I was introduced to a most interesting personage for me; the Chief officer of the prison and police station. His character was a mixture of good nature, shrewdness, and, what he called: "strict discipline". He pointed out to me, that his discipline was so effective; because, he applied to each prisoner, what, on careful study, he found best for that individual. He had picked up one of the ideas of Reform Schools. He was profuse in giving instances in confirmation of this his theory. He insisted, that *face* not *mind* reading should be made a habitual study of the chief officers of prisons. He narrated one of these instances in the presence of a prisoner, and I had an opportunity for a little face-reading myself. I thought, the face of the prisoner informed me, that humoring an officer in his idiosyncrasies was a very successful way to gain his favor. The chief officer was indeed very familiar with his prisoners, and one of them interposed, during the conversation, the remark: "Yes. But, Colonel! You don't know everything by reading my face." The officer replied: "that God only does." The prisoner quickly replied: "But not from reading faces." With this both laughed. I thought, the laugh hit the officer most, and left the prison. The officer informed me afterward of a queer fact in that prison, to-wit: that they had one-third more inmates in Winter than in Summer. I was about to give my surmise for the cause of this, but the officer, who had evidently read this purpose out of my face, interrupted my reflections and said: "dont waste thought on this matter. It has a very natural cause." I looked up inquiringly, and he added: "We keep warm rooms in Winter, and they commit light offenses on purpose, to be sent here and fed." I remarked, that he was evidently a mind as well as a face reader, and that that made him a good prison officer."

I was invited to a town ball in Pilsen. While sauntering through the hall, during an intermission of the dancing, and not knowing of the rule, that, at the coming dance, ladies had the privilege to invite partners, I was seized by a damsel, whose vigor I soon became aware of. She dropped me finally with the remark: "Sie sind ein Deutscher; danke schön!" I waved my hand with a kiss, and once more was a free man. I kept out of the dancing hall after that. These Pilsen people are kind-hearted to a fault. There was, at that time, a part of the garrison, Italians. And one of the officers, with whom I became also acquainted, could not talk enough of the kindness, he had received; he cried: "I fairly love this people." I interposed: "Yet, you hate their Government?" He replied: "Only when it intrudes on Italy." This silenced me, for I could not deny, that it was wrong in Austria to seek to rule over Italy. The Italian officer found out, that I was a Freemason, and, on my telling him, that I was on the way to Italy, and expected, to spend my winter there, he tendered me letters to his friends in Venice, Padua and Ravenna, which I carelessly accepted, not knowing, that these letters might bring me into trouble with the police. The police never saw them and they did me infinite good in Italy; and increased my knowledge of masonry besides.

From Pilsen I traveled to Prague, and there I had to observe, the misery mankind carry forward, in the shape of national antipathies, engendered by mutual misunderstandings. I tried to find why the Bohemian Czech hates the Germans and vice versa. And I had to answer myself: It is for the same reason, that the Northerners and Southerners hate each other in the United States; to-wit: their way of doing good to each other is spiteful, and we often do grievous wrong to each other, under the pretence of doing good. The only difference between the two is, that the troubles of Bohemia are of long historic standing, and are therefore not likely to cease entirely; while with us there are constant changes, going on in population, which will enable our Statesmen, if they are wise, to obliterate the former memories. At Prague I had to regret at almost every step, my lack of local historical knowledge; and yet I saw plainly that I knew a little more than most persons I conversed with. Even in the Convents and among public personages, I had to notice this, and I thought that it arose from the simple fact, that here was a people divided into two parts, each of whom studied only its own history, and neglected, or misconceived, that of the other part. My observation taught me, that the best thing, that could happen them both, would be to become acquainted with each others history and geography; that then they would soon find, that much of their hatred has really no cause. Now you have only to go to the one, to hear all of the bad qualities of the other. And you may hear of the good qualities of both, by listening to the self-praise of each respectively. It is just so in the United States as to our parties. Listen to their self laudations, and apply a little equation to them, and you have the capacity of both for good. Reverse it, however, and listen to their calumnies of each other, and you have a deeper insight into American wickedness that is so disagreeable; because so much of it is untrue.

My closer introduction into Bohemian Society, I owe to a letter of introduction to a Catholic Priest, who was one of the Superiors of the Archbishops' Seminary in Prague, which I had received several years previous from a former resident of Cincinnati, the now almost forgotten, Pastor Hammer. I went to the Seminary and presented my letter, only to find, that I could not find him, I sought, at Prague. An assistant of the superior of the seminary, gave me however much information about Prague, and enabled me to see all the important places therein. He introduced me also to several persons, that were useful to me.

I afterwards found Rev. Hammer, who then resided in a village near Carlsbad, and gave me a very kind reception. Hammer was one of the first Catholics, with whom I became acquainted, when I arrived in Cincinnati in 1833. He gave me then already an advice, that I found very useful and correct since; to wit: that I would understand Prague much better, after I had seen Vienna. I followed the advice a few years afterwards and found it strictly correct. I understood, how absolutely necessary both the two cities are to each others prosperity.

At the end of January, 1866, I reached Vienna, where I had letters to influential gentlemen from persons in Stuttgardt, that had met each other in the General Convention for the unification of Germany. These letters were to Messrs. Weniger and Schwede, both officers of the Anglo-Austria Bank; also to Tafel, who was an offi er of the city of Vienna, connected with its public works. The latter gentleman was the son of the well-known member in the Frankfort Parliament in 1849, who is the uncle of our Mr. Tafel, a well known personage in Cincinnati. I had also letters to Schuselka, who was then a noted member of the Austrian Parliament. I also had letters to Dr. Kolatschek, an eminent writer on political economy. The Bankers, Ladenburg, attended to my small pecuniary matters. I stopped at the hotel "Golden Lamb", that was recommended to me by my cousin, Richard Rümelin. It was good, but rather expensive I attended, as "hospes" all the lectures at Vienna University, that I could get time to attend. At the public reading room I found the current publications, and arranged for having sent me copies of several, to my library in the United States. There was then studying medicine in Vienna a son of our old family physician, Dr. Schneider. Through these several gentlemen I was introduced to many other persons of note, and was told of proper places for good eating and drinking, and sights worth seeing. They also entered my name, as visitor, upon the books of several societies; the best of which was, in my opinion, the Society of Jurists, whose reading room was very useful to me. I spent a month in Vienna, then went for a week to Pesth in Hungary, where I had letters to Deak; also to Kossuth's special friend Szell. I knew personally Pulsky from his visit to Cincinnati in 1849. Szell's family extended their hospitalities to me. Their handsome daughter spoke excellent English. Szell explained to me much of Hungarian politics, and now I understood better, why Kossuth kept himself abroad in Italy, near Turin. I admit, that they were too fine spun for me, after I saw Deak, and became acquainted with the several points. They were simply differences, similar in their character, as those were, that divided Calhoun from Van Buren, or Silas Wright. A nation is constitutionally weak, whose great men antagonize each other.

Statesmen, like Deak, have a patriotism. that I would call chaste; because it is untainted from selfishness or personal aversions. Deak's ground was simply: "That Hungary was a part of the Austrian Empire by a federal agreement, and, that the Emperor was right or wrong, just to the degree, to which he was true to lawful relations, that emanated from this federal basis, and were so to speak, the logic of it. Deak was the only Statesman, I met in Europe, who understood completely federal law, and comprehended, for that reason, federal politics as to all other countries, including that of the United States. I corresponded at that time with New York papers, and gave the main points of my conversation with Deak. I think, it was the N. Y. Evening Post, with which I corresponded. I did not get copies, while on my journey, and have not preserved any. My folks remember reading them, and I having written them.

In the latter part of February I returned to Vienna, and from there went to Italy via Gratz. I did not reach Italy, until early in March.

At Gratz I got into that excellent Hotel "Archduke Charles", to which I had been recommended by my brother-in-law, who had also given me his card for presentation to the Prince of Würtemberg, that resided in Gratz. It was the same Prince, that is well known for his high military capacities, and fine diplomatic abilities. He pointed out to me the many good things, to be enjoyed in Gratz, and I had opportunities, to witness some fine military maneuvers under his command. I of course ascended the beautiful hills, surrounding Gratz, and was gratified with the splendid views, that they afforded. I was gratified exceedingly also by the reasonableness of the Styrian population, and the excellent female attendance at the hotels, that exists there. The folks seem to say to strangers: "Come, and stay with us, we will treat you well, and never overcharge you, nor ever claim any extra pay." The point of attraction to me was the Mausoleum, in which Ferdinand II., the bigot, that caused the 30 years war, is buried. I had been told, that over his coffin the pigeons come every day by thousands, and use the Mausoleum, where he is buried, to deposit their excrements upon it, and I wanted to go there and see it done; and I wanted to add to it my curses upon the man, that caused the loss of ten millions of men to my native land, and held back its civilization for at least two hundred years. It was bigotry and treachery, like this, that has kept Germany divided to this day. Hurrah! for the pigeons at that Mausoleum!

CHAPTER LXV.

MY JOURNEY THROUGH ITALY IN 1866.

From Gratz I went to Triest; mainly: because, I had read in American papers, that it was the only place in Europe, that had a modern growth, in the new world's sense. I found a much less healthy growth, than I had been led to expect; but many evidences of mushroom growth, namely: a rush for all, that can be squeezed out of the thing, with least service or benefit to the respective locality. In that rush certain Italianized Germans, and half breeds of various kinds are harmonious, and the result is, that a stranger, when he gets there, is fleeced as much as possible. I stayed there but one day, after taking a fine view of the Adriatic Sea, from the fortifications on the hill, north of Triest. Then I left for Venice, taking in Miramare, the residence of the unhappy Maximilian and his wife. on the way. He was not at home, but we were shown the palace. Little did I dream, that the man, who was at that time the least disliked and most honored Prince of the Habsburghs, would, within two years, become the innocent victim of a lot of co-operating treachery from England, France, Mexico and the United States. I was in Miramare in 1866 on a flying visit, and at that time Maximilian and his wife were regarded as more likely to intervene for saving the life of innent prisoners, than, that they would ever have to undergo Capital punishment themselves. They were then governing Lombardy wisely, and if Lombardy had been asked to choose a King, they would certainly have selected M. in preference to any other German Prince. I must believe, that it was *not* wrong in Maximilian to go to Mexico, and I am sure, he would have been to Mexico of much more benefit, than any of the Rulers, is has had since. I have expressed my views upon the Monroe doctrine in a paper published by the Quarterly of the University of Tubingen, and cannot repeat them here, but this I will say: that the doctrine has never received a consistent application, nor a uniform construction; but the worst application of the doctrine was Seward's hostility to Maximilian, and his brutal execution through Huarez And I will add, that the least excusable part in all that tragedy, was played by Huarez. He played the callous Indian and stoic nativist!

When I arrived in Venice, it was a painful sight to me! to see there Austrian military! Maximilian was, by a strange exception excluded from the government of Venice. The longer I staid there, the more I saw: what a blessing a ruler like Maximilian would be for Venice! He would be a true statesman to it, and govern it free from Austrian and Venetian prejudices. The greatest curse, that could be inflicted on Venice, would be a govern nent, that would attempt to re-establish the old so-called "Republican Rule." It would, if that were possible, postpone forever the solution of what is called the Eastern question. It would stop off at once any further healthy development in that part of Europe. Venice can be truly great again. only as a member of a federally united State.

In Venice I met the first smiles of Spring. Otherwise everything was dull, as if a catastrophe was near at hand; but what it would or should be? nobody ever spoke about. The rivers we had to cross, were high. At Padua, I had letters to the German professors, that lectured there, and they were anxious to make my sojourn pleasant. I learned from their lips, that they all of them wished for calls from German universities. I suggested to them, to look a little to the United States. The idea was new to them, but they were rather pleased with it. They all looked upon their stay in Padua as precarious.

I had been told that I would find the name of an ancestor of mine on the walls of the principal halls of the Padua University, recorded there, because he had written an approved essay on "Melancholy". I spent some time in hunting it, but there were too many names, to find this one, within the time allotted to me then in Padua. It left on me the one useful impression: how much better the relation of universities to general culture were centuries ago

And it awakened in me the hope, that international education would soon get a good revival; and that then would come the right international political expansion: a world-citizenship would exist, such as had never existed before.

As I passed from Venice to Bologna, I noticed, that there was much railroad building going on. At that time—1866—the laborers on the railroads in Italy were principally Germans. A dozen years afterwards, I saw Italians working on railroads in Germany, and not a German doing it in Italy. From Padua to Ferrara, I had to travel by stage The Adige and the Po were dangerous to cross; the boats, we had to use, were rather insecure. At Ferrara I stopped a few hours in sight seeing, and then left for Bologna. We were asked frequently for our passports. We thought it a relic of barbarism, and if anyone would have suggested to us, that passports would ever be introduced into the United States, we would have called him a fool. My passport had the visa of the Austrian Secretary of State and the Papal Nuncio in Vienna, and we passed along without any detention. My masonic certificate helped me quietly often.

At Bologna, the landlord of the hotel I stopped at, on seeing my name, recollected that my father used to stop, forty years ago, at his father's hotel in Würtemberg. And I recollected, after hearing his name, that I used to be there, with my father, and often played with him, we being of the same age. He treated me, of course, very well, on hearing this, and assisted me in seeing the city well. He took me to the library of the University, and showed me the beautiful graveyard of that city. I little thought then, that I would, in 1881, stand near a fine monument, under which my youthful friend was buried. The monument was too costly and pretensious for such an humble person. In Germany should have been his grave.

We had much trouble and delay on going to Pistoya by railroad, but we were richly repaid at our stoppages, by the grand outlooks we enjoyed, from the Appenines over the planes of Italy. We arrived in Florence in due time, toward the latter part of March, and felt safe and happy. So far I had travelled, so to speak, solitary and alone; that is to say: I had no personal companions. The first evening in Florence, at dinner, I found myself seated adjoining to a lady, that turned out to be from my native city. She was the daughter of the best cutler there, and travelling with her husband, on her marriage trip. He soon introduced himself to me, as a fellow adopted-American citizen, who had lived many years in Matamoras, Texas, where he had made much money during the Civil War, and was now enjoying the world at large, expecting eventually to settle in Hamburgh, his native city. As may be expected, we three soon became a conjunctive trinity, with a woman as the ruling unity. We went out, even the first evening, to take a look at Florence, and to become familiar with it. Next day, on going about, we were joined by a fourth personage, no less a man, than a distinguished ex-officer of Lübeck, Germany. I found, on conversation with him, that he knew the Reimer-Ruge heirs, for whom I had been agent in their West Virginia lands, and he soon recognized our Hamburg friend, as an old acquaintance. Toward evening, our conversation, in English, brought a fifth member into our company, namely: an Irishman, who claimed relationship with me, when he found I had once been clerk of an Irishman in Philadelphia. We five stuck together in sight seeing in Florence, and afterwards in Rome. Once in a while there were temporary additions, but on the whole we remained the original quinary.

The eight days we spent at Florence, were to us one round of gratification. Going sight seeing, as we did, meant for us all gaining double, yea treble, in fact quintuple knowledge. We all brought something to the general stock, and we became common connoisseurs, if only in our own mutual estimation.

Every morning each of us paid in 10 francs to the common treasurer, the Lübeck ex-city-officer, who spoke fluently Italian, and he disbursed, for us all, carriage hire, lunch, extras, and took the brunt of all settlements. Never was there a better Democratic administration. Everything was done under our eyes, and the surplus or deficit was settled every evening. There was mostly a surplus. And we, who were served, had a fine time all day. We saw more, enjoyed more, and both better, than was ever done, or ever will be done again. We were all pleased with the arrangement, and expected it to endure forever; viz: while it lasted.

One day, however, as will always happen, our conjunctive arrangements, came to a fall by a culmination, nobody expected. Our groupe had swollen to the number nine — exactly four too many — and among the new additions were a Prussian State Councillor and a Prussian Judge. We were delighted at first, for they proved both to have full information and it very exact. At dinner they were a little fastidious. But after dinner they returned to their communicative ways. All at once the *two* Prussians differed. The difference was very positive, but to us unimportant. We others were appealed to, as arbiters, but declined. The dispute went on and was undecided, when we were about to quit for the day. The State Councillor saw, that the departing hour had come. Our Treasurer had paid the over-plus to each, so the Judge asked: "When and where do we meet to-morrow morning?" We all looked at each other. None gave a reply. Then they all looked at me with an inquiring look. I blurted out, what I thought to be the wish of the original five: "Nowhere, if you please." In less than a minute we had separated, and each was going to his separate hotel, never to meet again. The original Five met nevertheless next morning at 9 o'clock, to spend the day together, and in the evening agreed to go next morning to go to Rome together. We took the route via Pisa and Livorno, of which journey more the next page. Here I deem it well to state, that a Russian and his lady gave us also one day in Florence, much trouble. They formed two of the dissolved *Nine*. She was unusually handsome, and he was correspondingly jealous, which made matters disagreeable to us all. After dinner the couple left unexpectedly by taking a special conveyance. We never thought of them in the settlement in the evening. There was a surplus. We all got our share. Whether the Russian got his, we never knew and never cared. Who cares for a jealous fool!?

We left Florence early and arrived at Pisa about 9 o'clock.

There conveyances were ready for us, to see all the glories of the place, to-wit: the Leaning Tower, the Dome, il Baptisteria, Campo Santo and Camponile. The arrangements were perfect, and by 3 p. m. we were ready for dinner, and by 4 o'clock, we were on our way to Livorno. There we took rooms over night, saw the great sights, including the waterworks. After a good night's sleep, we departed, next morning, by steamer, to Civita Vechia, where we dined, and arrived in Rome, by railroad, early enough for 6 o'clock dinner at Hotel Minerva. My good countrywoman was the only one of us five, that got sea-sick, but she soon got well again in Rome; her lifelong desire having now been fullfilled.

We went from Livorno by sea, because the land journey, by stage, was reputed unsafe. Indeed, a large portion of Italy was then unsafe for life and property. The larger cities, being under good municipal government, were the most safe. I saw, in 1874, the chief bandit, that caused us apprehensions in 1866, at work, in chains, in Campo Santo, near Rome. He was the handsomest man I ever saw in my life. I must say: that I always considered the tales of highway robbery, of which we heard in 1866, as largely exaggerated. I suspected then, that the exaggerations were a part of the policy of secret orders, that expected, in that way, to counteract all attempts to subject Italy to some foreign yoke. I know, that these reports strengthened, at that time, the belief of many cabinets, that the rectification of Italy could be accomplished only by an inner reformation, through full Italians. It was believed, and I agreed with it, that it would take enormous foreign armies, at excessive cost to do it, through France or Austria, or any foreign intervention; while through Italian self-vindication, it would be done cheap and better. And it proved so eventually.

At Rome, I realized an observation I heard from a professor in Heidelberg, in 1843, to-wit: that all strangers go to Rome, expecting to find the Rome they have in their heads, but they never find it. As I walked through Rome, each of the respective ruins revived in my mind memory of some Rome, that I had been told of in school. I never could place that Rome before me in any one particular period. And in this, there is, a running disappointment, whose sting gets finally dull, as we fully realize the immense difference these is, between the present Rome, and all the Romes that preceded it. We then realize fully, that Rome really represents 24 centuries of attempts to subjugate the World, and that the ruins embody either the admiration or the hatred of mankind at these attempts. I tempered my hatred, by remembering, that Roman subjugation always meant a superior administration of public affairs to the conquered country, and why should we not bless them for that?

We came, as said, to Rome at the close of March, and remained over April. We enjoyed, of course, all the glory of the Carnival, Palm-Sunday and Easter, including the Pope Pio Nonos universal blessing, to the whole world, from St. Peters Cathedral. I noticed, however, that the poet described the best in Italy, in the words:

"The imperturbable sang-froid of nature."

I saw, that amidst the great crowd, that prayed and thanked, Nature paid no respect to God's vice-regent; it reigned and blessed in silence, as it had done for millenniums before.

Through the Pope's banker, Charles Kolb, a countryman of mine, I obtained a private audience with the Pope, to whom my name was known, because my cousin was the Minister of Würtemberg, that negotiated the concordat between the Pope and the King of Würtemberg. It was defeated in the Chambers of Würtemberg, upon the ground, that such a contract should not be made *with the Pope*, but by the free will of the State. They adopted it as a law, without changing a word in it. This was a surprise to the Pope, as he had been made believe, that the King and public authorities of Würtemberg were his friends. Mr. Kolb thought it would be agreeable, to me personally, as well as agreeable to the Pope, to meet the relative of the Minister, who had negotiated the concordat, with his Cardinals, and lost his office for it. As I could not converse with the Pope, not being master of Italian. my audience was rather an empty formality. I was glad, however, to have seen the Pope face to face, pretty much for the same reason, that I had seen Kossuth, Deak, Jackson, Alexander H. Stevens, and other great personages; it steadies a person to have seen them face to face.

From Rome we went by railroad to Naples. We spent there a week. We visited the ruins of Pompeii, ascended Mount Vesuvius on horseback, and returned the same day. By steamer we crossed to Capri. There we entered the blue Grotto, and enjoyed the Bay of Naples in an evening sunset.

There were then still exhibited miraculous sights in the churches of Naples, but I paid no attention to them. I went up, of course, to the spot in the convent, of which is said: "To see it and to die, is enough happiness for any person." I had engaged rooms at Hotel Geneva, on the invitation of the hotelkeeper. A step I do not usually take;

because passengers are apt to be disappointed by such a course. I
found the hotel, however. an excellent one, and was pleased with
my entertainment. I had, on arrival, my pocket picked, but having
not much money with me; only having enough to pay hotel and
such like expenses. Still, my loss was annoying, because I had not
with me any letters of credit on any bankers in Naples. I called on
Meuricoffre & Sorvillo, and they generously relieved me, on my giving them a draft on bankers Ladenburg in Vienna. The draft
was paid, but I had to pay it only two years afterwards, and then
without interest. These Italians are much misunderstood among us.

I had intended to go to Sicily, but had heard so much of robberies and general insecurity there, that I relinquished the idea, and
my companions agreed with me. So we concluded to return to
Würtemberg by steamer from Naples to Genua, and thence by
land via Milano, Verona, Innspruck and Munich to Heilbronn.

CHAPTER LXVI.

MY RETURN VOYAGE TO AMERICA IN 1866.

Our sea voyage from Naples begun in the evening. The run was
delightful on the Bay of Naples. We had a fine sunset and also a
grand moonrise. But during the night, the weather became
extremely tempestuous, and my fair countrywoman, became so sea-
sick by morning, that she begged to be taken ashore at Livorno,
which was done. We proceeded through the country to Genua by
railroad; and this we did by going from Livorno to Bologna, and
thence to Milano. We thus missed seeing Elba as well as Turin
and Genua, as we had intended.

At Milano we received the first intimation, that hostilities were
impending between Austria, Italy and Prussia. Next we were told,
that Italy would be the theater of the coming war. We received
strong hints, that we had better get out of Italy into Tyrol, or else
we would not be allowed to get out at all. We left Milano in the
middle of April, 1866, and, sure enough, we were met at Brescia, and
Verona by large bodies of Austrian troops, under the command of
Arch Duke Albrecht. The Italians were gathering under Gen. La
Marmora. On the other side of the mountains, in Germany, the
Austrians were forming into line, under Gen. Benedeck. We, however, were not molested on our journey, by either of the armies; our
passports showed us to be mere travellers. We were even allowed
to see the sights at Trent. There we saw the church, where the
Great Council met. We were allowed plenty of time also at Innspruck. In Munich we met considerable excitement, and still more
at Stuttgardt. At these points the popular mind was deeply excited
against Prussia, for allying itself with Italy, against Austria. Prussian funds were at a discount. Bismarck played a dark part there.

At my native city, the feeling was also strongly anti-Prussian;

but that did not mean being pro-Austrian. Prussian paper money was not regularly received by merchants. I lost several per cents on some I had taken. Rumors began to circulate, about May 1st, that France might yet be the ally of Austria, but public feeling in Würtemberg, was adverse to any French alliance.

I had purchased my return ticket on the Bremen Lloyd Steamer for the 20th of May, and I thought it necessary, to so arrange my travel, as to have at least one day at Bremen, for my social farewell from friends and relatives. I hastened to get away from Heilbronn by May 15th. My journey, by railroad, to Mayence, passed without interruption, but there my progress was impeded by military trains. At Coblentz, a train, with a large number of cars, with Prussian troops, interrupted our progress. We encountered, at Cologne, about 7,000 troops, some resisted to being sent forward at once. On starting, in the morning, from Deutz, our train was delayed an hour, until an emuette was quelled, and cavalry had driven the infantry into the cars. We reached Hamm late in the evening, and there saw a serious popular commotion, in consequence of the suicide, committed by an apothecary, that was drafted in the army, two days after his marriage. We got at last to Bremen, on the 17th, in the afternoon, and there considered ourselves, for the first time, outside of all army movements.

At Bremen we were, during the whole of the 18th of May, in the midst of friends, and they got up, on the 19th, a small celebration of my 52nd birthday. At this festival, congratulations arrived by telegraph, from Heilbronn and Stuttgardt, also from friends Weniger and Schwede in Vienna. We all felt deep sorrow at the now certain war. It seemed to us, like a relapse into barbarism, that Germans should fight Germans. The general feeling was, that Prussia was most to blame.

On the 20th we left Bremen, with a stiff northwesterly breeze, and reached South Hampton 30 hours afterwards. There we were detained a day. We left by Bremen steamer for New York, where we arrived ten days afterwards. At New York I was detained but a day, and arrived at home the first week in June.

During the rest of the year 1866, I did, what the mass of the American people did, to-wit: I tried to get to rights, among so much that was wrong. The first thing that I did, was to write articles, under the headings: "Blamed Germany" and "Money", for the German Monthly, published in Chicago. The object of the articles, was: to take out of German-Americans the conceit, that Germany was particularly wrong in the war. The article on money, was to disabuse the popular mind of the idea, that America was particularly *right* as to money. I resumed also my position as occasional correspondent to the "Crisis" in Columbus, and the "Commercial Advertiser" in New York. I wrote also, that year, articles for the

"Fackel", a paper published by Ludwig. The articles had the heading: "The Puritan in China." I had the five articles published in pamphlet form, and extensively circulated. This little book gave me a larger reputation, than anything, that I have ever written. It went to show, how unjust Puritan clergymen were toward other religions, especially the Chinese, and that their injustice arises from the self-infatuation, with which they underrate others, and overrate themselves. They do not, for instance, perceive, that "Taoism" is as to Buddhism in China, what Methodism is in America as to Christianity, namely: the carrying to sharp—false—extremes, doctrines, that were originally moderate, if not wise. In my speech, at Harvest Home, in my neighborhood, I exposed the same error with reference to political parties. I showed, for instance, that States, Counties and Townships, were adopted in the United States, for divisions and sub-divisions, from mere imitations of other home countries, without fully comprehending the necessities, that caused the original establishments of such organs. Our ideas were therefore mere fancies, and the organization of our local institutions was slipshod; and they would therefore have to be reconstructed in the course of time, as defects would show themselves. We got to the Statesright Doctrine, by assuming principles to be in our Constitution, that were really not there; and our Civil War arose out of these very political assumptions. Taoism in China, and Methodism here, have carried the agitation on religious doctrine to extremes in a similar way.

I wrote, by request, a series of articles on County Reform for the Commercial, and was paid for them $100, without me making any demand. I was astonished at this liberality of Mr. Halstead. It was the first money, I had ever received from a newspaper, for articles written by me. Mr. Halstead renewed his liberality afterwards, by paying me, for letters I wrote on my Southern tour, $150. I responded that Fall to an invitation by Democrats for a speech, at Plaineville, Hamilton County; another at Wooster, Wayne County, and one at Hamilton, Butler County. These speeches made some stir, for their party-free tenor, and their reasonings from statistics, that could not be denied; they made impressions upon the public, that last to this day.

CHAPTER LXVII.

I AM DRAWN AGAIN INTO POLITICS.

The candidacy for Congress — 1866 — of the Arch demagogue, Sam. Carey, with Dick Smith, as his opponent, excited the public mind deeply for its incongruity with anything like decent politics. The whole thing was, in my opinion, an intrigue on the part of Carey. He found the Democratic party, that he had so bitterly opposed all his life, a convenience for his plan. He took advantage of that party, because it was perfectly ravenous for power. A large portion of the Democratic party revolted, however, against this prostitution of their party. And they importuned me, to run for Congress, and thus, if possible, defeat the nefarious scheme. I declined to have myself used for that purpose, but I was willing to go before the people and to discuss the question fairly. Cary was the advocate of an out and out Greenback policy; in other words he was for an irredeemable paper currency. I was willing to support any public man, regardless of his party affiliatious, provided, he was not guilty of such a downright fallacy or wrong. I did not care for being drawn into the political arena, especially not into a Congressional contest; but I could not stand by, and allow a man, who had all his life made temperance his hobby, now drop that subject entirely, and use it, underhandedly, for a stepping-stone for his political ambition. S. C. had been all his life the bitter foe of every principle, advocated by the Democratic party. He had been the persecutor of the emigrant element of our Union, and it was certainly hypocritical for him, now to be the candidate of the very elements and very party, he had fought for years. I asked: if this would not degrade our elections, into a mere scramble for office, between bad public men? Would not that cause a total popular demoralization? I claimed, that there was a reaction, and a very proper reaction, among the great body of voters, against the present utter demoralization of the people on the subject of money. And I insisted, that it had come through the abuse, in the issue of greenbacks, during the war. And I asserted, that the crucial question then was: whether this awakening should be sized by political dissemblers, and be turned into a brazen paper money harlotism, or whether the old Constitutional principles of money should be revived? Had there been no resistance then, and we would stand now, not only before a silver fraud, but before a sweeping anarchy on the subject of money on all points. Sam. Carey was elected, but he failed utterly in his attempts to mislead the people.

I enjoyed many prosperous events in 1867. We were receiving every month good news of the progress of our son Edward in Europe. Edward had been, besides Tübingen, also in Berlin. My daughter Caroline, who had been sent over also, was progressing well in my native town. Edward and Caroline had joined in a journey through Austria and Italy, and were coming home through France, England and Scotland. My son Louis was preparing for High school in Cincinnati, and my younger children were attending the Common schools in Dent, and were assisted in their education by our usual family readings in German and English.

Other happy events in the families, with whom we associated, gave us much joy. Two ladies were married to two young gentlemen, whom we esteemed very much, namely: Hochstetter and Laist. Less deserving of favorable mention were my continued connections with the railroad interests, already mentioned. We had to experience the truth of the old proverb:

"While the wise think, the scamps think also, and act first."

My railroad connections had involved me in an investment of $2000 in a Coal Company, near Zanesville, that called itself Delcarbo, and that placed me in an equivocal position. I had made the investment, from the sole motive of relieving the Railroad Company of her being overcharged in her coal supplies. A new directory, that came into the Delcarbo, made an effort, to overcharge the Railroad Company even more, than the coal dealers had done, that formerly supplied it.

They were defeated, because the coal fields turned out, not to be as good as expected. The investment proved therefore a double loss, to-wit: of the money invested, and in reputation. I did not lose as much as the others, because I gave early my $2000 stock to my son Edward, when he married, and he sold it also soon for $1500, to get his furniture and other things he wanted. It warned me for life against any future investment of that kind. That was all I gained.

One incident occurred during 1867, which fed my mysticism in reference to the gypsy prophecy. It will be remembered, that she prophesied to me, that I bore a charmed life and that any person, who would injure me would sooner or later have to suffer for it. The incident I referred to, consisted in the fact, that the leader of the mob that intended to burn my house over my head under the excitement, following the assassination of Lincoln, committed suicide in the winter of 1867. It was, however, but for a moment, that this matter mystified me. It soon passed out of my mind, as one of the disagreeable events connected with our war. That war embodied a monstrous amount of mystification.

I have regretted ever since, one act of mine in 1867, namely: the enlargement of my house in Dent after the model of a mansion I had seen near Florence. I let my pride, which made me wish to have the finest house in the neighborhood, run away with my judgment. I ought to have seen, that it was not an enlargement of my house I wanted, but rather a diminution. My family was rapidly growing smaller by the marriages of my children. It cost me several thousand dollars, without really adding to my and my family's comforts. It in fact added burdens to my wife in house cleaning and general household duties. But notwithstanding all this, I liked, for years, to stand on top of my house and take a good look over the fine outlook it afforded for many miles, and say to myself, that I had at least carried an excellent plan for a house, from Florence to the hills near Cincinnati. And it is, as I write, in 1892, a feeling of reproach to me, that now I have sold this my house and farm, and that none of my family are likely to live in it after I am dead. I feel, how evanescent everything is in America. We

have not even a persistence of attachments to the very homes we
built up and beautified!

CHAPTER LXVIII.

AMERICAN POLITICS BECOME BARREN IN 1868.

The year 1868 was, politically speaking, for the United, States a
barren one. Society, as well as government, were wide of the mark,
in their policies; even the wisest suggestions fell stillborn to the
ground. The great leaders of the Republican party, wanted confirmation of their party rule, while the better elements of society
saw, that the true interests of the country needed a government,
that would give to the best minds the reins. The more brutal Republicans made Grant their hero. They lost sight of the great historic truth, that the military leader in a Civil War, can never be the
right civil ruler afterward. The wiser and more honest republicans
were for Chase, and he was then willing to be the leader. Neither
party wanted Johnson, the accidental successor of Lincoln. They
had an inner sense: that men that gain power, through a fatality
are not the proper factors in a country's destiny. The democratic
partisans had, unfortunately, but one desire, and that was: to get
into power. Pendleton was their first choice, but he had a very decided opposition against him, within his own party. Seymour had
a large body of supporters, but his poor health was a serious objection to him. A large element of the party had memories of a former
successful combination between democrats and republicans, and
this element looked again to Chase, as the man through whom they
could accomplish their objects. Chase had for his main supporter,
in this course, Alexander Long, of Ohio. He had aided Chase for
U. S. Senator in 1849; and he had a large body of followers in the
democratic party. It will be seen, from all this, that the fates were
spinning their web most busily in and about Cincinnati; and that
none of us could very well avoid being drawn into the current. I
knew too much of Chase's weaknesses to be his ardent supporter,
but I knew also too much of his value and capacities, to oppose his
becoming the leader in a movement, that might defeat Grant. I
helped therefore, all I could. my neighbor and early friend:
Alexander Long, in his agitation for Chase.

The situation was very complicated; the several cliques were
each trying to secure the more influential presses in the several par
ties. Such a clique had possession of the Cincinnati Enquirer, and
the representatives of it, were busy in fixing up the democratic convention to suit their plottings. They were smart enough to have
influences toward Grant *and* Chase, though their favorite object
was, to secure the nomination of the Democrat most favorable to
them. At the democratic convention, the ruling spirit of that paper,
had begun his course. by avowing himself to be the friend of Pendle-

ton; but he was really for anybody, to whom he could say: "I made thee President!" Wash McLean was this leader, and he found, on the morning of the convention, when votes had been taken on the nomination, that power was about slipping out of his hands, and that on the next ballot Chase would be nominated, *and he being known to be opposed to it!* He now approached Long, and asked for a delay of ten minutes, to give time to see, whether there was really no chance for Pendleton? The name of Pendleton was really a blind to his real designs. It acted on Long, because, as he was the townsman of Pendleton, he could not well stand in the attitude of refusing to give him the last chance. Long felt sure of Chase's nomination. Wash McLean used the ten minutes to rally Seymour's friends, and to get him the nomination. This shift really made Grant President, because Seymour was sure to be defeated at the election, and this enabled Grant to win. Long had mentioned the offer of McLean to me, and I had warned him instantly and persistently against it, but for reasons stated, Long went into the trap, and was fatally ensnared by it. Chase was defeated, and could never again rally a party around him. But Wash McLean had also played his last trump, by his trickery in this instance.

I must now call attention to the queer state of affairs in this Presidential election of 1868. There was, in both, the democratic and republican parties, a majority of the voters against the two respective candidates, Seymour and Grant; and the result, that was brought about, in the election of Grant, was really the product of a very small minority of the people of the United States. This state of things existed already before the election, and the public speakers had really to condone for the wrongs of their respective parties. They had really to invent reasons: why the great body of the respective parties should vote in violation of their better convictions? Everybody admitted, indeed, asserted it, that the game of blind man's buff, that was being played by both parties, should cease, but how to bring it about, nobody knew, nor could suggest. The country entered thus into the administration of Grant, blindfolded, as to all the great questions, that were likely to arise.

The main question had been, for some time, the money question. We have seen, how perplexed the body of the people were, through intrigues, gotten up by such demagogues, as Sam Carey. The resumption of specie payment, which all the good people desired, seemed further off than ever. I suggested, through the Commercial, the adoption of a compromise, framed after the "Seisachtia" of Solon. It meant, like the proposition of the wise Athenian, to settle the existing indebtedness in the United States, both public and private, on the *de facto status*, that had existed then, and for at least 15 months; and had, therefore, attained a rightful basis by the common acquiescence of the people and their government. My suggestion was denounced as a fraud, because it did not adhere to the ancient dollar, but meant to substitute for it a dollar, whose value had been fixed by actual common acquiescence. I tried to show the fallacy of this accusation, but failed, because the public mind had been induced to believe, that public honor required a reform by which the hundred cent dollar should become again the standard of all settlements. Thus the plan of Sherman was adopted, which meant, first of all: the payment of all existing indebtedness on the hundred cent basis, when in fact it was incurred on the $66\frac{2}{3}$ cent basis, which, expressed in figures, means that for $666,000 borrowed $1,000,000 should be paid. It meant in the next place; that the real question, to-wit: the reinstation of the actual policy of the Constitution, as to money, shall be left unsettled and transmitted into a confused future: the very one we have now before us in the popular cry for the free coinage of silver, and the issue of 2 per cent bonds, as the basis of security for a National Bank Currency.

I must beg the reader to remember that there was, under Sherman's policy, no real resumption, nor indeed any real settlement of the money question; and our money both as paper and coin remained unsound, and is unsound to-day. One part of society is still at a disadvantage to the favored part. The respective individuals have changed, but the principle at stake has remained the same. The Government is, moreover, not performing its Constitutional functions: "To coin money and regulate the value thereof."

I then, as now, saw that the way out of the difficulties, that surrounded us, consisted in learning by the experience of the past, and to adopt a permanent policy by the wisdom it teaches. I might refer to the various articles I wrote upon this subject at that time, but will simply mention that I wrote them for the Cincinnati Commercial, and the Commoner, and that I published occasionally pamphlets and made public speeches upon the subject. I feel grateful to the editors of those papers, for affording me opportunities for these publications; and must mention now especially Mr. Hassaureck, as editor of the Volksblatt, and besides Henry Reed, then editor of the Enquirer; both agreed with me.

In my family affairs in 1868, there was a cheering progress through my two younger sons. I got Louis passed into High School, and I took Rudolf to Wittenberg College, at Springfield, Ohio. My daughter Carrie returned, June 4th, from Europe. I attended three weddings, namely: the two already mentioned, and that of my niece, Annie Seifert.

I continued my relations with the C. W. & Z. R. R., but it was well understood, that the tie was loosening. In my private affairs, I kept fully in view, that I was growing old, and that a reduction in all my business and property relations, was to be my aim. The collection of rents, on my city property, was becoming every day more burdensome and precarious; and taxes, assessments and repairs, costlier and more certain on a rising scale. I thought I saw ahead an embodiment of our public wrongs in socialistic mistakes. I remembered an old adage, whose source I cannot remember, that says:

"Falsely presumed *best* governments end in having the worst institutions." And another:

"Neglected political reforms eventuate in anarchic conditions."

I kept up an extensive correspondence with literary friends in Europe, and this enabled me to pursue my comparative studies in the different literatures and gaining constantly in positive knowledge.

March 26th, 1868, I lost an old friend, namely: the banker Adae. His death left a void among us Germans of Cincinnati, that was never filled again. He had faults, that marred very much his influence for good. One of these was: that he lived, both at home and while travelling, on too high a scale. He failed, therefore, to gather capital sufficient to be a safe banker. After his death, this weakness led to the failure of the firm.

This year I wrote my book: "Wine Makers' Manual." Robert Clarke & Co. were my publishers, on their own account. I received a percentage on the sale, by annual account. It yielded but small sums, and yet I was satisfied, because the book was a good one, and was really of service to the public. It did not increase my popularity among the temperance people. Copies of it are being sold yet; but I receive no percentage any more. Why not? Who can tell?

CHAPTER LXIX.

I FEEL MYSELF IN A GENERAL DECLINE.

The year 1869 was, in most of my affairs, a slacking off in business and activity; and indications were multiplying, that with my LX. year my life had passed its climax, and that I was then on the decline. I felt no chagrin at this, for I had expected this change of my life to come sooner than it did. It mortified me however, a little, that much less sincere efforts for the common benefit made by others, of my cotemporaries, were more successful than mine, both in wealth and reputation. I concluded that there was a tendency going on here, that enured to those who fell in with this tendency. That could consist, in my opinion, in nothing else, than an unscrupulous co-operation in carrying on, our so-called: public institutions, that were chiefly the helpmates of semi-public money corporations and interests. I was opposed to that.

My reading and thinking was directed to find the full truth on these matters, both in American and European publications. It pained me to have to find, that, what the first contained, were almost all special pleadings and casuistic reasonings; whilst the second gave positive arguments from principles and axioms that were right, and had a general application. This made me conscious of an omnipotence of social forces over political government here. And it explained to me: why there is among our prominent men such a hankering for gaining positions in corporations and public jobs. Yea I perceived now the truth, there was, in my cousin Boettinger's remark: that there are really no politics in the United States at all, but much social imperiousness, both in private and public affairs, party rule included. Our politicians are only Politicians in a bad sense. I read, as I may as well mention, besides the daily papers and periodicals published here, also the North American Review, Harper's Magazine, Littell's Living Age, Unsere Zeit, the Vienna Reform, Popular Science Quarterly, Stein's Verwaltungs Lehre, and last, not least, Holtzendorf's "Principles of Politics"; and of course I compared my readings with the information and literature, from which I had been instructed in early life; as well as later, through conversation and reading.

I may be asked: what use was all your reading and study? I answer, that: the influence of the forecast, wisdom and knowledge of such men as Benton, Wright, and also of the still earlier American writers, such as Franklin and Jefferson, was waning in the United States more and more; and I thought I discovered in this fact a falling off of a connection, that used to exist here, between home learning and works of literature in the world in general. And I deemed it my duty, that, so far as I was concerned, I would at least resume the old connection with the worlds scientific development. I may express this my desire in one word: I was determined to remain *cosmopolitan*. This my literary tendency, was followed in my lecture in that year on: "The Humbug of Anglo-Saxonism." And in it I wanted to show, that the worship of Anglo-Saxonism, was an aberration from the true cosmopolitanism. The latter, and not nativism, I regarded as the basis, upon which, we gained our independence, and made it, the basis of all our real national glory I contended therefore, that Americans have no need, to carry forward into the new world, a special mythical derivation of its nationality. *It* was certainly made up of the world at large. The "Anglo-Saxons", whatever the word may mean, deserved no such honorable distinction. It was a mere invention in England, to hide the humiliation the Anglo-Saxons felt, when they were conquered by the Danes. At first I was abused for my lecture, then came some vindication; and I have not seen another eulogy of Anglo-Saxonism in our press since. And I am very glad of this!

My son Edward returned from Europe on May 18th. He was improved in many ways. The lectures he heard, on jurisprudence, in the German Universities, improved his knowledge of law. We were very glad to see him back among us, and he soon after entered the law office of Judge Coffin, and subsequently took up a general law practice.

In the year 1869 I lost, by death, two dear friends; first, my cousin Böttinger, at Lyons. Of him I have already spoken, and have now to add: that his wealth was distributed among about two dozen of his relatives, of whom the most important was his younger brother Henry, who was a disciple of Liebig, in the science of chemistry, and was employed in several large establishments in England. These relatives all bless his memory. The second was Timothy C. Day, who at one time played an important part for good in Cincinnati, in its politics. I wrote a necrology of my friend Day for the Commercial, which I have read again lately; and I still think, that Cincinnati has never given him the credit he deserves for his hostility to the Miami Tribe, and similar secret political societies. And to this I must add: Cincinnati has never done its duty toward counteracting the tyrannies, that originated in such political combinations. Is there a Cincinnatian, who can claim his city to be a real *res publica*?

My oration, at the German Pioneer's celebration, in May 1869, was first a surprise to those who heard it, then a success, when published. And it is still quoted, so far as it has been brought to the notice of our public, as having contributed to a better understanding of the true value of immigration to this country. The surprise of the audience arose from their believing at first, that my speech violated one of their constitutional prohibitions, which forbid any politics being discussed before them. I showed them, however, in a few words, that immigration is not really a political, but a social question. And this brought out an important point in our public affairs; to-wit: the one already several times alluded to, that we are much more socialistic in all our public conduct, than we think. Very few, here, understand that our party government is really a setting aside of political government, especially that contained in our constitutions. I am indebted to my friend Kapp, who has since died, for the success of my lecture, because he brought to public notice the main idea of it: that immigration has an immense value to the United States, that can be expressed in dollars and cents. *Engels* calculation having the same basis; to them I referred in my speech.

I attended the free religious convention, held in August 1869 in Louisville, over which President Fillmore presided, and for the same mixed reasons, that brought the great majority of those that attended there.

Thirty-two years previous, I had gone to Louisville to get married, and the convention was a very good opportunity for me to go there, once more, with the wife I had then married, and to enjoy ourselves, for a day or two, in Louisville. The convention was not so much a religious, or otherwise *free* assembly; it was a means of collecting together those American citizens, that wanted to find a less narrow bond of union, than the one the republican party provided, under Puritan leadership. William Corry accompanied me, and so did my Israelite friend Loth, and we three certainly represented a body, that worked—do not laugh,—"without distinction of party, race or previous servitude." I recorded in my diary, that I delivered a speech, which was well received; but my memory does not serve me either as to its contents, nor purport; and as I have preserved neither synopsis nor copy, I will say no more about it. I expect the reader's thanks, for this.

My diary informs me moreover, that I did, then and there, a much better thing, than make a speech, to-wit: I took my wife and myself to the old minister of the gospel, a Presbyterian, Rev. Dr. Humphries, that married us in 1837. He received us kindly, renewed his blessings and divine admonitions. I thought that our revisit of Louisville was a very good demonstration for free religion, even though our physical decline was very visible.

CHAPTER LXX.

REVIVALS OF EARLIER DAYS.

The year 1869 was in many ways a renewal of old friendships to me. On my journey to New York, I saw again: Messrs. Roelker & Möllmann, Bankers, that aided me years before in the negotiation of the sale of the Tunnel Railroad Bonds; also Bernard Roelker, called the "Chancellor", for he was one of the few representatives in the United States, of the study of law, such as are found in German Universities. In Columbus I met again my friend, Mr. Klippard, Secretary of the State Board of Agriculture. The sweetest revivals of older friendships, I found, however, in my own rural home, through persons, who came there uninvited, trusting to a cheerful welcome, for memories of: "Auld lang syne."

Such a one came to me on September 12th, 1869, in the person of F. L. Fleischman, who lived in Cincinnati in 1833, and married, like myself, a Cincinnati girl. He started the first Lager Beer Brewery in Cincinnati, and made the first literary German address in Cincinnati. In 1843 I met him in Stuttgardt, as American Consul. He had been appointed such by General Harrison in 1841. There he befriended me, by presenting me officially, as an American citizen, to some of the high Dignitaries of State, some of whom, however, remarked, that they knew me before, as one of their countrymen. After his recall to Washington, and his appointment to the Topographical Bureau, I met him later again, at the Congressional Library in Washington, and we renewed our acquaintance. When he came to see us at Dent, in 1869, he stayed with us for dinner, and we exchanged memories enough in conversation to last us for years.

Another old acquaintance came to see me in 1869; no less a personage than R. B. Hayes, then Governor of Ohio, and one the best we ever had. He afterwards became President in 1877. I learned to know him at the Cincinnati Club, in 1850, when Halstead, Noyes, Mussey, Victor Smith, etc., were members. The Club then met on Seventh, near Vine street. I voted for Hayes for Governor of Ohio, every time he run, for I regarded him as a model Governor. He expressly filled the bill. I did not, however, vote for him for President in 1876, because a man, much fitter than he, for *President*, — Tilden — run for the office. Hayes was then the reverse of what he was in 1869, to-wit: a "marplot"; for he kept out of the Presidential Chair the man of all men, then needed therein. Nevertheless, Hayes and myself remained friends.

The year 1869 remains memorable to me, most, on account of the fact, that then the outrage upon Municipal Government was perpetrated, to-wit: the building of the Southern R. R. at the expense of Cincinnati's money, and, what is worse, at the cost of the integrity of the city and its voters. I now more than ever feel, that I was right in my opposition to that measure. Being a firm believer in the construction, ownership and administration of public roads by the respective Governments interested in them, by honest methods, I am only the more jealous and adverse to any counterfeit public construction policy. And such was the bill for the Southern R. R. It authorized the direct taxation of the tax payers of Cincinnati for thirty millions of dollars on the pretense of an indirect benefit to them. This railroad thus built, is now administered for profit by a corporation under a lease, in which very few citizens, if any, have any honest interest. The road is situated out of Ohio. The States of Tennessee and Kentucky are the main beneficiaries of it. They exercise, in fact, control over it, but contribute only a very trifling sum to its construction and administration. The laws of Ohio, Kentucky and Tennessee, under which the road exists. are declared a 'contract between these States'; but this contract has never received the sanction of Congress, as the U. S. constitution requires. We have thus a railroad law, full of abnormities, and I repeat: that this is an outrage, because a fully legal and normal way could and should have been found to establish the road.

The father of all this iniquity was Alexander Ferguson, a native of Cincinnati; but he is only one of hundreds of others, who were born in Cincinnati, and made it the object and study of their lives, to get up projects, by which their personal and individual interests are secured at the cost of the city of their birth. And I say, it is a harrowing thought to me, that the most distinguished sons of Cincinnati are most noted for making themselves rich and powerful, at the expense of their native city. That accursed covetousness is gnawing at its vitals now.

Another reminiscence of that period, more pleasant than the one just spoken, was the founding of the German Pioneer Society, in May 26, 1868; followed, in 1869, by the establishment of a Monthly

Journal, under the editorship of Dr. Brühl.   At his request I contributed the biographies of the following early pioneers: Henry Roedter, Dr. Oberndorf, Engineer Roebling, L. Rehfuss, C. F. Adae, also the history of the founding of the Volksblatt, as well as other articles.   These compositions tried me hard, because I had reasons for using the opportunity, thus given me, to get even with these several persons, for some one or other injury they had inflicted on me.   I followed nevertheless the old rule: "De mortuis nil nisi bonum", but not forgetting Heine's rule: "that, in writing the life of a cotemporary, an author should bear in mind, that every human being's history contains. if well presented, one or more useful lessons, that should be brought out for the benefit of society." I think, I have have done the latter and forborn the former, in the articles mentioned. Subsequently I became myself editor of the paper, of which we will hear further along. I can say now; the establishment of the Pioneer Society and its Journal was an indefinite response to a feeling among many German immigrants, that a certain reverence for immigration to, and work in this country, is — per se — due to them.   This feeling was, in my opinion, carried too far, when it ripened into an assumption, that the older immigrants are also to be treated as superior.   I think, there should be due discrimination. We should not forget: that Europe has lately and for centuries, brought up generations, that were superior to their predecessors. This rising scale of civilization, has in pursuance of immigration imprinted itself on America, and we find it also in the different pioneer immigrations. I think, we should never loose sight of the points, just mentioned. It is the fundamental reason, why America should respect Europe, from the landing of Columbus to the latest free immigration and commercial intercourse.

As a matter of some interest I will mention: that I was in 1869 chosen a member of the Board of Education of Green Township, the only Township office, I ever held.   I had been District Director for many years previous, and my election, to the Township Board, was a promotion, of which I felt very proud.   I aided, while in that position, the efforts, that were then being made, to bring the schools in Green Township into a much better condition.   I said, in my diary, in support of my action: "The District Directors have promoted me into a Township office. So I will promote our Township schools.' My usefulness, in this particular, is the only public usefulness of mine, that never was questioned.

CHAPTER LXXI.

UNTOWARD INFLUENCES ON MY AFFAIRS IN 1870.

In 1870 I passed out of the service of the Zanesville Railroad entirely, and I was glad of the opportunity afforded me.   I had done a good deal of service for the railroad, and even risked money, as already explained, but at last I went out of it, without serious loss. I have already adverted to the loose manner, in which railroad enterprises are started and prosecuted in the United States, and I wish to say a few more words on this disagreeable subject. It is disagreeable, because I parted from it with the conviction, that the greater part of the time and means, I devoted to them, has been rendered useless, both to me and the public, for the want of correct legislation on the subject, and the neglect, to provide proper public administration over it.

I cannot now name a single function that could be performed, either by me or my colleagues, upon a strictly correct basis. Being acquainted with similar public affairs in my native land, especially as to railroads, I can say that *there*, all this, is entirely different. There is not a laborer, employee or officer, in their kind of institutions, that is not required to act upon correct conditions, and to follow appropriate orders. Nor is there a dollar of money received or expended in them, except for legally prescribed considerations. And if now we sum it all up, we see: that railroads, here, begin in defective organizations; that they are defectively constructed and financiered, and that they pass finally into a defective administration; all being conducted by a mixed body of laborers, employees and officers, who have, the engineers perhaps alone excepted, no definite functions prescribed to them by law. They have, using a homely term, to shift for themselves as best they may. Of course all their operations are, more or less, mere speculations. I parted out of the Zanesville railroad with regrets, that I have had to labor in such a medley of defectiveness very hard; and at last without any corresponding success to those concerned. And I felt bound, in writing this my life, to devote a page or two to this subject.

Similarly thwarted have I been in some other public matters, which I shall now mention. Early in the year 1870, I was spoken to: about assisting in efforts to bring McMicken's bequest for a University in Cincinnati, into complete fulfillment. I was asked to present my views before the Legislature, in a public address. I consented, and spoke before the evening session of the Senate, at which the Governor and members of the lower House were also present. I explained, that a University could easily be established in Cincinnati, if only all the public means then available, for this purpose, and partly in operation, were combined together in one Collegiate Institution, for higher academic purposes. The Legislature adopted, a few days afterward, these views, and passed an enabling act. The University Board has since made several efforts to carry out this enabling act, but has always again relapsed in a mixture of indifference and insufficiency, that seems to be its second nature. The trustees and the faculty have not their proper functions, and the public stands still puzzled by this inadequacy. I think it arises from a want of comprehensiveness of the public organization, as well as administration, that is requisite in this matter. The schools, both high and low, have, not yet, in Ohio received their proper unity; that is to say: the Universities, Colleges, High Schools, Intermediate and Common Schools, are without proper action, interaction and reaction; each has a separate sphere, and there is really no conjunctive administration. There should be a real State ministry and County and City officials under it. In other words, we should have a State department over our entire school system, and it should direct all school administration, including Colleges and Universities. The local boards would then get upon a higher plane, and so would the schools also.

I was very much pleased, when, at the beginning of the Winter, notice was given, that the faculty, of Cincinnati University, would give a course of free lectures to the public; and I attended them regularly; much pleased by the manner of treatment and the subjects discussed. But the course was entirely too limited, and never was participated in by the general public. I took from the whole procedure, that the University was still troubled by the defectiveness already adverted to. I had urged upon the board the previous Winter, the giving of a course of lectures on Sunday, similar in character to those I had participated in, at the University in Würzburg, in Germany; but my suggestion was rejected with the usual excuses; and I left the subject with the apprehension, that we shall have similar futile attempts for some time, unless we effect, through the Legislature, a thorough reorganization of Common and High Schools with our University, as already suggested.

March 4th, 1870, the Auditor of State, a republican, appointed me to be: special examiner of the treasury of Butler County. Rumors had come to his ears of a defalcation there; and he appointed me, as he wrote to me, because he had special confidence, that I would examine strictly, and report fearlessly, though the suspected treasurer was a democrat. I regarded the appointment, under these circumstances, as a mark of confidence to me, and as very honorable to the Auditor of State; and I accepted it. I saw very soon, after arriving at the treasury, and while beginning my examination, that it would take much fortitude to undertake the job, and to carry it through firmly. The treasurer, and the clique around him, counted on my party relations to them, that I would yield to their requests to temporize; but when they found themselves mistaken, they surrendered, under the advice of T. C. Campbell, a former member of Congress. He, at last, brought me the keys to the vault in the treasury, and the "combination" to open it. I had ordered from Hall's Safe Factory in Cincinnati an expert mechanic, to break the safe open, if necessary, and was just about ready to do this, when the keys were brought. When now we opened the safe, we found it gutted of all money, except a bag of coppers and some Mexican bonds, the property of a relative of the Campbells, being only placed in the treasury for deposit as a favor from the treasurer. On examination of the Treasurer's and Auditor's books, it was found, that the whole defalcation amounted to about $110,000. At a meeting with the County Commissioners, I insisted upon immediate steps being taken to sue the Treasurer and his sureties, and to hunt up and prosecute the guilty persons, that were the accomplices of the Treasurer. I named as a proper attorney for this purpose, Mr. Ramsey, of Cincinnati, but there were in the County Commissioner's office two Commissioners, one a tricky Englishman, and the other a slippery German, and they constituted a majority of the Commissioners. They caused delays, by which the proper time went by, and eventually the County lost the whole amount of the defalcation. I reported at once my proceedings to the Auditor of State, but no further decisive action was taken; the result was as heretofore stated. I received for services and expenses $250, and was publicly attacked in the papers by the hired tools of the defaulting Treasurer and his friends. It convinced me that, what I have expressed generally, was true also of Ohio, to-wit: that "government in the United States will prove weak, whenever it has to make an effort to subject the *ruling social forces*, especially those who manipulate party politics, to correction or punishment."

The State officers were willing and anxious to aid me, but the statutes, in the premises, were found faulty and weak, just as I have already pointed out, as to railroads and other public concerns. The Legislature never examined even into my recommendations; and they rejected my proposition to establish an administrative Court, with the necessary powers, to have at their command regular expert inspectors and examiners, and to issue disciplinary degrees and orders, so as to subject the whole public service, and every public account to frequent scrutiny and correction. Some denounced my propositions as "utopian"! What next?

April 27th, 1870, I was appointed, with Mr. Staley, by the Probate Court, one of the examiners of the Treasury of Hamilton County. We found some irregularities, but no defalcation. One main impediment to our investigation was the long standing imperfection, of the County's organization and mode of administration; under which all examinations proved more or less illusory. It consisted in the old obsolete grand duplicate system, under which all tax collections had to be made. Under it, it was utterly impossible to state definitely and promptly, how much money there should be in the Treasury at any given time? The Auditor's and the Treasurer's books never squared, nor did the amount, that should really be in the Treasury correspond with that of a complete rendering of the accounts. And yet the Cashier could show promptly, that he had the amount on hand, which the Auditor reported to us, and that his balance was correct. We reported these organic defects, to the Probate Court, and recommended a system of keeping accounts, such as is in force in the U. S. Treasury Department, by which no money comes into the Treasury, nor goes out of it, except by the knowledge of the Auditors, by which the uncollected taxes were also fully reported. The old influences, that prevail usually in County affairs in Ohio, prevailed also in Hamilton County then, and succeeded in smothering our report. Some better influences got control in the Treasury afterward, and introduced partial reforms; but the obsolete defective grand duplicate system, still prevails over the whole, and is in the way of all thorough reform.

In the Fall of 1870 there were three National Conventions, which I attended. 1) the Free Religion Convention in Cincinnati. In it I delivered the lecture, that appeared in the 'Index' afterwards, and had the title: "Will the coming man attend church? It gave me much notoriety, but also misjudgment. The pious called me an Atheist, and the irreligious called me a mocker at the church. I had to feel also the unveracity of Mr. Vickers, who was the Clergyman of the Unitarian Church, in which the convention met. In public he depreciated my lecture, but when I spoke to him privately, and wanted to correct some of his misconceptions, he told me, that he approved my lecture, and had made the depreciating remarks only, to reconciliate Rev. Challens, a bigoted man. Several Congregationalists, who were present, were taken aback through my lecture. In it I really meant to discuss the biggest question of the day, to-wit: "The future culture of adults." I meant to show, that Church service and attendance was not sufficient, to furnish that culture. My lecture is among my papers, were I read it lately again, and still approve it.

2) The Prison Reform Convention, also in Cincinnati. In it I met again my fellow commissioners in the establishment of the State Reform Farm: Messrs. Foote and Ladd. The first named rather surprised me, by introducing me very pompously to the Convention, as "The Father of the State Reform Farm system". I had to disclaim his eulogy, and state: that I got the idea in Mettray, in France, and that I succeeded only partially, in having the model I followed, carried out in Ohio. Foote really spoiled my intended remarks, for I could not well deliver them, after my explanation. I had to learn practically, how hurtful indiscrete friends can be.

3) The Immigrant Convention called, in Indianapolis, by such well disposed Americans, as Oliver P. Morton, then U. S. Senator, and Governor Baker, of Indiana.

At that Convention, I met Oliver P. Morton the first time. I found him a truly big-minded great man. The Republicans wronged themselves by taking Grant instead of Morton for the Presidential term of 1868 to 1872. Much unclean work would have been avoided, if Morton had been President, these four years. Moreover, many fatalities, that were neglected, would have been solved and placed in the right direction. I may have been partial to Morton, but the reader will please remember, that we were political opponents, and that I had a good reason for my judgment of Morton, and that was: that he understood well the limited objects of the war, which should be accomplished and no more. He did not want the perpetuation of the war party. He was the right man to organize peace, while Grant, and all other such persons, could only be eager persons, to reorganize and perpetuate strife.

At that convention, I met, for the first time, Dr. Morwitz, of Philadelphia, owner and publisher, of the leading German paper: "The Democrat" of Philadelphia, and of some other 30 country papers, with names too numerous to mention. I found him to be a very practical person, indeed, only too much so; because he gave, the practical, a priority, which, I think, is not always a safe criterion I admit, however, that he was faithful to whatever principles he entertained; I only think that he gave them too much a secondary consideration.

The convention did, as I think, one Good: namely: it brought out the fact, that the immigration question is, in the United States, more one of feeling than of judgment, and that consequently its respective agitation is oftener the product of temporary impulses, that become prejudices, than of any wise reflections on the facts.

The largest number of my contributions to the Press, in that year, went to the "Commoner.". Indeed, I may say: that I was its co-editor. Mr. Corry, the owner, left much of the work to me, because he took, an all absorbing interest, in a patent brick machine, in which he lost ultimately considerable sums of money. Some of my articles had no special print mark, by which to recognize them, a fact that I regretted lately, when hunting them up for use in writing my life.

To the "German Pioneer" of that year, I furnished five articles; towit: the biographies of Schroeder, of Miamisburgh, and Philip Reuss, in Cincinnati, and the three essays: "The Coffee Houses;" "The Future of Germanism in America;" and "Immigration and Emigration." What I said about Coffee Houses is true to-day, they are much in their own way, by the low rank they occupy, as to their mode of catering to social enjoyments.

My reading of the year consisted, as to books, of: Louis Napoleon's Life of Caesar; Winans's—of Baltimore—book on *Ancient Religions;* L. Von Stein's Political Economy; and Krause's Philosophy. I wrote for Torrence, Mayor of Cincinnati, a bill for Treasury Reform. It would, if it had passed, have taken away many unfair emoluments from treasury officials. It was, of course, defeated.

I made, that Fall, a very interesting journey from Cincinnati to Detroit, Chicago, Quincy, St. Joseph and St. Louis. I came back through Indianapolis and Richmond, Ind. At St. Louis I met several friends of my youth yet alive; to-wit: Cronenbold, Bernays and Mrs. Strothhote, formerly Miss Graeser. At Chicago I introduced myself to C. Butz, the publisher of the German Monthly. Also the editors and publishers of the Illinois Staats Zeitung. I was received with ostentatious politeness. I would have liked quiet interviews much better.

In these several cities I was struck with the ephemeral character of much of their development. Their population, their trade, their political status and their social condition, had very little permanence in it; and I thought, that for all of them, it was hard to determine, what would most likely be their future. I only felt certain of one thing: that the people, then there, knew themselves, and their city's future, least; they thought little of the future; they kept ever repeating: *All right!* It was always untrue.

The failure of my son Rudolf and my daughter Amalia in their examination for High School, started me to send them and my daughter Lizzie, with my wife, to German schools, either in Stuttgardt or Heidelberg. The thought once entertained, I adhered to it, and it was finally carried out 1872, as will be stated hereafter. In the Fall of 1870 we moved part of our family; to-wit: Caroline, Amalia, Rudolf and Louis, into the west house of a building of ours on Seventh street, south side, near Western avenue. It was a bad move; for children must not be left to themselves, in the way it was done then and there. I have some very disagreeable remembrances of that period, but they are no longer of any interest to me or the reader. The general happy drift of American life flowed over my mistakes, and washed them away.

CHAPTER LXXII.

MISHAPS PREVAIL IN 1871.

The first mishap occurred early in January. We gave up the intended journey to Germany, on account of private news we got: that war was impending in Europe. That abandonment led to our move on Seventh street, as has already been explained. In May I learned of the death of my brother-in-law Faulhaber, and I feared, that my sister's children would now be placed more or less in a suffering attitude, as his main support, his pension, ceased. These apprehensions of mine became but too true. Their inheritance was, however, not as small as I feared. Eventually one of the daughters got an excellent situation in England, and is now doing well there.

In the Winter of 1871, it was early ascertained, that the Southern Railroad would want at least six million dollars, in addition to the original ten millions. And that meant higher and higher taxes for some time, which, with falling rents and the difficulty of collecting, made my own outlook, as to my income, more and more precarious, and embarrassed me as old age approached. What I had long apprehended, now stood fully before me; to-wit: that not only the whims of Kings are dangerous, to human society; but also those of popular votes. In fact the latter are more so, because the popular mind, once set on an object, of which they expect to realize advantages, will hardly ever again abandon it, until compelled to do so by some very bitter experience, which always comes too late; whilst Kings can be brought under the influence of superior minds easier and earlier, and thus be induced to abandon their projects, when convinced that they are wrong. I feared therefore, that the evils, that were coming up in the affairs of the Southern Railroad, in the shape of more indebtedness and higher taxation, would be even worse than I had predicted, when this measure was adopted in Cincinnati. Schiller's words came to my mind:

"With the perfidious powers of fate,
No safe compact can be made."

Our Civil War had taught many of us, that there was some danger ahead, for our society and government, in consequence of the ease, with which the public mind could be inflamed into excitement; and how, when inflamed, it could be used for the most stupendous false distributions of wealth, through financial measures in regard to money and taxation. And as this sort of manipulation was employed in starting and conducting the Southern Railroad, and its administration, it meant, all the time, robbing the tax-payers of the City of Cincinnati, and to divert the wealth, thus taken, to the pockets ef undeserving individuals. I saw that this process, thus inaugurated, would encourage similar schemes as to other popular measures; since it was all a false conversion of private wealth, of which rogues were largely the beneficiaries.

The German Pioneer had formerly, as already stated, claimed and received my labors gratuitously. I had done this largely at the request of the first editor, Dr. Brühl. In 1871 Dr. Brühl resigned, and he received a successor, whose name I do not recollect, who did not satisfy the wishes of the society. And in 1872 it was proposed to me, that I should become editor, and receive the pay attached. I took the position reluctantly, because I doubted. whether the course I should pursue, would please the great body of members. I had also been of the opinion, that the paper cost the society more than it should. I agreed to assume the editorship, with the understanding, that a change of administration should take place. that would save at least $300 a year to the society. The change consisted in joining the collections with the editorship, to pay for both only the former total cost of $600. Of the pay only half were to go to the editor, and the other half o the collector of dues. I employed my sons for the latter function, and carried on the editorship myself, and thus divided the $600 between us. I edited the paper the most of the year 1872 and part of 1873.

During March, 1872, I undertook, as coarespondent of the Cincinnati Commercial, a journey through the South. I passed through Louisville to Nashville; thence I went to Chattanooga, Atlanta, Augusta, Crawfordsville, Charleston,—Montgomery, Mobile, New Orleans, Oxford, Jackson and Memphis, and from thence I returned to Cincinnati. I corresponded on the way, as stated, for the Cincinnati Commercial. Of the papers, in which my letters were published, I have preserved copies in my library. They are now in the City Library. As already mentioned, I was paid, by the Commercial, for my letters $150, which covered part, at least, of my expenses. This my journey was of great interest to me, because I now obtained much correcter information of the South and its prominent public men.

I had been on a much less extensive tour in the South, in 1858–59, on business for the O. L. I. & Trust Co. In 1844 I had visited Jackson, at his home, near Nashville, Tenn. But my journey in 1872, took place at a time, when the incidents of the Civil War were fresh in everybody's mind, and my journey not only covered more territory, but also a much wider acquaintance with distinguished persons than the previous one. I will only name: A. H. Stephens, Forsyth, Toombs. Tramholm, Semmes, Lamar and Jefferson Davis. I have now very little to add to my letters, to which I must refer. I saw then the Legislatures. of Tennessee, Alabama, Georgia, South Carolina and Mississippi, in session. Incidentally I met Dr. Hartenstein, who lived formerly in Cincinnati, in Jackson, Miss., whom I had not seen for 20 years. I mention him, because he gave me a great deal of intelligent information, that was of value to me in my correspondence. At Memphis I met a school-mate of mine, whom I had not seen for fifty years. He was lying on his death-bed, and died while I was with him. It was a sad meeting, because I met him in much poorer circumstances, than any of my other schoolmates had ever experienced. I assisted his wife to join her Eastern relatives, after burying her husband. The name of this my deceased schoolmate was Anton Hoffmann. He was one of 19 children, born within half a square of my father's house. We had been intimate friends in our school days. I wept at his death, as if I had lost a brother.

In June following, I was summoned to Washington to give testimony before the Committee, charged with the framing of Legislation for the reconciliation of the two sections of the Union. Some one must have made the committee believe, that I had a secret as well as a public object in my journey to the South, and that I might be made to reveal matters, not otherwise accessible. When I came before them, they were soon undeceived, and I was promptly dismissed to my home, which was very gratifying to me. They paid me the travelling expenses, about $150.00, which was an entire waste of so much public money.

Governor Hayes appointed me, in 1872, without previous knowledge on my part, as one of the Commissioners on Mines and Mining. It occupied my time nearly the whole Summer. My colleagues were Andrew Roy and Capt. Skinner. I afterwards ascertained, that I owed my appointment to the fact of being part owner of the Miami Coal mines, already referred to. The Governor presumed from that fact, that I understood much on the subject of mining, and that I would be able to assist materially in the drafting of Legislation upon this subject. I need not, after what I have said already on this investment of mine, state, that this was a misconception of the Governor. I told him so, and asked to be excused, but he insisted and I acquiesced. I took then immediate steps to secure from the chief officers of mines and mining, in Prussia, full technical information. I also applied to several professors, whom I knew to be instructors in mining academies in Germany. The information I obtained, in this wise, was very useful to me during the inspection of coal mines through the State of Ohio, and my report made, in 1873, to the Legislature, gives the result of the conclusions arrived at by me from this double source of information.

To it I must add, that the law, establishing the Commission, was introduced at the instance of Mr. Roy, my colleague, for the purpose, of giving a favorable report, for establishing the office of Mining Commissioner, for the State of Ohio. My report was not in conformity with this purpose, and Mr. Roy made a minority report. It contained the recommendations, that were previously determined upon. These were adopted by the Legislature, and he was appointed Mining Commissioner for three years, at a salary of $3,000 per annum. The office still exists, and is not of the full value it might be; for the reason already given on other subjects, namely: that the government and administration of the State of Ohio, is disjointed, and has not the proper interaction with the rest of the State functionaries. I regret this, because the same reason has made my labors on this subject largely a waste of time and work.

In September, 1872, I was made testamentary guardian of Mr. Heldemus' children. My duties continued for several years. I had much trouble in the matter, but I am glad to be able to say, that I have been useful to my wards, with small cost to them.

During the year I had a brief debate in the Chamber of Commerce of Cincinnati, with Louis Campbell, the well-known Congressman, of the third Congressional District, in Ohio. He was afterwards Minister to Mexico, in 1874. The subject of the discussion was, on a proposition of his, on the currency and the tariff. I was applauded, and I make free to mention this, because it was, again the first sunshine of popular favor, I had received for a number of years. The applause pleased me for this reason, but also, because I felt, that I really deserved it; since I opposed the popular leaning to the folly of an unlimited issue of paper money.

In the Fall of 1872 I was a candidate for County Commissioner, on the basis, that was in vogue 40 years previous in Ohio, that of running at the request of personal friends, merely on public faith, without previous party nomination by a party, and without paying for any electioneering expenses, and having even tickets printed and circulated among the voters. I got 5000 votes from persons that scratched out other candidates' names on party tickets, and inserted mine. No one in Hamilton County ever received, before or since, that number of votes, as a mere personal support. I was not elected, but I think I was much honored, by being voted for by so many party-free men.

In March, 1873, I was surprised by receiving a message from one of the Catholic Priests in the Church, corner of Vine and Liberty. He requested me to call upon him. I called, and he handed me $65, given him, for me, from a person, who stated to him in the confessional, that he felt bound to make this restitution of money, because it was taken wrongfully from me, it being all he could spare then. The Priest asked me: "whether I felt like forgiving him any and all wrong that I had suffered?" and I told him, to say to the man for me: that I remembered of no such loss, but forgave him heartily, whatever sin there may have been. I returned part of the money to the Church.

In August, 1872, we were, one Sunday morning, distressed by seeing our son Louis prostrated on the porch by hysterical paroxysms. He was then 20 years old. I had employed him as collector on the "Pioneer," and the extreme heat, with some indiscretions, in eating and drinking, brought on this fit, from which, however, he soon recovered. This attack brought anew to mind, our former plan: to send the four children: Rudolf, Amalia, Lizzie and Louis, to Germany, with my wife. It was carried out in September, 1872. They went via New York, London, Paris and Strassburgh to Heidelberg. There Louis studied law and government, Rudolf medicine, the girls, Amalia and Lizzie, attended excellent institutes for females. Louis' health improved immediately in Germany. I think the visit did my wife also much good, as it freed her from many onerous duties for several months.

My son Edward and Carrie and Lulu remained in Dent, with me. We missed, of course, the female head of the family, but got along pretty well after all. At the end of the year 1872, we drank the egg nogg missed at the beginning of the year; we said: "All's well, that ends well."

CHAPTER LXXIII.

PRESIDENTIAL ELECTION 1872 AND OTHER PUBLIC MATTERS.

I had intended to pass the Presidential election of 1872, with the single remark: "that it was held;" but I must state besides: that *Horace Greely* was the democratic candidate, by Gratz Brown's intrigue, and that is was in my opinion, a sad outcome of a cause, that excited, in the beginning, such high hopes, that would have been largely realized, if *Trumbul* had been the nominee. I was then and am now sorry, that I ever took part in it. With Schurz as President of the Convention, with a large majority of members desirous of reforming our actually bad party government; we had a right to expect from that convention, that its action would not only be up to the mark, but that it would give assurance doubly sure to these honest aims. Instead of that, a trickster, raised in the slimy politics of *then* Missouri—Gratz Brown—was able, by combining with a few tricksters in other states, to nominate Horace Greely, and turn the whole body into a mockery of itself. I shall never forget that adjournment. It was a fleeing of the convention from itself. The hip-hip-hurrahs for Greely, were really cries of despair at Greely's impotency to effect any good reform.

I left the convention, determined not to support the ticket nominated. I also resolved then, that never again would I trust to such bodies for bringing out the man, that should resuscitate the country from its critical situation. Such bodies may add some additional strength to a man, who is the right man, *before* the Convention meets, in the hearts of the people, because they know and esteem him; but they are worse than useless, if the convention has to *choose* between men, and decide. Such conventions cannot perform the functions of statesmen, because they are but ingrained partisans. There is no record in history of any great man being brought out by them for a country in an emergency. Indeed we may as well understand it, first as last, that great men are impossible in such assemblages, composed as they are of small men. Men like Gratz Brown get to the top of them by sheer impudence. That is the logic of the Cincinnati Convention of 1872. Carl Schurz stood, as President of it, helpless alongside of Gratz Brown. It was left to those, who despised the trick played, to resist it, and to prevent its success at the polls. That was done by the after-convention in Louisville, that nominated O'Connor against his will. I wrote at the polls my own electoral ticket. As I did it, I could not help reflecting on the fact, that I was violating the Constitution in nominating electors, but I thought, that nominating conventions commit the same wrong. So I excused myself.

The result of the division of the opponents of Grant was, that he was elected. Both Grant and Greeley are now dead. Greely died first and we may well regret his premature end.   He should have remained editor and died as such—honored by all.   As such he gained all his honors; and all his faults were forgiven; because, the tripod was his proper place; that for Candidate for President certainly was not.   Grant died later; and the people are still at fault as to his character; he had in him three characters; one bad, derived from his father; another — good — imparted by his mother; the third, — sharp as steel— gained by him in West Point.   They are still -- 1891 — at a loss, where to bury him, and erect a monument to him.   I would advise: leave it to history, to sift the facts of his life, and give the true lesson, they leave behind.   It will be: that heroes in Civil Wars cannot be great historic characters.   Their monuments convey no good lessons to posterity.

In April 1872, a well disposed member of the Legislature of Ohio, Mr. Wilson, introduced a bill under the title: "To establish a Board of Control in Hamilton County."   It contained provis'ons, that reminded me of the election of *one* Tribune in Rome; but the Board contained *five* members, which gave it an English tinge.   The inefficiency of the measure sprang from the fact, that it established a new extra authority, that was weak, because it had no adequate powers: it could not therefore act as check on the regular authority, that had very strong powers.   It proved therefore a fifth wheel to the wagon.   Mr. Wilson's bill was received by the public under the vague idea, that it meant a comptrollership.   The Board with its five members was elected by general vote, the members served without pay, not even their expenses being paid.   They had but one power — a negative one, — to-wit: no bill could be paid, without the approval of this Board.

At the first election, Messrs. Harrison, Gerard, Longworth, Brannon and myself were elected upon a ticket, made up by a self-constituted committee, without any consultation with the regular parties, nor the persons nominated. I at least had no previous notice of the nomination.   We were not even asked, to pay for the tickets, through which we were elected.

The author did not know the old principle, announced by Solon: "that a local government, to have vigor for control and inspection, must not be hampered, but freed; and therefore it ought to have powers to initiate reforms as well as to check abuses."

At the organization I was elected President, and Bacon, clerk. Early the defects of the law showed themselves.   The County Auditor, who understood, how to hinder reform, claimed, that all bills, that did not have to be approved by the County Commissioners, need neither be sanctioned by the Board of Control.   This left to the County Auditor his old autocracy, over a large part of the County's expenses.   The County Commissioners, including Sater, coincided with the Auditor, and sought either to block our way, or to enveigle the Board of Control into some controversy, that would make it unpopular.

The business entailed on me considerable labor and expense, which I bore without complaint, and would gladly have borne many years, if the benefits, expected from the Board, had been squarely named in the law. What chagrined me, was, that honest attempts at reform should be reduced to a minimum, because we were placed unarmed, so to speak, in the midst of a lot of County officials, that were armed "Cap a pie", and were determined, to thwart us. Our main impediment was the special attorney, as Law officer attached to the Board. The United States will yet find, that in such public servants, they have a lot of dangerous masters.

During the Winter, of 1873, I drafted, our Board approved, and the Legislature passed, an amendatory statute in reference to the Board of Control. It obviated some of the difficulties of the original law, but left also many uncorrected, because my draft was altered in Columbus.

I only wonder, that they left the provision, prescribing, how the annual county budget should be prepared. Previously there was no such regulation, and the tax levy was each year the blindest financial act conceivable. The provision for a Budget nettled the County office-holders, because they had now to proceed by chart prescribed. They submitted, however, gracefully (?) and made out the Budget. Then they claimed it as their work, and bragged of it; underhandedly they spoiled it. I thought of the proverb:

"Convince a man against his will,"
"And he is of the same opinion still."

CHAPTER LXXIV.

PRIVATE AND FAMILY MATTERS.

As I already stated, my wife had gone to Europe with four of my children, in the year 1872, with the understanding, that I was to follow them in the Spring, provided arrangements could be made at home, for the three remaining children. I anticipated to secure this in some way without trouble, but several matters interfered, and for a while seemed to defeat my object. Such was my discovery, that my eldest son Edward had fallen in love with my neighbor's daughter, Belle Bradford. Her parents were Irish. The discovery came to a definite conclusion, by my remark to him: "Eddy, I must admonish you, that you are paying Miss Bradford attentions, which, unless you mean to marry her, should be discontinued." He promptly replied: "I *do* mean to marry her;" and that is all the parental consent he asked and received. In May following, the couple was married. And I left, after the wedding, for Europe, to join there my wife and four children. It was agreed, that the young couple, with

Lulu, should occupy our house in Dent, until our return, which they did.

My journey, to the old country, was now made possible by my giving up the several public positions which I held. I resigned the secretaryship of the Miami Coal Co., and my son Edward was given my place. I assigned to him, as a part of his marriage portion, $2,000 stock in the Coal Co. He wisely sold the latter for $1,500, and used the money in purchasing a house and lot.

I also resigned as a member of the Board of Control of Hamilton County; but the Board would not accept my resignation, it allowed me leave of absence for a year. I saw no reason for declining this kind offer, for I thought the Board could well spare me.

The editorship of the "German Pioneer" I assigned, with the consent of the directory of the society, to a Mr. Knortz, a young German, that was then playing the part of "a literary man of all work" in Cincinnati. I regarded him, at least, fit to be a temporary substitute, and that's all he wanted the situation for; but instead of staying a year, he abandoned the place during my absence, in the Fall, abruptly, and this compelled the directory to employ somebody in his place. Their choice was F. A. Ratterman, who continued until my return. Ratterman caused an increase of outlays, contrary to the understanding, under which I became editor.

May 5th, I left Cincinnati, and May 10th, I was in New York. I went by the steamer Victoria, of the Anchor Line, in eleven days, to Glasgow, thence I went to Edinburg. Both cities I saw thoroughly. I had never been in Scotland, and found the people there much higher civilized than I expected. There was thrift there that pleased me much. I understood now, Walter Scott, Robert Burns and the fine Scotch periodicals I had been reading, much better than before. While I was there, the Annual Presbytery met, and I attended its sessions.

The clergy spoke in the Scotch brogue; Knoxism stuck out everywhere. It was on Sunday, I heard a very fine sermon. But after all, I retained the opinion, that it was a great pity, that Knox ever imbibed Calvinism; it intensified his own inborn bigotry. He and his countrymen needed softer, not harder religion, and Burns is, after all, a much more genial Scotchman, than Knox. Walter Scott held the golden mean.

From Edinburg I went to London, where I staid but two days. I visited some relatives I had there, and then left for Paris. I stopped at my old Hotel Violet. Oh, how changed was everything! The French friends I called on, hardly knew how to take me. An American? A German? or merely as a personal friend? They were at a loss too: how to take their country, themselves and their government? I went to Versailles to see the National Assembly with no idea of witnessing any particular event. As I entered, Thiers was speaking. My neighbor, in the gallery, evidently disliked Thiers; he uttered objections to his "balancing" policy, and expressed himself in favor of his resignation. I returned to Paris, wondering what the evident dissatisfaction would bring forth? After dinner at 7 P. M., I went upon the boulevard, to take my coffee; and there I found the proclamation of General McMahon, announcing his assumption of the Presidency, in the place of Thiers. Next morning everybody was clear headed as to France's future; as if a fog had passed away. But fogs soon arose afterwards again; and fogs are still rising in France; fogs caused by perplexing memories and irritating comparisons of the past with the present. McMahon rode through the streets, and his appearance acted like sunshine for a while. but the old clouds soon covered the horizon again. I hastened to Strassburgh, to meet my wife and two daughters. They had taken lodging on the place called "Broglie." They were happy to see me. Next morning my nephew. Victor Heerman. a captain in the German army, called on me. And we took a stroll together over Strassburgh. the vestiges of the bombardment were still to be seen. Between the Germans and the French there were continued strained relations; but under Manteuffel's wise course, these were rapidly passing away.

And here I allow myself to say: that during my sojourn in Paris, I said to myself again and again. that I would consider it as the happiest hour of my life, if I could realize, before I died, that France and Germany had found a way, for reconciliation and a lasting peace. I could not rejoice at the situation I saw before me, in Paris or in Elsace. I saw, that while I had become an American, I had fortunately gained in cosmopolitanism; and not lost any. I stood opposite to both France and Germany, as a citizen of the world, and not of any special nationality.

I had been in Strassburgh frequently, and liked the place and its people. I was glad that my wife had chosen there her residence with my daughters. My sons, Louis and Rudolf, remained in Heidelberg, where they continued their studies. My nephew introduced me to several of the German army officers, and I formed same pleasant acquaintances in the University. I can name especially: Professors Schmoller, Laband, also Geffken. I knew also some of the resident burgher families, both in the city and the neighboring villages. I spent in Strassburgh two months and enjoyed my sojourn greatly. I heard Schmoller's lectures on political economy, Laband on general jurisprudence, Weber on philosophy, Geffken on municipal government. I paid also a flying visit to Heidelberg, where I heard Kuno Fisher on Schiller and Goethe; also Treitschke on Greek history. I found, that both my sons had profited much by their attendance on the lectnres. Every Sunday was used for a journey to relatives in Würtemberg, my native State. We also enjoyed the German Theater in Strassburgh, and the Public Gardens. In the latter part of July we determined to divide ourselves into two groupes: Myself with Louis, and my daughter Amalia, should go to the World Exposition in Vienna; whilst my wife, Lizzie and Rudolf, should make Reutlingen their place of residence, until my return. Rudolf was to attend at Lukas' Pomological Institute, and take instructions in fruit culture. We were all, however, the first two weeks, to travel in Switzerland, and visit our relations at St. Gallen, Zürich, Burgdorf and Aarau. That plan worked well for all except for Rudolf; he had the spleen, and objected to learn in vacation; he stuck to his Americanism.

Besides the places named, we also saw Basle, Mühlhouse, Bern, Interlaken, Giesbach, Luzern, Rigi. Thence wife and Lizzie, with Rudolf, went to Reutlingen. Myself, Louis and Amalia went, by Lake Constance, to Lindau, thence to Munich. There Louis and Amalia saw, for the first time, grand sights of art. Then we travelled to Regensburgh, where Walhalla was the chief attraction, though the Cathedral and the great convent, with its imperial treasures, were not neglected. Thence by railroad to Passau, and from it by the Danube to Linz, and finally to Vienna. As I travelled along with my children, I could not help reflecting: how highly I would have prized, in my youth, such a journey, with my father as guide and instructor. Such a journey would, forty years previous, have been almost impossible, because of the absence of railroads and steamboats; and the necessary cash.

In Vienna we lodged, through the arrangement of my friend Schwede, with a Baron and his lady, who were, in consequence of the loss of office in Italy, living in reduced circumstances, but retained their modest dignity and noble behavior. Both he and she were of great benefit to us; so was my friend Schwede. We saw the exhibition thoroughly, and it was perfect in all its arrangements. We spent a week in seeing it, including Schönbrunn, Ladenburg and the adjoining places of public resort. I also made a short visit to Pesth. On the 18th of August we returned by railroad via Linz, Salzburgh, Munich, Augsburgh, Ulm, arriving to the minute at Esslingen, where we were joined by wife, Lizzie and Rudolf. We now jointly went to Stuttgardt, where we spent a few days, and then we went to Heilbronn, my native city.

We now made our preparations for the return of my wife, two daughters and Louis to America. They left August 28th, having previously a jolly time among our relatives. I accompanied them as far as Mayence. They then departed down the Rhine, and arrived safely in the United States the latter part of September. I returned to Heilbronn, and spent there several weeks with my elder brother. Then I called my son Rudolf to me, and went with him to Würzburg University; we got there September 21, in time for the vintages. We enjoyed the excellent grapes, that were getting ripe; we stopped at the excellent "Hotel De Baden".

At Würzburg Rudolf remained with me the rest of the year 1873. He studied medicine, and attended the clinical lectures at the Hospital. I heard lectures on law with Professor Held, Philosophy with Professor Stumpf, Political Economy with Professor Gerstner, and History with Professor Wegele. We learned early in November of my wife and children's safe arrival home. Our correspondence was active all Winter.

At Würzburgh, my cousin Böttinger, younger brother of my other cousin in Lyons, already mentioned, kept the largest brewery. He had lived a checkered life, after his parents had died. After leaving school he became an apprentice to an apothecary, then he studied Chemistry under Liebig and became his favorite scholar. By L's recommendation he became chief manager of Bass's great Brewery in England, and, as such, received a large salary. He led a frugal life and married an English lady. Subsequently, after he had saved up about $250,000.00, he retired from Bass's employment, and returned to Germany, with his wife, son and daughter. As stated, we met him in Würzburgh on our arrival; he was then erecting an entire new brewery, that had all the modern improvements and was expected to yield him a large fortune. Contrary to his expectations, this was long delayed, and in the mean time he made several visits to Munich, while the Cholera prevailed there. And at one of them, in February, 1874, he took the cholera and died. I felt, as if I had lost a brother.

As stated: both myself and son pursued our studies in Würzburg. We had also much pleasure through the excellent reading rooms, that were open to all, who attended the University. We made several excursions to the towns and villages near by; one was to Anspach, where "Casper Hauser" lies buried; "the enigma of his time," as it says on the gravestone, under which he is buried. His life and death are an enigma still. The half year I spent at that time at Würzburg, was the most instructive period of my life.

CHAPTER LXXV.

RETURN TO AMERICA, 1874.

I left Würzburg in the Spring, a little after Easter holidays, at the commencement of the Spring vacation of the University. Before narrating my return voyage, to America, I must state, that I met with some very sorrowful events; among these the most sorrowful was the death of my brother's wife. She had been ailing for some time; indeed, ever since they had paid a visit to us, while in Strassburgh; but our minds were not prepared for so early a decease. Our minds were all alive to the effect her death would have upon my brother. His grief, of course, was far more severe, than

mine, and when he stood, alongside of me, at her grave, I thought
him the most lonesome man I had ever seen in my life; for, as
already stated, she was all in all to him.   Her practical piety was
the staff of *his* rather theoretical piety.   Before I left on my return,
I called on him, and more than ever, realized: how lost he stood alone
in the world.   He married again and that wife died; and he married the third time.   Both these wives were excellent women, but
neither could supply the strength and the support, the other was
to him.   He died, since I commenced writing this, my life.   I had
expected to see him again and it pains me much, that I have been
deprived of this expected pleasure.

Before I left Würzburg, I spent a farewell visit to my native
city; there I saw, in the faces of my eldest brother and his wife
written the coming final close of their lives.

My brother seemed to have forebodings of a singular nature. One
morning he took me by the hand and told me: that this would be
the last time we would be together and he made me go with him to
the old house where we were born.   We went over all our play
grounds; so also to our common schools and family gardens, and
finally the graveyard where our parents were buried.   Then he bid
me farewell, prophesying distinctly, that we would never meet
again, and we never did.   I cannot, however, agree to one of his
closing remarks: "Brother! You should never have emigrated.
We should have become partners and thus perpetuated our family
name and family thrift in the business."   I think, that after all, our
lives have had about as happy a course as was possible under the
circumstances.   My emigration and his staying in Würtemberg were
both the logic of our respective characters.

My return voyage to America was from Würzburg to Fulda,
where I wanted to see modern Catholicism, with its best face, and
saw it.   Thence I went to Eisenach, where I visited the Wartburgh,
and had a good view of the place, where Luther plagued himself
needlessly about the *devil*.   Thence I went to Weimar, taking Gotha
and Erfurth on the way.   At Weimar I had an appointment with Dr.
Roelker, my most trusty friend in and about Cincinnati.   We met
for the purpose of seeing together those scenes, where Göthe and
Schiller and others of the great minds of Germany, had spent their
adult years.   Such joint meetings of two elderly persons, both of
whom have seen much of the world, and have had large experiences
in life, are apt to be extremely useful; ours at least, were so.   Doctor
Roelker was deeply versed in Goethe's life; I took special pride in
Schiller's.   So we exchanged views and interspersed them with
reflections on American politics.   Roelker startled me, by asserting:
"that men like Goethe and Schiller have been and are impossible
in America, because they would receive there, neither the right
kind of opposition nor support."   This gave me food for thinking

for several days, after I left Roelker, and travelled alone westward. I am still often thinking of the remark; I rather think he is right. What opposes in the United States the fructification of the ideas of such men as Goethe and Shiller, is a narrow nativistic prejudice. Its support is an admiration adopted without definite understandings and conceptions. Neither this prejudice nor this admiration can be the basis for disciples of really great men.

At Erfurth, I stopped over for a double purpose. I wanted to see the place, where my brother-in-law and partner grew up; and I wanted to see the town where Luther was a monk and sang for alms in the streets. I attained both my purposes, and more besides; for I learned what a thrifty place Erfurth is still, though several things, which they used to think indispensable to their welfare, had ceased to exist. This makes me remember, that we in Cincinnati, have also survived several times, political institutions and social conditions, which, those pecuniarily interested therein, tried to make us believe were necessary to existence; but they and we bravely survived their entire disappearance. I need not specify any particular instance. Hobby riding is common in both places.

At the Wartburg I was disappointed; because I saw nothing there, neither inside or outside, that looked like, or suggested even, the presence of the devil. Luther met no devil there. He brought *his* with him in his mind. Indeed, the fine view I saw, from over the land, signified to me, that of all places on earth, the devil would avoid this one. Poor Luther, he must have had some phantom, which he mistook for the Inferno. As a Lutheran, I am glad to have escaped all further trouble on this subject. The devil is "Nobody" in my religion.

From Eisenach, my route took me to Cologne, where I had been often before. Still I found new points of interest, of which I'll name one, namely: that my youngest nephew was there, and when I asked him: why Cologne looked so well? he said: "why uncle, the people here are ever new." I doubt, whether he understood the full import of his words? From Cologne I went to Brussels, whence I had not been long enough away, to find much interest in it. This time I took, however, a good look at it and was delighted with the place; especially for its historic interest. I wondered: whether the time wasn't very near, when another historic event would make it still more interesting? I next went to Antwerp, where two nephews of mine were clerks in a large commercial house. They showed me the city; and the more I saw and heard, the stronger grew my conviction, that this place should be the main sea-port of Germany to the West. From Antwerp I took a trip to LaHague and Rotterdam. Everywhere I saw indications, that Holland must come under closer commercial relations to Germany, if both countries are to have all the commerce with the world, and each other which they ought to have. From Rotterdam I returned to Brussels and thence by way of Calais and Dover to London, where I spent several days in sight seeing. I found London much improved since 1865. The National gallery pleased me exceedingly; so did the several parks. Visits to friends and relations, who lived chiefly on the suburbs on the hills, let me see how extended, and extending London is. I was astounded at the large number of Germans, that were either employed by large firms or were the heads of them or partners; I noticed, that London was more liberal on the subject of immigration, than any of the larger cities of the United States. I thought I saw also: that this country had labored under a mistake, when it took, for purely American Ideas, the arguments and principles expressed in 1876 in our Declaration of Independence. They were indeed adopted in the U. S., but previously too in England, centuries ago. I think it can be easily shown, that England and other parts of Europe have since contributed more to their extension and permanence, than the people of the United States have.

I recollected then, that O'Connell spoke a great truth, when he said: "the good in America is not new, and the new there, is not good." The fourteen days spent at London, suggested to me, in many ways and forms, that that city is more on the road of international progress, than any city in the United States. I admit, that this is specially true of its reformed municipal administration; but it is also true of national Legislation and executive political conduct. The chief cause of this difference is, in my opinion, that the ruling minds in England regard themselves bound to obey, the general human progress in our age more than those of the United States do. The great thinkers of England, its most advanced merchants and manufacturers, the professors in the Universities, the writers for the best periodicals, are far more colaborers with French, German, Italian, and other literary and scientific movements, in which it is acknowledged, that there is and ought to be a common progress all over the world, than is the case in the United States. During my sojourn in London I called on Rev. Conway, a former resident of Cincinnati. He occupied a very high, but somewhat *mixed* position in English literary circles, and I was rather in doubt, whether this gentleman had found then, his own self-poise. April 20th, I left Liverpool for New York in the steamer City of Brussels. We crossed the ocean, from Queenstown out, in ten days. May 9th, I was at home in Dent.

CHAPTER LXXVI.

GATHERING UP MY AMERICAN AFFAIRS.

Very soon after my arrival, I resumed my functions with the Board of Control. The business of the Board had augmented, in pursuance of the law I had drafted. The tax levies and County Budget were to be passed upon; the attorney of the Board played a queer game with Sater, the County Commissioner. This had delayed the regular annual report, and I was charged with drawing it up. I had it completed by June, when the papers published it; a copy of it is in the City Library. I continued, throughout the rest of the year, to attend to the business of the Board of Control. I ultimately, in 1875, declined a re-election. I may, in closing the subject, state the fact, that the Board of Control saved to the County, in the first three years of its existence, $40,000, and it cost the County not quite $1,000 a year for a clerk.

My farm occupied much of my time, after I returned. My absence had caused some neglect of it, but I soon succeeded in getting affairs again into a fair routine condition.

I had expected, in coming back, to resume the editorship of the Pioneer, for I felt myself bound to keep it in the closely economic working order that I had instituted two years previous. I found, however, that Mr. F. A. Ratterman, who had been appointed in the place of Mr. Knortz, desired to retain the place and become its editor. He had impressed many with the belief, that he was most fitted to be the Historian of Western German Pioneer Life. I concluded, that I might as well leave this position to him, and accordingly I tendered my resignation. About ten years afterwards, the question of a further continuance of the Pioneer came up again, and we shall, when we come to that, hear, what was the final determination.

My sons had, during my absence, been engaged in securing for themselves, a growing law business; I made their office my place of business. There too the Board of Directors of the Miami Coal Co. met; and for a while yet, my son attended to the collections for the German Pioneer Society; but on my final resignation, as editor of the Pioneer, this ceased. The new administration grasped for exclusive control.

My son Louis still lived with us in the country, and occasionally he helped about the place; but he had evidently not much inclination for a farmer's life. Late in the Fall, December 12th, he engaged himself to Miss Livingston, without previously consulting me; but he early informed me of the fact. She is the daughter of Phoebe Gilmore, one of the early settlers of Cincinnati. Her eccentricities once engaged much of the gossip of Cincinnati. I had known her fifty years, she was one of the kindest women I ever knew. The wedding took place soon after New Year. Miss Livingston proved very agreeable on more intimate acquaintance.

I will now recall the fact, that my son Rudolf remained in Würzburg, and we were gratified to hear, from various sources in Würzburg, that he made rapid progress in medical science and surgery.

I can testify, that he was an expert in drawing money from home. No regular German Student could ever have excelled him in that.

In 1874, I had to attend the funeral of two of my early friends, first: old Squire Heinzelman. He and his family were among the earliest German settlers of Cincinnati. One of the Masonic Lodges of Cincinnati is called after him. I had known him over fifty years. I met many at the funeral who had been in Cincinnati that length of time, and I noticed for the first time, very markedly, that I was no longer counted among the younger members; but that I distinctly belonged to the *old*. The second was, that of Liedel, in English altered into "Little," which is incorrect in spelling and in sound. He was one of the earlier barbers of the city. He was that, in the German sense, which includes surgery as well as shaving and hair cutting. Both of these gentlemen were rather proud of having arrived in Cincinnati before us, and occasionally they let us feel it.

Towards the close of the year I began writing my book, called: "Treatise of Politics as a Science." I had read and heard a great deal on the subject, and entered choice extracts and sayings in a scrap book of mine; but there it stood in a much scattered way, and it was rather hard to find a particular statement, when I wanted it for my own use. I noticed that Prof. Boehmert had, under similar circumstances, gathered his instruction into a book, and found it convenient for his lectures. I concluded to do likewise, and consequently I commenced to compose the volume already named.

I kept up my exchanges and correspondence with friends made in Europe; and their transmission of periodicals were of much use to me in writing the book; they assisted me in producing a coherent work. Robert Clarke & Co. were my publishers.

A society, called: "Friends of Inquiry," took me now into favor, and succeeded in getting much more work out of me, than I thought was in me. They met under the Unitarian Church, northeast corner of Eighth and Plum. I acted with it, because I saw in it a sign, if a feeble one, of a fair awakening in Cincinnati to the fact, that public affairs are here very defectively, indeed corruptly conducted. Mr. Lotze, a son of an old friend of mine, was one of the pillars of the society. So was Mr. Bernheimer, a free thinking Jew and kind hearted man. The society finally adjourned *sine die*, without accomplishing much. Their trouble was, that they never took a full view of the situation, but kept listening to specious statements. To be a reformer in the United States, requires, before all, the reformation of the reformers.

The year 1875 was to me, what is called in America, an "off year," which means: that a break has occurred between the past and present order of things, without the interval being normally filled. I become this year, May 16, grandfather. Charles was the name given the grandson. I was thenceforth permanently on the list of "old folks".

In April I stepped out of the Board of Control, and all public employment, by declining a renomination and re-election by any party. The people accepted my declination, as a matter of course, because I had become an odd person to both parties. They were willing for me to be a leader or member in either a Democratic or Republican party; but neither had any use for me or any other party-free man. My colleagues tried again the experiment of running without nomination, but they had to find, that the irregular regulation forces had again assumed their primeval powers.

With the help of our clerk, Mr. Bacon, I wrote a report of the Board of Control's three years work and its results. I showed. in figures, the value of the exercise of our veto power. But as our savings meant: withholding of that amount of spoils from the governing elements, we received but angry looks from them, and stupid stares from all, who did not comprehend the situation. Hamilton County relapsed into its old fatuities, from which it has since been only exceptionally jostled. The County personifies old malformations in a conservative way; and North America is that one of the New World's children, that costs most and is least thankful to the common mother.

I completed my book: "Politics as a Science"; paid to Robert Clarke & Co. $250 for 250 copies bound in book form, which I distributed gratis to persons, chiefly editors, of whom I believed they would actually read it and then give, either through the public, or private letters to myself their judgment. This expectation was realized in many instances. The reviews that came from Europe showed a deeper insight in the subject matter, than those, that came from American writers, but the former seldom perceived, that I prepared my work for an American public. The Americans misconceived the treatise to be a pessimistic reflection on this country's politics. What I desired most earnestly, was to awaken our public mind to the fact, that party government had superceeded constitutional government in the United States; and that party government was really an illigitimate child of our Union.

One of my critics called me: "a myriad-minded man", which I took to be too flattering; another said, "I was a dissappointed politician', which I regarded as rather severe. The best criticism came from the pen of Fred Hassaurek. I had to admit his strictures to be fair, and his praise moderate. I objected only to his want of understanding the main point of the book; namely: that all the great issues of our times can be solved only by equalizations, effected through public administration, that counteracts the inequalities caused by social forces. I had adopted this idea from L. V. Stein's Works and found it corroborated by every public event of our age; this point is least understood in the United States. It's only illustration here has been and is the Post-office. It pained me: that Mr.

Hassaurek should still adhere to the now obsolete conception, which the Democrats once, myself included, entertained: to wit: that the true standard of the best government was "a minimum of public administration." He died holding this error and transmitted it to his paper, the *Volksblatt*. And when I stood at his open grave, it was my deepest sorrow, that it was so. Hassaurek had his faults, but still more, his abilities; his best point being: that he could see and confess a mistake. The letter from Hecker on my book gratified me, because I knew he studied politics in Heidelbergh University. Most gratifying to me was J. B. Bigelow's correspondence; for it bore in every line the impartiality as a fair critic, and the kindness of a sincere friend. I filed the criticisms in a copy of the book, which I kept for myself.

I was much gratified this year by the transmission of a check for $400, by my old friend E. Gest, for compensating me for assuming temporarily the Presidency of the Street Railway, Route No. 9, in Cincinnati. I had incurred expenses, but had assumed, that as in other railroad transactions, I would simply have to stand it. I was more pleased at my mistake, because railroads, with this exception, had been a sore point of loss to me.

One of these was: that I was made to pay $250 to the Westwood Narrow Guage R. R., in violation of my contract. I subscribed this sum, on the condition: that the western termini, should be within a thousand feet from the Harrison turnpike, near the Seven Mile House. Mr. Schwartz, to whom I made the subscription, was the most persistent opponent to this extension; because: he wanted the railroad to stop on his premises. I made the subscription in the presence of Wm. E. Davis, the Treasurer. Both these persons are now dead. This instance of wrong convinced me more than ever, that public works, such as railroads, must never be treated as private concerns. It reminded me also, of the gypsy prophecy already mentioned, for both the gentlemen, who forced the subscription on me, came to grief. In the United States prevails the falsest Socialism.

During the year I paid a visit to the State Reform Farm, and was well received by the Superintendent, Mr. Howe, and his lady. I cannot say, that all I saw pleased me, nor can I admit: that there was all there, that I would liked to have seen; but it was, nevertheless, true: that at the farm much good was being done to hundreds, if not thousands of youth, that needed reform. An old friend, at whose house, in Lancaster, myself and family had often enjoyed hospitalities,—Mr. Lobenthal,—came with me to the Farm. He was born a Jew, but married a christian lady. He was ever a free minded man. He had known, from the first, all my reasons, why I recommended the establishment of the State Reform Farm. He said, as we left the Farm: "the Bishop's remarks to you were, after all, correct;" then added: "in this country we lack the well educated public servants, that devote their lives to public institutions for moderate pay and under a strict economic supervision." I had known Mr. Lobenthal for thirty years, as a business man, fellow democrat and excellent citizen. His death, soon after, was a great grief to me and my family.

CHAPTER LXXVII.

MORE CHANGES IN MY FAMILY. 1875—1876.

My son Louis was, as indicated, married to Miss Livingston Sept. 7th. I secured him a house to live in, in Cheviot. He added to our family one more branch and we were glad to have him live near us; he succeeded in getting a good practice; his mother- and sister-in-law lived with him and contributed toward the establishment of the house hold and the family expenses.

In December my son Rudolf came back from Europe. His departure and journey from there to America was replete with Contretemps, so that I wrote into my diary: "Mon enfant terrible est revenant." When he was born, I wrote in my diary: "He is born under the sign of the lion, I hope he will turn out to be a lamb." When he came back we saw quickly that he was no lamb; all his steps were hasty and arbitrary. We needed great patience. Thank God, we had it. His matriculation with honors, at the University of Würzburgh had so swelled his animus, that he felt it due him, that he should make a start as Doctor in the city. I thought he should have remained on our farm, and made his start there. His persistence led not only to considerable expense, but various vexations. He is the most German of my sons.

I continued during the year, my contributions to the papers previously mentioned; but did it in a slackening ratio. I wrote for the *Commercial* on "MONEY"; for the *New York Bulletin* on miscellaneous subjects. I begun also my book: "Critical Review of American Politics". I saw soon, that, writing it, was to be a severe task; and my reading up for it, soon convinced me, that with all our histories of the United States, we have really no history yet, in the true sense. I was at a loss, where to begin; but I adhered and gathered materials for the work.

My promiscuous reading this year, consisted of: Sismondi's "Literature of the South of Europe," and the philosophic works of Doctor Carus, Professors Hartman, Dührman and Draper. I also read the British Monthlies and Quarterlies, and our own periodicals and newspapers. I had to fall back also on materials I had myself collected for years. These I now hunted up, and arranged for re-reading them. Thus I entered on my work, and had at least a tenth part written out in 1876. I made, of course, inquiries of my literary friends in Cincinnati, such as Henry Reed, Wm. Corry and Mr. Jüngst, and others; the last named had himself written a very interesting book.

During the year several of my neighbors died, and I did the usual neighbor's part, in their illness and funeral. It intensified the general feeling of agedness, that came over me that year. My family at Dent was becoming small, and I had to contemplate more reductions. My house begun to look too large. At this time I came upon a letter of my father's, in which he wrote me: "Be careful! that you are prepared in time for that period in your life, when the demands upon your means increase, but your strength diminishes." I could not get the needed help on the farm, and the farm gave us, of course, more trouble every day; and my vineyard brought in less revenue. I had done a thing I never did before; I had sold a small property in Cincinnati, and expended the proceeds. I felt good, that I had more to sell, and yet didn't like the fact of the sale I had made.

We ended 1875, and began 1876, by drinking, as usually, our egg-nogg. The year 1876 put to me more frequently, than any other, the old question that has perplexed mankind oftenest; to-wit: Whether it is best to have, at all times, a definite aim in life, and to pursue it zealously; or: to have none such, and to follow the rule expressed in German by the phrase: "Man muss sich gehen lassen;" or, in English: "Pursue the even tenor of your way!" I found it difficult in my youth, to follow either method persistently; but in America it became to me almost impossible. Here we are rushed forward in our courses by irresistible impulses. We are, as the English say: "Under the whip." And *going ahead* becomes second nature to us all. But we were, neither as individuals nor as a nation, fully conscious of the change, that had been going on among us. And, every once in a while, questions came up, that reminded us rather pointedly, that a second nature, or perhaps better said: second Constitution, had taken effect, and that we were at a loss, which to obey.

Such a doubt came in 1876, when Grant was a candidate for a *third* term. Grant was eligible under the Constitution of 1787; but not so under the precedent set by Washington, Jefferson and Madison. Besides, many Republicans disliked him. They landed, as is well known, in the nomination of Hayes, by a compromise. The Democrats had the question before them, through the determination of its main element: to have a presidential candidate that would represent the inflexible purpose of restoring the government to its pristine public policy. They succeeded in nominating Tilden upon an uncompromising platform. I had made up my mind early, that the main thing to do was: to break up the tendency, to make the choice turn upon the party, and not the man; for the party criterion changed entirely the constitutional mode as to presidential elections, and upon that ground it should, in my opinion, be opposed. Grant was therefore, with me, any way out of the question, for he not only meant, squarely, the continuance of doing every thing by party, but a continuance of it in the meanest form; to-wit: the headship of a mercenary soldier and his staff. Thus minded, I kept aloof from all routine party movements; but furnished my—party-free—contributions to the press, chiefly through the New York Bulletin and the Cincinnati Commercial, both of whom stood upon the party free ground. I devoted most of my time, however, to my farm and my vineyard. In the latter I had mostly to do my own work; which was a hardship on me, as I lacked the necessary strength.

Whilst thus at work, on June 21st, 1876, there came to me, in the afternoon, my old friend John Bigelow, and, without preliminary remarks, put to me the question: whether I would not be willing to drop my work, and go at once with him to St. Louis, and there assist in securing the nomination of Tilden? I agreed to do so without a word; provided: I was to bear my own expenses. After drinking a bottle of wine, of my own vintage, we started for the city. The same evening we started for St. Louis, where we arrived the next morning. The last hundred miles we travelled in the same car with O'Brien, the main opponent, in the democratic party, of Tilden's nomination, with whom I had become intimate, whilst I was assignee of the Ohio Life Insurance & Trust Co. He was then Sheriff of New York, and met me very cordially.

On the road Mr. Bigelow and myself gave each other mutual explanations of the situation in our respective states. I told him: that, in Ohio, we were much hindered in our choice of President, because we had there ourselves four candidates: Allen, Thurman, Pendleton and Paine. I told him I was for neither of the four, but on the contrary, was in favor of Tilden, as the best man under the circumstances. I said to him further, that his coming to my farm had decided me, to confront the quadrilateral Ohio obstinacy, and to beat it with Tilden, by forming a combination of all prominent Germans, that I could gather in St. Louis in a public declaration, that the Germans in the United States were in favor of Tilden.

After I arrived in St. Louis, when, after much difficulty, I had secured lodgings, I called on the German editors, with a view to ascertain the situation. I found that *Daentzer*, of the Anzeiger, had himself thought of such a movement, and we readily agreed to co-operate with each other. A meeting of the prominent Germans was called that same afternoon. It convened, and I was made President on the motion of a gentleman from Baltimore, with whom I had had no previous understanding.

In the mean time, I went to the Ohio delegation and subjected myself voluntarily to their animadversions on my conduct. They complained, that I was co-operating with the New York delegation. This implied: that I was thereby violating some duty to my own State; but I told them: that as long as the State of Ohio had not united upon a candidate, I felt myself free to support Tilden. I declared then, moreover, that I was convinced, that Ohio did not mean

to unite on any candidate of its own, but was waiting to trade;
hence I felt free to work for the candidate I thought best. I said,
finally: "It is a national matter, anyhow, and I am determined to
prevent Ohio from being any longer the marplot in the nation's politics". I left as a free man, to do my duty, according to my convictions.

The German meeting had appointed a committee for the purpose of having their declarations formulated. That committee met
under my presidency and did it's work. It adopted a preamble and
resolution and reported them to the meeting, that adopted them
unanimously and sent them to the convention. where they met with
almost unanimous approval. The resolutions were the expression
of the German sentiment throughout the Union, and responses of
gratification came from all sides. These resolutions, more than
anything else, gave the final strenght to the nomination of Tilden,
and accordingly. he was nominated on the 27th of June. Adding
Hendricks for Vice-President was a mistake, which thwarted eventually the entire course of action for Tilden.

It is true, that Carl Schurz and Hecker declined to have themselves named as unreserved supporters of the resolutions, and this
was very probably acceded to as a reservation of the freedom of
action to those Germans, who had hitherto acted with the Republicans. That reservation was also a mistake; and a very mean one.

CHAPTER LXXVIII.

MY WORK IN THE CAMPAIGN OF 1876.

The nomination of Tilden, known in Ohio at least, to be somewhat my work, gave me a prominence in the Democratic Party in
Ohio, much greater, than was agreeable to me. I was called upon
to deliver public adresses, and did so, mostly in German, at Defiance,
Columbus. Lancaster and other places in Ohio, as well as in Indiana.
I had even to speak at Philadelphia, and saw then the Centennial
Exposition, with all it's faults and extravagancies. Occasionally at
hotels my bills were paid. but generally I paid for everything
myself; for my time or labor I never charged or received anything.
What troubled me most, was my apprehension, that folks would
take me for a re-instated partisan Democrat, who had came back,
because he had seen the error of his ways. And I took extra pains,
to discuss public questions in such a way, as to prevent that
impression being made. For me Tilden was not the candidate of
the party. And I made it my main duty, to press this point on all
occassions. I let them know my settled conviction. that the only
danger to Tilden's election was the too obtrusive party clamor for
the reinstation of the old Democracy. I told them, but few months
previous, that the great point in every good citizen's mind was: can we
find a Democratic Party, that we can trust? By that the people
certainly did not mean the old party without being reformed. It

pointed to the oft repeated phrase in the platform: "Reform is necessary". And after sixteen years, I still declare: Would that that democratic partisanism had been kept better in the background! Then Tilden could not have been cheated out of his election. Nor would any weak-kneed or treacherous supporter of Tilden have dared to vote for that fraud—"The Commission"—by which Hayes was finally placed in power. The constitutional election of S. Tilden was set aside by an unconstitutional formality, pushed through Congress by the co-operation of intriguing politicians of both parties.

To me it is as disagreeable to make this remark, as it is true. Indeed I must say: that nothing is so painfull, in writing my life, as having to testify to conditions in the United States, which bring out the temporary prevalence of base politics and ethics, such as existed in 1876–7. I refer here specially to the fact. that there was created a semi-judicial body, by an enactment, which every lawyer knew to be unconstitutional. The pretence was a desire to have the truly elected President counted out and defeated. It was a specimen of public acting, which wrong ambition always resorts to, when they want to alter the facts or bend them to their purposes, to wit: they create special tribunals for doing that, for which the regular tribunals would not serve them.

In 1876–7 there were such regular tribunals: the Senate and House of Representatives, by joint meeting of Congress. Their clerks would in their presence open and take account of election returns and then the House of Representatives alone could take preliminary and final action as to the proclamation of the President elect either by the people or the House of Representatives. The enactment named was clearly a subterfuge for circumventing, the popular decision come to in the State's election of 1876.

Hayes felt impelled to admit this, while under primary honest impulses; he prevaricated, however, under the promptings of the zealots of his party, and he took the Presidency, under cover of the false decision of the unlawful commission. Oh! how it pains, to have to write this of one, I must call: friend. To see the truth, is: in such cases, a grief, and Kassandras' words,—by Schiller—come before us, and we ask:

"Again restore me to my former blindness,
And the clouds that then obscured my mind."

My bitterest thought, however, is my conviction: that party treachery in the Democracy, also played its low trickery, and lost the country Tilden, the President, who would have initiated the reform, then most needed.

In my family-affairs everything prospered in 1877, except our efforts, for securing for my son Rudolf a steady practice. My two elder sons did reasonable well as attorneys; my three younger

daughters were perfecting their education very satisfactorily. The
eldest of them Amalia was married October 10th, to a Mr. James
Slocum, a well to do druggist in Lancaster, Ohio, now in Knoxville,
Tennessee. We had also two grand-children born to us, one named
after me, Charles, and a grand-daughter named after my wife,
Louisa.

As already pointed out, these private joys were counterbalanced
by public mischiefs. The Southern R. R. bill passed March 15th in
spite of the exposures of its falsity. I had made an adverse, elaborate address against the bill before the Committee on Municipal
Corporations in the Ohio Legislature; and I spoke against it also on
the 13th of March at a mass meeting at Turner hall. I may say
now, that while I do not deny, that it hurts one's feelings to fail in
stemming a vicious current in the popular mind; yet I must, in
honest truth, add: that it has it's pleasures to remember the good
men did, who stood by us at that time; and I thank Fred. Hassaurek and Wm. Corry for their aid.

And now, as I close, the narrative events in 1876, the question,
spoken at the beginning, comes back to my mind and I have to say,
as to it: Both courses are proper if persued—"cum grano salis"; but
neither is safe if carried too far. Forecast is necessary to fulfill our
destiny, and so is submission to fate. Cromwell's motto: "Trust to
God and keep your powder dry", expresses the true idea. I would
express it: "Trust to convictions; but keep wise a guard on your
impulses".

This main point on such occasions, is to form character so as to
enable the respective person to act both intelligently and virtuously;
for in that combination consists the wisdom of Longfellow's words:
"Learn to labor and to wait". In Goethe's couplet again it is as a
witicism:

> "Study the world both great and small
> But leave the end discreetly wise,
> To God's will after all".

But Christ sums it all up, in his advise to his apostles: "Be as
wise as serpents and as harmless as doves".

And now I must say a few words, about the two Constitutional-
isms. Each plays a dubious part in the United States, namely:
that which is written down as public will and that which our parties
are blindly evolving. Their dual existence makes both have a
vicious development; for it intensifies their respective faults and
prevents the employment of their virtues. This biformity in our
Constitutionalism causes most of the duplicity in our politics. It
led to that, for instance, between slavery and liberty, that brought
our civil war; and it will eventually destroy the Union. Our public
men should labor, persistently, to counteract it.

CHAPTER LXXVX.

HARD POLITICAL REFLECTIONS. 1878.

The year we are now entering upon, 1877, was to me a year of review. I had, as stated, written out my book: "Critical Review of American Politics", but now came the harder task, to act the critic on myself. That meant largely rewriting it, as well as reconsidering it. Many a time I felt, in the course of the year, like abandoning it, but eventually I continued it to the end. It was slow work; it took all the year and then the prospect, that another year would have to be added. Still I was never seriously discouraged; for events were running with my reflections and furnishing the historic commentary.

Tilden's treatment by the Democratic party, followed as it was by the election of Hayes, was the consequence of the false conduct of the election as a partisan campaign. A party, that is conscious of self-deception, cannot have the requisite fortitude, to expose and rebuke a fraud perpetrated by it's more determined members, because at every consultation there will be many to whom a halt is more agreeable, than a firm forward step. I urged in letters to prominent members of the House of Representatives, that they should declere: 1st. That there was no lawful election for President when the Commission elected Hayes. 2nd. That by the fundamental law of the land it was the right and the duty of the House of Representatives, to see to it, that the fraud attempted through the Commission, should be defeated; and 3rd. That Tilden, the rightful President, should be declared elected and placed in power, by the House.

As to the *modus operandi* I pointed out, that the Sergeant-at-arms should be empowered to take all necessary steps, by and with the advice and consent of the Speaker, to secure the ends expressed in the resolves against any and all attempts to prevent them. My advice was not heeded. Instead of it, the *cowards* and the *cheats* cried: "Let Tilden take the initiative! Let him come to Washington and declare himself elected! The people will stand by him!" Fudge! no one would have stood by him, in such a violation of the proprieties of the situation. His declaration or proclamation would have been mere idle wind and gasconade. The institution of a Returning Board, or "Commission," as it was called, as the final judge, with the Senate and the House sitting by as witnesses, was the perfidious proposition of those in the Democratic party, who, really, never wanted Tilden put into the presidential chair. As first proposed, the casting vote would have been given by the heaviest piece of human flesh ever grown in America; there was, at least, some weight in that fleshy preponderance; but even that good was taken away; for his heaviness was made U. S. Judge, and thus withdrawn. Then a substitute was put in his place; and thus the fraud was perfected. It will be seen, that after the efforts of the people to organize a reform movement, it was a failure. And that failure sunk deeper into the minds of the American people, than anyone supposes, because it has been followed by similar failures.

The Democratic party of Ohio, resumed its old business, at the old stand. It nominated Bishop, born and raised in Kentucky, who finished his partisan education in Ohio. First: by calling himself a war democrat, and then transferring himself and sons into leaders of the Democratic party. He was elected by 25,000 majority. The Baptists gave him really the majority.

During the year I made some effort to get for the German organ, the Volksfreund, an abler manager and publisher; by trying to induce Mr. Morwitz, of Philadelphia, to become the purchaser; but this effort failed, and finally Mr. Haake bought out the stockholders, and is now the owner. I am sorry, that I could not bring Mr. Morwitz in, as he would have made a much superior paper, to what there is now. July 5th, 1877, I was entered in the Probate Court, by the request of the heirs, administrator of John Eggers' estate. I took the position, in compliance with the desire of old friends, feeling certain, that the matter could be administered and settled at an early period. I soon converted the assets into money, about $14,000, and expedited it to the various heirs in Europe, by sending to each the respective amounts in bills of exchange on London. It was always my rule, in such things, to act promptly, and to close up the accounts. My promptness, in this case, saved me from serious loss. I had temporarily placed the money with the same banker, who held my own funds. This banker, J. C. Heman, failed two months after I had sent the money to the Eggers' heirs. It confirmed me in my rule: never to keep money belonging to others, a single hour after I get it, but to transmit it at once to the actual owners.

My daughter's Amelia engagement to Mr. Slocum made it appear proper, that I should aid him by my counsel in his plans to settle in Knoxville, in such a way, as to make his marriage feasible. So I went to Knoxville in March, to investigate an enterprise, which was claimed to answer the purpose. I found the thing proposed to be a partnership or purchase of a furniture factory. I examined into the concern and soon felt it my duty to advise against the project in toto. I recommended to my expected son-in-law, to stick to his own profession: "Practical Chemistry and an Apothecary." I promised aid in the purchase of a dwelling house. He adopted my suggestion, and the marriage took place in January, 1878.

My taxes for the year 1877, were $1680.00, which was 2 6 10 per cent on the legal valuation, and was 30 cents of every dollar I received in rent from the property taxed; and I paid assessments for streets and alleys besides. It was then, therefor, rather a grim joke on me, to hear nativists talk of tax-ridden Germany and tax-free America. I prayed for them: "Lord, forgive them, for they know not, what they are doing." Germany is less and fairer taxed, than the United States.

I declined, at that time, again, as I had done for fifty years before: to become the owner, in whole or in part, of a political paper. I could have had the *Volksblatt* several times, at low prices, as compared with what it afterwards brought. I also declined the repeated offers of Mr. T. C. Day, to join him in either buying established, or to start new ones. I was aware that Mr. Day, was sure to succeed in any newspaper enterprise, he would undertake. The *Enquirer* was never a better paper than under his management. The Philadelphia parties, already named, would have liked me to join in the purchase of the *Volksfreund*, and it would have been a large pecuniary success, but I declined their advances, as I had done all similar offers before, including the *Commoner*. And it may now be proper for me to state, why I, a constant writer for the press, have thus persistently declined to become the owner of any? It was, because I had sincerely sounded my own capacities and become convinced, that being owner and manager of a newspaper, requires one sort of character and writing for it quite another. The latter suited me, and I suited for it; while for the former I had neither taste nor specific qualification. There was then and is now, in my opinion, an incompatibility between the two, which I could not ignore. I would as leave be School Commissioner of the State of Ohio and at the same time seller of school books; as be the seller of news and the teacher of political principles, for personal aggrandizement, at the same time. I must add here: that I regard an effective educational system of the adults of society, as the great problem of our age. And I believe that this must be accomplished through the organization of the press of the country in a way, in which it is no longer a combination for money making and at the same time, an educational organ for society.

CHAPTER LXXX.

MISCELLANEOUS EVENTS. 1877—1878.

Death entered our family August 4th, 1877, and took from us our grandson "Mark Foster," Edward's son. He had been named after the family name of both parents of my wife. The first loss of a grandchild is, to the grand-parents, a rough reminder, that life and descent in family, do not proceed in a regular line; and that very often grandparents outlive grandchildren, of whose future they had formed too favorable opinions.

An old neighbor's widow, Mrs. Schweizerhof, died April 11th, and I attended her funeral. She had been a valuable servant in a family, very nearly related to me, in Heilbronn, between 1820 and

1830. Her husband was drill-sergeant of us boys in 1827, when about seven hundred of us were enrolled and drilled in military exercises by the orders of the King. They married about the time I emigrated to America; and after their marriage they emigrated and settled in Cincinnati in 1833. When I arrived, they were keeping a good boarding house; and her good cooking, and his strict order, made it a very pleasant resort for very many of us young gents. We got there many a good meal; such as our mothers used to provide. I spent many a pleasant hour with them. Schweizerhof drilled the Lafayette Guards in 1836, of which company I also was a member; and I was accordingly twice under his command; first as a boy in Germany, and then as a young man in Cincinnati. They were afterwards our neighbors, for thirty-five years, in Green Township; and when I attended her funeral, I felt as if I had lost a member of my own family. This bringing together, in America, persons of different classes in Europe, is one of the better influences America exercises on her immigrants.

One of the oldest settlers of Green Township, Mr. Hutchinson died in July. He lived not quite a mile from us. Forty-five years before, his family had the most promising future in the neighborhood. When he died, this promise had shrunk into very small proportions. The Hutchinson farm had dwindled from 160 to about 20 acres. A son-in-law, his wife and two children, resided on the place yet. While thousands of dollars represented the former wealth, there were but hundreds remaining; and the prospect was, that in a very short period. no Hutchinson born would reside on the place. To me, a descendent of a family and of a country, where estates remain in the same family very often for several centuries, the rapid decadence and disappearance from the Township of a family of note, is a matter of deep significance, as to the future of America. It affects me tenderly, because I stand before a similar status, as to my own family. America has not yet found a way to have a permanently settled population. And I think, that the geography of the country, indicates, that it will be a very hard problem to accomplish. Our present mode of living and economy is certainly not the way to it.

Wm. E. Davis, a personage. for whose public prominence, I bear some responsibility, died also in 1877. I had given him the first State office he ever held, that of Superintendent of the State Reform Farm. Soon he electioneered himself into the clerkship of the State—Senate. He entered the war in 1862, became a Union soldier, next a subordinate officer; then a prisoner, and a "victim of Southern cruelty." This gave him a high position in Republican newspapers, and that opened to him a career in that party. He was made Pension Agent, and afterwards Assistant U. S. Treasurer. It was a bad day for him *and* the Government, when I turned him from an unquestionably good school teacher, into a questionable State officer. My only excuse is: that there was no way provided by law, that would have guided me, in finding the proper man, for the public position I had to supply with an officer. He was not a person that could resist the temptations to corruption, that then existed in the Federal public service. When he died, he was found to have defaulted, as to some school funds, that were placed into his hands, and, I felt very much aggrieved, at this outcome of his career; but he is only one instance, of the many thousands, that our war has ruined. To presume, that a man is a good character, because he volunteered and became a soldier, has proved often a violent presumption.

I had at the end of the year 1877, completed my book "A Critical Review of American Politics" and submitted it to General Durbin Ward for revision, because he had the reputation of being an excellent critic. He returned the manuscript, with sundry marginal notes, all containing the words: "I don't like this". There were no corrections nor any suggestions of amendment as to style, spelling or reasoning. So I cut off the marginal notes and attended to my own revision and correction. We will recur to this matter again, when we come to the printing of the book in England. I only wish to say now: that I did not care for General Ward's likings or dislikings; what I wanted were the sincere criticisms of an accomplished scholar and a person familiar with historic details.

In March and April I wrote a sketch of my life at the request of Hon. Gustav Koerner, the renowned *German* of Belleville, Ills. He wanted it for the book, he was about publishing under the title: "The German Element in the United States of North America 1818-1848". The book appeared at the end of the year 1879, and the biographical notice of myself was on pages 186 to 192. I had expected, that the sketch I wrote, was to be simply the basis for being written out more fully by Mr. Koerner, including his judgment upon the facts and details furnished. Instead of that, it was, as printed, a mere copy of what I had written, with a few introductory and closing remarks. The general tenor, of the book, showed a well disposed spirit and it was a high honor, to be mentioned therein. The personal integrity and high character of Mr. Koerner gave to all he published additional value.

The year 1878 had for me too many echoes, from 1867, to enjoy it. Neither of our parties were able to lift itself out the quagmire of its false public relations. Both succeeded in perplexing themselves, and degrading their opponents; and it may be said, that American politics were on the inclined plane to false conditions. Hayes could not gain the reputation of integrity, which he knew, he needed, to be the right President. Soon it became evident, that he would adhere to his pledge: that he would not be a candidate for a second term.   His enemies insisted, that this was not his voluntary course.   His administration was a weakness to all concerned in it, including himself, because he could not relieve himself of the fact, that he was occupying the position that belonged to another person. The question of a successor to him caused innumerable intrigues pro and con in both parties and nothing but fear of being compromised for the contest of 1880, kept these intrigues from breaking out into turmoils in 1878 already.

The Democratic party was in its own way. It never gained the unity it needed. Tilden himself was not permitted to occupy the position of leader and the Tilden memories were in the way of all other Democrats, assuming that position. No intelligent Democrat doubted that Hendricks was not a true friend to Tilden either in 1876 nor since. The Democratic party was therefore without the distinct leadership it should have had. Whenever Tilden would get into due prominence, Hendricks would heave into sight in the distance, like a bad ghost. It is interesting, in this connection, to note, that Lord Hartington played in England a similar part towards Gladstone. Hendricks was like the R.R. engineer, that gained a reputation by constructing a convenient curve at a locality by which a high grade was overcome; and ever afterwards he kept suggesting curves even for localities, where no high grade had to be overcome, and straight lines were best.

The pleasures that I lacked in 1878 in politics, were made up to me in family affairs.   I had two granddaughters born to me in that year, namely: Emily, Louis' daughter on February 11th, and Edith, Edward's daughter on March 19th. The consummation of the marriage of my daughter, to James Slocum was also a gratifying event. I was able to give my son-in-law assistance towards making a fine start in his business, the purchase of a lot, and the building of a house thereon.

During the year 1878, my correspondence with relatives in Germany was unusually active. The only drawback was, that, in receiving letters, very frequently the admonition appeared, that the one sent or received was likely to be the last.

CHAPTER LXXXI.

POLITICAL OCCURENCES, 1879.

The year 1879 was to both parties, and all who cooperated with them, or even ventured only within their eddies; what all periods are, when public persons fail to take the definite steps, wisdom suggests; and resort to mere temporary expedients. This causes years of blunders followed by years of regrets, that still plague the country.

I may as well mention one of my own at once, I had kept myself for several months out of personal participation in active politics; but about May, I was called upon to assist in defeating the renomination of Bishop for Governor. I demurred at first, but yielded in the end. I was chosen a delegate to the state convention to be held on June 14th. It was a many sided fight. My personal choice was defeated; but so was Bishop; and Ewing, who had at first had the fewest votes was nominated. I had refused to vote for the latter, and was in a brown study, how I could consistently vote for Ewing at the poles, for he had committed acts, during the war, in Missouri, which I could not overlook. Suddenly I heard my name mentioned for State Auditor, and before I could get out a word, either for or against it, I found myself nominated unanimously. Instantly I was seized and held up before the convention by the arms of four men, who had before denounced me for not voting for Ewing. My declining words were drowned in exclamations for my nomination; and I was taken to my seat as the accepted and accepting nominee of the convention for Auditor of State. This was hardly done, when it was industriously telegraphed all over the state, and I received congratulations for the same in return, within an hour. A day or two afterward I received notice, that I was expected to contribute toward campaign expenses $500, which I of course remitted. After that followed my stumping the state, and all closed with a common defeat in October, which served us right. I had but one satisfaction: I run ahead of the ticket in Hamilton county; for which my thanks. I had hardly expected it.

After the election I retired from the general field to the more pleasant home localities. There, at Dent school house, we had public debates on several important questions. I startled the community by remarking, that we were committing a double error as to education; first: in not perfecting the present school system by giving it coherence and unity, from the university down to the common school: and second: by abandoning to the press and the parties they represented the *education of adults* in our society. The public was surprised at the statement, but no antagonistic efforts or responses were made. I have since, as occasion offered, spoken upon this subject; my latest address was made in 1891.

Hays' ill considered signature to the profuse Pension Bill for soldiers in the civil war, was a sore dissappointment to many of his friends; they had regarded him as a consistent conservative man, but they now found him to be a very loose political spendthrift.

My son Rudolf was again and again a cause of anxiety to me and always by surprise. He moved on February 20th, at the kind call of Dr. Roelker to Madison, Ind., where he soon got a remunerative practice. I aided him with money and also by letting him have our family horse. My daughter Caroline moved down and enabled him to start house-keeping, which gave him a quiet opportunity to have a better practice. My wife went there also on a visit. Everything looked promising, and we thought he was established for life in Madison. The change that came over the spirit of our dreams afterwards, we will meet with in succeeding chapters.

The failure of *Heman* occured in March. It was indeed a sad surprise to us all. I had known him for forty years, first as school teacher, then as newspaper owner; and was his creditor ultimately as banker. I had discovered only one bad point in his character, namely: a dangerous dubiousness as to public questions. We could never be friends unreservedly, but lately had become rather intimate together. I used his bank to deposit my private means. He aided, unsolicited from me, my son Edward, by giving him the notarial business of his bank. When he failed and our accounts were settled, I lost by him only about $15. I felt no resentment towards him for this loss, but I regretted exceedingly, that a man, who had received a good education and had so many opportunities, to build up solid foundations for wealth, threw them all away and ruined his character, by neglecting his business for months before his failure. He is still alive, but life is, unless I am much mistaken, a severe burden to him.

Several deaths, during the year, set me to thinking deeply over my own life, and the memories, in reference to Mr. Goepper, again came to my mind, when his death occured in the summer 1879. He died very wealthy and his sons had had great success in the business transmitted to them by their father; but I must repeat once more, that his ingratitude to me is one of the bitterest feelings, that I am carrying to my grave.

The death of my former colleague in the House of Representatives and noted Democrat 1845–1846, General McMakin, pained me exceedingly. He died June 12th., and I attended his funeral. He used to give me much trouble, in the legislature, to keep him "in the traces", as the phrase is, that is to say: to make him stand up to the more advanced policy of the party; but as the Romans say:

"Tempora mutantur, et nos mutamur in illis".

A few years, before he died, he upbraided me, for lagging behind, in sustaining the Democratic party, and he said: "I think I have a right to prompt you as to your duties, if only as a mode of repaying you the kindness you showed me in prompting me to stand up for the more advanced policy of the Democratic party in 1865–1866". We both laughed. Neither asked the other, why he laughed? But we parted in good humor with each other; wishing happiness and long life to each other and not forgetting to send our kindest regards to all the members of our families. I felt so good in parting with him then; because it convinced me, that we had been sincere friends throughout our lives. Mrs. McMaken and my wife were steadfast friends for over forty years; and that fact doubtless cemented our friendship.

The death of Mrs. Molitor brought up similar checkered memories of a social intercourse, that had been kept up for fifty years, between our two families. Mrs. Molitor was the widow of Stephen Molitor, with whom I had in the first years, 1837, I was in Cincinnati, very friendly relations, as to all political affairs; and she was, at the same time, a very intimate friend of my wife. When the war broke out, in 1861, all this friendly intercourse was changed, so far as Molitor was concerned; and while he lived, into feelings of animosity, which prevented us from even meeting together socially. This ill feeling continued for over fifteen years, and I was surprised, when I received her call, to come to see her, and to make her will for her. She at that time confessed to me, that she regretted the causes, that had kept us apart so many years. She told me also, that *she* had not felt unfriendly, during all this time, towards my wife and myself; and she only staid away, out of fear, that it might lead to an estrangement, between herself and her husband, if she would associate with us. This confession made me feel bad, because I had not believed, that Germans could thus hate each other, on account of political differences. An hour before dying, Mrs. Molitor handed me a sum of money, for her youngest daughter, Emilly, and told me, not to mention it, but to keep an eye on her daughter's condition, and to give her money from time to time, as in my opinion, I should deem right and proper. I have paid the money long ago, over to the daughter, being satisfied that she and her husband are now in circumstances, that make it no longer necessary, for anybody to watch over their lives. I am satisfied, they will get along without any extra support. On her deathbed, Mrs. Molitor whispered to me: "Have you forgiven Molitor for his harsh conduct towards you?" And on my nodding affirmatively, she pressed my hand and sunk back upon her pillow, as if a weight had been lifted from her mind. I may say here, that I have never ceased to respect Molitor, but I left it to time, for him to get right, in his feelings toward me, which I think he actually did. It did me good, to have his wife's confirmation of the change in his feelings. I had suspected such an undercurrent in Molitor's meditations as to myself; because I had held too many unreserved conversations with him, on American politics, for me to believe, that he could be, my out and out foe.

In June, 1879, the news of Louis Napoleon's death reached the United States. They were to me painfull, in many respects, but most so, in consequence of the callousness, with which our American public looked upon the afflictions of Napoleon and the French people. I had learned from relatives in Augsburgh, much about Napoleon's early education; so too: of Swiss friends, as to his later youth and middle age; and I had also special opportunities, to know his character, during his sojourn in America, England, and even while imprisoned in France, for his invasion at Strassburgh. The facilities were renewed, after he had succeeded in making himself Emperor. I had thus learned, that fate had most to do in forming his character and history. He was politically, neither innocent nor guilty, in the common sense, and therefore, to me, a person to study carefully and honestly. This I had done, by reading very carefully his life of Caesar. I understood from it, that he was a competent judge of political situations, when nations are swaying to and fro, under mixed sentiments, as to patriotism and righteousness. And when Napoleon died, I looked back over the events, that led to his fall; and in my mind there arose doubts, whether the statements made on the side of the Hohenzollerns, should be readily accepted as the full truth? And I then re-read the well-known passage in Napoleon's Life of Caesar:

"It is worthy of remark, that when destiny pushes a society towards a fall, there is a fatal concourse towards it; as well through the attacks, as the expectations of those who want a change, and so too of those who believe in it, and those who resist it, as well as those who would stop it all."

Poor Napoleon! He wrote the lession of his own fall. I asked: Why not pity him!? Why should Americans not see, that the history of their late war contains the same lesson!?

CHAPTER LXXXII.

THE ELECTION OF 1880 AND OUR JOURNEY AFTERWARDS TO EUROPE.

To my mind it was clear in 1880, that both our parties were drifting into mischievous errors, when they should have steered into patriotic and wise policies. The Republicans claimed a prerogative for *remaining* in power; the Democrats claimed an ancientry for *regaining* power, whilst in fact neither party was, as party, fit for power; that in fact they had rights to act officially, only so far as they stood in the attitude of civic authorities. The citizen, who, after peace has closed a civil war, persists in enmities, is a worse traitor, than he, that became an enemy of his countrymen before the war.

Let us retrace our steps to 1876, and the convention at St. Louis, that nominated Tilden for President. He and his friends embodied, in all integrity, the cause of a common return to the Government of the Constitution, by a common self-reformation of both parties. I know, that Tilden had individually, performed this self-correction, and that he desired the leadership of the Democratic party, only for enabling him to lead the Democrats to the same dutiful compliance. That desire inspired all his strong friends in working for his nomination.

Tricky partisans defeated the consummation of these purposes, after the election of Tilden in 1876. And this hurt those most, that had labored the hardest and the sincerest in the righteous cause. And of those I claimed to be one.

The reader must certainly realize, how we felt, when, as already stated, the result of the election of 1876 was rendered naught, and Tilden was plagued, for the four following years, by insincere requests to be the candidate in 1880. We anticipated the stranding of the Democratic party in some desperate ultimatum. And it came, in 1880, through the nomination of Hancock, by the Democratic National Convention. Nevertheless, we could not despair at the very outset; so we held ourselves prepared to do yeoman service and work faithfully to the last. And when, under these circumstances, the editor and owner of the Cincinnati Volksfreund, asked me, in 1880, to write for his paper, in aid of the success of the Democratic party; he gave me unrestricted leave to write, as I should think best. I concluded to exercise the privilege thus extended to me, and the result was, that a series of contributions appeared, that had my initials attached. I have the file of these contributions now before me, and I feel myself justified to claim, that they are a full and free expose of American politics, as they then stood. I know very well, that my labors were, in the then public condition of the public mind, like those of Sisyphus; but I recognized also, that American politics are like bottomless casks, that hold nothing except their own spoiled tastes. This is the main idea of my closing contribution, November 2nd, 1880. I then anticipated defeat, but felt nevertheless; that my labors had not been altogether in vain. Let us recapulate a little of the history, that preceeded the election. It took till September, 1880, to get the party into line. I made my first speech on September 12th, in Cincinnati. From then I was actively engaged until the middle of October, in Ohio and Indiana. Everywhere the people were anxious to learn; why American politics were so full of the quicksands of partyism? My last speech was October 29th, at Madison, Ind. My son Rudolf was present, at the meeting. Every word I uttered, was really meant for him. He had contributed, towards making it as large a meeting as it was.

All through October very little was done by either party, and one could easily notice, that the defeat of Hancock was a foregone conclusion. There was a time, when Hancock's name would have caused strong enthusiasm; but that time was passed and could never return. The heroes of a civil war are always short-lived in their fame, and Hancock's was only shorter than the rest; because he stood in no attitude, by which he could be fully honored for the military capacities, that he displayed. The Republicans might have owed him some compensation for his victories; but the Democrats did not. Hancock felt this and got into equivocal attitudes, just before the election; this added to the causes that were leading to his defeat. I had formed in August already, the resolution to go to

Germany and other parts of Europe as soon as the election should be over. By the advise of my wife I took my daughter Lulu with me; she being the only one, that had not yet been to the old country and become acquainted with our relations there. And according to the program all our arrangements were completed a week before the election.

On election day I voted, as soon as the polls were opened. After breakfast we left for Cincinnati. We bid farewell to our folks in Cheviot and Westwood. The grandchildren, as they looked wonderingly at us, brought tears to my eyes. In Cincinnati we took at once the cars for Cleveland, where we arrived in the evening. There we took sleeping cars and were next morning in Buffalo.

November 1st we spent seeing the Falls of Niagara. We departed for New York at 7 P. M., and arrived in New York next morning. At Buffalo already; and again at the Falls, we had learned by rumors, that the Republicans had gained the victory and that Garfield was elected. These rumors were confirmed by the morning papers, which we got November 4th, on our arrival in New York. We spent two days in New York. I called on the editorial staff of the N. Y. Staatszeitung, also on B. Roelker, Moran Bigelow and others. I expected to meet Bigelow in Europe in the Spring.

On the evening of the 4th, I took Lulu to the theater at Niblo's Garden; on the 5th I went with her to the German Theater.

Saturday, Nov. 6th, we took the Bremen steamer Mosel, Captain Nienhaber, the gruffest captain, I ever travelled with. Nov. 17th, we got to South Hampton. Here we stopped at the Dock Hotel. It was a poor, but nevertheless dear concern. The hotel keeper came on board, and we followed his invitation, which we should not have done, as hotels, to whom the owners invite in this way, ought to be avoided.

Our sea voyage of eleven days was a rough one in many ways. The captain was a disagreeable North German The fare consisted evidently of the leavings of previous voyages. The sea was rough, from strong westerly winds. We were promised to cross the Ocean in nine days. At South Hampton we arrived at midnight, and our disembarkment was delayed until four in the morning. Nov. 17th, we saw South Hampton, Nettley Abbey, including the great Hospital. I meant to show my daughter Romsey, Palmeston's former residence, but the weather was too rough, to be any further out of doors. We staid all night at our poor South Hampton hotel. Next morning we left for London, where we arrived at 3 P. M., and were soon at Hotel Royal. I called at once on my countryman, Mr. Roman, for letters; he was my brother's brother-in-law, and he and his wife are natives of Heilbronn. The next twelve days we spent in London in sight seeing and visiting relatives, which included Roman and his family, and also Rommel, who had married my niece, a daughter of my youngest sister.

Lulu became quite a Londoner and I really begun to think, that she might meditate to take up her residence there and marry some of the young gentlemen, to whom she was introduced, but nothing come of these thoughts; for Lulu did not coincide with them. Mr. and Mrs. Roman as well as Mr. and Mrs. Rommel showed us every attention, we could expect; indeed we were treated with unusual hospitality.

I had much trouble to find a publisher for my book: "*Critical Review of American Politics*"; but finally took it to Trübner. I had to pay him altogether about $750.00 for my book of about 650 pages. I was to get, for that sum, 250 extra copies of the book for Robert Clarke & Co., in Cincinnati, and of the other copies, I was to have received half of what was realized from the sales in England. But Trübner never even rendered me an account. I suppose, that I must charge it all to the gipsy's prophecy, and that Trübner must do likewise, for his failure to sell a larger edition in England.

We left London in the morning of December 2nd, and got to Paris late in the evening. Instead of stopping at my old hotel Violet, as I should have done, in return for former good treatment, we went to Hotel Calais, where my wife stopped in 1873. There we got good rooms; but poor meals. We stopped at Paris for about eleven days, and saw it thoroughly. It was a delightful time, to Lulu especially, after I had bought her a new bonnet, the price of which was 40 francs. It seemed to me to be too high; but the milliner said pointedly: "N'oubliez pas que vous ettez en Paris." And I did not forget it. I found in every purchase I made in Paris, that heavy taxes were levied there, to pay the spoliation, that had been levied on France by Prussia as condition of peace. Dec. 13th, 1880, we arrived in Strassburgh, and there spent several days in friendly intercourse with my nephew Victor Heermann, son of my youngest sister Sophie. He had advanced to the first captaincy in the German-Prussian army. He was very well liked at the court of the Governor of Elsass. He was as full of the war against France, as our officers of our civil war, were against the South. And we let him tell us all about it; indeed we prompted him for more interesting details. From Strassburgh we went to Baden-Baden, and there saw my sister Sophie with her youngest daughter. Both gave us a warm reception. Lulu and her cousin became friends very quickly. Girls feel a relationship quicker than boys. We went the same evening to Carlsruhe, and there enjoyed a real gratification by seeing, at the court theater, "Geyer-Wally", the new piece, written by Mrs. Hiller, a highly distinguished authoress, that was then in high favor with the Grand Duchess, the daughter of the Emperor. We stopped at Hotel Germania, the new Hotel, one of the finest in Europe, and spent three days at Carlsruhe. My step-sister Mathilda and her two daughters entertained us very affectionately. Monday morning, December 20th, we travelled safely and pleasantly to Heilbronn, via Mannheim and Wimpfen, at both of which places we stopped over, to see the points, that were of interest to me, during my residence there in my youth, 1830. At Heilbronn we were hospitably received by my brother Edward.

I thus lived once more in the old parental mans'on. It was full of memories of my family, but my brother and I, were the only ones left of some twenty-two members of the whole family, that were there in 1832. We saw the old year out and the new year in, under the ringing of the bells of the Cathedral, in which I was christened. We saw yet the church, in which my father and mother were married. It has since been pulled down; and as I stood there with my daughter that night, the queer question arose to my mind: Am I still at one, in attachment, to all these surroundings. as I was in 1821, when I stood there the last time with my mother? And the answer came from the bottom of my heart: Yes, in all priority of patriotism and affection, as a son of my native city, and without diminishing one particle of my love and esteem for my adopted country, including my wife and children and friends and fellow-citizens there.

CHAPTER LXXXIII.

OUR TRAVELS IN EUROPE IN 1881.

1881 was a year of travel for us. chiefly showing Lulu places and relations, which I had, but she had not, seen before. We commenced on the first day of the year. After breakfast we left Heilbronn by railroad for Würzburg, seeing on the way, historic scenes at Weinsberg, such as the Weibertreu or "Woman's Faith", also the places of horrors there committed during the "Boor's" war. Then the Fränkish Hohenlohe districts, where the old nobility may still be seen in their old homes. At Würzburgh we were in the town, where the "Bürger" element has governed and is still governing. We stopped at the hotel I lived at formerly, and where my son Rudolf boarded. We visited the lecture rooms, where I formerly listened to professors; we visited also the theater and drank of the excellent good wine raised in that neighborhood. We expected to see our nephew Böttinger. then the owner of the brewery his father built; but he was with his wife's parents at Barmen. spending New Year. On Sunday morning we heard in front of the palace the music played by the Royal band. It was the grandest sight and enjoyment, Lulu had yet experienced in Europe.

We saw at night at the Theater, played by one of the finest actors of Germany, the farce called: "The Flick Schneider". January 3rd. we returned to Heilbronn. There we found brother Edward in bad humor, which was not a very agreeable sight to Lulu, but could not be helped. Next morning we left for our long journey to Italy and return, which we expected to occupy us a half year at least. The first point was the town of Marbach; there I had two things to show to Lulu; first: the house where Schiller was born, and the monument erected on the adjoining hill; second: the schools and the rooms, where I was a scholar in the years 1824, 1825, 1826 and 1827. I saw that Lulu, like most Americans, had no mind for attachments to family localities. Her love of country, embraces too large an area to leave much room for tender attachments to small places. She thought we Europeans had too much of that kind of sympathetics.

At Stuttgardt Lulu had to become acquainted with many of our relatives, before unknown to her. There was my brother Eberhardt' and his wife with several daughters and sons. One of the latter–Alfred–had just married a brand new wife, a very neat useful person. There too my cousin, Eugene Rümelin, nearly eighty years old, the highest Judge in the Administrative Court of Würtemberg. She also met, for the first time, my cousin Alwina, the daughter of my mother's brother. She was the only one, of the relatives of my mother, that we met. I bought at that time Myer's guide book for Italy and an English-Italian dictionary. Lulu now began to feel that she was actually going on a very interesting long journey; eine Weltreise.

Whilst yet in Stuttgardt I got from London the proof sheets of "American Politics". Trübner offered me his own proof-reader and hinted, that I would find my book much improved on final appearance. I apprehended, that the process would be one similar to that mentioned, as to Durbin Ward, and declined the offer. I will admit however, that I would have liked a proof-reader to follow me, that would have confined himself to corrections of my diction, composition and grammar. Lulu did that by reading the proof sheets after me and applying some of her Cincinnati High School erudition; and I was glad to have her do it; and thanked her for it.

From Studtgardt we made many excursions to places, where I had been much in my youth; to-wit: Ludwigsburgh, Denkendorf, Hohenheim, Maulbronn and Nürtingen. I found, that while these localities were of pointed interest to me, they were of much less interest to my daughter. To her, those places are of interest, where *she* played and worked. I found too, that it is difficult, if not impossible, to preserve attachments to causes that perished; because they turned out to be mistakes. On the other hand I found, that one can not love folks, that clear you of errors. The association with persons, prominent in the great European folly of 1848, became irksome to me, because I was at a loss what to say to them. At first I called on them at Stuttgardt and other places, but soon saw, that they did not care to be reminded, even by the visit from a friend, of their former mistakes. Partisan friendships are not real friendships.

But to return to my narrative. Early in January we set out on our contemplated journey over South Germany to Italy, but went along slowly. We took in Esslingen, Ulm, Augsburg and Munich on the way. At the latter city we stopped indeed some time, which was a mistake; for Munich is not a healthy place in Winter. I picked up the illness there, that plagued me in Venice. At Esslingen we called on Baron Von Soden and his excellent lady, both former residents of Cincinnati, and still remembered there for their useful services to the German-English schools and other social usefulness. They gave us a very pleasant greeting and entertained us kindly. From Esslingen we went the same day to Ulm. There we saw the sights of the town, and ascended, of course, the Münster, then undergoing repairs, and it struck me as remarkable, how safely reconstructions were being made in this ancient chathedral. This showeth: how well done the original construction must have been. In the United States they would have had to tear down and then rebuild entirely. Our hotel in Augsburg: "The Three Moors", the city hall with its historic details, pointed out to us, that there was once a very interesting past in the center of Europe, and that the present importance of the West is an innovation against it. The Fugger dwellings showed us, that the better solutions of the conflicts between capital and labor, are those, in which capital steps forth in advance, and of its own accord, to alleviate social embarrasments. Great pleasure was afforded to us by our attendance on the Augsburg Theater, at which we saw the new opera "Carmen" played. The new Opera House proves, that our age can, provided, it does its public business through a good administration, accomplish finer results than any accomplished in antiquity.

Munich we found to be an over cold place, even for January. We staid there nevertheless two weeks, because the Theaters, the Art Galleries, the St. Peter's tower, with view to the Alps, Circus Renz and the new Rathskeller, with its good eating and drinking, held us fast. We left Munich January 25th, and arrived the same evening at Innsbruck. The hotel, we stopped at, was grand, but cheerless for its, then, emptiness. My foot, that had been troubling me for weeks, now gave me notice, that it was time for me to make an attempt to have it cured. It had got quite sore from my wearing warmly lined india-rubber shoes, brought from America, that were too large for me and chafed me at the instep. A Tyrolean apothecary gave me. a cooling salve and it relieved me at once, enough to do some walking and sight showing for Lulu. We saw the "Landes-Museum". I discovered at Innsbruck, that, as already permised, Munich had given me an illness along on the road, that I had better have attended to; but I thought I'll wait, until we get a little further South. On the 27th of January we reached Trent, after a tedious journey of five hours. I had never stopped there before. My foot pained me so much. that I concluded to stop over one day anyhow. A shoemaker remedied somewhat the defects in my shoes and I could, after remaining one day, walk about the town. I went, of course, first to the church, where the Council of Trent spend months, in vain, wrangling about questions, for which there is no positive solution, because they turn on doctrines and faith, not knowledge; there can therefore never be any final rule adopted, as there is in the arithmetic rule "twice two makes four".

We departed from Trent, to Verona on Jan. 28th, and arrived there the same day. At Verona Lulu became sick My foot was much better. I called on an Italian House with letters of introduction, that were really pressed upon me by persons in Cincinnati. The letters were evidently disagreeable to those, to whom they were addressed, but the ill-will wore off very soon, when they found, that we wanted nothing of them, except common courtesy. The incident confirmed a view, I had long held, to-wit: that you must not accept letters of introduction from casual acquaintances, nor give them to such. I had never stopped long enough at Verona, to see the town thoroughly; my visit there from the 28th to the 31st of January, proved of great interest. I called to mind all, that Heine wrote about it, and perceived now, how well he describes and reasons.

I think, Verona should be visited in the spring, not sooner than May. January 31st we went to Milan. This place I had visited before in 1866, while Arch-Duke Maximilian was still in grateful memmory, but I took a new interest in seeing it, first, because my daughter was with me, and second, because I had heard so much of the improved condition of Milan, as regards commerce and manufactures. The international exhibition, then going on, there, brought this improvement very visibly before us. I found the same cousin, whom I had met there in 1866, still there employed as a chemist; and he pointed out to us, how the many new enterprises had been brought there, through the new foreign elements, that had immigrated into the city. I saw very plainly, how different this immigration was to that of the United States. To Milan came chiefly those, that brought modern technical improved knowledge and enlarged commercial thrift; while to America were for a long time, and are still largely drawn those chiefly, who expect to live by crude and rough work. Moreover, as my cousin pointed out, there are now in Milan renewals of the ancient reciprocal migrations between Italy and Germany, that enhance the existence of both. He said very wisely: "The migrations are inter-migrations." I added: "Yes, and intermigration is the best spirit of our age." We stopped at the Hotel Milano. It was rather a good house, but I could have suggested a few improvements.

February 6th, we journeyed to Turin, where I renewed my acquaintance with Kossuth, which I had formed about thirty years previous in Cincinnati. I had since seen Deak, and could now well see the marked difference there is, between these two Hungarian patriots. Kossuth's failure must be respected for its nobleness and ideality; but Deak's success, must be approved for its measured correctness. Deak is a model guide; Kossuth a warning!

February 7th we went to Genua, February 9th to Pisa. At both these places we frequented the well-known places of interest. I had visited both places before. Lulu was well pleased with them, because they had more of a modern look. February 11th, we arrived at Rome. We stopped at my former hotel "Minerva". We remained in Rome twelve days. This city is always both a marvel and a mystery to visitors. I saw it first in 1866 under Pio IX., now it was under King Humberto, and the Pope was half deposed, and half re-ascending. Rome presented a much more pointed appearance, than it did in 1866. The twelve days we spent in Rome and vicinity were a constant strain upon our reflections on the history of Politics, Church Affairs, State-craft, the Arts and Mechanics. When I left Rome before, it was a relief to my mind; it was so also in 1881. I was glad, that the old Rome was gone, and that the new Rome had come; but I was so pestered with thoughts as to the future Rome, I wished for, that it chilled up my gladness. We left Rome the day after Washington's birthday, for Naples, where we remained nine days. Naples presented to us a much more distinct aspect of pleasure than Rome. It is nature, we come to see in Naples. When we first arrived, it presented to us Nature in its somber garb of transition from Winter to Spring; but it put on the bright habiliments very quickly. We felt at once, that man is here, like a child, ever pursuing nature like a butterfly. Nature always steals from a stranger a day or two longer, than he meant to stay. We left it rather reluctantly after going up to Mount Vesuvius, seeing the ruins of Pompeii, and closing up with the Blue Grotto and the Bay of Naples, and we left Naples itself, fully satisfied, of having reserved its grandest sights, to the last.

On the ides of March we turned on our journey's return voyage, and we left by railroad for Florence, making the journey in one day. We stopped over a few hours in Rome, and saw the most magnificent carnival procession, that had been there for many years. Our R. R. route between Rome and Florence took us through regions, over which fifteen years previous no sensible man would have travelled, unless guarded by a strong military force. In Florence we spent two weeks, and every day with gratification. We met there Mr. John Bigelow and family, who had spent the Winter there. We were also introduced to Carl Hillebrand and his family. At both houses we were treated hospitably, and were made acquainted with many other distinguished personages. Mr. Bigelow is a well-known statesman and author in the United States, who has taken a very beneficial part in American politics. Carl Hillebrand is by birth a German, but a distinguished French and English scholar and author; and at the evening parties given at his house were always persons of high reputation. For Lulu these meetings had a special gratification, because the wife and daughters of Mr. Bigelow were the first American ladies she had met since she had left home. She was evidently liked by them.

From Florence to Bologna we travelled through another strip of country, that was a few years previous considered dangerous to every traveller. Now we were rushed along the wildest parts of it at the rate of forty miles an hour.

We stopped at places for refreshments, with many rough looking fellows standing about; but not even the roughest made us now afraid. I thought of the wonderful change possible in Europe, if only the right kind of restoration shall be effected there. At Bologna we spent five days at Hotel Brun, formerly kept by my fellow-country-man and playmate. To my grief my health was not good, nor would health return by the use of common remedies. Still I managed to go with Lulu over Bologna including Campo Santo, and there we saw my playmate's beautiful monument. It indicated to me nothing, except that he must have died rich. The high cost mentioned to me, of the marble trophy, was an impediment to my recollections of him as a youth. I could not think really, that my playfellow was under it. I wished it away and a simple gravestone in its place. March 20th, we departed from Bologna to Padua, travelling upon a splendid railroad over lands and rivers, that I had crossed in 1865 at the risk of my life. At Padua, I felt the sickness, that had troubled me for a whole month coming on more and more. We saw the sights of Padua rather superficially, but still we managed to see them all, including the University. March 22nd, we journeyed to Venice. There my health broke down completely, after taking rooms at Hotel Bauer. I have no doubt, that the universal dampness, that prevailed there, precipitated my illness. I meant to hold up, until I reached Vienna; for I feared Italian doctors. But it came otherwise. I had to go to bed, have a physician called, and take his medicine and follow his prescription. To my great satisfaction, the physician, that came, was a German, called Keppler. I took his prescription readily, and soon fell asleep, and slept for forty-eight hours. When I awoke, I felt sort of well. I was weak as a cat; but still felt better. The German nurses, that attended me, told me, how incomprehensively I had talked in my dreams. Lulu was not in, when I awoke. She had asserted her independence, and gone sight seeing, without a guide. But she got along very well with the guide-book, which I bought in Stuttgardt.

Next morning, the doctor advised me to get up, and venture out, after eating a frugal meal. I did, and recuperated rapidly. being careful in my diet. The doctor told me, to "eat meat moderately, and drink red Hungarian wine." He sent me a moderate bill of forty francs, I sent him fifty francs, with my special thanks for the wine he ordered me to drink. I needed not to go sight seeing in Venice, having seen it all thoroughly fifteen years previous. Lulu's walks over the town, during my illness, had been more extended, than I had expected. She had, evidently, a nack for travelling alone; so it needed, but two days, to bring up the remainder of the sights; and we left Venice for Triest, in the latter part of March, and arrived there in the evening. after a one day's journey. We saw Maximilian's palace—"Miramare"—on the way, and again pondered on his sad fate in Mexico. At Triest we spent but a day. I wanted to show the place to my daughter, as a city, that contained, in marked distinctness, two populations; to-wit: Italians and Germans, who carry on their business at a minimum of quarreling, and do it very successfully.

From Triest we went to Gratz. There we stopped at Hotel Elephant. I had stopped formerly at Hotel Arch Duke Charles. I think the former was the better hotel of the two. At Gratz I took a special pleasure, to see again, and to show to my daughter, the principal Church, the Mausoleum of Ferdinand the Second, the notorious instigator of the thirty years war in Germany. And to point out to her, the fact, I mentioned before, that the pigeons were there in large numbers, performing, by the deposit of their excrements, what history ought to have done long ago, in a cleaner way; namely, covered him all over with infamy. We ascended the fine high hill, called: the Citadel of Gratz. I got very tired in ascending it, but it was a healthy fatigue, and the sight from it completely invigorated me. Dinner tasted very good after it. April 1st, we went to Vienna, and I felt stronger and stronger every day, as I walked about in my native land. We took eight days to see the city of Vienna. It had improved greatly in public buildings, since 1874, when I was last in Vienna. But in private places, and all along some of the streets, I saw signs of a waning prosperity and civilization. The stanza came to my mind:

"Wrong ways long pursued, are sure to end in evil."

April 9th, we took a jaunt to Pest, in Hungary. In the car we had with us two, rather young Jesuite Fathers, who, when hearing: that we came from the United States, conversed freely with us on religion and government. Lulu enjoyed every hit these Jesuits gave me. As I did not think them hits, but adroit evasions, I did not take it amiss; still I reflected some on the fact, that my daughter sided with two Priests, rather than with her father. We returned to Vienna April 11th, and there resumed sight seeing. We went to the palace Schönbrunn, also to Ladenburgh, ascended Leopoldsberg, and, of course, saw several plays at the Hofburgh Theatre and the

Grand Opera House. My former friends in the city, Weniger and Schwede, we were told, had left the city. A Professor Auer, to whom we had letters of introduction from the same parties, that gave us such, to persons in Verona, was very friendly the first day, but there was something in his behaviour, that kept us from calling on him again. We departed for Prague, pleased with Vienna; but we could not avoid seeing, that its population had gone through some sorrow lately and was still grieving over it. I grieved with them. April 16th, we arrived, in the evening, at Prague. There we met my old friend Weniger, who had become president of the principal bank. He was married and was conceded to be an excellent bank officer. I called upon him and he paid us all the attentions his official duties allowed him. He took us on Sunday to the Spring Festival, held in the country about a mile outside of the city, where we saw the elite of Prague. Lulu had thus an opportunity to see a Bohemia May-day, celebrated in all its ancient glory. Prague was to Lulu of great interest. It was to her an entirely new sight. We were in Bohemia, where all persons and things looked a little odd. From Prague we went to Dresden, where we stopped two days at Hotel de Saxe. We saw Faust played at the theatre. We journeyed through Hoff to Nüremberg. At Hoff we stopped over night at the one good hotel there. It was a regular old fashioned German country town tavern, with a solid treatment and excellent fare. It is one of the best within a radius of a hundred miles and it was a great treat to us. I enjoyed it as a good morsel preserved for us out of olden times. Next day we went to Bamberg, where we spent a day. We there visited, of course, the graves and monument of Emperor Heinrich and Empress Kunigunde in the church. They were the celebrated couple, that kept the pledge of carnal purity throughout their entire married life. We saw also the palace of King Otto, who was elected King of Greece and went there with his wife to carry on the government, but resigned, when he found, that his marriage was not to be blessed with heirs. He and his wife are also buried at Bamberg. Such two dead Barrenesses gave us a deep insight into the infatuations of such grand personages. From Bamberg we passed in the afternoon to Nüremberg, where we stopped at Hotel Bavaria, and spent two days, seeing all the items of interest in the churches and public buildings, including a civil marriage by the mayor of the city. From Nüremberg we went in one day, stopping two hours over in Heilbronn, and then to Stuttgardt. There we took temporary lodgings at hotel Textor. After a few days we engaged two rooms with a Mr. Roller for two months. Our coffee and breakfast we took at our rooms; our dinner at Hotel Textor; our suppers as opportunity offered. Lulu took music lessons of Miss Mölik, which improved her playing on the piano very much. She visited with me the theatre several times a week and enjoyed especially the society of my good cousin Alwina. We had little idea, that the latter would die so soon as she did; she died within the year 1891. I, though sixty-seven years old, did not think, that I was too old to learn. I entered myself as student in the Polytechnicon and heard the lectures of Professors Schall, Vischer and Denzel. Schall's lectures were on political economy; including taxation, money and credit. He was at that time one of the King's counsellors, and his lectures were very instructive to me. They were delivered early in the morning before breakfast. His private conversations had a special value for me. Vischer's lectures were on Aesthetics and he illustrated them by explanations and reviews of poets. He used for that purpose Shakespeare, Goethe, Schiller and Lessing. Vischer was then an old gentleman of over eighty years; he died lately. Every lecture was a treat. They were largely attended by ladies and gentlemen of the highest Court circles. Dentzel's lectures were of a high ethical character. I heard not only these of him, but also his extra readings on the "Niebelungen". The Professor and myself were surprised to learn, at our mutual introduction, that he was the son of Rev. Dentzel, who was the clergyman that instructed me, fifty-three years previous, in religion, preparitory to my confirmation. I also had many opportunities at the Polytechnicon to witness chemical experiments. In one word, I do not think, that I ever spent two months in my life, in which I learned as much as in the lectures named.

CHAPTER LXXXIV.

OUR SOJOURN IN STUTTGARDT IN MAY AND JUNE 1881.

Proofsheets of my book published in London reached me now regularly and I corrected the proofs promptly and returned them with corrections.

One day in April a letter came from Schwede in Vienna, inquiring: whether we could not meet at some place? The letter apprised me for the first time, of the fact, that we had missed each other. the spring previous in Vienna. I regretted it exceedingly; because Schwede was one of the acquaintances I made in 1865 and prized highly. I wrote him, that I would meet him on the 4th until the 6th of June in Munich. He accepted the invitation promptly, and we had a joyous meeting. We both regretted our missing each other a few weeks privious in Vienna.

Towards the end of May I saw, that it was high time to perfect our arrangements for returning to America; and on May 23rd I wrote to Messers Stevenson in Glasgow for berths for myself and daughter in the steamer Devonia, that left Glasgow August 4th. At the same time I laid out the travels we still had to perform, so as to carry out the views as to Lulu's education. I made up the following programme: We will stay in Stuttgardt until July 1st, so as to finish Lulu's piano lessons; and I my lectures at the Polytechnicon. also arranged for visits to relatives still unvisited. We fixed thus to go from Stuttgardt to Tübingen, the University of Würtemberg; then to Schaffhausen, so as to see the Falls of the Rhine; thence to Zürich. to visit my wife's relations; thence to Lucerne and to ascend the Rigi; all in time to get to Bern, the Capital of Switzerland, and see there the Swiss National Festival in July, and at the same time call on relations in Burgdorf near Berne; then to visit Thun, Interlacken and the Giesbach. Then return to Bern and go thence to Freiburgh, Lausanne and Geneva. Then return by way of Freiburgh to Aarau and finally to Basle. From Basle our route took us to Baden-Baden to bid farewell to my sister Sophie; also at Carlsruhe to see my sister Mathilda. This programm was to be carried out so as to bring us to Heilbronn, for final visit by the 11th of July; without the loss of a single hour and all without undue haste. We then meant to remain in Heilbronn five days, and see all of our numerous relatives, and partake of several entertainments. Among others, we proposed to have an excursion to my step-brother at Oehringen, where he was, what we call "County Auditor." My brother Theodore was to join us at Heilbronn, for the purpose of going with us down the Rhine as far as Cologne. This arrangement was fully and punctually carried out.

The most important incident of these journeyings was the fact, that I heard, on July 4th. in the Reception Room of the Swiss National Government, the sad news of the assassination of President Garfield. The news had been telegraphed from Washington, and were read to those present, by the Swiss President's Secretary.

I was deeply shocked at this atrocious crime; but I heard its announcement, as if it sounded like the logic of the events, that occurred in the United States, since March, 1861. Napoleon's remarks, about the concourse of events, towards a fall, came to my mind, and I saw in our American future, more gloomy forebodings, than bright outlooks. I put away my apprehensions, by saying to myself: Don't forget, that you are sixty-seven years old; you may see matters too darkly.

CHAPTER LXXXV.

FROM HOME, FOR HOME.

We started on the 18th of July, from Heilbronn, for our American Home, by railroad to Frankforth, where we arrived at noon. We called, after dinner, on my nephew, Emil Rümelin, and his young handsome wife; we saw then the most important sights of that city. My nephew Heerman accompanied us also. On the 20th, we were in Mayence; on the 21st in Cologne. There we met the grandson of my brother Edward, Otto Sailer, and we saw Cologne together. On the 22nd, we were in Brussels, whence we made, on the 25th, a detour to Antwerp, La Hague and Amsterdam. My brother Theodore, had returned home from Cologne. We went via Dover to London, and arrived there on the 26th of July.

There we stopped at Hotel Royal again, and took pains to close up, whatever remained for us in and about London unsettled. I paid the small balance due on my book "American Politics." It cost me altogether about $800, and I must say, that Mr. Trübner treated me very unfairly. I do not regret having published the work, nor the gratuitous circulation in America; but I do feel that Trübner had not rendered me anything like an adequate service for the money he obtained from me.

London was made specially cheerful to us, by my niece, daughter of my sister Sophie, who was married to a wool merchant, Mr. Rommel. She hadtwo children. They lived in the eastern environs of London, and we enjoyed our visit to their pretty home greatly. Mrs. Rommel reminded me much of my deceased mother. Another delightful opportunity to share German-English society, we obtained at Alphonse Roman's family home, which he called "Neckar Lodge," after the river, that runs past our native town. Roman's aunt was my elder brother's wife. My brother regarded him almost like a son. We spent some time at other places of public interest; we saw, for instance: Windsor Castle and Hampden Court. July 31st, we left London, and got, the same day, to Edinburgh. There we spent three days in looking all over the city and its points of historic interest. On the 2nd of August we went to Glascow after breakfast and arrived there before dinner. On the 3rd we spent looking over Glasgow and on the 4th we embarked on the Devonia for New York. Our European journey was over!

It lasted almost nine months and did us both much educational good. With this European tour of Lulu's, I had finally carried out the purpose, that I had silently formed in 1845; to wit: that I would, before I died, take all my children to Europe, show them our relatives and give them an education there. My three sons have attended European Universities and they are, in my opinion, guarded against false patriotism, because they have learned, what real patriotism is; that it does not consist in disparaging other countries and people. And I may add, that I feel certain, that this guards them against any false Germanism also. I am now more than ever convinced, that American civilization needs the preservation of its ties with European civilization. An isolated America is a lost America Mastery of European governments over American society is wrong; but influence on America by good literary men and by scientific instructors is right. And the former is a good reason for the latter; because there may be useful positive knowledge without abstract religious belief; but there cannot be useful abstract religious belief, unless it has been fortified by positive knowledge and enlightenment.

CHAPTER LXXXVI.

ONCE MORE IN THE UNITED STATES.

We reached New York, August 16th, 1881. There Miss Whorum, the sister-in-law of my son Louis, met us at the Hotel St. Nicholas, and she and Lulu and myself, did New York, as the saying is, to-wit: we drove out to Central Park, and the Water Works, and saw the harbor and the bay, with adjoining towns, from the ferries. I called on Schurz, then editor on the Evening Post, who received me with a query on his face, as if he wanted to know, first of all: what made me call on him? I replied also by a query on my face, and then left to call on other friends. I also visited my friends: Roelker, Moran and Stern. On the 18th of August we; namely: Miss Whorum, Lulu and myself, went to Philadelphia and thence to Baltimore. There we got into a neglected hotel and made haste therefore to leave it and to call on the sons of deceased cousin, Pauline. We found them well employed in the street railroad building. On the 20th, we went to Washington. There we called on George Mark, nephew of my wife; and he, having been long assistant in the Congressional Library, introduced us to Librarian Spofford and assisted us with his knowledge of Washington, and showed us the town and its more important places, including the Congressional burying place. August 21st, in the evening, we left Washington for Cincinnati and arrived there next day. We went homewards to Dent the same afternoon.

I had concluded, to fall right in with my American home life again, and my neighbors in Green township agreed to take me back on that basis. August 25th, I attended, as every year for twenty years, "Harvest Home". I listened more attentively to the speeches, than the rest of the crowd; for I had to make some show as an excuse for having been a stranger nine months.

August 28th, my daughter-in-law Bell, brought me a grandson and agreed, that she would name him after my father; to-wit: Benjamin, if I agreed, that he should also have the name she selected, namely: "Oscar". I agreed to this and he has the two names, but that of Benjamin is very much neglected in practice. Copies of my literary child—my book "Critical Review of American Politics", appeared about a month after my arrival and I distributed them gratis to the several state libraries and principal newspapers, leaving the rest for sale at Robert Clarke & Co. I delivered a speech before the Sons of Inquiry in September, on the subject: "Education of Adults". I had spoken upon the same subject before and could now only reiterate its importance to American Society.

My rehabilitation in Cincinnati would not have been complete, without a speech before the German Pioneer Society; so, being invited, I made one in November, which I had published at my

expense and sent copies to many persons, whom I presumed, it
might interest. I have also filed copies among the papers deposited
in the City Library.

The year 1882, stands in my memory, as that one, in which I
became fully conscious, that not only were there some new species
of weeds in our fields, but also that old ones prevailed more largely
than ever before. Weeds have a perennial existence here. The so
called "White-tops" ruined in 1881 many a meadow; and even in our
day, after persistant efforts, it seems impossible to exterminate
them. How to kill weeds on our land and abuses in politics, are
evidently to be hereafter, the most onerous problems in America.
I was invited in January 1882, to write for the Quarterly published
at the Tübingen University by its Faculty, an essay on the Monroe
Doctrine. I complied, and the article was promptly published. I
have the article, in the file of the Quarterly named, in my library.
My household affairs and farming concerns engaged my attention
anew on my return from Europe, and I allow myself to mention
here, as a gratification for myself, that at no time in my life, did I
seriously neglect my duties to my family, my farm and other civil
relations. It is true, that I took a deep interest in public matters
and read, studied and wrote and spoke about them much; but I
never seriously neglected my home or means of gaining my liveli-
hood. I never was a dependant upon public support; and I ever
regarded it as the first duty of a citizen, that becomes what is called:
a public person, to secure to his family, himself included, civil independence and civic integrity. Whoever fails to do this, will in the
United States, sooner or later, become an abject dependant on the
social powers, that control here public affairs. I was always strictly
independent as to this, and I have ever guarded my freedom of
thought; because I have never depended on the press or my cotemporaries in this country alone. I have ever endeavored to remain
informed of what was being promulgated in other countries. And
thus have I always striven to find the abstract right of a question,
and then having found it, to make due application of it to existing
circumstances. Nor did I ever read only the literature of some
political party alone, or in any special language exclusively. And
I may say: the same as to any particular science or any special professional study. I do not speak of this, because I claim any superiority for myself over my contemporaries. I only wish to state, that
we were different, and the difference arose from the unavoidable
causes, which I have explained in this, my life. I think that these,
our differences, should be mutually respected. I certainly did this
to my fellow citizens, but not many did it to me. They misjudged
me and made false accusations; at the same time they exalted themselves without any valid justification, and they claimed superiority
for being born here, a claim I have always denied.

I kept up my promiscuous reading after my return from Europe in 1881, and so too my literary labors; the latter however with less strength and inclination, as I grew older and the numbers of the members of my family circle decreased. I found it more difficult to form new acquaintances, as death reduced the number of my *old* ones. Age will tell! We become stiffer, and blending with others is more difficult. I came therefore, as we say in German: "More to myself". But I did this not as a cynic or hermit. My correspondence with friends and relatives on both sides of the Atlantic, were as active as ever, and so were my interchanges of political views with thoughtful men in other lands. There were, however, many occurrences, in this period of my life, to prevent its being too monotonous.

CHAPTER LXXXVII.

INTERRUPTIONS IN MY FAMILY LIFE.

In May 1881, I received a letter from my son Rudolf in Madison, announcing; that he wanted to take unto himself a wife, and these indications soon developed into a significant reality in the shape of a call on us by him, accompanied by Miss Marmet, whom he introduced as his bride. His call included a request for my wife to come down to Indiana, and to use her motherly eyes in looking round for a proper house for the new pair to live in. Next it developed in a further call on me also, to go down to Madison and to inspect, with Mr. and Mrs. Marmet, the situation. Well, it all ended in our becoming aware, that we old folks should help the young folks with money to get them a roof over their heads. To me fell the solidly useful part; and I agreed to buy a certain house in the center of Madison and to make the advance payment of $2,000.00. The Marmets were to furnish the other half of the purchase money, and to complete the household furniture and adding "modern improvements"; a much meaning word in America. October 18th, the marriage took place in Cincinnati; Mr. and Mrs. Marmet were to furnish the wedding; we Reemelins—about a dozen—to attend it. It was an unnecessary costly affair, in a public house. At it, I made, as I say in my diary: "an out and out laughing speech, while inwardly I felt like weeping". The happy pair retired to Madison, with the intention, as I thought, of making it their permanent residence; but the calends of the future wrote it otherwise, of which more hereafter.

A very provoking affair gave us considerable annoyance during the Summer. A daughter of my eldest sister Lina, married a Mr. Gallas in Rhine Bavaria, about five years previous. We had heard nothing of them since. In 1882, we received a letter from them, inquiring: whether we would recommend their immigration to the United States? I replied, that I could not do so, without knowing more of their capacities and purposes. Shortly afterwards, before my letter could have reached them, we received the news, that they had arrived in this country and would wait for letters from me at a certain merchant in New York. I wrote again and sent copies of my former letter; but we were informed, when our letter had hardly been despatched, that they were on the way to Cincinnati, and would on arrival call for word from us at a place he designated, but not naming the time, when he would arrive. I at once left my address at this place and stated besides in a letter, how they could reach us at Dent. I also gave them the name of a good hotel in Cincinnati, the one where the omnibus to Dent stopped, and, of course, then waited for further news. We were next informed by letter from Mr. Gallas, that he had been at Cincinnati; had done well in selling rights under his patent and thanked me, for naming to him so good and so cheap a hotel. A month subsequent to that, Mrs. Gallas, my niece, wrote, complaining of our inhospitality and informing me, that she was sick of cancer and was unable to travel. I wrote her a letter, explaining all we had done and inviting her to come to us. To this letter we received no reply. I cannot, while noting down these facts, see, how my wife and myself should under the circumstances have lacked in any hospitality. We certainly desired to render them all the help possible. We received, a year afterwards, news of her death, from other persons. Further comment seems unnecessary.

The "Taxpayers League," a body of volunteer reformers, that had been formed, while I was in Europe, invited me to join them in 1882, which I did, early in the year; though a little doubtful of the propriety of such organizations in a Democratic government. I asked myself then, and often since: whether the semi-organic should be allowed to regulate the organic? I concluded, after much reflection, that, as public affairs were, in the United States, then already conducted by semi-organic public organs, or parties, it would not be wrong to add another such organ, as a negative and for corrections. Moreover, I knew the members of the Taxpayers' League, to be gentlemen of good character, and I became, therefore, an active member, and did considerable work during the year. Mr. Edmund Dexter, was our leader, and a liberal contributor to the funds. Rufus King was also much help to us by his wise counsels. The Society was eventually superceded by the "Committee of One Hundred," of which I also became a member, but left it several years ago. I learned to my sorrow, again, that, of which very few persons in the United States are aware, to-wit: that the main justification for political organization and government, consists in its being a counteraction to social selfishness and ambition.

These several bodies grew up in the United States, for the reason that many abuses existed, that had crept into our city and county administration, through public officers and corporations, that were the tools of contractors and jobbers, that had succeeded, in making the tax-paying public their milch cow, either for getting rich, or enjoying a luxurious living.

The waste of the primeval forests, a subject, on which I had written often for the "Ohio Farmer," caused the starting of another such semi-organic society: "The Forestry Association." I became also a member of this. Of it, a Mr. Leue, a German by birth, and school teacher by occupation, became Secretary, and he succeeded, after a time, to get a law passed, for organizing a State Forestry Bureau, with a Forest Commissioner at its head, with a good salary. Mr. Leue became that Commissioner, and he was, under Ohio's public administration, a further appendage to our disjointed state organism. His reports contained many suggestions of reform; but they were never read with the interest they deserved, and may be said to have fallen dead born upon the public. I contributed a few articles, that met the same fate. I repeat: the difficulty of such separate and disjointed public functionaries is, that they are not in proper interaction with the other organs of the government. Besides, our public lands are not managed, as they should be, by one public organization, and there can hardly be, therefore, the right kind of official action, under such disjointed ways. The lands have passed, and are passing, from the general public ownership of our federal government. They should not be misused and robbed of their general utility, and pass into a private ownership, that has absolute, indeed, I might say, sovereign rights of possession and use. And it may justly be said, that one of the most hopeless tasks of American society now, is to get the lands of the land into rightful legal relations. *It involves the future of the country!* Mr. Leue has now ceased to be State Forestry Commissioner. He has charge of the parks in the City of Cincinnati.

August 9th, a grandson was born to us in Knoxville, Tenn. It cost me the usual silver spoon I sent to my grandchildren. I was repaid, by the pride I enjoyed, in being a grandfather. It occurred to me then, that there is a queer duplicity in this relationship; to-wit: that, while each grandchild counts a peg up in the family; it counts a peg down with the grandparents. August 27th, 1882, we celebrated the fiftieth anniversary of my arrival in Philadelphia, in 1832. We had a goodly company of Reemelins to dinner, and had a good time generally. On such occasions, the retrospect on early hardships, is more pleasant, than the outlook for enjoyments in the years yet to come.

August 31st, I made my speech on the history of Green township at the Annual Home Festival, near Cheviot. This speech was published at my expense in English and gratuitously distributed over Green township; I translated it into German and sent the manuscript to the Quarterly published in the University of Tübingen. The Quarterly published it and sent me a very liberal compensation for it. In it I gave the names of three hundred and twenty early settlers of the township up to 1840, and I gave other data, by which the people of the township could, for the first time, realize the actual course of their development. They could see, for instance. by comparing the list of the three hundred actual settlers with the number twenty of those still remaining alive and residents, that there was a greater mortality and a more extensive emigration from the township, than they were aware of. They could arrive at the real truth on these subjects by the other table, that gave them the respective increase in the decennial periods since 1800. There they could see: that the increase of population was growing continually less and that it now has reached only about 2½ per cent in a decennial period. Moreover could they learn, that there was one period, when the population did not increase at all. Some of my hearers and readers complained of the sarcastic tone that, they said, prevailed in the speech. I certainly did not intend to perpetrate any sarcasms. I meant to submit a frank statement of the actual development of the township with the view to cure:

"Our pride, our erring pride".

In October I delivered before the German Literary Club of Cincinnati a lecture on the Suez Canal, whose main object was to remind us: that the motto:

"Westward the Star of Empire moves",

is no longer true in the exclusive sense, in which we use it; that, in fact, there is coming, for Europe, a Southern and Eastern revival, that will far outstrip all Western outputs. October 31st, we had Mr. "*Silver*", the temporary German Imperial Consul to dinner. He afterwards was sent to Samoa and he gave a new impulse to German colonization there. He made a good impression on me, by his fine intelligent knowledge of history, and bright forecast as to the future.

December 4th, I became suddenly extremely unwell. We sent for Dr. Davis, our village physician, who remedied my severe illness in a short time; but d d not conceal from me, that this sickness of mine meant a *first* hard spell of disease, that would be followed in time by others more severe, relatively, as I took good or ill care of myself. I entered New Year with this admonition well in my mind. It did not frighten me; but it made me more cautious in my living.

CHAPTER LXXXVIII.

FATE AND MYSELF AT CROSS PURPOSES, 1883.

I had intended, to make the year 1883 the last of my, public and private, strong activities, and the first, of the years of rest and quiet, preparatory to my death; but instead of this, I was sort of forced into a continuance of existing engagements, and even into entering new ones. I kept on writing for the "Merchant and Manufacturer", the German papers, and also the "Socialist"; I also continued in my school directorship, including my teaching history to the children every Friday afternoon; but queerer still, I allowed myself to be persuaded to go, at my own expense, to Columbus, and become the lobbyist, to assist an old acquaintance, that had often acted foully towards me, in getting for him money long due to him, for an overflow of his factory in Cincinnati by a break in the State canal. Dietrich was the name of that individual. He had once become very rich by a railroad speculation, but had, by adopting expensive habits, become very poor. The $6000.00, I helped to secure him, served to help him along, to live out in comfort the two years, that he lived afterwards. His life was unusually varied in its immigrant vicissitudes, as to poverty and riches.

A pleasanter turn in my life came to me through my nephew, Prof. Emil Rümelin, who published in the Tübingen Quarterly an essay on Federal Law. It was to me a most welcome contribution towards a better knowledge on the subject. I wrote for a New York paper a commentary on it, and received the thanks of several American jurists. The essay contained true federal law.

Armin Tenner, an enterprising publisher in Berlin, called on me, when he was about to publish his book "America", with the request to write for his work three articles; to-wit: "Taxation", "The Railroads" and "The Post Office System", all with reference to America, and he offered to compensate me for them. This offer was a novelty to me, for I had hitherto been seldom paid for anything, that I wrote for the public, and then only after it was published. I devoted therefore to this task extra care, and was most happy over the good opinions, expressed over my three articles by critics.

The Reemelin birth record was this year augmented by the arrival of my grandson Herman. I got the idea some way, that he was going to be my smartest grand-child, and it looked that way for some time; but defects in his physical constitution developed and the good boy died in 1890. I shed more tears than, I ever did before. Death crossed my path in 1883 often, by the decease of interesting cotemporaries. Alexander Long's departure after a long illness pained me deeply. I had known him for over forty years, and always, with all his faults, for a genial soul. In 1884 he was a good country school master in my neighborhood; he soon progressed, if progress it was, into an active township politician and valuable aid-de-camp, to the leaders he supported. In 1848 he became himself a leader as a zealous pro-slavery and anti-negro man. And as such he was elected to the Legislature. There he reversed his course and voted for the repeal of the black laws, and supported Chase for United States Senator. When in 1861 the war broke out, he aided much in securing enlistments and helping the enlisted; and to these labors he owed his election to Congress in 1864. There he now made, to the surprise of all, a speech for *peace* and was for several years the leader in a peace movement. I must also mention his persistent endeavors to make Chase the nominee of the Democratic party in 1872. He died 1883, when unexpectedly his, original, vigorous health broke down, in a law case, in which his tender feelings as a father were outraged. He left his family in very good circumstances. What shall we say of such a career? As stated, he was at all times my personal friend. He was in his public life never fully right nor fully wrong. He knew of no such criterion. His motives were absorbingly partisan, on the Democratic basis. As such he was a representative man of the characteristics of the time. These characteristics were: that clean citizenships had degenerated into unclean partisanships.

In one word: the success of one's party, and not its being *right*, was the measure of the respective conduct. A victorious Democracy was his highest joy, a beaten Democracy his greatest sorrow. Summing it all up, we have to say then: party politics being crooked in his time, his ways also were more or less crooked in spite of his better tendencies. Knowing him as I did, I could not, help liking him personally; but with my sense of the proprieties of public life, I had oftener to differ from, than to agree with him. I attended his funeral and there pondered deeply on the queer fate, that made him die before me, when he should, by natural law, have outlived me.

In 1883 I was enabled to carry out a long desired journey through West and East Virginia, as well as through East Tennessee. I went from Cincinnati up the Ohio river to West Huntington. There I called on JOHN C. BRESLIN and family, who were then living in rather good circumstances, he being employed in a remunerative R. R. office there. Breslin had been with me in relations, that alternated between warm friendship and cold disdain. Through me he secured his first office — the Clerkship in the Senate of Ohio in 1846. In it, he was a faithful and competent officer. This beginning secured him in time the position of Treasurer of State, and while he held it, I could no longer be his supporter, because I saw things occurring, that made me doubt his fidelity to the state. In 1858 I was, as already stated, placed on the commission, to examine into the Bliss, Breslin and Gibson defalcation of $500,000 in the State Treasury of Ohio. It was a trying task to me, because my mind was impressed with the belief, that Breslin was originally honestly disposed, and that is was a lack of proper organization of the administrative offices of Ohio, that led eventually to his degradation. When I met him, in 1883, in Huntington, as a trusted R. R. officer, through whose hands large sums passed, it did me good to perceive, that my original faith in him was recognized by those, who now employed him, although they knew of his defalcation to the State of Ohio. I left for Lynchburgh, Virginia. relieved of the oppressed feeling, with which I had met him and his wife. Breslin has since died and is very nearly forgotten, which is about the best thing, that can be done for him.

The country I travelled through, between Huntington and Lynchburgh, and thence to Knoxville, Tenn., is delightfully romantic. We learned there, what a beautiful country the United States are, in most of its parts. The journey was a great pleasure to me, because I saw that portion of the United States, that I always regarded, as being for the United States, what the Jura mountain region is for Europe; namely: the pivot of its general development. It had first too much importance in American history, and afterwards too little. At Knoxville I saw my grandson, Edward Slocum, for the first time; in my eyes he was, of course, a fine boy. I enjoyed also, being with my daughter and her husband. At Knoxville I made many pleasing acquaintances. Among them was the charming great old man, that goes by the name of "Historian of Tennessee."

The greatest mistake of the year, if not of my life, was my yielding to be a delegate to the Democratic State Convention on the 20th of June, and there to support Hoadly for Governor. When I started in, I thought him the fittest man for Governor of Ohio; after his election, I soon saw, he was one of the unfittest men for that position in Ohio. It was a double disjointer of action and character. He did not suit the party, nor did the party suit him; and it was hard to tell: whether this was, in consequence of his being too big for the party, or too little. In fact, it was an entire mistake, to bring about that conjunction. My only apology, for my share in it, is: that I never realized my error, until I heard his speech of acceptance of the nomination. I then saw: that we were deceived, and every additional day in the campaign, confirmed this my impression. In Cincinnati it had none but ill effects. The county ticket, nominated that Fall, was another abomination. The material nominated was bad, but the mode of the nomination was worse; and the whole of it came so, because we all seemed to have entirely forgotten the lessons of the earlier existence of the Democratic party, namely: that parties need competent leaders, to put them to rights, and to cure them of their wrongs. Hoadly never taught the Democrats to be right; nor did he ever lead them away from their wrongs; and the two years, during which he was Governor, was just so much time, and money and labor lost, for Hoadly, as well as the Democratic party. In my mind it operated as a revealment.

My hardest plague in the year 1883, was the appearance, in the United States, of my nephew, Robert, only son of my stepsister Mary. For him, we had taken extra pains, to put him on the right way, from his very landing. But on landing, he never even called at the address I had given him; but he went to a distant relative of his, who neither cared for him, nor respected him. He got, however, in debt to him. And thus it went on. Ever appealing to us and others, to provide for him, and ever acting counter to our pr viding. We even took him into our family; but we soon saw, that would not do, for he annoyed the ladies of our household beyond endurance. He was not in Cincinnati a day, before we secured him a place in a factory, with a good salary. In less than two weeks, he left it, without giving any reason for his departure! Finally, there was no other resource, than to inform him, that our patience was at an end, and that he need not ever call on us again.

I have still to mention, that early in October 1883 we moved into our house on Clinton street in Cincinnati, and remained there all winter. We left the hired man in charge of our country property. Our horse and carriage we took to town with us and kept them in a livery stable; we moved our furniture and our wine, preserves and vegetables to the cellars in the city. Our house on Clinton street was a very convenient house, and, in many respects, the very house we needed; but still it remains true: that it was an extravagant act in us to leave, only for a few months living in the city, our permanent country home. It meant, that we had abandoned economic reason for mere fancy convenience. Such annual movings back and forth, twice a year, are very expensive. They cost not only money, but they cost also by the deterioration of the furniture moved and also in having a double set of hired folks. Moreover we experienced in many ways, that frequent changes in habitations are unhealthy.

CHAPTER LXXXIX.

VICISSITUDES OF THE YEAR 1884.

This year occured the great flood in Ohio—seventy-one feet above low water mark. The year came in with a cold of twenty-six degrees below zero. In politics, Pendleton got most unexpectedly the cold shoulder from the Ohio Democracy, through the purchased election of Henry Paine for the Senatorship. It brought to my mind, the time, when thirty years before, Pendleton first entered the Democratic party and expected to have a continued successful career. He came into the party wrong end foremost and he was put out of it by the same improper relation. This brought to my mind, how often I wished for Pendleton a more congenial relation to the party, than he had in it; because I was satisfied, that it would be better for him and the country, for them to stand in their real relations to each other. Throughout the thirty years, Mr. Pendleton never took political ground from the standpoint of inner convictions; and for that reason he was constantly presenting to the public plausabilities, where he should have presented his inner convictions of right, after a careful study of the respective questions. We hear much of the phrase: "Republics are ungrateful", but we had better first ask, whether republics owe office and emolument only; because the respective persons enter public life for purposes of ambition and wealth? Yes, more we would ask: must a republic be grateful to persons, to whom it really owes no gratitude, but really rebuke? We ask this, not because we did not feel the wrong there was in defeating Pendleton with H. B. Paine, and doing it by bribery and corruption. No, we say this; because then there was done a double wrong, that might, if Pendleton had always been right, have been saved to the State of Ohio and to him.

We spent our time, in the Winter of 1884, by renewing our acquaintanceship with many former friends. I met many such, each afternoon, at Vogel's saloon, on Elm street, at the north end of Washington Park. I can name now: Kolb, Renau and Martels, as well as Dr. Buckner. I had also found some new family acquaintances through my wife and daughters. Of these families I will name the Wildes, Herancourts, Snyders, Marmets, Roedters, Ballaufs and Franks, not to forget my brother-in-laws folks, the Seiferts.

I found employment for my pen in many old channels, but also in, comparatively speaking, new ones. The German Pioneer Society celebrated the 22nd of February, as usual, and I participated in the festivities. At the annual Spring Festival of this society, May 26th, 1884, I made a lengthy address, and I had it printed at my expense and distributed. I attended also regularly every fortnight, and fulfilled there my duty of delivering an address on some chosen subject each year. Of these addresses I have preserved no copies. I was in 1884, as in other years, invited to the annual festivities of the General Literary Club in Cincinnati, whose proceedings are in English. And here it may be proper to mention, that I attended often the Masonic Temple as a member of Cynthia Lodge, to which I have belonged for many years. Once I made an address in German before the Masonic Lodge, on the corner of Twelfth and Walnut streets.

It is, of course, understood, that we had in the year 1884 the celebration of my seventieth birthday, and that at it were present all our children and grand-children in and around Cincinnati. We moved back to our Dent home on March 17th, and soon found ourselves overwhelmed with Spring work. We had kept a good hand on the place, to milk the cows and to send us to the city the milk and vegetables, as well as canned fruit. He boarded himself at very moderate cost.

On the 29th of March, rumors reached us, that there were portending serious troubles on account of the numerous murder trials, in which the State prosecution failed to convict. On the 31st the news came, that the Court House was burned and the Jail broken open. Many were surprised at the diabolical spirit abroad.

I was not. I saw, in it, the logical result of the general public conduct of the preceding years; still it pained me, that so much wrong and violence and disorder, as well as corruption, should have so little counteraction. Party power ruled without proper check on the part of the public authorities; and thus our society, and its political institutions, were constantly disgraced. I had pointed out, ever since 1881, the mischief that was working underneath. I knew: that it was coming to the surface; but did not expect it to come, in my time, nor that Cincinnati would be its field of operations. Pendleton's defeat for the United States Senate, showed, that the master spirit of it—corrupt ambition—was at work in Ohio; but I could not think it possible, that our masses could be incited into the burning of their own Court House and into the committment of murder and rapine. This brought to my mind the significant warning of Goethe: "that the main thing to do, by a people and their government, was to keep down the brutality and the meanness of the bad elements in society"; and it was plain to me: that this duty was being very much neglected in the United States, and especially in Ohio; for reasons, which have been oft repeated in these pages.

The failure of the banking institution in New York, with which Gen. Grant was connected, took place on May 9th, and exposed the great extent of the infatuation, that served the bad men of the country in their purposes of spoliation. It was a counterpiece to the burning of our Court House, and revealed the deviltry, that occupied our streets. That Grant was really a fatalist, in the worst sense, was now evident; and the haste, with which his callousness was forgiven, proved, that our voters are no longer judges of the character of our public men.

It is time now, to remind the reader, that 1884 was the presidential year and therefore the field of operations for the general fatalism, that then pervaded in American society. In the Republican party, President Arthur might have served, as an averting force, from the false partyism, that was enveloping the whole country; but Blaine and Sherman, with Harrison in the background, were determined, that such wholesome aversion to evil, should not take place. They wanted to derive some benefit to themselves first. In the Democratic party the early declension of Tilden, in June, threw *it* on its few reserved capacities; and soon all eventualities ran towards Cleveland's nomination for President and Hendricks for Vice-President. The Democratic party was at a loss, what to do! In the Republican party, the lower elements had control of the machine; and it turned out very soon, that it would be impossible, to lift the party up to the proper perception: that Arthur was the man, through whom the country might be relieved of the false public spirit, that persistently lingered in our politics and prevented the full unification of all the states and their people. Arthur had, with
17

with the assistance of Pendleton, secured the first important step towards this, through the Civil Service Reform Measure, which, if he had been continued as President, would then have been far more effective, than it has been since, under Cleveland and Harrison. I had for these reasons made up my mind, with many other Democrats, to vote for Arthur, if the better Republicans had succeeded in nominating him for President. We believed in the rule of action. which the science of politics teaches; to-wit: "that whenever the administration in power explicitly advocates the main reform measure of a country, good policy requires, that it should be supported in it and kept in the lead, in establishing it". It was plain then already; that whoever the Democrats would elect, he would have to attempt the introduction of Civil Service reform, in the face of the clamor of the office seekers in his party, for removals and appointments, on the old "spoils" basis; and that, even at best, only a very lame half-way reform policy would be pursued. This would necessarily have a double bad effect, first: it would make part of the Democrats indifferent to reform, and second: it would induce the reformed Republicans to re-unite themselves with their former friends. In short, the Civil Service Reform would have to pass through the most perilous test, that can befall a reform measure namely: a vacillating persuit of it by half-way friends; and this would have the further consequence, that there would be, for some time, an alternation between half-way Democrats and half-way Republicans, which would finally perplex and tire out the people, so that the whole matter would end in a relapse into the old system of the loaves and fishes. I became a supporter of Cleveland, after Arthur had been defeated in the Republican convention. I did not know Cleveland personally, and I had strong cause to mistrust his special supporters in Ohio. I could not expect, that Cleveland would take the decisive course as to Civil Service reform, which it had to have, to be a success. As to other great measures, such as the Revision of the Tariff, I had seen in the conduct of the Democratic House of Representatives, in 1882-1883, enough to satisfy me, that the Democratic leaders did not understand the full import of Tariff revision; that they failed to see its full necessity and were afraid to undertake it. The great necessity of bringing about, in the whole country. an equilibrium of all taxation, so as to have a comprehensive financial policy for all parts of our government, including the States and Municipalities; that great issue, they were hardly prepared for. Nevertheless, when Cleveland was nominated, I deemed it my duty' to support him, with Hendricks to boot, and I did so. I made speeches in many of the towns of Ohio and Indiana, and used my pen as efficiently as I could, whilst many of those, whom the administration. after the election, favored with offfices, sulked in their tents.

CHAPTER LXXXX.

In June my son Rudolf surprised me, by informing me, that, though successful in Madison, he had determined to leave Madison, and to sell the house, I helped him to buy. He did it merely to please others; and had arranged to move into a *rented* house in Cincinnati. It hurt me deeply, that I was never consulted in this matter, nor informed of it, until after it was irrevocably adopted. In July he carried out this determination, and I felt, that the act was disrespectfull towards myself and my wife.

During the Summer months of 1884, it became plain to me, that I would again be asked in the Fall, to move, for the Winter, into the city, so as to afford to our female folks, society more to their notion, than Dent offered to them. So I concluded to try to dispose of my Dent property altogether, either by a direct sale or by exchanging it for city property. Several houses were offered and looked at. Two on Everett street, one on Eighth and one on Richmond; but no trade could be made. The prices asked *me* were too high, in comparison with the price I asked. It was then suggested, that we should rent a flat, corner 9th and Vine. This was very distasteful to me, because I always disliked to live in a rented house. Hence I concluded to build a flat myself on 341 Vine street, and so to build it, as to rent out a part. I did so at an expense of \$4,000.00. We moved into the second story flat in December and rented out the third story to a family, without children, at \$25 per month. I wonder to-day, that my health did not break down, on our moving, into a new build house in mid-winter. I had gone through severe strains of my health, while making speeches in September and October by often travelling at night. In November I worked hard, as Fellow Commissioner with Mr. Staley and Prosecuting Attorney Pugh, in examining the books and papers of the County Commissioners by the appointment of the Judges of the Court of Common Pleas.

March 20th, 1884, my grand-daughter Sallie was born. She is the first child of my son Rudolf. My grand-son, Carl Reemelin Slocum, was born October 11th, 1883, in Tennessee.

In October 1884, we were agreeably surprised by the arrival of Miss Erich, who was the bridesmaid at our wedding in 1837. We enjoyed her visit very much. My reading during the year 1884 was in the current literature of the country and besides in the European periodicals; to-wit: the Rundschau, Littell's Living Age, North American Review, Blackwood's Magazine, British Review, Popular Science Monthly, Tübingen Quarterly and the Political Science Quarterly. An effort was made in 1884, to establish a rival to the Enquirer. It was a failure, both as to the man, who was to be editor, and also, as to the manner of the conduct of the paper. The idea was: to rival the Enquirer by conducting even a more intense party organ and in catering for news. They might have known from the first, that the Enquirer, in these respects, cannot be outdone. There was also a lack of pecuniary means. Mr. Underwood, of Kentucky, was the unfortunate leader in the movement; I kept wisely aloof from it.

The most noted paper I wrote in 1884, was that written for the Columbus Law Journal, at the request of Mr. Jahn, the owner of the Journal. Its main point was, that we are as little prepared to codify, as we are, to perform any other politically scientific act. We are critics of the past; but we can settle nothing anew in our own age; nor work well for the future. The reason of this is no other, than, that we have long ceased to decide any public question by state-reason. We have plenty of partisans; and attorneys-at-law; but jurists are very scarce; and so are statesmen.

The year 1885, brought the lesson for me, that after a person passes the seventieth year, here, a reputation, of being *old* and *wise*, follows, that is oftener in a person's way, than in his favor. I was called upon, by some of the Hamilton County delegation, to the General Assembly of Ohio, who presumed themselves to be reformers,—to draft, in general outline, a Bill: to have for this county but *one*, instead of *two*, Municipal governments and Administrations. The "Bund für Freiheit und Recht" passed a resolution to the same effect. The Hamilton County delegation presumed, that I meant: subjecting the country portion of the County under City rule. When I told them, that no such wrong course could be undertaken by me, they were amazed, and asked: "What is it then, you do propose to write?" I told them, that: "I meant no subjection at all; but, indeed, to do no more nor no less, than make *one* good Municipal Government, and to put *it* into the place of the two wrong ones, that now existed." And it now came out, that very few persons understood the history and constitutional development of the City and the County; and that accordingly they misunderstood entirely the remedy that was needed, to correct existing abuses. Those, who had asked me to prepare a bill, now became lukewarm, and I soon perceived, that they had really meant me to write for them a wrong public measure, and one that would have been an additional misconstruction. I handed them, however, the bill I had prepared, in general outline. I then took up the even tenor of my way, and wrote articles containing correct views on Municipal Government, for the "Merchant and Manufacturer," a weekly paper published by my friend Mr. Smith.

As already stated, I had determined to go on, to build a flat on my own lot on Vine street, and was much in trouble with my architect, my contractors and their employees, in their endeavor to drain

my pocket. I had got the ugliest disposed contractor I ever saw,
and he persisted to thwarth me on every point, and to delay finishing
the flat until very late in the fall.   I got some lessons on the questions of "Labor vs. Capital."

I had received an invitation to speak before the Farmer's Club
in N. Y. City. It was a society of millionaires, who loved nature as
well as money; they also had a desire, being "Nature's noblemen",
to hear addresses from literary amateurs on Gardening, Vine dress-
ing and Farming. I was to speak on Wine making and Grape culture; because I had written two books on these subjects. I did so,
on February 19th, with Depuy Lanier, and hundred others, of like
manifold culture, as my audience and critics. I dare say, that, however we differed on the subject of my discourse, we were unanimous:
that the eatables and the wine of the entertainment were good. I
certainly enjoyed them.

My address was published by the order of the society. It received,
in the discussion, that followed, some hard hits as well as some mild
encomiums. I have lost the last copy I had, and can only now say
in original general outline, that I meant to enforce the view: that
all, the different parts of the United States need, to have good grapes
and wine is: "to find the special culture of all vines, which science and
experience shall, after carefull experiments. finally point out, as the
one respectively correct; and that the opposite idea, that good grape
culture can ever come by letting nature have its way, is an infatuation". I was generously paid my expenses, including my hotel bill,
which was all I could have asked. Mr. Lanier sent me to Cincinnati, also as a special gratuity, a box of fine Rhine wine, as a
memento of my native land. I learned: that "Capital" is more
generous than "Labor". Next day I called on my personal friends:
Messers Bigelow, Moran, Roelker, Gest and the editors of the
Staats Zeitung. I met also Bigelow, Tilden's devoted friend.

During the winter I frequently took part, in Cincinnati, in the
proceedings of the German Pioneer Society, the German Literary
Club, the Taxpayers' League, and the Bund for Liberty and Right.
I was made assignee of A. McFarland & Co. This business harrassed
me much during the year, in consequence of the severe litigation
that was connected with the matter. Elderly persons should not
undertake such tasks. I was glad, when my final report was in, and
the Court had passed upon it, and finally discharged me. I have to
say. however, that the future historian of Ohio, will have to say of
the Ohio Assignment Laws, that they are just as falsely economic,
as they are wrong in principle.

CHAPTER LXXXXI.

SOME POLITICAL AFFAIRS, 1885–1886.

The Presidential election of 1884 brought Cleveland into the
White-House from the Governatorial mansion of New York. His

majority for Governor was prodigiously large; that for President, was ridiculously small. Cleveland was but little known outside of Buffalo. American politics had lost all proportions; they had become dissimilar—grotesque. The political shams, by which Tilden was cheated, had unbalanced the popular mind. Uncle Samism had any way made caricature in North American politics indigenous; and the Republican press had very adroitly impressed the popular eye with the view, that Cleveland's figure was grossly fat. And they used the impression for passing off on the public, as true pictures most distorted pictures of Cleveland. I saw Cleveland the first time at Columbus, Ohio, at the celebration of Senator Thurman's birthday and was amazed at the audacity, with which false pictures of Cleveland were even then sold in the streets. There is absolutely no such coarseness in his face and figure, as the public prints represent. But it cannot be denied, that there is a quaintness in our party politics, which has evidently hung itself around Cleveland and which he cannot shake off, nor can his opponent Harrison, though the latter is certainly, for his littleness, much more liable to it.

In Ohio, we have felt this lowering of the political standards much more acutely, because, in our earlier history, we had been specially jealous of any degeneration as to principles. I had taken a very prominent stand and the Germans had stood by me with few exceptions; when in 1852 I had fought the corruptionists, that had organized the Miami tribe. I cannot go over this matter here again. I must say, however, that events proved, that our Miami tribe was but a local case of a general political degeneration, that was going on, more or less, in every State of the Union, and that it exhibited itself most pointedly in the lowering of the estimate, which the respective inhabitants put upon the character of our candidates for the Presidency and Congress. And this showed itself also by the indifference, with which our people would look upon the defeat of great men by little men. A people, that permits small men to get into ruling positions is not fit to be a Democracy.

And I must admit, that there were indications in the election of Cleveland for President, and also in that of Henry B. Payne for United States Senator, that alarmed me, and made me apprehensive, that public matters were on the down grade here.

I was glad therefore, in the Fall of 1885, when I was invited to attend the lectures of a Mr. Reich before the University of Cincinnati on "The Science of Politics". He was a native of Hungary, that had received a fine academic education, and he showeth this degradation pointedly.

The lectures were open to the students and the public generally, including many ladies. I regarded their delivery as an indication, that the faculty of Cincinnati University were about to follow the course adopted by several Universities in Europe, and that out of the lectures would grow an improvement in academic education.

The lectures might have done a great deal of good in this line; to-wit: The general education of adults and in a much better way than has ever been done here before. Mr. Reich was fully appreciated by the general public and it was hoped, that his services would be permanently secured to the university; but these expectations were not realized and Mr. Reich has left Cincinnati, feeling rather disappointed towards the directors of the university.

I may be allowed to further remark on this subject, that it is much better understood by the literary men in Europe, especially those of Germany, than it is done by our folks here. The Germans have a very expressive word for the same; to-wit: "Ausbildung der Erwachsenen". This phrase expresses the leading idea in this matter; namely: that our adults need a *finishing* of their education, after they leave school, such as fits them for the new range of duties and functions, which they have to perform in public and for society at large; namely: to revive here, what Aristobelos, Socrates, Epicure, Plato and others had done in Athens in antiquity.

By request I translated into German for the Pioneer anniversary of 1885, the *Pioneer* song of the poet *Gallagher*: "Fifty Years Ago". It has become since the regular song at the Pioneer festivals; but they have, against my advice, adopted another than the original music, which I very much regret; because, this original, being that of the poet himself, is much better than the one they adopted. The old song comes into our minds in singing and the new music thwarts the full enjoyment of the song in German. My success in this translation from Gallagher has encouraged me to make a few other efforts in translating English poetry into German; some for the German papers. These effusions have made various impressions upon the public and I have preserved copies; but they could not persuade me entirely, that I had really a call for being a poet.

In the latter part of August I attended, at Milwaukee, the convention of the prominent German liberati connected with the press. I met there many old friends and was very much gratified by seeing them again; but I left for home, convinced, that the association, which was formed by the convention, was not the proper outcome of the call; because the convention's object was: to bring together the German literary men from all parts of the Union for mutual enjoyment and refinement, while the association has for its object local gratifications and social pleasure, which other societies furnish as as well, if not better.

On my way home I attended the annual meeting of the Association for the Advancement of Science at Ann Arbor, Michigan. I was much disappointed. The whole procedure was too much point—no point. There was too much spreading of subjects and scatterment of audiences, so that the thousands present got never a general view of the proceedings. The best thing about it was, the good bracing air and the gentle hospitality of the people. My lecture was on City Government. I had it printed at my expense and distributed generally. I have some copies yet among my papers.

The general tone of social and political life was at that time very deceitful. The northern part of the United States had gained, in the war, against the Southern States, a reputation for a love of liberty and liberal institutions, as well as enlightenment, which was largely undeserved. The Republican party, that was then in power, did not love freedom half so much. as it hated the opposition, that the South had made to protective tariffs, and to all those wrong politico-economic measures, asked for by speculators in the North, that wanted to become rich, without work, on credit operations. These measures were embodied in National Bank acts.

The Republican party had also indicated its real character by the peace it forced in 1860. It rested on principles, that were drawn from the old rules of war, such as Sparta imposed on Athens, after the Peloponnesian war; which gave, to the victor, those absolute powers, which are prohibited in our federal constitution as repugnant to the reason of federal law. Hungary has successfully denied them to Austria in its late peace transactions. England no longer claims them over Scotland and Ireland.

The Republican party entered. besides, after the war, into a general public policy, that violated many of the tenets of progressive political science. And in those points it has set a most pernicious example to the corrupter elements in the Democratic party; and they have, unfortunately, often followed it. And that circumstance is, to-day, in the way of true reformation in the Democratic party. I refer here specially to the many corruptions in our municipal governments, to the general profligacy in the use of Public Credit, and to the notorious monstrosities, in State and Local taxation; which very often amount to taking from property-holders over half of their income. There are continually new offices created, to which large salaries are attached; and they are given, without reference to qualification, and merely as party patronage. The men in power, are, in nine cases out of ten, unscrupulous politicians, and without any technical education or experience to fit them for their positions. A well and systematically organized public administration exists only in a few instances. There are no regular administrative Courts, and it is, every where in the United States, very difficult to bring corrupt officers to justice, punishment or removal. Wise disciplinary orders are very difficult to obtain.

This state of things is mostly due to the temptations, which the civil war has engendered, and which ambition and avarice has since magnified. Neither the science of finance, nor that of politics, are cultivated here as regular scholastic studies. A few persons only read up in them privately. I enjoy, just now, the perusal of the late publications of L. v. Stein, on Finance, Politics and Administration.

By way of diversion, I allow myself also to mention here, that in 1886 two grandchildren were born to me; namely: Walter Guy in the house of my son Louis; and Otto Emil, in that of my my son Rudolf.

In the same year died in Europe my brother-in-law Ferdinand Heerman, the husband of my sister Sophie; also in Cincinnati Francis Seifert, brother-in-law; in Stuttgardt my brother Eberhardt, and soon after his widow. In Westwood died my son Louis' mother-in-law. The adage came to my mind:

"In the midst of life we are in death."

Thus my life presented, in all its retirement, considerable manifoldness; since I still attended also to my farm and vineyard. I took, however, a calmer view of men and things, than formerly, and found, that I had taken a much greater interest in many affairs, than they really deserved. For instance: "Party Success" appeared to me now of very little value; indeed, I saw: that, in most cases, party victories were a curse to the people. I became more certain every day, that elections were hardly ever real democratic rulings; on the contrary, often democratic foolings. I became satisfied, that administrative officers should be entered in the lower grades, by proving the prescribed qualifications, and then rising to the higher places by deserved promotion.

I wrote, for the celebration of the 22nd of February, by the German Pioneers, a counter poem to that written years previous by F. Hassaurek, in which the argument was: that it makes no difference how we act, at last the refrain will be: "All is Over in Fifty Years." My argument was the reverse of that; to-wit: I held: that we must be very careful of all our acts, and see to it, that they should be true and right. And the refrain should be: "Only Lies and Illusions pass away." My poem was published in the Pioneer, the same as Hassaurek's song was formerly. My work received much attention; because it was regarded as an outcry against the indifference, now prevailing, as to the future of American politics. About the same time, I delivered a speech before the Committee of One Hundred, in the same tenor. It was published in the Commercial, accompanied by cutting criticisms. They did not cut me.

My main labors, in the political field, were done, in 1886, in the Bund for "Liberty and Right." I cannot here detail all the several acts done, or arguments made and published in that Society; but may state generally: that it all was a work of patience, without a copper of actual or expected compensation. It was not, as some deprived it, a mere German movement. On the contrary, very active measures were taken, to have a united action by all the elements of our population. We, of the Bund, at least, had never rejected any tender of cooperation, by our English speaking fellow citizen. But we have again and again been repulsed, by them, when we sought to cooperate with them. This proves, that the English have been less liberal than we Germans.

The primary object of the Bund was to confederate the many, separate and separatistic societies, that were opposed to the Law and Order League. We meant thus to do away with the one-sided opposition, that made an indefinite *liberty* the barren watchword. We wanted to make *right* the co-eval standard. We wanted no liberty that was not right, nor any right that was not free. We had for that reason two opposing factions to encounter; first: Those who wanted only one watchword, and *that* indefinite; second: Those who wanted two watchwords, neither of whom had either liberty or right as a standard. It must be plain, that our justification consisted in our pureminded existence; because it was a standing protest against the meanest of politics: those pursued for pay and offices under deceiving phrases and names.

In the Spring election of 1886 certain Democrats, that ever calculated; but also ever miscalculated, conceived the notion, that by drawing me into their net they could prevent their defeat; so they suggested my name for City Comptroller. To their surprise I declined. I did not want to play a part in such party politics.

During the Summer a State Convention was called at Sandusky to see, whether the Bund for Liberty and Right could be extended into a state organization. I attended as one of the delegates from Cincinnati. The convention showed, that the popular mind was fully awake to the double betrayal of the people, which was going on through the two great parties of the country. But it showed also, that there was still much uncertainty, as to the right way, to counteract this partisan duplicity. When I suggested, that, what was wanted, consisted simply in an actual square return to the governments in our constitutions; those present stared at me as if they had never heard of such a proposition before; and the same vacant stare met me, when I asserted: that we had not for years had that formation of a legitimate will: that on the contrary we had been governed for years by a bastard public will, and that was formed in party caucuses and party conventions. I saw now very plainly the distinction there was between me and the great body of those, who listened to me on those questions. I was even apprehensive, that my participation in the Bund for Liberty and Right, was exceeding my rights as to our public conduct, because it might interfere with the formation of the public will, which the constitution prescribes.

But here were the masses, who believed it not only their right, but their duty, to participate in the conduct of parties, that actually prevented the actions prescribed by the constitution as to the formation of the public will! I saw therefore, that we were engaged in a work, that required, not only great patience but fair discrimination.

We delegates from Cincinnati went also over to the city of Cleveland, and presented our credentials to the organization, that claimed affiliation with the Bund for Liberty and Right. Their meeting was, however, chiefly called for social enjoyment of a low order. We held conferences with our friends as to our matters, but received very few satisfactory explanations. They asked us to address their meeting, which we did, and then returned to Cincinnati the same evening.

I took a decided interest in the proceedings for contesting H. B. Paine's seat in the United States Senate, but I discovered early, what events proved to be the fact: that Paine had backstair friends among Republicans, who needed Paine, or persons of that ilk, in the Senate.

CHAPTER LXXXXII.
SUNDRY MATTERS IN 1887.

September 15th, I delivered, before the German Literary Club, an address to the memory of my parents' dear friend "Justinus Kœrner", the well known main originator of spiritualsm in 1820. I had the address published in pamphlet form and sent copies of it to his friends in Germany. I had known Kœrner in my youth; he was the liberal friend of my nearest relations.

The wedding of my daughter Lizzie, took place October 5, 1886. I gave her an outfit and lot on Laurel street in Cincinnati, which was somewhat more than the other children received at their marriages. It was the purpose of my gift, to enable the new couple to live without having to pay rent. They lived in the house a little over a year; then they moved into a rented house in Cheviot, where they got rooms at less rent, than they received from the Laurel street house. This behaviour chagrined me some. I thought they should have at least spoken to me, before they moved out of a house I gave them for a special purpose. I charged it, however, to the queer variations of social conduct, which American society is bringing forth. Lizzie's wedding took place at Dent in the parlor, where her sister Amalia was married before, and where many a family event, including our golden wedding, was performed. In October 1886 we moved into the city. to 341 Vine street, and there led the retired life, described as to former years. We got our milk and vegetables chiefly from the farm and enjoyed the German Theatre and many other social festivities.

It is with some reluctance, but yielding, at last, to an inner sense of propriety, that I advert to a very disagreeable circumstance of my life in 1886-87. It will be remembered, that in 1875, on my return from Germany, I found F. A. Rattermann installed in the editorial chair of the German Pioneer, as a substitute for Mr.

Knortz. I explained in previous pages, why I concluded, at that time, that Ratterman had better be retained permanently as editor, and that I should resign in his favor. I stated then, that we should meet with Ratterman again, later on, and that has now come.

When in 1886 we had moved into the city, I was informed, that I had been placed by the German Pioneer Society, on a committee to enquire into the causes: Why the receipts from the Pioneer were constantly growing less, whilst the expenditures grew larger. The latter had grown to over $1,800 a year; the former had sunk below $800 a year. We saw, that such an annual deficit of $1,000 would soon lead to the ruin of the society. On inquiry we ascertained, that the false situation had several causes; 1st: that part of the excessive outlays were due to false economy in the editorial department, and 2nd: that the other causes were due to a general decline in the number of the membership. We deemed it therefore, but proper: to suspend for a time the publication of the paper. It was, in fact, already a month behind time in its issue. At the same time we advised: that the society should advertise for proposals from persons or publishing houses: at what definite cost to the society, they would publish the Pioneer hereafter either monthly or quarterly? The committee presumed, that Mr. Ratterman would be suited by such a proposal, as he was well acqainted with the possibillities of such a publication and would like to continue it on his own account. We also expected, that some of the daily or weekly papers would, perhaps, submit some proposal of their own; but, to our amazement, no proposal, from either, came. There was therefore nothing left to the society, except to stop the publication, until further orders, and the resolution, to that effect, was passed at the next meeting of the society. Mr. Ratterman took this action as a personal attack on himself. He accused us with being his enemies. Thus the matter remained for a month or two. Ratterman now started a paper on his own hook. His purpose was to take revenge on the committee, by publishing in the new paper, attacks on me. This he made his special point in a fragmentary publication of the Volksblatt. I exposed the misstatements of this article, by stating the real facts and suggesting: that Ratterman's publication was not only defective in general facts, but contained also misrepresentations. Ratterman now changed his course, by raising a new false issue. He denied in his paper, that I was the author of the project in 1835, to found a German university in the United States. In this matter also Mr. Ratterman's statement was very deficient, as well as incorrect. I stated this at the time publicly, and asked: why Mr. Ratterman tried now, the second time, to shift the issue? I charged it to the fact, that he was entirely wrong upon the questions involved in the publications of the Pioneer. His new paper was published for a few weeks, but was soon after, to my regret, stopped at a loss to Mr. Ratterman and some persons, whom he had induced to contribute money to his new enterprise. Everybody now saw, that it was proper in the Pioneer Society to stop their paper and to invite for proposals for its further publication, as it did. It also proved, that Mr. Ratterman was not the proper person to conduct such a publication for the society, at its expense.

For a while, the personal relations between Mr. Ratterman and myself were strained; but this wore away in time. My feelings towards him were always kind, and I was glad to see, that he too now again reciprocated them.

In 1887 I was charged by the Bund for Liberty and Right, with the defense of the people of Cincinnati against the attempts of the Gas Company, to subjugate them, for a hundred years, under the pretense, of furnishing to them cheaper gas light. The offer before the Legislature by the Gas Company was, to relinquish 45 cents of the then price, provided its franchises were extended hundred years. This mode of dealing with Cincinnati is an old trick of the Gas Company. It means simply to get a higher price, than they should get from the City Council, by pretending to be generous themselves and tendering as a voluntary reduction, what was really an unjustly high price; they knew that that same game secured to Conover the original franchise. C. got then his franchise under the pretense, that *he* was bringing something cheaper to Cincinnati, while the fact was, he had *nothing* to bring. He never paid anything for the franchise, but he and his company made thousands in the course of time, by selling a poor gas to our citizens at higher prices, than in honesty should have been charged. When I stood before the committee in 1887 and showed by simple statements, that there is not a dollar in the gas works, which the *city's franchise did not create*, I saw how the scales fell from the eyes of the members and that they perceived it to have been a mean act, not to have let the city itself have this wealth. They saw also, how false all these pretenses of the Gas Company were, when they tried to make us believe, that *they* proposed to do something *for* Cincinnati, when all the time they were trying only to gain something for themselves. I opposed just such propositions, that were pending in 1887, fifty two years previous. After the discussion was over, we retired, and the committee took a vote and rejected the Gas Company's perfidious proposition. Now the Gas Company reduced of its own accord, and without an extension of its franchise, the price 35 cents per one thousand feet, and this reduction was accepted by the people, simply because the Gas Company was too rich and too powerful, to let the people hope, that they could force the Gas Company, by legal proceedings, down to 75 cents or double the reduction the Gas Company have now accorded to the city. In 1892 the Gas Company beat the city by a similar shift. The people still pay $1, where they should pay only 75 cents.

The Bund for Liberty and Right inaugurated a reform movement with the trustees of the Cincinnati University; and I was charged with the duty of presenting it; to-wit: that that body should, like such institutions in Europe, introduce Sunday lectures for the general culture of adults. I attended a meeting of the Board and explained our proposition. In reply, the head of the faculty claimed: that the professors were overworked or at least not prepared for such labors. I explained, that we did not mean to ask, that this new work should be done by the present professors or out of present available means. What we desired was: that the trustees should take the matter into consideration and that, if they approved it, they should submit, to the people of Cincinnati, feasible measures to carry it out. The trustees could not well refuse, to at least take the matter into consideration. They considered the matter and sent a written reply to the Bund for Liberty and Right. In their reply they begged the question, on several points, and evaded besides the real issue, by insisting upon it: that they never had been or never meant to be a real university, as long as they had so much difficulty to carry through, even the very limited collegiate course now carried on. I think, the difficulty lies within themselves. Their late special lectures, and success therein, proves this.

The Street Railroad question was then also a much mooted issue, before the public. I was placed on the Committee, charged with a visit to the Legislature: to advocate the principle, that the making of regulations for the running and stopping, as well as the police within the car, should not be under the exclusive control of the company, its officers and employees; but that the City Council, the Mayor, the Board of Public Works and the Police, should participate in the discussions, previous to the adoption of rules, as well as in their enforcement. It was an agreeable surprise to me: that, when I had stated these propositions before the Committee, their correctness was unanimously admitted. I found, however, that there is, in America, a long range between the admission of the correctness of a proposition, and the taking of measures, for carrying them out and enforcing them. Ever since that time, the City Council and the Board of Aldermen, have been procrastinating; but the Street R. R. Companies have been acting. And to-day the street cars are run under rules and regulations, which they adopted from their own sense of propriety, without ever asking the consent of the public authorities of the city. I, who am born in a free city of Germany, and received there my education until my eighteenth year; and having read carefully the chronicles of my native city, in which are related the struggles that that community had with the nobility and clergy, in and around our town, say now: that my native city never failed so completely to save the liberties of the town against their would-be tyrants, as our authorities in Cincinnati have done against

the machinations of the Gas Company and the street railroads; not
to forget its political parties.

CHAPTER LXXXXIII.

BUND FUER FREIHEIT UND RECHT IN 1887.

My membership of this Society was a marvel to many of my
friends. They could not see any good in a body politic, that gave to
its members neither public money, nor position, nor office. They
could see no value in my independence from party dictation, whilst
I co-operated with an association, that had no party tests. They had
failed to notice, however, that agreeable as this freedom was to me,
for the reason stated, it was also accepted by other members of the
society, for opposite reasons. They kept themselves in line with
their party, and they took especial pains to do nothing, that would
affect their standing therein. They were zealous only, when our
action was against their party opponents; but lukewarm, when it
mitigated against their own. In brief, they were conservative to
anything, involving their parties, but radical, when it worked the
other way. And the result was: that the policy of the Bund was
gradually less and less vigorously supported. To me, this was apparent in 1887 already; but it did not change my adhesion. The
Bund was still, for me, the way out of party tyranny, for all. I adhered to the measures, that had received the Bund's sanction; and
I went to Columbus, before the Legislature, for that purpose, even
as late as 1890, at my own expense. In the Spring of 1887 and 1888,
when we moved back with our family to Dent, I could not, of course,
be very attentive to matters coming before the Bund.

My farm, garden and vineyard claimed and received my special
diligence. We had had, as hired man, during the winter, "Charlie",
as he was called. He was of little use, when the master was not supervising him. We found, therefore, everything considerably out of
order in the Spring, and very many repairs were necessary. The
Spring work was much behind, and I had to remain on the farm, as
much as possible; only on special occasions, d d I allow myself to
be engaged in any public matters. Such a one was my appointment
by the Court of Common Pleas, as one of the appraisers of the real
estate of Mr. Jeffry, deceased. As part of the property was in the
city and the other in the country, it took us several days to attend to
the matter. We closed it however up and made our report to the
Court by May, I had then gotten my country home affairs in some
sort of order. I had discharged the hand I had in the winter; had
rented out, on shares, a part of my farm; had bought me another
horse and got me a new hand. So I felt myself able to accept also
the appointment of the Probate Court as one of the examiners of the
County Treasury. Mr. Jones became my associate in this examination. It occupied us several days to count the money and examine
the books, and a week more to write our report.

The popular mind was uneasy about the time, when our report came in, about the failure of the Fidelity Bank. We reviewed therefore our own report, to have every part clear and indisputable. Our report was favorably passed upon by the Court. Some were rather apprehensive, that the Fidelity frauds, had in a secret way, permeated the country treasury, but we found nothing of the kind. Other excitements followed however; indeed, I may say the year was full of excitements. For instance, an old friend of mine, a Mr. Althouse, committed suicide for no conceivable reason, except that a running sore, he had on his forehead, was held to be incurable and he thought life no longer desirable.

In August the Bund required me to go with a committee to the Philadelphia Centennial, and at the same time to meet with the new American party, that was proposed to be formed upon a basis, that seemed compatible with our co-operations. Mr. Spiegel, Mr. Abbihl and myself, were to go together, but Mr. Spiegel soon found an excuse for not going, and Mr. Abbihl and myself therefore went alone. We met after some search, the brand-new Americans in an office on Chesnut street, not far from 8th street, but, we saw very soon, that they had only added a few more pseudo Americanisms to the old ones, which only confirmed our previously ascertained apprehensions. We saw in their propositions neither liberty nor right; and accordingly returned to Cincinnati and reported to this effect. Our report was accepted by the Bund, and, after approval, it was published. A copy of it was sent to the Nativists in Philadelphia. It may be well to remind the reader, that the fact, that American politics had become a "caricature" of their former selves, was also true of these Nativists.

CHAPTER LXXXXIV.

OUR GOLDEN WEDDING IN 1887.

October 3rd, 1887, we celebrated our golden wedding. The whole Reemelin-family in the United States, was present. We old folks lived our lives over again by refreshing our memory. Such a festival caused conflicting feelings between the Past in our minds and the Future before us, and its odd Presence of parents and grandparents. There is a shrinkage of life in the very fullness that surrounds us; but also an expansion and we cannot understand, either, right. I had expected to die thirty years previous. My wife too had looked death several times in the face. And there we were, in a way, healthier than ever before, enjoying ourselves, and being enjoyed by our children and grand-children, in a town, on a farm, in a house and a garden with large trees and surrounded by a vineyard, that owed their existence largely to our industry, habits, capacities and tendencies, acquired in Europe and yet it was, in America, we were sitting; and at last strangers, in this, our home. Thus we felt that day, but we felt it in a harder sense the Winter following. A week after our golden wedding we moved into the city, on 341 Vine street, for winter quarters. This time we left no hired folks in charge of our Dent property. We had enough of the thanklessness of such people and the losses they inflict: but the old proverb proved true: "In trying to get out of the rain; folks get into the trough". We left our cattle to neighbors. To one a fresh milch cow, he agreeing to treat her well and to return her in a fair condition in the Spring. To the other we left a fine young cow, that we expected to calf in the Spring, but still able to give considerable milk during the winter; we gave him a ton of hay, for feeding and milking her until she became dry. Our horse we sold to another neighbor on credit at half price. Now for the results: The fresh milch cow was allowed to go dry, by neglecting to feed her, then we were asked to take her back in mid-winter. The other lost her calf by neglect and was generally injured. The horse was overworked and threatened to be thrown on our hands, unless we submitted to a reduction. In short our neighbors' irgratitude was worse than our hired man's thanklessness. In farming life half time, half care, half work, indeed all half measures are wrong economy. They cost more than they come to. We learned therefore the lesson: "Stick close to your place, or sell it out-right"!

We lost time and money showing our farm to pretending customers. And when at the end of winter we moved back in the spring of 1888; we became fully alive to the fact, that we immigrants were in the United States, without that public or private help, that is necessary to possess farms and lands on anything like advantageous conditions. To do that, one must himself be the owner, supervisor and laborer over it. Th s perception of ours made us more than ever eager to sell the place. None of our children would take it as a gift, on the condition, that they live on it and maintain it as a property to remain in the family. It was a queer thought, to us old folks, that here were thirty-two and a half acres. the remainder of a former posession of 174 acres, and our children refused to take it off our hands, even without paying a dollar, and all of them well knowing, that the land was well preserved, as to fertility, and that it was an excellent opportunity for an industrious family to make a good living on it, in fact, grow wealthier and healthier. A property, that was in excellent condition for a long future for such a family and yet not one of that family willing to go on it and stay on it. I asked myself very seriously: whether the general economy of a country and a people can be right, where such results prevail? I had to look, on our very golden wedding day, upon my children and grand-children as predestined emigrants from their own home; or, if the words suit better, predestined exiles from their country; for Dent was, in the closest sense, their country.

I may be told, indeed I have said it to myself: that I co-operated in producing this state of things; in educating my sons to be lawyers and doctors, and my daughters to be ladies. I admit it; but must interpose, that I did it, in obedience to the inexorable social and political conditions that surrounded me, and that I obeyed these conditions, only as far as I had to. I always gave my children, besides a professional education, also one, that would have made it very easy for them to become farmers or gardners, on our homestead, and to live well on it. I always provided, in such a manner, for all my children, so that their sole dependence would never be their professions alone. The situation, that confronted me in 1887, as to my farm, was not, therefore, caused by me, or by any plan of mine, nor any neglect. It was the result of surroundings, which existed, in pursuance of National, State and Municipal organizations, over which I had some, but at last, a very limited control. We were all in incidentally prosperous social conditions, that must, of necessity, be to a great extent, temporary and transitory.

We stood then before this result: This wealth we had to leave, without being able to give it proper stability, application and permanence. We all thought ourselves, for forty years, to be creating permanent wealth for our descendants, when we cleared off the forests, built our houses and barns; fenced in the fields, and planted orchards, gardens and vineyards; but now we found: that we were wasting our time and money, because our descendants did not, in fact could not, make them their habitations, we intended them to be. In the 32½ acres, which I thus possessed, and was willing to turn over to my children, is represented an outlay in cash of not less than $10,000, for buildings, and an amount of labor, worth at least $5,000 more, which is all lost as a future possession for my family. We got about half back in the price of the land. Think! Please! We people, as we call ourselves, never meet in public, but what we sing hosannas to a progress, that is largely fictitious, if not regressive. We are, besides, ever casting invidious comparisons into the teeth of the people of the old countries, from which the people of the new world have emigrated; but we are close-mouthed as to the wrongs and errors, that we have planted here. Have not folks a right to ask: whether we have done our duty, as to the establishment of our governments, and the organization of our public administrations? Will this people ever change, from one that is racing along in temporary and transitory conditions, into a cautiously settling people, that will make the homes they are building, their and their children's permanent habitations; or in scripture phrase, will have them in condition: "that will let them live long in the land that the Lord, their God, hath given them?" What answer can we make to these queries? I know of none, except this: We became, by our emigration, rash fatalists, and we were relieved of this destiny, only so far, as capacities, acquired by education or experience, aided us to free ourselves from it. How much each of us respectively affected in this self-delivery from this evil tendency, each of us has to settle with himself. My autobiography contains my answer. The readers have it before them. I have no other excuse or claim in the matter. It brings a test, that I cannot avoid: nor would I, if I could. I proceed then:

In the Fall election of 1887, I had again to go through with the painful choice between two party tckets, that were both equally pretentious in their claims to be entitled to govern the land. They differed only in the degree and kind of the misgovernment and spoliation they would respectively perpetrate, if placed in power. I gave my support to the Democratic side, because my vote was, at least, so much opposition to the worst evil in our present public conduct; to-wit: the employment of private corporations for doing public works or conducting public affairs. I cast this vote against these evils, because they involved the enriching of special covetous elements of our society, at the cost of their neighbors. I knew very well, that the Democrats were not entirely free from this wrong, but I knew also, that the Republicans and their party were far more guilty of it, than the Democrats. I estimated the whole amount of this spoliation, through social privileges, amounted to, at least, one thousand millions a year, and I showed years ago, in my book: "Critical Review of American Politics", that seven hundred and fifty millions of this sum flowed unjustly to Republican favorites in pursuance of certain special Republican party legislation on the subject of money and indirect Taxation.

I ask: _can this be rectified, by continuing our voting Babel? Think of it! Only in the fewest instances are statesman-like views taken by our people. Hardly any person is made an officer in either of our governments or their civic administrations, except by the partisan criterion! Then reflect, that we have no general, far seeing financial policy; that our entire taxation is without the proper equilibrium and that we are throwing burdens upon the future society with a recklessness, that would frighten any other people. Then bear in mind, that the cost and risk of efforts, to secure the rights and possessions of our population through courts of justice, is constantly increasing through a very numerous body of lawyers, which must be engaged, to have any success in court at all. Bear in mind also, that the protection from personal insults and injuries, through public and police authorities, is entirely inadequate, though that which we have, costs an enormous sum. Reflect in this connection also, that in all our larger cities, merchants and others have to employ an extra police, and that there is a secret organization of detective police throughout the land, that grows rich on rewards offered by parties injured!

I was drawn incidentally into what is generally called the Anarchists' trials at Chicago. Some Socialists presented a memorial to the Bund for Liberty and Right asking it to intercede for them before the authorities of Illinois. On my motion, the Bund laid the memorial on the table, which was equivalent to declining to have anything to do with the affair. I stated: that, in my opinion, there was to much manufacture of false buncombe public will from the beginning in this matter. Chicago was made to believe, that it had to act for the whole of mankind and *that* placed the mayor and police in a false relation. The trial was unduly sensational and this was now in the way of a fully wise executive clemency. Asking him to intercede would be only adding another false interference. I contended besides, that society is in the Anarchic state, when its political authority is, as here, brazenly usurped by unlawful political parties, who claim to rule.

We are pointed to ancient Greece, mediaeval Rome, modern Paris, and our South American Republics, for specimens of unstable Governments and vicious Societies, whom we are to avoid; but it seems to me, that the wrongs perpetrated by our parties, represent much meaner anarchies and vices, than any of the political or social bodies, we are warned against. And these perceptions of mine became my convictions in 1888.

CHAPTER LXXXXV.

THE WAYWARD YEARS OF MY LIFE.

During 1887 two grand-daughters were born to us, first: January 12th, Isabella, daughter of my son Edward; second: November 1st, Agnes, daughter of my daughter Lizzie. The name Isabella, is the same as that of the ship I came in to America in 1832, but my grand-daughter did not get her name for that reason, the coincidence was subsequently remembered and stated by me.

The last, but one, day of 1887, a sub-marine telegraphic dispatch, brought me the sad news of the death of my eldest brother Edward. I was somewhat prepared for these news, but nevertheless, they brought on me a flood of tears, that would continually begin again, when I tried to stop their fiow. He was, what we call in German: "Mein Grosser." He directed, as such, my first steps, as well as plays. I obeyed him readier than I did my father. He was five years my senior. My first sensation of terrible fear, came to me, when, one morning, somebody halloed to me, when I was standing near the river: "Your brother is drowning!" and when I rushed up to the place, I saw him drawn out of the water—to all appearances—dead. His revival then, brought a feeling of joy to me, that I can never forget. I remembered too, how disconsolate I was, when my elder brother was taken away from home, and sent to Carlsruhe, to be an apprentice in a store. I was then—1821—the oldest son at home, and perfectly at a loss in all my conduct. Similarly I felt, when I read the sub-marine dispatch. I saw, that the main link, that held me to Germany, and my folks there, was now broken, and that I must look upon my American family for my future base in life. I sent a return dispatch, announcing our common grief. Next I wrote by mail, and enclosed the condolences of my whole family; for all of them had known Uncle Edward, and loved him. One of my sons, and two grandsons are named after him. He sleeps the long sleep in the graveyard of my native town. His grandson carries on the old wholesale grocery business, founded in Heilbronn, one hundred years ago, by my father; the firm still bearing father's name. We had thus nominal persistence, but in fact, irreversible change. It was a rather sharp reminder of our consanguinity, when I perceived, that I had made my will within a few hours of his death. His daughter wrote me, that he thought of me, while dying, and that his last letter was written to me, while trembling in his last throbs. I received it next day, after the telegraphic news of his death, and saw but too plainly, that his hand was, when he wrote it, hardly able to send me his last farewell.

The year 1888 was to me on the whole, so tedious, that I shall treat it as briefly as possible, so as to make it less weary to the reader, than it was to me. It begun with troubles, which might have been avoided, if I had only called to mind again, the Gypsy's prophesy. I rented to a Mr. Daeutzer, a pretended Actor and Theatre Manager, the second story flat in my house on Vine street, on the recommendation of Mr. Balke, who had an interest to get him to Cincinnati as he manufactured theatrical utensils. His conversation and outer appearance favored the good statement, that had been made to me. I had conceded to him with that view a very low rent. Eventually all my preposessions proved erroneous and I was glad, when I was clear of him and the scamps, male and female, that came with him. I lost considerable in rent and more in the after repairs and cleaning that he ought to have done. After he was gone, I reflected, how helpless a property holder of Cincinnati stands before such a prevaricating renter. But I reflected too, how false *theatricals* are, as means of education, when mere adventurers have them in charge and there is no supervision by men of high culture.

My next trouble was, through a Mr. Wegner, who had become editor of the Socialist paper and had been introduced to me when he became a member of the Bund for Liberty and Right. We were placed together on the committee, that was to investigate some wrong with the State administration of the Miami and Erie Canal. Our investigation proved, there was really no wrong in the administration. He next used the acquaintance, he had thus gained with me, for pursuading me to edit for him, his paper during, what would be, he claimed, only a temporary absence. I continued to edit the paper for one week, without any sense of wrong, but when his absence continued for two weeks I ceased my work. Mr. W. really never again returned to his place as editor. This affair became known and some decried it as proof, that I was a Socialist. I never contradicted it, and it died away. I was not sorry to have done a favor to the owners of the paper; but regretted, that I had been deceived by Mr. W. It was a brief period, but a lasting warning to me. It gave me an insight in this phase of social political developments in America, which I would not have got otherwise. This removed some prejudices I had, but suggested other dissagreements between us. I understood fully, that there is a difference between agitations made for effect by an advocate of a special cause, and an agitation that arises in the progress of events from inner convictions; that there are really social questions that should be solved by a people through their government and public administration. I certainly sympathized with any socialism, that had the latter aim from conviction, but I do not wish to have anything to do with any social party, that merely agitates for the purpose of getting power and wealth for selfish purposes. The latter is a wrong disturbing element.

In 1888 there were several demonstrations for making it the Centennial American year. That might all have been very proper, if it had been the result of self-reflection on the real history of the United States, that would have been used, to bring before the public mind the lesson, which the history of one hundred years of Ohio was then teaching. Unfortunately, the reverse was the case with these demonstrations. A lot of people got the control over the respective celebrations, that knew only, how to spend a great deal of money, under the cover of its being a Centennial year, and then to combine, with themselves the festival's speakers and writers, that deemed it their privilege and special vocation to cater to an excessive popular pride. They had but one idea, and that was to self-over-estimate themselves intensily, and to get their audiences in the same humor. The church folks were particularly intrusive with their misjudgements, as to the true relation, religion had to ind vidual, social and political developments. When our Bund therefore, perceived this misdirection, they deemed it their duty to make a contrary demonstration so as to bring these people to their senses by asking them to consider some of the realities of the situation. The Bund appointed a committee that should present to the managers the desire of a large portion of the Cincinnati public, that the Exposition should be open to the public on *Sunday* afternoon. The same committee, that was sent to Philadelphia was re-appointed; to-wit: Mr. Spiegel, Abbihl and myself; and this committee, again with the exception of Mr. Spiegel, presented the above named request and asked for a day, when they would be heard by the Board of Managers. This request was granted and a day fixed for the hearing of our committee. The Law and Order League now asked leave to be also present and to present their views, which the Board of Managers granted and thus arranged for a joint meeting of our committee with that of the protestant clergymen, who proposed to be present.

I think I may say, that in the discussion had, on the appointed evening, our committee scored a victory; because its moderate demands, and even-tempered arguments, carried convictions to almost all that were present. This drove the reverend gentlemen to be unusually reserved, in their opposition; and induced the managers also to play sharp between us. They came in, after holding a private consultation, with their decision, in the following words: "We decline your request, for business, and not for religious reasons." That meant: that to us, of the Bund, they denied the Sunday opening of Exposition; and to the pious and the clergy, they denied the *reasons* that had really induced them to make their declination. Everybody saw, that there was really a double evaison.

During the Winter, the proposition, to have for Hamilton County, but one Municipal government, was again presented for action in the Legislature, and the Bund for Liberty and Right was asked to revise their first bill, and to prepare a more extended memorial for signature by the public. I prepared the memorial, and had it printed, and various copies of it were signed by the public, and then sent to the Legislature. The memorial was opposed only by a few individuals, who had talked themselves into the belief, that some wrong would spring out of the correction of the Municipal law over Hamilton Co. They held a meeting, which was attended by a few persons. They were kind enough to allow me to present my views, and then passed condemnatory resolutions, that showed only, how completely they misunderstood the entire subject. The then Mayor of the city, the Board of Public Affairs, and the Members of both branches of the City Council affixed their signature in favor of it. Thus supported, our Committee was ready to go to Columbus, and present anew their arguments in favor of the proposition. The Committee of the country portion of Hamilton County also appeared before the General Assembly. They confused themselves and the public, by declaring, that they were opposed to our Bill, because they did not want to *annex Hamilton county to the city.* They looked perfectly blank, when they were informed, that their mistake was the same, as that which had troubled England for centuries, because it never understood, that William the Conqueror had for dynastic reasons ruptured, the old shire organization, by injecting into it a county organization; and afterwards mixing with both also a city organization. The result of the discussion before the committee was, that the majority of the committee, being Republicans, became afraid, that this would bring to them a public issue, which the

Republican party had better avoid, as it might lose them votes. The question was adjourned with the promise, that we would hear of them, whenever they had arrived at any positive conclusions. This, of course, meant simply adjourning the question for an indefinite time. We never heard of the subject again. *Old* confusion beat again *young* distinctness.

On Sunday, March 11th, I made an address on the late political reorganization in Germany. It was made before the meeting held at Music Hall on Walnut street, by the Germans of Cincinnati. I had not been originally invited as a speaker; but, on the eve of the meeting, Mr. Paetow, one of the managers, called on me to make a few remarks. I complied, as I was about going to the meeting anyway, and expressed the few sentiments, that were then on my mind. To my astonishment, the audience applauded them highly. I had expected rather a cool reception, because I was known to be not fully satisfied with the treatment, Hanover, Würtemberg, Bavaria and Frankfort had received, in the terms of peace imposed upon them in the imperial reconstruction of the Germanic Union. When I stated: that late events had changed my views somewhat, and that I regarded myself standing before accomplished facts, which comprised simply a perfected reorganization of my native land, which I could not help from approving, because it was a solution of a very perplex issue, that gave to fatherland an assured peace, they applauded so vigorously, because my frank admission pleased them, and I saw the cause of this pleasure of theirs clearly to be their gratification at my submission to their views. But when they also applauded my words: "What had been done, was still only a beginning toward a still better union", I saw, that it was not the import of the words they applauded, but the fact, that I spoke the first time again, after an interruption of several years, in accord with their popular speakers. They overheard the warning, I gave them, against their assuming, that Germanic Nationalization had reached perfect on.

I was much occupied during the year with writing an expose of the three articles, written by Professor M. R. M. Smith, of Columbia College, for "The Political Science Quarterly" under the heading: "Control of Immigration". The articles were on their face, a seeming fair and polished study of the question; but on closer view they were found to be written with Nativistic prejudices. I sent my review to the Periodical, in which the professor's article appeared, but the editor returned them to me, and claimed, that I misunderstood him. So I sent the paper I had written, after it was printed in pamphlet form, to the committee in Congress, that had the subject in charge. And they sent it to the Congressional library, after they had read it. I retained copies thereof among my papers. I received approving letters from many distinguished persons, to whom I had sent copies, and flattered myself, that the paper had prevented the passage of several pernicious anti-immigration measures, that had been proposed. The main idea of my review was: that the only immigration, that is worthy of unexceptional acceptance is: "Free individual immigration". I am convinced, that this idea cannot be refuted; it has worked and will work itself yet into the public mind, as the true basis of legislation.

My speech at the Marietta Centennial, gave this same idea in a new form. The question, the Committee of Arrangements there, asked me to discuss, was: "The part that German-born and their descendants had in the settlement and development of the states formed out of the northwestern territory? I first took especial pains to see, whether the specific question, could be at all definitely answered, and I made researches, both by verbal and by written inquiries; but I had to accept, finally, the conclusion: that such an inquiry will always prove specifically unascertainable, and that we can only arrive at the general fact, that no *one* of the emmigrating elements to the northwestern territory can make out any special distinctive superior claim for its part in the settlement and development of the states formed out of it. And on that conclusion my Marietta speech had to rest; because it was the truth. The delivery of my speech was rapturously applauded by the audience, composed chiefly of Germans and their descendants; and it gratified me; because it was bearing testimony to my fundamental idea, that it is to free indiscriminate immigration, as contradistinguished from colonization under state direction, that belongs the whole merit of the settlement of the Western states. Its reiteration from the lips of persons, that heard me, was balm to my feelings, wounded, as they had been, by the incessant repetition of the New England falsehood; that the influx of Puritans from New England, with their prayers on arrival, their adoration of the pilgrim fathers and their sectarian homilies, was the only meritorious immigrant element. I heard one such speech then in Marietta, from the lips of Ewarts, and felt, that such special laudations of New England immigrants, are gross misrepresentations of immigration as a whole. I am grateful to the Marietta folks for their invitation and fine hospitable treatment; but, more so, for their giving me an opportunity to nail down as a calumny the *Yankee* claim of a special merit of New England in the settlement of the West. For the publication of my speech in German, I am indebted to my friend Paetow. I have retained copies of Paetow's paper: the Anzeiger. My speech was published in English by the State Festival Committee in its official report. They kindly sent me a copy.

I must say a few words on the Presidential election of 1888, and my course on it. I measured Cleveland (never having seen or conversed with him) more by the wrong tendencies he checked, than by the good ones he promoted; but I desired positively to have him re-elected. I was also gratified. that he had affiliations with the Civil Service reformers, outside of the Democratic Party, and so too was it with me, as to his anti-protective tariff policy. He certainly did not go too far for me. On the contrary, I desired him to go further; but, as I knew that his political position was, as it was, in consequence of the peculiar historic drift matters of taxation have had in the United States, I understood, that Cleveland's move would in itself reach further, than was expressed by him in words; that, in fact, it would culminate eventually in a reform of our entire revenue system, including Federal, State and Municipal affairs. I assumed, that the end would be, the establishment of a better financial equilibrium, and the removal of the present wrong of surpluses on the one side and deficits on the other. I took some steps to bring these views before Cleveland's eyes. I do not know, whether he ever saw them? In a public debate, in my neighborhood, my mode of explaining the subject, won a decisive victory. Several Republicans expressed their satisfaction; and at other places, where I spoke, my arguments tended, as appeared to me, to clear the minds of my hearers of doubts and prejudices on the subject of free trade. They saw too, that immigration is a local, not a federal question.

The degeneration of American Politics, of which I wrote before, had however, gone too deep into the very marrow of the popular mind, to allow me to hope much from the Presidential election of 1888.

Cleveland's defeat, in November, 1888, was painful to me, but not unexpected I apprehended, that he would lose votes, from the entanglements Gov. Hill had inadvertently caused; so too I apprehended secret defaults from disgruntled Democrats, who never liked Civil Service Reform, even in its meagerest form. I knew also, that many, whom he had favored with office, were ingrates: and I felt sure, therefore, that: while Harrison's name would hold all Republicans together, this would not be the case with the Democrats as to Cleveland. I saw Cleveland in Columbus, Ohio, 1890, and understood then: that he was certainly not a master mind.

We had moved, in October previous, into the third story of 341 Vine street, much improved as it was by the additional conveniences, we had made therein. We had also rented the second story to what we believed, permanent honorable tenants, but were gravely disappointed by these renters and their successors. We had Christian Prager, the son of a neighbor, as hired man at our country place, paying him ten dollars per month wages, and ten dollars per month boarding besides. We kept our horse and cow there, and he called for us, when we wanted to visit Dent, as we directed him by mail. The arrangement cost much more, than it should have done, but it was better than leaving our farm without any one present on it. Christian did much preparatory work for the next year, but it inured, as matters went, more to his father's benefit than to ours. His father rented our place on shares, in the Spring. We got, all through Winter, our milk sent regularly to the city, which was very pleasing to us all. We had brought into town with us, from the country, our hired girl, Maggie, an excellent girl, provided you let her have her own way. She acted on our life, as too much salt acts on soup. We had come to the conclusion, that in household affairs, it is best to make as little change as possible. I remember well my saying, when we were all together again, on Vine street, that we must not let a fair opportunity pass, to make it our home for the rest of our lives. We had a fine supply of our wine, made from our own grapes, at Dent, for entertaining friends and our own table use. We had our egg-nogg on the last night of the year, and we passed with it over into the New Year of 1889. I say in my diary: "Glad the year is over, it brought but little good. When living is but living, it is no enjoyment."

CHAPTER LXXXXVI.

A NEW YEAR, BUT THE OLD TROUBLES.

On New Year day, 1889, we went from the city to our home in Dent, and there enjoyed happy hours, with three of our children, and a dozen grandchildren, and also two daughters and one son-in-law. We returned to our city home the same evening. How young was life in the country! how old in town!

Our expectations, that our sojourn in the city would aid us in disposing of Dent, were not realized. We had many inquirers; but, low as the prices were, which we asked, still lower were those offered to us. The discrepancy was even greater, when we offered to trade for other real estate. The traders claimed extra high value for their property and conceded only the lowest to ours. So the perception gained steadily with us, that we had better move next time back to Dent for good, and adhere to our resolve, until death part us forever. And I remember, how this word, death, entered into all my thoughts of the future, as a surely approaching certainty. But it did so without dread. And so too I recollect in my reading, All I read had a deeper meaning, and words, that previously would have made but a light impression. now caused in me, deep reflection. Such words came up one day in January, while reading in L. Stein: "that there must be in all knowledge a three fold interrelation; namely: to know, to possess and to have ability, and that this must conjoin to make either of real value". In other words: that "neither knowing alone, nor possession alone, nor capacity alone suffices". My article on "Free Immigration", appeard in the Volksblatt the second Sunday in January. I had, by request, delivered it before the Turners, the evening previous.

Mr. Paetow. who publishes an independant paper—The Anzeiger—was. at this period. frequently on a visit to our house. We regarded him as a valuable associate, because he suggested new thoughts. Mr. Paetow was the only party-free editor in Cincinnati. I got my social enjoyments, among my countrymen, by calling every week day in the afternoon at Hager's saloon, corner 9th and Walnut streets; and there enjoyed the society of cursory friends, and with it a glass or two of good beer. My American friends regarded this "as a very unbecoming occupation, for a man of my habits and talents". I told them that I liked it, because it required only good habits and talents to enjoy it.

The usual children diseases made their appearance in the households of my sons and daughters; and that interfered with free intercourse between the families, but, as all got over them without much trouble, the interference never lasted very long. The German theatre was our regular Sunday evening recreation. It cost, counting by German standards, rather much. Each reserved seat cost about 75 cents. In Germany, two marks would suffice; but as most of the pieces we saw were comedies or farces, we laughed these compunctions, for these higher prices, away. Submitting to high priced social enjoyment is one of our obligatory Americanizations. The German Literary Club afforded me, about once a week, a pleasant intercourse with many of my German countrymen of cultivated minds. Mr. Hager generally supplied us with a good lunch at the close of the meeting. I called several times on the oldest friend of my youth, Dr. Schneider We both felt our meetings to be a great treat to us; because they went back over fifty years. We were the only two survivors of prominent Germans, that lived in Cincinnati in 1833. I took at that time, January and February 1889, much part in the meetings of the German Pioneer Society. I noticed there a tendancy to carousing festivals; and determined to counteract them in two ways, first: by bringing about meetings of a more ethical character, and where I could not do that, to prevent any meetings at all. This year, when certain leaders were determined to use the German Pioneer Society for the usual carousal on the 22nd day of February. I succeeded in preventing this abuse, by getting our Society to join the English-speaking Pioneers. We thus kept the leeches off our back, and did not turn leeches on the others. I think by a similar process, of merging our entertainments with those of our other fellow citizens, we would, in most instances, be the gainers. Wise affiliation is always of mutual benefit.

I kept scrupulously aloof from interfering with any of the movements as to Harrison's cabinet. by persons who solicited me to recommend them to the President. They supposed: that my official intimacy with his father, Scott Harrison, would justify my interference. I entertained no such presumption. I did make an effort, however, towards securing to Mr. Halstead, the position, for which I deemed him specially qualified. I did this, by writing a letter to President Harrison, recommending Halstead for Minister to Berlin, and this letter I sent to Halstead, authorizing him to send it to the President, if he liked. Mr. Halstead replied: that he would not send my letter to Harrison, but asked me to let him retain it, as a personal memento. I made no reply. Halstead's subsequent defeat in the Senate was a mistake all around. Had Halstead been sent to Berlin, he would have been more useful *there* than he has been *here* since. An absence from home was needed by friend Halstead. At Berlin he would have been surrounded by better associations, than he is here.

These clashings, within our parties, and the counterplots, with which the lower partisans, in each party, aid each other, in putting down the better characters in both parties, lead me to think: that we have reached here, within the first hundred years of our history that condition of public life, which it took Rome five centuries to' reach; namely: that condition, when the mean and brutal in society, that which Goethe calls: "das Gemeine," gets completely the upper hand. I see in Senators, like Teller and Cameron, Payne and Gorman, the modern Catalines; as I have seen in Gran tthe modern Marius, and in Blaine Sylla. I felt the great body of American society to be only one big field, on which demagogues contest with each other, for offices, jobs and privileges. I had read and studied history too well, not to know, that such degenerations in nations are never the result of sudden incidents, or local causes, but they are the result of general intensifications of mischiefs, such as come out of partisan hostilities. These reflections were to me keys for unlocking the corruptions, that exist in every detail of our public administration, and I understood: why all our financial affairs are one series of tax abuses, of violations of good faith as to credit, and extravagent appropriations of public means for private gains. To arrive at such conclusions, is in itself painful; but it becomes agony, when we see such a brazen harlot, as the Republican party, brag of the very evils it has wrought, and claims perpetual power and unlimited patronage for its nefarious purposes, and this all under the pretense of being the embodiment of anti-slavery movements.

I had, at this time, many of my old pamphlets bound, and got for them a new book case. It made my library more accessible to me, than ever before. It revived in me the love of reading in books, and I commenced to reduce the number of newspapers, that I took, and I rejoiced in the great improvement it made in my reading and my literary enjoyment. We moved back to Dent, about the first week in March, but it took us until April 5th, to get fully moved out. I felt, that delay, in my health.

I was much perplexed, as the Fall election of 1889 approached: What a party-free citizen had better do, under the existing circumstances? The year 1889 will in the future be known, as the one in which both the regular parties of the country looked no longer to their own strength at the polls, but looked beyond their own ranks. Underhand trading, with influential persons, for extra support, either upon plans of their own, or those of personal combinations, which had been formed, now became the rule. In the Democratic party, such a co-operative agency existed in Ohio, between Brice, John McLean and Campbell. In the Republican party, Sherman, McKinley and Foraker relied upon their previous combinations respectively, and expected to have them under their directions, without any serious interruption. And to all appearances, it looked as if all their calculations would run smoothly towards final success in the November election. But a surprise came through the ballot box accusation, made against the nominally Democratic candidate for Governor, J. E. Campbell. That attack was followed by a defensive line on the part of the Democratic candidate, in which he was completely successful in defending himself against the attacks made by Halstead in the Commercial Gazette. They exposed Foraker to counter attacks, in which F. made a very weak defence. The result was, that at the October election the Democratic party gained a complete victory and even carried a majority in both Houses of the Legislature. I say of this victory in my diary: "It is too early, to define fully the real import of the nominal victory, which the Democratic party gained at the November election. We fear, that when the whole truth is known, it will be found, that the people of Ohio have been duped once more, and to this I have to add, that it would in the amount of deception have made very little difference, if instead of a Democratic victory, there had been one for the Republicans. The persons duped, the measures by which it done, or to be hereafter done, or the reasons advanced for them, would have been nominally different; but the actual injuries inflicted on the moral tone of society, on the integrity of our governments and the administration of the county, would have been the same." My prognosis was, as will be seen later, but too true.

In October 1889 occurred the most distressing accident known, by the terrible distressing catastrophe of the Main Street Cable, by which two of our acquaintances lost their lives. Most painful to us was the death of Mrs. Hofstetter, nee Hartman. She had been for many years a visitor of our family in Dent, before her marriage and we had remained intimate, until her death. She had received her education in one of the finest institutions, for females, in Europe; had been lady's maid in one of the most distinguished families in Russia and had resided two years in Russia. It was a terrible shock to myself and wife, when she lost her life by the catastrophe named.   We all felt, that our life had received a deadly shock.

CHAPTER LXXXXVII.

FURTHER REFLECTIONS ON THE POLITICAL SITUATION, 1890–1891.

The foregoing remarks, on Ohio politics, also apply to Federal politics. The processes of these indications were there only more intense than in states like Ohio. While in the latter a dozen of ambitious men were intriguing against each other, there were hundreds doing it in the National arena. And we may as well understand first as last, that since all these intrigues had to proceed against an inner sense of propriety, they were in the way of any correction of our party ethics and general political integrity. This generated an intense hypocricy in all political conduct, because the necessity to *appear* right, was at last much stronger,, than the inner repugnance to the wrong. Our government had thus become a mere demagogical gambling between two standing parties, neither of which was a fit public organ to govern; nor had they the respective numbers of voters within themselves, that could have given them the nominal majorities, which they needed to be even nominally only the government. And for this reason we were drifting to a shiftless future, because we were still indefinite as to the real nature of our government. Who of us could tell? which side of the following questions is true? Do our parties rule our government? or does the government rule our parties? We have laws made by one party against its opponents, but who knows? whether these laws are mere expressions of an arbitrary will, which we are bound to obey and carry out? In brief: are we not merely playing with such important words as "Republicanism" and "Democracy"?

I have never before felt it so difficult to discharge my civic duties as now. Both party nominations looked to me like usurpations; for in them the qualified men have less chance than the unqualified. Time seems, to me, to run in the United States with the powers of evil. We have many efforts, throughout the country, to break up lotteries, because they engender a false economic spirit, but the worse lotteries, those of our parties, we make no effort to suppress.

And yet: I could not help asking the question: Which lotteries are the most dangerous of the two? Those of our parties? in which there is gambling for offices; or those of companies, in which money is played for? I asked the question, not for myself alone; for I was the father of three grown up sons, and felt the responsibility,

In the election of 1889 I had no difficulty to decide; whom *not* to support, what perplexed me, was: whether I could be justified in voting *for any* party nominee. I reasoned, that voting *for* any

party candidate, was an admission, that the system was right, and
that I could not do, without sanctioning courses, whose politics
must deteriorate more and more the government of our constitutions; because they set aside the principle, upon which they were
founded. That principle is: that in our constitutions is prescribed,
not only the general character of our governments, but also the
extent of the respective powers and functions Our party rule rests
upon an entirely different assumption, namely: they assume, that
there is, within our parties, an evolution of a public will, that gives
to the party, successful at the polls, the right to establish a public
policy by this their arbitrary will, and to engraft it on our statutes,
and thus giving it the force of law.

And in reference to this matter, I must insert here, what Mr.
Van Buren told me in 1842; to-wit: "The country has been saved
several times from drifting into political precedents, that would
have gradually become a sort of common law or unwritten constitutionalism. similar to that in vogue in England. The first time,
this occured, was in 1800, when the Vice-Presidential succession.
which was inaugurated under Washington, was stopped by electing
Jefferson. straight from the body of the people to the presidency
over John Adams. who claimed succession under the rule of "safe
precedents". Mr. Van Buren added: "In 1828 a similar so called
safe precedent for succession, by which the Secretary of State was to
follow his chief, was broken up, by electing Jackson, who had held
no civil office previously, over Henry Clay, who was the Secretary
of State under J. Q. Adams. Mr. Van Buren predicted from this:
"that nominations by the respective National party conventions,
would in time become dangerous to the Union, because they eventually mean the setting aside of the constitutional f rmation of the
public will; and the substitution for it, of a spurious party will."

In my opinion, we stood in 1889–90 before this very crisis: None
of those, who then were working the machinery, by which men got
offices or jobs or rewards, thought for a moment of the Constitution,
its forms or methods, as the proper ways and means in politics,
except so far, as they needed them to make them legal at all. Nor
did any of them ever propose to urge before the people, any actually
needed reform; on the contrary, their propositions or platforms, as
they called them, were fictitious, with the view to give power to
their respective parties. The Bund for Freiheit und Recht was the
only party-free organization, and even it was it only as to a part of
its members.

CHAPTER LXXXXVIII.

ALTERNATE GENERATION BECOMES THE RULE IN OUR POLITICS.

The kind reader will remember, that I doubted, years ago, the
capacity of our people to generate continually such government

and public conduct, as should secure to American society that constant progressive development in political institutions and public service therein, which the Constitution obviously requires by its organism and rules. I could have no reason for this doubt, except the fact, that we had ceased to be one legitimate people, and had become divided into two illegitimate parties.

I read in 1889, while reflecting on the political situation in the United States, in the Library of Universal Knowledge the article on "Alternate Generation", Vol. 1, page 332, and it struck me, that the method of reproduction therein described, of certain of the lower orders of animal life, in a regularly recurring series of ancestral orders, bore a resemblance to our political methods in our partisan organizations; because they fail too to have normal generation and relapse continually into ancestral forms and processes, by alternations of a lower order.

Our political parties and their organs, were certainly a much lower order of public life, than the organs provided by our Constitutions. And their alternations between each other, in their special policies, were so many indications of some inherent weakness, in being for our nation the fully competent generative organs. So too were Harrison, Cleveland, Blaine and Hill, Campbell and McKinley partisan incompetent leaders. To me, the general tendency of our politicians: to form parties, for reform purposes, was obnoxious in 1854 already, and I opposed the formation of the Knownothing as well as the Republican parties then specially, because they were in no good sense public organs. I was even then willing to abandon the Democratic party, and to take up and perfect our constitutional institutions. I opposed all movements, by which a constitutional method was abrogated, and a party method was substituted. I, for instance, have ever deprecated the setting aside of State electors for party electors, in the Presidential elections.

In the canvass of 1889, I felt how difficult it had become in the United States to be a free citizen; and how easy it was to be a party slave. I noticed also, the various disintegrations this caused, even to families. As stated, I had, for instance, felt it my duty, to withdraw from all entanglements with party affairs. And it annoyed me greatly, that my son Louis, whom I loved affectionately, had become a member of the Democratic Executive Committee, and thought himself doing yeoman duty, by serving upon it. Still more it pained me, that he was mentioned, as likely to be appointed, by Governor Campbell, to a lucrative office, which was expected to be created by the passage of a Ripper Bill, as removals, by Legislative act, were called. They were to me, mean alternate political generation. I still remember the deep pang I felt, when such a probability was first mentioned to me. I felt certain, that others were urging him, for the purpose of involving us in the wrong.

I had taken extra pains, to place into the Constitution of Ohio a clause, by which the Legislature was prohibited from making any appointments, except of its own officers or servants; and I opposed bitterly all those bills, which the Republicans passed between 1862 and 1885, merely for the removal of Democrats, and the appointment of Republicans. I declared them to be relapses into the mean politics practiced in early times, by the Federalists and Whigs, who had adopted them from English politics. Indeed, I had repeatedly declared: that there could never be any really good public administration in Ohio, if it was possible here, to revolutionize, at any time, the entire public service, by the arbitrary will of the General Assembly. And I held it as wrong in a Democratic Legislature, as in a Republican.

One of my most cherished measures was the proposition to establish in Ohio, an administrative Court, whose function should be, to pass upon all questions of removing, suspending, disciplining and fining public officers. I insisted, also, upon a more thorough and systematic examination of all accounts and official routine. I took the ground, that the Democratic party must cease to be merely the alternate of the Republican party, by being the non-partisan blank of these nonentities, that draw pay under various pretexts, but really are the marplots of all regular organic developments. The Democratic party should immortalize itself by revising and reforming, as well as unifying Municipal Government in the States, by general State laws, as the Constitution thereof really requires. This would secure local self-government and give to public affairs in Ohio a new and better conduct, for the general benefit of all our people. I insisted, that the Democratic party should cease to be a mere opposition party of the Republican party and a mere kicking-out agency of Republicans, with the view to get the offices themselves. I held it at that time, and do now, a positive duty to discard in our municipalities, all partyism, that is not the public servant, within the written constitutional statutory provisions.

In December, 1889, I wrote articles for the Volksblatt, under the heading: "Gebrechen und Schwaechen im Amerikanishen Regierungs-Wesen, (Failings and Infirmities in American Government). I was warned from Columbus, by Democrats, that I was injuring my son's chances for getting an office, through the Governor or Legislature, but I adhered to my writing, and I hoped it wonld keep my son Louis from any further intimacy with those Democratic elements, whom I knew to be destructives of all organic order, and I meant by this especially: Gov. Campbell. I knew that that person would prove the marplot of the Democratic party, and I wanted to save my son from bitter disappointment; for I never loved him more dearly, than when I penned these articles. At that time, I recalled to memory, the sorrows I passed through, when he came near dying, then not quite five years old.

I became more and more impressed with the fact, that the chief harm of our parties consisted in their obstructing, among the adults of society, their getting such a finishing of their education, as would enable them to perform the additional public functions, which modern progress had given to them in relation to the formation of an intelligent, virtuous and wise public will much better, than they now do. Public speaking, the daily press, convivial intercourse in clubs and societies, public entertainments and exhibitions etc., are now conducted with so little culture, because they are mostly sunk to bring mere alternate generations of ancestral varieties of social culture, without the modern finish, which a more extended international commercial and literary intercourse gives; and thus prevents in so many parts of the world the decivilization that that threatens them.

I wrote, about that time, for the Commercial Gazette an obituary notice on Jeff. Davis. In it, I took bold ground against the illiberal treatment Davis had received form ultra-Republican partisans. I had known Davis personally for over 30 years, and I believed him to be misjudged by the North, and felt bound to say so in my paper, even at the risk of being abused for it. I was not denounced, but, on the contrary, papers both North and South gave me favorable notices. I took this as an indication, that the world still accorded to me, my old freedom of acting and writing, and that the North was beginning to prepare itself, to treat Southern statesmen with some fairness, especially those that were dead.

CHAPTER LXXXXIV.

DEATH COMES NEAR TO OUR FAMILY.

My son Rudolf passed towards the end of the year 1889, and during the first two months of 1890, through a very severe case of Typhoid fever. Dr. Comegys, who attended him, had once very nearly given him up. We were all apprehensive of a fatal ending for weeks. At the same time, we were all ourselves severely troubled with various ailings, and for the first time we contemplated, how near we were all the time to eventualities, that would dissolve our family: and place all and every thing, within it, in a critical situation. I could not help feeling the uncertainty there was in this American family life of ours.

The thought struck me, that this uncertainty was sure to prevail in a country, whose inhabitants are immigrants; unless counteracted by methods of education, through which their aims, occupations and modes of living are placed upon a higher footing and correcter rules. Experience should be gathered and used for self-knowledge and self-guidance, with a view to secure habits of life, that would conduce to settledness as the characteristics of the People.

That I, at my age, should, in 1889, think of approaching death, was a matter of course, but that my youngest son should have to face it, and that my youngest daughter, should also have to pass the ordeal, and in the most painful form, confounded all our calculations. My good wife, though herself troubled with ill-health, bore it with the most consoling equanimity; I perhaps with the least. And I thought, that the reason of this was, that in me there was embodied more of family zeal for its health and happiness, and that I felt more intensely my responsibility for it. I certainly did not believe in the popular doctrine: that a desire to form and perpetuate a healthy and prosperous family in the United States, was incompatible with the liberty and equality, which are claimed to be the corner stone of American institutions. I detested in fact, the public policy already spoken of, which ripped up in party alternations our political organs, and redistributed them to party tools. And so too did I condemn as absurd, the insidious practice of our politicians, to seduce the public into an acquiesance of party rule, by placing on the respective partisan boards, members of both parties. The practice is but a doubling of false government, and a degeneration of public administration.

At the very time, when I was meditating on those questions from the standpoint of my own and other immigrant families, the submarine telegraph brought the news of *Georg H. Pendleton's* death in Europe; and this brought the subject before me in the aspect of the life and conduct of families, of whom we had a right to presume that their family ambition was much more definite, than mine would be; that it would of course, be more conservative.

The lessons presented by Pendleton's life were necessarily a part of my studies, while writing my own. George, as we called him familiarly, was my junior in American politics both by the standard of personal participations as a voter, and that of a student of them as a science. We were both adopted members of the Democratic party in the sense, that neither of us came into it by birthright. To a full understanding of this matter it must however be stated, that my joining the party was much more the logic of actual relations, than that of Pendleton's. I regarded it my actual duty to be a Democrat, soon after my arrival in 1832; whilst P. decided to become a member of the party for reasons adopted from considerations of the political situation in the United States about 20 years afterwards; when many Whigs believed it smart policy to leave their party and to become nominal Democrats. P. was one of these new converts, but he had never been an actual member of the Whig party. He entertained, indeed, some advance views, that made him disinclined to adopt the party of his father. There was another difference between us, which must be stated. P. affilliated naturally with the F. F. V. of the Democratic party, to-wit: the supporters of paper money, corporations and established wealth and official power; whilst I was for metallic money, unprivileged credit and a public service purified of the false excrescences derived from British mal-administrations and blemishes grown out of party government there. P. and myself were therefore antipodes in the Democratic party for historic reasons; that preceded his entry and had even personal points in them, for it will be remembered, that his father and myself had a sharp public discussion in 1840 already. I expressed this matter in 1852 very briefly by saying: "Mr. Pendleton's joining of the Democratic party had in the main for its objects, the taking of a short cut for securing political power to himself and family, which he could not gain by remaining a Whig or Federalist". That object P. secured by co-operating, from 1853 to 1863, with the corrupter elements in the Democratic party. He became in rapid succession State Senator, Congressman and United States Senator.

A change came in 1864. Pendleton's friends forsook him; and his real friends would not make up with him. The immigrants felt shy of him as the native versus the immigrant. P. saw that he must create some merit for himself, and he took up civil service reform. That did not mend matters. It enstranged him entirely from his false friends and this jostled him out of his career. The Payne intrigue took advantage of it, and secured the Senatorship to themselves. Cleveland saw: that it was his duty to lift up the fallen man, and made him Minister to Berlin; but fate struck at him a still more fatal blow by the accidental killing of his idolized wife in New York. This aggravated his own mortal disease; and he lies buried in his grave as the victim of the alternate generation in American Politics already explained.

I had in the later years of his life, become a sincere friend of Pendleton. I saw, that with the loss of Van Buren's and Benton's influence over the Democratic party, Douglass had seized the reins and seduced Pendleton for awhile. But the latter soon saw his mistake and recoiled; he took up Civil Service Reform, and saved for himself at least one good memory.

CHAPTER C.

A YEAR OF CHANGES. 1890.

I entered this year with a foreboding, that it would be my life's last year. I did this because I became, in it, seventy-six years old, which is exactly the age at which my father died in 1856. Before the close of the year 1889, I had an opportunity to put in a quiet disavowal of certain feelings, that were attributed to me in Green Township, by certain ultra-religionists. They accused me of being a bitter opponent of christian charity. It came in this wise: Mr. Gamble, the head leader and ostentatious giver of charities in Green Township, sent his soliciting committee around the township for contributions, and it came also to our house.   I happened to be at home, and I took them down in our cellars, and gave them free leave to determine pretty much for themselves, how much of the various vegetables we had there, they would regard as a proper contribution from me. They filled their own bags and also one of mine, and were about departing, when I offered them several bottles of wine. One of the ladies of the Committee doubted the propriety of taking the wine, but the other two concluded, that they had often sick persons to whom it might prove good. This occurrence was talked about, and brought relief to me from the oppprobrious charge. It proved a double correction.

The Old Year passed out, and the New Year came in with the form usual in our house; namely: that we drank each others health in excellent egg-nog, and then fired the customary salute to the New Year, before going to sleep. We got up late on New Year's morning, having overslept ourselves. Louis and family came, and we had a good time together. But our conversation turned finally, on what the Legislature was going to do, and I learned from him, that there would be great changes in the city government, and that he expected an appointment under the new organism. I became alarmed, and wrote in my diary: "I feel downhearted as if some mischief were brewing."—

I was, as above stated, on and off, much engaged in drawing up a Bill for reforming Municipal Government for Cincinnati. The main instigator was the Municipal Congress, of which Mr. Davis on Eighth street, in Cincinnati, was the leading mind. He struck out widely for reform, and presented some very excellent views, but after all, he had not studied the history of Municipal organization, and had no right conception of the organic symmetry, that is needed for a Municipal Government. He was unacquainted with the Municipal systems, that existed in ancient Greece and Rome, but somewhat familiar with those in England and the United States. He had therefore no scientific groundwork. My plans were based upon the Municipal reforms, carried out in the larger cities of Europe, and when I mentioned this fact frankly, it aroused opposition to my plans, for which no very clear grounds were given. The Municipal Congress is the parent of the phrase "City Charter on the *Federal plan*," which at once exposes the fact, that they were bewildered in a contradiction of terms, because a charter is a grant of power given by some supreme authority to some community, whilst a Federal organization implies a union agreed upon by sovereign parties or cities. The hanseatic union for instance, was a Federal plan established by free cities, by and for themselves. The confusion that existed here in the popular mind, and which came out in the phrase, "City Charter on the Federal plan," was the hinderance, that finally defeated the adoption of any correct Municipal legislation: and it brought forth eventually the late illegitimate production, that was talked about among our people as "the New Charter."

I tried to get before the General Assembly and the people of Ohio, suggestions, that would, if they had been properly considered, saved Cincinnati from the muddle in which our city affairs are now. The "Bund for Liberty and Right" passed the resolutions I had drawn up for that purpose, which declared: that the right thing to do was: "to reframe the Municipal laws we had, so as to make them applicable to large cities and then to bring them all under a Municipal organization such as science points out in history."

I was again admonished, "to cease my agitation for a perfect reorganization, because it would endanger my son's chances with the Governor." The suggestion did'nt please me any better than before, nor did it deter me for one moment from adhering to my belief: that we needed a reorganization such as statesmanship points out, and to avoid all partisan measures, such as the "Ripper bills."

January 12th, 1890, I read before the Turners my lecture on "Philosophy and philosophers," in Turner Hall on Walnut street. I did this in obedience to a call from the Turners, the same as I had done for several years previous. The audience seemed to be rather pleased with it. I had it published in the Volksblatt, and distributed copies among the people. I retained copies of it among my papers: and filed them in the City Library.

Governor Campbell's message appeared, when the Legislature met. It was his first message; his so-called "Inaugural address: but it was the duplication of previous stump speeches, and contained nothing but glittering generalities. I saw very plainly, "that the Governor himself had no policy, and that he had arrived at no definite conclusions on any of the questions, that were floating about in the community. It was only another instance of the general course now pursued by our public authorities, namely: that they talk and write, not because, they have anything to say, but because, in the usual routine, a day or occasion has come for a customary talk or writing.

In the middle of January I heard, that my son Louis' wife had bought a house on Wesley avenue, and that they expected to move into it very early. We were ourselves about that time thinking about trading off our property in the country, and no doubt this purchase of my son's wife, drew our attention to Wesley avenue, and it led to our subsequent purchase, a couple of months later.

I did but little literary work during the first month of the year. I wrote, however, an article on "Taxation", also one on "Military Organization". In the latter I showed, that there is in the United States no proper provision for sustaining the police forces in a sudden emergency. I referred to the burning of our Court House as a proof of my assertion. On the question of taxation, I pointed out, that there is no general order nor system in our taxation, and that for this reason there is no equilibrium in our finance; also that we are absolutely without any regular Budgets and that the several public authorities are largely acting at cross purposes with each other.

Towards the end of January the rather persistent sickness of my good wife alarmed me very much. I took a lesson on the topic of the mutual dependence in family life; and I came to the same conclusion, that Pope did in his essay on Man: "To reason right is to submit". My wife gradually regained her health, and we continued to live in the country and to enjoy our quiet family life.

The public underwent a considerable perturbation on the notorious ballot box issue, through the investigation going on in Washington on the subject. It was, like most public acts in America, a caricature. This matter had played a very ridiculous part in the Fall previous, and when it now came before the public, it was but a continuance of hunting for misleading information, and it finally ended in the re-illustration of the old Roman saying:

"Parturiunt montes; nascitur ridiculus mus".

The whole story may be told in a few words: There was in 1889 a certain scamp, who dealt in patents; he had a patent ballot box to sell, and he believed Congress could be got to buy it, and that he would make a million; provided he could find the necessary Congressmen to assist in the scheme; and then he would engage one of the principal dailies in Cincinnati, to work up a pretended exposure of the whole matter against Campbell and thus defeat him and save the Republican party. Upon this plan a pretended counterexposure was to be sprung and a double advantage taken, beside killing of Campbell at the election. The dirty scheme failed.

About this time I received the fourth volume of "Treitschke's History of Germany in the XIX. Century," and there learned, that there too, like here, were played many episodes, which are best described by the phrase, "much ado about nothing"; but the book also teaches: that when a people's practical men continue to search for the essential points in their affairs, and keep employing their common sense in it; there is a sifting process going on, that brings finally into public position more and more the clear-headed men; such, for instance, as "Moltke", and then finally the clearing processes are placed under their direction, and the solution is reached. The history, I was reading, interested me so intensely, because it brought before me events, that transpired within the last years, before I emigrated to the U. S. I knew many of the persons named in the history. Some of them were relatives of mine; often acting loosing parts in the semi-comedy or semi-tragedy; as the case might be.

In the month of February came the sad news of the death of my brother Theodore. His eldest son wrote the letter in the tone of patient sorrow and simple narrative. In the letter lay a half-finished note, written to me the day before he took his final sickness, and in that note he referred back to the period, in which I advised him to come down square to the life of a teacher, and to give up all his political pursuits after mere theories. He had written down, how happy he became through following my advice, and how under it, he was promoted to a first-class professorship. But there his note stopped, and it left me to form the conclusion, that he meant to thank me for his becoming a public teacher; that he was fully qualified for that position, and had left the wild course of a leader in wild politics, for which he had really no qualification. They could indeed bring to himself and family only innumerable sufferings, including imprisonment and suspension from office and pay. Of course, my mind recurred to our mutual life in youth and I reflected on the fact, that we two brothers had, out of six of us, been longer school and playmates together, than the others, and how also in our later life we were more frequently together, and imparted to each other much useful information.

I cannot pass over the fact, that my dear brother became very pious in his later years. He would press upon me, in conversation and by letters, that I too should join him in his religious regeneration. I, for a while, attempted to explain to him, that his fears as to my religion were misconceptions; but, when I found my efforts to be in vain, that, in fact, he became irritated, I ceased to write or speak to him on the subject and our intercourse became thenceforth much pleasanter, and I was just rejoicing, that our entire fraternal affect ons had been fully restored, when I received the announcement of his death. I believed from the note inclosed, that such was undoubtly the fact, and that he died with similar feelings.

It was a great gratification to us that year, that the health of my son Rudolf was constantly improving, and that he was sure eventually to regain his accustomed health. My eighteenth grandchild was born in the Summer of 1890. We called him James, after his grandfather Schoenberger. The mild winter gave many opportunities to be much out of doors and he developed finely. In the Spring I did much work about the farm myself, but I had to learn, that having passed 75 years and approaching my 76th birthday, made it advisable, that I should work slowly and avoid the severer tasks. At this time of my life I could not help making comparisons between the condition under which, well to do elder folks pass into old age in Germany and in the United States. In the Old Country they are always sure of finding easily the help they need as they grow weaker; while in the United States they are in the fewest cases successful in this respect. It was at least to me a sad coincidence, that with my failing strength, had also come a greater difficulty to secure hired help; and what pained me still more. was the conclusion forced upon me by much positive evidence, that the want of proper help in my old age, did not spring from any diminution in the number of persons, that were capable to render it, but that it came from an unwillingness to serve others and to perform hired labor. All these various inconveniencies and hardships made me more willing, nay, anxious, to dispose of my farm.

But selling or trading a country property like mine, meant much humiliation and pecuniary loss besides. The troubles, that induced me to sell or trade, existed all over the state; indeed, the whole Union; and what made me willing to sell, made others unwilling to buy. And in the same way it affected exchanging country for city property. I could have once sold my farm for $10,000, when it was less improved than in 1890; now I dropped to $9,000 in the beginning of the year. In the month of February I had dropped to $8,000, and by March, I had to reflect seriously: whether I had not better accept an offer for exchange of city property, that would have secured to me, at least, $7,000.

While I was thus laboring about the disposal of my property an inquiry reached me from Berlin: whether I would not write for their paper:—"Das Deutsche Wochen Blatt",—some articles on America, with the understanding, that they had a right to use or reject, what they pleased, and to pay me only for such as they published? I composed two articles, but evidently they did not suit their taste; for they did not appear in their paper, neither did they give me any explanation. They however sent me their paper and I found it interesting, so far as it referred to European affairs. At the end of three months they sent me a bill for the paper and I saw, that all they wanted of me, was to become a subscriber. But, as that was not my desire and as I did not want to extend my reading matter, I finally kept returning the paper until they stopped sending it and that ended our intercourse over a year ago. It was evidently the end of a mutual misunderstanding.

In the mean time, the Legislature had gradually got to work and partially succeeded, by some public discussion, but by still more caucusing, to abolish, in the various towns and cities of the country, many local Boards, and to substitute for them new Boards; and this meant, that out of the old Boards, Republicans were removed, and that in the new the offices were given to Democrats. Only in a few instances Republicans were appointed. The Governor received, in most instances, power to make the appointments. The power of removal was not fixed by any uniform rule, because the presumption was: that the Governor and his appointees would remain harmonious for several years. The abolition of the Board of Public Affairs, and the establishment of the Board of Public Improvements, in the city of Cincinnati, brought into this matter the most important and most remunerative five offices in the State. There was considerable contest, as to who would get the respective appointments. My son Louis was much talked of, and soon I became satisfied, that he would be one of the successful candidates. I then felt it my duty, to speak to him squarely, and to inform him of the relation that I had determined to hold to him, in reference to this matter. I therefore wrote to him the following letter:

Dent. Ohio, February 12th, 1890.

DEAR SON LOUIS.—After severe reflection, I have to inform you, that I cannot go on your bond. You are, as I see the situation, co-operating in a public course, that must lead, if persisted in, to the ruin of the country and your own besides; and I cannot allow my personal affection for you, to rule me into doing an act, that my conscience does not approve. Now please understand. I do not mean, by this, to prescribe your conduct, I simply determine upon my own, by refusing to comply with your request. My refusal is but doing, what my father did to a brother of mine, when he was seventy years old. My age is 76 years, within a few months, and I have for my denial more reason, than my father had. He claimed, that parents must, in old age, weigh every act of theirs, by the consideration, that what they are doing, will most likely reach beyond their own lives, and that it affects the heirs more than themselves. I need peace of mind, and must avoid every additional burden on it. And you must see, that this consideration would, even if I approved your purpose, justify my declination. I ask you to consider this, and to restrain any ill humor, that may arise in your mind, by the filial love, that you have, I think, always had for me.

I remain, as ever, affectionately your father,

CHARLES REEMELIN.

This, my letter, brought me a letter in reply from my son, and from it and conversations, I could easily see, that both he and his wife, as also my wife and family, did not approve of my conduct. I understood from this, how completely the ethical basis has gone from under American politics. Nobody understood any longer, that a father should refuse to support a son in an unquestionably false political course. I am at a loss for words to express my sorrow at this dilemma. To me it is incomprehensible, how a father can support a son in a wrong political act!

I got towards March into negotiations with a man and his wife, just from Alsace in Germany, about renting my place. Both looked, at first, like perfect Godsends, to be for us the help we needed, both on our farm and in our kitchen. Their coming to us meant most evidently a new deal; but we soon found out, that it meant no improvement at all. He at first talked, as if he understood everything and if not, would be anxious to learn. She indicated the same disposition, only more so. A trial of two weeks satisfied us, that he had never been an agriculturist and regular hand in his life; he knew very little about handling cattle and I had to show him everything about the horses. She had evidently been the daughter of a family, in which hired persons did the work and left her but little active co-operation. It must, however, be admitted, that she was much hindered in her work, by a baby boy, that she had brought with her, about two years old. who instantly begun to yell, every time his mother moved more than arm's length away from him. And such yelling. as he brought forth, I never heard before nor since. We stood their pretended superiorities and confessed inferiorities about two months, when they moved to a neighboring house, where they hired a room. My wife then got her hired help from a neighboring family. I retained the husband of the Alsacian family, and *he* did my work on the farm, with my assistance, he boarding himself and living with his family. In one month he wore out my patience. I discharged him and fell back upon a hired hand, who, if incompetent, made at least no false pretences.

CHAPTER CI.

THE BAD WINTER AND SPRING OF 1890.

During fifty years, of a country residence, we had the most detestible Winter and Spring in 1890. It rained every day, and often several times on the same day, but the rains. with all their continuances, were failures, as it never once rained right. It was under the circumstances almost impossible to do any good garden or farm work; and this was also much in the way. to sell or trade my place. Nobody wanted to go into the country, ever weeping as it was.

About the middle of March I went to Washington, as a delegate from our Bund to a convention, which was to serve, as a mediator between ultra-Germanists and ultra-Americanists. The president of the Bund was also along, but he represented the Turners. We did in Washington some mutual admiration, and cosy beer drinking: but accomplished nothing in the line of our duties. How could we?

Congress was divided on the subject and so were the people; not so much, because they were divided in opinions distinctly formed, but because everybody was at sea upon the subject. Each person could write down their respective opinion on some special point, but were they were afraid of taking up the whole subject of Free Immigration, as it was and should be in modern times. The great change therefore, that had taken place in the popular mind, since the earlier part of this century, was never fairly considered; nor were ever the causes of this fully looked into. Neither were the different phases of it properly examined. The fact was and is: that well minded men, who had common prudence, were afraid to look into this chaos, and this left the field to the prejudiced and imprudent. We had in Washington several meetings and once or twice had careful discussions; but soon the state of things just described became uppermost again; and then the first opportunity, to avoid coming to definite conclusions, was seized and an adjournment took place. When the majority found, that its presence could be of very little use, it returned to its respective homes. We of Cincinnati reported to the Bund our proceedings. The minorty of the convention went before the Congressional Committee and presented their views, but they had no effect on the Committee and the whole thing died out finally, without any good results.

I tried to get a clause inserted in the Report to this effect: "The immigration of land speculators, office seekers, fortune hunters and religious zealots from the Eastern to the Western States, has done infinite harm to the latter; and we ask the Nativists, who oppose Immigration from Europe, to consider this fact in their future tracts."

I met in Washington, an old acquaintance, a Mr. Fleischman, whom I had known in Cincinnati fifty-eight years previous. He was but a wreck. His life had its bloom in Cincinnati in 1838. He had married into one of the first families of the city, and was drawn about 1836, to Washington on account of his fine technical knowledge, and there he received in 1837 a remunerative public position. Under the Harrison-Tyler administration, he was made American Consul to Stuttgardt. When the Democrats returned to power he was recalled; but he was employed in the departments at Washington, and held in high esteem in Washington society. When I met him in Washington in 1890, I think that he realized, of his existence in America, the truth of the couplet:

"Life is but a bubble,
"Life is but a dream,
"And men are the passengers,
"That paddle down the stream."

On parting, he slapped me on the shoulder and said: "Reemelin, you did better than I did." I think he meant to say: that my economic and social farm life was better, than his turning public servant at the seat of the United States Government. He had visited me in Dent in 1882.

I met in Washington also the grandson of Hassler, the Swiss Scientist, who in pursuance of Benton's recommendation, was employed many years usefully, in making surveys and preparing coast maps, both for marine purposes, and also for the lands. He was of great assistance in getting up correct mapping of the geography of the eastern part of the United States. I called on my old friend, A. R. Spofford, Librarian of Congress, with whom I had co-operated for mutual benefit in the Literary Club of Cincinnati. He had got old, but retained a fresh memory of our earlier associations. He had prospered also pecuniarily.

When I got home to 'Cincinnati, the first thing handed to me was a letter from an office seeker, that offered me $100 for securing him a place under my son Louis. I returned the letter through the mail, after writing underneath the man's signature: "You are a scoundrel". I thus learned, that my son was installed into the Presidency of the Board of Public Improvements. Other annoyances of that kind followed, and I was thus made acquainted with the meanness, to which our partisan politics had sunk. and I more than ever regretted, that my son Louis had taken that position. I knew, he would be subjected to unjust suspicions and that the public would believe almost any charge, that might be made. I read in the daily papers every morning the proof, that my fears were well founded. The Republican papers particularly teemed with false accusations and what annoyed me most, was the frequent mention of my name in an invidious manner towards him. I knew, most positively, that he was never bribed, and that was my only consolation.

Mrs. Seifert, my sister-in-law, had gone to Europe, for health and recreation, and she claimed of me at that time advise and introductions in aid of her journey. I sent them promptly and was very happy in the thought, that my sister-in-law, her son and two daughters were, from all appearances, "doing Europe", as the phrase is, with great satisfaction to themselves. Her letters were excellent descriptive epistles and afforded good reading. Many of them refreshed memories of my own travels and they revived in me my inclination to travel. I was, however, in no condition to carry out my inclination. I got distressing news from Europe of the illness of my cousin Alwina. I wrote her oftener, than any of my other cousins; and now I was told, that she was sick from an incurable disease. To go to Europe and to see her on her death bed was an impossible thought to me. She had just written me a letter, that showed on its very face, how sick she was, and how well she remembered me.

March 26th, I looked for the first time at house No. 26 Wesley avenue, owned by Mr. Murray Shipley. He had intimated to my son Louis, whose wife had purchased of him the house and lot adjoining on the south side, that he might trade for my farm. After looking at the house, I offered him $2,500 to boot, provided, certain improvements were made therein. Mr. Shipley is a master in wearing out a man who lets him know, that he is anxious to trade, and I suppose, he knew, that that was the case with me. He talked off and on, but finally I yielded $500 more and left open several points, in which I was more or less worsted in the final bargain. Well! what else could I do? Wife, my two daughters, and myself were determined to leave the country and to move into the city; and we did not want to do either, without having got entirely clear of our country place; so we finally came to a trade and then commenced a series of movements, back and forth, between the city and Dent, that entirely unsettled my life for the season. I unfortunately got, besides, a severe fall in the barn, by which I injured my shinbone severely. My leg got into a state of inflamation, that at one time threatened to endanger my life. I was forbidden by the doctor from moving much about, or to undertake any trips to the city. My wife had determined to move into the city alone and to leave me in the country with at least one of my daughters to be with me. And she had carried out her resolutions and, of course, I carried on in the country a most miserable existence, principally, because I could do very little work and had no proper male help at all. I did attempt occasionally some work in the vineyard, my sore foot being much in my way. Once I swooned away in the vineyard.

CHAPTER CII.

MORE FATALITIES, INCIDENTS AND ACCIDENTS, 1890.

Towards the end of March I experienced one after another of those annoyances, that render social life in America, and in the country especially, so disagreeable. One of them is: that you are in a neighborhood, in which they are always some who expect to be employed by you on jobs, and to receive a large compensation for light work. A neighbor of mine upbraided me for not having given him any work that Spring. He was the man, I used to employ to haul my coal and to do other jobs, by what is called "back loads." I told him, that we were on the eve of moving and that that prevented us from employing him. I gave him however, a small job—a back load—that he usually charged me fifty cents for, he now charged me $2, and when I complained of the overcharge, he claimed, that I ought to compensate him for the loss of the hauling, that he did not get in consequence of our moving. There was such a barefaced impudence in this claim, that I could not help laughing heartily at it and admitting the overcharge. It was the beginning of a long series of facts, by which I was made to pay imaginary losses for our removal to the city. They are so numerous, that I think it best not to mention any more. I received during the same period a copy of an article written by my cousin, G. Rümelin,—who had been Chancellor of Tübingen University. The article was headed by the word "Zufall". In English the word meant, accident or incident, as the reader may please. It was found among his papers after he was dead. I had received notice of his demise, but a week previous; and the person, who sent me the article did it, as I supposed, for the purpose of sending me, besides a notice of my cousin's death, also the proof, that my cousin had written an article with which I would, most likely, not agree. I read it, however, with great interest, as I have all the products of his pen; but hardly felt grateful to those, who published it and sent it to me. It was not up to his other works in penetration, and contained besides defective reflections. He seems to have been aware of this, and for that reason did not publish the article himself in his life time. He seemed unaware of the concept on, that there is really *no accident* in the world, and, that that, which appears to be such, is really an event, whose causes are either partly or wholly unknown or unclear to us. He evidently also neglected to analyze the much clearer word: "Schicksal", which is really oftener employed to express that, for which he uses the word "Zufall". And it no doubt was adopted and got into use, because the German mind had long ago found out, that there is a "fitness"—a Schick— in all fatalities and they wished to express this idea. I wrote therefore this explanation to the editor, who sent me my cousin's posthumous article; but I received no reply. I noticed, however, that another critic expressed the same view in a monthly journal, and dismissed the subject from my mind. Since I have thought, that the word "Gottes Walten" is also a significant German word in this connection. It is also an indefinite expression.

March ended in a snow storm. I stopped at the Gibson House over night. In the evening I attended a meeting of the Bund for Liberty and Right, and I saw there more and more, that the words of scripture apply here: "All is vanity and vexation of spirit." I noticed, that there were cliques forming within the Bund, that would, if this tendency was not stopped, end in the dissolution of that society. These cliques were striving at a control of the Bund, that was in itself equal to a declaration, that the square honest original character of the Bund, that of being a union of free-thinkers and actors for the general enlightenment of society, and a solution of public questions, as they may arise, should not be maintained. The cliques meant evidently the opposite; namely: that a part should subject the whole to their decrees. I knew enough of the original members of the Bund to foresee, that that meant simply a gradual withdrawal of the better elements of it. I am sorry, to have to state, that my foresight was found true in the end, as we shall see.

April 1st, 1890, I realized several times, that most of April fooling is self-fooling. The paper in Berlin, that had written to me for a correspondence on the U. S., was much troubled about the main point of my correspondence to them; to-wit: That the people of the U. S. are infatuated with a seemingly inexhaustible prosperity, and had, in consequence of this, fallen into a self-conceit, that would, unless checked, end in a self-overestimation, and a depreciation of other nations, that would eventually render all high civilization, in the U. S., impossible. — Evidently, the formation of an intelligent, virtuous and wise public will, had, under these circumstances, to become more and more impossible. Now on April 1st, 1890, I received a number of newspapers, in which they were compelled to adopt this same conclusion, in consequence of the likelihood of the passage of the new protective Tariff, by Congress. And, in a similar way, I was written to from more than a dozen other places in Europe, the letters indicating, that their judgment as to America, was at fault.

The discharge of Bismark, by the Emperor of Germany, caused much excitement here, when the news arrived, and there was much division of sentiment with regard to it. I thought, that Bismark ought to have resigned of his own accord, some time ago. He must have known, that he was in the way of the Emperor, becoming Emperor in the full sense. Bismark's reign, had, moreover, blotches in it, such as the maltreatment of Arnim, etc. These prevented the Emperor, to draw around himself all the elements, he needed, to be the Emperor at all. Bismarck was too *major domo.*

Mankind was trying hard to forget, that Bismark was after all an unscrupulous tool of the former Emperor. His presence in the young Emperor's Cabinet, brought this fact back to the memories of reflecting minds. He raised, after he was dismissed, memories of former difficulties, and he must in time find, that, from that time on, a review and rejudgment of his history was going on, that must end in new conclusions of his character, in which many of the old eulogies will not again be used. The sooner Bismarck retired, the more he would have escaped harsh reflections on his former conduct.

Toward the middle of April, I got the severe fall in the barn, already mentioned. It wounded my shinbone so, that it bled profusely. I neglected the wound, and my hired man disappointed me at the same time, so that I had to do more work, than I should have done at my age. One day my neglected wound began to swell rapidly, and we had to take extra steps to secure a physician. Dr. Williams however drove past our house; he came to my aid in time. He applied poultices and cooling salves, and stopped the swelling, that was becoming very dangerous. The wound proved, however, a very painful one, and very difficult to heal. It compelled me ultimately to abstain from all work; and that was hard on me.

My daughter Lizzie wounded my feelings at this time by starting plans for building a house in Cheviot. She proposed to borrow the money of me, and giving a mortgage on the property, I had given her, as a marriage portion. Of course, this did not mend my humor. I had an inveterate dislike, during all my life, against building on borrowed money, and I, of course, particularly objected to my daughter doing so. I wrote her a letter against her plans, but she persisted in building, and that again increased my ill-humor. But finally I dropped the matter out of my mind, and was afterwards agreeably surprised by the nice building she erected, and that none of the diseases and other misfortunes, that I had feared, would happen to either my daughter, or any of her family, especially not to my favorite granddaughter, Agnes.

I learned incidentally in the beginning of May, that my son Louis was in debt, both for his house, and also for current expenses. I regarded it as a mortal offense. I foreboded from it nothing but evil. I charged it all to his party relations, especially to Governor Campbell. Under the circumstances, it aggravated all the previous complications about the office, that he got from the Governor. My granddaughter, Emily, his daughter, came to our house at this time, and looked very unwell. Dent, and its healthy air, restored her health without much use of medicines or other remedies and my love for her restored my equanimity as to my son. I felt nevertheless, that I was a sick grandpa myself and I was getting crossgrained, and thought, that everybody else was getting crossgrained towards me. All this made me anxious to get away from my old home, and to move elsewhere. My old German home was ever uppermost in my mind. We had not then finally come to a trade with Mr. Shipley, but all my troubles run in his favor, because it made me more and more disposed to close at almost any price. I did some writing for the German paper in Marietta, under the assumed name of "Old Kunradt". I also took occasionally a turn at politics in the Bund for Liberty and R'ght, and I published some articles in the "Volksblatt" under the heading: "American Illusious." I should have used the opposite expression "*American Realities.*"

My neighbor's son Hoffman kept nibbling at me with offers to buy a part of my farm, and when I add to this, that I was also negotiating in a general way, with my conceited hired man, the one, that had the irritating baby boy, the reader will understand, with what anxieties, I crossed over from April into May, and looked forward to the expected hot season in June. We begun May with an experiment, that is so frequent in America, and always dangerous; namely: a change of hired girls. We had for several years a very excellent housekeeper, she had but one fault: a predisposition to a soured temper. We had got used to enduring it in wisdom, but all at once, without any known reason, as far as we are concerned, it broke out in a violent form, and she informed us, that she was going to leave our house. From neighbors we learned, that she was going to get married. The new girl, we now hired, was the daughter of a neighbor, and was therefore not so much an experiment, as it looked at first. She adhered to us, until we finally moved, and even for a good while beyond it; so that we may say, that the whole t'ing went over without any serious difficulty. We had during the Summer very few visitors; indeed, we were not in a condition to have any. We were glad, however, to receive one from one of our usual Summer visitors, a Miss Hartman. I may say of her: that he was an old country acquaintance, since she came very near *from* my bitrh place, on the Neckar. We could talk therefore over old country matters, and thus keep out of American mischiefs. We had so long known each other in our families, that our conversation -flowed on, both delightfully and continually. During the first week of May, Emma, my son Louis' wife brought out to us, Mr. Shipley. I showed him our place all over, but he evidently saw very little of it, though he had both eyes open. Mr. Shipley is one of the folks, that ought never to own land, for he has not a particle of rusticity in him, and I doubt very much, whether he has any rural feeling, if that has to include a love of the land, we live in. Mr. Shipley left without intimating, on what terms he would trade. He simply said, on going, that he would be glad to see me at his house in the city. I promised to come. and that meant, that I was prepared to l e bled. I went, and we came to a trade, and it meant, that my farm was to be undervalued about $2000.00, whilst his house was over-valued a like amount. It was a $4000.00 advantage, to Mr. Shipley, and away went my Dent property. My creation! How could I have the cruelty to yield thee up? I was certainly to blame, but what was my wrong any more than the fault so general in America, to-wit: a callous submission to the common fate of being a roaming people!

CHAPTER CIII.

I BECOME SEVENTY-SIX YEARS OLD.

My seventy-sixth birthday brought, as a matter of course, all our grandchildren, that could be made to come, to our house, and I felt very happy, whilst in their midst. I think they enjoyed themselves also, being with us old folks; but when they were gone, I fell into a brown study. I cast a retrospect, not only on my own life, but on that of my forefathers, so far as I knew it. All ending in the question: What is human life, after all? I had often asked myself the question, but I have never answered it. because the unsolved problems have outnumbered the solutions. And when I learned, May 19th, 1890, on my seventy-sixth birthday, of my brother Theodore's death, when he was seventy-five years old, I took it in deep silence as notice to me, that my time was running short, and that I had better quit asking questions, and make my preparations towards my grave. I wept at this; but did not feel bad.

With June began a most unsatisfactory existence for me. I had, without proper reflection, agreed with Mr. Shipley, to stay in Dent over Summer, and maintain a general supervision over the place. This saved Mr. Shipley the expense of keeping a hired hand on the place, which was, no doubt, the motive for suggesting to me a continued residence on the place, with the obligation of taking care of it. With me the simple motive was: that I was, at last, very reluctant to leave the place, and to abandon the gardens and other things, to the mercy of the neighborhood. While I was making the agreement to stay on the place, my wife had, wiser than I, made all her preparations for moving into the city at once, and when I returned home in the evening, I found that I had committed the grave fault, which all economists warn against, namely: "to make your arrangements without your host." I had to ask myself, what is to become of me? My shinbone wound grew every day more painful, and less likely to heal. It did this, even with the care and attention of my wife; how would it work, if she were gone? We saw then very plainly, that we had got under threefold bad relations; namely: a protracted stay in Dent, a hasty moving into the city, and a very protracted healing of my wound. Dent suffered in all this most. The garden was neglected, the vineyard also; and everything about the farm got into precarious conditions. The end of it all was: that I made an agreement with one of my neighbors, by which he pastured his *and* my cows on the place, free of charge, and that he guarded our garden, orchard and vineyards, indeed the whole place, whilst I and the rest of the family moved, with a part of the furniture, to the city. We reserved, to ourselves, to have sent to us the vegetables and fruit from the garden, also some milk, and, that any or all of us might come out to Dent, any time we pleased. There was furniture enough there, to accommodate us, on such chance visits. The neighbor, thus placed in charge of the farm, was himself an honest, careful and capable man; but his daughter, who had been our hired girl, gave consistency and propriety to the whole arrangement; and thus our whole family moved into the city in mid-summer; and neither of us in the right physical condition for such a movement. To me it brought the special advantage, that I could have the daily assistance of my son, the doctor, in reference to my sick leg and general health.

There was one drawback, however, to it all, and that was: that it would necessarily bring us, and me especially, more in direct contact with any political complications, that might arise out of Louis' adherence to the Presidency of the Board of Public Improvements; and these complications came sooner even, than we expected. The hot weather in June, brought on mischiefs, in reference to the Water Works, and other parts of public administration. This again quickened, into sharp activity, the odious conduct of the Republican, as well as the neutral papers, to heap accusations and condemnations upon the then obnoxious Board of Public Improvements. A public press can act very mean.

I thought, the first thing to do, as against this course of the Republican party, was, to get before the people information, that could not be questioned. And I fell in, readily, with the proposition, made by the Municipal Congress: To ask the Governor of the State, and the Mayor of the city, to co-operate in an investigation of

both the old and the new Board. The Governor was not then in an-
investigating mood, nor did it suit him *then* to co-operate, in anything, with the Mayor of the city; so he searched the records, for
some evasion, upon which he could decline the petition of the
Municipal Congress, that had been supported also by the Bund for
Liberty and Right. And he found it in that clause of the law, that
requires all cases of complaint against the members of these
Boards, to be brought before the Probate Court of Hamilton Co.
So he declined the afore mentioned request, and wrote a letter to
the Municipal Congress, and the Bund for Liberty and Right. In
this letter, he took special pains, to advise the public, to have patience, and not to assume guilt, where none had yet been proven.
The Mayor of the city never took any steps at all, to co-operate with
the Governor, in the matter. but started, through the Board of Revision, a viciously one-sided investigation, against the Board of
Public Improvements, that in the end proved of no use to the public
whatsoever, because it was secret and prejudicial, as stated.

The meanest, however, in the conduct of both the Governor and
the Mayor was, their falsification of the object of the investigation,
asked for by the Bund for Liberty and Right and the Municipal
Congress. In the first place, the Bund never asked for any investigation, that was not joined by Democratic and Republican authorities; and included both the old and the new Boards to be examined.
In the next place, the Bund only asked for a preliminary examination, and it for the purpose of aiding both the public and the
authorities, to determine: whether they should be brought to punishment, or censure, or removal. The perfidious course pursued by
the Governor and the Mayor, inflicted serious loss on the city, and
led subsequently to all the injustice and wrong, that is still agitat-
ing the public mind, and causing untold evil. I beg the reader, to
reflect, just for a moment, on this whole matter. How different the
result would have been, if the request of the Bund and the Municipal Congress, had been complied with?! I certainly think, that it
would have brought peace very early to the public mind, and
thereby avoided implications and false directions, that have inflicted undeserved evils on numerous families, and done not a particle of good to anybody, and least of all to those, that have caused
all this mischief, because they had not the right public spirit, but
were guided by their own personal ambitions and hatreds towards
their enemies, or what they took for such.—

Let us now review, for one moment, the results, that have flowed
from the course, that the Governor pursued. His great wrong, consisted in withdrawing from the public gaze, the original wrong there
was in the so-called "Ripper" bills. And, speaking of Cincinnati,
that means the removal of the Board of Public Affairs from office,
by an arbitrary Legislative act, that had no reason, except partisan

persecution on the one side, and party favoritism on the other. Why has Governor Campbell labored so hard, to cover that wrong up, from public discussion? Is there any other motive? except the fact, that in that act he was guilty, with all of the Democratic party, that supported that measure. And now, let us consider, wherein the wrong lies of this concealment? In my opinion, it consists simply in this: that it removes the real issue, and permits false issues to be put in its place. That real issue was: Shall the people of Ohio take steps, to break up forever, all arbitrary legislation, that rests upon the doctrine: that the temporary majority of any Legislature, may tear up, change, alter and refill all regular public offices; in other words: upturn and set at naught all regular public administration in the State of Ohio.

The false issues are: that the Governor of the State, or the Mayor of the city, or any leader in any party policy, may invent, publish and circulate, any pretended accusations, or insinuations, for the purpose of having a foundation for inflicting arbitrary removals upon those, whom they respectively hate. This sort of oblivion, as to public questions, is the painful part of this whole business to me. I was from the first opposed to so-called kicker legislation. I foresaw and foreannounced, that it would prove ruinous to the state and all concerned in it. I announced to my son the very first moment, it begun to take shape, that it was wrong in principle, and it would have none but fatal consequences. And for the purpose of making upon him a full impression, I cited to him the old German proverb: "Wer sich in die Kleien mischt, den fressen die Säue." Had the true issue been kept before the people, and persistently argued, it would have sooner or later led to the formation and enactment of a public will, by which this legislative abuse would have been permanently abolished, so it would not have troubled the popular mind any more. We shall meet with this question later on.

CHAPTER CIV.

I TRADE MY PLACE FOR A HOUSE IN CINCINNATI.

As stated, I closed the bargain with Shipley for trading my home place for the three-story stone front house, No. 26 Wesley ave., in Cincinnati. My place looked very forlorn to me, the night after I closed the bargain, and I felt forlorn in it from that moment. I worked next morning in the vineyard, though I knew, it was for Shipley's profit and not mine. I ate some very good strawberries, because it was stipulated in the sale, that I might do so; and they tasted better, because, I thus enjoyed, what was honestly my due. By the first of July I had become a permanent resident of Cincinnati, but not all ties with Dent were severed. I still had there rights and duties, that would not expire until the October following. I had sold my horse, loosing $50 by the sale. He was the best horse I ever owned, and I felt ashamed, as the new owner led him away. Four months afterwards, as I was standing on Race st., near Washington Park, conversing with a gentleman, I felt a knock on my shoulder, and on turning around, I found, that it was my old grey horse, that had recognized me. He whinnowed, as I turned round to fondle him. He was in an express wagon, and hitched to the lamp-post. I begged mentally his pardon for selling him. When he was driven away, I pondered: whether that horse's affection for me did not prove that, what we call instinct in animals, is something near akin to our ideas of the soul? My residence in the city, during July, proved very miserable to me. The weather was extremly hot. I missed my cool drinks at the old well. I got no right sleep. My foot, though much improved by the medical treatment from my son Rudolf, and good nursing from my wife, still pained me severely. I could not use it at all, without risking a new inflammation.

The birth of my eighteenth grandchild, afterwards called Irene, was a real joy to me. I gave her, of course, just like all the other grandchildren, a silver spoon with her name engraved. She was a pretty baby, and I kissed her with the feeling, that after all, my life was not without new joys. She reconciled my son Edward to life again.

July 15th, I made my last will and testament, by the aid of Gustav Tafel, who declined to receive anything for his services. I sent him a copy of my books on the Science of Politics. The book pleased him, as his gratuitious service pleased me; namely: they represented personal esteem, and not mere pecuniary compensation. All July my foot plagued me. I was, in fact, imprisoned in Cincinnati. July 29th, I slept again in Dent, and enjoyed a good country sleep. Louise was there with me. Our visit was for the purpose of holding a final sale of personalty upon the farm, on August 1st—my father's birthday. Mr. Dunn was our auctioneer, with his brother as assistant. Dunn has a great reputation for getting high bids; I found him to be a splendid distributor of adieus and generosities from a departing—selling-out—proprietor, to his neighbors. The sale was a very cheap scattering of my household goods and farming utensils, among folks eager to have them. I spent some wine among the crowd, without distinguishing between temperance men and publicans, and it was gladly drunk by all of them. One old neighbor took his goods away without paying for them. He used to vote against me for School Director, and that was his way of showing his gratitude. When the auctioneer, as well as the crowds, were gone, my wife and myself looked at each other. Our looks said plainly: "Glad! 'tis all over." I remembered, that our auction was on my father's 110th birthday—August 1st, 1780. His picture hung in Dent, while the sale was going on. And with his, was also my mother's picture, hanging there before us on the wall; and, before both, we drank to his and her memory.

When we got into the city next morning, we learned of the severe illness of our daughter Lulu, and on the same day we heard the scandalous stories, with which our son Louis was being published by his personal enemies. I wrote into my diary the old proverb: "Misfortunes seldom come singly", and then I added: "How unhappy do I feel to-day!" This feeling was intensified, when I heard Lulu's excruciating cries during the operation, Rudolf had to perform on her, to save her live.

My reading was in Cincinnati chiefly confined to Treitschke's work on Germany. I knew the Professor personally, while he was Professor in Heidelberg. The part I read, was about affairs I lived through between 1822 and 1832. I saw very plainly, how natural it was, that emigration to America should become, for many of us, the best solution of our troubles, but I had at least to see also, that it was the worst for many of us. I saw too, that the present situation in the United States, is much the same as that, which existed in Germany, at the time named. That is to say, there were then in Germany as numerous unsolved social and political questions, as there are now in the United States; and again: that there were in Germany nearly as many tyros in politics, as there are now in the United States. And finally, that there might be now in the United States, as many correct solutions of political evils, as there were in Germany at the time named; provided, our great men would, like most men in Germany, abandon their partisan prejudices and specious notions; and adopt the teachings of real Statesmen.

I had severed, by the fall of 1880, my connection with the Bund for Liberty and Right, as soon as my son Louis' difficulties with Gov. Campbell began; my severance was the proper course. I didn't want, to *appear* even, as influencing the Bund in its action. I had signed the request of the Bund for an impartial investigation, but from there on I kept aloof from its proceedings. My signature to the request, was so basely misinterpreted by the Governor; and used as a subterfuge for his outrageous conduct, that it convinced me, that I had to be extremely cautious in every step I took. But it was not, only the base conduct of the Governor, that imposed great caution on me, but still more, the baseness of the partisan press, opposed to my son Louis. It again and again eulogized me, for the very purpose of founding thereon some calumny against my son. I can truly say, that there never was more infamous conduct, than that pursued by my son's enemies, against him. He had not deserved it at their hands. His great fault, was that of most of his countrymen; to-wit: vaulting ambition.

About August 20th, my foot began to show decided tendencies towards healing. I felt like new born, and risked even to attend the funeral of my old friend, Dr. Schmidt, on Ninth street, between Main and Walnut. I once could hardly call him my friend. When first we became acquainted, he listened too readily to misrepresentations that Stallo and Roeder spread about me, they being then my opponents. But later, when we learned to know each other better, we became steadfast friends, and associated freely with each other. During the war we became again estranged; because he was bitter as gall against the South, whilst I held: that the North as well as the South, were to blame for the war. My removal to the country, kept us much, from seeing each other for several years. But when, in 1871, I became the editor of the Pioneer, and he had got cooled from his fervor for the war, we met again occasionally, through the call of Dr. Schneider, and by 1880, we had become very intimate and friendly, even so far as to bear each others contradictions. At his funeral I wept freely for my dead friend, and forgot, that we had ever differed. I made a few remarks at his coffin. I remember him now only as a man of sterling integrity in his social dealings.

Of General Noyes, who died about this time, I say in my diary: "He was one of the men that succeeded in politics, when he should not." To this I must now add, so as to do him justice: that I am convinced, that he would have been a much better man, if our politics had been better. I knew him, when he first came from Boston to Cincinnati. I heard him frequently before the Literary Club. His aspirations were Yankee, in the better sense of the name; that is to say: he desired good local government, and understood very well, the low character of our general politics. The war changed him, after 1863, for then he got into associations. which made him eager to have a successful career at any cost, even if he had to become corrupt himself. He served the Republican party in its meanest acts, including the defrauding of Tilden of his election, and he was made Governor of Ohio for it. Next he used local politics for gaining a living, and then he left the office he got, under doubtful circumstances. He got, two years before he died, into a good local office again, and died with a somewhat redeemed character. American politics played, in his life, the seducer, that covers his vices under prodigal generosity.

The early part of September, 1880, my wife went out to Dent, to gather the grapes, and to send them in to what I call "produce merchants", in Cincinnati. It was done to keep me from going out there, and risking a relapse as to my foot. She thus risked her own health and life to save mine. I felt a little chagrined, in the first place, at this her sacrifice, because I wanted to perform myself this last instance of labor in the vineyard, which I had planted and worked in for years. I wanted to turn the grapes into a good delicate wine;

and disliked the thought, that the grapes, that I had worked up, should be sold to merchants, at a price, that would yield them 100 per cent profit. Nevertheless, I appreciated my wife's generosity. And some times, when in my presence, American women were blamed for a disinclination to work, I used my wife's grape cutting experiment, to refute the scoffers.

By the middle of September, I got finally the last three barrels of self-made wine, I had before 1890, from the country into the city. I now felt, that I had indeed bid farewell to Dent forever. I determined to forget all the disagreeable parts of my life there, and to remember only those, that were pleasant; and I did. Dent is to me to-day, a memory of youthful labor. There I was indeed a useful man all 'round, and yet I must say in conclusion, that I now think of Dent, only: to wish I had never sold it.

I now dislike to go there and see it, neglected and wasted, as it is, by the man I sold it to. I feel, as if it was a sinful act, ever to sell it to him. And these repinings overcame me entirely, when I was informed on July 10th, 1892, that my house in Dent, in which I had lived from 1851 to 1890, had burnt down entirely the night before, in pursuance of extreme negligence.

All September and half of October, in 1890, I was troubled with making a final settlement with Christian Moerlein about a house, I rented to him for a saloonkeeper, who sold his beer there for 10 years. M. had paid the rent punctually, but had allowed the house to get totally out of repairs, and to be disfigured by all kinds of neglect and injury. M. always admitted, that he would have to make up my loss to me, but he played with me at cross purposes in a small way. I learned, how small a big brewer can be, but also, how they allow themselves to be misled by favorites, who gain their confidence. In short, I became aware, how choke full America is getting of false relations! It was plain to me, that if he had pursued a square business way with me, he would have saved himself at least $200.00, and a similar sum to me.

I resumed in October my social meetings with friends at Hager's, on the S. E. Cor. Walnut and Ninth. I also attended meetings of the Bund for Liberty and Right, besides those of the German Literary Club. Both had lost all interest for me, and so it was as to my reading of current publications. It became actually a burden to me, to read them. I fell easy asleep, while reading them. I wrote for that class of papers only, when I had strong reasons, to do so. My reading of standard works became of greater interest to me, and I enjoyed it serenely, because I felt like coming home to original learning again, and thereby finishing my education.

CHAPTER CV.

EVENTS AT THE CLOSE OF 1890.

Towards the middle of October, I went to Columbus to see: whether I could do something to avert the worst injustice, the Governor meditated, from my son Louis. It proved of no avail. What pained me most, was the changed character of the Legislature as compared with the Legislative bodies, of which I was a member nearly fifty years previous. I found, that there was no longer any consciousness among members of its being a dishonor for doing a mean act in the interest of party. They openly said: that they could not understand, how I could denounce the Ripper bills as wrong, when my son got a fat office by them!?

To me such remarks were odious, because they proved, that all correct ideas of the true character and rights of the legislative power had been sunk in Ohio in a ruthless party government The Republicans supported Campbell, because his conduct would prove a precedent, which they could cite, when they wanted their Governors to exercise for them some tyrannic power; and certain Democrats labored for Campbell, because he helped to remove their personal enemies. Thus the Legislature became the mere tool of party animosities and personal hatreds. Most bitter for me, were however, remarks, such as Judge Thurman made to me, when he said: "I did not believe Gov. Campbell's charge of dishonesty against Louis Reemelin. because I know, that his father cannot have a dishonest son." I protested against such an exoneration as strongly. as I did against Campbell's accusation. The latter was made without a particle of proof; whilst the former was a mere wanton hypothesis, uttered as a flattery, that really concealed an insinuation; both were evasions of the true issue. Campbell deserved rebuke for his perfidy to his own appointee, and I certainly owed my son a square defense against it, to the utmost of my capacities. What chagrined me most in this defense. was the villany, that made the charge of dishonesty against my son appear, as if preferred for some public defalcation or misconduct; whilst no such charge was really made or could be made. And this false presentment of the matter, was repeated several times by newspapers, that knew better.

November 3rd, my grandson Hermann died, and of course. the funeral absorbed all my attention. He looked so beautiful as a corpse. Innocence itself spoke out of his face. I was so glad, that I had seen and caressed him yet, a few days before he died.

The news of the death of my old friend August Eggers in Bremen followed a few days after. He had for several years previous exercised a highly beneficial influence on me, because he forced me: to never rest satisfied about any question, until I had probed it to the bottom, and found the abstract proof of the proposition. E. had a fine acute judgment himself, and his education was very good. He introduced the works of L. von Stein, Professor in Vienna University to me, and assured me, that he was an author, from whom I could learn the best knowledge on political organization and economy. And my five years of intercourse with Mr. Eggers and his cultivated lady were the best spent years of my life. I had visited them in Bremen, since they returned to Germany, and there saw, that their natural home was in their native land, amidst their own relatives, and not in the United States. They both remembered however with pleasure, the many hours and days we spent together in Cincinnati.

The result of the November election was, with the exception of the elections of Hamilton County, an indication, that a sort of American revolution had broken out all over the Union, through the Farmers' Alliance, or People's Party. It looked like an awakening to the bad status of all our public affairs; but when closer viewed, it was nothing more than an intensification of prejudices, misunderstandings and discords. Such revolutions always break out, when public contests are no more than quarrels over the possession of power. The public is then like an habitual drunkard, that has no longer access to his accustomed stimulants. In other words: the people have lost their capacity, to act politically right; to have any right design or merit, because they are habituated to do wrong, under leaders that cater to their passions. Fatalism then takes possession of the crowds in squads, and their whole course runs finally out into a new aggravated form of the evil they ought to undo, if only they knew how. It is but a wavering between evils.

The appearances, the so-called "Farmers' Alliance", or as it, later on, called itself, the "People's Party," had caused the many upturnings, that came out in the previous November election. But there were no benefits from the new organization in the better sense, because the new party was only starting a quodlibet of new, sophistries.

I lost no opportunity to meet this seemingly new, but really old American political agitation. And when a discussion arose on the Tariff, before the German Literary Club, and a similar disposition was shown, to discuss the question only sophistically, I used the opportunity to show, that, what was wanted, was not only an opposition to the so-called McKinley Bill, which was an ultra protective measure; but that we needed much more, to-wit: a discussion over, and an expose of, the totally false public mind, prevailing in the United States, as to taxation, assessments, fees, excises, imposts and duties. And I was glad to see, that my remarks, made a good impression on the Club.

I went, November 13th, to Columbus, with the view to attending on the banquet given in honor of Allen G. Thurman's 77th birthday.

I heard both Thurman's and Cleveland's addresses. That of the latter soon overshadowed that of the former. Whether this was design, or mere result, I could not tell; but Cleveland's nomination, for the Presidency, soon was the main topic of private conversation. And it was plain to me thenceforth, that the assembly as a whole, really embodied the general disingenuous character of our party politics, which is rapidly making it impossible in the United States, to have at such meetings any squarely beneficial action, in aid of public judgment as to the public men, to whom prominence should be given, at the respective period. The effect upon me, as to Mr. Cleveland's re-nomination, was rather dispiriting; because I heard enough talk, to satisfy me, that Cleveland was really not the man, who would be the choice of the party, from a well-formed public opinion, as to his fitness; but from an indefinite feeling of resentment, for his defeat in 1888. This perception troubled me severely; because I now saw, that the United States were then in the position, that is most fraught with danger in republics, to-wit: they cannot elect the most fitted for chief magistrates, but are misled by some singular qualities of the persons they favor, that are perhaps, of only very little value, in a President of the United States. I became, consequently, more and more convinced, that we are now getting more and more at fault, as to the course we should pursue, as to the nomination and election of our President.

The national conventions of our political parties are really conspiracies against the people. The motives of the delegates are, to nominate and force upon the country, a tool for their party, that will favor them personally. The constitutional idea, that only an elector, chosen by the people, for his knowledge and integrity, should have any power in the matter, is entirely set at naught.

The Legislature had, among its several fugitively considered bills, passed a law, constituting a Legislative Committee, that was to travel over the State, with a view to find, by hearing from prominent citizens their views of municipal reform, proper material for preparing and perfecting a Bill, for the reorganization of the larger municipalities in the State. I appeared before that Committee, in company with Mr. Davis, of the Municipal Congress and the representatives of the Labor Party. I soon saw, that the better way to do, would have been, to stand there in my own person and representing only myself. Both Mr. Davis and the Labor Party men gave me an opportunity, to bring this about, by the very prominence which they gave to themselves and the associations they represented. I explained the object of my Bill, for reorganizing the city of Cincinnati, and the County of Hamilton, as one municipality; and I submitted freely to the cross-examination, I was subjected to, before the Committee. The inquiries made of me satisfied me, that there was much more to do before that Committee, than a presentation of well-prepared propositions. I saw, that several of the members were co-operating with certain cliques, and that only, what chimed in with the purposes of these cliques, would have any chance before that Committee. And I saw also: that the purposes of these cliques, and of their friends, had personal and party ends to subserve. I did, therefore, my duty as to the presentation and adequacy of my measures squarely. and left to time the future development. One of the members of the Committee—Senator Morrison, of Cleveland—impressed me at first, as if he was well disposed towards real reform; but I had to find in time, that he was quietly laying low, waiting his chance of getting a good fat office for himself, out of the expected legislation. The reporter of the Commercial Gazette took the manuscript of my Bill, and promised to have it published next morning; but the promise was not fulfilled, and I was thereby deprived of an opportunity, to have the Bill published by any other paper, because it was no longer news, after the day of its presentation. My Bill was type-writen. in three copies. One I handed to the Committee, another to Senator Brown. Both put it permanently to sleep in their pockets. We shall meet with the subject again; for I kept a copy of my Bill, and showed it, as a fair opportunity offered. One gentleman predicted its defeat before the Legislature; because the bill contained no inducements to support it, such as new offices, or revenge on enemies, or rewards of friends.

The list of sad events in the year 1890, was closed to me by the news of the death of my brother Eberhardt's widow. And, as will happen on such occasions. the mind runs back to early days, and so came to my mind the memory of the baptismal festival of this my brother. It was a very noted assembly. Ten uncles and aunts were present; our grandmother Rümelin presided at it. flanked on the one side by my father, and on the other by my mother; five of us brothers and sisters sat at a little table in a corner. And of them all, I alone am alive! And alive in America, 4.000 miles away from the scene of the festival! Was this all Providence, or all fate? I think every fact is the sequence of logical antecedents. Why should we want to make of it anymore? Why invent conceptions and words for events, and thus prevent the real comprehension?

The last work in November, 1890, I did, by participating frequently in the sessions of the Investigating Committee of the charges made by the Governor against the Board of Public Improvements, and persons and things connected therewith. I attended the sessions so far as I could spare time from my composition of the Life before the reader. The investigation was but an other instance of the utter chaos, that prevails in our politics. The real crime, which it concerned all to suppress, because it affected the very virtue of our State, and of the people that make it up: — the

Ripper Legi-lation — was hardly named before the Committee and entirely ignored as a subject of investigation; but all personal squabbles were examine 1 into, and presented in nauseating quantity and detail. Nor was the principle urged, that it is wrong to alter a Municipality or its organization for party reasons. And again there was no square opposition made, to the many acts of the Officers of Corporations, to excercise an improper influence on the Legislation of the State, as well as of the City Council and other authorities in our large cities. I asked leave therefore, from the Committee, to submit a paper, that would bring up these very points, and expose the false popular mind, that caused the conduct, which the Committee had come to investigate and to report upon. The Committee gave me leave and I exercised the privilege granted, by submitting my paper published in pamphlet form, and leaving several hundred copies on the table of the Committee. The press treated the paper cavalierly, by not publishing it, but I had copies distributed among the people, and thus had the satisfaction of knowing, that the public was informed, that at least one man thought over, and wrote and published upon the real question before the Committee. I filed also a copy of my paper, with others of my works, in the City Library.

I paid about the first of September, my taxes. They amounted to $668.54, being for the half year of 1890. I ascertained by actual accounts that this meant, paying 33 per cent. a year of all the gross revenue I derived from the property taxed. I was subjected, besides, to assessments and road taxes, which, being irregular, it is impossible to give the amount as annual percentage. In France the Socialist Prud'homme wrote: "Property is robbery." He meant that the property holder was robbing the public, by the mere fact of owning property. In the United States it would seem, that the state is the favored partner in this robbery. We should deeply reflect upon that fact, in consequence of Henry George's proposition to have but one property tax for revenue, from which to supply public wants. The question suggested by the French Anarchists in 1790, is likely to become an intensely interesting one to the present holders of property in the United States. I, took the whole matter to be only an additional proof, that our reformers take exceedingly limited views of the whole subject, by continually talking of taxation, and omitting persistently assessments, fees, excises, duties, imposts and personal exactions, such as Military service and Road work and charaties.

December 14th, my sister-in-law, Mrs. Seifert, arrived with her son Willie, from her late travels in Europe, and took lodgings with us. I had invited Mrs. Seifert to our new City home, full of the old memories of fifty years ago, when she came with us to Cincinnati, as the bridesmaid of her sister, just married to me. I anticipated her spending a joyful Winter with us; but did not think of the minus and plus, that is always hovering around, when old folks lay their plans. I refer here to a minus of health, and a plus of disappointments. Well! She came, and brought her son Willie along. We welcomed them, and listened with pleasure to their descriptions of their journeys in Europe, during the past year. Unfortunately, we had several illnesses in both families, and frequent series of bad weather. Nor was public life agreeable.

Christmas became the chief subject of conversation. We had the public entertainments, among those particularly, the German Theatre. My attendance upon several public Societies, was also talked of, I was also bothered by Mr. Shipley's neglect, to have the valuation of the house I had purchased of h m on Wesley Ave , properly put down in the Public Records, and on the Grand Duplicate. He had not been in Cincinnat during the Summer and Fall, and had not taken notice in time of the excessive entry made, as to the value of his property on Wesley Ave., by the Assessors. And he was therefore in default, and this included my property. Under the slipshod ways of doing public business, not only Mr. Shipley, but all who purchased of him, were prevented from a proper payment of their respective taxes. I had as stated, paid all my other taxes; and all my habitual conduct and economy on the payment of taxes, were thus broken into. I utterly despise being in default as to public taxes; but not so Mr. Shipley. I hate all unsettled private affairs. Mr. S. inclined the other way. The kind reader will understand therefore, that among my regrets for having disposed of my Dent Property, not the least of them was, my self-reproach, for having traded with Mr. Shipley.

Christmas passed off pleasantly. I sent the customary Christmas Dollar to all my grandchildren, and I received from, and gave presents to my wife and children at home, including this time, my sister-in-law and her son. New Year's night we had a New Year's party of neighbors, friends and relatives. We went into the New Year amid cheers and greetings, and it was past 2 A. M. on January 1st, before we went to sleep. I could not help casting a retrospect over the year just passed, and to ask myself, how far the old proverb applied: "All's well, that end's well!" And I could not help perceiving, that much the greater part of our life and surroundings, had not only not ended at all, but were evidently only continuances of rather disagreeable pre-conditions. Of course, I found, that the old proverb has only a very limited application, and that it really means merely, that we ought to be thankful: that things are as well as they are, and *that* thankfulness I felt, that night, on retiring to rest.

CHAPTER CVI.

A CURSORY RETROSPECT. 1891.

My grandson, Charlie, was with us to start the New Year. I I was glad to notice, that being over fifteen years old, he was evidently waking up to public questions. I saw to my regret, that he did not take a very favorable view of the course of his Uncle Louis, but as he judged conscientiously, and had evidently made up his mind: to think for himself. I had to respect his conclusions, though they differed from mine.

The first work I did, was to write out anew my Bill for constituting the County and City *one* Municipal Government. I had it afterwards type-written and sent copies to the Chairmen of the Committees in the Legislature, that had charge of the subject. The Bill was a carefully reconstructed paper, and I was assisted in my work by several publications, in which the subject was very properly and thoroughly considered, and I did have some hope, that some one in the Legislature would study my bill with the sincere desire to understand it and to perfect it; but I had my misgivings also.

I had agreed early in the Fall to deliver before the Turners a lecture under the heading: "Reasons why our Parties act injuriously on our Politics." I began to prepare for the lecture at once, after New Year, and I did deliver it, and it was published in the German papers. I sent copies to several of my friends in Europe, and also to some newspapers. One of them took very respectful notice of it, and while some of its criticisms were rather severe, it confirmed on the whole the general argument contained in the paper.

My connection with the Bund for Liberty and Right dragged on my hands. I could not, under the situation, as to my son Louis, participate in the proceedings as unreservedly, as I would have preferred to act in public on all occasions, and there were influences growing up in the Bund, that were constantly leading to the disintegration of the organization of the Bund. I saw this very pointedly, when the Governor's message appeared in January, 1891. It was an out and out piece of demagogueism. I wrote an article against it for the Commercial Gazette, and ridiculed *his* idea of "independent cities." I would have preferred to have the Bund for Liberty and Right take up the subject and bring it pointedly before the public; but for reasons stated, I made no motion towards such a purpose before the Bund.

It has ever been a marvel to me, and is so now, that so few Americans take up the subject of Free Cities, and their relation to all our several governments, including that of the United States. This neglect leaves this important subject to the demagogues of the land, who, like Gov. Campbell, get it into all kinds of false positions. One of the difficulties of Americans is, that they fail to understand, that both cities and counties are Municipalities, and should be therefore an integral part of all law and constitution making on this subject. We see this difficulty in the American mind, when we take into account the fact, that cities are not mentioned in the U. S. Constitution, and in not more than three of our 45 State Constitutions; and the result has been, that whenever we approach our public with distinct measures upon this subject, we are confronted by a bewildered public mind.

I made early preparations for securing reserved seats for my wife and myself in the German Theater on Sunday nights, and we enjoyed the comedies that were played there. They were the brighter moments in our existence; our aged earnestness needed refreshing in the hilarities of the stage.

January 12th, my good wife had a severe fall on the pavement, on the corner of Clark and John streets. The ice there was very slippery, and if her comb and her hair had not protected her, when she struck the ground with her head, there would have been fatal consequences. The fall nevertheless unsettled her general health, that had not anyway its full strength, in consequence of several strains upon it, whilst leaving our farm in Dent and moving into the City. In the latter part of January, she became quite sick, and all through February she was compelled to keep in bed. Rudolf attended her faithfully, and Lulu was assiduous in her care for her mother; so was also Caroline. For several days she was in a critical condition, but by March 1st she was, to the gratification of us all, up again, and about the house. Spring brought new hopes and pleasures for us all, as she regained her strength.

All January and February we had, what most people call: a mild Winter. I called it a mean Winter, because a Winter, in which there is neither snow nor ice, looks to me like a pitfall and harbinger of evil. I attended, as I did the year previous, the Wednesday meetings of the Literary Club and similar Societies. Once or twice I visited Cynthia Lodge, and there renewed my acquaintance with ancient Masonry.

I have now to mention also the fact, that previous to my wife's severe illness, my sister-in-law, Mrs. Seifert, was sick several weeks. For a while her sickness caused us severe apprehensions. After my wife got better again, both Mrs. Seifert and her son concluded, that they had better go to Indianapolis; and they did so, as soon as Mrs. Seifert was well enough to travel. There Mrs. Seifert regained her health, and made us once or twice flying visits. She has since settled in Boston permanently.

All winter I was painfully affected by the miserable course pursued by our politicians, both in the Legislature and in Congress, as well as the fallacious policy, that a large portion of the public press maintained in reference to the Silver question. I got through the Bund, a resolution, condemning the Free Silver Coinage of a dollar, that was at best worth only seventy-five cents. We condemned also the forced Silver purchases and the issue of a paper money, based on the false Silver dollar. I regarded the whole proceedure as proof, that there is a dangerous subjection of the public integrity, to the corruptly minded elements of our society. The trading that was going on, between mean Republicans and mean Democrats looked to me as strong proof, that we are mixed up in our public conduct, and that a straight forward honest public conduct labors more and more hard, under the oppression, that is now proceeding in the U. S.; and prevents all proper political development. Our public men are often falsely related to the money powers.

The exposure of Senator Cameron's conduct in speculating in Silver, while the Bill for Free Coinage was pending in the Senate, is an evidence of the demoralization now going on in high circles in the United States. He confessed the fact before the Committee of Investigation, and was allowed to retain his seat!! I could assign for this instance of depravity no reason, except the notorious circumstance, that there were in that Senate, many members, for whom their seats were either purchased outright, or obtained through corrupt considerations. They keep down better men.

February 12th, I received the sad news of the death of the wife of my step-brother Otto. Of all the sisters-in-law I had, the death of this one came most unexpected. It made me think more seriously, than ever, of my brother's loneliness. He was expected to retire soon, on full pension, from his present office, and then to live a long life of peace and quietness, with his wife, who had proved to be the most suitable companion, that he could have chosen. He is now left alone, but this loss is even greater to his sons and daughters, than to him.

CHAPTER CVII.

PUBLIC AND PRIVATE SORROWS.

The death of General Sherman called to mind with me some of the very earliest historic lessons I learned in America. One of the first was, the one already mentioned: "No General can ever get an unquestioned fame for deeds done and won in Civil War." I had known Sherman in Lancaster, Ohio, twenty years before the war, and when nobody ever expected of him any very distinguished career. I had followed him through life, until he entered the service of Louisiana as a Military Instructor. Then I had lost sight of him, and he seemed to be forgotten; but our Civil War, that brought so many to light again, that had fallen into obscurity, brought him also forward to the light of day. His employment by the South, at that time, raised the very difficult question, whether it is right in any man, who has eaten the bread of others, to become their foe in war? The decision of the Northern mind then was: that the duty of patriotism to the whole Union outweighed every debt of gratitude or allegiance, that any person might owe to that section of the Union, if it should claim the right of secession. There is no doubt, that Sherman himself took the rule to be: an unswerving fidelity to the Union. And he took it relentlessly. It is well known, that in the Germanic Union, the rule is for local allegiance. When he entered the lines of the Northern armies, there were some in the U. S., who doubted both his capacity as a military man, and his honor as a citizen. But he overcame these doubts, and marched through the South, and saved his reputation as a leader of armies. His conduct towards A. J. Johnson relieved him of all doubt, as to his being a perfect gentleman. So, when he died, and I read the death bed scenes, I remembered the already often mentioned lesson in history; and concluded, that his fame rested under a cloud, and, that the future historian would still have some anomalies in his character to consider, and it would still be an open question, whether his fame would be entirely without a blot. That doubt was reawakened lately through the criticisms of the English General Wolseley. The fact, that the General named is in the British service, will prevent his opinion getting a firm hold in the American mind. And yet, the fact, that the final tests: the ones, suggested by historical citation; to-wit: That the fame has to be scrutinized by the historian under the light of having won it in a civil war, makes me doubt, whether the future historian will give him such a unquestioned high reputation, as he still holds at this time in the U. S. as a citizen, a military man and husband of a catholic wife.

My son's fate, under the attacks of Governor Campbell, assisted as they were by both corrupt Democrats and corrupt Republicans, was, all through the winter of 1891, the all-absorbing question for me. He applied to me early in the winter for some pecuniary relief from his most pressing difficulties, and I gave it to him, and charged it to: "Fond perdue". I did it upon the principle, I heard my father often announce, to-wit: that, when a member of a family gets into difficulties from a general error prevailing in public affairs, it is the duty of the head of the family, to come to his assistance and to treat the sum advanced, as a common outlay, for the family.

He consulted me afterwards, as to the brief, to be presented to the Supreme Court of the State, and asked me, to become security for the costs and I signed the bond, believing, that I was simply doing my duty, when I assisted in bringing the question of the legality of the abolition of the Board of Public Improvements, and the establishment of the Board of City Affairs, before the Supreme Court of the State for final decision. I at the same time suggested, that besides the questions raised in the original brief, there should also be others raised, that involved more then mere technical points. I refer to the real question of "*Free Cities.*"

My suggestions were not adopted by the attorneys, from considerations of practical legal considerations, that were based upon previous decisions of the Supreme Court, and I acquiesced in this course, though having some doubts of the correctness of such a policy. I was therefore agreeably surprised to learn, March 12th, 1891, that the Supreme Court of Ohio, had decided, that the act of establishing a Board of City Affairs was unconstitutional, and expressed also the opinion, that the said act should be condemned for its general wrongfulness. When I heard of the decision of the Court, I felt, that we need not despair of Ohio entirely, when its chief judicial tribunal lifts itself above mere technicalities, and proves itself impartial and sound on the general principles of jurisprudence. The Court lacks full penetration as to "free Cities."

Towards the close of winter I received more and more the impression, that the Bund for Liberty and Right, had lost its usefulness. I therefore took an independent position towards it, so far, as paying my own expenses, for any, that I incurred for matters that concerned the Bund, and I drew up a set of declarations as to what steps should be taken preparatory to the coming Spring election. The Bund passed them, but in such a way, as to satisfy me, that steps were in contemplation, that meant the running of a special ticket at the April election, then impending, and to give my name a prominent place on that ticket. Such a course was not acceptable to me. I was satisfied, that we should avoid even the appearance of having organized for the purpose of gaining political power for ourselves. I said frankly, that in my opinion, the making of a ticket for the voters, was usurping functions, that should only be exercised by authority of the Constitutional authorities of the land. Moreover I insisted upon it, that such an act on the part of the Bund was an obstruction to the inauguration of the rightful reform, that has to come, if there is to be a legitimate regeneration of politics in the U. S. I felt therefore, that, having made these remarks, I had to withdraw, and leave to time the further developement. Similar considerations induced me to keep from attending the celebration of Washington's birthday by the German Pioneer Society.

The health of my wife continued to improve all through March, and by April we felt, that for the present, the worst was over. She essayed even some visits to my daughter and also my daughter-in-law, in Westwood and Cheviot. She had occasionally relapses of weakness, but as they always yielded again, we regarded them more as signs of persistent recovery, than of any dangerous weakness.

AM BROUGHT TO REVIEW RELIGION.

Religion was always a critical subject to me. I knew, that my parents differed upon it; and I became cognizant of the circumstance, as I passed through school, that my teachers were not strict believers in the current religious tenets. And when I was confirmed in church, 14 years old, I believed more firmly in my Uncle's prediction: "that a great change was at hand as to religious faith", than I did in the catechism, they had made me learn by heart. These points stuck to me through life, and I was ever on the lookout for every sign, that pointed in this direction.

When therefore in March 1891, Mrs. Wilde, a friend of our family, handed me a copy of some posthumous works of Rev. Julius Rupp, of Königsberg, and told me: that they contained many religious truths, and that their author was the correctest leader in the freest religious movement of our age, I read his works, and felt gratified, to find therein the following leading idea: "There is an inner necessity for all to seek to discover and to learn religious rules of conduct for their guidance through their lives." Also: "With this search for the capacity of self-government must proceed the acquisition of more and more positive knowledge, and the faculty to reason right, both abstractly and conjunctively."

These ideas of Rupp, brought to my mind, as congenial thought, some remarks, I had made on a Fourth of July celebration, 30 years ago, at the State Reform Farm of Ohio. I then said among other things: "Religion means of all things, first and last, liberation from vice, folly and error." Also: "The truly religious person is free, even in a prison." And again: A human being might to all appearances be free, and enjoy himself highly; and still be unfree, if he was vicious in his disposition, and preferred error to truth." I felt, no doubt, a congeniality with Rupp, because he took, like myself, fundamental grounds on the subject of religion. God was to Rupp, evidently not a person. nor a separate being, and just as little: a lawmaker or ruler. by issuing decrees or orders. Nor was religion to Rupp a personal revelation through some individual. Rupp used words, that proved to me, that religion was to him, what it was to the late Sir Matthew Arnold—the promulgation of a universal rule of conduct. worked out by educational processes, in perennial development. The use of my native language by Rupp, contributed, no doubt, also to my accord with his general religious views. I cannot think fully on Religion without such words as: Wesen, Sein, Walten, Lehre. They are to me, what many Greek words are to the authors of antiquity, to-wit: a part of the general language — Weltsprache — as we call it in German, which will make it in time possible, to drop words and ideas, that mislead so much in religious culture, as, for instance: God as a person — or a divine rule, — doctrine — to be — ich. They always perplexed me, when using English.

I regard Rev. J. Rupp therefore a clearminded leader in the impending readjustment of belated, merely disciplinary, theology by progressive scientific ascertainment. I believe besides, that he has been, by his teaching and by his writing, a reliable aid in the religious readjustment, that was going on in the XIX. century, by which religious instruction would be freed from the impediments, which existed, wherever Religion is the specialty of a particular mind, country, race, or period, and is not like Philosophy, Ethics, Science, Law and Finance, a part of a universal world culture.

I did not, however, disguise from myself, that Rupp still clung to phases of religious ministrations, and expressions, as to Divine Government and direction, which interfered with the true conception of cosmical unity and identity in Religion. R. made constantly distinctions between "inner and outer life", "spirit and matter", and spoke of them, as if they where anchors to his faith and religion, without which he feared to be drawn over a cataract into an abyss. This gave to R's works a pietistic turn, that marred his otherwise succinct treatment of the several matters.

I understood fully, that the history of religion tells us distinctly, how the true progress of religious developments has been always hindered by such relics of ancient devotional fervor; but I know also, that with minds like Rupps and those of his disciples, the religious truths will in time overcome the errors and superstitions, especially, where the conception has taken fully hold, that religion must be an international culture, in a much broader sense, than that of the catholic church. I mean in the sense so often brought forth by Rupp, viz.: "that the best progress made by religion, has always consisted in correcting previous errors and defective knowledge." Schiller points to a similar process in the development of jurisprudence, by showing, that wise corrections of wrongs have always preceeded really effective law reformations. The true perception is in fact contained in the word religion itself; to-wit: that it must be a perpetual educationary process, and a reminder of eternal an integrity of the world and its action, interaction, and reaction, past, present and future. Rupp himself comes very near this perception in his sermon, entitled: "Consecrated Religion"; but he misses it by trying to draw a distinction between natural religion and "eternal order", as if he really understood, what he meant by both or either of these phrases. The first he calls "A creation of Nature"; the second he designates: "as the capacity to determine between good and evil", and then qualifies further, by the remark, that it means: "The progressive in love for the good and the Eternal." We meet here a remnant of the great error, that intense theologians have so far always made; to-wit: that they attempt to restrict the word "Nature" to some special emanation of human developement in the ethical; whilst the right course would have been, to hold with Aristotle: "that the vital principle is an abstraction of our own making, and that Nature's attributes are qualities, that cannot exist apart from material objects." I admit, that Rupp is freer from delusion, than most other religious teachers known to me. Indeed, I believe, that his definitions are actual aids to a better understanding of the subject. Indeed, we wondered, as we read them, that he did not come squarely out with the declaration: that mankind's knowledge of the universe, its government, laws and forces, are still too imperfect, to comprehend them fully, and to name or define them correctly. Hence it was, that the Names, Definitions and Attributes given, are still expressed in more or less vague words and terms. I had, through my knowledge of the dead and living languages, and comparisons between them, reached this and similar conclusions, as to Rupp's works.

In the Commercial Gazette of August 15, 1892, I found the following, as part of remarks, made the day previous, in Wesley Chapel, by Rev. Charles R. Brown:

"I believe thoroughly," said he: "in the sermon, the Sunday-school, the prayer-meeting and all the regular church services and appointments. These are necessary for the cultivation of a proper devotional spirit, and also for intellectual and spiritual instruction and enlightenment. This kind of teaching and exercise is essential for the inculcation of right principles. But I also believe thoroughly, in the immediate application of these principles in all the practical affairs of life. My idea of religion is: that if it is not made an every-day, practical matter, it can not make much impression in a church situated like this. Wesley Chapel can succeed only by being made an institution of all-around, every-day salvation. It ought to be honeycombed with educational, industrial, musical and entertaining appliances. It must work as Christ did, helping and promoting the temporal condition of people along with its directly spiritual work."

The movements here indicated, are certainly steps in the direction I have pointed out in my lecture on "Finishing the Education of Adults," which follows at the close of this my biography. To it I refer, for further explanation.

By impressions made on me early in life, I had become able, to detect even such slight attempts at concealing defective knowledge, under noble expressions, as those made by pure-minded Rupp. This faculty is not always a pleasure; on the contrary, it is often disagreeable to exercise; as for instance on the following sentences in Rupp's writings: "Hail to man, that, however all may turn in eternal change, there is in every soul an eternal life; that is not subject to change"; again: "that however human inclinations may rise or fall, the Eternal Father's eye again unites in love the enstranged relations through its holy presence and unchangable faith." These are pure and refined thoughts in elegant language; but it is, nevertheless, expressing matter in misleading similitudes, that are borrowed from certain temporary parts of the world; but are totally inapplicable to the Eternal All. The full truth is still absent, as to the culture that religion must be, to be religion in the full sense.

I thank him for having made me review religion. It has confirmed many of my conceptions, cleared others of doubt, and suggested new inquiries; but the best service it rendered, was in pointing out for me more distinctly the true merit and the right way for religious culture. I know now, that to acquire it, through religious culture, is a consummation of intelligence, morality, knowledge and wisdom. I understand therefore, that all religious defects have sprung from a lack of provisions and institutions for the readjustment of old tenets to new knowledge and morality. That lack has always caused: first, a laming of the necessary progress; next anamolies, and finally useless disputations, that ended often in bloody conflicts. My leading religious idea is, that these consequences could and should be avoided, by making religious culture an unbroken progressive disciplination of mankind in a much higher *international* sense, than the Catholic Church even had it in its best days. And if I were now asked: whether I regard myself as a religious man? I would say: that I do; though I do not believe in any special religion. I certainly believe into a constant religious culture, such as I have explained.

CHAPTER CIX.

A POLITICAL REVIEW.

In the middle of March, 1891, I was called upon by some friends, to make a statement, before the Judiciary Committee of the Legislature on the subject of Temperance Legislation, or, as I called it: "Temperance Prevarication". I attended March 12th. and reviewed the history of the subject for the last fifty years; showing how two extreme factions have prevented in Ohio the coming to a permanent rightful policy on the subject. I distinguished between these factions respectively, by designating the one: "that body of men and women in our state, who want righteousness without liberty"; and the other as: "the one, that wanted liberty without regard to propriety and right." There were other persons present to reply to my remarks: but they had not much to say. And they admitted finally, that my remarks had produced a strong impression on the Committee, and that most likely the proposition, to fix up a new jury system for the Police Court, in aid of Temperance Legislation, would be defeated. I had stated in my speech, that this proposition was but another instance in proof of my main argument.

The statement caused in me very serious reflections on the general political experience I had had in the the U. S., and to ask myself in all sincerity: what testimony I had to bear to the value of Constitutions and Legislation generally in Ohio? My reflections were in great part comparative, for I had, after participating, in Ohio, in Constitution making and Legislating; seen many Legislative Assemblies in many of the states of our Union, and also in Great Britain, France, Belgium, Switzerland, several German states, Austria, Hungary, Servia, Bulgaria and Italy. Some of these I had seen several times, and had formed acquaintances among their more prominent members. With these Assemblies in my mind, I had to say: that I saw none, that were inferior to our present Ohio Legislature, except those mongrel Legislatures in Mississippi, South Carolina and Louisiana, that distressed the South after our Civil war; but that there were several superior ones, as for instance, the two Legislative bodies, that I saw in Switzerland in 1848 and 1853. I saw there, what charmed me most, the good temper and eminent high culture, that members of Legislature must have, if they are to be elected to, and to have influence in good legislative assemblies.

I had also received in the middle of this century, much instruction, as to the proprieties of Legislators, from my uncle, who was for many years, a member of the Legislative Assembly of my native state, Würtemberg. He told me in 1843: "Any man that would make a sharp party speech here, would be disgraced." It was a remark, that I carried with me, even, when I was a partisan myself. And I confess, that it often tempered my partisan zeal. I do not claim, that I never made a party speech, but I can declare: that my party speeches were much checked by my memory of the remark narrated. And with this confession before me, I have a right to express my judgment and say: that in this respect Legislative bodies in the U. S. stand lowest, by the standard of rightful conduct. The real merits of a question are now seldom brought out in the U. S. And I hope, that I may be allowed to add here, that I have had to look over, and review, pretty much all I have said and written in composing this, my life, and that I wish to say at the close of it: that all, that I have spoken, that gratifies me still, was made from the general standpoint of right; but that I now deprecate all those words, in which I allowed my party feelings to get the better of me. I regard as coming within the first named distinction my speech on the annexation of Texas; but that as to the second, I regret ever having made the speech against the repeal of Black Laws in Ohio The remarks I made at the Fourth of July celebration on the State Reform Farm, I like to read still for the high tone and ideality, that is displayed there. I think it will not be deemed improper in me to state here besides, that I confess to have derived, a few years ago, much benefit from the lectures, I heard from Professors Geffken, Schmoller and Laband in Strassburg, and also from Professor Held in Würzburg, on Government and public administration.

With what has just been said before us, I feel at liberty to state: that all through the winter of 1891 the political situation in Ohio, so far as the general Assembly of the state, including a part of the authorities of Cincinnati and the press of the Republican party was concerned, caused me harrowing reflections; not only on account of the mischiefs, they involved for my son Louis, but mainly for the general political degeneration, which then evidently prevailed in this state. I had been for nearly sixty years a supporter of the Democratic party, but was always aware of the inconsistencies with political science, which the word Democratic involved, as it is used in this country. I never gave up my vigilance, against the use of the word, by corrupt demagogues on the one hand and infatuated zealots on the other. I nevertheless adhered to my faith, that after all, up to 1856, the Democracy was the safer of the two regular party organizations in the United States. I must mention here also a few of the instances, that staggered this my faith afterwards, viz.: the repeal of the Missouri Compromise in 1853; the election of Buchanan to the Presidency in 1856, and the passage of the Ripper Bills by the Ohio and other Legislatures in late years; as well as the corruption in our Court house cliques, in earlier periods.

My son's imbroglio with Gov. Campbell, was one of the by-scenes in the political drama 1889—92. My participation in it was from the beginning, and throughout the whole of it, against my will, because it placed me, all the time, in a delicate position. The public continually presumed, that my only motives of conduct in this matter were my parental feelings; but this was untrue from first to last. In no single instance did I loose sight of the principle, that the public interest must in all such questions be the paramount issue, and that we must always be on our guard, not to let our personal feelings ever overbear our public sense of right.

I desire to show, the necessity just expressed, at the hand of the miserable history Cincinnati has been made to undergo during the period named.

It was universally admitted, that Cincinnati needed a correction of its municipal institutions, both as to their organization, as also its government and administration. It had within itself the well-known political capacities, that could have secured this correction. But these were purposely and maliciously ignored. The Legislature was sought to be made the organ of the lowest kind of partisan legislation by both parties. It was chiefly charged upon the Democratic party, but the Republican party perpetrated often also the election of a large number of men, who were just as false to the great interests of society and just as eager for party wrongs. In one word, the whole legislature was filled with political hypocrits, that believed, that the legislature had a right to pass laws, by which the public wealth and public interests would be made subservient to persons, who pretended to be very zealous for party interests and party arbitrariness. I can testify, that I know of only about a dozen members, with whom the public integrity as to right, justice and wise public economy, were the standard of their thinking, speaking and voting. There were many appeals made to members, to rise above their party prejudices and vices; but they almost invariably turned the appeals aside upon the ground, that the other party had been and would continue to be guilty of these wrongs. The acts of their predecessors in all their deformities, were thus the justification of their own respective misconduct. Their entire conduct rested on deceiving by catchphrases.

CHAPTER CX.

OFFICE SEEKING DOUBLY ASSURED.

Most people had seen the evils of making party zeal the basis of securing offices to political aspirants, and movements for breaking up this abuse, became popular. But as these movements were blind strokes on the part of the People, they were taken advantage of by sharp-sighted politicians, and they suggested: that the way to counteract the evils of intense partyism was: to make it doubly sure, by entrusting the new public administrations to many-headed Boards, and to prescribe, that in each Board *both* of our standing parties shall be represented. This double alternation mystified the people, but secured the trade in offices, and gave the traders therein double assurance. Office seeking was duplicated.

We have seen how this pretended reform began, and how it multiplied and fructified. These, our neutral politics, generated Boards in alternation with Corporations, who were paid highly for very poor services they rendered to the public. It drew elements into politics, that believed in venality as a means in public careers; but had no idea, how to organize and carry on efficient municipal public service. The Committee for Municipal Reform, whose chairman was Corcoran, proved to be a mere sham body. that had a scheme fixed up in advance, which was held back for months, and was only finally introduced, when the Legislature was dumbfounded by the multiplicity of propositions, that had been shelved unfairly. Then the old plan was sprung upon the Legislature, and as much as possible was pushed through under deceitful names, such as "New Charter", and "Tax Equalization." Only a few members in both houses of the Legislature knew the real contents of the measure and the bill passed in an indecent hurry, near the close of the session. In it power was given to the new Boards, that no honest friend of republican government would ever knowingly vote for. In it was, for instance, as to tax valuations and equalizations, the old abuse of special legislation, that was meant to be killed by the Constitution of 1852; and thus most arbitrary powers were conferred in a special Board, that has existence only in a part of Hamilton County. To me this complex system, of unconstitutional municipalism, was very odious, because I not only knew, from my studies and observations, that such multiples of municipal complications are condemned by the science of politics; but I had also heard, from the lips of the best professors of several universities, their advice, that one of the highest duties of modern reformers is: to simplify all municipal government, by abolishing the complexities, which had grown up therein, in the course of time. That Cincinnati should, in consequence of the facilities our parties furnish to bad men, to foist themselves into high positions, be subjected to the very opposite course, and, instead of abolishing, increase false municipalism and establish tyrannic public organs, pained me so much, that I had to withdraw from all participation in public efforts to oppose these iniquities. Party politics had so vitiated the public mind, that the sounder a reform measure was, the less acceptable it was to our people. They had become enamoured with the specious opportunities, that demagogues had, to play hide and go seek between City and County, in alternanation. All they had to do, was to fall in with the respective reformatory pretences, that were gotten up, as the one or the other municipality was the object of attack or defense. It was an actual occurrence, that repeated itself frequently, to-wit: that this self same people of the two municipalities imagined themselves to be two people, with inherent causes for enmity. This got such mastery over their minds, that small politicians had for years made money and held offices, to the general injury of both City and County; the real interest of all concerned being all the time, that all public matters should be simplified and made beneficial to all. It looked then (1890), as if the bitterest thought I shall have to carry to my grave, will be the conclusion: that there exist in Hamilton County and the City of Cincinnati, prejudices and misunderstandings, as to municipal government, which will long be in the way of all correct reform therein. Their source is no other, than our partisan contests, in which candidates for public favors, use for every election respectively, false pretexts to carry their schemes. And just as they invented pretexts to carry their schemes, so too did they invent accusations and nicknames against their opponents, so as to get themselves into offices. Most of them were drawn from their own guilt. Our municipal politics were made up, as novels are, of heroes and scamps, written out for a purpose, but borrowed from actual life, only magnified or belittled, as was needed for the plot. And this made it here almost impossible, for the people to arrive at correct conclusions, in reference to men and measures. In other countries, they neglected the political education of adults, but here they intensified their false education, and preverted the popular mind. For every election there was a specious twist in the presentation of the many issues, which always prevented the public, to see the real truth, to-wit: that under our party government it was almost impossible, for either party to take the right ground for itself, or to expose the real faults of its opponents. It was therefore a most thankless task, to be for this people of ours, either an advocate of real reform, or the antagonist of frauds. Bad men, especially such as had grown rich as lawyers, or railroaders, or jobbers generally, had the decided advantage over them; and the good men, had really no weapon for attack or defense, except a faithful persistence and patience,in sticking to their cause and that of the society and people,with whom they lived. Their opponents had versatility in serving causes, and ubiquity in their habitations, that gave them a capacity for vacillation, that was impossible to men of sterling integrity and settled habitation.

CHAPTER CXI.

SOME PERSONAL INCIDENTS AND THEIR LESSONS.

A sterling character died in Cincinnati, in March, 1891. His name was Rufus King. I attended the memorial service held, in his honor, at the U. S. Court-room, March 28. I had known him for half a century. I agreed with him in few things; but esteemed him as the most valuable man to consult with, in public interests and personal views to general principles.

He was always on his guard against hasty conclusions; but his mind was open to points new to him. At the same time he had considerable tenacity of opinions, and I will mention one instance in support of these statements. About forty years ago, we had a conversation as to the teaching of German in the public schools. He expressed an opinion adverse to it; his main argument was, that "learning German would interfere with learning English." He insisted, that English being the language of very nearly all in the U.S., it should be the standard, by which all questions on the learning of languages, should be decided. I claimed, that the reverse was true, and that every new tongue was an additional aptitude in the use of language, as well as in learning it. I then took the extreme ground, that mankind would be much less capable, in the gradual perfection of that, for which language existed; namely: human intercommunication,—if the education in languages were confined to only one, and I pointed out to him, that the perfections of language had all consisted in adopting from the various ones, superior expressions. And that in all these matters, the English had gone furthest. He admitted his mistake, but returned to it, by advancing the idea, that it would interfere with the unity of American civilization. I met him here also, by a square contradiction, and asserted, that no nation could, now or ever, be truly civilized, that confined itself to only one language. He now yielded, and adopted more liberal views. Then I added to my former argument, the one, that the suppression of German in the United States, would impoverish the country socially, politically and religiously, because it would deprive the several minds of people of the means of interconversation. He now demurred, by interposing, that in our intercourse, my knowledge of the two languages sufficed; but he surrendered entirely, when I showed him, that the main question was one of numbers, and that it was undeniably true, that the more persons were cognizant in a given country, of more than one language, the better it would be for all. He became, afterwards, a quiet supporter of a free expansion of the teaching of languages in our public schools. Mr. King became thereby, a mediator for general improvement, and justified Wm. Groesbeck's statement, at the funeral obsequies: That "he was the most valuable citizen, Cincinnati ever had."

I had for years cooperated with him in various special organizations, such as the Taxpayers' League, the Committee of 100, etc., and I served with him on other committees. I liked best, to do so, in matters relating to higher education. The law, by which the consolidation of all the various trusts and endowments for universal education in Cincinnati, was made the settled policy of our university, was originally drawn by me, and then perfected by Mr. King. I then saw, that he not only willed, what was right, but understood the subject. He was also aware of and opposed steadily the great hindrance of city and county affairs, to-wit: the hangers-on to our schools, colleges, university, public trusts and works as well as improvements, for the money, they could make from them, or the fame they could gain in them. And he said once to me: "Our country is becoming a very different nation, from what was the idea originally, when independence was achieved. Individual selfishness is combining in such a variety of corporate power, that public government and administration is dwindling into pettiness before it, and making it less and less a Res publica." I cited to him, in support of his statement and the principle it enforced, from Shakespeare:

"Things growing to themselves — are growth's abuse."

King thanked me for the citation, and applied it to our politics, and an understanding of the drift of American political development. The speeches made at the memorial services, turned, in my opinion, too much on King's capacity as a legal mind; and I appreciated every remark the better, the more it brought out his general usefulness as a civilian and honest leader of his fellow-citizens in their public concerns. I learned lately, with great interest, that a life of Rufus King, with a good portrait, is about to be published.

At the close of March, I attended one of the free lectures, given by the Cincinnati University, and delivered by Prof. Eddy, on the subject of the "Moon and the Tides." I was highly gratified by this discourse, because it was carrying out a procedure, I had so frequently urged upon the Trustees of the University. My journeys to Germany in 1865 and 1873, had made me acquainted with similar free lectures at some of the Universities of Europe, and I judged, that, as they benefited me then and there, that so too, would they be advantageous to Cincinnatians. The lecture pleased me besides, because it was fully up to similar lectures, which I heard from the Professors in Europe. It made me have new hopes of Cincinnati.

There were about 250 ladies and gentlemen present, and all paid strict attention to the Professor's teaching. That part, in which he demonstrated the indestructability of "Matter" and "Energy" excited due interest in me. It sounded to me doubly clear on hearing it again in Cincinnati, after I heard it first at Würzburg. I reflected on the inevitable clearing such lectures must have on minds like those present in Cincinnati, and I argued from it, that the continuance of these lectures must act as an entering wedge to the acquisition of more scientific knowledge by the adults of Cinnati. I asked myself, why it should not gradually become the leaven, that would leaven the whole lump. I believed it would, and was very assiduous in attending all the free lectures, some five in number, by the Professors of the City of Cincinnati. I was very pleased with one of the lectures on "Plato's Republic", and I was thankful to Prof. P. V. N. Myers for reviving in my mind one of my best studies of my youth. One point of Plato's Republic, that of regulating population by law and administration, would, I think, be radically changed by Plato himself, if he would take the subject now up, with the knowledge, we now have.

May 4th, 1891, the official position of my son Louis ceased, and I did not know whether to be glad or sorry for it. I certainly wished that he had never taken it. I am now more than ever convinced, that taking office, that is created by arbitrary Legislative power, is always a blunder, if not a misdemeanor. I had supposed, that w.th his going out of office, there would be an end of the controversies and quarrels, that arose out of Campbell's conduct. But, while I am writing this, there is renewed excitement, in consequence of the candidacy of Campbell for re-nomination for Governor. It gratified me much. that he was defeated; but I did not think so, because of any ill-feeling, I may have on account of the treatment my son received at his hands, but for the much better reason, that I regard Campbell as utterly unfitted for so distinguished a position as Governor of Ohio. He never learned a political truth, and he never unlearned an error.

About the 10th of April, I received, unexpectedly, a letter from Gustav H. Schwab, Treasurer of the "People's Municipal League," in New York City, inquiring of me about the great question of the day—Municipal Reform.—It seems, a friend of mine in that city, Albert Roelker, had told the Directory of the League, that I was acquainted with the history of the free cities of Germany, and the principles, upon which they were organized, and that I was a proper person to consult, as to what was the best way to create similar Municipalities in the United States. April 12th, I sent in my reply, which I had type-written, at my own expense. It contained a dozen or more pages, and I retained a copy among my papers. It is too long for insertion here. April 20th. I received an answer to it, in which it is said: "Your letter contained so much, that is of the greatest interest, and has such a pertinent bearing upon the subject, in which we have such a great and common interest, that I desire to lay it before our Committee for further consideration." I have heard no more of it since; but have filed one copy, with my other papers, in our City Library.

The reader will, of course, understand, that such a request from New York City, gratified me exceedingly, and that I used the opportunity, to present some of my views, for the purpose of having them publisped at large. I do not wish to appear callous to such honors. Municipal reform is, in my opinion, the best field for winning glory in the United States. I said of it in 1891:

"In Ohio the old tendencies to a deterioration of Municipal "Government, under reform pretences, still have their sway, and a "full awakening of the popular mind, is hardly to be expected soon; "because the coming gubernatorial election, is rapidly absorbing "public interest. Sham issues will be thrown, as tubs to the whale, "*id est* at our people. It would not be fair, to call this a fooling of "the people, by partisan demagogues, unless it is understood to "mean self-fooling; because at last, the great body of the people "participate largely in whatever political fooling there is going on "in this our commonwealth."

CHAPTER CXII.

NOTABLE MATTERS IN THE SPRING OF 1891.

I am writing this chapter within a few days of my 78th birthday. I wish to insert in this chapter, only the more notable events. In the last days of April, I got the sad news of the death of my dear cousin, Alwina Heinrich, in Stuttgardt. She was the niece of my mother, and resembled her much. I never saw her without remembering my mother. With her death, the last link between my mother's female relations, and myself is broken. I have frequently referred to her in my life, and can only now express my deep grief, that I could not have seen her once more, as I intended to do soon: but find now to be impossible.

About this time I received a very pointed reminder: that authors are apt to overrate the value of their writings. It came thus: the German Pioneer Society had got tired of paying storage and insurance, on the thousands of extra copies it had ordered printed for many years of its paper, "The *Pioneer*." Of these, several yearly issues were from the editorial pen of Doctor Brühl, the largest number from that of F. A. Ratterman, and I had contributed some volunteer communications, as well as editorials.

The Pioneer Society had given many away to other Societies: but they kept accumulating, nevertheless of the issues of later years, and finally it took special rooms to keep them. The society now ordered them sold. But little or nothing was realized on the sale; and the Pioneers got desperate, and ordered them to be distributed gratis. After several weeks, they were thus disposed off. Thus a series of publications, that were presumed to have a great value, were largely wasted. We writers looked blank at each other. I kept on writing my life and realized, as consolation, the American Negro's addition, to the sermon on the mound: "Blessed are those, that expect nothing; they will not be disappointed."

On the 10th of April. I went with my son Louis, and his two sons, to the Catholic Ladies' Seminary in Clifton, to pay a visit to his two daughters there. We were pleased with the general air of comfort and propriety that existed there. On our return home, we came within a yard of being run over and killed. The presence of mind of my son Louis, was the only thing that saved us.

The same runaway team, from whose violence we were saved, killed my old neighbor Trum. His life was lost, and mine endangered, because our suburban police had not enforced the laws against fast driving. It guarded against infractions of the Sunday law—in a way!? I was weak from a wound, caused by a fall in my barn. My son was careful of his driving. Trum was well, though my senior and he was proud of his faculty to drive. It was a queer saving; and a queer killing. The Police did least in the first, and most in the latter. It was just so, as to our civil war. There too, that part of our society, that should *prevent* mischief, i. e. the political force in the Constitution, was least usefull. Was it not so, because *it* was least organized and active? I attended Trum's funeral, and heard the remarks, that were made on all sides. They treated his death as an unavoidable misfortune, and mentioned others, that he had had: for instance, the heavy losses Trum had met, in the failure of Bishop Purcel and his brother, all, as if Trum's old age, made such events a matter of course. I could not get clear of the impression, that the fault was our defective suburban police administration, in consequence of the incompleteness of our township organization for the protection of life and property. There is in these communal bodies, a reckless pursuit of wealth and pleasure on the one side, and on the other a defective discharge of public duties, by the public authorities. The adults of society are assumed to be able to protect themselves, and to need no guardianship, which was true in the fewest cases. Trum overrated his strength in driving his horse, and the rural ward authorities overrated their capacity, to enforce the laws, and to use due foresight in discharging their respective functions. The youth of the country-towns, and those in the city, intermingled promiscuously, and both believed themselves entitled to various liberties, for which there was really no foundation. There was besides a clashing between country and City authority.

When, in the evening, we arrived in our city homes, we felt very grateful: that we were safe, and needed no further discrimination between country and city life. My 77th birthday, was celebrated in the city more quietly, than it used to be done in the country.

It came upon me, when I had much less vigor of body and mind, than former times. I have already named my bodily ailings. Those of my mind arose largely out of the utter degeneration of our public rule, that was then oozing out all over, but especially as to Silver coinage. Both parties were false to true political economy in this matter; neither carried out in good faith the international ethics as to money, to which the United States stood pledged before the world, by publishing themselves in their Constitution as a Government, that would coin honest money. The Republicans ordered monthly an excess of four millions of Silver money, and did it, openly confessing, that it was done, because they could hold by that course, partisan votes, that otherwise would desert them. A part of the Democrats asked for a free coinage of Silver, because they hoped in that way to gain votes, which they would otherwise loose. The very results, which I had predicted of party rule, had occurred, and I might have used the fact as a personal triumph; but such self glorifications were ever foreign to me, and I sorrowed over the shame, that this our partisanism had brought and was bringing upon the country. Most painful is was however to me, that the facts transpiring would, utterly ruin in the course of time, the reputations of the few statesmen connected with it, such as Sherman, Edmunds and Fessenden, because the false glory, that deceived cotemporaries would then be exposed, and leave them in all the nakedness of their real characters. The Silver frauds Sherman consented to, can never be forgiven.

When I reflect, besides, on the many arbitrary fluctuations, that have resulted from paper money issued in the United States, since 1862, and then read the condemnation of Buenos Ayres for their unstable currency, it makes me realize, how unjust our press can be against other nations, and how oblivious of its own misdeeds. I wish, that the United States were less able to commit wrongs with impunity, than they actually are. Oh! that impunity to do wrong!? What a fatal gift it is to America!? It engenders false pride!

CHAPTER CXIII.

POINTS OF INTEREST DURING 1891—92.

During the months of May, June and July, 1891, I dictated to some lady novices in type writing, the foregoing pages of my autobiography, deeming that better, than for them to copy my manuscript. And it did prove better for the ladies, but, as to myself, the advantage was problematical. They worked at lower wages, and that was a lefthanded compensation to me; of which the least said is the easiest mended. I paid the ladies their prices, and afterwards did the proof-reading. It ended all in a complete breakdown of my health, and in a tedious case of erysipelas. And as it was about type-writing, so it ended about printing. I saved money by the final contract, but it cost me untold labor and time. My life was actually worn out by unfair delays. The gipsy's prophecy of evil for hasty confidences were now more then ever realized, and my heart bled, that the last hours of my existence should be so much embittered by these faults in my character. I noted from it the lesson, that "men's uncorrected faults cause many bitter hours." My wife proved then, as always in such cases, a good nurse and my son Rudolf a good physician. I felt by September quite like an old man. Kind friends kept telling me, that I looked as young as ever. I had, however, to wear blue eyeglasses; I had to give up my favorite drink—wine; and was allowed only a moderate use of beer, in company with friends. I got quite in the habit of acting as an invalid.

My intended journey to Germany was postponed indefinitely; but clearer than ever I saw, that there I ought to spend the last days of my life. I declined several invitations from our ladies, to join them in journeys to resorts of pleasure within the United States. The ladies went without me, and soon my condition at home, and theirs abroad, testified in favor of my judgment on this point. Indeed my dear wife became quite reconciled to being my support. We both accepted as correct the Russian Proverb:

"The world is beautiful everywhere, but at home it is best!"

I did it in the sense, that in America, at least, my home was Cincinnati.

I had now plenty of time to consider the propriety of publishing my autobiography, and to invite proposals from printers and publishers, as to the best method of doing it. The subject was as disagreeable as "American Politics", with this difference: as to my book, I could burn it up, and forget it, but *Politics* intruded, whether I liked them or not. Besides, as already pointed out in the preceding chapter: "Politics, like chickens, come home to roost."

On showing, in 1891, a type-written copy of my autobiography to a friend in the East, who was, like myself, party-free, he accused me of speaking of American Politics in too dark colors, and claimed, that I made some invidious comparisons." I told him, that I had avoided comparisons studiously, and had made them only in refutation of specious nativistic boastings. I claimed, that this course of mine was the performance of a duty by me, as an adopted citizen, who, in writing his own life, had to speak of American developments, from the true comparative standpoint; namely: "Have the U. S., in their commercial, social and national intercourse with the world, progressed as much in morals, finance, politics and public service, as a reasonable, well informed person had a right to expect of them?"

That duty I claimed to have performed, by bringing out again and again the fact: that the United States have had superior advantages as to the production of wealth and its nominal local value; but, that this circumstance presented a distinct issue, that enters only to a certain degree into the points of inquiry, we have before us; because, as to it, no other nation comes within the comparison; whilst in the other points named, all civilized communities had nearly the same opportunities. The true comparative standpoint is therefore: Which nation has resisted the general progress most? And, on this issue, every reasonable person must say: that the United States have antagonized modern progress more than several other nations, we might name, if to do so, were compatible with our only object in the matter, to-wit: to bring to the American mind correct knowledge of itself, to-wit: that America is the dearest child the world has got.

When I had presented these views, my friend handed me back my autobiography, and retracted his accusations. He also conceded the propriety of the comparative standpoint, I had presented. He asked me, however, pleasantly, not to use his name. This I agreed to readily, for I always meant to rest my views, on my own authority. He thanked me for showing him the advance copy, as stated.

All through the winter and spring of 1891, evidences multiplied, that in the legislature of Ohio the corrupter elements of *both* parties were working in cooperation with certain cliques, both in Cincinnati and Cleveland, that worked in the interest of the — would-be — ruling municipal officials. Their aim was to defeat all real reform in Ohio municipal law, and to smuggle through sham reforms. They succeeded, by representing themselves as the advocates of a superior reorganization; and they appealed to historic memories, by talking of their bills as "New Charters" and "Magna Charta" and such clap-trap. They enlisted many persons, by turning them into lobbies to Columbus, and paying their expenses; whilst they gulled others, by misrepresentations of the measures, proposed by their antagonists. The members of the Legislature in both houses, who were not in the ring, were utterly confounded in their views. In the end a measure passed,—nem con—that contained not only numerous fortifications of boss rule, but also increased revenues for it, and longer terms of office. There were besides in many parts promising "futures". At the head was a bloated boss mayor. and in nooks and corners were those nuisances of municipalities, those supporters of mixed judicial and fiscal and administrative boards, whose powers, to do good, are very limited, whilst those for evil are large and unlimited. They are the revivals of mediaeval times, when cities had some walls against outside robbers, but none against those, that grew up within. Ohio is, as stated, entitled to the credit, if there be any in it, of prescribing for these boards, that no one shall be a member of them, that does not belong to some one party. Secret affiliations with *several*, seems to be the main recommendation.

After the spring election of 189I, there were surprises as to the real nature of the new municipal law. Bad men had more facilities for doing wrong; good men had more impediment to doing right. Municipal tyranny wore new liveries, and had new names, but real municipal reform had fewer hopes than ever. ·

The worst sign of political degenerations, prevailing in 1891, was however, President Harrison's six weeks electioneering tour, for securing his renomination in 1892. Former Presidents had refused to undergo such a run of personal exhibitions, believing them improper. A few Presidents had paid visits to localities, on being invited. Harrison's volunteer journeyings, with several speeches a day, upon his own advertisements, were to all discerning minds positive proof of a mutual degradation between the traveling President and the sight-hungry public, in comparing the year 1791 with 1891.

Blaine, Harrison's Secretary of State, was reported, as opposed to the Presidents preambulations, but he showed his opposition only, by not bidding his chief farewell, when he departed on his tour; nor welcoming him on coming back. In 1892 the full truth came out; for Blaine then announced himself to be the rival of Harrison. It was another sign of a decline in official propriety at headpuarters.

These two men had, for three years previous, the management of our foreign relations under their care; and their conduct lacked the wisdom and statesmanship, which a decent respect for the opinion of mankind requires.

In the case arising out of the murder of 11 Italians by a mob in New Orleans, the constitutional rule as to treaties for the protection of citizens of foreign states, was palpably violated by a persistent ignoring of the duty of the national government, to take jurisdiction over the case against the murderers.

In the Chili affair, the course of the President and his Secretary was reversed. There the Chilian government was forced, to do its international duty, by the U. S.; but it was done by mean ways.

Putting these cases, and that against England in the Alaska Seal Fishery question, together, and it cannot be gainsayed, that the U. S occupied a totally different relation to international law, than they did a hundred, yea, even fifty years ago. The boast, that the U. S. are the greatest people on the globe, reads now like mere *vain glory*.

When, in 1891, Chicago succeeded, by a congressional intrigue, in foisting upon the United States, its project of a World's Exhibition, and did it, by connecting with it, a celebration of the discovery of America by Columbus, in 1492, it raised in my mind many conflicting feelings. I was certainly in favor of World Exhibitions, for I had attended four of them, to-wit: the one in London — May 1851; that of Paris in 1867; at Vienna in 1873, and at Philadelphia, in 1876. I am also heart and soul for the objects of these exhibitions, as promulgated by Prince Albert, namely: the "international dissemination of knowledge and attainments, now extant in the world, as to the arts, sciences, technics, mechanics and the means of better and quicker intercommunication between all mankind." And so too was I an admirer of Columbus and his great work. But I was adverse to mixing the two together indefinitely, and confounding both manifestations, and doing it by importunities, that cast a doubt on the sincerity of Chicago in the matter, and must prevent the complete carrying out of both. I had observed too in the conduct of Chicago, and its special friends and managers of the program, the employment of artifices, that indicated, that Chicago's special interests and local aggrandizement, was much more in their minds, than the desire to understand and carry out the objects named. And I doubted therefore: whether the world-wide humanitarian spirit did or would exist, that has been found indispensible, to impart to the whole movement a lasting and wide-spread beneficial effect? And I soon ascertained, that no such spirit prevailed in Chicago, but that instead of it, ruled a feeling of rivalry, as if somebody was to be overcome, or at least surpassed. The real idea, that a new future was to be initiated and promoted for all mankind, in which there was to be no national hostilities, but many new international co-operations and facilities, was almost totally absent; and of course the whole thing had rather a backward, than a forward look.

What quickened, however, a conflict in my feelings, as to this matter, most, were my memories of the relations, the United States used to occupy towards all international issues. When I left Europe, sixty years ago, my emigration meant a wider, and not a narrower individuality, and it carried with it expanding interrelations as to old and new countries. I carried in my head, with all my fellow-emigrants, a *world-citizenship*, and the song, we loved most to sing ended in the refrain:

> "Our Fatherland must greater be",
> "Unser Vaterland muss grösser sein."

And the word "greater" referred, in the main, more to mental than territorial expansion.

My travels since, especially my visits to the World Exhibitions, have not narrowed, but widened my mind; and I feel so strongly for the objects named for World Exhibitions, and am so sharply against all compressions into Chicagoisms; because I can not forget, that

real progress there is in being an immigrant, and therefor an original embodiment of the ideas, that are the basis of all free migration
and all well organized and conducted World Exhibitions. Goethe
says, significantly:

> "Dass wir uns darauf ergehen,
> Darum ist die Welt so gross."
> "That we pass all over our world,
> That 's why the world 's so great."

Our age's signature is international expansion, and not national
contraction, and World Exhibitions mean no mere municipalism,
even if it were as wide as that of Rome; they are for the world and
mankind. Nothing short of cosmopolitanism satisfies us, not even
Pan Americanism. True Americanism has a World Citizenship for
its basis; and it is a distressing thought to me, to know, that the
United States have not yet risen to the best conceptions of international progress. They never understood Columbus.

In August and September I suffered from new attacks of erysipelas, and I became a confirmed invalid. The ancients called this
disease St. Anthony's fire, a significant name, especially the fire.
All I had to undergo in this illness, reminded me, that the country
has also a political ailing like it, and that it is likewise as hard to
cure. There are also many relapses, and all from the same cause,
namely: a want of complete knowledge of the nature of the disease.
In our politics, we have certainly no adequate remedy for theirs, by
Saint or otherwise.

In September, 1891, I received from the officers of the State Reform Farm an invitation, to attend the celebration about to be given
there, in honor of my former colleague, Hon. John A. Foote, who
had lately died at Cleveland, O. On the advice of my physician I
declined the honor. I mentioned, however, in my letter of declination, some facts, that occurred during the original organization of
the State Reform Farm, and among them the one: that several items
which had been deemed, in the original plan, essential to it, as a
self-supporting institution, were never carried out in Ohio. I expressed also my regret, that this had been so, because it was a reminder of a false tendency in our public institutions, to-wit: that
important functions are lost sight of, whilst the offices and their
pay receive too much attention.

In the following October, I was, with other citizens, much annoyed, and very seriously injured, by the untoward action of the
Board of Review, one of the boards instituted by the acts, already
spoken of, for the reorganization of the city government of Cincinnati. These annoyances and injuries reminded me forcibly of
remarks often made by teachers of political science, viz.:
that, in Republics, the people are most in danger, when mischief plodding persons are able to use their well reputed

townsmen as tools in their false schemes." Such was obviously the case then in the attacks made on us tax-payers by the Board of Review. Ostensibly the board was to equalize assessments made by the regular assessors; but, when it became known, that the board was an irregular body, one of the kind, that our partisan legislatures create, when they want arbitrary work done, I felt, that I was to become the victim of this new public organ, that was clearly created for reasons, in which financial science was out of joint. I had not received any notice of any intended increase in the regular valuations for taxation, nor had we heard of any complaint, such as the law speaks of. On the contrary, we had been led to believe, that the increase, made by the assessors already, were regarded as sufficient. How then could I take the new valuations, reported at the last hour in the Commerial Gazette, otherwise, than as arbitrary attacks, made on us under erroneous, if not dishonest impressions?! The board was composed of well-meaning men, that had the reputation of honesty. I at least do not question it. But I must say: they were not familiar with finaucial science, nor with fiscal practice. They did not accept as right the universal principle of political economy: that in taxing real estate, income is in all cases, in which it is ascertainable, one of the criteria, by which to assess its value, and to fix the tax charge. Not over one-fourth should ever be imposed in taxes, except for special, very cogent reasons.

I appealed to Court for relief. My sons Edward and Louis acted as attorneys. The case, briefly stated, amounted to this:

I had a piece of improved property on Sixth street, in Cincinnati. Before 1891 the lot and building were valued for taxation at $8,000. Then the valuation was increased to $12,000, by the regular assessor, and so reported to me. The Board of Review increased it to $20,500, without any complaint being filed, and without notice to me. I had, as stated, been led to believe, that the assessor's valuation would not be disturbed. It was, in fact, a valuation, that was high. It would have made me pay $308 tax, out of a gross revenue of $1,040. The valuation of the Board of Review made me pay $592. No other government on earth would have imposed such taxation.

I called on the Board for redress against this gross injustice. They informed me: "that I came too late;" and intimated, that the Courts could not and would not relieve me, unless I could prove fraud. And the result of my suit proved, that the Board's statements were made in accord with the opinions expressed to them by the Courts and the County Solicitor, before trial.

I will not here give my opinion of the case. But I feel bound to state, that I believe, that neither the Board of Review, nor the Court, is concious of the atrocious wrong, that has been inflicted on me. And it is this blindness, that constitutes the guilt of the State officials. It is an arbitrary tyranny, that is so atrocious, because

there is absolutely no remedy, except by the grace of the Board of
Review.

The State of Ohio has existed for ninety-two years; it is forty
years in the life of its second Constitution, and yet its public organs
are still uncertain, whether the Legislature can enact a special Board
and give it power to double the tax on a piece of real estate, and to
upset thereby any one of its citizens in his or her economy; indeed,
to impoverish them. That the Board of Review can do that, and
that the County Auditor or Treasurer can not be enjoined from collecting such an arbitrary imposition, was the decision in my case.
And when I left the Court, after being informed of the decision, I
left it minus the implicit faith I once had, that the State, whose
Constitution I once helped to make, was:

"The land of the free, and the home of the brave."

I once smiled, being rather pleased, when called by a friend:
"One of the fathers of the Republic of Ohio." I would still smile, if
the appellation were repeated; but with other feelings.

Let those of my readers, who have any doubt upon the subject,
reflect upon the situation we Ohioans are placed into, as to our means
of support of our families; if the claim of the Board of Review were
finally maintained. The Legislature can then create, for any locality
in Ohio, a special Board, and confer upon it not only special powers
of its own, but those of overriding all regular boards, which it may
declare defunct. It can thus oust a regular public organ, that is a
part of a regular system, that prevails over the whole State in pursuance of the State Constitution; and substitute for it an irregular
organ, that exists only in one locality, and is even there no part of a
system, nor an embodiment of a system, but a thing of several incon-
gruous functions, that can thus be ever infringing upon all the normal branches of municipal government, be they judicial, legislative,
executive, or administrative in their bearing. Can this be right in
Ohio?! If so, then we are not free!

Consider now, that such a Board cannot perform an act without
straining the construction of its powers and usurping authority; so
that in all its conduct, it exemplifies the ancient parable of the
teamster, that locked the wheels of his wagon on going up hill. For
seven months now has the action of the Board of Review perplexed
me and others almost to distraction, because its professions are
never fulfilled, and its evils are ever protracted. Worst of all however, is its conduct as to the reasons it assigns for its action. They
are all mere suspicions, or at least suppositions. It claims, for instance, that the increased valuation I complain of, is justified, because I have paid for years less taxes, than I ought. But I can show,
by positive proof, that I have paid, for twenty years, higher taxes,
than was right and proper, as compared with others. I do not blame
anybody specially with this injustice. I assert it as a fact! I rather

think it to be inseparable from such municipal goverument, as we have had for the last twenty years. Our legislation has been our tyranny. And a mean one at that; mean in qualification.

CHAPTER CXV.

A PHRENOLOGICAL INQUIRY.

In the early part of December, 1891, a phrenologist — Mr. Edgar C. Beall—called at my house in Cincinnati, and expressed a desire, that I should permit him to measure my head and face. I yielded to his request; and gave him an interview.

On the Sunday following appeared the subjoined article in the Commercial Gazette.

I insert it here, in aid of the general object of my biography. It has the same, yea, a better right therein, than the "Gipsy's prophecy." Both are attempts to understand my life from facial indications, but the phrenologist does it on a scientific basis. My own belief is, that the nature of human beings change according to modes of living, thinking, learning and acting, and all facial prognosis has value corresponding to the effect it has to improve character. Both, Mr. Beall and the Gipsy, did me more good than harm. Many thanks to both. The article is herewith submitted:

CHARLES REEMELIN'S CHARACTERISTICS.

The word conscience, as generally understood, and as defined in the dictionaries, means a faculty, which distinguishes between right and wrong. There is no single element in the mind, however, in the sense just stated, because the whole intellect, which consists of a dozen different faculties, occupying the forehead, may be concerned in moral discrimination. For example, it is right for a man to use his own hat, umbrella, purse, horse or house, but how can he distinguish his property from that of his neighbors, if he does not exercise the various faculties of form, size, weight, color, locality, etc. Sometimes the recognition of the right depends on only one or two of the intellectual powers, and in other cases several may be employed.

Thus an engineer, by the mere perception of a colored flag, learns, that it is his duty, to stop the train. Again, in seeking religious truth, many of the greatest men have strained their minds to the utmost, without arriving at perfect unanimity of belief. Hence it is plain that no one mental element can always decide, as to the lawfulness of our acts. But there is a faculty, which loves the right and prompts us to do it, in the same sense, that appetite impels us to eat, yet can not tell us, what is wholesome.

This love of equity is not, in any sense, a species of knowledge, as the word conscience etymologically implies, but is merely a blind sentiment, that needs to be directed by knowledge or reason, as much as the propensity to hate, to hide, or to hoard. Conscienti-ousness is the better name for it, and is the term chosen by Spurz-heim, to whom the world is indebted for the discovery of its cere-bral center.

It is located in the superior parietal lobule of the brain, and when large, gives symmetrical height and breadth to the cranium a little above the "parietal eminences," at the point indicated in the accompanying likeness of Mr. Reemelin. In this instance, how-ever, the height is not remarkable, from the fact that the head is one of the brachycephalic or short type, in which all the convolu-tions tend to expand laterally rather than upward.

Here one has a typical German. The temperament is well bal-anced, showing great natural capacity for physical labor, while the strength of the nutritive system and activity of the brain are very far above the ordinary. The head is rather large, measuring 22½ inches in circumference, and the general shape is a compromise be-tween a cube and a globe. On the whole, it illustrates the French idea of the German head, which they call "la tete carree." The base of the brain is massive, and all the faculties, which relate to the preservation and enjoyment of animal life, are developed in a high degree.

He has strong social feelings, a deep, steady love of nature, and much regard for the few friends, whom he finds congenial. But his attachments are never developed by the mere accident of associa-tion. His affection goes out first of all to certain principles, and then to the persons, who share his views. To these, if they prove worthy, he will be as staunch and true, as the oak to the tender vine. Loyalty is always his first thought.

Few men have such tremendous energy. He not only dares to face the most formidable foes, but beats down and exterminates the obstacles in his path. This is shown by the unusual diameter just above the ears, which, by the calipers, is 6⅝ inches. However, as he is a moral philosopher, this executive force will be chiefly spent in legitimate labor, or in warfare against the evils and errors that afflict the race, and not in senseless anger over trifles, or in cruelty to the weak. On the contrary, he has almost a woman's tenderness for children, and with his combination of small self-esteem and large benevolence, he can interest himself in a forlorn urchin upon the street, or take the world's woes as the sorrows of a single great family to his heart.

The sense of property is also strong. Mr. Reemelin does not think of money, as a mere momentary convenience, but always associates with it the idea of an abstract power, which deserves re-spect. He feels the impulse to garner his grain, and this instinct gives the cue to his intellect in much of his philosophical thoughts; thus leading him to the study of political economy. If he had less reasoning power and benevolence, he would be a selfish man. As it is, he will be saving, in order to do greater ultimate good. No doubt he will be more ready to give time, labor or advice than money, but he can not be called stingy; and in his methods of doing business, he would be exceedingly frank and truthful. He hates even the appearance of falsehood. Secretiveness is weak in him, and he may always be known by the colors he carries.

To many he will seem stubborn and obstinate, but he has no excess of firmness. He will yield a point, if he sees that he is in error, but he is not a man of superficial judgment, and not many opponents could instruct him. In this respect he is a little like the Scotchman, who said he was "'willin' to be convinced, but would like to see the mon who could convince him."

The sense of justice gives the key to his character. He loves truth for its own sake, and neither asks nor desires any reward for doing right, other than the pleasure he feels in the discharge of his duty. He believes in deeds, rather than creeds, and is not religious in the ordinary sense. But he is devoted to his conception of the highest and noblest aim, which is to improve the race by a rational philosophy of life.

Pride has no place in his feelings. He is never impelled to put himself above others, and the qualities of haughtiness, arrogance, disdain and conceit are totally foreign to him. He has only the assurance which is born of conviction, and if he desires to lead, it is not to tyrannize, but to teach.

Intellectually he is both observant and thoughtful. He appreciates both knowledge and wisdom, and having small continuity, shows great versatility of talent. He has been a manufacturer, a merchant, a linguist and a statesman. But his upper forehead shows his greatest intellectual power, which is in abstract reasoning. Altogether he is a scientist, a philosopher, a philantropist. and, above all, an honest man.

The temperament most favorable to honesty is the mental motive, in which there is both brain and bone. Men noted for their uncompromising integrity generally have rugged or striking features, such as Lincoln, Wendell Phillips, or the poet Whittier, in contrast to the voluptuous softness of contour and tissue of the vital constitution. Firmness and solidity of bodily fiber naturally go with the desire to do solid and substantial work. Yielding tissues are, on the other hand, better adapted to light, and it may be, crooked performances. As a rule, therefore, other things being equal, a very soft hand will need more watching, than one that is firm to the touch.

If the eyelids conceal much of the iris, there is ground for some suspicion as to truthfulness, although the individual may be merely shrewd. But the most important sign of deficient moral principle is the gable conformation of the top head on a line upward from the ears."

The reader will find the likeness spoken of in the preceding phrenological report, in the frontispiece. I give it for completing the phrenological inquiry; but also to show: that I give facts, irrespective, whether they flatter me or not.

I had told the kind phrenologist of the prophesy of the gypsy, and how it became engraven in my memory, by coincidents during my life; and he called the gypsy's work: "guess work." I then explained to him the german word: "Schicksal," and argued: that it expressed, in my opinion, best all auguries, in which a human being's character was attempted to be read, either out of the features of his face, or his hand. All anybody could find in that way, were predispositions, and history would afterwards have to record partial verifications, or contradictions, or alterations, as the case might be. And this the word: "Schicksal," which I would translate in English by the new word "fit-fate," would express, because it combined both these ideas, and was therefore truer; since human life is made up of fate and destiny, as well as tendency.

I informed the phrenologist also, of the controversy my cousin, Gustav Rümelin, the late Chancellor of the University of Tübingen, got into, just before he died, by the publication of an essay, on "Zufall," (accident,) in which he denied both fate and destiny; that I however claimed: that in all life logic prevailed. that was either fully known, or in part unknown; in other words: Some was conscious, some unconscious conduct; but all was logical.

And since it has occurred to me, that we may also apply this explanation to what our phrenologist called: "guess work," or by others: "chance words." Persons speak and write and act definitely or indefinitely, according to the state of their knowledge. And men are fatalists or not, just to the degree their hopes, aims and conduct rest on clear or unclear views. We shall see all this better through the next chapter.

The words cited from Shakespeare on the title page, are a'so important in explanation of this point.

It was originally delivered in January, 1892, before the German Literary Club of Cincinnati. It has since been translated into English. which makes it somewhat a different document. This will appear at once, if we notice: that the title of the subject of the paper in German is: "Die Ausbildnng der Erwachsenen."

CHAPTER CXVI.

IS THE GIVING OF A FINISHING EDUCATION, TO ADULTS, STILL THE MAIN TASK OF AMERICAN SOCIETY AND GOVERNMENT.

The undersigned takes the affirmative on the question, and quotes in support of it, the rule contained in Article 7, of the Ordinance of 1787.

"Religion, morality and knowledge being necessary to good government and the happiness of mankind, schools and the means of education shall forever be encouraged."

In this clause there are no distinct requirements, for either the common school education of youth; nor for academic education of adults. Neither are there mentioned, besides religion, morals and knowledge, as means of education, a sense of *order* and *economy*, which many persons regard as absolutely necessary, to complete the cycle of faculties necessary for a rational instruction, and as a guard against onesidedness in popular culture. Without these guards, we are apt to give, to some one of the means of education, undue importance: and this would lead to the neglect of others that are essential; and we would fall into sweeping assertions, such as Almendingen made, when he said: "*Order* must be means and object at the same time; because where it rules, there can be a prosperous status of right, and the State can fulfill its functions, even if all its citizens were devils." And thus it is too, with the observation of Greely: that "The History of the United States will show, that all the political errors may be committed in that land, without endangering its welfare, provided there is in it a continued general distribution of wealth over society." And we have to put into the same category, the assertion of Sam Lewis, of Cincinnati "that a common school education suffices, without any culture of adults, to form a fully good national character", and "that Religion alone is sufficient for the maintenance of a high civilization." We regard all such expressions as too one-sided.

Culture, both of youth and adult, is the best wealth, a people can have, if it is all-sided, and proceeds in connection with progressive World Culture. All nations, that cut themselves off from other people, and treat them with disdain, lose in civilization, and relapse eventually into barbarism, even though they were ever so populous, and occupied ever so large a territorial area. Only allsided culture secures to a community permanent welfare, because it guards against prejudices and extirpates errors. Great differences, as to culture, between the several parts of Society, vitiates social order.

I have never doubted, that the framers of the Ordinance of 1787, meant it well for the United States, when they promulgated the rule, we quoted. We were, however, not so sure, whether they understood completely the matter involved, and their relation to it. Their first mentioned means for education — "Religion" — led to self-contradictions in cotemporary American State papers; we find, for instance, in the first amendment to the United States Constitution, this clause: Art. 1: "Congress shall make no laws, respecting an establishment of Religion, or prohibiting the free exercise thereof." There was much discussion over the contradiction this clause contained to the requirement of the Ordinance of 1787; that "Religion is necessary to good Government, and the welfare of mankind": but the discussions were endless, because they were conducted without a full understanding; and for that same reason we are discussing this subject still. Out of this condition has also grown this distinction between the United States and other nations, viz: Whilst of the latter each have a special religion, which they claim to be classic and orthodox; the former has many fragments of religions, none of which the Constitutions recognize, either as classic or orthodox; in other words: religion is no part of the established public will. Please reflect. that the provisions of the ordinance of 1787 have, as to education, never received a definite construction; nor have they ever been religiously carried out. And we are evidently not fully conscious, that the constitutional prohibition of all laws for an establishment of religion, was really a guaranty of perpetuity of existence to the then established sects. It was actually a suppression of all true religious culture. Merely forbidding or ordering religion, is ordering or forbidding good and bad; it means, therefore, a public standstill, and private indifference.

It cannot be denied, that the Sects and Churches have ever since construed the clause of the Constitution, as authority, for them to continue their respective practices of religion forever. in spite of any and all opposition; but it is equally undeniable, that the better construction is: that the Constitution does not forbid a religious culture becoming general here, that shall be accepted as the one true way to carry out the requirements of the Ordinance of 1787. We are now stuck fast in the ideas, as well as common law practices, that originated in England, in the XVI. century; and they certainly gave religious freedom only to sectarian religion. and did it on the same parallel, that made their parties the custodians of civil liberty. But the State and Society became unfree there and here. Sects and parties rule them, for in their hand was and is both civil and religious culture; they were masters of the situation.

And with this, our perception of the control, which sects and parties exercise here over educationary processes, we perceive also, that these processes are scattered over the whole Union, in seeming harmony and unity; but having no real coherent polity. Most public schools receive indeed public support, and the State Legislatures exercise over them a general guardianship; but the United States Congress has also donated large bodies of land, and has in many other ways, such as the aforesaid clause in the Ordinance of 1787, acted as the founder of institutions of learning, but the entirety is really more a confused mass, than an organic totality.

To my mind, it is a most obnoxious thought, that the present promiscuous religious exercises of religion shall be regarded as having by the Constitution, a guarantee of perpetuity for sectarian religion, and that the true religious culture, which the ordinance of 1787 certainly foreshadows, and which every cultivated mind has now taken hold of, and entertained more or less, is to be deemed as forbidden by the Constitution.

Of that culture of the adults of society, whose object it is to impart to the entire life of a people, and especially its culture, a higher tone and a better subsistence; about that, there is here neither a fair understanding nor agreement. There is not even an official name in common use for it; and we hardly know: whether to treat the matter as a political, social, or private affair? And equally unclear it remains, as to whose guidance the subject shall be entrusted, or at whose expense it shall be conducted? The words of Seneca: "That the True, the Virtuous, the Beautiful, need culture, because they do not grow of themselves; whilst the false, the ugly and the mean do not need it, because they grow of themselves", were forgotten: indeed the reverse was adopted and became the leading idea. They assumed for themselves, that they would, in and of themselves become the greatest, best and wisest people on earth, and that these characteristics would include also being the richest people, as a matter of course. And they assumed, as the logical proof of these excellencies of theirs, the fact, that they had less government, and fewer public officers, than any other country. And they summed it all up in the motto: "That government is best, that governs least." The assumption itself proved eventually an untruth.

The deep significance, these assumptions must have had for American Society, you will perceive at once, as I shall name the several ways and means, which the people of the Old World, and in part also those of the new, have adopted for the culture of adults. It will prepare your mind too, for the main differences, between culture of adults and that of youth. The most marked of these is: that in the culture of adults there is much less school education and much more personal self-culture; and yet also much more reciprocal instruction; than in the education of youth. The schoolmaster is no longer the main figure, after the culture of adults begins. And men and women, as they gather experience and understand facts, become more ready, both to learn and to teach, and to impart it mutually. The Home and the Family are no longer all of the world for them; a new one, much wider, indeed one, that is at first immeasurable to them, arises. It is unlocked for them, but each unlocks it also for others. Conversation is felt to be a great want, and they realize, what a reality of culture there is in the practical application of knowledge by adults, to every-day life, since beside education, there is to be instruction also. The individuality forms into sociability, and it becomes eventually political forecast — there is a comprehension of the necessity of looking ahead and providing for the future, in other words: the political comes forth. And political means: thinking ahead with philosophic reason.

Let me now name these means of culture in regular order. First we name: bodily and mental exercises for public necessities, under the guidance of well-disciplined officers, let us call it *military* culture. We become familiar with it, when the sense of public duty exists in its most marked form.

Next comes learning from speakers, by private or public speaking or conversation, such as listening to sermons from the pulpit, or to speeches from some other public standpoint, and also in lecture rooms or public meetings. It includes music, with its teachings of harmony in sounds, and of their enjoyments and convivialities.

The third educational medium is the Press with its many varieties of publications, such as public reports, books, journals and pamphlets. America was once Primus in this, now it is anarchic in its relation to the Press.

The fourth group is still more manifold; it embraces Theaters, Circuses, Zoological Gardens, Museums, Libraries, Exhibitions of the Arts and Sciences, public holidays and celebrations. They include Harvest Homes, Vintages, Church Fairs and National feasts, such as our Fourth of July and Washington's Birthday. And I suppose I may name also, journeys, public baths and walks and personal recreation. In all of them, the children may share, and give us, by their presence, lessons of innate patriotism, by letting us feel, that we belong virtually together. World exhibitions must not be forgotten.

And, if now we pass to the consideration of the conditions, in which these several means of culture present themselves to us here at this time: we cannot help noticing, that they are not in the public relation, they should be to each other, nor to culture generally. I mean by this, that there are in the schools for youth neither the right primary, nor secondary, nor final modes of interculture between the different ages, the respective instruction, nor the conclusive studies and exercises. There is no right coherence in their administration. And memory has not therefore the needed lasting continuity, nor is the capacity. to form mature judgment, sufficiently tested and cultivated, whilst prejudices have gained a pernicious tenacity. And for these reasons every species of culture lacks the needed action, interaction and reaction of the whole on the parts, and of the parts on the whole. And there is not therefore the correction of errors, the remedying of defects, nor the rectification of mischiefs, that ought to be in every society.

And if now we cast our eyes upon the first named means of education for adults, we perceive at once, that we have *not* the necessary military organization and discipline; because he have habituated ourselves to think of this matter according to certain popular ideas, that rest on mere negations. And we have, in consequence, all kinds of military, even a hireling soldiery but all imperfectly organized. And we have too the motley combinations of discharged soldiers, that float about society on pensions, granted as a subsidiary party policy. But we have no organic disciplination of adult youth, nor any cultivation of a right sense of public duty and service.

Our Federal Constitution, and most of our State Constitutions, prescribe military organizations, such as I named last; but they are not regularly organized, and mostly entirely neglected. And we have a right to conclude. that these provisions stand in the respective Constitutions, more in pursuance of the recommendations of Washington, Franklin and Jackson, made in former times, than as a result of a popular study, or understanding, of the questions to-day. Seventy years ago, we had still some well-drilled militia soldiery; but about sixty years ago, we allowed the word "militia" to fall into disrepute, so that it became a term of ridicule and reproach. And we never recovered the true idea of armed forces, raised from truly patriotic motives, on the basis of military duty f⟩r all, and for statesmanlike views. We allowed also the old antipathies against standing armies, to overpower our minds, so that we became so blinded on the subject, that we never saw, that we had in our so-called "regular troops" the very lowest specimen of a standing army, which the world ever saw. Low, not only in its inadequacy, but also in its great cost, namely: forty-five millions of dollars a year, for about 28,000 men. We have thus lost all true appreciation of a proper military establishment; and we regard, erroniously, the armies of France, Prussia and Austria, as "standing armies," that impoverish these States and endanger their liberties! whilst our own, *i. e.*, regular army, and our pensions, cost one-third more than the costliest of the armies just named. This false judgment is the more remarbable, because we have in our excellent *West Point Academy* the proof, that we might have, if we really wanted it, an, every way, good military establishment; and one free from the faults of former standing armies.

It must therefore be pointed out to you, that there is in this country a disinclination to have public things done by ways and means, that are carried forward on the advice of science, and persevered in; because found correct by experience. And that this disinclination exists, in pursuance of a belief prevalent among us, that progressive development does not here proceed, as it does all over the world, namely: by finishing the education of the adults of the respective nations; but by an intensification of the inferior pecuniary interests and the struggles they beget. This intensification has here taken the name of "Americanism." It is an anomalous name—formation any way, as it expresses no marks or token of either the hemisphere, the country, or some *one* of its distinguished localities or citizens;

such as Bi-Continent, Grand Montana, Columbia or Washingtonia would express. It has been extensively used by demagogues, to give vent to antagonisms, that are fictitious, and prevent here the best development of the age, to-wit: cosmopolitan, international politics, which I have just described. I call it "World culture," as distinguished from mere national culture, such as the Egyptians, the Persians, the Greeks and the Romans had in antiquity, and France, Spain and England had subsequently, and Germany has lately adopted. The national distinction has come out in our times sharpest in the respective various military organizations. And our abandonment of our constitutional military requirements has made us an oddity on this subject. We have committed all kinds of outrages on scientific military organization. The worst was the rejection of the bill, prepared by Van Buren's Cabinet, in 1837, for the constitutional organization of the military forces in the United States. The wrong there was in this rejection, came out, in rendering the Mexican War in 1845, excessively expensive, and unnecessarily protracted. And, as we lingered along in our fatal indifference, we came into the Civil War of 1861, totally unprepared, and won in the end only by a series of eccentricities, both as to systems and persons; so that we have confounded the military judgment of all that have so far written on the subject, and will perhaps do so for some time, at least until the historians shall come in aid of the military critics and explain the cause and effects of our neglect in this particular. We will then understand too, that we cannot get a good police force without a good military force.

We now turn to the *second* main medium for the culture of adults; public instructions by sermons, orations, etc., etc. We actually believe, as to them, that our present methods of public discussion are the very best extant, *because* liberty of speech is here guaranteed to all. I regard this reason as a mistake, for the question involved is not so much liberty, as education and the standard by which we must judge of it. We want to be certain, that the respective speakers understand the subjects they are discussing, and moreover, that they know how to present their arguments. So too is it essential, that the orators are men of integrity, and not partisans. In every Government, including Democrats, the turning point in this matter always is: whether there are actually unprejudiced teachings and consultations, and whether all share in them? Such are possible only, where there are proper preparatory studies, as well as sound after-explanations. Our people have deprived themselves of these, because they have, as to politics, divided themselves into Parties, and as to Religion, continued their old Sects. There is not, therefore, really any people's Government or consultation possible; it is Party and Sect agitation, that ever ends finally in preventing reform. All the speakers have lost their right courses, and also their reckonings; Parties and Sects use only their respective casuistries, that is to say, they work, with seeming arguments and fair looking reasonings, only for *their* special objects and aims. The audience hears only the casuistries, they learn them by rote and repeat them to others. And of course there are no really instructive discourses on either Politics or Religion. There may be harangues on some specific moral precepts or tenets, or policies, and so too on some specious party policy or purpose, but never for any correction of their errors or predispositions; they are, in fact, confirmed in them. And it is absolutely true, that the scarcest beings, in the United States, are persons, that think and act pure in politics.

You will, perhaps, ask now: How can we get out of these our distracted conditions? And I can only say: You must endeavor to realize the original object of the constitution; it is: to be: *one* People. It is easily done, provided you are for it decidedly. But it is difficult, indeed impossible, if you persist in your partisanisms and sectarianisms. *With* them you cannot be an honest people. Cast them off then!

I think moreover, that it will facilitate your decision to present to you a brief statement of the real situation you are in.

You think you are participators in the formation and enforcement of a public will, by your mixing in with party elections. But you are not doing anything of the kind. You are only participating in party quarrels and chicanery between parties, that mean to impose their party will upon the people on false pretences. In other words: You let yourselves be led by your party nose to assist in hindrances of the formation and execution of a rightful public will. You hinder the formation and enforcement of a good public will, when you should be its best civic supports.

To be One People again, you must reform yourself politically, in the sense expressed in the Ordinance of 1787; and the main point in it is: that public culture shall not be conducted through the moulds of parties and sects, but through the civic rule of the Constitution and the order of States, conducted by statesmen and educated public servants. Public discourses must not be a mere inculcation of party resolves or sectarian dogma. And in Congress, and all legislative bodies, the standard of debates must be State righteousness and not party wrongheadedness. They must all, however, be carried on publicly before the House or its Committee, and not in the caucus of the respective ruling party.

You! Gentlemen! will perhaps interpose here, and say: "You are asking of us the impossible; for it contravenes all our habits and rules, thus to fall back upon the primeval idealities of our Constitution. We are unable to regenerate the idealities of our constitutions; for we are too captiously real, to be iderl." We are partisans and sectarians, and have really ceased to be citizens.

I cannot accept this interposition, as a full answer to the accusations I have made; but I may admit, that it is, as a confession, useful, so far as it leads to further serious inquiries into the real situation. And if then we come face to face with the realities of the situation, and understand them, then there will be no longer, as now, impossible reforms. They dishearten us now on the Silver question, on election frauds, and our tariff and tax•laws. The old adage is still true: "Where there is a will, there is a way." We lack the right will. To get it, we must gain the right cognition. Then only will we see that our people, as well as our Governments, have not only broken faith with our written constitutions, but also with the promise implied in our Declaration of Independence: that we would march onward in an even pace with the general progress of mankind in ameliorating political ruling, including party manipulations.

I cannot discuss these subjects extensively; they lead us into Comparative Politics, which are a subject by themselves. I may, however, point out, that a parliamentary party government, that works with a written or federal constitution, must avoid all deviations from it with the greatest care, because it is, therein, much more troublesome to retrace false steps, than it is in unwritten civil constitutions. The false steps represent social infidelities. The social and political wrongs occur at the same time, and there must be a co-operation in reforms between the social and political powers and forces, which is next to impossible, because it requires a coincidence, that rarely occurs: since it involves the cooperation of two public wills, that are unlike in their very nature. Constitutional prescriptions may make it possible.

The consequence of the prevailing false ways, in the United States, are these: that the political discourses delivered, contain very little, if any, political logic. They argue from special social partisan premises, which the science of politics condemns; and there can be, therefore, no sound culture of adults in such discourses. They excite their passions, but do not enlighten their judgment. Our party organizations are nought but a hitching up of the party teams for the respective leaders. And we may see, to how small an extent there is in these teams, any popular judgment, by the fact, that the respective partisan crowds listened last Fall, in Ohio and New York, eagerly to the speeches of their candidates for Governor, both of whom misstated the real issues involved in the election; and everybody knew it. They came to hear and to applaud their own political falsities, and did it, and nothing else.

It was, in certain respects, somewhat different in the listenings of congregations to sermons from the pulpits; but only so far as the sermons were subject to a better prescribed culture and discipline, than the stump speeches were. We must ever remember, that most of our sects antedated our Constitutions, and our parties; and that their pulpit orators are limited in their indoctrination; and that consequently there can not be as many deviations as there are in our parties. Compare the two, and we have this general picture as to politics: We have a President that is the plaything of his party: a Congress intriguing for party power; States that are the battle-fields for party fights; Cities that are the places where party shad-ows are the longest. They are all abortions of institutions, which the fathers meant to create by our constitutions. They meant a party-free President; a Congress that would be, in truth, a States Council; States and Cities that gave the Union its equipoise. And finally, they meant an organic People, bound together by a common patriotism and progressive enlightenment, superior to any that ever existed before; for in it civil liberty was to be the leading motive and standard.

We come now to the central point in all "culture of adults" at this time — the *Press*. Every one admits, that the American Press is, so far as the publishing business is considered, in a gratifying progressive development; but the reverse is the fact, when we esti-mate its value by the use made of it from the standpoint of having it as the main organ of culture for the people. And the reason for this fatal difference can be no other, than the fact, that here the Presses, that are most animated in their conduct by social desires for riches and power, give tone to the general conduct of the whole Press, and force their cotemporaries into the common track of prostituting our public affairs to these desires. There are doubtless many presses, especially among those, that are party and sect free, that discuss public questions in honestly instructive ways, but no-body will say, that they are the most influential in shaping the pop-ular mind. This position is conceded to papers of a very different character; namely, to those, that cultivate semi-culture, because it is more profitable and suits better to the general character of the money-making papers, to-wit: that of being the venders of sensa-tional news and personal foppery. These sort of presses play the trick well, that represents their course as being American par excellence, and as such are sure to be imitated by the whole Press fraternity, and to become masters — master minds — in the modern sense. This claim is also fortified by invidious comparisons as to the size and the quantity of the reading matter, and the number of pa-pers sold here as compared with Europe; but we regard all such comparisons as misleading. They bring us to false inquiries, and lead us away from true ones. In one word, it is to us all a false "*stimulus*", and around it cluster, "censorships", "Liberty of the Press", as catch phrases; with which to suggest extreme party measures, and to enable editors and correspondents to play the re-spective parts of political demagogues, or the puritanic zealot, as the case may be.

But for us the Press is neither a sanctuary, nor a deviltry, nor even a modern substitute for the ancient court fools. We know, however, that something of all this may occur in it, just as our people shall become qualified or not: to solve the problems it has as to the Press. We may be glad that it has not yet made of itself a sort of infallible church, whose politics we would have to carry out, whether we like to or not. There is indeed danger, that certain party organs would like to assume this very position; for *they* have been in the way, so far, of all the national economic developments, by which themselves, railroads, telegraphs, banks, and similar institutions of general utility, might have become public servants in the best sense; that of freeing the people of social upstarts.

We have to lift these institutions out of their present negative position, and place them upon positively right ground. And that we shall secure, provided we shall prescribe, beside the present, not very effective prohibition of and punishments for pernicious acts of our presses. also: positive behests for certain wholesome conduct by them. I mean by the latter, a healthy increase and perfection in measures. such as our weather reports and the papers written by professors, expert engineers, and well educated and disciplined administrative officers, that are published in scientific papers, which bring to the whole people knowledge and capacities, as they need them for the discharge of their duties as citizens, heads of families, and chief owners of business establishments. Then the Press will, so to speak, *cease of itself* to be the tool of avarice and ambition; its self-reformation will bring a general reform. It must form itself into a public service, of which our ancestors hardly thought, and ourselves have hardly yet clear conceptions. for which, however, our descendants will bless this generation, provided the policy we indicate, is soon adopted and persisted in. The fruitful elements for this action are around us; they need but to be sifted and applied to make them effective for the common good.

The Press was, for a long time, the country's darling; it has come to be the country's terror; but our Society is too well tempered, to weaken itself by measures, that would destroy the liberty of the Press, or infringe on our people's equanimity. One thing, however, is certain. and that is: that no Press can ever be the right public organ for the spread of intelligence here, whose owners, editors respectively, use them like the old Banditti did their hirelings; viz: for the subjugation of their fellow citizens. This must be counteracted; and the best course is that: by which statesmen in all ages, and especially in ours, have converted. in their respective States, their impudent would-be masters, into public servants; towit: by bringing within the regulation of public administration, all those parts of their occupation, that are really public affairs. This has been done as to money, public conveyances, the mail, schools, etc.; in each case by special methods and to certain extents; but all upon the general principle I have stated. It has been done in the Press as to public reports, documents, etc., but not sufficiently definite; and as a result we have a party Press, that abuses its liberty and rules the country, when it should serve it. Let public administration embrace Telegraphs, Railroads, indeed all ways and means, by which *authentic* information and instruction can be brought to the common use of all our adult population. Then the wings of the would-be masters would soon be clipped, and we would have furnished in proper continuity, regularity and quality, the authentic information and instructions as to religion, morality, knowledge, economy and order, which is now needed more and sooner, than ever, to enable our citizens to be the rulers, which we mean by calling ourselves a Democracy. Don't forget, that a self-conceited people can never be this correctly. I cannot, for obvious reasons, go into details; but may say: that every public act in the premises should be done without infringing on Liberty. Now the Press has all liberty, and of course takes liberties with our people. Democracy is a pitfall and a snare. We must free the people from this incubus of the Press, as we did in the other affairs named.

The fourth group of means for cultivating adults embraces: Theaters, Circusses, Zoological Gardens, Museums, Collections of Antiquities, Travel, etc. Connected with them should be Art Exhibitions and public congregations, in aid of improved knowledge and technical capacities in Agriculture, Mechanics, with popular plays and festivities, in honor of public days, like the Fourth of July, or celebrations of the birthdays of distinguished persons, like Washington. We refer specially to those, that have an international reputation. International co-operation is most needed.

The applications of the principle named, are too manifold in this group, to give a detailed description of the several means, as to its present status here. We can only say: the Country has, as yet, no definite policy as to such public affairs. We are still too much engaged in attending, to what we regard as the "necessaries" of life, to take the full view of this group of the aesthetic enjoyments and refinements of our society, which are indispensable to a good public conduct of them. We differ also, as yet, too much as to the public proprieties at such public meetings and popular concourses, to have our public authorities charged with their conduct. Our police are not well enough organized and disciplined, to let them have full control. And our public is still much too intensely in love with its fancied liberties, to take readily to rules and regulations, as to individual conduct, such as must be adopted, if in these celebrations we are to have the better high enjoyments, and mental and physical displays at them. We have consequently, still much more control over them, by persons as owners and directors, than is compatible with their best public development. We permit also, far too much, that money-making shall be the leading motive of all exhibition-. There is therefore in all such public affairs, an excess of grossness and temptation. And that complicates matters, since they are already complicated by the difference of opinion in our public, as to what constitutes *sin*, and what is a mere misdemeanor or impropriety. The religious sects are predisposed to oppose even the most innocent amusements. They would, if they dared, pass laws, requiring all to attend church on certain days and at fixed hours.

And if now we take up the subject in its general bearings, we cannot avoid coming to the general conclusion: that the culture of adults has not yet received among us the full consideration it deserves, and that our adult population is not instructed in Religion, Morals and Knowledge, as the Ordinance of 1787 prescribes. Nor is there the right kind of political information promulgated to qualify our people, to act well their part in popular Government. The Ordinance says expressly: that it was enacted "for extending the fundamental principles of civil and religious liberty, which form the basis, whereon these republics, their laws and constitutions are erected." And again: "to fix and establish these principles as the basis of all laws, constitutions and governments, which forever hereafter shall be formed in said territory."

These words do, certainly, not point to the establishment here of any special religious, moral or political governments; they must mean all this in the philosophic sense of a general religious culture, that embraces the best of human conduct. as history is made and recorded. I think, that we would do the framers of the Ordinance of 1787 a gross injustice, if we were to take their words in any narrower sense. To us the chief value of the earlier American State papers consists in the cosmopolitan tone, in which they were written. They were free from sectarian and partisan narrowness.

Compare, if you please, the writings of men like Washington and Madison, with those, which the Press furnishes us to-day from Blaine and Sherman, and other partisan politicians, and you will at once see the difference there is between them, which we have just now pointed out to you. It points us to the variance, that has grown up in the culture of adults, between then and now. The men, first named, grew up under circumstances, that confirmed their rectitude in thinking on political questions; the second named grew up under conditions, that awakened crooked ideas in their minds. Liberty and Right was the object of the first, and they created both, for their country, by securing, pro primo, Independence from England, and then, also, by creating good institutions for the internal concerns of the country. The second wanted to be rich, and to live in a rich country. For them a material prosperity, expressed in money, was the object and standard in politics. They were superficially educated, and deceived themselves and their followers; they confirmed each other, mutually, in their self-deceptions, and, worst of all, they intensified social egotisms and prejudices.

National economy was for both means to end; the first named, it served as a widening of their culture; the second used it for contracting their political views. And the consequence was, that, under the guidance of the first, the country's institutions were constantly improved, but under the lead of the second, they were gradually spoiled. There was in the course of time more and more opportunity and temptation, to mislead the people with fine sounding words and promises. This concealed from them the real problem of our system of government, and favored the invention of wild political issues. They used, for this purpose, the false shine, that was on everything in consequence of the immeasurable wealth expressed in paper money; it corrupted the political sense of our people more and more, so that the popular mind stood confused between the two extreme conditions, that were over the whole country, to-wit: Undeserved increase in wealth on the one side, and undeserved impoverishment on the other. This meant in politics, the undue preference, by the voters, of partisans for office; and the undue neglect and rejection of party-free persons. And these two extremes have led to the alternations of political crises with social crises, that plague us. The peace and quietness, that springs from the right culture of adults, exists here now, only in exceptional instances.

There arose, out of this state of persons and things, manifold hindrances in the political and religious culture of the United States; they all culminated in extremes about money, and these gave avaricious moneyed men the control in alternation. One part of them *had* nothing but money, whilst the other part *wanted* only money. Money surpluses and money deficits led to moneyed gambling, that disgraced our mercantile classes, so far as stock speculations were concerned. It might be interesting to expatiate over these matters, but my discourse is already too long, and I must turn to the one point, that I should have spoken about already; because I believe, it is on the point of the tongues of every one of my readers; to-wit: "Whether schools for Youth, and pulpit sermons for the adults are not sufficient, to satisfy all the wants of culture for a population, like ours?" As stated already, this question contains a dangerous error, that has a long history, on which we cannot enter now, but may say: that the error is the reaction from the opposite ancient error, that the culture of adults was deemed all-sufficient in itself, and needed no precedent education of the country's youth.

I cannot agree to either. The first effort at education, outside of the family, was undoubtedly verbal intercommunication between adults. Schools in the community developed much later. The words of Christ: "Let the children come unto me", indicate, that children were then excluded from conversations between adults. We have a right to assume, that children's schools soon grew into an exclusiveness, under which the culture of adults became neglected, because no longer deemed necessary. Then came in apprenticeships and fellowships in Mechanics and Commerce, and Colleges, Gymnasiums, arose. The adults were believed not to need further education. *There* was the fatal mistake; but its great mischief did not become apparent, because all-sided education never ceased entirely after all. The social convivialities grew up and were continued, and so were Theaters in special localities, and so too was there always some superior personal self-culture.

The church and the nobility always also kept some adult culture alive, and so did the professions. All these customs influenced more or less the rest of Society. The discovery of the art of printing brought new additions to means in culture, and gave to all manifoldness, which again took new directions on the discovery of America. The culture of adults and the ways and means for it, were thus here more and more lost sight of. Indeed there arose a tendency to depreciate individual book-learning of all kinds. Society at large was anti-church to a large degree, and the part, that was not, confined itself to Bible reading, and insisted on its being the only, or at least the principal education for adults. The primary education of youth soon absorbed all public educationary proclivities, and it became a sort of national axiom, that the common schools for youth were to be the cornerstone of all the institutions in the new world.

But with all my esteem for elementary schools, I cannot regard this axiom as correct. It is too exclusive. The incessant culture of all members of Society, is the great problem of human life. It must of course vary according to age and other circumstances, but must be, in one way or other, *continuous* and connected, as well as interactive. There is a time, when school teaching by school teachers must pass into self-teaching and its mutualities. Gathering experience must then be the leading idea, but it must be done under guides, that have a general, besides their school education. It must not be only a bodily, but also a mental and aesthetic disciplination. Adult life has educationary wants, that cannot be supplied in the schools, but must be furnished after arriving at mature age, day by day, or, perhaps better stated, evening by evening, in those various social ways, in which politics and ethics can not be entirely ignored, nor form the exclusive object of promiscuous intercourses.

The latter error was oftenest committed in the United States; and the culture of adults degenerated generally into some extravagant sectarian or partisan ultraism, in which true culture could not live. It is certainly an evidence of a low state of culture among our people, that a large portion of it refuses to visit Theaters, because they hold them to be *per se* sinful, whilst they encourage Base Ball, and visit this game in crowds. The first has been recognized for thousands of years as excellent means of culture, if they are managed by persons of culture, while the other is known to be based on the ideas of the old Roman Gladiators; or, if you like it better, on the wild scion of modern bull fighting proclivities. The latter sprung up as a kindred thought to that illusion, which deems all our natives exempt from all further culture after they leave school; whilst they hold, that no immigrant, even the educated adult persons, can ever claim the same exemption, and that they require an entire re-culture, to qualify them for American citizenship. This · absurd presumption, is the now largely prevailing mischief, that plays its wicked part in all our public life. It hinders the very culture, which alone can save this land and people from the perils that now hang over them. It is no other culture than that required by the Ordinance of 1787; to-wit: that religion, morals and knowledge shall be cultivated. Were this culture once unreservedly established, it would extirpate the intensifications of sectarian dogma and partisan tenets, which spoil all our conduct, because they are but confirming us in our prejudices.

And here, at last, I have to state, in plain positive words, what has been leading my mind all along in this chapter, to-wit: my convictions, that our public in the United States is to-day more at sea as to their education, than any other of the Nations, that claim to be in the front ranks of civilization. We are not clear as to Politics, nor do we know definitely, what Religion is? Our sects and parties are afraid of all scientific development in such issues. And this is the reason why the words, we have cited from the U. S. Constitution and the Ordinance of 1787, are dead letters. I would revive them, so that our public should arrive at more definite conclusions as to their full import.

If now we throw, what we have said in our discourse, into one general outline, we have to point to a people divided into sects and parties; that, falsely cultured, as it is, deems it securing liberty, to be thus divided. It mistook also, caught in a similar delusion, our distracted military organizations, for means, that would save us from the tyranny of *standing* armies; and it thought also, that public harangues, filled by the heated spirit of sects and parties, could impart to a people the culture it needs to have in Religion, Morals and Knowledge, as well as in its policy for the future, the temper and capacities, which modern civilization requires.

And thus it came, that those who called themselves free-thinkers, believed, that a free surrender of the Press, of Theatres, Public Expositions and enjoyments, indeed all the means for the culture of adults, to speculators, that were hungry most for money or power, is the true way for causing in a people the right sense for the beautiful, the true and the virtuous, and the wise.

To us, all such one-sided conceptions. appear radically wrong. We know, that keeping up in all things due measure and degree, is the true idea; and that this can be maintained only, where and when, all sided culture furnishes the standards for all conduct. This not being the case here, on the contrary, the country and people being subject here, in a large degree, to the mean and brutal in our Parties and Sects; we concluded, that we are correct in our leading thought; to-wit: that "The giving of a finishing education to adults is still the main task of American Society and Government."

As shown: neither the education of youth, nor the culture of adults, had here their systematic public interrelation; but the culture of adults was neglected and left to chance. And of course all public action went on under a similar fatality. It lacked the sterling equanimity, which only this culture can secure. We had, on the contrary, partisan and sectarian agitations, in which imagined, rather than real, issues were urged, and pushed forward, upon fictitious grounds. The most noted instance was the question of Slavery. The agitation against it became, in the course of time, general, from no inner compunctions of conscience, as to the wrong there is involved in an ownership of human beings. No! the opposition to it arose out of party quarrels, into which the churches were also drawn, and then caused the general commotion between 1854 and 1860, and, finally led to civil war. Let the reader mark this! It is the key to our history; and it teaches us, that if we had had, during the first century, the complete education we have here urged. we should have had not only an earlier, but also a wiser abolition of slavery; and no civil war. I say this, being convinced of its correctness.

CONCLUSION.

I must now, by way of recapitulation and for the purposes stated in the Introduction, bring out, once more briefly, the principal perceptions, that lighted my path in the work before me. The most weighty of these perceptions is: that social order is out of joint in American society, because the social-inorganic forces govern in matters, that should be under positive political guidance and organic authority. Our public conduct is largely the reverse, of what the science of politics teaches, and so too it is, as to political economy. We give, both the initiation and decision of public measures, to social combinations, such as parties, etc. And our executive and legislative organs are, to a dangerous degree, the merre tools of combined pseudo-political elements. This arises out of the anomaly, that we have in the United States both public and private successes in the obtainment of wealth, office and distinction, which carry with them very little actual merit, honor and respect, because everybody knows, that many persons get rich here and secure office and places of honor, without possessing the capacities or the qualifications, which mankind has almost universally deemed necessary for these positions. And this circumstance causes false relations between them, society, the public authorities, and trade: so that there is neither right discipline in the public service, nor strict proprieties in trade, and just as little social decorum. Religious doctrines, public policies, and political principles, are advocated to suit patrons, or special interests, and seldom from convictions. All this increases the confusion there is as to religion, politics and honor; and we alternate between zealotry and indifference. And this is complicated by the other anomaly, that there are constantly occurring here failures, in political, commercial and other business, and even professional careers, that do not receive the customary blame, because the public is conscious, that these failures are mostly caused by our general lack of economy and finance, which ever causes crises, that overwhelm the weak that are innocent, as often as the bold, impudent, guilty adventurers. And thus we alternate between undeserved successes in land spoliations, or money, stock and bond speculations, and partisan contests; and undeserved failures; all feeding a largely vicious public mind, with false political notions. Among these notions the leading one was and is: that being born here, or residing long in the country, constituted *per se* a claim to distinction and preference. It kindled in many an excessive pride. But we know, that neither being born here nor immigrating, are *per se* either commendable or reprehensible.

The other perceptions, which I must mention yet, came to my mind, in consequence of the prominence now given to Columbus, in connection with the World Exhibition at Chicago. It is really with me a memory of the ideas that were current, when I arrived in Philadelphia in 1832. Columbus was then the hero of the World's unity in civilization. Everybody believed in the motto:

"No pent-up Utica contracts our powers,
The boundless universe is ours."

The Americanism that meant the United States to be the one ruling power in the Western Hemisphere, and it, in antagonism to the Old World, was not born; but there were very definite conceptions current, that the United States would, in the course of time, be the medium, through which this globe of ours would embody one mankind in unity, under one general civilization.

The United States did not then speak of itself always in superlatives, such as: We are the freest, richest, best governed, least taxed, fastest growing and bravest people of the world. All that has come since and perverted the public mind. To me it was ever clear, that the superlatives emanated from self-conceit, that needed invidious comparative standpoints, for the antagonisms it wanted to create in American society, such as party feuds, knownothingism and sectarianism. These all culminated in civil war, 1861. That war then bred its own mischiefs and conceits, and we have been blustering in them ever since, at a tremendous cost of civic comity. The citizens, that in private life, social intercourse and commercial dealings, were affable, generous and polite, were, as publicans, turned into ruffians, intriguers and mercenaries, and our public life became a field for vicious turmoil. The fate of men and things now turns largely on the specious use of the word "Americanism," that has become popular here under the conceits named.

Let us understand, once for all, that such an infatuated Americanism means not only a stoppage of all true progress in America, in the direction of the civilization named; but that it is in fact a reaction to all the errors and faults, which developed in antiquity, when the self-overestimation of races induced them to war upon other people, and to think, that conquering them made themselves great. It was the same mischievous solecism, as that, which lurks in the word Americanism, as certain demagogues use it, for blinding our people as to themselves. This public course perplexed me so severely, because in my individual intercourse with my fellow citizens, I experienced many friendships from both natives and immigrants; and I confess, from the first more than the latter.

I ask the reader to reflect on the undeniable fact, that since 1840 this people has been gradually more and more ruled by appeals to its nativistic prejudices. Has this any other cause, than the abandonment of our original position, that we were to be the foremost leaders in the modern cosmopolitan civilization? Our Presidents, up to Harrison and Tyler, held that view and were free-minded. Take now a fair view of our late troubles with Italy and Chili. Was not every step we took, an appeal to popular prejudices? And coming now home to our own internal issues, I must inquire: whether the leaders in our politics, the heads of our parties, have lately in any instance presented the real issue on the Silver question? Is not the whole discussion a variety of appeals to prejudices? And is it not also as to the latest act of our Government, the Quarantine regulations against Cholera? Did not our President have the stoppage of immigration more in view, than that of the cholera? And does it not prove an utter perversion of all sound educational ideas, to have to read lately from General *Clarkson*, a man well known to me to be an unusually bright politician, the following:

"It has been one of the marvels of the first century of American history, that the great mass of American Colleges, by the use of European text books on all economic questions, have taught our American boys, European instead of American ideas on Tariff, Finance and other subjects."

The General not only opposes, as he says: "Vicious or pauper immigration;" but he would ardently exclude European text books, written by Professors of Colleges and distinguished authors on economic questions. He would, it appears, confine American youth to "American ideas." To do that consistently, he would have to admit the absurdity, that the sciences are, as studies, national subjects; in other words: that Mathematics, Arithmetic, Medicine, Jurisprudence, are, as studies, national. Indeed, General Clarkson, had he been alive in 1492. would have opposed the landing of Columbus, for fear, that his coming would bring: European Ideas on Navigation or Geography into the New World.

It hurts my feelings to point out these evidences of degeneration here; for they remind me: that I have had, again and again, to struggle, within myself, against the temptations, that would, if I had yielded, have made me fall, with the rest, into a false exclusiveness. I resisted, and can now close, this my autobiography, with an inner assurance. that I am still true to the freedom from national prejudices, with which I left my native land, sixty years ago.

And knowing thus, how hard it is, in this country, to resist temptations, to intensify prejudices, especially those that grow out of misunderstandings, as to our magnificent general growth, I felt the supreme difficulty, present and coming generations have already, and will have every day more, to attain the self knowledge, and integrity, that can enable them to effect the reforms, that will be necessary to save the country from a dreary fate, such as Rome had, after it had fallen under the rule of quarreling factions. I feel weary of the reflections, that thus arise in my mind, and I ever again throw them off; but they return, whenever I see one of my grandchildren; indeed, any youth I know and take an interest in; and then I cannot help seeing, in all its actual deformity, our financially debauched land, under a viciously disposed government, and public administration, all in the midst of a politically spoiled people. And I ask: Can this people ever work itself out of its present degeneration, if it goes on in its self-exclusion, from the World's progressive civilization? I take hope, of course, from some good deeds, such as our liberal international postal treaties; but hope grows dim again, from procedures, such as I have named. and which are ever occurring again. And then, as now, an answer fails me to my queries; I write:

THE END.

INDEX.

—

INDEX.